Time of Peace

Time of Peace

September 26, 1930—December 7, 1941

By BEN AMES WILLIAMS

HOUGHTON MIFFLIN COMPANY · BOSTON

The Riverside Press Cambridge

1942

The characters in this book are fictitious;
any resemblance to real persons is wholly
accidental and unintentional.

CL

PRINTED IN THE U.S.A.

Preface

IN 1930, it was inconceivable to Americans that they would ever allow themselves to become involved in another European conflict; but by midsummer, 1941, there were few who had not accepted the inevitability of our entrance into this war, and weeks before December 7, millions of us, rebellious at the hypocrisy of our undeclared naval war on Germany, were ready to vote for a formal declaration.

This book has as its background an attempt to show the successive changes in our national mind as it passed from the one extreme to the other. To that extent the book is a historical novel; and it would be possible to document it as completely as if it dealt with the Napoleonic Wars. There is in it hardly a line of conversation expressive of personal or national opinions that is not a paraphrase of editorial comment of the period, or of some book or magazine article, or of dated correspondence and diaries, or of an actual conversation. If some of the things said seem from our point of view today almost treasonable, they did not seem so at the time they were said or written.

We have had innumerable interpretations of the world events of these ten years, and scores of writers have attempted to portray public opinion in France, in Germany, and in England during this period; but to know, even in retrospect, our own minds is certainly equally important. We have believed many things which were false, we have believed many things which we did not know we believed, and we have thought we believed other things which we did not believe at all. The attempt herein has been to record some of these beliefs and opinions accurately, as of the period when they were held and expressed.

This book is the fourth of a group upon which the author has been for a number of years engaged, and which have sought to deal with our American wars, not on the battle front, but in the minds of civilians at home. *Come Spring* saw the Revolution from the point of view of a small community in the remote Maine wilderness. *Thread of Scarlet* looked at the War of 1812 from Nantucket Island. *The Strange Woman* saw the end of that war, and the approach to and the progress of the War Between the States; but the central character usurped that book and to some extent defeated its original intent. This work is an approach to the war in which we are today engaged.

The people in this book are, of course, completely fictitious persons, and no portrait of any individual is to be found in these pages. Upon the life of each character, the War of 1914–1918 left its imprint, and upon each one the approach of this War of Mankind made its mark. But that is true of everyone past adolescence in the world today.

B. A. W.

September, 1942

I

Heads Will Roll

(September 25–26, 1930)

1

(September 25, 1930)

WHEN Mark Worth left Tony un-
dressing and came downstairs, he saw that the tall clock on the landing
had stopped. The absence of its eccentric tick-tock, tick-tock, tick-tock,
two beats and then a pause, like the hoofbeats of a galloping horse, was
a clamorous shouting in the unnaturally quiet house. The ancient time-
piece usually ran well enough; and it told the time, not accurately but
cheerfully, and as though to say: 'Oh, I guess it's about quarter past the
hour—if that matters.' After all, Mark thought, clocks must occasionally
find themselves bored and rebellious at the necessity of spending their
entire existences being right to the second!

He paused in front of the clock, remembering a poem he had read or
heard about a grandfather's clock like this one which stopped, never
to run again, when a certain old man died. With a hurried movement
he opened the case, wound up the weights, and touched the pendulum.
He watched it for a moment, fearful that it would stop again. He was
perspiring faintly, and yet he was a little cold.

He closed the case and the old clock set a rhythm for his steps, tick-
tock, tick-tock, tick-tock, as he descended the stairs. When he came into
the living room he could hear Tony moving to and fro in the room
above. The youngster always seemed to do a great deal of walking
around while he was taking off his clothes. That had been true of him
even as a baby, when Mark and Nan used to like to put him to bed
together, and Tony was forever escaping from Nan's arms to run to his
father, or from Mark to run to his mother, squealing with delight at
this game till at last Nan pretended to lose patience, and caught him
and held him while she peeled off his clothes and pulled on his Doctor
Dentons and tucked him in bed.

Mark had watched his son often enough during the process of undressing to be able to guess in a general way his movements tonight. Tony might take off his coat and pause to study the bird chart on the wall, and then walk across to hang his coat on a chair and stop on the way to inspect the model aeroplane on the table in the middle of the room, which he hoped some day to complete. He might stand on one foot and take off one shoe and drop it, and then sit down to take off the other, and while doing that he might notice, on his desk at the other end of the room, the latest issue of one of the air magazines, and cross—with one shoe off and one unlaced but still on—to lay the magazine on the floor and sit down and look at the pictures in it while he wriggled out of his other clothes. Tony was already air-minded, to such an extent that his school work suffered, although he was just past his eleventh birthday.

Mark after a moment went into the kitchen to speak to Elin, washing the dishes in the sink there. 'I'll say good night to Tony,' he told her. 'Then I'm going to the hospital. I may not be back tonight, but I'll be here for breakfast, unless I telephone you.'

Elin turned to face him, wiping the suds and water off one arm and then the other with her hands. She was a young Swedish girl who had come to this country when she was twelve years old—her father and mother being dead, her older brothers and sisters married and with homes of their own—to live with an uncle in Somerville; and when she finished high school she went for a year to a school of domestic science and then into service. Nan was her first mistress. She was now twenty-one, with the warm blond beauty of her people, and she had an unquestioning friendliness which made everyone like her. Nan, the day she engaged her, came home to tell Mark: 'She's had no experience, and I haven't the faintest idea whether she's a good cook or not, but I knew I wanted her the moment she smiled. Of course I'd be thankful for anyone who can make toast without burning it, after some we've had; but she's really a sweet girl, Mark. I shan't blame you if you fall in love with her. I don't know when I've liked anyone so much, on three minutes' acquaintance. Maybe it's because she so obviously liked me. She's coming Thursday.'

Elin came Thursday, and that was two years ago. She was a good cook, she kept the kitchen and the house immaculate, she served the meals in a fashion which made it a pleasure to sit down at the table, and she found time to do most of the laundry, and to darn Tony's stockings and his father's socks too. Mark from the first liked her as much as Nan did, and she was devoted to them all.

Mark, when he entered the kitchen tonight, saw that she had been crying; for she too loved Nan. He wondered absently whether tears were an anodyne for pain. She said in a quick solicitude:

'Maybe you'd drink a cup of coffee, Mr. Worth, or eat a little toast before you go? I could make it in a minute. You didn't eat a bite of dinner.'

This was true. Mark and Tony had been alone, Nan's place achingly empty at the foot of the table; and Mark had watched his son assimilate food in a sort of wonder. Evidently not even grief and terror could spoil a boy's appetite.

'I'm not hungry,' he told Elin now.

'You ought to eat something. You'll be sick your own self.' Her eyes were entreating him. He understood that she was anxious to show him her sympathy and her solicitude, and this was the only way she knew. Not because he was hungry, but to give her the happiness of serving him, he said:

'Perhaps you're right. I think I might eat—dropped eggs on toast, a cup of tea?'

'I'll make it strong,' she said happily. 'The way you like it.' She was beaming through her unshed tears.

He felt in her the instinct to comfort him as though he were a child; but he was not a child. He was almost forty, with a son eleven years old and a wife lying tonight desperately ill. He was a man, with a profession and a house and a car and a family, and other men came to him for advice and counsel and help. But he himself needed help tonight. He felt terribly alone, and he was grateful for Elin's solicitude.

'Yes, strong,' he assented. Then the door from the hall into the kitchen opened, and they turned and saw Tony in his pyjamas. The youngster looked at his father, and laughed in a sudden relief.

'I called and you didn't answer and I thought you'd gone without saying good night,' he confessed.

Mark put his arm around the boy's slender shoulders. 'I'll go up with you now,' he said, and they went out into the hall together.

All the lights in the house were on, no shadows anywhere. 'I turned them on,' Tony explained. 'I like it bright, the way you do.' Nan had always insisted on candles for the dinner table, shaded lamps everywhere. Mark sometimes laughingly protested that half the time he did not know what he was eating till he put it in his mouth, tasted it. Once, to point the jest, he had brought a flashlight to the table and used it with elaborate ostentation, to Tony's hilarious glee.

Father and son ascended the stairs side by side, and Mark's arm rested across the boy's shoulders. On the landing, Mark saw that the clock had stopped again. Perhaps he had wound it too tight. He set the pendulum swinging, stood watching it. He did not want that clock to stop, never to run again, never to run again, never to run again, never to run again . . . His eyes were scalded by a sudden hotness in the outer corners. He squeezed them shut and felt the tears beneath the lids.

Tony led the way into his room, and climbed into bed and pulled the covers to his chin and looked up at his father. His eyes seemed tonight to be tremendous. He said, as though the thought were a comfort:

'Father, you've always come with Mother to say good night to me, haven't you?'

'I surely have.'

'I always know you'll both come in and open my windows and turn out the light and everything,' Tony said, and Mark smiled, and the boy asked, in a lower tone, as though the answer would be a secret: 'Is Mother pretty sick, Father?'

'She's pretty sick,' Mark assented.

Tony's whisper was like a muted bell. 'Is she going to die?'

Mark hesitated. In the moment's silence he heard the tick-tock, tick-tock, of the old clock on the landing. 'She may,' he said honestly.

Tony's eyes widened. Mark opened the windows. It was raining, but this room was in the southwest corner, and the rain came from the northeast, so it did not beat in. Mark opened the windows wide. He turned out the wall light. There was a reading light fastened to the head of Tony's bed. Mark asked: 'Are you going to read awhile?'

'I guess not,' Tony said. 'I guess I'll go to sleep.' He added reassuringly, like a promise: 'I'll go right to sleep, Father.'

Mark bent and kissed him. Tony's arms around his neck tugged tight and then let go; and Mark said with half a chuckle that was also half a sob: 'You're all right, Tony.'

Tony lifted his hand, touched his father's cheek. 'You're all right yourself,' he said, grinning weakly.

Mark went toward the door. Tony would turn out the reading light when he was ready, pulling the end of the string which dangled within reach of his hand. As Mark approached the door, he wanted to hurry, wanted to run, to escape the question he knew was coming; but he held his step steady. He reached the door. Then Tony called:

'Father?' Mark turned. Tony smiled at him pleadingly. He said: 'Promise to wake me up when you come home?'

If Mark and Nan were going out to dinner or to the theatre or any-where else for the evening, Tony from his baby days had always exacted that pledge from them. Nan used to laugh at him and call him absurd, but they regularly promised to wake Tony when they returned, and they always kept the promise. Usually, when before going to bed they came into his room, it was only to touch the boy's shoulder, to say: 'Hello, son.' Then Tony would murmur in his sleep: 'Are you both home? Are you going to be home all night?' He seldom really woke; seldom remembered, next morning, what either he or they had said. But he always exacted the promise.

Tonight, Mark did not expect to come home at all. 'I'll wake you when I come,' he said.

'What time will you be home?'

'I don't know exactly, Son.'

There was a moment's silence. Then Tony pulled off the light so that his father could not see him. 'Well, if you have to stay with Mother, I'll be all right,' he said. 'Don't worry about me.' And he added: 'Give Mother my love.'

The last word was husky, so Mark knew Tony was almost crying. 'I surely will,' he said. He was glad Tony had begun to cry. The youngster would go to sleep more easily if his eyes were bathed in tears.

2

(September 25, 1930)

The clock was still running when Mark went down the stairs. Elin brought a tray into the living room, set before him eggs, strong dark tea, an extra slice of toast, a little marmalade.

'That looks fine,' he told her. She stood by and he said: 'Elin, if Tony wakes, you might go to him. Of course he's a big boy, but—things always seem worse in the dark.'

'I'll leave my door open, and his, yes, sir.'

'I'll probably stay at the hospital all night. He may wake and want to know whether I've come home.'

'I'll hear him. Don't you worry about him.'

He ate clumsily, his fingers stiff and awkward. He spilled a little egg yolk on his coat, and Elin brought a damp cloth and wiped it clean.

'Sorry,' he muttered.

She said: 'You're pretty tired. But you can get some rest in the hospital.'

'Oh, I'm all right,' he assured her. He drank the hot, sweet tea, sipping it slowly. He knew suddenly that he dreaded going to the hospital. Nan was delirious. She would not even know he was near her; and she was so small and haggard, and when she coughed his breast was torn, and the pulse beating in her throat was like hammers beating in his head. The hospital seemed to him a hideous place. The cold floors had a greasy look, a greasy feel; the very silence was funereal. The smell of cleanliness disturbed him. There were in the hospital none of the lusty, sweaty, healthy smells which made the world so sweet in a man's nostrils.

The doorbell rang and Elin went to answer it and Bob Ritchie came in. Bob and Nell Ritchie were their most intimate friends, living just across the street. Bob and Mark had been in Dartmouth together, and at Harvard Law, and they were in the same legal firm—of which Bob's father was the head—now. Bob was one of those men for whom other men felt an easy affection, for he was slow to see ill in anyone. His was the lawyer's mind, precise and logical, finding irrelevance in everything but fact. He spoke now calmly, in a normal tone which Mark found heartening. Most people when they spoke of Nan did so in hushed whispers.

'Hullo, Mark,' Bob said, asking directly: 'What's the news tonight? Nell called the hospital, but you never get any satisfaction from them.'

'Why, there's no good news,' Mark admitted, rising to shake hands with Bob while Elin took the tray away. 'Except that Nan's still alive, and Doctor Hethering says every hour she lives improves her chances.' He added: 'I'm going to the hospital now.'

'Anything you want me to do?'

'I'll let you know if there is.'

'Right. Nell and I are on call, if you need any errands run or anything. We're not going out this evening.' Bob added in a matter-of-fact tone: 'Nell sent you her love.'

'Thanks.' They shook hands again—since there were so many things they wished to say and could not—and Mark went with Bob to the door.

When the other was gone, Elin brought Mark's hat and coat and held the coat for him; and she fetched the car keys from the desk where he always put them. If Nan had been the last to use the car, the keys might be anywhere; in the car, in her pocketbook, in the pocket of her coat, on the mantel, on the dining-room table, on her dressing-room table, anywhere. But Mark always put them in the same place, with a methodical monotony. Nan used to tell him that if he didn't put them somewhere else just once for a change, she would scream!

He took them now with a muttered word of thanks. Elin, her hands clasped to keep them still, said reassuringly: 'I'll listen for Tony.' He nodded, not risking speech, and went out through the French doors.

3

(September 25, 1930)

On the side of the house toward the garage there was a brick terrace with a pergola roof over which wisteria climbed. Mark followed stepping stones to the garage. They had built the garage after they bought the house three years before, when the stock market was gathering momentum for its last skyrocket flight. Mark himself did not speculate. His surplus earnings had gone into payments on the house; but he shared, during the later twenties, the general feeling that all was well with the world. Even since the market collapsed, now almost a year ago, his income—bar some difficulty in collecting his fees—had shown a healthy increase. Lawyers were as busy in hard times as in easy ones.

The lives of most of the men he knew had been shaken by that crumbling away of paper values; yet Mark thought the collapse of the market might be in the end a good thing. Through the twenties, people his age and younger had thrown themselves into a feverish riot of extravagance and dissipation, drinking too much, making light love to each other's husbands and wives, laughing too much and mocking the wrong things. He and Nan tried to keep their heads, tried to hold fast to those things which were good; but they had not wholly escaped the contagion.

All that madness was perhaps an echo of the War, but now since the crash the madness was ended. The War too could be forgotten, for wars were done with. The War to End War had proved that victors and vanquished were alike the losers. It had ended everything that went before; and now all the nations, conquerors and conquered, were struggling, like men caught in a mire, trying to get back to firm footing again, trying to get back to a normal way of living. This would take time, but they would manage it somehow. The folly of war was proved, once and for all; and by and by the old ideals would come to life. People would be proud of keeping their given word, of working hard and saving and planning for an earned security in their old age. Looking up at Tony's open windows, Mark thought that his son's generation would cleanse the world and teach it honor and beauty again.

He was reluctant to start for the hospital, and he stood a moment by the garage, thinking of the years he and Nan and Tony had had together here. The house, this home of theirs, stood a few feet below the level of the road, and behind it the ground dropped steeply to the lake, not a hundred feet away. There was a sort of summerhouse beside the lake, octagonal, with open sides and benches all around, and a table in the middle where on fine warm days they sometimes served cocktails before a dinner party. There were a few fish in the lake, yellow perch and chub, and Tony sometimes fished from the bank below the house. They could swim if they chose, but the shore just below the house was reedy, so it was pleasanter to go to the bath-houses around on the other side, a mile away. Mark sometimes went there with Tony. He had taught the boy to swim.

The house itself was shingled, and it was stained a weathered brown. The living room had many windows and an ample fireplace; and the hall was wide, with a graceful stair up to the landing where the grandfather's clock stood. The dining room was small, and not more than eight people could sit without crowding at the table there. Upstairs, their room and Tony's were almost alike, long and narrow, with windows on two sides. The guest room and the room where Elin slept were on the other side of the hall. The attic was a studio, with a skylight. Nan was an amateur with brush and pencil, and Mark thought some of her things good. He had been pleased with the house when they bought it, and Nan had been ecstatic.

He looked again at Tony's windows. If the boy were still awake, he would hear the car go out; and Mark watched the window for a moment, thinking Tony might appear in the black rectangle, but he saw nothing. Those windows were dark, but the rest of the house was brightly lighted. Every bulb in the living room was burning. Elin stood in the French doors, watching him.

Seeing her reminded him that he must go on. He went into the garage. It was built against the lot line, and the city ordinances required that it be fireproof; so it was of cement, with wire-netted glass in the windows, and doors sheathed with metal. It was an ugly garage, built as cheaply as the fire laws would permit. Mark had assumed a considerable financial burden when he bought the house, and the garage was a makeshift, nothing more.

He took his seat in the car. It was two years old and they had talked of buying a new one, but the house was not yet paid for; and till the mortgage was paid off, Mark would not feel that the house was really theirs. The money for a new car could be applied to the mortgage; and the old car was as comfortable as an old shoe. When he touched the starter now, it answered instantly.

He backed out into the street. Rain lashed the windshield, and he set the wiper going. As he passed in front of the house, the windows on the stair landing were bright, and he caught a glimpse of the old clock in the corner of the landing.

He wondered whether it would ever run again if Nan should die.

4

(September 25, 1930)

Nan had been a lovely girl and woman, but she was little and wiry, full of nervous energy which never let her rest; and about two years ago Mark had noticed that she was losing weight. He accused her of dieting, but she pointed out that she was eating tremendously; and he had to admit that this was true. Nevertheless, she seemed to him thinner all the time, and her eyes became increasingly prominent, like those of a deer. He urged her to see a doctor, but she would not do so; and in the end, he was driven secretly to consult Doctor Hethering on her behalf.

Doctor Hethering was about sixty years old, with white hair and mustaches and twinkling blue eyes. He had begun his professional career as a surgeon, and won a brilliant success, but while he was still a young man his wife died, leaving him with an infant daughter. When the little girl was seven years old, her foot was crushed by a streetcar. Doctor Hethering himself operated, and as a result of his anxiety to save as much of the foot as possible, his procedure was less radical than it should have been. The result was that a second and a third operation were necessary and his daughter's leg had finally to be amputated just below the knee.

At almost the same time, the panic of 1907 swept away the fortune Doctor Hethering had begun to accumulate; but these twin catastrophes, which might have embittered a lesser man, bestowed upon him a fine philosophy. He became a general practitioner, and he devoted himself thereafter to service rather than to success. His fees were ridiculously low while his capacities were first-rate. He was one of those physicians who by their very presence heal the sick; or, if they cannot help the ailing, they know how to comfort those who must endure irrevocable loss.

Doctor Hethering heard Mark's story and came to see Nan. He found that she was suffering from hyperthyroidism, and said an operation would relieve her and restore her to health; but Nan—to dread the operation was, Doctor Hethering told Mark, a symptom of the disease— laughed at his word and flatly refused to heed Mark's urgencies. There was no enlargement of her thyroid gland, and she pointed this out as proof that Doctor Hethering was wrong.

'It's just that I'm so busy,' she insisted. She and Nell Ritchie were active in all sorts of community affairs. 'I'm on the go all the time. That's why I don't gain weight. And besides,' she added triumphantly, 'I don't want to gain weight!'

Mark could not persuade her; but he asked Doctor Hethering many questions, and watching her with an informed eye, he saw a dozen evidences to confirm what he had been told, and felt a growing concern.

A few days ago—with Bob and Nell Ritchie and Ed and Mary Halstead—they had driven out to Lincoln to have dinner with Tom and Emma Sheffield and to play Badminton afterward in the court Tom had built in the old barn. Tom was in the Trimount Trust Company, in the loan department. The Lincoln place had been his father's, but his father was dead; and when Tom and Emma went to live there, Tom's mother and Emma were from the first at odds, till eventually Mrs. Sheffield moved to an apartment in town. Neither Tom nor Emma ever saw her now, Emma insisting that Tom must choose between his mother and his wife. Emma was extravagant, so that Tom had once confessed to Mark that they regularly spent more than he earned; and Mark, though she was pretty and gay and amusing, never forgot that she had separated Tom and his mother.

At Badminton, Ed Halstead and Nan teamed up against Tom and Nell Ritchie, and then, since Mary Halstead was soon to have a baby and could not play, Nan became Bob's partner against Mark and Emma. Afterward, the four men played, and against Mark's remonstrances, Nan insisted on going out-of-doors—it was a raw, rainy September night—to cool off. She refused a wrap, and she developed next day a severe cold which kept her abed. The day after, she was wretched; and Mark insisted on bringing Doctor Hethering to see her.

Nan told the Doctor, hiding her fears behind a jesting tone: 'I'm perfectly all right; just a rotten cold. But Mark's a regular old woman. I told him not to bother you.'

Doctor Hethering assured her that it was no bother. He sat with his hand on her wrist, took her temperature, asked her a few questions, and said cheerfully: 'You'll be better by tomorrow morning, but I'll drop in anyway.'

Nan looked at him sharply. 'You think I'm sick!'

Doctor Hethering smiled. 'We'll have to get rid of this cold,' he said. He gave some directions and departed; but when Mark went downstairs with him, he said in a low tone:

'I'll come back this evening. Has she complained of any pain in her chest?' Mark shook his head. 'Well, that's fine, but I'll come back,' the Doctor repeated.

He did return that evening, and when he had seen Nan he sent for an ambulance. She was by that time too ill to protest; and she could no longer hide from Mark the terror in her eyes. He went with her to the hospital, saw her settled there, talked with Doctor Hethering afterward.

'I'm just taking precautions,' Doctor Hethering explained in a reassuring tone. 'At home, she might be hard to manage, but here we can take care of her.'

But Mark was not deceived. Nan developed pneumonia, and Mark, knowing that the poison in her system must have weakened her heart, was shaken with fears which he tried not to let her see.

For three days now, when he came to the hospital, Nan sometimes knew him, sometimes did not. She seemed to shrink and contract from day to day, like a balloon deflating; and though she had been beautiful, her face became like the face of a stranger, drawn and flushed, her skin almost translucent. There was an extraordinary purity in her appearance, as though she had been burned clean by fire.

5

(September 25, 1930)

Mark left his car in the parking place across the street from the hospital and went indoors, shaking the rain off his coat and hat, nodding to the nurse on duty at the desk, turning toward the elevator. He found Doctor Hethering with the floor nurse; and the Doctor saw him coming, and came to meet him and took his hand. Why was a doctor's hand always so dry and hard? Was it from scrubbing up so many times a day? Mark asked at once:

'Is there any change?'

Doctor Hethering shook his head. 'No. No change,' he said. He hesitated, added then: 'She's asleep, or seems to be. We can give you a room. You lie down. I'll call you when she rouses.'

Mark nodded, glad it would not be necessary for him to go into the room where Nan lay, to listen to her coughing and to her quick, audible breathing, to sit and watch the faint stir of the blankets across her breast, to see her head forever turning fretfully upon the pillow.

Doctor Hethering spoke to the floor nurse and she opened a door and turned on the light. They entered a room bare as all hospital rooms were; the bed with the crank at the foot, the dresser, the closet, the bedside table, the bell button on its cord lying beside the pillow.

'You'd better lie down,' Doctor Hethering repeated. 'Sleep if you can. You look as though you were short of sleep.'

'I suppose I am.'

'I might give you something to make sure you sleep a while.'

'No. No, I'll stay awake.' Mark smiled ruefully. 'I have a feeling that once I really go to sleep I'll be hard to wake.' He asked after a moment: 'Doctor—what do you foresee? What are you expecting? What is the situation?'

'It's just as I told you. Every hour we can keep her alive is clear gain.'

'How long will that go on?'

'If we bring her through tomorrow night, I'll begin to think we're going to win.'

Mark lay down on the bed, his arm across his eyes. 'Tonight, and tomorrow, and tomorrow night,' he said under his breath. 'It's a long time.' He asked: 'Doctor, is she suffering as much as she seems to?'

'No, no. She's delirious. She doesn't know anything.'

'Isn't delirium a sort of pain?' Mark's eyes were closed. The Doctor did not speak, and Mark said: 'I suppose in a way I'm delirious myself. This moment, this hour, tonight, doesn't mean anything to me. It isn't real. The real part is all in the past; the things I remember, things Nan and I have done together.' His voice changed, almost as though he were smiling. 'I keep hearing her voice, laughing, and saying things; and I can see her expression when she said them.' He said apologetically: 'But you don't want to sit here and listen to me talk.'

The other told him: 'Go on and talk, Mark! It's good for you.'

A gust of wind threw rain against the window, and Mark looked that way. The door opened and a nurse came in. She said: 'She's awake.'

Mark stood up as Doctor Hethering rose. 'You wait here,' the Doctor suggested. 'I'll send for you.'

So Mark stayed where he was. After a little, the nurse returned. 'You can come in now,' she said, and smiled in friendly reassurance. 'I think she'll know you.'

She held the door open, and Mark stepped out into the hall. It was only a few paces to Nan's door, and their feet as they moved that way were almost soundless; but it seemed to Mark that his heels woke echoes in the corridor. The white uniform of the nurse ahead of him was a moving blur as she led the way. When she paused to open the door for him, he blundered into her like a blind man, and he murmured: 'Oh, I'm sorry!'

She was a woman in her middle thirties, with many experiences like this one behind her. As a girl, just beginning her profession, she had hardened herself defensively against the tragedies of which her work forced her to be a spectator; but since she grew older her warm heart had taken command, and now she suffered with her patients—and most of all, with those who loved them—sharing this suffering which she had learned to ease. With a gesture almost motherly she touched his arm, squeezing it affectionately; and she said, lapsing as she was apt to do in such moments into the tender way of speech native to her people:

'Never think of that, man dear. Go in to her with a smile in the heart of you, now, for her to see.'

Her words and her tone and the touch of her hand put strength into him. There were so many good, kindly people in the world. His head lifted, and then he was in the room. A shaded lamp on the dresser gave the only light. Mark nodded, approving that, thinking that Nan always preferred dim illumination. He came to the side of the bed. The oxygen tent had been opened, and Nan's eyes looked up at him. They were her eyes, and from her lips came Nan's voice; thin and small and frail, yet Nan's, just the same. She said softly, a faint mirthful note in her tones:

'Well, Mark, you were right, weren't you? I was sick after all.'

'You're a lot better,' he said.

She whispered: 'How's Tony?'

'Asleep. I left him in bed.'

Her eyes closed, opened, and then closed again; and her mouth twisted in a tender, wistful smile. 'You opened the windows,' she murmured, half teasing, in a cadence almost like singing, 'and you turned out the lights, and left the bed light on so he could read, and kissed him

good night . . . and he said: "Wake me up when you come home." '
Her voice faded, came again: 'And I will, Tony—and hello, Tony . . .
and are you going to be home all night . . . sound asleep, talking in his
sleep . . . open the windows wake me up when you come home . . .
good night, Tony . . .'

Doctor Hethering touched Mark's arm. He turned blindly, understanding that Nan had dropped into delirium again. The room was too
dark. He could not see. The nurse took his arm, leading him; and then
Nan's voice spoke behind him.

'Mark.'

'Yes, darling.' He returned to the bedside.

'Mark,' she whispered. Her hand moved and found his and clutched
it weakly. 'Mark,' she said, smiling with closed eyes. 'Take care of Tony.'

She was for this moment beautiful again. He said: 'We'll take care
of him together, darling.'

'Take care of him,' she insisted. 'Be good to him, Mark. He's all you'll
have of me.'

6

(September 25, 1930)

Mark found himself in the hall, and the nurse, her white uniform a
blur to his dimmed eyes, went beside him along the corridor. His feet
lagged with weariness and his heels pounded, waking echoes, filling the
world with those echoes deafeningly.

'Now lie you down, my dear,' the nurse said when she had led him
back to the bare room. 'Rest you till she needs you again.'

But Mark suddenly dreaded being left alone. 'I think I'll go say good
night to Mrs. Halstead,' he decided.

Mary Halstead had come to the hospital the day Nan was taken ill,
and her baby, a boy, had been born that night. Mark and Nan counted
the Ritchies, the Halsteads, and the Sheffields their most intimate
friends, and the four couples were much together. There was a fine
courage in Ed and Mary, and they knew how to take good fortune and
bad with an equal composure. Ed was not a college man. Beginning as
an office boy in the bank of which Mary's father was the head, he had
worked up to a position in the securities department when he and Mary
met. Her father disapproved her marriage to Ed—for no good reason
unless because her mother, ambitious for Mary to marry wealth, worked

upon him. Nevertheless, Ed and Mary were married, and Mary was quite prepared to live on Ed's small salary, but her parents, though they formally countenanced the wedding, did not readily forgive her; and a month after their marriage, Ed was discharged with no cause given.

'We thought we'd have to wait a long time before we could afford to have any children,' Mary sometimes smilingly explained, speaking of those times. 'But business was bad and Ed couldn't get a new job right away, and we thought three would be company, so we had Edwin as quick as we could.' Ed after some weeks found a place in a brokerage house, serving as a 'customers' man,' and when his clients found he never recommended pointless switches from one stock to another simply to fatten his commission account, they trusted him. In 1924, he fell ill with pneumonia; and Ann, their second child, was born so soon afterward that Emma Sheffield, who had a bawdy tongue, said they should have named her Delirium.

When Mark came to Mary's room tonight, the nurse was about to take the new baby back to its own place, and Mark had a chance to admire it. 'Have you named him yet?' he asked.

'Yes, we're calling him Burt, after my grandfather,' Mary explained. She looked smilingly down at the small head on her arm. 'We seem to have a baby every time anything unpleasant happens to us. It was Edwin when Ed got fired from the bank, and then Ann after Ed's pneumonia, and now Burt when the stock market went pffft! But babies do take your mind off things, you know.' And she asked gently: 'Is Nan . . . Is there any news?'

'Just that she's still alive.' Mark added, remembering Nan's last word: 'She thinks she's going to die. I saw her just now. She was conscious for a moment, and she told me to take care of Tony.'

She did not speak, but he found comfort in her wise silence, glad she refrained from empty reassurances. He stayed a moment, sitting beside her, and then her nurse came to make her ready for the night and Mark left her.

Alone in the room which had been put at his disposal, he lay down and closed his eyes. To do so was to shut out the things he did not want to see, and to summon other things upon which it was pleasant to look. He could see in his memory Nan's long, fair hair falling across her shoulders while she brushed it, sitting before her dressing table, brushing it conscientiously, a hundred strokes, from the scalp clear down to the end of every hair. She used to brush it so after he was abed, and he would lie watching her, laughing at her, teasing her sometimes because she brushed her hair so long, because it took her so long to be ready to come to bed. 'No lady can prepare for the night in less than an hour!' she used to say. She had been threatening for a year or two now to bob her hair, declaring that it was a nuisance, that it would be so much easier to handle if it were short. Almost everyone else had bobbed hair, but Mark had been able to persuade her to leave it as it was. She protested that it made her look like an idiot to wear long hair when everyone else's was short; and she had it thinned out, but she did leave it long.

But now it was short. The nurses had cut it, close to her head, even closer than Tony's hair was cut. When they cut her hair, it was for Mark in some ways the end of the Nan he had known. Even after her countenance was ravaged by sickness, her hair had remained the same, making her real to him; but when her hair was cut, that reality was destroyed. She was no longer Nan. She was a boy with a haggard face, lying still and small in the big hospital bed.

Doctor Hethering came to find him. 'She knew you,' he said.

'Is that a good sign?'

'Every time the clock strikes another hour, it's a good sign.' The Doctor sat down, and Mark watched him without speaking. After a moment, the older man said: 'She speaks often of that boy of yours, speaks always of him and you together. Sometimes she seems to confuse you two in her mind, as though you were one person, or were brothers, instead of father and son.'

'We're pretty close to each other, Tony and I.'

'And she talks a lot about someone named Ruth.'

Mark put his arm across his eyes. 'That's the daughter we didn't have,' he explained. 'You told us we'd never have her, after Tony came; but we sometimes spoke of her.'

Doctor Hethering said almost hurriedly: 'I like the looks of that boy of yours.'

'So do I,' Mark agreed. 'I suppose all fathers feel the same way, but he seems fine to me.' The rain lashed against the window, and a sudden memory came flooding back to him. He lay silent awhile, said at last: 'I remember the day he was born.'

He looked toward the other man, but Doctor Hethering was gone, the door just closing behind him. Mark watched the door for a while, thinking the nurse might appear to summon him again; but when she did not come, he closed his eyes and lay still, all his muscles slack, remembering.

7

(September 26, 1930)

He remembered the night Tony was born, on the ninth of September, eleven years ago, with a northeast rainstorm lashing at the windows, just as the rain lashed the windows tonight. Mark's mother had come on from Ohio to be with them for the great event, and Mark thought of her now. She had been of another generation, the generation which lived and was happy and saw its children grow up before the War. She was gentle and fine; and there were old ways alive in her. 'When I was a girl,' she used to say to Nan, smilingly, that summer while they waited for Tony, 'women who were waiting for their babies did not go out-of-doors in daylight.' But she did not blame Nan for her gaiety, understanding quite well that times had changed. 'Everything changed with the War,' she sometimes said.

She died three years after Tony was born, but Mark tonight remembered her, and he remembered the pleasant world before the War, the world Tony had never known, and he thought his mother had been right. Everything changed with the War. Probably any war meant an end to the world that had gone before. With every war, many things ended—and for millions of men, everything ended, if death was an end. When war began, it was like opening a new book and reading the first page; but the difference was that you could not turn over to the end of the book and see how it came out. You had to read it a day at a time, torn with fears and hopes and hates. Yes, his mother was right. After the War everything was changed.

The change had begun, Mark thought tonight, even before the War. It had begun with the coming of the automobile, and the enactment everywhere of speed laws which as the new invention developed became ridiculous, so that everyone broke the laws. Mark remembered Tony's first automobile ride, in Bob Ritchie's car. Tony sat in the front seat with Bob, and that night when he was preparing for bed, he said:

'Father, when you see a cop, you have to slow down, don't you?'

That was what had happened to people in the years since the automobile came. They habitually broke the laws, and when they saw a cop, they slowed down. Even good citizens broke the traffic laws, just as later they broke the prohibition laws; and they laughed over their success in avoiding or evading punishment. Mark could remember when he himself was a boy in Ohio, and some enterprise was proposed, and one of the other boys said: 'No, we can't do that. It's against the law.' That always ended the argument. If a thing was against the law, you didn't do it.

But that was all changed in the years since Tony was born.

Mark believed that when otherwise good citizens regularly disobeyed a law, the law should be repealed. Respect for the law was the foundation of the state; but the law must deserve respect. If bad laws were made, then the public disobeyed them, and respect for the law was undermined. No one respected laws as such nowadays. Tony had observed on his first automobile ride that if you saw a policeman you must slow down. That was true because every man who drove an automobile regularly broke some law, and it was left to the discretion of the officer to arrest or not as he chose. You were governed by men, not by laws; and if you faced prosecution for law-breaking, your friendship with the enforcing officer or with his superiors might save you.

Automobiles and overzealous legislators had brought about that lawless mind among men. The prohibition law aggravated it. This world in which Tony was passing from boyhood into adolescence was one in which good citizens regularly broke bad laws.

Mark, half asleep, thought of these things, and he thought back to the night Tony was born. The afternoon before, it had begun to rain. The wind had been northeast for a day or two, and Mark knew the rain was coming; and it worried him. When Nan's time came, she must go to the hospital, and that was five miles away, and they would have to telephone for a taxicab to take her there. Mark did not know much about having babies, and neither did Nan, and Mark's mother thought it indelicate to go into such matters in detail; so Mark and Nan were at once ignorant and badly frightened. When Nan woke up that night and woke Mark, and his mother said it was time to take Nan to the hospital, midnight had just struck, and the rain was coming hard. It slashed against the windshield of the car in which they made the trip to the hospital just as it slashed against the windows of the room where Mark lay now.

That night, driving to the hospital, he had thought, somewhere in the back of his mind, that Nan was going to die. He knew Nan thought so too. He and she clung together in the taxi, and he remembered now the set of the driver's shoulders and his head and the cap he wore, a little too small for him. He and Nan had watched that cap in silhouette against the blurred glare on the windshield all the way to the hospital, holding each other tight, very young and very much afraid.

Afterward at the hospital when Tony was being born he had stayed with Nan. He had not wanted to stay with her, because he was sure she was going to die and he did not want to see her die. But she needed him, so he stayed till toward the last they gave her the anaesthetic. When she relaxed and was still, he went into another room and knelt down by the bed there and prayed; and after a while he heard a small squeaking, mewling sound in the hall and he came out, and the nurse showed him something which was hardly to be recognized as a face at all, and told him this was his son.

That was Tony, and Tony was asleep at home now, and he had promised to wake Tony when he came home.

Tony was asleep, and Mark, lying here with his eyes closed was half asleep, half dreaming. His thoughts were half dreams, half memories: memories of Tony becoming pink instead of red, of Tony's eyes beginning to focus, of Tony learning to sit up, of Tony beginning to crawl, of Tony standing up and holding on to chairs and tables, of Tony walking, of Tony's first word. His first word was 'beel.' He meant 'automobile.' He would stand at the window and, holding on to the sill, watch tirelessly the cars gliding by; and for every one that passed he shouted in a gleeful triumph: 'Beel!' Mark and Nan used to watch him and laugh together.

The night Tony had a head cold that settled in his ear, creating a pressure on the ear drum, causing sharp pain, Nan was half sick with a cold herself, so it was Mark who slept in a cot beside Tony's bed. When the pressure in his ear increased sufficiently, the pain woke the little boy; and he might cry out sharply. But at the cry, or at his movement, the pressure each time was relieved. He woke thus every ten or fifteen minutes all night, woke with a cry which roused his father there beside him; and each time Mark asked in the darkness:

'All right, Tony?'

Each time Tony answered: 'Feela fine.' He was not yet old enough to speak more precisely; and he was hoarse from the cold, so that the words were a choked croak.

Mark remembered those hours as he lay here tonight; remembered how each cry had dragged him from the deeps of sleep, how each time he slept again. He must have slept for a while with his dreams now, for when he opened his eyes Doctor Hethering was nodding in the chair near the bed. If Doctor Hethering were asleep, then Nan must be still alive. Every hour she lived was gain, was at least a partial victory. The rain beat hard against the windows.

If Nan died tonight, Mark wondered, what would his life be? He remembered that he had asked himself the same question the night Tony was born; and he had thought then that his life would end if hers ended. Tony had then no place in his thoughts. The baby being born that night was still impersonal, an enemy who threatened Nan and threatened Mark through her. If Mark thought about the baby at all that night, it was with a careful reserve, an attempt to remember that Nan's suffering was not the baby's fault. It did not occur to him that she might die and the baby live.

But tonight, there was Tony. If Nan died, he would still have Tony; and Nan had bidden him take care of their son, and Mary Halstead had said, awhile ago, that children took your mind off your troubles. Mark knew he would find comfort in Tony, if Nan should die. Tony even now was the source of many happy hours; when he came in the morning to wake them, when he called downstairs that he was ready to be put to bed, when he spoke sleepily late at night if Mark went in to say good night.

Mark had taught Tony to swim, he had tried to show him how to swing a golf club, he had patiently played tennis with him, patting the ball back across the net, applauding whenever Tony succeeded in returning it. Once, when the Sheffields went to Europe for the summer, rather than leave the farm empty, they had asked Mark and Nan to live there; and one night Mark and Tony camped out together, near the spring down over the knoll, where they could not see the house and might have been way off in the woods somewhere. Mark cooked supper and then they cut twigs off a hemlock tree in the border of the wood below the spring and made a bed, working through the long summer twilight; and then Mark spread the blankets, and drew Tony in his arms, spoon-fashion, and tucked the blankets around them. The mosquitoes were bad, and Mark did not sleep much; but Tony woke not at all in the night, and he was still asleep when at first gray dawn Mark slid out of the blankets and started the fire. The smoke helped to drive away the mosquitoes, and Mark woke Tony in time for him to wash his face and hands at the spring and to brush his teeth while Mark cooked breakfast. When they came back to the house, Nan was still asleep. It was not yet seven o'clock. She laughed and called them both idiots, but Tony said it had been wonderful; and Mark supported the youngster in this assertion. He was desperately sleepy all that day; and he went to bed at eight that night, but he had always remembered the occasion happily.

If Nan died, Mark thought tonight, he and Tony would be alone in the world, but they would do many things together. He had his profession, and Tony his school; but the boy's summers would be free, and Mark decided that they would go fishing, or take canoe trips, or play golf. They would do whatever Tony wanted to do. By and by Tony would go away to school, and after that he would go to college, and then to law school; and then he would come into the office; and they would work together, preparing cases, trying them. Mark had a sudden vivid picture of himself at the counsel table, Tony at his elbow.

Mark thought he and his son would grow even closer together if Nan died. If Nan had died when Tony was born, Tony might have died with her; but if she died now, Tony was left to him. His world would not be empty, for he would have Tony still. To that thought he clung.

8

(September 26, 1930)

Mark did not open his eyes when the nurse came in, but he heard her whisper as she roused Doctor Hethering. Mark lay still, so they thought him asleep, and Doctor Hethering went out with the nurse. The Doctor did not return, but presently another nurse, younger, came to the door, came in. Mark opened his eyes and she crossed to where he lay. She said in a careful tone, a little awed by her errand:

'Mr. Worth, Doctor Hethering thinks you had better come to her now.'

Mark felt his heart begin a slow pound, so that for a moment he could not move; but then he sat up, wearily, and stood up, waiting for a moment to get his balance, rubbing his eyes. 'I must have been asleep,' he said. 'What time is it?'

'A little after four,' she told him. She opened the door of the lavatory, and turned on the light. 'Would you like to freshen up?' she suggested, anxious to help him, not knowing how: 'you'll feel better.'

He splashed his face with cold water, then followed her out into the hall. In this moment he felt nothing, but he perceived everything. He saw three nurses, standing by the floor desk where the charts were, careful not to look toward him. The nurse who had summoned him opened the door of Nan's room and he went in. She followed him in, closed the door behind her.

Doctor Hethering was beside the bed, his back toward the door. The older nurse stood on the other side of the bed, facing Mark as he came in. Doctor Hethering turned as he entered, and Mark went toward him, looked down at Nan. He saw at once that there was a difference in her breathing. It was dry and harsh, and her respiration quickened while he listened. She seemed to snatch at each breath with a physical effort, snatching faster and faster, breathing deeper and deeper. Then suddenly she appeared to stop breathing altogether, and for seconds her breast did not move, and there was no sound, till softly she began again, snatching at each breath, slowly at first, and then faster and faster, deeper and deeper.

He looked at Doctor Hethering, a question in his eyes. Doctor Hethering did not answer that question with words, yet the answer was plain.

Mark stood uncertainly, feeling that something was expected of him, not knowing what to do. He took hold of the foot of the bed, and he looked down at his own hand and saw the knuckles whiten as his clasp tightened there. As though his touch upon the bed disturbed her, Nan's face contorted in a grimace of pain, and she coughed feebly four or five times, and then seemed not to breathe for a while; and then she began again that soft breathing, its tempo accelerating while the breath rasped harshly in her throat.

Mark looked at Doctor Hethering again and he moved away from the bed toward the door, Doctor Hethering following him. He said in a flat, toneless voice:

'She's worse, isn't she?'

Doctor Hethering did not evade the question. 'Yes.'

Mark felt that there was something he ought to say, something he ought to do. Silence was unbearable. He asked in a low tone:

'Why is her face so flushed on one side and not on the other?'

'It sometimes happens so.'

Nan made a low sound like a tormented groan, and Mark went back toward the bed again. Looking down at her, he felt no grief nor terror, but only a profound and almost impersonal pity.

He stood there for a long time, for a time of which he was not conscious at all. It was broken only when now and then Doctor Hethering with the nurses did something meaningless to Nan, tending her, seeking to ease her, trying this device and that in a desperate battle against the rising tide which would drown her presently. Mark could not always watch her. Sometimes he closed his eyes. That was good, because when he closed his eyes he could see Nan as he remembered her, as he always would remember her. This was not Nan on the bed, suffering and dying. This was someone else, in torment that seemed to have no end.

After a long while he looked around the room as though seeing it for the first time. The window was gray, for day was coming, outside. Day was coming across the city, and presently men and women would be waking, and the crowded streetcars would be trundling in from the suburbs, and automobiles would be flowing in a steady stream along the streets as people hurried to their daily tasks. The world was all about him, heedless of him and of Nan dying here. He remembered that other morning when Tony was born; a morning like this one, with rain against the windows and dawn coming gray across the clouded skies. He remembered how he had prayed that morning, on his knees beside the bed in the room where they had left him to wait, and he found himself praying now. He must have swayed where he stood, for the older nurse touched his arm, said quietly:

'Sit down, man dear. Here's a chair.'

He sat down gratefully, yet resenting the attention, resenting the hospital all about him, the whispering nurses, the Doctor, the scrubbed cleanliness everywhere, the faint smell of disinfectants; resenting all these trappings of sickness and of death. Death was a solitary business. A man or a woman ought to be allowed to die alone.

His chair was close beside the bed. He leaned forward, resting his head on his crossed arms on the foot of the bed. Nan was so little that her feet did not reach this far. The bed was longer than she needed. She needed so little room in which to die.

9

(September 26, 1930)

When he and Doctor Hethering came down in the elevator together, the hospital was beginning to awaken after the hushed silence of the night. They emerged on the ground floor, and Doctor Hethering asked:

'Can I give you a lift?'

Mark said: 'I have my car.' He buttoned his coat, turned up the collar around his throat, pulled his hat low. The Doctor asked:

'Are you all right? Would you like someone to drive home with you?'

'I'm all right, yes,' Mark said. They came out and stopped for a moment in the entry, sheltered from the storm. Mark looked at his watch. 'Tony won't be awake yet,' he said. 'He doesn't have breakfast till half-past seven.'

He stepped out into the rain. Behind him the Doctor stood watching him cross the street, watching him go through the parking place till Mark found his car and stepped into it. He fumbled in his pocket for the keys. He had some trouble in finding them. They were in his right-hand trousers pocket where he carried his loose change; but the first time he felt there, his fingers, still too numb for full perception, did not pick them out. He found them at last, started the car, meshed the gears.

He drove home slowly, with an exaggerated care, like a man who has had a drink too many and is suspicious of his own reactions. He kept to the side of the road, following the curb, using it as a guide. It was near and he could see it. Objects a little way off blurred and became indistinct and meaningless; but the curb was a friendly guide, reassuring, kindly, comforting. Whenever he had to pass an intersection, it was an ordeal before which he hesitated, an adventure into which at the last moment he plunged recklessly, stepping on the throttle, leaping across to safety on the other side. He was so absorbed in these successive adventures that he missed his own turning and drove half a mile beyond before he saw a traffic light which reminded him that he had come too far. He went around the block, because that was easier than turning, and so at last crept home. He drove the car carefully into the garage and turned off the ignition and sat for a moment, breathing hard, as though after prolonged exertion.

He stepped out of the garage and looked up at Tony's window. The window was open, so Tony must be still asleep. Mark went along the stepping stones toward the terrace, and Elin opened the French doors from the living room to admit him.

To find her waiting here, to know she shared his grief, was deeply comforting. When she saw his face, her eyes filled. Without speaking, she helped him off with his overcoat; and she took it and his hat and went to the closet in the hall. She came back with the morning paper, put it in his hands. He asked, in a voice he did not know:

'Is Tony still asleep?'

She said, so softly he hardly heard her: 'Yes.' Then in a stronger tone, clinging to the comfort of the commonplace: 'Your coffee's ready. You drink that, and I'll wake him and you can have breakfast together.'

That was what he wanted, to have breakfast with Tony. He went into the dining room, and Elin brought steaming black coffee. He said: 'Let Tony sleep as long as he can.'

As though understanding that he wished to be alone, she retreated to the kitchen. He laid the paper beside his plate and lifted the cup, but the coffee was scalding hot. He could not drink it quickly.

But there was no hurry. He let it stand, and glanced at the paper beside him. A headline caught his eye.

HITLER PLEDGES
WAR ON TREATY

Cries that Heads Will
Roll when Fascists
Come to Power

Mark felt an incredulous amazement at those words. He lifted the paper and glanced through the first lines of the story under the headline.

> BERLIN, Sept. 25—Adolf Hitler, Fascist leader of Germany, today in Leipsic at the trial of three young Reichswehr lieutenants for high treason, declared that the aim of his party is the overthrow of the Republic and the repudiation of the Treaty of Versailles.

Farther down the column Mark found the quotation upon which the secondary headline was based.

> The Fascist chieftain declared passionately: 'Whenever my party by legal means shall have seized power, there will be constituted a new German Supreme Court. November, 1918, will then find its expiation, and heads will roll.'

Mark thought in a sharp scorn that men, decent men, had not talked in such terms since the French Revolution. This man was clearly mad. Mark tried to remember whether he had ever heard of Hitler before today; and he had a vague impression that he had noticed the name as that of the leader of some small party in Germany. But von Hindenburg was President of the German Republic; and that stout block of a man— who during the War had seemed to the American mind a Moloch devouring helpless millions—now commanded the respect of the world. No one took seriously the shrill cries of the lesser German figures opposed to him; and certainly the name of Adolf Hitler had never made the slightest impression on Mark until now.

He turned the page with an impatient gesture, almost amused. No one talked of heads rolling in the sand today! Hitler was either crazy, or he was a relic of those old days of drawings and quarterings, of burnings at the stake, of torture and death, which the world had put forever behind it a century or more ago. He was an atavism, a throwback to the Dark Ages; but there was light in the world today, and the bleached and pallid monstrosities which dwelt in darkness no longer could survive.

Mark tried to forget, looked at other news; but he could not concentrate on the paper. His thoughts, touched with unwilling terror, kept reverting to that barbarous phrase. Heads will roll! If men thought in such terms, and talked in such terms, then war might come again, a great blood-letting, death to millions.

It might even come in Tony's time!

The thought was intolerable! Mark crushed the paper and thrust it harshly aside. He finished his coffee and went up to wake his son, remembering Nan's words. Tony was all he had left of her now.

II

Time of Peace

(September 1930–June 1931)

I

(Winter 1930–1931)

MARK found it strangely pitiful that Nan's going should leave on the surface of their lives so slight a trace. In the office, absorbed in work, he forgot his grief for hours at a time; and at home, at breakfast with Tony or in the evenings till Tony went to bed, he and the youngster might be as merry together as they had always been.

But after Tony had gone upstairs, calling his father to kiss him good night and to fix the bedclothes and the windows and to leave the light burning so that he could read awhile—Tony always demanded these attentions, as though he knew it pleased Mark to have him do so—the house seemed silent and empty and forlorn. There would be for a while the sounds in the kitchen where Elin was putting all in order; and then she would go quietly up to her room. Sometimes Mark in his loneliness wished to call to her to come and sit with him, but he never did, and after she was gone upstairs, the house was still. Mark usually read late, knowing that he would not sleep easily. He had always been apt to wake early, at the first coming of day; but now he woke before daylight, and lay awake to watch the windows turn from black to gray and then to the bright hues of dawn.

He clung to these wakeful hours, feeling that they were somehow a tribute which would please Nan. He was unwilling to admit that she who had been so much a part of him could depart forever and leave him whole. He would not let himself believe that a life may end with no more disturbance to the scheme of things than the vanishing of one among the myriad stars.

2

(Spring 1931)

In the spring and early summer of the year after Nan died, Mark and Tony took a long automobile trip together, travelling some four or five thousand miles; and they were six or seven weeks upon the road. They left Boston early in May, and to do so involved taking Tony out of school. This sacrilege against the educational gods would not have been possible but for Mark's decision that the headmaster of the Heights School lacked the tact and wisdom which a good preceptor should possess.

Mr. Farthing, the headmaster, was a small, nervous, gray-haired man who had been born with an abiding conviction of his own inferiority to other men. He became a school teacher because he could enlarge himself by a sadistic lingual cruelty toward the boys in his classes; and in his occasional contact with their parents he discovered that most adults are defenseless when the welfare of their children is in question. He founded a school of his own, beginning humbly; but by accusing solicitations in which he pointed out to parents of boys in his charge that their son's education was being handicapped by the lack of proper physical facilities, he raised funds to enlarge his plant. He organized a Parents' Association, holding monthly meetings, at which he harangued these men and women who listened submissively for their sons' sakes. Mark and Nan at first attended, till Mark came to the conclusion that an equal amount of energy devoted by Mr. Farthing to the boys themselves would have been better worth while.

One evening in March, after Tony had said good night and gone upstairs, the doorbell rang. Since Elin too had retired, Mark himself went to the door, expecting to see Bob and Nell Ritchie, who often came over through this winter when he declined all formal invitations. Nell was apt to drop in during the day to inspect the house from cellar to attic. 'I like to keep an eye on things,' she told Mark, and when he said Elin needed no overseeing, she said: 'It's no trouble, and even the best servants must be watched, you know.' Nell was so full of a relentless energy that she was sometimes a nuisance, and Mark had once told Elin he would put a stop to these visitations if she wished him to do so; but she assured him she did not object. 'Mrs. Ritchie likes to feel she's helping,' she explained. 'And she might see something I've missed. He thought some servants would have resented Nell's intrusions, but it was like Elin to accept them as helpfully intended.

Tonight, instead of the Ritchies, it was Mr. Farthing at the door. He had come, he announced at once, to ask Mark to see to it that Tony's home work was more conscientiously done. Tony studied for an hour or so every evening after dinner, and at first, when he ran into difficulties, he had often asked Mark's advice; but Mark found himself helplessly rusty on such things as algebra. Elin heard their perplexed discussions at the dinner table and offered to help, and thereafter Tony sometimes went to her in the kitchen with a puzzling problem. Later, at Mark's suggestion, she began to come into the living room to go over Tony's work with him, and Mark enjoyed watching them at the big table, their heads together. They were like children, sweeping sometimes into gales of laughter at their own mistakes or shouting with an equal triumph when a problem was solved.

He had assumed that Tony's work was well done; but even if it were not, he was completely unwilling to become Tony's taskmaster; and he told Mr. Farthing so. Mr. Farthing said in a hurt, accusing tone that no school could accomplish much if the parents of the pupils refused to cooperate, and Mark told him tolerantly: 'Oh, I won't work against you; but neither will I work with you. I'm not at all sure an eleven-year-old boy ought to be expected to study at home. Tony's in school eight hours a day. I think that's enough time for a boy his age to devote to education.'

This precipitated a discussion, cool on Mark's side, resentful on the other's; and Mr. Farthing's eventual good night was frosty. Mark had afterward a half-guilty feeling that he should have met the little man halfway; but the incident, and the palpable narrowness of Mr. Farthing's mind, set him wondering whether Tony's time might not be better employed under some other direction. The thought of sending Tony away to boarding school—while he himself stayed on alone in this empty house—was intolerable. He sought alternatives, and a fortnight after Mr. Farthing's call, it occurred to him that he might put Tony for a year or two under a tutor.

The idea held a strong attraction. If Tony had a tutor, he would not be held down to a school's rigid schedule, and they could go away together for a week or so, winter or summer, whenever Mark chose. The prospect was enticing and Mark embraced it. He decided that Tony should tutor next year.

But he had not considered the possibility of taking Tony away from the Heights before the end of this school year until one morning late in April old Mr. Ritchie, Bob's father and the senior partner in the firm, sent for him. Mr. Ritchie was a tall, gaunt man, with a huge block-like head and a grim solemnity of countenance which never varied, and which served to accentuate the humor apt to underlie his words. When Mark went into his office, he nodded toward a chair and Mark sat down, and the older man said:

'Well, Mark, it's been a long, hard winter.'

Mark, expecting some discussion of the business of the office, was surprised; yet he realized that what Mr. Ritchie said was true. During this winter since Nan died he had worked hard all day and slept ill at night. He had lost weight, and Mr. Ritchie's words made him realize suddenly that he was desperately tired.

He said: 'It's over now. Spring's on the flood today.'

Mr. Ritchie shook his head. 'We'll have some raw weather yet.' He spoke severely: 'I've been keeping an eye on you, young fellow, and it depresses me. You've held your nose to the grindstone till it's rubbed raw on the end. I want you to get out of my sight. There's no work ahead that the rest of us can't handle. Get out of here. Don't let me see you around here till the first of July at the earliest.'

Mark for a moment did not speak, astonished at his own quick delight. 'I've been thinking I'd take a long vacation this summer,' he admitted.

'Take it now,' Mr. Ritchie said vigorously. 'Take that boy of yours and go fishing, or somewhere. Seeing you around here is more than I can stand!'

'I can't very well take Tony out of school,' Mark suggested, but even as he spoke he felt a faint amusement at his submission to the convention that a few weeks of school were important; and the older man exploded:

'School be damned! It will do him a lot more good to spend a couple of months with you than with a pack of school teachers.' He added: 'And it will do you good, too. You need him, and you need to get out in the sun. Go South, play golf, swim, fish, loaf!' He banged his desk. 'But whatever you do, get out of here. We'll have you sick on our hands.'

Mark snapped his fingers in decision. 'You've talked me into it!' he said cheerfully, and shook the other's hand, and went to clear his desk; and on the spot he dictated a letter to Mr. Farthing, announcing that

Tony would not finish out the school year. He was maliciously amused when he thought what that little man's reaction would be.

3

(Spring 1931)

Mark, even before he left Mr. Ritchie, had half-decided what he and Tony would do. This decision resulted from an encounter which had occurred a few days before. Happening to go alone to the Parker House for lunch, he saw Jerry Crocker, also alone, and asked permission to join him.

Crocker was a few years younger than Mark. A boyhood injury to his foot, as a result of which he limped a little, had kept him from active service in the World War; but he became a war correspondent, and it was in France that Mark had first met him. Afterward Jerry served for eight or nine years in the Washington bureau of one of the New York papers, and he made three trips to Europe to write articles for national magazines on the postwar ferment there. Perhaps because of his slight lameness, he was profoundly shy; but except in feminine company, when he seldom spoke at all, this manifested itself in a defensive violence of expression. His wide knowledge of international affairs had developed in him a profound hatred of the sham and hypocrisy he found in public men, and of what seemed to him their abject stupidity; but for honest blundering he had a surprising compassion. His diffidence may have been responsible for the fact that he made a fetish of privacy; and although he lived somewhere in Greater Boston his telephone, if he had one, was not listed, and even his address was a secret from all but one or two close friends. His native New England thrift, coupled with a shrewd sense of values, had led him into the stock market in 1926 and a complete lack of illusions had rescued him from it in 1929, before the collapse of prices there. Now he had a modest income which he supplemented by writing occasional reviews of weighty books on foreign affairs.

He and Mark met only by chance and at long intervals; but Mark not only respected the other's informed mind, but felt a definite liking for Jerry. He sat down now and ordered, and Jerry asked how he was, and Mark spoke of Nan's death; and Jerry murmured some word of awkward sympathy, and asked whether Mark had any children, and Mark told him about Tony, his eyes lighting as they always did when he spoke of his son.

Jerry had reviewed for the *Atlantic* a recent book, *The Strange Death of President Harding,* and Mark spoke of it, and they agreed that the corruption in Washington during Harding's administration was a part of the moral chaos into which the country descended after the War. Mark himself was just now reading the memoirs of Marshal Foch, and they discussed that book, and this led Mark to remember something he had half forgotten. 'By the way, Jerry,' he asked, 'on your trips to Europe, did you ever run across this man Hitler?'

Crocker looked at him acutely. 'Yes,' he said. 'Why?'

'I had never noticed his name,' Mark confessed, 'till one day last fall. He made a speech, said his party wanted to tear up the Treaty of Versailles, said that if he ever came to power the Germans who signed that treaty would have to stand trial. For treason, I suppose. He talked of chopping off their heads.' He added: 'I've been watching the dispatches about him since. He sounds to me like a dangerous man.'

'He is,' Crocker agreed. 'Dangerous as a rattlesnake. I wrote a piece about him for the *Times,* six or seven years ago. I was in Munich. He had founded the Bavarian National Socialist Party, imitating Mussolini. I heard him make some speeches.'

'What do you think of him?'

'He's a self-important little bastard,' Crocker said with characteristic vehemence. 'He's a great talker, sprays everyone within twenty feet of him when he gets started, screeches like a woman. But he can swing a crowd!'

'I thought the days of orators were past.'

'Don't fool yourself!' Jerry retorted. 'Man, they're just beginning. Orators used to get results, as long as they could find an audience. Then the world got too big for them; but now the radio has given the orator back his audience. If he can get a coast-to-coast hook-up—if he's a candidate for President, say—he can talk to just about every voter in the country, all at once. In the next campaign, bet on the man with the best radio voice. Whoever he is, he'll be elected—and he'll go on being elected till he loses his voice, or till someone better comes along.' He added with a wry grin: 'You know, elections in the past haven't pulled out the votes. I don't suppose a majority of the people eligible to vote in this country have ever cast their ballots at any election; but from now on the radio will get them to the polls. Democracy has never been tried, but now it's going to be. You and I will call it mob rule, and we'll say that the President, whoever he is, is no better than a demagogue; but if we believe in democracy, in majority rule, we'll have to grin and bear it.'

'You really think the best radio speaker will win?'

'Sure.'

'Regardless of whether he has character, or intelligence, or ability?'

'Sure,' Jerry repeated, and he grinned in sardonic reassurance. 'But it may not be so bad. One of the old Romans said that an orator was a good man skilled in speaking. If he was right, and we elect an orator, we'll get a good man anyway.'

Mark smiled, understanding that the other spoke with his tongue in his cheek. 'If Hitler's an orator, is he a good man?'

Jerry answered strongly: 'He doesn't have to be! He starts with the audience already on his side! The hay-brained, blovalating, so-called statesmen who wrote the Treaty of Versailles—after unnecessarily starving Germany for six months, starving thousands of children to death—built his platform for him. I saw those starving children. I was over there. If you turned down their eyelids, the whites of their eyes were a sort of blue green, as if they were already dead. Long before they actually died, they were beyond help. Their physical organization seemed to run down, or atrophy, or something. You could keep them alive for a while, but sooner or later they died. It was a sight you don't forget, and you can be damned sure Germans won't forget it. So they're ready to listen to Hitler now.'

'That was during the War,' Mark reminded him uneasily. 'It was the blockade that beat Germany.'

'This was after the armistice,' Crocker retorted. 'They still kept Germany on starvation rations after she'd surrendered; wouldn't even let her fishing boats go into the North Sea till the treaty was signed.

'And I tell you, Germans remember it. So Hitler's got his platform ready-made. He doesn't even have to remind his audiences about that. They remember it.

'So he talks about Versailles, and when he isn't screaming about what was done to Germany at Versailles, he's screeching about what the Jews did to her during the inflation years. He's as full of speeches as a hen salmon is of eggs, and he throws promises around like cockle-burs—and naturally some of them stick. Mind you, he's talking to people who are still broke, bankrupt, with no jobs. They've nothing better to do than listen. If you wave a piece of raw meat at a pack of starved wolves, they'll pay attention. Well, that's what he's doing. He tells those people that he's going to unite all Germans everywhere, smash France, grab some colonies, kill all the Jews, and raise Hell generally—and the crowds he talks to love it.'

'Does anybody believe him?'

'Sure, every dimwit in Germany believes him, and there are plenty of them. Oh, maybe not as many plain damn fools as there are in Congress, on the average; but plenty. Then a lot of capitalists are on his side, thinking he'll save Germany from Communism; and England is for him, hoping he'll make Germany strong so she can stave off Russia. Foch wanted the Allies to go ahead and smash the Soviets after Versailles. We wouldn't play, and Clemenceau and Lloyd George liked the idea, but couldn't finance it; so all they did was land troops in Siberia and in Odessa and support Germany in the Ukraine and on the Baltic, trying to help Admiral Kolchak, but the Soviets smashed the lot of them. England will back Hitler or anyone else who will stand up against Russia today.

'So Hitler's got the mob on his side, and the capitalists, and the tacit backing of England, and of course that means France. The sensible Germans are against him, but he's put all the roughnecks in Germany in uniform to beat up his opponents, and they're scaring the others into line.'

Mark asked uneasily: 'Will he ever come to power?'

'Come to power? Why, man, he's practically there! His Storm Troops are the strongest gang of organized thugs the world ever saw, and he himself is the loudest-mouthed blatherskite the world ever saw—and the most persuasive.'

'Is he an able man?'

Jerry hesitated. 'I didn't think so when I was over there,' he admitted. 'But he's made himself the most powerful individual in Germany, so he must have something. No one whose head was stuffed with hay could do that.'

'I was disturbed by his "heads will roll" speech,' Mark confessed. 'But probably that was just a piece of bombast!'

'Don't fool yourself! The guy's not playing marbles. Maybe his gang haven't cut off any heads yet, but they've done everything else in the mayhem line, and they'll do more.'

'This talk of his about cancelling Versailles, that would mean war,' Mark argued. 'But Germany's disarmed and bankrupt. She can't start a war.'

'All Europe's bankrupt,' Crocker assured him. 'The Allies made Germany stop spending money on armaments, but they've gone ahead themselves, spending like water, while Germany has had economy forced on her. She's better off financially than any of them now. She's a bankrupt, but with plenty of concealed assets.'

Mark said thoughtfully: 'I suppose lack of money never prevents a war. The financial experts said the last war would be over in six months, said no one could afford to keep it up longer than that, but they were wrong.' He suggested: 'But doesn't the drain of her reparation payments take all the money Germany can raise?'

'That's due to stop,' Jerry assured him. 'Germany's telling the world now that she can't pay any more, and if necessary she'll throw her finances into chaos to prove it. She won't go on paying reparations—any more than the rest of them will pay their war debts to us. We'll be left holding the bag.'

'I can't believe that England will ever repudiate her obligations.'

'Don't be that way, man,' Crocker told him scornfully. 'England's policy since the armistice has been aimed right straight at that target. She'll try to get us to cancel—has tried. But if we won't do it, sooner or later, she'll welch. Make up your mind to that. Her angle is that we sold them a lot of war materials, cashed in plenty on the war, and that now we're trying to collect for a dead horse!'

'But two fifths of our loans to the Allies were made after the armistice!'

'Sure. We pay and pay and pay—and in the next war we'll hold the bag again.'

Mark looked soberly at his plate. 'The next war?' he echoed. 'You think another war is coming?'

'Sure.'

'How soon? My Tony's not yet twelve years old. I hate to think he'll have to get into it.'

Jerry said in dry, ironic passion: 'A good many other people feel the same way, but they can't help themselves. Who was it said: "In time of peace, prepare for war." In other words, save your money, build some ships and planes and guns, and raise some boys to be soldiers. Make cannons—and breed cannon fodder! That's what these piping times of peace are for!'

4

(May 1931)

As a result of this talk with Crocker, Mark was persuaded that
Tony's young manhood might see war again let loose upon the world—
by Hitler or some other. That would be hideous enough; and yet was
not the thing most to be feared that blind confusion of mind, that
passive acceptance of lies, that sheeplike willingness to be led by the
nose which had characterized the years from 1914 to 1917? The threat
to Tony's life was dark and terrible; but even worse was the threat to
Tony's capacity for clear thinking. If a man, by choice or not, died
for a cause he understood and loved, why, men had gladly died for
such causes from the beginning and would again. But Mark was
unwilling that Tony should be led blindly into the chaos that might
be ahead. He determined that if it was in his power to do so, he would
teach his son to see straight, to think for himself, to form an independent judgment untainted by the infection in other minds all about
him. There had been talk enough since the last war of the Allied
propaganda which had then bemused the American mind. Men—men
in high places—had frankly admitted that to accomplish what seemed
to them good, to lead the United States into the war, they had lied.
If another war came, that machinery of lies would again be set in
motion; but it seemed to Mark that there could be no slavery so depraved as the slavery of the mind, no submission so abject as that which
permitted a few men to persuade millions that they thought thus
and so.

From that submission, from that slavery, he wished to save Tony;
but if Tony were to learn to think for himself, he must be equipped
to do so; and if his thinking were to be sound, his conclusions must be
based on a broad and a firm foundation of knowledge and of understanding. He raised this point with Jerry, urged the other to come to
dinner some evening. 'I'd like to have Tony talk to you,' he said. 'It
would do him good, help him see straight and think straight when the
time comes.'

But Jerry declined. 'I stick pretty close to home,' he said. 'And anyway, telling people things doesn't teach them anything. They've got
to do their own thinking. One big trouble with the world today is that
we believe a lot of things we hear or read, where if we had the sense

God gave little apples we'd know we were being kidded.' And he urged: 'The thing to do with that boy of yours is to teach him all you can about his own country. He's an American. Well, damn it, let him see for himself what that means. I spend about half of every year travelling, myself; travelling here at home. There's a hell of a lot of the United States outside of New England—and everybody knows it except New England.'

This had long been Mark's opinion, and Jerry's advice recurred to him when Mr. Ritchie insisted that he and Tony go away for a while together. Jerry was right. If a man were to learn to look at the world with a level eye, he must first know himself, and know the country of which he was a citizen.

Mark made his plans, and the evening after his talk with Mr. Ritchie, he told Tony they would leave at once, take the car, spend weeks upon the road. 'I want to show you where some of your ancestors came from, son,' he explained. 'And where I was born, and where I lived when I was a boy; and I want you to see at least a part of this country you live in. I don't want you to grow up to be one of those New Englanders who think there's nothing south of Washington or west of Albany.'

Tony was delighted at the prospect; but he was much more interested in the fact that they would drive than in the places they were to see. He urged that they buy a new car for the trip, but Mark told him smilingly: 'There's lots of mileage in the old car still. If we bought a new one, it would be old by the time we came home.'

'The one we've got is apt to go to pieces under us,' Tony argued. His enthusiastic interest in automobiles had never faltered. 'The brake linings are gone, and we get a knock on every hill, and there's a broken leaf in the right rear spring, and the spring shackles rattle, and . . .'

Mark chuckled. 'I'll have it put in shape,' he promised. 'It will get us there and back.'

After dinner, Tony raced away across the street to tell the Ritchie children his great news. Betty was a year or two older than he, and since girls mature more rapidly than boys, she was already intolerant of Tony's young eagernesses. Will was Tony's age, an outsized young-ster who outgrew his clothes so fast that Nell was constantly protesting, as if it were Will's fault. She was apt to tell older people, in his pres-ence, what a trial he was to her, while Will sat grinning and suffering unspeakably. Will had not yet learned to control his own members; and he was forever tripping over rugs or lamp cords, or knocking things off tables. His clumsiness was another of Nell's favorite topics; and he so often heard himself discussed with strangers that he sought to avoid being put in the position of a helpless listener, slipping away at the first opportunity, or sitting in wretched silence when he could not escape. Nell, after her audience was gone, sometimes reproached him for 'sitting there like a bump on a log,' and she demanded: 'Why can't you be at ease with company, the way Betty is?' The result was that Will heartily disliked his elder sister.

Jan, still in pigtails and with a rich crop of freckles, was two years younger than Tony; and when he permitted, she followed him like a shadow, stoutly taking his part against Will in their occasional arguments, intensely loyal. She and Will and Tony could be content together; but Betty held aloof from them and went her own way. She was already pretty in a masklike fashion. Of the three, Mark liked her least, and he was even a little afraid of her poised assurance. He and Will were on good terms; but Jan—perhaps because of her fondness for Tony—was his favorite among them.

While Tony was across the street this evening, Mark spoke to Elin, telling her his plan. 'We'll be away about six weeks,' he explained. 'You've taken mighty good care of us this winter. You're due for a long vacation.'

She asked in an almost breathless haste: 'Will you want me when you come back?'

'Heavens, yes!' he laughed. 'We can't get along without you, Elin!'

'I wouldn't want to work for anyone else!'

'What will you do while we're gone?'

Her eyes were alight with many plans. 'Well, there's the house to clean first,' she said. 'I'll take down the curtains and wash them, and there's some painting needs to be done, and we ought to varnish the linoleum in the kitchen.'

Mark was touched by her eager happiness in these projects. 'As though the house were her own,' he thought. 'And of course in a way it is. Loving a thing and taking care of it is one way to own it.' He left all such arrangements in her hands. 'I wish we could take you with us,' he admitted smilingly; but she laughed and said she had too much to do here at home. He nodded, liking her use of the word. This was her home, of course; the only home she knew.

He put the car in the shop for a complete overhaul. Their departure was thus delayed forty-eight hours, and he had time to receive and to toss aside Mr. Farthing's stiffly indignant answer to his letter. Elin worked tirelessly putting their clothes in order, darning and mending,

washing and ironing, packing Tony's bags. The night before they were
to start—Mark wished to get away at dawn, ahead of traffic—they
stowed all but the last bags in the car. Elin woke them while it was
still dark, and gave them breakfast. At the last minute Tony threw
himself into her arms and kissed her soundly, and Mark was tempted
to do the same thing. When they were in the car, she urged: 'Now
be careful, Mr. Worth. And have a good time. And I'll have everything
nice for you when you come home.' Mark, as he backed out of the
garage, thought Nan might have given them a like good-bye.

5

(June 1931)

They made Washington in one long first day upon the road and
spent four days there, taking one of those days to drive to Gettysburg.
Then they pushed on toward Richmond. The immediate subtle changes
in the character of the landscape impressed Tony, and he said presently:
'This is the first time I've been in the South, except just when we went
out to the cemetery at Arlington.'

'You've Southern blood, you know,' Mark reminded him. 'We're
taking this trip not only to show you places, but to give me a chance to
tell you something about your forebears. It's a good thing for a man
to be conscious of his ancestors, because as long as he lives he'll be
recognizing in himself some of the traits they displayed.' He added
smilingly: 'I don't mean just knowing that you are descended from—
William the Conqueror or Henry the Eighth, or someone like that.
Most people, who brag about being descended from some eminent man
in the fourth or fifth generation, forget they are also descended from
say fifteen other men and women who lived at the same time and who
were perhaps completely commonplace. They draw their family tree
upside down, with the big name at the top, and call themselves kin to
all the great man's descendants; but the useful and interesting family
tree is one in which—instead of the branches being descended from the
trunk, the trunk is descended from the branches, so that you can look
at it and see who all your ancestors were. They all survive in you, the
great men and the small, the good and the bad, you know.'

And he said: 'You come from good solid people, Tony. Most of
them were educated men. My mother's paternal ancestors landed in

Massachusetts in 1630, and they were usually either lawyers or ministers. My great-grandfather on Mother's side went to Ohio in 1798, and my grandfather, her father, went from there to Mississippi in 1835. That's the New England strain in you. My mother's mother's people came to Virginia about 1660, and after two generations they went to Georgia, and after a hundred years or so, some of them went on to Mississippi, where my mother and I were born.'

Southward from Richmond they took for their itinerary the path of that migration of the generations, exploring roads that led down to tidewater between Richmond and Norfolk in the region where their forebears had lived, avoiding tourist routes, but seeking out plantations secret and beautiful, while Mark, from the wealth of his own knowledge of history, re-created for his son the prodigal and gracious loveliness of these regions in the years before the War and made Tony see the land as it had used to be. Thence they went to Augusta, Georgia, where one of Mark's mother's ancestors had been a judge and a great man more than a hundred years before; and from Augusta they turned west to Mississippi.

'Your great-great-grandfather went West about 1820,' Mark explained. 'He settled in Beacon, Mississippi, where your grandmother and I were born. My mother, your grandmother, went North from there to Ohio University, in Athens, because her father's father had lived near Athens, and she had relatives there. She met my father there. He was an Ohio farmer's son. They loved each other, and he came South and they were married and he planned to stay in Beacon. He read law—that was the way most people studied law in those days—in her father's office; but a year after I was born, her father died and they moved to Ohio.'

Beacon was a little town, a few hundred white people and twice or thrice as many negroes, halfway up the eastern tier of Mississippi counties. Mark himself had not been here since he was eleven years old, but he and Tony were welcomed by many kinfolks, uncles and cousins by the score, who contested for the privilege of entertaining them.

They stayed with Tom Yerkes, Mark's second cousin, president of the Beacon Bank. He was a fat, bald, amiable man in an alpaca coat and a broad black hat, a widower with a married daughter and two sons who had homes of their own: and he lived alone in a ramshackle big house with an old negro named Jake and an enormously fat Sally, Jake's daughter, to cook and tend for him. One day Jake brought his mother, old Mammy Lou, a wrinkled, ancient crone who had been Mark's nurse when he was a baby, to pay her respects.

Their days were full with visiting, but in the long evenings Mark and Tom Yerkes sat and talked for hours; about the scandalously low price of cotton, and about the deficiencies of negro labor, and about politics—Tom was sure Hoover would be beaten next year unless prosperity ceased to hide just around the corner—and about European affairs and whether the war debts should be cancelled; and their talk was larded with tales about the sayings of the negroes, at which the two men laughed together. Tony—for whom on this trip an eight o'clock bedtime was forgotten—might sit and listen to them till his eyes blurred and his lids fell and old Jake came to lead him away to bed.

They went together one day—Mr. Yerkes and Mark and Tony—to Longstreet Dent's plantation, a few miles out of town. Mark had spent some happy days there as a boy. Tom Yerkes and Mr. Dent—whom Mark called Uncle Long—had business together; something about Uncle Long's notes in the bank, and the difficulty of raising money to make a new crop of cotton when most of last year's crop was still in the warehouses unsold. Uncle Long had a shock of white hair and a merry blue eye and a mouth full of gold teeth which were the envy of every negro on the plantation. Tony, listening to the business talk that first afternoon, wondered why Uncle Long wanted to make a crop when they all seemed to agree that he would lose money by doing so; and he asked the question, and Uncle Long said:

'Why, sonny, I've got right around seven hundred darkies here on the plantation, and if I don't make a crop they don't eat, and they'd scatter like dead leaves on a windy day, so I'd never get them back again. If every white man in the South quit raising cotton, there'd be millions of darkies starving, begging on the streets. We have to do it, whether we make or lose.'

Uncle Long kept them for supper and the night; and though Tom Yerkes went back to town next morning, Mark and Tony stayed a day or two more. Mark relived his boyhood days here, and he showed Tony the very gun—an old army musket made over to peaceful uses—with which he had on one of his visits shot a meadowlark.

'It was the first bird I ever killed,' he said. 'I wasn't as old as you, Tony, but Uncle Long gave me this old shotgun and two shells and let me go hunting alone. I saw the meadowlark on the ground and put the gun to my shoulder and walked toward it till it flew and then—by some miracle—killed it.'

Tony murmured: 'Gosh! I've never even shot a gun!'

'Maybe we can go duck shooting next fall,' Mark suggested, and he laughed at his own memory, and added: 'I shot at a blue jay flying overhead that same day. I missed the blue jay, but the kick knocked me down and made my shoulder black and blue.'

Back in Beacon for a few days more, he found and showed Tony the swimming hole in the river where he had once seen a water moccasin with a large bass in its mouth, the bass unable to escape, the snake unable to subdue its prey, so that their struggles drove all the swimmers out of the water.

'I wasn't in the water,' Mark remembered. 'I hadn't learned to swim.'

Tony laughed and said: 'I'll bet if you had been in the water, you'd have got out mighty quick.'

'I'll bet I would,' Mark agreed. 'I always hated snakes. I'll tell you another snake story.' They drove out into the country to the river where he and his Southern cousins had used to set trotlines to catch catfish. 'We had to put them out after dark and take them up before daylight,' he told the boy. 'That was so the negroes wouldn't find them and steal them. One morning at first dawn I was pulling in the line over the bow of the boat, and there was a water moccasin, drowned, on one of the hooks. When I saw it, I dropped the line and just then a wildcat screamed on the bank quite near us, and I squalled and jumped the length of the boat, falling all over the other boys. I've never been so scared before or since!' They laughed together at the picture he painted.

When at last they said many good-byes to the Beacon folk and started northward, Tony was full of questions about what he had seen; about the way Uncle Long cussed the darkies, and how they seemed to like it, and about the slow, easy way everyone talked. 'And Father, Uncle Long and Mr. Yerkes and most of the men their age chewed tobacco all the time,' he commented.

Mark chuckled. 'That's right.'

'I never saw anybody chew tobacco before.'

'You've seen a lot of things on this trip you never saw before,' Mark agreed. 'That's why we came, Tony.' And he asked: 'Did you like the people?'

'Gosh, yes, they're wonderful. Everybody was so glad to see us, and wanted us to visit them and everything.' He grinned at his own memories. 'And I never saw so many good things to eat.' Then he added doubtfully: 'But they're all awfully poor, aren't they?'

Mark laughed. 'I suppose they are. I never stop to think whether they're rich or poor—and neither do they.'

Tony drew a deep breath. 'Gosh,' he said. 'It's certainly not like New England.'

'That's what I wanted you to see and to understand,' Mark assented. 'You know, people—literary people—used to talk about the great American novel, which someone was going to write some day. But it will never be written. America's too big and too various to be neatly packed into the pages of any one book. Boston and New England are—you may almost say—a country by themselves. So is the great industrial region, from Massachusetts to Delaware, and west through Pittsburgh. So is the Border South; and so is the Deep South.' He added: 'And you'll find the Middle West largely different from any of them.

'We're headed now for Hardiston, Ohio. I lived there when I was a boy, except that we came down to Mississippi every winter to visit. You've seen where my mother's side of the family came from; New England and the South. Now we'll see where my father's people lived. His father came to this country, with his father, my great-grandfather, in 1839.'

'From England?'

'No, from Wales.'

Tony looked up quickly. 'You lived in Wales for a while, before you went to college, didn't you?'

'Yes. My father was consul, in Cardiff, and we were there for a year or two. Of course we saw a lot of England, too; two months in London, and Stratford, and Kenilworth, and so on.'

'Did you like it over there?'

Mark said: 'No. We were homesick.' He added thoughtfully: 'You see, son, we didn't like English ways. Everyone over there either looked down on everyone else or looked up to them. We thought they were snobs. And there were so many dreadfully poor people, pale and thin and undersized. We were citizens of a young and impatient nation, and of an even younger Mid-Western community, and when anything seemed to us to be wrong, we thought something ought to be done about it. What we didn't see was that the British had already learned the wisdom—as Henry Ford said in the book of instructions which came with his Model T Ford—of letting the car alone as long as it ran.

It's no part of the British habit of thought to attend to tomorrow today; but if today needs attention, they muster an extraordinary energy and an unshakable resolution and attend to it!'

Tony said quickly: 'They had to get us to help attend to things in the War! Germany would have licked them if we hadn't!'

Mark smiled. 'We helped, yes,' he agreed. 'But England wasn't beaten, Tony. England still had her fleet. France might have been beaten.' He added thoughtfully: 'As a matter of fact, I think France was beaten, despite our help. I think Germany won that war. Of course, she lost a lot of men and a lot of money, but most of it was borrowed money and she went into bankruptcy and never paid it back; and her high birth rate soon made up for the men she had lost. But France lost not only men and money, but things—factories, machinery. I think France is weak today. I suspect that if she ever gets into another war with Germany, she'll be crushed.'

Tony looked sharply at his father. 'Do you think there'll be another war when I grow up?'

'No,' Mark said, too vehemently. 'No, not in your lifetime, son. And certainly, if there is, we'll not be in it. We learned our lesson, once for all.' He was not so sure as he wished to seem to be, but Tony need not yet know his forebodings.

On the way North they stopped overnight at Chattanooga and drove up Lookout Mountain, and Mark told Tony the story of that battle. Then they traversed the beautiful bluegrass lands of Kentucky, and crossed the river and came into Ohio; and as they followed the winding road through the lovely hills toward Hardiston, Mark spoke of his boyhood there.

'We moved North when I was a baby,' he explained. 'Beacon's changed since then, and so has Hardiston; but the people and their ways have changed more than the places.' He smiled. 'You see, Tony, I was born in the Victorian age. Prohibition has taught us all to drink nowadays, but when I was a boy in Hardiston, self-respecting men didn't drink in the presence of ladies, and ladies didn't drink—or smoke —at all.' He hesitated and said, after a moment: 'I've seen other changes, too. When I was a boy, we had none of the so-called modern conveniences. I've seen the first interurban traction lines come—and go—and I've seen the first coming of the telephone, and of running water, and of electric lights and automobiles and moving pictures and radio. For people of my age or older there's nothing new in this, but for you it may be worth remembering. You're probably wondering how we ever got along without them? Well, we got along without them very well.'

'Did people drive around in carriages?'

'Or walked,' Mark assured him; and he said reflectively: 'I sometimes think we were better off. There weren't so many things we worried about getting and keeping. Today, advertising has made us all feel that there are certain things we can't do without; but I tell you, Tony, there are a lot of things we can do without and never miss them. There are so many things we never wanted till someone told us how wonderful they were. We're a nation of salesmen, but I sometimes think we'd be a lot happier if we never let anyone sell us anything, if we just bought things as we found we needed them. Our manufacturers spend more of their energy persuading us that we want what they make than they do in making what we want.'

6

(June 1931)

Hardiston, by comparison with Beacon, was a metropolis; a lively town of five or six thousand people in the southern Ohio hills. Tony had seen his grandfather twice or thrice before, on Daniel Worth's occasional visits to their home in Boston. Mark's father was editor of the *Hardiston Journal*, a solid, chunky man not as tall as Mark, with an arresting habit of thought, and a way of commenting on the simplest matters in such terms as to open even Tony's eyes to new points of view. He was a tremendous reader. Tony had never seen a house so full of books as this one. They filled the shelves and littered the tables and the desk in his grandfather's study; there were trunks and boxes full of them in the attic, and they were gathering dust and mold in piles in the cellar.

In Hardiston Tony was surprised to find that a fair proportion of the people he met had been in Boston and had seen parts of Boston— Bunker Hill, Faneuil Hall, the church where the lanterns for Paul Revere were hung, the Library and the Art Museum—which he himself had never visited. He spoke of this to his father and grandfather, in some surprise, and Dan Worth chuckled, and Mark said:

'Yes, of course. Middle-Westerners travel all over the country, if they can afford it. When I was a baby we went South every winter, and before I went away to school, I'd visited in Ohio and Indiana and Kentucky and once in Philadelphia.' He added: 'Father and Mother made one trip East, and then they sent me to a boys' camp in Maine for two years, and then to school in West Newton.' He smiled. 'I remember how surprised I was to find that the boys at school had never been outside of New England—except perhaps to go abroad. The boys in school seemed to think Ohio was half wilderness, half farms. When I told them that there were more schools and colleges in Ohio than in Massachusetts—I didn't know whether it was true or not, but I was on the defensive—they didn't even take the trouble to call me a liar. They just laughed!'

'They're sort of the same way still,' Tony confessed. 'I never thought Ohio would be the way it is.'

Dan Worth remarked: 'The New Englander is a mental turtle!' And Mark assented.

'That's true,' he admitted. 'I know a lot of otherwise intelligent men who know nothing of their own country; but they know London and Paris, and Berlin and Munich and Rome. That's probably why their attitude toward foreign affairs is so different from that of the people here in the Middle West. An Ohio man feels at home anywhere in his own country, but many Bostonians are more at home in London than in Cincinnati, or Chicago.'

Mark's father commented: 'Back about 1808 there was some talk that New England might secede from the United States. That talk came to nothing; but in many intangible ways she has done so.'

Mark smiled, and Tony watched the two men, his eyes turning from one to another. 'What you say is true, of course,' Mark agreed. 'But there's another side to it. With the Spanish-American War, the United States became a world power; a citizen of the commonwealth of nations, with responsibilities as well as privileges. At least that's the New England point of view. I know very few people here would agree, but possibly New England is right and you are wrong.'

'Possibly,' the older man admitted. 'But the danger in that point of view is that it's apt to lead us to try to reform the world. I never had much sympathy with foreign missionaries—religious or political. For one thing, they're apt to become bigots, sure that they're right and that the other fellow is wrong. And for another—any man who wants to help other people ought to try to improve himself first. After he's done a good job on himself, he'll find a few problems still to be settled close at home.'

During their days in Hardiston, Tony and Mark and Dan Worth took long walks through the surrounding countryside, and Tony saw the log house in which his grandfather had been born, and Mark showed his son the places that had been familiar to him as a boy; the swimming holes—Tony was astonished that anyone would swim in the coffee-colored water—and the bends where he had fished; the caves and gulches where they had used to go on picnics or where he and his father had cooked their lunch on all-day tramps together; the secret springs of icy water, the farm south of Hardiston where he had spent many of his boyhood summers with his grandfather, the creek where he had learned to skate.

Once, passing a farmhouse, Dan Worth told Tony that Morgan's raiders had stopped there; and Tony asked who they were, and his grandfather said: 'They were Southern soldiers, cavalrymen, who made a swing up through here during the War.'

'Gosh!' Tony exclaimed. 'Do you remember the Civil——' He corrected himself, recalling his father's warning before they reached Mississippi. 'I mean the War Between the States?'

The older man chuckled. 'No,' he admitted. 'But I sometimes think I do, because there was so much talk about it when I was a boy. People don't forget wars quickly. That's the trouble with most of us. We remember the exciting times, and tell tall stories about them, and forget the quiet fruitful years between. Even your histories give most of their space to wars. As a matter of fact, real history is the history of the way of life and the way of thought of the average man. Wars are just an interruption in his progress toward whatever goal there is at the end of the road. I'd like to write a history sometime, a history of what ordinary men did and thought from decade to decade. I'd dismiss all wars with a paragraph something like this. "From 1861 to 1865, and to a diminishing degree for fifteen years thereafter, war and its aftermath distorted the lives of most Americans; but by 1880 they began to resume their normal ways."' He smiled at his own thought. 'But no one would read it, or study it. We like to read about fighting, and heroes; and every so often we get the fidgets, want some excitement, and then the first thing you know, here comes a war.'

Tony found his grandfather sometimes puzzling, sometimes amusing, always interesting. He liked to spend the day with the older man at the *Journal* office, where men were forever stopping to talk awhile; and when at last he and Mark started East again, Tony found that it was the newspaper office which he remembered with the greatest interest.

'I was editor of the *Journal* for four months once,' Mark told him, when he spoke of this. 'I used to work in the office when I was about your age, just getting into my first long pants. My job was to sweep out, and to build the fires, and I learned to set type and to run the presses. Then I went East to camp, and to school, and then to Wales, and then to college. The summer after my sophomore year I worked on a newspaper in Oklahoma City. I finished college in three and a half years, and went home to Hardiston at the end of the first semester, senior year, and ran the paper while Father was in the State Senate.'

Tony asked: 'Did you go to Law School before you went to war?'

'Yes.' Mark added: 'Mother was in Wellesley then. I used to go out from Cambridge on the trolley to see her. We were already planning to be married; but when the United States went into the War, I decided to enlist. So we didn't get married till I came home.'

Tony was silent for a while, considering this. He asked then: 'Did you want us to be in the War?'

Mark hesitated for a moment, remembering. 'I had the Middle-Western point of view,' he said at last. 'New England people—most of the men I knew—thought Germany was damned when she invaded Belgium. I didn't feel that way. You see, Tony, it's a mistake to speak of the laws of war, to think treaties can override national necessities. War is the negation of international law, just as a fist fight between two men is the negation of criminal law. In criminal law, a man who thinks his life is in danger may do anything, even to killing another man, without being held legally culpable. It isn't even necessary that his life be actually in danger, if he can prove conclusively that he thought it was. Probably all nations in war think they are fighting in self-defense. In the World War, Germany had persuaded herself that if Russia mobilized, since France and Russia were allies, she would have to attack France quickly and overwhelmingly. The quickest way to do that was through Belgium.'

He added after a moment: 'Most of the fellows I knew thought I was pro-German because I didn't blame Germany for invading Belgium, and because I didn't believe the atrocity stories. Any war is an atrocity, of course; but I didn't believe that the Germans were killing women and children for fun. I tried to keep my common sense, to see the truth back of the lies—propaganda, they called them—which a lot of people believed. I was a Middle-Westerner, you see. The Middle West felt as I did. In April, 1917, just before we went into the War, I came out to Hardiston for a few days. On that trip I talked to fifty-eight strangers, on the train, on trolleys, on street corners. I asked each one: "Do you think we should go into the War?" One man said: "Yes." He was a member of the Ohio National Guard. The others all said: "No, positively no." '

Tony protested: 'But if you felt that way, then why did you enlist?'

'After your country is in a war,' Mark assured him, 'every decent man wants to do all he can to win, as quickly and completely as possible. In Hardiston County, in spite of the way they felt, they oversubscribed every Liberty Loan four or five times; and there were so many volunteers from the county that almost no men were ever drafted from there.'

'What did Mother think about your enlisting?'

'She said I must do it if I wanted to.'

The youngster's eyes were wide. 'Were you in a lot of battles?'

'Our trenches were shelled pretty hard one night, the first time we went into the lines—if you call that a battle. And after the Germans were on the run, I was in one attack. I'd just got my commission then.'

'Was it pretty bad?'

Mark for a moment did not answer. He remembered Corporal Knowles, who went insane under the shock of that first barrage and never recovered. He remembered the cold sweat of fear upon his own forehead, and the coppery taste of fear in his mouth; and he remembered the smell of death, and the green-hued faces of the dead, and the screams of wounded men. 'Pretty bad,' he said mildly. There were some things which, God willing, Tony need never know.

'Did you kill a lot of Germans?'

Mark said thoughtfully: 'I saw Germans—except wounded and prisoners—just twice; and they were a mile or so away. That was during this attack. It wasn't as exciting as you might think. We just walked ahead, over some low hills and across some fields; and guns and trench mortars and machine guns were banging away at us. About half of us were killed or wounded, but we didn't see anyone to shoot at. Mostly it was just walking forward, feeling terribly alone. The nearest man would be maybe fifty feet away to one side or the other. The worst time was when we went through a forest of little low evergreens where you couldn't see anyone, and the machine-gun bullets were cutting twigs all around you. Not being able to see made it bad. It wasn't so tough when you could see other men around you, scattered across the fields.'

'Did any of the bullets hit you?'

'No. Men were hit, killed, or wounded, all around me; but I didn't get a scratch, not till later.'

Tony looked at him with wide eyes. 'What happened?'

Mark smiled faintly. 'It was after our—attack was over, in a lull. I'd gone back to regimental headquarters to report, and a salvo of shells from one of our own batteries hit the post. I got a splinter in my eye. It's never been as good as the other since.'

'Gosh,' Tony protested. 'Your own men shot you! What did they do that for?'

'Well, we weren't trained soldiers, you know. We were amateurs, and we had to pay for our ignorance. We made a lot of mistakes. A lot of us were killed who need not have died if we'd been better prepared.'

'Were a lot of your men killed in that attack?'

'A lot of them, yes.'

Tony asked again: 'Did you kill any Germans?'

Mark said with a smile: 'No, not as far as I know. I never fired a rifle or a pistol—except on the target range—all the time I was in France. In that battle, the only one in which I took part, not a shot was fired by our outfit. We never saw anything to shoot at. The Germans who were killing us were out of sight, far away. All we did was walk forward and jump down into the trenches the Germans had abandoned.' Mark added: 'But I did drop a grenade down into a dugout. I've often wondered whether there was anyone in it, wondered what they were like, whether I'd have found them good company, in normal times. I hope there was no one there, but I never did know.'

They drove East through West Virginia and came to Gettysburg again, and to Harrisburg; and they saw the hideous ravages of man in the anthracite fields around Mauch Chunk, and spent a night at Poughkeepsie, and next day sped toward home.

'So now you've seen where your ancestors lived,' Mark told his son, as they came into familiar surroundings. "Don't ever forget that you're more than a New Englander. Out of your eight great-great-grandparents, two went from Massachusetts to Ohio, two went from Georgia to Mississippi, one lived in California, one in Oregon, one in Minnesota, and one—your mother's great-great-grandmother—came from Germany. Two of your great-grandparents came from Wales. Your grandparents came from Mississippi and Ohio and Michigan and Minnesota. You've all those blood strains in you, Tony. You're not a Westerner, nor a Southerner, nor a New Englander. You're an American.'

7

(June 20, 1931)

Mark had telegraphed ahead to Elin that morning from Pough-keepsie; and through the last hours of their journey he was increasingly impatient to reach home. These weeks of constant daily companionship with Tony, in which they drew so close together, had been rich and happy ones; but he was, he admitted, tired of touring. It would be good to come once more to the familiar house, to find Elin waiting to welcome them. He was eager to see her again, thinking how her eyes would shine with gladness. When they turned the last corner, Tony cried: 'Blow the horn so she'll know we're coming!' Mark did so, sending long blasts of forewarning ahead of them. Elin must have been on the alert, for she came running out to the driveway, crisp in her fresh uniform, glowing with happiness at sight of them. Mark had forgotten how beautiful she was. Tony sprang from the car into her arms, and Mark, watching them, conscious of his own great pleasure in seeing her again, remembered what Nan had said, long ago. 'I shan't blame you if you fall in love with her.' He smiled. That would never happen, of course. Nevertheless, he was glad to be at home again, glad to clasp her hand; and they all talked together while she helped unload the car and carry the bags into the house.

Mark had paid little attention to the newspapers during his absence. Reading strange papers made him feel like a stranger. But he knew that Germany, as Jerry Crocker had predicted, was pleading for some relief from reparation payments. Two weeks before, Chancellor Bruening had told the world that the German people could endure no heavier taxes, that 'the limit of deprivation has been reached.' The *Transcript* the night they reached home carried a report that von Hindenburg had appealed to President Hoover to intercede; and Mark was not surprised to find in Sunday morning's paper the announcement of the Hoover proposal for a moratorium. War debt payments due the United States in the coming year would be suspended if the Allies in turn would waive payment of German reparations during the same period.

The Ritchies came over that morning to welcome Mark and Tony; and Ed and Mary Halstead dropped in for a moment. Ed, with the point of view of a man whose interest centered in the stock market, was jubilant over the moratorium. It meant, he predicted, the beginning of a new period of world prosperity.

Mark said thoughtfully: 'But it's only putting things off, Ed. They've got to pay sometime. As Coolidge says, "They hired the money." '

'They'll never pay,' Ed insisted. 'Before the year's up, we'll cancel the war debts. Business is going to boom. We can afford to.'

'Will the Allies cancel the reparations payments too?'

'If Germany can't afford to pay, they'll have to.'

Mark said, 'If you're right, it amounts to something like a consent decree of bankruptcy for the lot of them. Their national credit will be lost.'

'It amounts to a fresh start,' Ed insisted. 'Mark, this is the first step to a new era of international cooperation; it's the birth of a new and more prosperous world.'

III

The New Deal

(September 1931–September 1933)

I

(September 1931)

WHEN he began to think of finding a tutor for Tony, Mark wrote for advice to his friend, John Harmon. Harmon had taught mathematics at the Allen School in West Newton when Mark as a boy came East for a year there, and although he was even then in his later forties, an abiding friendship developed between him and Mark and still persisted. Harmon was a teacher nowadays in the high school in Belfast, Maine. He and Mark seldom saw each other, since Harmon rarely came to Boston and Mark had no occasion to go to Maine, but they corresponded at irregular intervals. Since Nan's death, Mark had found satisfaction in exchanging letters with half a dozen men—his father, of course, and Tom Yerkes and Uncle Long in Mississippi—and John Harmon was among the number. To write a letter to an old friend, he found, was one way to forget his own loneliness, one way to fill the long empty evenings.

He had written in the spring to tell Harmon of his intention to take Tony out of school. 'I suppose you'll say I'm wrong,' he admitted. 'Probably you school teachers stick together. But Mr. Farthing doesn't seem to me the sort of man to be an inspiration to boys. I think of having Tony tutored.'

John Harmon replied with a paraphrase from *The Virginian*. 'I don't blame you a bit,' he said. 'A middling doctor is a poor thing and a middling lawyer is a poor thing, but deliver any boy worth his salt from a middling teacher—if you can.'

When now Mark wrote to him again to ask how best to locate a tutor, Harmon was ready with a suggestion. 'There's a boy who used to go to school to me,' he said. 'His name's Bob Preble, and he's doing post-graduate work at Tech, studying internal combustion engines. He's one of a big family. His father married young, never finished high school, has kept one jump ahead of the sheriff ever since, leading a life completely devoid of alternatives. Bob went to work cutting lawns and shovelling snow before he was ten years old, and he worked his way through the University of Maine and he's still working his own way. I'm writing him to come and see you. He's a good man.'

Bob Preble at first sight was a disappointment; frail, undernourished, shabby, wearing heavy spectacles, and already almost bald; but Mark led him to discuss the research on which he was engaged, and Preble lost himself in his own enthusiasm in a way Mark liked to see. He came to the house at nine, five days a week, and worked with Tony till two. Their common interest in matters mechanical drew him and Tony together, and in the evening Tony was full of talk about the things Preble told him, and about his work, which Preble succeeded in making completely interesting.

'It's not like school, where you just have to learn things out of a book,' Tony told his father. 'Mr. Preble shows you how the things you're studying all sort of fit in together, and what they mean, and why it's a good thing to know them.'

Once satisfied that Tony's education was in good hands, Mark gave himself up to complete enjoyment of the fact that Tony was no longer tied down to a rigid schedule, so that they could be together when he chose. Not from any sense of duty, but because it was the keenest pleasure he knew, he spent much time with Tony; and they might talk for hours, as gravely as two men, about questions—whether concrete or abstract—which the youngster raised. During these two years before Tony went away to school, father and son drew always closer together, and the bond between them tightened and grew strong.

2

(Winter 1931–1932)

Mark's close companionship with Tony did not exclude his friends. Through the winter after Nan died, he had declined all formal invitations, preferring to spend his evenings at home, enjoying watching Tony and Elin at their studies together; but in this second winter Nell Ritchie insisted that it was ridiculous for him to live like a hermit. She and Bob came over one evening in early September to invite him to dinner for a day the following week; and when he started to decline,

Nell interrupted him. She was a small, energetic woman with sandy red hair; and she had a lively tongue, and a profound confidence in her own executive abilities. Her eager, active mind often led her to break into what others were saying before they had finished. Dave Rollins, who spent as much time as possible every summer sailing, once said of her: 'Trouble with Nell, she's forever fore-reaching on you, cutting across your bows.' Strangers meeting her for the first time, finding it impossible to finish a sentence, were apt to be reduced to a blinking stupefaction.

'Nothing of the kind,' she said now as Mark started to demur. 'You put me off all last winter, but it's time you came out of it. You can't stay at home every evening.'

'I like it,' he assured her. 'I like to be with Tony and . . .'

'Tony's growing up,' she retorted. 'You can't monopolize him always, Mark. And besides, you're still a young man, and you're a natural-born husband. You'll get married again, some day. You might as well begin looking around.'

Mark grinned at Bob. 'Women must enjoy marriage,' he commented. 'They're such good press agents for it. The sight of a man without a wife is like a red rag . . .'

'It's for your sake—and for Tony's,' Nell assured him. 'He'll be going away to school in a year or two. You'd better begin to make a normal life for yourself again.' And she added: 'Will's going to Hadley next year. Why don't you send Tony with him?'

Mark tried to hide a sudden panic. The thought of losing his daily companionship with Tony, of going weeks at a time without seeing his son, was hard to face. 'Oh, Tony's all right where he is for a year or two,' he said lamely. 'He'll be ready for college by and by, of course; but I want to keep him with me till . . .'

Nell protested: 'Nonsense! It isn't good for him, to be studying with Elin every evening. Boys need a man, and they need other boys. Besides, she's much too pretty to be teaching a boy at Tony's impressionable age.'

Mark laughed outright at that. 'Pshaw, Nell! Tony's only . . .'

'He's older than his years, being so much with you,' she retorted. 'And if it comes to that,' she added briskly, 'Elin's entirely too pretty to be keeping house for you, Mark.'

Bob said sharply: 'Oh, Nell, don't talk like an idiot!'

'Well, it's a lot better to talk like one to Mark's face than behind his back,' she insisted. 'Plenty of other people are saying the same thing.'

Mark smiled. 'I don't care what people say about me. Never explain.

Your friends don't need it, and others won't believe it.' He added: 'But Tony's not studying with Elin this winter. I've a tutor for him, a young fellow named Preble. Tony will study at home till he's old enough to go away.' He saw Nell about to speak, so he added hurriedly, to end this discussion: 'All right, I'll come to dinner. When did you say?'

He was not surprised to find himself assigned, at Nell's dinner table, to an attractive woman whom Nell introduced as Mrs. Flood, of Chicago; and he amused himself and excited Nell, by devoting himself to Mrs. Flood with some assiduity. They talked together throughout dinner, ignoring everyone else, and Mark saw Nell watching them with a triumphant light in her eyes. Mrs. Flood was pleasant and pretty and intelligent and he enjoyed the dinner, enjoyed recapturing her in the living room afterward. He stayed till all the others were gone, and submitted to Nell's eager cross-examination. 'Isn't she lovely? Her husband's dead, you know, and she's rich as Croesus. Did you like her? Are you going to see her again?' When Mark told her that Mrs. Flood was sailing for Paris within the fortnight, and that they had made no plans to meet, she went upstairs in a sputtering indignation and left Mark and Bob alone.

Tom and Emma Sheffield and the Halsteads had been among the guests at dinner, and Mark said thoughtfully: 'It seemed to me Tom looked badly tonight.'

Bob agreed. 'He's jumpy,' he said. 'He's in the loan department, you know, and most of their accounts are under water.'

'I'd hate to wake up some morning and read that he'd jumped out the window.'

'There're a lot of suicides in the papers,' Bob assented grimly. He himself, for all his level head, had been tempted into the market in the last stages of the sky-rocket rise, to his loss; but he counted the experience a cheap lesson. 'What bothers Tom most is that he's having to call loans on fellows he knows, friends; and they—or some of them—blame him.'

'Tom would take that hard,' Mark agreed. 'And—I imagine he has worries of his own. Emma's extravagant, keeps him in debt all the time.'

Bob said in sudden heat: 'If I were her husband I'd take a golf club to her. She has no more conscience than a rabbit.'

It was so unusual for Bob to speak unkindly of anyone that this criticism of Emma meant a great deal; but Mark admitted to himself that it was just. Yet, because of his loyalty to Tom, he was reluctant to discuss her, even with Bob. He rose and said good night.

Mark that winter felt an increasing concern over Tom, and once he suggested to Tom himself that the other was working too hard, was finding his responsibilities at the bank too burdensome. 'You ought to take Emma south for a month,' he urged. 'Play some golf, rest.'

'Can't afford it,' Tom said. He grinned unhappily. 'And besides, I want to stick around for the finish. You know, if things don't get better pretty soon, there'll be hell to pay, Mark.'

Mark nodded. 'Hoover's moratorium didn't cure things after all, did it.'

'Not by a thousand miles.' Mark saw that the other's lips were white with sudden pressure. 'People are still scared, scared worse than ever, afraid of what's going to happen. They're hoarding gold like a lot of damned French peasants, Mark. I'll bet our depositors have half a million dollars in gold tucked away in their boxes today.'

'I saw Hoover's appeal to the hoarders to stop it,' Mark assented.

'That did no good. He just advertised the idea, started other people doing it.'

They were at the Sheffield Farm in Lincoln that Sunday evening; Ed and Mary, Bob and Nell, and Mark. Young Tommy Sheffield, an only child, now seventeen, joined them at supper and at Badminton afterward. Tom and Mark while they talked watched Tommy, paired with Mary Halstead, give Ed and Nell a beating; and then Emma called to Mark to join her in challenging the victors. They too were vanquished; and Emma, flushed and hot and panting from her efforts, said laughingly:

'That's enough for me! Mark, take me up to the house. I want to powder my nose.' She held fast to his arm, leading him away, while a new set began. Mark went with her, a little ill at ease as he was apt to be when he was alone with Emma. Her manner always subtly exaggerated the intimacy of such moments. At the house she disappeared for a few minutes, came back refreshed and with highballs for them both; and Mark, defensively, spoke at once of his concern for Tom.

'I know,' she agreed. 'I've talked to him and talked to him, trying to make him be sensible, but Tom takes things so seriously.' She said in an affectionate tone: 'But I'm as much worried about you, Mark, as I am about Tom.'

Emma's girlhood had been distorted by the fact that although most of the girls she knew had enough to spend so that money was not important, in her own home every dollar had to go far. Her father had none of that Midas touch which is so mysteriously possessed by many men otherwise without capacities; and her mother resented this fact

and constantly reminded him of his inadequacies. Instead of making a
virtue of necessity, of making the most of what they had, she—and
Emma under her influence—used every possible device and contrivance
to hide the truth; and Emma's mother impressed upon her the wisdom
of marrying—above everything else—a man with money. Tom's father
was a wealthy man, or seemed to be; and Emma and her mother agreed
that Tom would make an ideal husband. Tom might not have succumbed easily to their shrewd campaign, but when the war broke out
in Europe, he decided to go to France and drive an ambulance; and in
the emotional fervor of leave-taking he and Emma were married.

While he was still in France his father died, and the world discovered
that although Mr. Sheffield's income had been large, he had spent most
of it. His estate was sufficient to give Mrs. Sheffield a small competence;
but it all went to her, none to Tom. Emma was furious at this; she felt
herself cheated, and when she found that Tom's mother could not be
persuaded to confide the management of her affairs to her son, she hated
the older woman, and eventually contrived the breach between Mrs.
Sheffield and Tom. The fact that Tom had never progressed beyond a
minor position in the bank embittered Emma still more. She was at once
envious and greedy. She recognized the fact that Tom's friends accepted
her only for his sake, but she was careful to wear toward them a mask,
careful never to offend them beyond the bounds their tolerance set.

She had never really loved Tom, and she would have left him long
ago if she could have found a man ready to accept what she had to offer
and able to give what she demanded. As a result her manner toward
all men was intimate, her eye held a lurking hint of impropriety; and
tonight, alone with Mark, she smiled at him flatteringly.

'You don't need to worry about me,' he assured her, pleased in spite
of himself by her solicitude.

'I know how you miss Nan,' she insisted, in a fashion almost caress-
ing. 'I wish I could find some way to make you happy, Mark.'

Mark knew Emma's faults well enough. Nevertheless, she was pretty,
and her kindliness was warming and there could be no harm in it.
'Well, I have Tony,' he reminded her. 'That helps a lot!'

She shook her head, smiling at him wisely. 'You're a man who needs
a woman's love, my dear,' she declared. 'Nan and I always agreed on
that. She understood you, you know—and so do I.'

He laughed, faintly uncomfortable and yet admitting to himself
that what she said was true. She sat relaxed in a deep chair, one foot
tucked under her, looking at him with kindling eyes; and he remem-

bered something Bernard Shaw had written, something to the effect that any normal man, meeting an attractive woman even casually, felt at least a momentary desire for her. That was the sort of thing Shaw so often said, true enough so that you acknowledged the grain of truth even while you resented the bald statement. There were in men so many instincts which the moralists called depravity, but which were probably universal, all the same. Men of his own kind had learned to smother or to ignore these instincts, might even deny their existence. Men of the coarser sort gave them vocal or even physical outlet; and perhaps they thus escaped the distorting effects which psychologists attributed to civilized inhibitions. Every man, Mark suspected, had an inner life of his own, had thoughts and impulses which never manifested themselves in either speech or action. There had been occasions when some incautious word from other men, some reference, revealed to him that the things in himself which he had thought unique and of which he had been ashamed were a part of universal masculine experience.

Mark was sure that for his own sake even more than for Tom's, he would never accept the invitation in Emma's words and in her manner; yet he could recognize that invitation and contemplate the possibility of accepting it and admit to himself the momentary exhilaration which that acceptance would produce. This recognition made him cautious, and he found himself listening for the sound of footsteps on the pathway from the barn to the house, wishing the others would come. 'I seem to get along all right,' he said cheerfully.

She laughed a little, resenting his refusal to play the game she proposed even though if he had accepted her invitation she would have rebuffed him. Her resentment sharpened her tongue. 'Of course Elin loves you,' she said reflectively. 'Probably in many ways she takes Nan's place.' Her tone was light and mischievously accusing. 'None of us blames you, but after all, Mark, you need the affection and the understanding of a woman of your own world.'

He rose, resenting her reference to Elin, setting his finished drink aside. 'What's keeping the others?' he said, seeking escape. 'They ought to be through by now. Let's go see.'

'Oh, don't go!' she urged. 'They'll come up to the house when they're done.' She did not move.

'I'll have to break it up,' he insisted. 'I've a big day tomorrow, ought to be starting home.' They had all come together, Ed and Mary picking up the others in their car.

She said behind him, still not rising, a faint laughter in her tones as though she were amused by his flight: 'You don't need to go on the defensive. I just want to help you, Mark, to see you happy.'

'I'll see how they're coming,' he said, and went out, closing the door with an unintended emphasis. Halfway to the old barn that served as a Badminton court he stopped to look back, at first frowning thoughtfully; but then he laughed at himself, thinking: 'Don't be a damned fool, you fathead! You're imagining things! Emma's crazy about Tom—in her own way.'

The house door opened and closed and he saw her in the light on the veranda, but she could not see him in the darkness and—leaving the path for the lawn so that his feet made no sound, amused at his own absurd half panic—he hurried on to reach the barn and the others ahead of her. She came in almost on his heels and caught his eye with what he thought was derision in her glance. He turned to Mary Halstead as to a refuge.

When presently they started homeward, Mark and Bob sat in the rear seat with Nell between them, while Mary was with Ed in front. If it had been Bob's car tonight, he would have made Mary sit beside him, and let Mark and Ed share Nell in the rear seat, just as at formal dinners husbands and wives are by convention separated. But Ed and Mary preferred to sit together, and when the others dined at their home they always sat side by side, let their guests choose their own places.

'I'd rather sit by Ed than anyone,' Mary always said, when they teased her. 'Why shouldn't I admit it!' The frank devotion between them in this and many ways excluded even their closest friends.

So for them to sit together tonight was not unusual, but Mark saw that Mary pressed close to her husband's side, and he guessed that her hand was tucked through Ed's arm. Once Ed looked down at her and smiled, and she leaned nearer and kissed his cheek.

Nell protested: 'Hey, if you two want to start that sort of thing, park somewhere. Act your age.'

Mary said, smiling at them over her shoulder: 'Age? I'm not too old to be crazy about Ed. Don't you all think he's wonderful?'

They laughed at her, and Bob asked: 'Just find that out, did you, Mary?'

'Oh, I've always known . . .'

But Nell, with a shrewd instinct, interrupted her. 'You always were a fool about Ed; but you're not usually so shameless. Mary, something's worrying you. What's wrong?'

For a moment no one spoke; but then Ed said, his eyes upon the road, an empty mirth in his tone: 'Why, it's just that I got my walking papers yesterday. Business has gone to pot, and they're cutting down. I'm out of a job.'

They were quick with sympathy, but Mark saw Mary watch her husband with such a wealth of love and pride in her countenance, outlined against the glare of the lights on the road ahead, that he thought Ed the most fortunate of men. The passionate tenderness in Mary's tones was plain enough. Ed was lucky, any man was lucky, to be able to turn from the world to a warm sweet haven in a woman's ardent arms.

Bob asked Ed what he would do, and Ed said he had not had time to consider that question. The talk led nowhere; but Mary held fast to his arm and Mark himself was warmed and comforted by this glimpse of the love between these two.

3

(Summer 1932)

After the Lindbergh kidnapping a day or two later—although he recognized the absurdity of his own reaction, since no one could hope to collect a ransom of any consequence from him—Mark was beset by fears for Tony's safety, and reluctant to leave the youngster alone in the house with only Elin to protect him. He could not be at ease even during the day; and in the evenings, when Tony had gone up to bed, he was alert to any unusual sound. If he went out to dinner, he asked Elin to leave her door open. 'So you'll be sure to hear Tony if he calls you,' he explained. When he came home he went immediately upstairs to make sure Tony was safe in his own bed, and Elin's door was always open; but while he was in Tony's room he might hear her shut it softly, and he knew that she had been lying wakeful in the darkness, keeping silent guard, and the knowledge reassured him.

When spring was well come and he heard that the ice had gone out of Moosehead, he interrupted Tony's studies long enough to take the boy to Maine for the early fishing; and as soon as they were away from the city, he had a grateful sense of security. They stayed five days, driving up and back so that they were a week gone. On the trip home the car balked, the radiator began to leak and to overheat, they found it necessary to stop and refill it every few miles, and Tony said disgustedly:

'Gosh, Father, isn't it about time we got a decent car?'

Mark decided Tony was right, and the selection and purchase of a new automobile was for both of them the big event of the next week, and Mark found a keen pleasure in watching Tony's shining joy. When in June he asked whether Tony had any ideas for the summer, the youngster proposed another long automobile trip.

'It was wonderful even last summer,' he declared, 'and with the new car it would be perfect.'

Mark thought of Jerry Crocker, whose suggestion had led to the trip last summer which Tony now wished to repeat. He had not seen Jerry since that day, had had no chance to thank the other for his advice; and he wished now that he knew Jerry's address so that he could do so. He welcomed Tony's suggestion, half ashamed of his own absurd fears that his son might be kidnapped, and yet relieved that on this trip they would be constantly together, Tony under his watchful eye.

He consulted old Mr. Ritchie, thinking it possible that the other would object to the two months' absence he proposed; but Mr. Ritchie agreed at once.

'You're a wise man, Mark,' he said. 'Someone once said that he could do a year's work in ten months, but not in twelve. We Americans work too hard, and we take our work too seriously. That's why so many men have jumped out of windows, or forgotten to open the doors of their garages, this last three years.' He waved his hand in a gesture of dismissal. 'Go along. Forget law and business and politics and the Lindbergh baby and prohibition and everything else. Any man who lets himself think about all the things wrong in the world today will go crazy.'

'You ought to get away yourself,' Mark suggested.

'Lord love you, I'm going to,' Mr. Ritchie assured him. 'Newfoundland, the Serpentine, live in a tent, kill a few salmon—and not see a newspaper for a month! Where are you going?'

'We'll drive to the coast, I think,' Mark said, and he explained: 'I want to talk to people, strangers, hundreds of them. I want to find out what they're thinking, see if there's any common denominator in their thoughts.' He smiled, 'I want to try to read the American mind.'

The old man looked at him with a twinkle. 'That's a large order. Most of us don't even know our own minds.'

'I don't always know my own,' Mark agreed. 'But maybe I'll know it better when I come home.'

When he spoke to Elin about their plan, she listened eagerly, asked at last: 'How long will you be gone, Mr. Worth?'

'Two months, anyway,' he told her. 'Possibly longer. We ought to be back by the first of September.' And he asked: 'Why? Had you something you wanted to do?"

'I thought if you won't need me I'd go home to Sweden for a visit,' she confessed. 'I haven't seen my brothers and sisters since I was a little girl. But I'll be back before you are.'

'Fine,' Mark agreed. He added warmly: 'Only—be sure and come back. I can't get along without you, Tony and I.' His own words made him realize how true this was, how completely the pleasant routine of his life lay in her hands. Suppose she met some Swedish boy and married him! 'If you're not here when we get home, I'll come after you,' he told her laughingly. 'With a battleship if necessary.'

She did not laugh. 'Oh, but I will be here,' she assured him. 'I do not want to live anywhere but here.'

Mark said good-bye to her, when the time came, with misgivings; and through that long summer he and Tony spoke of her often, and Tony sent postcards to her in Sweden, and Mark once on impulse wrote her a long letter about their travels. When it was done he was half minded to tear it up; but that was ridiculous. There was no reason he should not write to Elin if he chose. Certainly he knew her better—yes, and felt for her a more definite affection—than for any other woman. He smiled at his own thought, thinking how scandalized Nell would be if he should tell her this.

He and Tony drove to the coast and back, going out through the South and Southwest, returning by a more northerly route. On a large-scale map of the United States they traced the roads they had taken, and when that trip was over there were a scant dozen states they had not at least glimpsed upon their journeys.

Everywhere, every time they stopped, Mark talked to men and women about the world in which they lived. Before the summer was half gone, he was satisfied that Mr. Roosevelt would defeat President Hoover. Men and women everywhere had felt the pinch of the depression. President Hoover had failed to mend matters. Someone else—anyone else—might do a better job. This was the general view.

But also, more than once Mark had reason to remember Jerry Crocker's prophecy; for again and again a man or a woman said: 'I'm going to vote for Roosevelt. I heard him on the radio last night. I like to hear him talk.' Jerry was right! The days of orators, thanks to radio, were come again.

Mark talked not only politics but prohibition—almost everyone was for repeal, and the Democrats by their platform stand would win many votes—and he talked business and found everyone with a panacea for the state of affairs. The market had turned upward in July when at Lausanne the reparations question was—or seemed to be—settled; but the tide of business activity still rose only sluggishly. Something would have to be done, and Mark heard a hundred remedies proposed. He was astonished to find that many sober men of business thought inflation might be wise. Tom Yerkes—they spent two days in Beacon on their way West—was one of these. The obvious way to put the prices of commodities up, Tom argued, was to put the value of money down. Mark did not agree, and the two men discussed the matter for long hours.

On that trip, all day together, Mark and Tony talked of many things. Mark liked to point out to the boy how men's ways, and their habits of thought and their very appearance, were modified by the nature of the region in which they lived. They discussed the easy, hospitable Southerner, and they catalogued the Mid-Western traits; frank interest in you and all your affairs and in your family and even in your thoughts. They came to know the ebullient Texans, like a nation of young giants sure of their strength and of their future; and they liked the calm, sun-bitten men of the Southwest with eyes narrowed against the steady sun, and with a bent toward picturesque costumes, wide hats, decorative vests, beautifully stitched high-heeled boots. They divided the Californians into two groups, the enterprising boosters who saw California as the answer to men's prayers, and the old people from Iowa and the other farm states who had come to California to live out their lives in a pleasant indolence under a smiling sun. Each individual, Mark told Tony, was the product of the scene in which he lived—just as the New Englander's cautious austerity and careful thrift were ingrained as a result of the necessity of preparing always against the harsh bitterness of coming winter.

Mark enjoyed that long vacation, but before it ended he found himself anxious to come back to the routine of his work again, to come home to the comfortable household over which Elin presided so pleasantly. They had no word from her—their movements were so uncertain that mail seldom reached them—but late in August when she should have returned from Sweden, Mark telegraphed her from Minnesota, giving the approximate date of their arrival in Boston, and giving an address to which she might reply. Her answer duly came, and his own relief surprised him. He had not realized how persistently he had feared she would never return.

In Minnesota, and again in Detroit, and in Hardiston when he stopped there, Mark heard rumors that many Middle-Western banks were in precarious condition; but he forgot this and everything else when they set out on the last reach of their journey. Their home-coming was a warm reunion. Elin was lovelier than ever, and seeing her and Tony together made Mark realize for the first time how much Tony this summer had grown. Now he was taller than she. That first evening at dinner they kept her in the dining room, Tony telling her about their trip, telling her a thousand things, till at last Mark asked her questions about her visit to her homeland.

She had found her relatives all well and happy, she said; and he asked what Sweden thought of conditions in Germany. At the July elections, the Nazis had polled seventeen million votes, more than any other party, and Hitler was their head. Elin said Sweden was glad to see Germany on the way back from chaos again.

'We do much business with Germans,' she explained. 'When Germany is prosperous and busy, then Sweden is prosperous too.'

'Are the tales true, about the things Hitler's Storm Troopers do?'

'I think yes,' she agreed. 'The rich people in Germany do not like it, but the poor people everywhere love him.'

'Do you think he will come into power?'

'Everyone in Sweden thinks he will surely be President after von Hindenburg, yes,' she said.

Mark thought she was probably right; but if that happened, Hitler himself had said that heads would roll in the sand. Mark had a grim prevision of a bloody world—in which Tony, when he came to manhood, might have to take his part.

4

(September 1932)

Mark came home convinced that Mr. Roosevelt would be elected President in November; but he was not surprised to find that Bob Ritchie and Tom and Ed and most of his friends either expected Hoover to win, or thought the contest would be close. The stock market had risen steadily all summer, and spirits rose with it. That prosperity which had for so long hidden coyly around the corner seemed to be returning, and there was a growing confidence in a Hoover victory. Mark told his friends—they met for lunch at the first opportunity—that they were wrong to count on Hoover.

'The trouble with you all, you're New Englanders, and you think the rest of the country feels as you do,' he said. 'I don't know whether Hoover will carry New England or not—but I'm sure he won't carry the country. I've been talking to dozens of Roosevelt's Forgotten Men. You're all forgetting them, but they're going to vote for him.'

Bob grinned. 'You can make some money if you're right,' he challenged.

'Don't say I didn't warn you,' Mark retorted. 'But I'll even give odds —ten to seven, say.'

Bob accepted the wager, and so did Tom; but Ed shook his head. 'Can't afford to gamble,' he explained cheerfully. 'I've given up all such luxuries.'

Mark had thought of Ed often that summer, remembering that the other had lost his job; and three or four times he had written Ed long friendly letters. He asked now: 'What are you doing?'

'Why, I've set up for myself,' Ed explained. 'A sort of investment adviser. I'm getting along, getting by.'

He said no more than that, but his tone was reassuring; and Mark thought that Tom too looked as though his mind were easier. After lunch Mark and Bob turned toward the office, and Mark asked about Ed's new venture.

'He's got a good start,' Bob explained. 'You know Ed never made suckers of his customers in the office. A lot of brokers and investment counsel, back in the boom times, kept switching their clients. They'd make them sell Public Service of New Jersey and buy Consolidated Edison, and then in a month or so they'd shift them back again and get the commission both ways. Ed never did that. If he advised a shift he had a reason—some reason besides his own desire to get a commission—and usually if he advised selling, he advised selling everything; so the men who dealt with him know he's honest. Now he's just running an advisory service on a flat fee, and a lot of his old customers are using him, and he's getting more business all the time.'

'Swell,' Mark agreed. 'He and Mary are about as fine as they come, Bob.'

'Right!' Bob assented. 'They're having another baby sometime this winter. They've rented their house, living in an apartment. Mary's doing her own work.'

Mark asked their address, and from the office he telephoned an order for flowers to be sent to Mary with a card on which he wrote: 'Just heard your good news. Fine. See you soon. Love, Mark.'

He had a note of thanks next day, bidding him come to supper Sunday night; and the Ritchies and the Sheffields were also there. Mary was radiant, and Mark told her affectionately: 'You're always a lovely woman, Mary; but babies are the most becoming thing you wear. You're wonderful tonight.'

She laughed at him happily. 'You always say that, Mark.' She summoned Emma and Nell to help her put supper on the table, and thereafter the evening followed a familiar pattern. They played casual poker —they had given up bridge after Nan died, since they were now seven instead of eight—and Mark, watching these friends of his, thought how clearly each person's traits emerged at the poker table. Bob played calmly and precisely, weighing the value of his hands, betting with a judicial care. Nell was more absorbed in making sure that the deal passed around the table in the proper order than in who won the pots. Emma was forever arguing as to whether the dealer had put up his ante, or as to whether the others put in the right number of chips when they called or raised a bet; but she always threw her own chips into the pot so that they could not be counted, and watching her closely, Mark saw that she often put in less than she should. Tom was more interested in talk than in the game; Ed and Mary more alert to the comfort and content of their guests than to the rise or fall of their personal fortunes. Mark wondered whether his own play was equally characteristic. He almost always lost; and from his point of view the game had been a success if his cards were good enough to allow him to bet freely on every hand and still break even. Probably that reflected some trait in himself, but he did not know what it was.

They broke up early, and in the confusion of departure, Emma said so that they all could hear: 'Mark, you didn't tell us a word about your trip this summer. I wanted to ask you a thousand questions. Why don't you take me to lunch tomorrow and give me a chance?'

Mark had not been alone with Emma since that evening last winter when her eyes even more than her words had been an invitation which he could not fail to recognize; and he was at once startled and attracted by her suggestion now. He looked at Tom as he answered. 'Afraid I can't,' he said. 'I'll be in court.'

'Then Tuesday,' she insisted. 'I'm not going to let you off.'

'Tuesday's out too,' he told her, wishing Tom would come to his rescue.

'Wednesday?' she challenged. 'You're surely not busy every day!'

Mark felt himself trapped, and he saw that Tom and the others were amused at his confusion. 'Why, Wednesday's all right, I guess,' he admitted, and suggested hopefully: 'Why don't you and Tom meet me at the Copley at one?'

'Oh, Tom never has time to lunch with me,' Emma assured him; and Tom laughed and said:

'She'd be sore if I showed up, Mark. She gets a kick out of having lunch with other men.'

So it was settled, and Mark was alone when on the day set—he was there on the hour, but she was fifteen minutes late, and he had begun to hope she would not appear—Emma came in from the street. She was so sleekly groomed that even his masculine eye remarked it.

'New hat?' he asked when they were seated at their table.

'Of course. New everything.' She smiled at him. 'This is an occasion, you know! You never took me to lunch before, so I dressed for it. Like me?' She was maliciously enjoying his faint embarrassment. Even during the nineteen-twenties, when to drink a little too much as proof of your scorn of prohibition, and to flirt with other men's wives was the rule, Mark had preferred Nan's company to any other; so this luncheon was for him a new experience.

'You look like a million dollars,' he assented, smiling. 'You could put on a one-woman style show all by yourself. This lunch is costing you something.'

'It's worth it to me!'

'How about Tom?'

'Oh, Tom!' She laughed carelessly. 'Of course, he forever complains about bills, never admits he can afford anything. He's always preaching poverty.'

'Tom's a fine fellow.'

She nodded. 'Tom's sweet. But he's too sweet, Mark. He was always his mother's boy. Like Oedipus. Oh, I don't mean anything sexy, but she taught him to be gentle and nice—and a man needs to be rough and tough sometimes.'

Her comment was shrewd, and it was patently true, but Mark faintly resented it. 'If he were rough and tough with you,' he said smilingly, 'you'd both be a lot better off.' And he added seriously: 'You could help him a lot, you know, by—not spending so much money.'

She tossed her head. 'I expect Tom to earn enough to take care of me. He knew I had expensive tastes, when he married me.'

'We all have expensive tastes,' Mark reminded her. 'But we control them.'

She laughed. The waiter was at hand and they ordered and she said: 'There, that's enough about Tom and me. I didn't come to be scolded! Tell me about yourself and your trip; everywhere you went and everything you did.'

He was glad to talk of impersonal things and did so, describing their travels that summer, answering her occasional quick question. Half a dozen times as his eye swung around the room he met glances of recognition from men and women he knew; and each time he colored faintly, till Emma spoke of it, laughing at him. 'You're cute, being so embarrassed,' she declared.

'Nan's the only woman I ever took to lunch,' he confessed. This was strictly true. Bob, if he had an attractive client in his office, might continue their consultation over the lunch table; but Mark had never done so. Nan had sometimes teased him about it, declaring that he must be afraid of being compromised.

Emma laughed. 'Mercy! Really? We must do it oftener! You're old-fashioned, Mark. Women don't take the veil, just because they're married, nowadays. Times have changed.'

'I don't think times have changed so much, not among our sort of people,' he said thoughtfully. 'Of course, magazines and books are apt to deal with emotional crises of one sort or another between husbands and wives. But——' He was silent for a moment, thinking. 'But for instance, I don't know, except casually, anyone who is divorced. Most people you and I know live pretty decent, respectable lives.'

'Heavens! There's nothing indecent about divorce!'

'I'm not so sure. I was brought up to think it was—one form of promiscuity,' he insisted, and he said, smiling at his own words: 'I remember when I was a boy in Ohio, there was a family in town, a man and woman who got divorced. No one was surprised when their daughter subsequently went on the stage. The one scandal seemed to follow the other quite naturally.'

She smiled with him, reached across the table to touch his hand in a light caress, carefully impulsive. 'You're sweet, my dear,' she told him, and laughed a little. 'But you really are old-fashioned, you know! I assure you, times have changed.'

In spite of himself he enjoyed that luncheon. Emma could be charming when she chose, and she chose to be charming to him. 'We must do this again,' she said when they parted. 'Every Wednesday? Is it a date?'

He laughed and said his Wednesdays were sometimes too busy for

such distractions; and she suggested some other day and he said he
could never be sure ahead of time. 'Then I'll call you up,' she proposed,
and when he demurred she said: 'It's good for you, Mark. You're lonely,
need a chance to let down and be a little gay sometimes. You've had a
good time today, haven't you?'

'Of course,' he agreed, but he would not commit himself for the
future, and that evening he decided not to repeat the experience. Tom,
no matter what he said, might resent it; or if Tom did not, ugly talk
might start. Thereafter, though Emma more than once suggested they
lunch together again, he made excuses. She teased him about it openly,
when they were with the others.

'Anyone would think I was making love to you,' she declared one
night at the Ritchies'. 'You needn't act so embarrassed! I'm the one to be
embarrassed, if you're going to make such a point of it!'

Mark grinned uncomfortably, and the others laughed with her, but
he saw Mary Halstead's glance at Ed, and Nell Ritchie said in faint
scorn: 'Oh, go ahead, Mark, give the gal a cheap thrill!'

Emma, to revenge herself for that, suggested laughingly: 'If you're
afraid of being compromised, Mark, Nell can come and chaperone us.
She'd make any gathering respectable!'

Nell said crisply: 'No, thank you, Emma! I'm not your guardian—or
Mark's!'

But later, after the others were gone, she told Mark: 'You're wise not
to let Emma make a fool of you. It's just a game with her, you know.'

'It's harmless enough,' he admitted. 'But probably I'm old-fashioned.'
He smiled. 'At least Emma says I am.'

Nell touched his arm with one of her rare gestures of affection. 'I like
old fashions,' she said crisply. 'And I like you—and Tom. But I don't
like Emma—any more than she likes me.' And she added thoughtfully:
'She really hates the lot of us, you know—just as much as she hates
Tom.'

Bob, always slow to speak unkindly, protested: 'Oh, Nell, she and
Tom get along.'

'Tom gets along!' she retorted. 'But Tom Sheffield would get along
with a—with a royal Bengal tiger! Tom's grand. But Emma's terrible!'

5
(December 1932)

Mark reluctantly at last faced the fact that sooner or later Tony must go away to school. Nell Ritchie insisted that it was absurd to keep the youngster at home another year. He tried to argue the point with her, urging that Tony was doing good work with young Preble, learning more than he would learn at school; but he found that Bob agreed with Nell.

'It isn't altogether a question of studies, Mark,' Bob said. 'Tony ought to have a year or two away before college. It's only fair to the boy.' He added understandingly: 'I know you dread being left alone, and worry about things happening to him; but we have to turn our children loose, more or less, from the beginning. If they climb a tree, they may fall and break their necks; but if we don't let them climb trees, they'll grow up a lot of sissies, different from their fellows.' He urged: 'Hadley's a good school, and Mr. Carbrey, the headmaster there, is a great man with boys.'

Mark was forced to admit that in keeping Tony at home it was himself, rather than Tony, whom he was considering. He asked the boy at last whether he wished to go on tutoring for another year.

'Oh, sure, I guess so,' Tony doubtfully agreed.

'Anything else you'd rather do?'

'Well, probably we couldn't afford it.'

Mark smiled. 'I guess we can afford anything that's important for you.'

'Why, I'd kind of like to go to Hadley with Will,' Tony confessed. 'Of course I'll be homesick, but I'll have to go away sometime, won't I, Father?'

'Hadley, eh?'

Tony grinned sheepishly: 'I guess Will's going there doesn't seem to you like much of a reason.'

'It's good enough,' Mark declared. 'I remember I decided to go to Dartmouth because I saw a football game where the Dartmouth captain was hurt and yet didn't want to quit playing and they had to carry him off the field. I thought all Dartmouth men were heroes, and I wanted to be one of them.'

He wrote asking whether there would be a place for Tony at Hadley next fall, and Mr. Carbrey suggested that Mark and Tony come up and see him and see the school. The result was that they drove to Hadley on a Sunday in early December.

Mr. Carbrey was in every possible way the antithesis of Mr. Farthing. He had become a teacher of boys because he loved boys, found his greatest happiness in being with them, believed in them and trusted them and admired them; and it would have been as impossible for him to hurt a boy with cutting and sarcastic words as it was impossible for Mr. Farthing to refrain from doing so. His home in Hadley was a rambling old white house of the sort which seems to have grown with use, shaded with elms, comfortable in the angle of the village street. He himself was a friendly little man in a dusty blue serge suit; and when Mark and Tony arrived, they found him at his desk in the main hall of the school building.

'This is a pretty busy place during school,' the Headmaster admitted, 'with the boys going past on the way to classes all the time. But I like to see them.' He tipped back in his chair, his leg over one arm of it, knuckling his nose. 'Well, Tony,' he asked, without preamble: 'Why do you want to come to Hadley?'

Tony said: 'Why, Will Ritchie's coming, and he's my best friend.'

Mark amplified that. 'And of course I've made some inquiries about you and the school, Mr. Carbrey. This is where I want Tony to go, if you can have him. He went to the Heights school, near our home, till two years ago. I've had him tutored at home, since then.'

'Have you considered any other schools?'

'No,' Mark told him. 'I want Tony to come here if he can.'

Before Mr. Carbrey could speak, Tony said with a certain eagerness: 'Mr. Carbrey, of course if you can't take me here, I can't come; but I want to come, and I'm going to come if you'll have me.'

Mr. Carbrey looked at him with a more attentive eye. Mark said: 'He won't be ready to come till next year, but I thought it might be wise to enter him, put his name on your list.'

'Oh, we don't have a waiting list,' the Headmaster explained. 'I just take the boys we think we want, when the time comes.' He rose and added: 'I hope you can stay to dinner. There'll be a sing this evening, and I'd like to have you see something of the school.'

They did stay. Dinner at Mr. Carbrey's home was pleasant. For the singing afterward, the boys gathered in the big living room in the Old Dorm, joining in familiar hymn tunes with a ringing zeal. When the young voices rose, Mark felt his heart tighten. These boys were so young, so completely unafraid, so valorous and brave! His thoughts were suddenly sombre, thinking that a threat against these boys, a threat that might kill some of them, and maim some, and wreck the lives of many of them was rising in the world. The threat was named Hitler. This wild crank who talked like a medieval potentate about beheading men was challenging Hindenburg's leadership in Germany. In November von Hindenburg had offered him the chancellorship on a parliamentary basis. Hitler declined, refusing to accept the qualification; von Papen's cabinet had since resigned. General von Schleicher was forming a cabinet now, but Hitler was the most powerful leader in Germany, and his ascendancy, his imminent rise to power, seemed sure.

Mark thought presently that some such reflection must have come to Mr. Carbrey; for between songs the Headmaster talked awhile. He stood near the piano, and he spoke in a quiet, conversational tone.

'I don't usually have much to say,' he reminded the boys, 'unless I have an announcement to make, or something of that sort; but I feel like talking tonight. In times like these, when there's so much uncertainty about the future, it's interesting to try to figure out just what we're doing here at Hadley. We seem pretty remote from the world. From September to June, we go about our business with only a few interruptions. But in a year, or two, or three, all of you will be in college; and in a few years after that, you will be out in this world which is going through a bad attack of fever and ague now.'

He smiled faintly, and said: 'That reminds me of the first time I ever came to Hadley. I came to apply for the position of Headmaster. Old Colonel Isaac Howes was the chairman of the board of trustees, and he was the man I had to see. It was in June, and it was one of those hot June days we have every now and then. I went to the Colonel's house, and found him in his sitting room. You all know the house, over across the Square, and some of you know the room. It was blazing hot outside and the sun was shining, and he had all the windows open; but he had a great fire going on the hearth, and he was sitting in a big rocking chair about halfway between the windows and the fire, with a shawl wrapped around his shoulders, and a palmleaf fan in his hand. He must have seen how surprised I was because he had a fire going, and yet wore a shawl over his shoulders; for he said to me: "Young man, you may think I'm a fool, but I'm not. I've got chills and fever, and I don't know which is coming next; but whichever it is, I'm ready for it!"'

A gust of laughter rocked the room, and Mr. Carbrey chuckled, and then he said more seriously: 'I suppose what he meant was that he was

prepared. We call this a preparatory school, and we think of it as preparing us for college. But of course college isn't an end in itself, although it's easy for us to think so, since you're busy here earning the
right to go to college, getting your various credits so that you'll be admitted. But as a matter of fact, college is preparation too. In a way,
much of your lives will be preparation. You will never know surely
what's coming next—just as the Colonel didn't know whether chills or
fever would hit him—but you'll need to be ready for whatever happens,
to prepare yourselves for whatever demands life may at any moment
make on you.'

He hesitated, added easily: 'I don't know just why I'm talking this
way tonight. It's just that I fell to thinking about the importance of
being prepared, and—I felt like talking. Now let's sing something else.'

He opened the pages of the hymnal and gave a number, and a moment later the young voices rose. Mark found himself tremendously
moved by the hidden meanings in what Mr. Carbrey had said, tremendously impressed by this wise man. After the singing he waited to say
good-bye, and he and Mr. Carbrey were for a moment alone. Mark said
at once:

'I'm wondering how you happened to say what you did awhile ago?
I've been thinking along the same lines lately. With this man Hitler
gaining strength in Germany, I'm no longer sure that the World War
settled anything.' Mr. Carbrey looked at him with a quick attention,
and Mark explained: 'I hadn't even heard of Hitler till he made that
speech a couple of years ago, promising that heads would roll when he
and his party came to power. Well, he's mighty close to seizing that
power now.'

The Headmaster rubbed his nose. 'Something of the same sort was in
my mind,' he admitted. 'The trouble with wars is that they're always
followed by peace treaties. It's interesting to speculate on what the state
of Europe would be today, if after victory the Allies had not sought in
any way—by territorial exactions or by other clauses in the treaty—to
crush Germany.'

Mark asked soberly: 'Then you too think another war is coming?'

'I don't know. I hope not; but Hitler has announced his intention
of tearing up the Treaty of Versailles, and he seems to have a powerful
party behind him.'

'Do you think von Hindenburg can hold him in check?'

'I don't know,' the Head added in a lower tone: 'Probably I'm taking
Hitler too seriously, but so many Hadley boys went to the last war, and

some of them died. The possibility that the boys here now may have to go to fight again in Europe is a little more than I can contemplate calmly.'

Mark nodded, thinking of his son. 'There's trouble enough in the world without another war,' he said. 'I don't suppose we've seen in our lifetime a year as bad as this year nineteen-thirty-two has been. The stock market—I hope—touched bottom; but Tony and I heard in the Middle West this summer rumors of trouble coming in the banks out there. France and Belgium defaulted on their debt payments to us, and I'm afraid England will eventually do the same. When governments fail to keep their promises, private morals may follow public morals into the discard.'

Mr. Carbrey nodded. 'It's been a hard year,' he agreed. 'The bonus army in Washington, the hunger marchers, prison outbreaks, the Lindbergh case, the suicide of men like Knowlton Ames and George Eastman and Ivar Kruger.'

'And hundreds of other men have died from hypertension,' Mark reminded him. 'Dropped dead of heart trouble, or from strain and worry. And the rest of the world is as badly off, with Japan seizing Manchuria and attacking China and no courage anywhere to stop her, and an incipient civil war in Spain, and Hitler in Germany. Mr. Roosevelt's election here seems like the beginning of a revolution to me. There's a story that he's said he'll either stand the country on its head or be the greatest president we ever had. I wonder which it will be.'

'The people elected him,' Mr. Carbrey suggested, smiling. 'Perhaps they're right. The many are often so much wiser than the few.'

'If Hitler drives the world to war, he and Mr. Roosevelt may be matched in the final struggle, just as President Wilson led the Allies in the later stages of the last war.'

'It would be hard to find two men more different,' the Headmaster reflected. 'Hitler with his ruthlessly destructive program, Mr. Roosevelt with his Utopian dreams.'

'I voted for Mr. Hoover,' Mark said. 'But I hope I was wrong; we'll need a good man in Washington, these next years.' He rose. 'But it's time for us to go along. What about Tony, Mr. Carbrey?'

The Head extended his hand. 'Thank you for coming,' he said. 'As for Tony, there's time enough. I'll think it over, let you know.'

6

(Winter and Spring 1933)

During the late winter months, Mark was concerned about Tom. Reports of bank weaknesses were spreading across the country, and the financial world was so closely knit that the collapse of a bank in San Francisco might affect Boston institutions. Tom's bank, he knew, had loans out on securities and on real estate which were by no means covered by the quick-sale value of the collateral; and Tom was in the loan department and wore this knowledge like an actual burden under which he bowed. The bank holiday came, and fear stalked the streets, and men gathered in whispering and nervous groups, talking in low, furtive tones together.

Mr. Roosevelt took office pledged to economy and to the maintenance of the gold standard, and he told the country that there was nothing to fear but fear. Even Bob Ritchie, who had worked for Hoover in the campaign, approved the new President's bold handling of the banking crisis. 'I'm willing to give him a chance,' he told Mark. 'He's got a tough job ahead. If he can swing it, more power to him.' But when Mr. Roosevelt moved to stop by law the hoarding of gold, Bob was sure he was wrong. 'Gold's a commodity,' he declared. 'I have as much right to buy gold and keep it as I have to buy wheat, or shoes, or an automobile.' And when in mid-April Mr. Roosevelt embargoed gold exports and abandoned the gold standard in international affairs, Bob damned him completely. 'It means inflation,' he predicted. 'That's the next step.'

Mark, without taking an opposite view, nevertheless argued that there was another side to the question. 'I've a friend in Mississippi, a small-town banker named Tom Yerkes,' he said. 'He believes a controlled inflation may pull the country out of the mess we're in.'

Bob said scornfully: 'There's no such thing as controlled inflation. That's a contradiction in terms. You inflate a little and it works—so you decide that to inflate a little more will work even better. Or you inflate a little and it doesn't work, so you decide you didn't inflate enough. Either way, you inflate some more, and some more after that.' He laughed, 'You and your small-town banker!'

'I'm no currency expert,' Mark assented. 'Maybe there's no such animal. But I've sometimes wondered if we wouldn't be better off with a currency unit that had a lower purchasing power. Other peoples think in terms of shillings, or of marks, or francs, or lire. Maybe we'd be a little wiser in financial ways if we thought in terms of quarters. A thing priced at sixty quarters sounds a lot more expensive than at fifteen dollars. Maybe we ought to start counting our pennies.' And he urged: 'We've been able to afford waste, up to now, because, if we wasted, we could always tap unused natural resources to make up for it. A man living on coconuts can afford to let some rot on the ground if he owns a whole grove; but if he only owns one tree—he'll be more careful. And if that one blows down, he'll plant another one mighty quick.'

'The English think in pounds—or guineas.'

Mark smiled. 'Don't fool yourself. You never heard an Englishman say the price of his new hat was a pound and a half. He'd say thirty shillings.'

'Our standard of living's higher than that in the European countries.'

Mark nodded. 'But maybe it's too high for our own good. And maybe it's coming down.'

His interest in events in Washington made him less attentive during these months to what was happening in Germany; but also there was always in the back of his mind like a shadow the fact that next fall—if Mr. Carbrey had room for him—Tony would go away to school. He had had no word from Mr. Carbrey; and in mid-May he decided he must know the other's decision; for in June he and Tony planned to go to Newfoundland to fish for salmon. Mark for two months had been gathering information as to what they would need, relying largely upon the advice of old Mr. Ritchie, and he and Tony had gone together to buy flies and gear. Every evening at home they fondled these new possessions with that passionate interest which only the true fisherman knows. Mark had difficulty in remembering the differences between the various flies. The Silver Gray and the Silver Doctor were so like that he was confused, and he was never quite sure which was a Black Dose and which a Mar Lodge. But Tony knew them all, and he could name at a glance the hook size on which they were tied. He practised tying the knots illustrated in the fishing tackle catalogue, practised at first with heavy twine and then with a well-soaked length of synthetic gut; and they spent the long spring evenings on the lawn where Tony learned to cast until he was handling line as well or better than Mark himself, beginning sometimes to be a little patronizing of his father's efforts.

'The trouble with you, Father,' he might say, 'you push out with your elbow. You don't have to do that, and the line handles better if you let the rod do the work. Stick a book under your upper arm, and let your wrist and the rod do everything else.'

Mark enjoyed these hours of practice together, and he was happy in watching Tony's enthusiasm, and amused at the boy's confidence in his own powers.

But as May neared its end, Mark decided Tony's school plans must be settled. He wrote to ask Mr. Carbrey's decision, and the Headmaster suggested that they come up to see him again. So on the last Sunday in May they drove to Hadley. As they drew nearer the school, Tony became silent by his father's side, and Mark, watching the boy's intent face, asked quizzically:

'What are you thinking about so hard?'

Tony hesitated. 'Well, I was just thinking, Mr. Farthing always said I didn't do very good work at the Heights, but if I come to Hadley, I hope I can do all right.'

'Why, Tony?'

'Well, I know it would make you happy.'

This was true, of course, and Mark was touched and pleased. Yet— Tony would be fourteen this fall, and perhaps his two years at home had robbed him of some measure of self-confidence, and certainly he was old enough to assume responsibilities. Mark said carefully: 'That's true, in a way; but it's a secondary consideration, son. After all, my job is to give you a chance to go to a good school; and when I've done that, I've done my job. The rest is up to you. If you don't take advantage of whatever opportunities I can give you, I suppose I'll feel badly for your sake, but not for mine. For I'll know that I've done all I could.'

Tony nodded. 'I see,' he agreed, his tone faintly startled. For the rest of the way he was silent, considering this new point of view.

When they pulled up at the school, Mr. Carbrey came to greet them. He said they must stay for dinner, and Mark accepted this suggestion, and they talked together a moment more and then Mr. Carbrey said:

'Well, Mr. Worth, I want to talk to Tony. Suppose you take a walk, come back in time for dinner.'

Mark, amused and yet a little piqued at being thus excluded from the discussion that would determine Tony's immediate future, did as he was told. He walked past the football field and down to the meadow, and across the meadow to the river, and sat awhile in the sun there, looking at his watch, thinking that time dragged, wondering what Mr. Carbrey was saying to Tony and Tony to Mr. Carbrey. He came back at last to find Tony and Mr. and Mrs. Carbrey together in the living room of their home, and the Head was asking questions about the projected trip to Newfoundland, and Tony was answering them; and during dinner school was not mentioned.

Afterward, Mr. Carbrey came out to the car with Tony and Mark to see them drive away, and Mark could no longer refrain from putting the question in his mind.

'Well, Mr. Carbrey,' he asked, 'are you going to be able to take Tony this fall?'

Mr. Carbrey answered, as though his reply were the most natural thing in the world: 'Tony's going to let me know. Good-bye. Thank you for coming up.'

Mark found himself silenced and drove away. When he was alone with Tony, he waited for his son to speak; but the boy sat quietly beside him, looking straight ahead, saying nothing. Mark made up his mind to let the youngster take the initiative, but after half an hour his endurance failed.

'Well, Tony,' he said, 'what did Mr. Carbrey have to say to you?'

Tony moved with a start, coming out of an absorption so deep that he had forgotten where he was. 'Oh!' he said. 'Oh, well . . . Well, he's . . . Well, he had a report on me from Mr. Farthing.'

Mark found his lips dry with anger at that man. 'I suppose it wasn't particularly complimentary,' he commented. 'Mr. Farthing thought you didn't do enough home work.'

Tony nodded. 'I guess I didn't do very well at the Heights,' he admitted. Tony was always honestly ready to accept blame without evasion. Mark was sure Mr. Farthing's attitude was distorted by resentment because Tony had left the Heights before the school year was finished, but he did not say so.

'What did Mr. Carbrey say about next fall?' he asked. 'Is he going to take you?'

Tony explained: 'Well, he said boys at Hadley usually worked pretty hard, and he told me I could come to Hadley if I wanted to. He told me to think it over and let him know.'

Mark did not speak, digesting this, trying to understand it, realizing the perfection of Mr. Carbrey's word. If Tony now went to Hadley, it was with an implied promise to do good work. Mark wondered what his son's reaction to this proposition would be; but Tony said no more, and Mark was forced to ask at last:

'What are you going to do?' He found a deep happiness in this question, in this deference on his part, in leaving the decision to the boy.

'I'm going to think it over,' Tony said.

Mark smiled to himself, finding that he had no desire to advise Tony or to urge him. Yesterday, or a month ago, he would have felt that the decision was his to make, and that Tony should turn to him for counsel, should accept his judgment; but now, seeing the situation through Mr. Carbrey's eyes, he realized that this was not true. The decision was Tony's, and the responsibility of that decision would be his.

7

(July 1933)

Mark watched his son, during the days that followed, with an increasing appreciation of the change taking place in Tony. Till now he had been a child; but now, suddenly, the boy began to reveal not only opinions of his own, but reasons for those opinions; and he began to assume responsibilities. When they set out on the long drive to North Sydney, en route to Newfoundland, the first time the gas gauge showed their supply was low, Mark stopped at a filling station. The attendant did not at once appear, and Mark said:

'Tony, you have him fill it up and check the oil and water. I'm going to buy a newspaper.'

When he came back, Tony reported: 'I had him look at the batteries and tires too, Father.'

'Thanks,' Mark told him. 'I meant to have them checked before we started.' He was pleased, feeling a pleasant excitement at this evidence of initiative in his son.

They stopped the first night at Ellsworth, and the second at New Glasgow. On the third day, when they had crossed the Gut of Canso and went on, Mark saw Tony watching his feet on the pedals and he said:

'I expect you know as much about driving a car as I do, how to shift and so on.'

Tony said: 'Yes. Sometimes I've sat in the car in the garage and practised.'

Mark, on impulse, pulled up beside the road. 'You take it for a while,' he suggested. 'Let's see if you can keep us out of the ditch.' The road before them was open, not heavily travelled, and wide enough; yet Mark saw his son's lips tighten, saw the boy suddenly pale. 'That is, if you'd like to?' he amended.

'Yes, sure,' Tony told him.

So they changed seats, and Tony took the wheel. Mark switched off the ignition. 'You might as well begin at the beginning,' he said. 'Start the car from scratch.'

Tony nodded. He pressed the starter, pressed the clutch pedal down, and went into low gear. He eased the clutch in, and the car bucked and the engine stalled.

'You need to give it a little extra gas when you let the clutch in,' Mark suggested. 'It takes more gas, just at first, to get it moving; more than it requires after the car is under way. Try again.' He added: 'And I usually throw out the clutch before I use the starter.'

This time Tony succeeded in putting the car in motion, although it hiccoughed two or three times, and then, when he stepped too firmly on the throttle, leaped ahead like a startled horse. He shifted into second, and then into high, and Mark said:

'There you are. Now just keep it moving at a moderate speed, and all you have to do is steer.' After a few minutes, while the car made a snakelike progress along the road, weaving from side to side, Mark chuckled and said: 'You remind me of a time when Mother and I went down to the Cape to see the Rollinses. We went out for a sail, and Dave Rollins let Mother take the wheel, and she kept it spinning one way and the other, till Dave said that when Mother steered she steered all the time!' Tony grinned, and Mark explained: 'Everyone does too much steering when they begin. It only needs a touch on the wheel now and then, to keep the car going straight.'

'It keeps trying to go off into the ditch,' Tony confessed. 'And when I pull it back, I pull it back too far and it's over on the other side of the road before I know it.' And he added: 'It's the same way with flying. Beginners always over-control.'

Mark had not known this, and also he was a little surprised that Tony should know it. 'Who told you that?' he asked.

'I've read about it,' Tony explained. 'I like to read about flying. Some day I want to learn to fly, Father.'

Mark felt a faint cold touch on his spine at the thought of Tony risking his life, risking death or mutilation, in an airplane. He made no comment, but when Tony had driven eight or ten miles, he took the wheel again.

'You don't want to get too tired the first time you try it,' he suggested, and Tony yielded without protest.

'It's a sort of strain till you're used to it,' he confessed.

They were two weeks on the Grand Codroy, fishing much of the time the Overfalls Pool, although they sometimes went upstream or down to try other waters. The river was crowded with fishermen, and the water was low; so that, although the great pool held many salmon, the fish were not taking. Mark in two weeks killed a dozen salmon and twice that many grilse, but Tony caught only four salmon. His youthful patience was not equal to the wearisome business of casting hour after hour without a strike, and he was apt to tire and sit down on the shore with his guide, and become absorbed in some other occupation for a while. Mark had a certain satisfaction out of the fact that he caught more fish than Tony, and he was amused at himself for this, amused to think that he was competing with the youngster. He knew quite well that for him the trip would have been a success, even if he had caught no fish at all, because Tony's enjoyment was continuous and complete whether he fished or not.

During their hours on the river they were not much together, since perforce they fished different waters; but when they started home again, Mark realized that even in these two weeks Tony had changed, had acquired an increased confidence and a new maturity. Probably this was natural. Probably the years between ten and fourteen were the second great period of change in a boy's life. The first embraced the years from his birth till his entering school. Tony had started in kindergarten when he was five years old; but he displayed an immediate precocity, and stayed only a month or six weeks before his teachers advised shifting him into the first grade. Mark, looking back, remembered that in that year, too, Tony had seemed suddenly to mature, to cease to be a baby; but since then there had been no period of rapid development until now.

But on this homeward drive he realized that Tony's boyhood was nearly over, that in a matter of months, a year or two at most, Tony would begin to feel himself a man.

He let Tony drive again, two or three times on the homeward journey, and before they came back to Boston he said: 'You know, son, you've learned a lot about driving, mighty quickly.'

Tony said: 'I want to. Of course, I won't be able to get a license until I'm sixteen, but I want to be all ready.' Mark smiled at the eagerness in the youngster's tone.

They had seen no newspapers during their two weeks on the river, but Mark bought a paper in North Sydney. To Tony the most interesting news was that two dozen Italian seaplanes, on their way from Italy to the Chicago World's Fair, were due in Shediac that night; and he wondered excitedly whether he and his father might see them in the air, and watched the skies that day. He saw nothing, but on the second day of their homeward drive they sighted one of the planes, which had apparently been delayed and had fallen behind the others, flying high on its way to Montreal. Its double hulls seemed strange to their eyes, and Tony thought they must greatly increase the difficulty of a take-off from water, and he explained to Mark that water-borne air craft had to overcome the suction of the water before they could take the air.

'You pull back on the stick till they get up speed,' he told his father eagerly, 'and then you push the stick forward and rock them back and forth till you get them up on the step, and then pretty soon they take off.'

'How did you find out all that?' Mark wondered, at once amused and impressed.

'I've read about it, and I've talked to pilots,' Tony explained. 'And Mr. Preble has told me a lot about flying. He can't fly himself on account of his eyes, but he's been up a lot.'

'I suppose flying will come naturally to your generation,' Mark assented. 'Like driving a car. I never drove a car till I was twenty-six years old. I'd ridden in them, of course; but I never drove one.'

They talked endlessly of planes and cars on that homeward journey, and Mark came to know Tony, to know the boy's secret thoughts and hopes and dreams more intimately than ever before. He had always recognized Tony's absorbed interest in automobiles, but he had not till now realized that this extended with equal force to planes and to flying. His better understanding of his son, achieved during these days, made him happy; and the day they crossed back into the United States again, in a suddenly expansive love, with that generous impulse which every father knows, he volunteered a promise.

'Tony,' he said, 'you're pretty keen about flying, aren't you?'

Tony looked up at him in a shy eagerness. 'Yes,' he said. 'I think about it a lot.'

'You've some hard work to do, in the next few years,' Mark said. 'I'm sure you'll do it well. But I'm going to make it worth your while. When you're all ready for college, Tony, I'll let you learn to fly.'

Tony sat up straight. 'Honest, Father?' His eyes were big with delight, and Mark smiled down at him.

'Cross my heart,' he declared. Yet his own doubts must have showed in his eyes, for Tony said after a moment:

'Gosh, you're swell! You're scared I'll get killed, or something, but you're saying that anyway, because you know how much I want it.'

'You've done a lot of nice things for me. I like to do things that make you happy when I can.'

Tony sat quietly beside him for a long time thereafter before he spoke again. Then he said, without preamble: 'Well, I've made up my mind to one thing, Father! I've decided to go to Hadley in the fall.'

8

(August 1933)

One day early in August, Mark with no pressing business on hand decided to walk up to the St. Botolph Club for lunch. In the Public Garden, swinging briskly along, he overtook Jerry Crocker, recognizing the other's slight limp while he was still some distance behind, and he greeted Jerry cordially.

'I've been hoping to run into you for the last two years,' he said. 'I'd have written you if I'd known your address, to thank you for that advice you gave me.'

'You're welcome,' Jerry assured him smilingly. 'But—what was the advice?'

'To let my son see something of his own country,' Mark reminded him. 'We took an automobile trip that summer, and drove to the coast last summer.' He laughed. 'I don't know how much Tony got out of it,' he admitted. 'But we had a great time. Where've you been keeping yourself?'

'Been away a lot this past year,' Jerry explained, and he smiled. 'I took my own prescription, spent three or four months in California last winter and then a couple of months in Washington, watching the New Deal deal them off the bottom.'

'You knew what was coming, didn't you?'

'Did I?' Jerry grinned. 'I'm a Jeremiah by habit; so when the times are out of joint, I usually predicted it.'

'You did,' Mark agreed. 'Hitler's chancellor, and he's begun to abuse the Jews, just as you said he would. And the silver-tongued Demosthenes of the air is in the White House.' He said: 'I'll buy you a lunch. Come on to the club.'

'I can't,' Jerry confessed. 'I'm expecting a call from New York, told them they could get me at the Ritz at one-thirty.'

'We'll go there,' Mark assented. 'I want to know what's coming next. On your record, you can tell me.'

So they turned into the Ritz together, and when they had ordered, Mark asked: 'Do you still think an orator is a good man skilled in speaking?'

Jerry grinned. 'I judge you don't rate Mr. Roosevelt very high.'

'I was ready to wait and see,' Mark said soberly. 'It seemed to me he did as well as anyone could have done, at first. He straightened out the banking mess, and repeal is on the way. But when he signed the bill cancelling the gold clause in federal and private contracts, I crossed him off my list. The government had promised to pay gold for its bonds. It broke that promise, defaulted on its debts just as truly as Germany and the Allies defaulted on theirs. There's no more national honor left in the world—and no more national courage!'

Jerry said grimly: 'True for you! The ideals we were brought up to respect are dead. And that silver-tongued nightingale in the White House killed them!'

'I suppose every man wants to be able to work out a planned security in his old age,' Mark suggested. 'But Mr. Roosevelt is on the way to making that impossible. Thrift is no longer either a virtue or good policy.'

'Face it, sucker!' Jerry advised. 'We're in the middle of a revolution, or at least in the beginning of one.'

'I know,' Mark agreed. 'Ever since I was a boy, labor has been demanding greater and greater rewards—and deserving them and getting them; but up till now the rewards of capital have held pretty steady. Now the pendulum is swinging on toward the point where capital's rewards will begin to shrink.'

Jerry laughed. 'Sure, and pretty soon it will be capital's turn to strike! Then there'll be hell to pay!' And he said strongly: 'Washington's all for labor, and down with capital. Capital is money that has been saved, but Roosevelt's a spending fool! Saving isn't in his dictionary! So now, down with capital, says he! If capital ceases to be productive; that's O.K. with Roosevelt. But it takes about ten thousand dollars of invested capital to give a man a job in modern industry. Machines are fixing it so a few men can produce just as much as a lot of men used to, and that throws other men out of work—and it needs new capital to make new jobs for them. We'll have unemployment till we tempt capital back into the investment market; and the only way to do that is to show capital a sufficient chance for a profit to compensate for the risk.

But Roosevelt's idea is that capital doesn't rate a profit.' He looked up as a boy came to their table with a message. 'Right,' he said. 'There's my call. Back in a minute.' He rose and moved away.

While Mark sat alone, reflecting on what the other had said, Emma appeared at the door and looked around and saw him, and came triumphantly to his table.

'What luck!' she exclaimed. 'I was afraid I'd have to buy my own lunch!'

He felt trapped. After that first occasion he had evaded her frequent urgencies that he give her lunch or tea; but she still persisted in calling him on the telephone and she wrote him many little notes, full of derisive amusement at his ideas of decorum. 'Jerry Crocker is lunching with me,' he told her, rising reluctantly to greet her. 'He's just gone to telephone.'

'Crocker? Who is he? Don't stand up!' There were four chairs at the table, and she sat down and began stripping off her gloves, settling herself to stay.

The waiter appeared and took her order, and Mark told her who Jerry was, and when Crocker returned she looked at him in the melting fashion she was apt to use toward any man she met for the first time. Her flattering manner overwhelmed Jerry, smothered him into a red and wretched silence. 'I know you two were having such an interesting talk,' she declared. 'Do go on. Don't pay any attention to me. I love to listen to good man-talk!' When Jerry dumbly stared at his plate, she began to question him, and Mark watched, grimly amused, wondering how long Jerry would endure this, surprised at the other's helplessness. Jerry, usually so vocal, answered Emma in choked monosyllables; but he seemed unable to contrive an escape, till Mark at last in mercy called for the check.

'I'm due back at the office,' he explained, and he added in dry amusement: 'I'll leave you two to finish your talk!'

But Jerry came hastily to his feet. 'I've got to go,' he said desperately. 'Got to get downtown. I'll buy you a taxi.'

So they left Emma, prettily reproachful at being thus abandoned. In the cab Jerry drew a deep breath of relief, and he asked guardedly: 'Who's the lady?'

'Do you know Tom Sheffield?' Jerry did not. 'He's a friend of mine,' Mark explained.

Jerry did not speak; but Mark wondered what his comment upon

Emma would have been if he himself had not thus put this curb upon the other's tongue.

He saw Emma again on a Sunday in mid-August. Nell and Bob had taken a house at Scituate for the summer, and Nell telephoned to ask Mark and Tony down for a picnic dinner on the rocks. When they arrived, Tom and Emma were there. 'I asked Ed and Mary too,' Nell explained. 'But they couldn't leave the baby.'

Emma at once referred to that luncheon at the Ritz, telling the others about it and with malice in her tones. Mark's persistent refusal to appear with her in public places had infuriated her. Having no longer any real fondness for Tom, and dramatizing Mark's loneliness since Nan died, she had imagined a great romance between them, imagined herself saying at last to Tom in a pretty compassion: 'I'm sorry, my dear, but this is a love bigger than any of us. You must give me my freedom.' When Mark avoided her, she at first attributed this to loyalty toward Tom, but by a process of reversal, she began at last to tell herself that Mark was pursuing her, and to blame him for wishing to betray Tom, who was his friend, and she came thus to feel toward him a secret enmity. By way of revenging herself upon him, she sometimes spoke of Elin to people who knew Mark only slightly, damning him by indirections. 'Of course people who don't know him think it's queer that he should keep that pretty Swedish maid in the house; but we don't think anything about it. Mark's our friend, whatever he does, and the girl is really bewitching, and you know how Swedes are, and of course a man alone . . .'

She described that encounter with Jerry and Mark now with an excessive amusement. 'I wish you could have seen those two, Nell,' she declared. 'They acted as though I were a chorus girl who had suddenly plumped herself down at their table, with the deacon of their church watching. Mr. Crocker was worse even than Mark.'

Bob laughed. He knew Jerry slightly. 'He's the shyest grown man I ever saw,' he agreed. 'And you always act as if any new man were Gary Cooper and you wanted to swoon in his arms.'

'Don't be ridiculous!' Emma retorted. 'And besides, Mark's not shy!' She turned on Mark in pretended indignation. 'You acted as if you thought Tom had detectives on our trail and they'd caught us in an assignation. It was perfectly insulting.' She told Tom: 'If you were half a man, you'd knock him down, just for what he was thinking!'

Her tone was sufficiently near jest so that they could laugh at her;

but Mark saw Tom's acute discomfort, and he remembered it when next day the other telephoned him at the office.

'I'd like to see you for a few minutes, Mark,' Tom explained. 'Sometime this afternoon. How about it?'

Mark said: 'Of course. Four o'clock?' But while he waited for Tom to appear, he thought of Emma uneasily. She had destroyed the old straightforward friendliness between him and his friend; and he wondered whether it was to speak of her that Tom came to him today.

But Tom, it developed, had come frankly to borrow money.

'I want to make some alterations in the house,' he explained. 'It's pretty run down, needs repairs and painting anyway. I'm thinking some of selling the place, if I can get a price; but it will sell better if it's put in shape.' And he said, swallowing a little: 'I've mortgaged it for all it will carry, Mark. But I'll give you my note. I'd like to borrow a thousand dollars.'

Mark nodded, embarrassed by the other's embarrassment, blaming Emma's extravagance for driving Tom to this. Tom said, smiling weakly: 'It probably sounds like a bad investment, but I'll pay it, Mark.'

'I'll be glad to let you have it, of course,' Mark said. In the three years since Nan died, his income had increased. The house was paid for now, and he had bought a few bonds. He could afford the loan. 'Never mind a note.'

'I ought to be able to pay you within eighteen months, or earlier if I sell the place. It's too big for us—or will be after Tommy goes to college.'

Mark said almost curtly, wishing this were over: 'I'll send you a check in the morning.'

'I'll give you a note,' Tom insisted weakly. 'We'll keep this on a business basis, Mark.' He tried to laugh. 'Six per cent all right?'

Mark chuckled reassuringly. 'Don't be a damned fool. That's too much. Three per cent if you like. You're as good as a government bond, old man.' He rose, anxious to end this interview which was an ordeal for them both, and clapping the other affectionately on the shoulder, went with him toward the door.

But when Tom was gone, he sat awhile in troubled thought. Tom's salary must be sufficient for their reasonable needs; yet Emma's demands, he knew, were beyond reasonable bounds. Probably Tom would never be able to pay this money, and if that proved to be true, it would be hard for them ever to come back to the old friendly footing. Emma had by her extravagance made this borrowing necessary; and for that, in Mark's mind, she must always accept the blame.

9
(September 1933)

The weeks before Tony would go away to school passed like the fanned pages of a book. There were so many preparations to be made, so much to be arranged. Mark had in anticipation a stinging sense of the loneliness that would be his when Tony was gone, and once he spoke of this to the boy, but Tony said:

'I'll be coming home every little while, Father, for Thanksgiving and Christmas and Easter; and we'll have all summer together. But school is my job for the next two or three years, and getting ready for college.' He added affectionately: 'I can't stay here with you the rest of my life! I'd like to, but you know I can't!'

Mark nodded, smiling a little. 'Yes, I know, son.' And then he confessed: 'When your mother died, I looked forward to all the things we would do together, but I always thought of you as still a little boy. It's natural for a father to think of his son as staying the same.' He added: 'You know, you'll change on the outside, and in some ways the inside of you will change too; but you'll never feel much older than you'll feel, say, by Christmas, after your first three months at school. I don't feel any older now than I did when I went to college. I'm just as easily embarrassed as I was then. I've learned to hide it better, that's all. But of course,' he admitted, 'you've changed already in these years since Mother died. You've grown up a lot this last year, Tony.'

'I've tried to,' Tony confessed. 'I know how lonesome you are without Mother, and I've sort of tried to take her place as much as I can, to be with you when you come home, and in the evening, so you wouldn't think the house was so empty.' He grinned in a shy way. 'It wasn't hard to do. I've always liked being with you.'

In preparation for Tony's departure for Hadley, Mark brought up one evening the subject of finances. 'How do you think we ought to work it, Tony?' he asked. 'Do you want me to give you an allowance for spending money?'

'How much is the tuition at the school?'

'Fifteen hundred dollars.'

'Gosh! Isn't that a lot? Can we afford it, Father?'

Mark said: 'Yes, we can afford it.' He felt as he always did a deep pleasure at the boy's use of the pronoun. He added: 'We can afford anything that's wise for you.'

'Will that cover everything?' Tony asked. 'The fifteen hundred dollars?'

'I think it covers everything at school, except perhaps your laundry and your spending money. And there may be some charge for books—I don't know about that—but it won't be much.'

'It sounds like an awful lot to me!' Tony laughed. 'Even five dollars has always sounded like a lot to me.' Then he said thoughtfully: 'I ought to be learning about money. How would it be if you gave me an allowance big enough so that I'd pay for what I buy, and get some idea of what money's worth, and how much things cost, and all?'

Mark looked at his son in a still surprise, recognizing again, as he did so often in these days, how fast Tony was maturing. 'Do you think you could handle all your bills, keep them straight?' he asked.

'I'd probably make a lot of mistakes,' Tony said, 'but I'd be learning all the time.'

The result of the conversation was that between them they calculated, as nearly as they could, what Tony's total needs for the year would be. Fifteen hundred dollars for tuition, plus travelling expenses, possible doctor's bills, clothes, books, and spending money brought the total— Mark's estimates were intentionally liberal—to something over two thousand dollars.

'And if you were paying your own bills,' he explained, 'you'd have to have a checking account, and you'd want to keep at least a two-hundred-dollar balance in the bank. And there's another thing, son.' As the idea developed, he saw in it more and more possibilities. 'You might take out some life insurance. At your age the rate would be low. Then, when the time comes that you want to get married, you'll have that feeling of security which comes from knowing that if anything happened to you, your wife will have at least a little money.'

Tony readily accepted this suggestion. He had a physical examination and took out two policies. The combined premiums came to about one hundred and twenty-five dollars a year.

'That means that about two hundred dollars a month will cover all your expenses, Tony,' Mark calculated. 'You'll have a margin, too. Suppose I send you a check for two hundred dollars the first of every month, and you can bank it and then pay your bills as they come due. I suppose your first school bill will come in October or November, so I'll have to give you a few months in advance; but you'll catch up with me before the end of the year, and after that we can go along on a regular basis.' And he suggested: 'I think you'll want to keep pretty careful accounts. You can do them once a month, when your checks come back from the bank—enter your deposits, and itemize the checks you drew—so you'll know where your money's going.'

'I'll try not to spend all of it,' Tony promised.

'Well, it's all yours,' Mark assured him. 'To spend or save, as you please. I think you can save quite a little, if you're careful.'

Tony grinned. 'I'll be a millionaire in no time.'

'Whatever you save is yours,' Mark repeated, and he said with a chuckle: 'Maybe I'll be borrowing money from you before we're through.'

Next day Mark took his son to the bank and opened an account for him with a deposit covering five months' allowance.

10

(September 1933)

When the time came, the question arose as to whether Tony should take the train to Hadley; but Mark said: 'If you don't mind, if it won't embarrass you, I'd like to drive you up. In that way we can take all your luggage in the car, and any pictures you want for the walls of your room, and so on; and it will be a satisfaction to me to see where you're going to live, and to meet your roommate.'

'Gosh, yes! I'd like that,' Tony said. He grinned and confessed: 'I'm a little scared going away from home the first time. Come along, sure. I'll like having you around.'

Tony packed all his things the night before. When he was ready for bed, as he had done for years, he called to his father, and Mark went upstairs to fix the covers, and to open the windows. Tony, lying in bed, watched him with sober eyes. 'It's going to be kind of queer,' he said, 'not having you at school to tuck me in and kiss me good night.'

'You'll get used to it.'

'Oh, sure.'

Mark sat down for a moment on the edge of the bed. 'I'm going to miss you,' he said.

'I'm going to miss you, too; but, Father, with me away, you can go out more. I know you stayed home a lot, just to be with me.' Tony grinned. 'You can't just be a hermit the rest of your life.'

Mark smiled and leaned down to kiss his son, and Tony clung to him fiercely for a moment. Then Mark started for the door. 'Are you going to read awhile?' he asked.

'I guess so.'

'Good night, then.'

Tony asked, grinning at his own words, which Mark had heard so many times before: 'Are you going to be home all evening and all night?'

Mark chuckled, but his eyes were brimming. 'All evening and all night, yes.'

'Wake me up when you come to bed?'

'Yes, of course, son. I always do.'

He said good night again and went slowly downstairs. The old clock on the landing was running cheerfully enough, and when he sat down in the living room he could hear its uneven tick-tock, tick-tock, sounding through the empty house. He did not read, but he sat a long time, staring at nothing, wishing he might keep Tony at home, wishing they need not be separated now.

II

(September 1933)

Mark woke early, and he came downstairs before Tony was dressed. His son's belongings were laid in an orderly heap in the living room, near the French doors, ready to be loaded into the car. There were two bags, a book-stand, an etching, a framed snapshot of Tony holding up the twelve-pound salmon he had caught in Newfoundland, Tony's tennis racquet, and the tin box containing the assortment of wrenches, pliers, screwdrivers, files, and the like, which were his particular pride. Mark stood looking at the pile of luggage, and Tony came racing downstairs his eyes shining with excitement. They ate breakfast together; and Mark asked:

'Well, son, glad you're going?'

'Sure. I'd rather be with you, but I'm glad I'm going, too.'

'I wonder if we've forgotten anything? Of course I can send things to you.'

'Elin's going to make cakes and brownies and things and send them back with my laundry,' Tony explained. 'I told her she had to take good care of you while I'm gone. She will too.'

Mark nodded, thinking that with Tony gone he and Elin would be alone in the house, thinking Nell Ritchie would surely disapprove. 'You know,' he confessed, 'I haven't realized yet that you're really going. Of course I've known it, but it seemed a long way ahead, and now here all of a sudden you're ready to start.'

Tony swallowed hard, but then he grinned. 'But when I come home,' he urged, 'we'll be so glad to see each other, we'll have just that much better times.'

Mark smiled, and then breakfast was ready. Afterward, Elin had a great box of brownies for Tony to take with him, and Mark saw that she was near tears at the prospect of the boy's departure. While they loaded the things into the car, Elin helped, and at the last Tony kissed her, clinging to her in a strong affection. 'Don't forget to send me a lot of brownies,' he urged.

Elin smiled and promised, and then they were in the car and then they were away.

When they came to the open road, Tony asked to take the wheel for a while.

'You're not old enough,' Mark reminded him. 'You're not supposed to even learn to drive until you're sixteen, and you're only fourteen now. If I did let you drive and we had an accident, it would void my insurance.'

'Gosh, Father,' Tony protested, 'we won't have an accident! I can drive all right now. All I need is practice.' So Mark indulgently yielded, and the boy took the wheel for a dozen miles, driving through the traffic in one small town with a calm assurance which Mark watched with amusement. It was Tony, in the end, who suggested changing back again. 'I did all right, didn't I?' he asked, when his father had the wheel, and Mark said:

'Perfectly. You've learned to steer the car now without weaving all over the road, and you didn't have any trouble with the gears.'

'They say if you can drive you can learn to fly a plane,' Tony said. 'I went out to the airport one day last week with Will Ritchie, and we talked to a pilot named Hadden.'

'You're anxious to learn to fly, aren't you?'

'Gosh, yes! But not yet. Mr. Hadden said I ought to know how to drive a car; and he said if I could handle a motorboat, that would help too. He said a motorboat was really more help than a car, because you learn to come alongside wharves and stop just in the right place, and everything.'

Mark thought if it were so easy, he too might some day learn to fly. It would be pleasant to compare notes with Tony, to be learning together, when the time came.

They drove into Hadley in early afternoon, and Mark was glad to see Mr. Carbrey again. His heart warmed at sight of the little man in his dusty blue serge; and Mr. Carbrey's welcome was a cordial one. He sent someone to show them Tony's room, and Mark and Tony between them began to unload the car and carry in bags and pictures.

The boy who would room with Tony presently arrived. His name was Frank Parks, and within a few minutes he and Tony were already on such terms that Mark began to feel himself an outsider. Frank was so polite to him that Mark felt himself senile, as though he were limping on a cane, with a long beard waving in the breeze. This, he thought, was bound to be true. These youngsters had so many common grounds on which he could not enter. He listened to their talk awhile, watching them unpack and stow their belongings in the bureaus and the closet. Their room was a big one, in one of the old houses in the village. There were two other rooms on the same floor, with two boys in each, and the six boys would share a common bath. The door of their room was open, and in the hall outside there was a constant cry of young voices, of voices which had a silvery quality, yet in which now and then deeper tones sounded.

This was youth, Mark thought, and he by comparison was old. Between him and these children lay a gulf which could never be crossed. It was right that this should be, just as it was right that between man and woman there lay always a division, a wall, so that each had his own life separate and apart from the other. Tony would enter this life among his fellows and find his place there, and Mark thought that in some ways he was losing Tony today, and losing him forever. He stayed on, heedless of the time, till Tony said:

'Father, you ought to be starting home, oughtn't you? Elin will be expecting you for dinner.'

'Why, as a matter of fact, I told her I wouldn't be home,' Mark explained. 'I thought you and I might have dinner together. Perhaps Frank would like to come along.'

Tony said doubtfully: 'Well, if we did that, you'd have to drive home at night, and I know you don't like driving after dark. I'd feel a lot better, honestly, knowing you were getting home by daylight.'

Mark recognized the fact that Tony wanted him to go, that school was a part of Tony's life in which he would always be an outsider.

There was sadness in the thought, and yet satisfaction, too. 'Well, perhaps you're right,' he agreed. 'If there's nothing more I can do to help you get settled here?'

'No, I'm all set,' Tony assured him. 'You go ahead.'

So Mark said good-bye to Frank Parks, and he and Tony went down to the car. He said: 'Write to me, when you have any time.'

'Gosh, I will!' Tony promised. 'And you write to me, too.'

Mark extended his hand. 'Well, good-bye, son. Take care of yourself!'

Tony took his father's hand, but then he stepped nearer and kissed Mark on the cheek. 'Good-bye, Father,' he said. 'Take care of yourself, too.'

Mark drove back to Boston slowly, adjusting himself to this new existence to which he was committed now. There had been a change in Tony, even in the hour or so they were at Hadley. Probably, he thought, Tony would not have kissed him good-bye if Frank Parks had come down to the car with them. It was the sort of thing a little boy would do, but Tony was no longer a little boy. Mark realized gratefully that for Tony to kiss him good-bye at the car, where a dozen of his prospective schoolmates might have seen, required a courage that was akin to valor. Oh, Tony was fine!

IV

The Watch on the Rhine

(September 1933–June 1936)

I

(September 1933)

WITH Tony gone, the house seemed terribly empty for a while. Mark rose at his usual time, and Elin had breakfast ready for him when he came downstairs and sometimes he kept her with questions, hungry for any company, for breakfast alone was astonishingly dreary.

Breakfasts alone were bad and solitary dinners were worse, and the evenings were worst of all, when Mark sat reading in the living room, and the house—except for the faint sounds of Elin's activities in the kitchen—was terribly quiet. He fell into the habit of calling good night to her when he heard her go upstairs. Her room was across the hall from his, and sometimes when he went up, perhaps to read for hours before he slept, he heard her still stirring there. On Thursday nights when she was out, he dined at the club and sometimes played bridge for an hour or two; but he was apt to be abed, though not asleep, before she returned. He might hear the click of her key in the back door, and then her quiet steps on the stair and the sound of the latch as the door of her room opened and closed. It was astonishing how much he could hear, in the still silences of the night; and sometimes his book lay forgotten under his hands and his thoughts followed her.

He thought that it was strange for two people to live as he and Elin did, alone together, under the same roof, yet remote from one another, meeting only in the dining room, seldom speaking except of household matters, yet each acutely aware of the other's presence so near. He wondered sometimes whether Elin was as conscious as he of the fact that they slept night after night not thirty feet apart, with two doors, closed but not locked, between them. He knew well enough her strong affection for him. She showed it in a thousand ways, and not only in her constant thought for his comfort and content. He had a warm respect and liking for her; and he sometimes remembered—smiling at his own folly—King Cophetua and the beggar maid; and he wondered what the beggar maid really thought of King Cophetua if she were as young as Elin and the King was forty-one years old—as Mark himself was now.

Sometimes, thinking of Elin, he felt a quiet amusement when he considered what Nell or Emma Sheffield would believe if they could read his thoughts. Mary Halstead might understand him better. She could comprehend a man's need for a woman's affection and tenderness, could understand that this need was much more than a simple hunger for physical possession. It was compounded of so many lesser—and yet greater—needs. It was the need to feel a loving presence near: to know as you sat reading in the evening that beside you sat another between whom and yourself deep currents of understanding flowed; to know that if you were troubled, another took half the burden of that trouble off your shoulders by sharing it; to know that if you wished to talk there was one who would listen; to be able to raise your eyes and meet other eyes and smile without words; to come home from a wearying day with the certainty that tenderness and understanding waited to greet you and give you rest and peace. Caresses, brief ardors, these were after a few years so small a part of marriage. It was the little daily things, the daily sharings, that bound two people together. Without them, marriage was not marriage. Without them, though a man might have been well and duly wedded with bell and book and candle, yet he remained a bachelor still.

Yet how few women knew this! Too many of them thought—or said—that man wanted from them only one thing. Having given themselves, they thought their duty done. Perhaps their attitude was a mere convention, an insincerity so long maintained that they believed it true. In the drunken nineteen-twenties, that long debauch which prohibition ushered in, and which had left its mark on so many of the people he knew, men and women who had till then been temperate or abstinent plunged into excesses to testify their contempt for the new laws, and the attempt to impose virtue by mandate set loose everywhere a reckless profligacy. Mark had seen more than one woman—Emma Sheffield, for an example—so openly provocative that he was half sickened, and yet at the same time felt there would be a grim satisfaction in seizing her with a hard and brutal violence. But that harsh emotion which such women provoked was neither love nor lust. It was more truly hatred and abhorrence; an instinct to hurt them which was as deeply rooted as the instinct to crush a snake.

Love was liking, and tenderness, and the happiness which came with understanding. By that definition, he confessed to himself, he might be said to be in love with Elin. He would for instance have been glad to have her sit in the living room with him in the evenings, glad to be able to talk with her when he chose.

Yet, calmly appraising his own emotions, he was sure that this was all. Certainly if jealousy were a part of love, he was not in love with Elin; for on Elin's nights out, when she came home, a man always came to the door with her, and Mark might hear their voices murmuring awhile, and Elin's low warm laughter. He wondered about that young man, who he was, what he was like, what Elin thought of him; and he liked that young man, for Elin's sake, before he ever saw him.

2

(Autumn 1933)

In October, Hitler announced Germany's withdrawal from the League of Nations and from the Disarmament Conference; but Roosevelt said the United States would keep its hands off old-world politics, and the League of Nations had never seemed to Mark important, so he was not much disturbed. His thoughts this fall were more concerned with Tony than with Hitler. Tony's first year away from home was for Mark a period of adjustment to the changes in his son. Early in October the boy enclosed in one of his letters a statement worked out on the model Mark had taught him, with each check accounted for, and explanations added. Mark studied this statement with misted eyes, trying to realize that this youngster, this baby who always wanted to be tucked in at night, and who always insisted that his father should say good night when he came home, had suddenly become even in a small way a man of business. He wrote Tony as gravely as possible, discussing each item in this accounting.

Tony came home at Thanksgiving, and Mark met him at the station. Tony cried: 'Hi, Dad!' and ran into his arms. 'Dad' was new. It had always been 'Father' until now, and Mark was sorry for the change. But otherwise, he thought at first, Tony was as he had always been. When he went to bed at night, he still called his father to turn out the lights and open the windows, and he still made Mark promise to wake him up when he came to bed. Yet before the week-end was over, Mark realized that in many intangible ways there was a change. Till now Tony had often asked questions, but he had usually been ready to take Mark's answer as gospel. Now he had opinions of his own, and reasons for them. Sometimes Tony was surely wrong, but Mark found that he did not win any of their mild arguments. Tony listened respectfully enough, but he remained unshaken in his own points of view.

For example, Tony noticed that one of the rear tires on the car was badly worn, so that the tread was gone, the rubber smooth; and he said:

'You ought to get a new tire, Father.'

Mark explained: 'I always run tires until the fabric begins to show through. As long as the fabric is protected by rubber, it doesn't rot, and the tire is as good as new, except that it doesn't give you quite the same traction.'

'I know,' Tony agreed. 'But it punctures a lot easier. If you keep driving it till you get a puncture, you might have to change a tire somewhere by yourself; and then, with snow on the ground, you'd have to wear chains, where if you had a good tread on the tire, you wouldn't need them except in deep snow. And besides,' Tony added, 'the fall is the best time to buy tires, because they don't wear out much in winter. The rubber has a chance to season and get tough. If you buy new tires in the spring, they're all worn pretty smooth before fall.'

The question rose as to why this particular tire had worn more than its fellows. Mark thought it was because this was the right-hand tire, carrying the burden of propulsion; but Tony said the wheel was probably out of line. This led them to a discussion of the life of tires and of cars; and Mark said he might trade in this car next spring, when it would be two years old, but Tony said quickly:

'Look, Dad, why don't you keep it till I'm sixteen? Then I'll be old enough to drive, and you can give it to me and buy a new car yourself.'

Mark was a little startled at the suggestion. The prospect of allowing Tony to adventure upon the highway at the wheel of a car seemed to him alarming. There were so many dangers on the road. Tony himself might learn to drive skilfully and well, but not all drivers were wise and careful. You never knew when some car with a fool at the wheel would come speeding around a curve, or out of an intersection, at such a reckless pace that it was impossible to dodge.

'I don't know, Tony,' he said doubtfully. 'You'll be sixteen while you're still at Hadley. Do the boys have cars at school?'

'Oh, no! They're not allowed to drive them there; but they drive at home, the fellows that are old enough.'

Mark smiled. 'As a matter of fact, son, I hadn't figured on giving you a car, not right away. For one thing, we just have a one-car garage. There'd be no place for you to keep it.'

'I could park it in the street,' Tony argued.

Mark did not contest the point further at the moment, and to avoid committing himself on that larger matter, he conceded the lesser question of the tire, agreeing to buy a new one next day. The whole incident at once amused and pleased him. It was the first time he and Tony had had a real difference of opinion; and Tony had held up his end of the argument. This was, he thought, a definite milestone, an intimation of approaching maturity in his son.

3

(Winter 1933–1934)

That fall, Tom Sheffield, now that young Tommy was at Harvard, sold the Lincoln house to Dave Rollins. Dave and Marcia planned to use it as a winter home. Dave had served in the last war, emerging without wounds but—Marcia always insisted—with shattered nerves. He had inherited substantial means, and Marcia likewise enjoyed an independent income; so he had no business or profession, and they usually spent their summers on the Cape, while in the winter they might go South, or to California, or to Honolulu, or to Europe. But now their daughter, Ruth, was sixteen, and Marcia wished to bring her out in Boston in another year or two.

Mark—and the others of their group—had known Dave and Marcia for years. Dave was subject to occasional nervous breakdowns as a result of which he might be under medical care for two or three weeks at a time, seeing no one except Marcia and his doctor. Afterward, he seemed to return to normal, and Mark had always found him a thoroughly delightful companion. He sometimes thought Dave would be more content, and better off physically, if Marcia did not coddle him so persistently. She was one of those women who are happiest in the belief that the persons they love require constant protection and care. 'Marcia's never so contented as when she's babying me,' Dave told Mark once in affectionate amusement. 'I play things up worse than they are, just to let her have a good time.'

They bought Tom's house without those repairs and alterations which

Tom had thought of making, preferring to do it over in their own way; and Tom and Emma took an apartment on Gloucester Street. Mark, inevitably, remembered the money Tom had borrowed from him to finance those repairs, and he hoped—for Tom's sake—that the other would repay it out of the purchase price. When Tom did not at once do so, Mark reminded himself that his friend probably had other debts more pressing, which must first be satisfied; and there were always those 'expensive tastes' of which Emma liked to speak, to be appeased. But if Tom could not pay back that thousand dollars, Mark wished he would come and say so, frankly and openly.

Tom did not do this, yet almost every Sunday evening the old group still drew together; Tom and Emma, Ed and Mary, Bob and Nell, and Mark. Dave and Marcia were often of their number now. Tom, as though conscious of what was in Mark's mind, wore a forced gaiety; and there was this fall, as though with Tommy away from home she released some restraint upon herself, a change in Emma, too. For one thing, she had in the past always limited herself to one cocktail; and Mark had heard her say, with that bald and shocking openness which in the twenties had been characteristic of the times: 'I don't dare take more than one. Tom has always wanted a daughter, and if he ever got me tight, anything might happen.' But now she began to take a second cocktail and a third. They never seemed to affect her, and the others wondered at her capacity. 'It's inherited,' she sometimes said. 'I had an uncle who for years drank a bottle of whiskey a day.'

But once this winter Mark saw her obviously affected. They had all gone out to the Lincoln house for supper with Dave and Marcia, and for Badminton afterward; and Dave, though he was himself abstemious, mixed excellent cocktails. Emma drank her share and more, and she became tearful, buttonholing Mark, leading him outside to tell him how unhappy she was at seeing their old home in other hands, to say how miserably lonesome her life had become since Tommy went away to college, to complain that Tom didn't really like her, that no one liked her. 'Not even you, Mark,' she sobbed. 'You don't really like me at all.'

He assured her that he liked her very much, and she clung to him, sobbing, and insisting in a maudlin self-pity that they all hated her. 'I love you, Mark,' she insisted. 'I've always loved you. I've tried to tell you, but you just won't ever listen. You're awful mean to me! Why are you so mean to me?'

She was soft and yielding and all submission, and her flushed cheeks and swimming eyes made her treacherously attractive. Mark put her in her car and she pleaded with him to sit with her; but he went to find Tom and said: 'You'd better take Emma home, Tom. She's not feeling very well.'

Tom made some excuse to the others and he and Emma departed. Mark told no one what had happened, but when he was driving home later with Bob and Nell, Nell said:

'Emma was cocked as a mink tonight, wasn't she.' They did not answer her. Bob rarely spoke ill of anyone, keeping silence unless he could find a kindly word to say; and Mark would not speak, but Nell required no answer. 'She gave me a long song and dance the other day about Tom's drinking. She said he never goes to bed sober. But he'll have to put her to bed tonight. The little fool had a crying jag.'

'Tom has had a rough time this last year,' Bob reminded her. 'I guess it's been pretty tough on . . .'

'She's not helping any, getting drunk.'

Mark said thoughtfully: 'Of course she knows we're all fond of Tom, like him a lot. That must be hard for her to take. She's on the defensive all . . .'

'You and Bob are just alike,' Nell retorted. 'Always standing up for people. I still say she's a mess!'

A week or so later Tom came to see Mark about that loaned money. He said straightforwardly: 'I ought to have come before, Mark. I know what you've been thinking, since we sold the house; and I don't blame you. But Mark, I had a lot of other debts, some that might have made trouble if I hadn't taken care of them. We've always spent more than I earned; not much more, but enough so that we kept going further and further behind. I knew you wouldn't sue me, or anything, so I paid the other bills first.' He laughed shamedly. 'Why, Mark, some of them went back five years. I've cleared up most of them now. The house was mortgaged. Dave paid me all it was worth, maybe more; but I've used every cent of what I got.' He added lamely: 'I can pay you fifty dollars now, and some every month. I'll clean it up as quick as I can.'

'I'm sorry you're in a hole, Tom,' Mark said. 'Take as long as you like, of course.' He wished to bid the other forget the matter altogether, but to do so would hurt Tom.

'I'll pay you something every month. We're not spending as much now, even with Tommy in college.'

Mark nodded. 'Work it out any way you can, Tom,' he agreed. 'Don't let it worry you.'

Tom said awkwardly: 'Emma wants me to thank you about the other night, Mark. She wasn't really as bad off as she seemed. Her stomach was upset, something she'd eaten, I guess.'

Mark was sorry Tom had mentioned that incident. 'Sure. I know. Forget it!'

'She doesn't drink much of anything, you know,' Tom loyally explained. 'She's not used to it.'

Mark said in affectionate reassurance: 'You don't have to tell me, Tom.' He took the fifty dollars—in currency—which the other gave him. 'And don't worry about the balance,' he insisted. He wondered how long it would take Tom to pay the total; a year, perhaps. But time was to prove him wrong, over optimistic, in this conjecture.

4

(Summer 1934)

Tony, during his first year at Hadley, grew with a startling suddenness. Mark did not notice this until spring vacation, but when Tony came home he was almost as tall as his father, and in June Tony was definitely the taller, lean and awkward and a little stringy, as boys after their last spurting growth are apt to be. He had grown faster than his own capacity to control his members. He was as awkward as a puppy, and Mark thought that some form of physical training would be desirable to teach the boy to handle himself; tennis, perhaps, or boxing lessons. He spoke of this to Bob one day. Bob sometimes patronized a gymnasium, working out for an hour or so before going home to dinner; and he suggested that Mark let Tony try the boxing instructor there, and took Mark to the gymnasium to meet him.

The instructor was Mike Hennessy. Somewhere in his forties, he was a stocky man with many small scars on his countenance that testified to long experience in the ring. His manner was pleasant, and he had a cheerful friendliness which attracted Mark. He spoke easily and well, and when Mark afterward commented on this in some surprise, Bob told him: 'He's a great reader, a pretty good man. He did some boxing while he was in the army—the British army, during the last war—and an American promoter saw him and brought him to this country, and he fought for a while as a lightweight here. He never got to the top, but he was always a dangerous man. He went back to Ireland to help

fight the Black and Tans, and his father and his brother were shot
against a wall—because Mike was in the field, fighting against the English—and their farm was burned. So he hates England, and you can't
blame him; but as long as you don't start singing "God Save the King"
to him, he's all right.'

Before making a decision on Tony's boxing lessons Mark wanted
Mr. Carbrey's opinion on the question. He had come to have a lively
respect for that little man's wisdom where boys were concerned. Having business one day in Springfield, he drove home through Hadley to
talk with the Headmaster. Mr. Carbrey was glad to see him and to hear
the news of Tony.

'I'm putting him in Mr. Woodring's corridor next fall,' he told Mark.
'The boys there are more nearly his size and stature, not only physically
but in character. Tony's a pretty positive boy, you know; he knows his
own mind.'

'He likes Frank Parks,' Mark suggested. 'Will they be separated?'

'Yes,' the Head said. 'Frank is older than Tony; but Tony's the
stronger character of the two. I think he needs contact with boys he
won't dominate quite so easily.'

Mark spoke of what was in his mind, and Mr. Carbrey agreed that
boxing lessons would be fine. They stayed awhile, discussing the times.
Mr. Roosevelt had pushed through Congress a bill permitting him to
devalue the dollar and it had become a crime to own a ten-dollar gold
piece. A dozen army pilots had been killed because the President set
them to the unaccustomed task of carrying the mails. Every nation except Finland had defaulted on the war debts. In Germany, Hitler,
crushing out a plot to overthrow his government, had shot General
von Schleicher, the former Chancellor, and Captain Roehm, commander of the Storm Troopers, as well as three or four score others.

But to both Mark and Mr. Carbrey, what was happening in Washington overshadowed European affairs. 'Most of the men I know think
Roosevelt has horns and a forked tail,' Mark admitted. 'I disagree with
practically everything he's done—especially his handling of the currency—but I try to remember that I may be wrong.'

'He had a ticklish situation to meet,' Mr. Carbrey suggested. 'Troops
had driven a Bonus army out of Washington, and in some of the farm
states men were in the mood for violence over the mortgage situation.
You don't hear of that sort of thing now. Mr. Roosevelt has ended those
disorders.'

When Mark came home, he reported to Tony Mr. Carbrey's plan

about his new room; and he asked: 'Do you think you'll like the change?'

Tony seemed doubtful. 'The fellows in that corridor are mostly athletes. I wasn't good enough to make even the second team in football or baseball, so I'll be sort of out of it with them.'

'Do you know the fellows?'

'Oh, yes, sure, I know all of them.'

'Like them?' Mark insisted.

Tony said: 'They're all right.' There was a reservation in his tone, and he added: 'The only one—there's a fellow named Charlie Spring. He's my age, but he's bigger than I am. He had a set of gloves, and he used to kid fellows into boxing with him, and he could lick all of them. I don't mean they had any real fights; but he'd get them to box with him, and knock them around pretty bad. He knocked out a couple of teeth, and there was nearly always some boy who had a black eye from boxing with him.'

Mark welcomed that opening for what he wished to say. 'I've been thinking you ought to take a few boxing lessons before you go back. You might find it good fun. I talked to the instructor at the Gym in town, if you'd like to try it.' He smiled. 'Maybe after a few lessons you could tackle Charlie on equal terms.'

'Gosh,' Tony protested, 'I doubt it. He's taller than I am, and heavier too.'

'Well, you've grown pretty fast,' Mark reminded him, 'and boxing would help you learn how to handle yourself. It's not a bad thing to know.'

Tony, somewhat doubtfully, in the end agreed to try it; and for the rest of the summer he went three times a week for half an hour of instruction. After the first two or three times he began to enjoy it; and when he came home he might tell Mark, proudly, how his foot work was improving, or that Mike Hennessy had praised his left jab. Mark himself had never learned to box, had never been an athlete in the more active sense of the word; but he saw Tony's shoulders thicken and broaden, and was pleased.

The night before the boy left to return to school, Mark asked him: 'Glad to go back?'

'Yes, sir, I am,' Tony told him. 'I've had a wonderful time this summer, but I get sort of tired of just loafing; and it'll be fun to see everybody again.'

'Still like Mr. Carbrey?'

'Yes, he's swell!'

So Tony went back to Hadley for his second year.

5

(September 1934)

A week or so after Tony's departure, Mark met Elin's young man. She spoke to him at breakfast one morning, and, though her tones were steady enough, her color was high.

'Mr. Worth, are you going to be at home this evening?'

'Yes,' he said, and then added, thinking he understood: 'Unless you'd like to go out. I can always dine in town.'

'Oh, no,' she told him quickly. 'It's only, I wanted to know if you could talk to Einar.'

Mark repeated the name. 'Einar?'

Her cheeks were bright. 'Yes, Einar Kemmi. He is Finnish, and he does not understand about American laws, in some business he wants to do, and I told him you might help him.'

'I'll be glad to,' Mark assured her. 'Have him come this evening.'

So that night Elin, blushing happily, ushered into the living room a tall young man with a shock of stiff pale hair, and broad high cheekbones under his blue eyes, obviously uncomfortable in a high collar and a heavy dark suit. He proved to speak English only haltingly, so Elin acted as his spokesman, making clear what he wished to say when he was at a loss.

Einar was a chauffeur, in private employ, and Elin proudly assured Mark that he could do anything with engines. He had saved some money, and with it had bought a small lot of land—Mark knew the location—and now wished to build there a public garage. His savings were almost sufficient—with the sums he could borrow on the land and on the building as it was being put up—to finance this undertaking; and he had come for advice on the legal complications involved in notes and mortgages and building loans.

Mark was disturbed by what he heard. The land the young man had bought was in an alder swamp which bordered one of the well-travelled routes through Newton; but it was half a mile from the nearest residential district and Mark thought it unlikely anyone would with-

out solicitation send a car there to be repaired. As for gas sales, there
were filling stations long established at the nearest corners. He suggested that the garage might not be a profitable venture, but he saw at
once that Einar was obsessed with this plan, that it was a dream toward
which he strove as the old knights strove to find the Holy Grail. Mark
asked Elin, whose manner toward Einar was evidence enough of her
proud affection for this young man:

'And when the garage is a success, then you and Einar will be married?'

'Oh, yes,' she said happily, and he wondered where he would find
anyone competent to fill her place; but she added in quick reassurance,
as though she read his thought: 'Only Einar knows I will always take
care of you and Tony.'

Mark smiled, and Einar watched them both, with quick, questioning
glances, trying to understand what they were saying. In the end Mark
decided that Einar would never be satisfied till he tried this plan of his,
so he said:

'Well, Elin, if Einar wants to do this, I'll handle the legal side of it.
You'll need a permit from the city, and I'll check the title to the land
and all that. But Einar's cutting it pretty fine financially. He's allowing
no margin at all, and there are always unforeseen items. I think he'd
better let me lend him say two hundred and fifty dollars. Then if there
is any slip up, he can handle it. It's always better to have some leeway.'
Before she could speak, he added: 'Let me have the pleasure of giving
you a hand.' He smiled. 'You've done a lot for Tony and me that we
can never pay for, you know.'

He was afraid she would protest. So few people were wise enough—
and generous enough—to allow others the pleasure of being generous.
But she agreed almost at once, speaking quickly to Einar, telling him
this wonderful news. She promised Mark: 'And we will pay you back.
You can take it out of my salary. I only need a little every week.'

Mark smiled. 'No, this is between Einar and me,' he insisted. He
thought with a stir of warm liking for this young man that Finland
alone among the nations of Europe steadfastly paid each instalment on
its war debts. 'Finns pay their debts,' he told Elin. 'I'm not worried
about being paid.'

He drew up a note—with no interest—and gave it to Einar to sign,
and wrote a check. The two young people went away to the kitchen together and he heard their happy voices there. He was not sure he had

done right. It seemed to him inevitable that Einar's project would fail
—but at least the young man would acquire wisdom from the experience,
would know better another time.

Probably, despite her loyal promises, this meant that he would lose
Elin. Once she and Einar were married, there would be babies coming,
and Elin would want a home of her own. But they would be happy,
those two. Elin's smiling eyes during the days that followed increased
his pleasure in what he had done.

6

(Winter 1934–1935)

Tony's three years at Hadley always seemed to Mark in retrospect to
have passed very quickly; and this was particularly true of his second
year there, when affairs in Washington and the progressive reorganiza-
tion of Germany and her increasingly ominous attitude filled Mark's
mind. Mr. Roosevelt's program of social and economic legislation provoked the abiding distrust of the men Mark knew best. Men of business and of the professions agreed that the President was unsound, unscrupulous, dangerous to the established order of things. Word-of-
mouth anecdotes designed to express scorn and contempt, to portray
him in ridiculous lights, were current everywhere. 'Have you heard the
latest Roosevelt story?' was the usual introductory question. Mrs. Roosevelt was an even more popular target; and there was among Mark's
friends and acquaintances no easier way to provoke a laugh than by
some derogatory remark about the President of the United States.

Mark himself was troubled by this, and he was struck one day by a
conversation—to which he was content to listen—between Bob Ritchie
and Jerry Crocker. Mark had not seen Jerry since that day more than a
year ago when Emma joined them at lunch. The three met by chance,
in the lobby of the Copley, and stood for a few minutes in talk together.
Jerry was just back from Washington; and Bob asked: 'How's Franklin?' His tone was dry with contempt.

'I didn't see the President,' Jerry admitted. 'I had some things to look
up at the Congressional Library. But I judge he has the situation well
in hand.'

Bob asked: 'Have you heard the story about the two sea gulls?' Jerry
had not, and Bob told the story and Jerry laughed politely, but he said
then:

'You might as well get used to him, Bob. Mr. Roosevelt's going to be President for a long time. He's got the votes, and he'll keep them.'

Bob said incredulously: 'You're not a Roosevelt man, are you, for God's sake?'

Jerry smiled. 'No. I'm what the English would call a member of His Majesty's loyal opposition. But telling funny stories about Mr. Roosevelt—or Mrs. Roosevelt—is empty business.'

Bob looked at him in astonishment. 'Are you standing up for that butterfly-minded nitwit?'

'He's President of the United States,' Jerry pointed out, in mild tones. 'I don't think much of his ideas, but I respect the office he holds.'

'I used to respect it!' Bob exclaimed. 'But he doesn't! Why should I?'

Jerry laughed. 'Didn't mean to start an argument,' he said amiably. 'But I think it's a mistake to ridicule a man we've elected to high office.' He lifted his hand. 'Well, I'll be seeing you.'

On the way back downtown Bob was silent for a while, but he said then thoughtfully: 'You know, Jerry was right about "respecting the office." Didn't Plato say the same thing?'

'I don't remember,' Mark admitted.

'I think he did. That's one of the weaknesses of this country, Mark. We—the majority of us—elect a man and then make up silly jokes about him. That doesn't get us anywhere.'

Mark felt a sudden affection for the other. Jerry's word might have been resented by most men as a rebuke. It was characteristic of Bob to be willing to recognize the fact that he had been wrong, to be ready to amend his ways. 'I see his point,' Mark agreed. 'There are some bad judges on the bench, but that doesn't justify contempt of court.'

Bob nodded; yet after a moment he exploded: 'But God damn it, Mark, how can any sensible man respect Roosevelt? I'll be damned if I can!'

Mark chuckled. 'Respect the office, then,' he advised. 'That's Jerry's rule.'

His own uneasiness over Mr. Roosevelt's policies was relieved by the fact that the Supreme Court declared unconstitutional the more flagrantly unsound New Deal legislation. Mark thought the Court was a fine balance wheel, a governor, which made it impossible for the machinery of government to run wild even with an inexpert or an injudicious hand upon the throttle. The decision on the abrogation of the gold clause in government bonds was a reproof which Mr. Roosevelt must heed and mend his ways.

Mark had come to accept developments in Germany with a certain philosophy. The men he knew, though they united in the universal condemnation of Hitler's violence toward the Jews, saw no threat to world peace in his program. When the Saar plebiscite returned that region to Germany, Hitler pledged his word that he would make no further territorial demands on France, and when he restored compulsory military service in Germany, he at the same time vowed to respect all other provisions of the Versailles Treaty. His promises were accepted at face value. France did not protest his actions, and the will for peace in Europe was manifest. Mark's anxieties slumbered for a while.

7

(Summer 1935)

During the summer before his sixteenth birthday Tony met Barbie Parks. He went in August to spend two weeks with Frank on the Cape, and he wrote his father one long letter while he was there. He said the Parks house was tremendous, and he explained:

> They're awfully rich. Mr. Parks made a lot of money in the stock market. He started being a bear just before the big break, and Frank says he made over ten million dollars. Frank doesn't get along with him. They're always arguing and Mr. Parks laughs at Frank and says he's a fool. Frank says his father was just a public burglar, selling short and robbing people. I like Mr. Parks all right, and Barbie—she's Frank's sister and she's swell—is crazy about him. Mrs. Parks is sort of silly, dressing as if she was about Barbie's age. Mr. Parks laughs at her a lot, too; and he never goes anywhere with her, just plays golf and bridge with his friends most of the time. There's a man visiting them, named Vance Ruthven, younger than Mrs. Parks, and he takes her to dances and things. Barbie doesn't seem to think much of her mother, and she calls Mr. Ruthven: 'Mama's tame cat!' Frank will hardly even speak to him.

There was much more about Barbie. Clearly she and Tony were on the best of terms, despite the difference in their ages. Mark was faintly disturbed by what Tony wrote about the Parks household; but apparently the boy had a level head, saw straight.

Tony wrote only that one letter, but a later postcard announced that they would drive up in Frank's car the Sunday night before Labor Day, would arrive about half-past ten or eleven. Mark sat up to wait for them; but at eleven they had not come, and he was uneasy, thinking of the hazards of the road. The hour till midnight seemed interminable, but not till a quarter of one did Mark hear a car outside, and young voices in the night, calling their good-byes.

Then Tony came in, brown from much sun, delighted to find his father still awake, full of talk about the two weeks just past.

'It was wonderful!' he said. 'Frank's got a keen boat, and there's a swell crowd my age down there. His sister's a peach! We got along great together.'

His quick tongue ran on, and Mark heard over and over what Barbie did and said and thought. It was the first time Tony had ever shown a concentrated interest in any girl, and in the first pause Mark asked:

'How old is Barbara?'

'Seventeen,' Tony said. 'She's only two years older than I am, but she calls me "Babe." Just kidding, of course. I'm going to write to her, and she promised to write to me.'

'Who brought you home?'

'Frank and Barbie and Joe and Betty Chase.'

'I'm sorry they didn't come in. Where did they go?'

'Frank and Barbie are going to visit the Chases down at Manchester.'

'Are they driving down there tonight? It's an hour from here.'

'Oh, sure.'

They sat late, and they went upstairs together. Tony was first ready for bed, and Mark heard his windows raised, heard his lights snap out, saw the doorway dark. He went to the door before turning out his own lights.

'Good night, son,' he said.

'Good night, Dad.'

Mark asked: 'Do you remember how you always wanted me to fix your windows and turn out your lights?'

'Sure!' Tony chuckled in the darkness. 'And if you were going out, I always made you promise to wake me up when you came home.'

'I suppose,' Mark suggested, smiling in the dark, 'I suppose from now on it'll be the other way around. You'll be out late, and I'll be asking you to wake me up when you come home!'

'I guess so,' Tony assented.

'Tonight, for instance,' Mark confessed. 'Of course I knew you were all right; but I couldn't have gone to sleep till you came home.'

'You don't ever have to worry about me.'

'I know, son; but I hope that if anything ever does go wrong, so that you're going to be later than you expected to be, you'll call me up and tell me.'

'Sure,' Tony promised, and he added sleepily: 'Good night.'

Mark did not go at once to sleep, thinking of Tony and of Barbie Parks, wondering what she was like. Probably it was ridiculous to take this, Tony's first enthusiasm over any girl too seriously. After all, the youngster was only fifteen.

But everything that concerned Tony was interesting to Mark, and would always be.

8

(September 1935)

Tony's sixteenth birthday fell on the ninth of September. His interest in automobiles had never faltered; and on a fishing trip to Ontario that summer—they drove out by way of Ohio to see Mark's father in Hardiston, then turned northward and shipped the car to Buffalo, picking it up there after a fortnight in the Nipissing country—he had done much of the driving. He wished to get his driving license before he went back to Hadley, and Mark went with him when he took his examination. He himself sat in the rear seat, Tony at the wheel, a police officer by the boy's side; and Tony, at the officer's direction, performed the few simple maneuvers required. When the driving tests were concluded, the policeman said:

'All right. Take me back.'

So Tony thought the ordeal was finished, and Mark saw the high elation in his son. Then they approached a cross-walk where an elderly gentleman was about to cross and Tony blew his horn, warning the old man to stop while he went by.

The officer said sharply: 'That will cost you your license, this time, young fellow. At a cross-walk pedestrians have the right of way.'

Tony said, in a crushed tone: 'Gosh, I was just afraid he didn't see me coming.'

'You haven't any right to make him stop,' the officer insisted. 'You're supposed to do the stopping, and let him cross.'

Mark saw the crushed despair in the very slump of Tony's youthful shoulders. 'I think you've taught the boy a lesson he won't forget, Officer,' he said courteously. 'He's naturally careful and considerate; but he was excited just then because he thought he had passed all the tests. He might not have made the mistake if he hadn't been feeling so pleased with himself.'

The officer said seriously: 'Well, any man driving a car is being tested every minute he's driving. You can't afford to take your mind off what you're doing.'

'That's quite true,' Mark agreed. 'And I think you were perfectly right to emphasize the point. But it was an error anyone might have made.'

He thought the examiner might relent; but the other said firmly: 'He can take another test later on, but I can't pass him now.'

When they were alone, Mark was glad to find that Tony blamed only himself for his failure. 'I know the pedestrian has the right of way,' he said contritely.

'It's hard luck to have to wait.'

'Sure,' Tony agreed. 'But I've waited sixteen years. I guess I can wait till Christmas.' He looked at his father with a quick, shy grin. 'You can get a new car then and give me this one for a Christmas present.'

Mark smiled. 'We'll see about that when the time comes.' He was quite sure Tony was too young to have a car of his own; but he would not debate the matter now.

9

(October 1935)

Ruth Rollins—she was two years older than Tony—made her début that fall at a dance at the Somerset. Mark had watched Ruth grow from a lanky youngster into a tall, rather pretty girl whom he liked very much. Early this last summer, he and Tony had driven down one Friday afternoon to spend a week end at the Rollins' place on the Cape. Dave and Marcia had had a dinner engagement, so only Ruth was at home when they arrived.

She offered them sandwiches, milk, anything they desired; but they declined, and Mark said it was a night too beautiful to stay indoors and they went out on the veranda. The moon was full, the skies a cloudless arch of blue, and there was a long swell rolling in, breaking whitely on the white beach below the house.

Mark lighted a cigarette and Tony perched on the veranda rail and Ruth lay on the couch and they talked politely for a while, and Mark began to detect in Ruth's voice a strange unrest. Once he said he was tired, might go to bed; and she sat up quickly, protesting: 'Oh, no, stay

and talk awhile!' He smiled and assented, and she rose and walked restlessly up and down the length of the veranda, swinging her arms, laughing at herself till they laughed with her. She was in slacks and sweater,
and suddenly she stopped, knelt, and then stood on her head, her slim
legs straight, her toes pointed. Mark applauded, and she came erect
again and made a flying leap to land prone on the couch, and kicked her
heels there and pounded with her fists on the cushions, and cried: 'I
want to do something, do something, do something!' Mark understood
the hunger in her which she herself was too young to recognize; and
Tony tried to stand on his head as she had done, and toppled over with
a crash, and they both laughed at him, and Mark said he had better
find a soft spot before he tried it again, and Ruth exclaimed: 'Come
down on the beach and I'll teach you.'

They raced away and Mark followed them and Tony spread his
coat on the sand, and set his head on it, and Ruth held his ankles while
he tried to learn the trick of balance, and he wavered so that she had
trouble holding him and at last they toppled over and she fell on top
of him. Mark, sitting on the sand with his back against a drift log,
thought they were like puppies playing together. Tony decided he
could never learn, and Ruth protested, in a laughing urgency: 'But
we've got to do something!' She began to march up and down the
beach, whistling the March of the Wooden Soldiers, marching like one,
her arms and legs stiff; and Tony joined in, and she called: 'Come on,
Uncle Mark!' So Mark took his place beside them and they marched
and countermarched, whistling the tune, laughing in the moonlight
till Dave and Marcia returned and from the veranda of the cottage
Marcia called in an amused surprise:

'Whatever are you idiots doing?'

So the spell was broken. Mark himself felt more than a little ridiculous, and Ruth at the first sound of her mother's voice changed completely. All her sweet exuberance was gone, and she turned with Mark
to walk sedately toward the house. Only Tony marched all the way,
whistling that same shrill tune.

Mark had never seen the girl again in that high humor. Nevertheless, he and she had come to be good friends, and he enjoyed the occasions—at the Cape cottage on the beach after a swim, or in the barn in
Lincoln watching others play Badminton—when he talked for a while
with her. She had spent a summer in Germany when she was fifteen,
liked Germans, and was more interested in the German and the Russian revolutions than in our own. He discovered one day that she was

violently opposed to hunting and fishing, to any wanton killing; and when he tried smilingly to discuss the point with her, he found in her a quiet firmness which made him drop the subject.

He was astonishingly pleased to find that she liked him, sought his company. Something about her touched him deeply; and he decided that this was in part because she seemed to him not particularly happy. She was devoted to her father, but there appeared to be no close bond between her and her mother. Mark asked Tony once whether she were popular with boys, and Tony said: 'Not very. Frank Parks goes to see her a lot in summer and talks about Russia to her; but she hardly ever goes to dances or anything. She was at one dance I went to down there and I danced with her and I was stuck for almost an hour.'

Mark said smilingly: 'I think I'd enjoy an hour with Ruth.'

'Sure, but not dancing with her!'

Probably, Mark decided, Ruth's mental maturity—the very fact that she could talk interestingly and intelligently with older men—made her less attractive to youngsters her own age.

He received an invitation to her dance at the Somerset, and on the engraved card she had written: 'Be sure and come, Uncle Mark. Love. Ruth.' He was touched and he decided to go. Till Nan died five years ago he had enjoyed dancing; but he had not danced since then. Tonight he found himself rusty at it, found his partners surprisingly difficult to handle. Nell Ritchie, though she was small, nevertheless dominated him, compelling him to follow rather than to lead. She had a wearying trick of resting too much weight on his left hand, so that his arm and shoulder ached with fatigue; and she talked steadily and leaned away from him against the curve of his arm, till once or twice he almost lost his balance. Emma Sheffield pressed so closely against him, her face buried under his ear, that he was embarrassed and glad to be rid of her. Mary Halstead, to Mark's surprise, danced rather poorly, so poorly that they were forever stumbling, and laughing at their own mistakes; but when the orchestra swung into a waltz they danced it with an exaggerated gusto which amused everyone.

Mark danced, too, with Betty Ritchie—a sub-deb this year, invited because of the friendship between the families—and he thought Betty was like a queen scornfully permitting a humble subject to kiss her hand, and was grateful when some awkward boy relieved him. He had never liked Betty. Jan was not here tonight, was still too young for such an occasion.

Mark caught Ruth's eye as she danced past him and he thought there was an appeal in her glance, so he touched her partner's arm and he and Ruth swung away, moving slowly on the now crowded floor.

'Having a grand time?' he asked, and she nodded, looking past him. He followed her glance and saw her father with two or three other men, champagne glasses in their hands. 'I never saw you look so well,' he said. 'We're all mighty proud of you tonight.'

'Father's having a good time,' she said in a tone Mark did not understand, as though she were frightened.

'This is a big night for him,' he reminded her.

She laughed, more than was necessary, her head thrown back; and he realized that she was strung tight, under some hard tension, and wondered why, and remembered that any girl was taut with excitement on such an occasion. She did not speak again, and he realized that they were dancing well together, in complete harmony, as though the music moved them both. 'I like this,' he said.

She looked up at him with grave eyes. 'I love you very much, Uncle Mark,' she told him quietly.

He laughed with pleasure. 'That's great. I love you too, Ruth.'

Her brow touched his cheek and she whispered: 'It's practically insulting for them to let me dance with you so long, you know. But I'm glad of it.'

Mark had a sudden certainty that she was unhappy, had an impulsive wish to hold her close and kiss her and tell her how wonderful she was. She needed just that, needed someone to praise and approve and love her. He looked around the crowded floor, trying to discover some young man who would give her the tenderness for which she was so hungry. The boy who touched his arm—a shock-headed youngster whose tie was awry—did not fit the pattern, but he was better than nothing. Mark watched them move away.

Then he saw Dave and crossed to join him. Dave's eyes were unnaturally bright and his face had a metallic look which Mark had never seen in it before.

'Fine party,' Mark said.

'A good time was had by all,' Dave agreed, his drawling tone heavy with something that was almost insolence. Mark thought possibly Dave had drunk too much, and he said:

'The only thing missing is a little fresh air. Where can we get a gulp or two?'

Dave winked at him. 'Don't tell me. Let me guess. I'll bet Marcia sent you to take me in hand.' Mark saw that he was not himself. Dave normally was a gentle, gallant, thoughtful man; but his very tones now were an offense.

'That reminds me,' Mark said disarmingly. 'I haven't danced with Marcia yet, haven't even paid my respects.' He moved away.

Marcia danced effortlessly, matching his steps to perfection. He said: 'I had a fine dance with Ruth. She's a grand girl.'

'She's sweet, yes,' she said abstractedly. Then she added, like a question: 'You were talking with Dave.'

'Yes.'

"How is he?' The question seemed to be forced from her by an uncontrollable anxiety.

'Dave?' he said evasively. 'Why he's fine, having a fine time.' Then Bob Ritchie took her away from him.

Mark went home a little after midnight, dancing half a dozen steps with Ruth to say good night, and he spoke to Marcia and then to Dave. Dave said elaborately: 'Oh, must you go!' Mark colored at his tone. It was sardonic, deliberately insolent. Dave clearly did not drink gracefully. Mark hoped as he drove home that Dave would not spoil Ruth's party.

10

(Autumn 1935)

Tony's letters that fall spoke often of Barbara Parks, who was a Freshman at Merryfield, near Hadley. 'She's coming over to the game, Saturday,' he reported once; and afterward: 'Barb was here Saturday. We went for a walk down to the river, after the game. She's wonderful, Dad. You'll get to meet her, Christmas.'

When in October Italy attacked Abyssinia, and there were rumors of war in every newspaper, Tony for the first time became conscious of world affairs. He wrote:

Do you think there's going to be a war? Everybody here is talking about it. I guess about ten per cent of the fellows would want to enlist if war started now, if they were old enough, but another ten per cent say they'd rather be shot than go in the army. Everyone's wondering whether Russia will fight along with U.S., France, England, and Ethiopia. Some say the war will be short and sweet, and that U.S., Russia, and Japan will stay out and make lots of money and that in another few years Russia and U.S. will beat the pants off Japan. No one knows a darn thing about it. No matter what happens, we aren't going to do anything but what we're told to do, and that's that. But I'd like to know what you think is going to happen.

Mark was startled by this letter, not only because he was surprised at Tony's sudden interest in world affairs, but because he was astonished at the immediate acceptance by Tony and his friends of the likelihood that in the next great war, like the last one, the United States would be involved. He took a long time to frame his answer to Tony. In college he had written an essay—he searched it out from among his papers and re-read it with a curious interest—on 'International Arbitration,' with a subtitle: 'The Hague Court as an Educational Agent.' He entered the essay in a prize contest conducted by the Lake Mohonk Peace Conference. His thesis was that the habit of submitting minor differences to the World Court at the Hague would grow upon the nations of the world till the Court was to international affairs what courts of law were to the individual; but he predicted that there would always be incidents so provocative that nations would spring to arms just as the individual under extreme provocation takes the law into his own hands. He spoke of this youthful essay in his reply to Tony's letter, sent it for Tony to read; and he explained:

It's chiefly interesting as showing what sort of boy I was when I was a little older than you are now; but it's pretty well obsolete. Times have changed—and not in the ways I predicted. I see little hope for world peace now except perhaps through world conquest, an enforced world union. But probably I'm as wrong now as I was then.

As for today—I doubt whether a general war will come out of what's happening in Ethiopia. Of course Italy is simply a burglar, a big boy taking marbles away from a little boy. Japan has been doing the same thing to China. Sometimes big boys interfere to stop the bully, and that might happen now; but I don't expect it. The great powers—England and the United States—could have made Japan stay out of China. They could have done it without fighting, probably. But they lacked the moral courage to do anything—and I doubt whether England will do anything now. Wars aren't fought for abstractions. England won't fight to defend Ethiopia. She won't go to war unless she feels herself threatened. In the long run most wars are, from the point of view of the combatants, self-defense. Italy even pretends this is a defensive war. Of course that seems to us absurd, and I don't think even Italy believes it. She's simply a highwayman. But innocent bystanders seldom risk their lives to arrest a highwayman unless he threatens them more directly than England is threatened now.

Maybe some day the great nations of the world—or some of them—will unite to enforce peace. It can be done, but only if those nations are prepared to fight to do it. If, for instance, the United States had been able to say to Germany in 1914: 'If there's a war, we're in it, against you, and we can land a well-trained army of half a million men in France in thirty days,' why, then there would have been no war.

But Germany knew that England had no real army, and neither had we.

We said nothing, and even if we had spoken, our word, since there was no immediately ready force behind it, would have had no weight. So war came. Probably war will come again some day unless we're so well prepared that no one is willing to risk having us as an enemy.

This neutrality act of ours is an invitation to the world to go to war. It is as if we announced in advance that we were leaving to the robber nations a free hand.

Tony must have been completely satisfied with that letter; or perhaps his own affairs made him forget it, for when he next wrote he did not mention Ethiopia. Instead he proudly reported:

Well, I've finally boxed with Charlie Spring. He asked me to. I guess I was scared, because I tried to get out of it; but he sort of kept kidding me about it, and said we were just going to spar a little, for fun. I had told Frank Parks about my boxing lessons, and Frank had talked about it; so Charlie knew it, and he kept kidding me, saying he wanted me to show him some of the fine points, so finally I said I would, and there'd been so much talk about it that when we went over to the old barn five or six of the fellows came along. We started off, just kind of sparring and going through the motions; but finally Charlie got excited, the way he always does when he boxes, and he began to really get hit, and I started jabbing him. He's a sucker for a left jab; so every time he tried to come in, I had my glove in his face. He's heavier than I am, of course, but whenever he started to swing his right, I'd catch him with a jab. I didn't think I was hitting him very hard, until his nose started to bleed; and then he got kind of mad, I think, because he kept coming at me harder and harder all the time. He caught me two or three good ones, but not many, and mostly on the side of the head. He's a swinger. I didn't use my right at all, because I was so busy keeping him off; but finally he was the one that wanted to stop, and he laughed and said he couldn't tell whether there was one of me or two, by that time. He said his eyes were toeing in! He was swell about it. I guess we're going to be pretty good friends.

That letter pleased Mark mightily, but this was not true of all the letters he had from Tony during the fall, for the possibility that his father would get a new car and give him the old one was very much on the youngster's mind. In every letter Tony had something to say about the virtues and the defects of this and that make of automobile; and when Tony came home for Thanksgiving, he could talk of nothing else. Mark would have been willing to avoid the issue, even if to do so meant driving the old car another year; but Tony by this time had firmly settled his own opinion of what they should do. He was bent on a new car.

'And the old one isn't worth much on a trade-in,' he said. 'So you give it to me, and I can drive it for a while. It's a lot cheaper than if you bought me a new car, or even a good used car.'

Mark said reluctantly: 'Well, I hadn't really figured on giving you a car yet, Tony. You're not allowed to have one at school, and you'll not be allowed to have one at college while you're a Freshman. Why not wait till your Sophomore year at college?'

'Oh, I'd do most of my driving in the summer time, anyway,' Tony argued. 'And I can use the car going back and forth to school. I can store it in Joe Merry's barn up there, between times, for five dollars a month.'

Mark was startled to find that his son had gone so far with his plans. He diverted the conversation into less dangerous fields.

II

(December 1935)

Nell Ritchie had never given over her insistence that Mark ought to marry again. 'It was all right for you to devote yourself to Tony as long as he was still a boy,' she conceded. 'But he's a grown man now, or soon will be, and the first thing you know he'll have a girl, and the next thing you know he'll be through college and married—and there you'll be, your occupation gone. I've told you before, you're a natural-born husband.'

Mark chuckled. 'Any special wife in mind for me?'

'Dozens.'

Mark said more seriously: 'I'm all right, Nell. Elin takes good care of me. I'm set in my ways. You'll have a hard time finding anyone . . .'

'Elin's one very good reason why you ought to get married,' Nell retorted. 'It's dangerous to go on depending on her, Mark. The first thing you know you'll be marrying her, just out of habit!'

Mark laughed. 'That might not be a bad idea,' he said, to annoy her. 'But I'm afraid she wouldn't have me. She has a young man in attendance—and strictly between ourselves . . .'

Nell cried quickly, interrupting him as she was likely to do: 'Really? Who is he?'

So Mark told her about Einar and his plans. 'I'm helping him, advising him,' he explained. He had seen Einar two or three times, and he often talked with Elin about Einar's enterprise. As Mark had feared, the garage was not prospering. Financing it had not been so simple as Einar hoped, and business was slow. Einar lived at the garage, sleeping in a cot in a half attic above it, cooking his own frugal meals; and Mark had thought of suggesting that Elin and Einar get married so that Einar could share Elin's room, but he decided the two young people would better work out their own salvation. He told Nell now: 'In fact, I loaned him some money to get the thing started.'

'You didn't! You helpless baby! You'll be getting yourself sued or something, the first thing you know. I knew you liked Elin, but I didn't think you'd be fool enough to give her money!'

'Lend,' Mark quietly corrected.

'You'll never get it back!' He smiled, and she said: 'Well, all right, then. But if they're going to be married, all the more reason for you to start looking around. You'll be lost without her.'

He asked in mock seriousness: 'What do you think of Ruth?'

'Ruth? Ruth who?'

'Why, Ruth Rollins.'

'Oh, you idiot!'

'She's a mighty sweet girl.'

'Of course she is!' Nell added abstractedly: 'She was sick after her party, you know, poor kid.'

Mark had not known that. 'What was wrong?'

'Just a nervous breakdown or something. Dave had one too. You know he has them, right along. Marcia took them both to Honolulu.'

'I knew they had gone, of course; but I didn't know why.'

She said accusingly: 'You didn't mean that about Ruth, of course!'

Mark smiled. 'You've only one defect, Nell. Among your many admirable qualities a sense of humor is not included.'

'You're not old enough to fall in love with a child,' she told him. 'But all the same, you're too young not to marry again.'

She urged her point on other occasions, and she did more than talk. If he went to dinner at their home, Mark was sure to find himself seated next to some attractive—and unattached—woman. Since Mrs. Flood there had been others. Once it was a pleasant spinster of thirty-odd, a Miss Frost, who lived in Milton. Before the evening was over she confided to Mark that she was secretly engaged to an Englishman who proposed to come to the United States in January and go into business here. It amused him thereafter to pay her many attentions—all of which he reported to Nell—until her Englishman arrived.

In October there had been a Florida girl, Marcia Rollins' unmarried sister, who laved Mark in flattering coquetry until he begged Nell to rescue him; and in December he had an interesting evening with a young German woman, a Mrs. Hueck, come to the United States to be near her son while he spent two or three years in American schools.

When Mark and Mrs. Hueck began to talk together, he found that she spoke English with complete precision. He found, too, that she held toward Hitler a loyalty at once passionate and proud. She said in response to Mark's question: 'He is the greatest man in the world today.' Mark saw her eyes glow. 'He has given us already a new Germany, has changed the whole world for us. He has given us back our hope and our self-respect.'

'It seems to us over here,' he suggested, 'that he is full of bitterness and hate. Do many Germans feel as he does? As bitterly?'

'Why should they not?' she countered. 'I was a young girl during the last war, and for two years I never had enough to eat. I worked with the little starving children, trying to save them. There was a whole generation of German children who were starved till they died—or till they were so weak that they will never be strong and well again. That is how the Allies made war on us, not sending soldiers to fight our soldiers, but putting thousands of men, comfortable in their ships, to shut off our food so that we women and children starved.' Her eyes flashed. 'That was a fine part for men to play, who call themselves brave; to sit in safety themselves and starve helpless ones.'

Mark would not risk outright argument, but he suggested mildly: 'England was fighting for her life, using every weapon she had.'

She looked at him with a keen, sharp glance. 'So were we,' she reminded him; and she said: 'Yes, there is bitterness in Germany. But now our Fuehrer leads us toward strength and joy again.'

'Is he not leading you into another war?'

'No. We want no war with anyone. We want only room enough in which to work and to live.'

'He's building up an army and a navy—and even an air force.'

'We will be the equal of any nation,' she assured him. 'That is our right. No one can deny it.'

'I don't think anyone today wants to keep Germany helpless,' he told her. 'But no one—unless it is Germany—wants another war.'

She spoke almost appealingly. 'You are all against us, you Americans. Why is that?'

'I think as much as anything because of the way you've treated the Jews.'

Her eyes hardened. 'The Jews!' she cried. 'We hate them, yes. In 1923, when we were helpless, they seized our banks and our factories and our hotels, everything. They wished to make us their slaves.'

Mark smiled faintly. 'I know what you mean,' he admitted. 'There's a story here in Boston of one of our merchants who was over there during your inflation, just as it began. When he left, he gave his waiter a ten-dollar gold certificate and advised him to save it till he could buy the hotel for three dollars, refurnish it for two dollars more, and keep the rest for operating capital. According to the story, the waiter did just that.'

She said crisply, 'Perhaps that seems amusing to you, but not to us.'

'I've a client in New York,' Mark admitted, 'a Jewish banker. He says he warned your German Jews, his business correspondents over there, that they must expect trouble. But they told him: "No one can touch us. We own the banks, the newspapers, the radio, the biggest businesses. All Germany is ours today."'

Mrs. Hueck said triumphantly: 'You see!'

'I see that!' Mark agreed. 'But I don't see why you have to beat them to death with clubs!'

She shrugged. 'That is all very much exaggerated. But we will make them give up what they seized when we were helpless.' Mark felt an iron will in her, strong and driving—and potentially dangerous. She added simply: 'When we were weak, all we had was taken away from us. Well, now we are strong! We will take back what is rightly ours.'

They talked for long. Afterward Nell asked him eagerly: 'Well, did you like Mrs. Hueck?'

Mark was almost startled by the question. 'Like her? I didn't think about that,' he confessed. 'But I respected her, certainly. If there are many Germans like her, they'll be hard to hold.' He said slowly: 'Nell, I think the world is drifting toward another war.'

12

(December 1935)

Tony's letters seldom failed to remind Mark that they needed a new car, and early in December Mark, anxious to please his son, decided on the purchase. The fact that Tony wanted the old car for his own was an issue he did not face, sure he could persuade the boy to give up that idea. He visited the salesrooms, and his own choice fell on a convertible coupe, but Tony must share in the decision, so he deferred any final selection and wrote Tony his plans. When the day came, he met Tony at the station and drove him home, and the boy said quickly:

'Well, Dad, I've got my license. I took my examination in Greenfield last Saturday. When do we pick out the new car?'

'Tomorrow?'

Tony grinned. 'Tomorrow suits me,' he said. 'We can park the old one in the street, till I go back to Hadley, unless it gets too cold. Then I'll put it in a garage somewhere.'

Mark said slowly: 'But, son, I figured I'd better turn the old car in. I think you're too young to have a car for which you'll have so little use.'

Tony protested: 'Gosh, I'd use it all right! I could have a lot of fun with it next summer.'

'It would be an expensive proposition,' Mark urged. 'You don't realize what it costs to run a car, because you've never paid the bills.'

'I know, sure,' Tony agreed. 'And that old crock is a gas hog too, and it burns as much oil as it does gasoline; but I can pay for it all right out of my allowance.'

Mark was silenced, too happy in the boy's home-coming to contest the issue then; but next day it was forced upon him. They went into the salesroom together. Tony's selection proved to be the same as his father's. When this was settled, the salesman said: 'I'll have one of the shop men take a look at your car, Mr. Worth, and see what we can allow you on it.' Tony caught his father's arm in protest and reminder, but Mark did not speak, and the salesman departed. When they were alone, Tony said urgently:

'Dad, don't I get the old car?'

Mark hesitated. 'I think you're too young to have a car!' he repeated.

'Gosh, Dad!' Tony protested. 'You haven't treated me like a kid, not since Mother died. And you know I can drive all right.'

'If they'll allow me two hundred dollars on the old car, that's quite an item.'

Tony's lips whitened a little. 'I'll pay you whatever they offer you for it,' he said stubbornly. 'I've got over eight hundred dollars in the bank, and two months' allowance coming in before my tuition is due, and I'd rather spend it on a car than anything else.'

'But, son,' Mark urged, 'these years in school are a good chance for you to save some money. The mere fact of having money in the bank is no reason for spending it.'

Tony said almost sullenly: 'I suppose it's your money.'

'No,' Mark assured him. 'When I send you a check the first of the month, it's yours. If you save it, it's yours; and if you spend it, it's yours. But I think I have a right to give you advice now and then on how to spend it.'

Tony laughed shortly. 'Sure, but if you give me advice and I don't take it, you'll be sore!'

Mark felt something like panic, certain that Tony was wrong, yet equally certain that the boy thought he was right. 'No, I won't be sore,' he promised. 'You and I can disagree about things without either of us getting mad.'

'Well, you gave me a bigger allowance than I needed,' Tony insisted. 'Either you expected I'd waste a lot of money, or you thought I'd save some.'

'I thought you'd save some.'

'Sure, and I have,' Tony pointed out. 'I could have fooled away five or ten dollars a week pretty easy, but I didn't do it. You never said I couldn't have the car. I've counted on it, Dad. That's why I've been saving money.' He colored. 'The whole question is, is the money I've saved mine or isn't it?'

'It's yours, son,' Mark told him helplessly.

The boy faced his father squarely. 'Well, then, I want to buy the car from you. If you don't want to sell it to me, that's all right; and if you don't want to give it to me, that's all right; and if you tell me I can't have a car, why, then I won't have it. I guess you're the boss, as long as I'm living on you. But if you don't tell me I can't have a car, then I want one. I can buy one myself, second-hand, after I've saved a little more, even if you don't want to sell me this one.'

Mark saw the salesman coming toward them from the elevator. The distance the man had to come was not great. It was scarce ten seconds before the other reached them; but Mark had time to choose his course. The essential thing was that he must keep Tony's affection and trust and confidence. He thought remotely that a son held all the cards. In any direct conflict between son and father, the father must always lose, because there were no fruits of victory when the vanquished was your son. A father was helpless. So long as he could lead, guide, counsel, and thus win his son's agreement, then he could dominate the relationship between them; but when he had to rely upon his authority, his victories were also defeats. In any outright issue between him and Tony, Mark knew that he must always be the one to surrender, because to refuse to

surrender meant losing some part of Tony; and that was worse than
defeat.

He had decided before the salesman reached them. The other said:
'Well, I tried to get them to do better, but there are a good many things
that would have to be done to your car to put it in resale condition.
A hundred and ninety dollars is about the limit.'

Mark nodded. 'I see,' he said. He looked at Tony and smiled. 'In
that case,' he said, 'I think we'll keep the old car. My son can use it to
knock around in, next summer.'

Tony's hand clutched his arm in a jubilant gratitude, while the salesman and Mark discussed the last details. When the other went to have
the new car serviced so that they could drive it away, Tony said raptur-
ously: 'Gosh, Dad, you're swell!'

Mark forgot that in this first outright difference with Tony he had
been defeated. It was a delight to him to see the happiness in the
youngster's eyes.

13

(Christmas 1935)

Tony was during the holidays almost delirious with delight and pride,
and as if having a car of his own were not enough, Barbara Parks came
over from New York to spend New Year's in Manchester, and Tony
brought her to the house. In her presence he was half intoxicated, laughing at anything or nothing, flushed, with shining eyes.

She let Tony drive her back to college on his way to school in his
own car, and that made Tony's happiness complete. Mark watched his
ecstatic departure with misgivings; and at the last moment he asked
Tony to wire him the news of safe arrival. Tony promised to do so, and
he drove happily away.

After the boy was gone, Mark went up to Tony's room, finding comfort in the disorderly traces of his son's departure. The room looked as
though a high wind had blown through it, and there was a litter of
odds and ends on the bed, the table, the chairs, the floor. Under the
table he saw a sheet of paper and rescued it and discovered that it was
a poem, in Tony's scrawling hand; and he read it, smiling to himself.
It was called 'The Dance.' In the throes of composition Tony had
paused to draw on the margin of the sheet three wing sections, and one
complete aeroplane; and at one side he had written a telephone number,

presumably Barbie's, and in the upper right-hand corner he had printed
her name. Also he had written, four times, the hour he was to meet
Barbara to drive her back to college, twice in longhand, twice in figures:
'two-thirty. 2:30. 2:30. Two-Thirty.' The poem, complete with elisions
and amendments, ran thus:

The Dance

Gay, tender, intimate smile when I cut in on you.
Soft cheek pressed against my own.
Fragrant hair that ~~causes~~ makes my heart pound.
Gentle softness of your body in my arms.
Whispered words of sweetness, ~~and flattery and shy~~
Shy hints of deeper feeling spoken not.
I thrill and love and hope.
And then I 'wail the power in fate
That makes you mean the same
To the mug who cuts in, ~~and dances~~ awhile ~~with you~~
                    gets your smile,
And leaves me to go and have a drink.

                              Anthony Worth

Mark read and smiled. No matter how great his devotion to Barbara,
Tony at least had kept his sense of proportion—and his sense of humor.
Mark wondered whether Tony might under the given circumstances
'Go and have a drink.' He thought not. He himself sometimes had a
cocktail in the evening, even when he and Tony were alone; and he
always offered one to Tony—who always refused. But Tony was free to
drink at home whenever he chose, and Mark did not think the boy
would make a secret of it when he chose to drink, at home or elsewhere.
He hoped Tony would not mix alcohol and gasoline.

Tony wired that evening to report a safe trip; and he wrote next day
that the car was stored in Joe Merry's barn to wait till spring vacation.
Mark admitted to himself a strong relief because for a while at least
Tony would not be exposed to the hazards of the road.

14

(January 1936)

Late in January, Tom Sheffield came to pay Mark thirty dollars on
account of that original debt, which was reduced by this payment to
seven hundred and ten dollars. 'I'm sorry it's not more, Mark,' he said,
and grinned ruefully. 'But I have to spread every dollar pretty thin.' He

added: 'I'll be able to clean it up when we get our bonus.' Congress
had passed the bonus bill over Mr. Roosevelt's veto a fortnight before.
Most people agreed that since public moneys were being poured out
with a generous hand in every other direction, veterans were entitled to
their share. Even Mark uneasily accepted this point of view. Economy
in national affairs was long since forgotten; and certainly in this election
year just opening, no politician could afford to lead the way in par-
simony.

'Don't let it worry you,' he told Tom. 'Take as long as you like.' He
smiled in a friendly way. 'I guess you know I'd tell you to forget it if I
thought you wanted to.'

Tom grimaced in a sort of pain. 'No, no, I'll pay it all, sooner or
later.' He explained with a wry chuckle: 'I'm not going to tell Emma
about the bonus, and she never reads the newspapers, so she probably
won't think of it. She won't know when I get the money. If she knew
I had it, it would all be spent ahead of time.'

Mark thought Emma, if she ever discovered that Tom had had this
extra money, would make his life miserable, but that was not a thing he
could say to Tom. 'This Congress is in a spending mood,' he said. 'Two
billion for the bonus, and that's just a starter. You know, I can remember—so can you, of course—the first Billion Dollar Congress. We were
rather proud of our ability as a nation to spend so much.'

'They're all out to buy re-election—with our money,' Tom agreed.
'Roosevelt's bonus veto may beat him.'

'I don't believe so,' Mark argued. 'The soldiers will forgive him,
because they'll get their money anyway; and he'll get the votes of practically everyone who's drawing government money. My father in Ohio
says he'll carry the state, get a big majority in the industrial cities, and
a whopping farm vote.'

'The Supreme Court found the AAA unconstitutional,' Tom pointed
out.

'I know, but the farmers blame the Court for that. They know Mr.
Roosevelt will work out some new plan. Of course he'll get the South,
too. He would anyway, but the cotton states are in his pocket now.
And I'm beginning to think he'll carry Massachusetts. I talked to our
chore man, the other day. He thinks Mr. Roosevelt is one of the lesser
gods.'

Tom stirred unhappily. 'What's happened to us, Mark?' he demanded.
'We used to be pretty self-respecting people, we Americans. We didn't
want charity.'

Mark smiled. 'We still don't,' he answered. 'It's not as bad as that. But our sensibilities have been blunted, Tom. The defaults on the war debts—and our own government's unilateral cancellation of the gold contract in its bonds—set us an example of broken promises and faithlessness; and self-interest has led a lot of us to condone these things. I went duck shooting at Merrymeeting Bay last fall. Half a dozen sneak boats lay together to watch for ducks to swing over our decoys; and the guides talked all day long about the easy money to be had from the government. They told stories about men doing road work, taking pay for it and dodging the work. They talked about shooting some of the Western cattle sent to pasture around the Bay, stealing the meat, as though it were a joke. These were State-of-Maine men, hard workers most of them, farmers, self-respecting men.

'But, Tom, they'll realize sooner or later that this waste comes out of their own pockets. My friend, John Harmon—I went to school to him, a long time ago—lives in Belfast. He says a surprising number of farmers and small workingmen are already waking up to it. He thinks Maine will go Republican next fall. Last fall the state would certainly have gone for Mr. Roosevelt, but if John is right, Maine has come to its senses—and the whole country will come to its senses by and by.' Mark smiled. 'We're still sound and sane, underneath, you know.'

Tom said gloomily: 'If we don't stop the way things are going there'll be the damnedest bust up the world ever saw, before long.' He rose, grinning in an embarrassed way. 'But I'm as bad as any of them right now. I'm going to take my bonus and pay my debts with it—or some of them.' He asked curiously: 'Are you going to take your bonus, Mark?'

Mark said: 'Of course.' He did not plan to do so, but he could not tell Tom the truth without offense. He was in fact faintly ashamed of his own reluctance to accept the largess to which he was entitled. His attitude seemed to him absurd and quixotic; but to take the money, since he did not need it, seemed to him worse. Certainly if his need had been as definite as Tom's he would not have hesitated. So he said: 'Of course,' and felt no guilt for the lie.

15

(March 1936)

One day in March, Jerry Crocker came in to see Mark. When the switchboard girl gave his name, Mark was astonished. 'Mr. Crocker?

Jerry Crocker?' he asked. She assented, and Mark went out to meet Jerry, led him into the office, said how glad he was to see the other man.

Jerry explained at once that he had come on business. 'I've decided to buy a house,' he explained, grinning in a diffident way. 'And there's some trouble about the title. I don't know whether you do anything in that line, but maybe you can send me to someone who does.' And under Mark's questions he explained: 'It's an old house, a hundred years or so; and as near as I can find out, everyone who ever owned it died intestate, and they all had big families, so there are a God-awful lot of heirs, I don't know how many.' He added with a wry grin: 'As a matter of fact I've already bought it, last fall. I paid the old woman who said she owned it, and then she died, but I didn't have the title examined, and now a couple of lawyers are trying to hold me up, representing people who own a piece of it.' He said wrathfully: 'They tell me that anyone who owns a share in a house can live in it, and one of them represents an old woman who is crazy as a coot, and he's threatening to move her in on me unless I settle.'

Mark would be busy at odd times for months, clearing Jerry's title. 'I'm going to be away all summer,' Jerry explained. 'So I'll leave the whole thing to you.' There proved to be more than a hundred individuals, descendants of the line of owners who have died without making wills, whose claims must be satisfied by persuasion or by small cash payments. The total amount involved was small, not worth Mark's time and trouble; but until Jerry presently left town, Mark saw more of him than ever in the past, and he was glad of the excuse for regular meetings with the other man.

A day or two after Jerry's first call at his office, Hitler's troops marched into the Rhineland. At the same time Hitler denounced the Locarno Pact, which a year before he had promised to respect; and he offered to France and Belgium a twenty-five-year non-aggression treaty, to be guaranteed by England and Italy, and to be supplemented by the demilitarization of the Franco-German frontier. In a speech to the Reichstag he cried: 'We have no territorial demands to make in Europe.'

Mark, reading the news in the daily press, found himself confused. Hitler's protestations were so reassuring, yet the implications of his every action produced throughout the world a deep concern.

'I don't know what to think,' he told Jerry, the next time they met. 'Hitler has torn up Versailles, a little at a time. Possibly the Allies would have been wise to tear it up themselves, long ago. They've made a treaty-breaker out of Hitler, and now, like a woman who has lost her reputation, he might as well have the game as the name.'

Jerry said drily: 'Sure, they're as much to blame as he! They're all a bunch of bastards. Show me one that ain't!'

Mark laughed, and he asked: 'Will France listen to his proposal to demilitarize her frontiers?'

The other grinned derisively: 'Don't be a damned fool! France is playing turtle behind the Maginot line. You wouldn't expect a turtle to discard its shell if its nearest neighbor were a wolf.'

'Do you think Hitler is sincere in proposing this non-aggression pact with France and Belgium?'

'Why not?' Jerry challenged. 'It's to his advantage. If France agreed not to attack Germany, and England guaranteed that agreement, Germany would be secure on the west. Hitler wants to move east. The *Drang nach Osten*, remember? If he could be safe from attack by France and England, he could do what he chose with Poland and the Balkans and Russia.'

'England would never let him do that.'

'Of course not. She'd be a fool if she did. England thinks first, last, and all the time of what's best for England. She's always been against the dominant European power, working to whittle her down to size. She built up France and the others against Spain, and she built up Prussia against France, and then she built up France and us against Germany, and for fifteen years she's been building up Germany against Russia. If Germany grows too strong, she'll build up Russia against Germany.'

'That sounds pretty cold-blooded,' Mark protested.

'Cold-blooded?' Jerry's tone was explosive. 'Of course it's cold-blooded! It's also plain common sense. Since Queen Elizabeth, there has been more national brains in England than in the rest of the world put together. Maybe some day, after we've played the sucker a few more times, we'll be as smart as she is.'

'You talk as if England had no conscience.'

Jerry laughed. 'Conscience? Blah! Blah! Blah! Ask the Boers. Ask the Chinese about the opium war. The balance of power is England's ideal. Let two European powers achieve a precarious equilibrium, and England will be satisfied. All she wants is to rule the seas. I tell you, the national intelligence of England is the shrewdest in the world.' He grinned scornfully. 'But as for her conscience, there's only one national conscience in Europe!'

'Finland?' Mark suggested, and Jerry nodded. Mark said thoughtfully: 'Some of my friends think the war debts should have been forgiven long ago—on the theory that they never will be paid.'

'Maybe they won't. But Coolidge said it. "They hired the money."
And even if we forgave the debts, they'd feel more contemptuous than grateful.'

Mark asked: 'What do you make of the naval treaty between England and Germany?'

'I told you, England is building up Germany against Russia. But, treaties don't amount to anything. No nation will sacrifice its own best interests to obey the terms of a treaty or an alliance that has gone stale.'

'Men keep their bargains. Even at a loss.'

'Sure. Men as individuals have a pretty high sense of honor, but men in political power will break their word for their country's good—and for my money they should—as readily as a trustee gets out of a bad investment.'

Mark nodded. 'I sometimes wish the world were run by boys, boys and young men,' he said. 'They're a fine, honorable, idealistic lot. It's only as they grow older, and perhaps become statesmen, that they learn evasions and sophistries.'

Jerry grinned. 'Well, I dunno,' he drawled. 'There are some boys out my way that I'd like to get over a barrel. Every time I go away I come home to find a few windows broken.' He added: 'But they're not as bad as these crooks who are trying to hold me up now, at that.'

Mark before the month's end had made progress in straightening out Jerry's tangled affairs; but Jerry did not suggest that he see the house itself. 'I live there alone when I'm in town,' he said. 'So it's all in a mess.' He was planning to spend the early summer in Canada. 'I'll do a little trout fishing up in the Laurentians,' he explained. 'Then I'm going West. No knowing when I'll be back. I'll give you a power of attorney at my brokers so you can draw any money you need. How much will it take to clear it all up?'

Mark thought fifteen hundred dollars would satisfy all the claimants. 'Most of them are just running a bluff,' he explained. He asked laughingly: 'Why don't you marry and settle down, Jerry? Now that you've got a home of your own.'

Jerry grinned. 'Why don't you?' he countered.

He departed; but he left Mark convinced that Europe was drifting toward war; and if war came, Mark was certain that somehow, sooner or later, the United States—and Tony—would be involved.

16

(April 1936)

When Tony should be graduated from Hadley in June, he would be ready for college. There was no question of his admission to Dartmouth. Even under the strict selective system, his scholastic record at Hadley would have made his acceptance there probable; but as the son of an alumnus he had a preferred rating and would certainly be admitted. There was a long-standing promise that when Tony was ready for college he might learn to fly; and in April Mark decided to share this great experience with the boy.

He had heard Tony speak of an instructor named Hadden, at the Norwood airport; and he drove out one day to see that young man. Hadden was older than he had expected, small and wiry, with dark, slanting eyebrows; and he spoke easily and well, with the accent of a cultivated Englishman. He said Mark was not too old to undertake the venture.

'If you can pass the physical, there's no reason why you shouldn't,' he explained. 'Straight flying's as easy, for most men, as driving a car; and it's much less of a nervous strain. Once you're off the ground, there's no traffic to worry you; and your road is wide, with no ditches, and no corners. In the air, the plane flies itself. You can relax completely till it's time to land. Even that's no harder than to make a good landing with a motorboat—except that a mistake is more serious.' He added fairly: 'Of course there's more danger in flying. Not much, but some. Because of that, I never urge a man to fly, but I think you would enjoy it.'

He remembered Tony and he smiled understandingly when Mark said he wished to keep his own flying a secret till Tony came home in June. 'I know,' Hadden agreed, 'I've a son of my own. He's too young to solo, but he flies with me. And my wife flies too.'

Mark said: 'You're a good salesman. I'll have my physical, see what the verdict is.'

The examining physician, Doctor Swain, was a plump, cheerful man who seemed not at all surprised at Mark's errand. Mark asked whether many men as old as he came to take out student pilot licenses. 'Perhaps you fly yourself,' he suggested.

'No, I've never even been up,' Doctor Swain said surprisingly. 'Never seemed to see any reason for it. It saves time, of course; but I've always had plenty of time.' He said briskly: 'Well, we'll look you over.'

Mark's only trouble proved to be with his eyes. That old war wound had impaired the sight of one of them; and this made the depth perception test difficult for him. At the first few trials he failed badly. Doctor Swain said: 'You don't come up to requirements on that, Mr. Worth.' He asked: 'Did you think of doing much flying, taking out a private license, buying a plane?'

Mark shook his head. 'Oh, no. I just want to do enough flying so that I can at least discuss it with my son.' He smiled and explained his promise to Tony.

The Doctor nodded. 'I see.' He hesitated. 'Let's try this test again. This time, before you try it, look away for a while, rest your eyes, then look back quickly. Sometimes it's easier that way.'

Mark, obeying these instructions, was able to do well enough so that Doctor Swain passed him, and a day or two later Mark went to Norwood for his first lesson.

He flew thereafter, through April and May, at every opportunity. At first he was confused and uncertain, suffering definite physical qualms; but when he had acquired ten or twelve hours of flying time, Mr. Hadden said casually one day:

'You know, of course, that you can solo any time you want to.'

Mark was by that time sure that he could take the plane up and fly around the field and set it down again, always assuming that nothing went wrong; but he was in no hurry to do so. His reluctance was not fear. Before he began to fly, he had assumed and discounted the risk involved. He was reluctant because of a natural and deep-rooted conservatism; and to some extent he was reluctant because he doubted his own ability to meet an emergency. But he did not try to explain this to Mr. Hadden.

'I think I can handle it all right,' he assented. 'But I can learn just as much with you in the plane; more, perhaps, because I know that in a pinch you'll take over. I'm not trying to make any records, to prove anything. Suppose for the present we go ahead as we are.'

Hadden was, he thought, disappointed at his attitude; but he made no objection. Mark continued to fly, coming to the field every fine day after he was finished at the office, and every Sunday afternoon. He told no one, for the present, what he was doing, uncomfortably sure that if his friends knew he was flying they would call him a fool.

He flew day after day, monotonously, till one afternoon toward the end of May something happened. Hadden, boredom in his very posture, sat in the front seat. Mark was practising landings. Until today, the moment of landing had always been for him a hurried one; the plane seemed to be moving dangerously fast, the ground raced past under his wheels, things blurred before his eyes. But today, suddenly, in the midst of the landing, everything slowed down. His first thought was that the plane was about to stall, and he gunned the engine, speeded up; but the runway was long. He made his landing.

Hadden asked wearily: 'What did you gun it for?'

Mark suddenly laughed. 'The plane, the ground, everything seemed to slow down,' he said. 'It happened suddenly, just as sometimes when you're playing tennis the ball seems to hang in the air and you have all the time in the world to hit it.' He added simply: 'You can get out, Mr. Hadden. I'm ready to go on alone.'

Hadden was perfectly matter-of-fact. 'All right. Take me back to the hangar. I don't want to walk so far.'

Mark taxied up the field and the other got out and Mark alone made three or four landings. There was no longer any hurry at the final moment. The ground came slowly up to meet him; he poised, drifted easily, settled down without a jar. He climbed to two thousand feet and tried a wing over, pulling up the nose, dipping a wing. The plane seemed to stand on its tail, shivering like a nervous horse; and Mark, looking down over his shoulder at the hangar far below him, wondered what was wrong, and realized that he had forgotten to kick the rudder. He laughed aloud at his own mistake and finished the maneuver. He put the plane through a dozen wing-overs, losing altitude to a thousand feet, and circled the field, and then with a series of slips came easily down. At the last, he slipped steeply, revelling in his new sense of time when everything moved so slowly, till he was so close to the ground that an instant after he levelled off the wheels touched. The plane seemed hardly to be moving at all when it met the ground.

Mark taxied to the hangar, wondering if Hadden had been watching, but apparently no one had paid any attention to him. He stopped at the office to say: 'I'll be out tomorrow if it's fair.'

'All right,' Hadden indifferently agreed. 'We'll be ready for you.'

17

(June 1936)

Tony's Commencement, the end of his three years at Hadley, was at hand. Mark expected to drive up Friday afternoon. He had long ago reserved a room at the Hadley Inn, a few minutes' walk from the school, and he was full of a fine anticipation. Elin was as excited as he; and he wished he might take her to see Tony graduate, but that was of course impossible.

The bright days, when the time came, were a happy time for Mark, moving proudly with his tall son beside him, or watching Tony with his fellows. The alumni luncheon in the Gymnasium, when the graduating class and alumni and parents all gathered together and the prizes were awarded, was a richly satisfying hour. Mark, watching the beaming faces of fathers and mothers all around him, thought Commencements more than any other occasions focussed all a parent's hope and pride and love. By the time boys and girls were ready to graduate from school, or from college, there was not much more you could do for them. You had brought them from helpless babyhood through infancy and childhood to the stature of grown men and women. They had the stature, but they had as yet nothing else. They looked like grown people, but you who knew them so well knew how young—despite their brave outward maturity—they really were. Yet they must go on so much alone, and so much was expected of them, endurance and wisdom and character; and you could help them so little. These shocks of unruly hair all about him here would thin and turn gray; and these smooth young faces would show the scars of time, more and more deeply as the years passed. Till today these youngsters had been yours to cherish and protect; but now, for their own sakes, you must let them face the buffets and the cold, impersonal fury of the world.

Mark remembered a man named Hitler, three or four thousand miles away; and what Hitler sought to do might some day send these boys, send Tony, to be cut down by machine-gun bullets as grass falls before the scythe; to be shattered by shells and choked by gas and to leap hopelessly from sinking ships into the strangling, icy sea; or to plummet from the skies in blazing planes, or to be rent apart by bursting bombs. Mark's jaw set in a hot, choking rage. There was no Hell too deep for any man who let war loose upon the world, upon young men like these.

The Commencement exercises were held in the old church near the school. The day was fair without being warm, and some of the windows of the church were open, and a catbird miaowed persistently outside one window. Mark sat in the balcony, and his eyes fixed on the top of Tony's head, rested there almost continually throughout the exercises. Doctor Spear delivered the address. He was a spare man with iron-gray hair, and he began lightly, but little by little he spoke of more serious things. Mark was afraid he might exhort the boys, tell them they were the hope of the world, give them empty, meaningless phrases. Boys— even such boys as these—were not in the mass the hope of the world. Most individuals had very little to say about what the world should do with itself. Now and then a man came along, a man like Hitler for instance, who, by the force of his ideas and by his ability to lead men to his way of thinking, did shake the world and break the old images and perhaps set new ones in their places. It was even conceivable that Mr. Roosevelt was such a man. Mark did not think so, but certainly a tremendous majority of his fellow citizens believed Mr. Roosevelt was a great man. But—how many of them were moved by frank self-interest? How many intelligent men, how many of the big men in the country, thought well of Mr. Roosevelt? No large proportion certainly. Yet was not the mass emotion of many men more to be trusted than the reasoned judgment of the few? Certainly very few national leaders had thought highly of Lincoln during his lifetime. Was it not Emerson who said there was more virtue in Andrew Johnson's little finger than in Lincoln's loins? It was the people, turning out by their hundreds of thousands and their millions to see Lincoln's funeral train go by, who planted the seed of the Lincoln legend. The truth, unperceived by wise men, had taken root in their simple hearts.

But they loved Lincoln for abstract reasons. He had drafted their sons and sent those sons to die on bloody battlefields, and yet they loved him. He had not, like Mr. Roosevelt, put millions of them on the public payroll, encouraged them to expect to live without working, given them much and promised more. If Mr. Roosevelt could make the millions suffer and still keep his place in their hearts, then there might be virtue in a comparison of him and Lincoln. It was no proof of greatness to be despised by the few and cheered by the many; certainly not when those cheers had been bought. Even Hitler had been able to persuade men to devote themselves to the dream he showed them. He had implanted in the youth of Germany the ideals of service and devotion and sacrifice. Mr. Roosevelt had only been able to awaken in his supporters a greedy appetite for money from the public purse.

Mark's attention was caught by the speaker. Doctor Spear was saying: 'You boys will, most of you, go on to college; and it's hard to predict what sort of a world the world of 1940, when you graduate, will be. Perhaps we will be by that time in another European war. In Germany and Italy boys your age—yes, and much younger—are being trained as soldiers, trained to believe that their highest duty is to the state, that their own lives are unimportant. We in this country have believed in the importance of the individual. The state, in our conception, is our servant; its duty is to make secure and orderly and comfortable our daily lives. The German concept is that the man is servant of the state, that his duty to the state stands above all. I don't know which concept is right, but the time may well come—I am not sure it has not already arrived—when each of us will have to decide whether he will not be happier in devoting his energies, or a major portion of them, to some cause outside of and greater than himself. To a great extent Hitler's power arises from the fact that he has aroused in young men and boys—boys like you—the noblest of emotions, the self-sacrificing willingness to serve.'

Mark was struck by the similarity to his own thoughts awhile ago, and Doctor Spear went on:

'We do not know what is coming, but we do know that our world is no longer what it was. We are not even sure what it is; and least of all do we know what it is going to be.'

He stood for a moment silent, and then suddenly he smiled. 'So if you look to me for advice today,' he said, 'you will be disappointed. I know the future no more than you. Yet I will give you one word.

'In this changed and changing world, try to find one thing, or two things, or three, of which you are sure. Ideas of right and wrong may change; but some things are always right, and some are always wrong. They are not necessarily the same things for every individual. Each must define them for himself.

'But get hold of one or two or three things which you are sure are true. Cling to them. Let them be the test by which you appraise each new idea that is presented to you. If you have even one truth of which you are forever sure, you will have a solid rock upon which to stand.'

He was done, and Mr. Carbrey began to deliver to the graduating class their degrees. The lines of boys filing to the platform to receive their diplomas had a strange likeness to one another. Even Tony, if

Mark's eye lost him for a moment, was not easy to find again. Mark thought this was as it should be. Tony was everything to him, but so were the other boys to other parents. They would go on to college, and work, and marry, and raise families, and take their small places in a crowded world, indistinguishable units in a mass, individuals only to themselves and to the few others like themselves who knew them and loved them. Not the individual was important, but the mass. That was democracy; the concept that the mass should rule.

But the United States was built on the theory that the mass should rule for the benefit of the individual. Mark thought there was a thin line of contradiction here, a contradiction hard to define.

He found himself a unit in a moving stream as the church emptied itself. Then he was outside, and then Tony's strong young hand gripped hard and happily on his arm.

V

Rehearsal in Spain

(June 1936–June 1937)

I

(Summer 1936)

MARK had not told Tony that he himself was learning to fly; and he had happy plans to surprise the boy, to dramatize the disclosure of his secret. Hadden, his instructor, since Mark had begun to solo, had been friendly and amiable and helpful in every way, so that Mark sometimes suspected the other's former manner had been a pose designed to hurry him toward self-reliance; and the pilot understood his wish now, and they had decided together exactly what to do when Tony first came with his father to the field.

For a few days after Commencement, the weather was evil, with rain and gusty winds; so Tony's first flying lesson was put off. He had time to take out his student pilot's license, and to buy a helmet and goggles; but at Mark's request he did not go to the airport.

'I want to go with you the first time,' Mark explained; and the fact that ill weather made flying impossible till Saturday played into his hands.

When at last they drove out to Norwood, Mark was even more excited than Tony, though he concealed it better. Tony knew Hadden of old, and while the plane was being warmed up, the three of them stood talking together. Then, when the plane was ready, Mark caught Hadden's eye and the instructor said to Tony:

'Come into the office for a minute. I've a book there I want you to read while you're taking lessons.'

The two disappeared; and Mark went at once to the plane and climbed in. His goggles and helmet had been placed in the seat ready for him. He put them on, gunned the plane, taxied down the runway, and swung into the wind to take off toward the hangar.

When he turned, he could see Tony and Hadden outside the hangar watching him; and he grinned happily, imagining Tony's ejaculations, amused at his own wish to display his prowess before his son. He opened the throttle and lifted the plane into the air. He was twenty feet up when he passed where Tony stood, and he looked that way and waved, and saw Tony throw up both hands and saw the boy's mouth open as he shouted something, and saw Tony's grinning delight.

Then he was away. He circled the field, climbing to two thousand feet; he did a few tight turns and wing-overs and was tempted to try a spin, but remembered Hadden's injunctions not to do that without a parachute; so he compromised on a power stall and levelled off at fifteen hundred feet and made a gentle glide thrice around the field, watching his altitude, keeping the motor warm with an occasional touch on the throttle. He had timed himself so well that he came in for a landing without the necessity of a slip and landed and taxied up to where they stood; and before the plane stopped, Tony was running toward him, climbing on the wing to grasp his hand, crying out in a high pride and happiness.

That summer before Tony went to Dartmouth would seem to Mark a short one. With his tongue in his cheek, he proposed a fishing trip to Newfoundland; but Tony said apologetically: 'Gosh, Dad, if it's all the same to you, I'd rather stay here and get in as much flying time as I can.' Mark was not surprised; and all that summer Tony went to the airport whenever the weather was favorable. Mr. Hadden said he was ready to solo after eight hours of flying, but at Mark's request the boy agreed to go on for more dual first.

'You and I aren't trying to prove how good we are,' Mark reminded his son. 'We're just doing this for fun, and we don't want to take any unnecessary chances.'

Tony soloed early in August. Hadden—his first name was Cecil, but Mark had a characteristic American reluctance to use such names as Cecil and Cyril and Cedric, which come more easily to English tongues —said Tony had a distinct natural aptitude; and he took much pains with the youngster, not only in the air but on the ground. Sometimes after their flying was done, Mark and Tony stayed in talk with him awhile. Hadden had been at first a pilot and then an instructor in the World War; and he told them tales of his experiences, while Tony listened with wide, shining eyes.

'I was stationed at a field up in Scotland,' Hadden said one day, 'teaching youngsters to fly Camels. The planes were tricky; and the field had been selected by politicians. There were mountains all around it, and there were freak winds everywhere, and if our luck was out we might kill two or three of these lads in a day, partly because the Camels were killers anyway, and partly because the field wasn't fit for flying. I remember one morning four boys crashed, and the other youngsters had the wind up. The C.O. sent me and the other instructor up to put on a show, to put the heart back into them; and we did, cutting grass with our wing-tips, flying through the hangars . . .'

Tony cried in astonishment: 'Through the hangars?'

'Yes, in the front door and out the back. We had a regular routine on these shows. And after we got through, the boys went at it again, thinking it was easy—and we had two more killed that afternoon!'

He told them of sending youngsters up to test the parachutes which were then a novelty. 'We had some old Camels that were ready to be discarded; and they went up in those. You had to close the throttle and climb out of the cockpit to jump; but sometimes the plane went into a spin before you could get out of it, and then you had to straighten it out gently, or the plane would fold up like a book, and you'd lose five thousand feet or so and have to climb back up and try it again. It took one lad three days to get out of his plane—and then the plane caught him on the way down.'

The stories he told were apt to end thus, in curt tragedy; and there was when he spoke of such things a harsh bitterness in Hadden's tone. Mark suggested once: 'I suppose the wastage of life was necessary.'

'No,' Hadden said flatly. 'If we'd started getting ready for war in time, and if we'd had proper training fields and proper planes, we could have cut training casualties seventy-five per cent. It was hurry, hurry, hurry, all the time; and hurry costs money and lives.'

Tony asked: 'If there's ever another war, will you be in it, Mr. Hadden?'

Hadden smiled. 'Not I, lad. I was nearly court-martialled in the last one. No, I'll never fight anyone's war again.'

He had tales, too, of the years since the war, the years when the aeroplane was a sideshow at country fairs, a contrivance clothed in wonder and in danger which only the boldest dared approach. He and Mark were apt to stand together watching Tony in the air, talking quietly; and Mark came to feel a firm affection for the man. Hadden spoke gently and serenely, but when their talk turned on the last war, and he remembered things seen and known, and the folly of ignorant and stupid officers which had always to be paid for with young lives, a bitter scorn crept into his tones. Sometimes Mark suggested that war might come again.

'It will not come for me,' said Hadden more than once. 'I'm done with war.'

He told Mark one day about a court martial with which he had been threatened. Reports of the inadequacy and unsuitability of the flying field at which he was an instructor had reached Parliament, had led to questions in the House of Commons, and a deputation came to inspect the place. Hadden by that time was in command of the field; but one of his superior officers—'A fat ass who had never been off the ground,' Hadden explained—conducted the deputation; and he told Hadden to send some of the beginner pilots into the air. The day was unsuitable for flying and Hadden flatly refused, explaining his reasons. He was put under arrest, and six pilots were ordered to take off in an exhibition flight.

'It would have been a court for me,' he said grimly. 'But two of the six crashed and were killed, so they didn't want the facts aired. I was transferred to staff, to keep me quiet.'

'What happened to the fat ass?' Mark asked.

'They sent him to France, where if he killed some more boys it wouldn't be noticed among so many. So that's why I say they can fight their own wars now.'

Mark and Tony on Saturdays and Sundays usually went to the field together, and if there were two planes available they might both be in the air at the same time. If not, Mark flew first and then Tony had his turn. At home Tony talked of little else, and Mark was as keen as he, but more because he caught the infection of his son's happiness than on his own account. He found an hour in the air to be a fine relaxing experience, from which he emerged rested and refreshed; but Tony was always tremendously stimulated after he had flown.

2

(July 1936)

Bonus bonds were mailed to veterans in mid-June. Mark, faintly amused at his own scruples, had thought he would not apply for his bonus; but Bob Ritchie said reasonably: 'Why not? You might as well. You'll have to give the money back to the Government in taxes anyway—whether you take it or not. None of the men who get the bonus will be able to keep it. It comes out of taxes. The Government just hands you the money with one hand and then takes it back with the other.'

'I know,' Mark assented. 'But a lot of men don't realize that.'

'Sure,' Bob agreed. 'Just because they don't pay any income tax, they think they don't pay any taxes. The Government picks their pockets with indirect taxation. You never get something for nothing in this world. The Government doesn't just print the money and hand it to you. It has to collect it from you, either before you get it or afterward. You might as well take the damned bonus. Being so high-minded about it won't get you anything but laughs.'

So Mark put in his application, as did most of his friends. Early in July, Tom Sheffield came to pay him the balance of that old debt. He gave Mark the amount in cash. 'I didn't put it through the bank,' he explained, 'because Emma and I have a joint account, and I don't want her to know about this.' He added in a deep relief: 'I've got my head above water now, Mark. For the first time in seven years I don't owe anybody a nickel except current bills.'

'You didn't have to hurry about this, you know,' Mark assured him. 'I don't need it. Why don't you keep some of it for emergencies?'

Tom grinned. 'No, thanks. I like the feeling of being in the clear. But for God's sake don't tell Emma.'

He was smiling as he spoke, and Mark smilingly assented; yet within a fortnight Emma learned the truth. The occasion was a Sunday evening at the Ritchies', and the familiar group was there, including Dave and Marcia. Mark had not seen them since Ruth's dance. They had spent the winter in Honolulu and on the coast, had not reopened the Lincoln house at all, returning East only to go directly to their place on the Cape; but they were in Lincoln over this week-end and Nell heard of it and captured them. Mark asked how Ruth was, and Marcia said she was fine. She was to go to Bryn Mawr this fall.

'She's tutoring this summer,' Marcia explained. 'She isn't awfully good at books, you know, and of course she's been a year out of school, getting her health back, so she's freshening up a bit.' She spoke of Ruth's illness with a sort of unction. Marcia was always perfectly well herself, but she liked to think of Dave—and now of Ruth—as invalids, making much of even little ills. Mark smiled understandingly.

'I'd like to see Ruth,' he said. 'We always did get along. She's a sweet girl.'

'She thinks you were made and handed down,' Marcia assured him,

and added laughingly: 'Come down and see us, some week-end, if
you're sure your intentions are honorable!'

'Oh, perfectly,' Mark declared; but her word made him remember
that impulse he had felt, when he sensed unhappiness in Ruth, to take
her in his arms and tell her how wonderful she was. He was interested
in his own feeling. Certainly he was not even remotely in love with
this child—and yet it was equally certain that in some deep, instinctive,
perhaps paternal way, he loved her. Perhaps it was the fact that she so
surely needed to be loved, needed some man's adoration, which drew
him so strongly.

Marcia named a date. 'Over the twenty-sixth?' she suggested. 'Bring
Tony along.'

Mark promised to let her know. Cocktails were going the rounds,
and Mark saw Dave take a second and then a third. Marcia saw this,
too, and she remonstrated in a protectively chiding tone: 'Why, Davy,
you never take three cocktails.'

Dave said lightly: 'What, never? Well, hardly ever.' Everyone
laughed, and a minute later he picked up his shaker and filled his glass
again.

When presently they came to table, Mark realized that a stranger sat
in Dave's place. The other normally was gentle and courteous and likeable; but now suddenly his tone had changed, his words were new.
There was a certain truculence in his bearing, a jeer in his voice. Mark
remembered Ruth's dance. There had been the same note in Dave's
voice that evening. Mark was not sure whether the others noticed the
difference, now, but to him it was plain enough. Dave was not merely
drunk, or on the verge of becoming drunk; he was completely changed.

Mark found himself Dave's particular target. Ed asked some question about the flying. It had produced between Mark and Tony a bond
stronger than in the past. They were equal in their enthusiasm, keen in
good-natured rivalry, each laughing at the other's minor errors and
applauding the other's good performances. But Mark did not say all
this now; said only: 'We like it, have a lot of fun out of it.'

Dave drawled: 'Who's going to scrape who off of what telephone
pole?'

There was a moment's shocked silence. Then Mark said agreeably:
'There's an element of danger, of course. But flying as we do, in good
weather, and always within reach of the airport, the danger's not great.'

'Sure,' said Dave in an ironic tone. 'Nothing can happen. You never
see anything in the papers about people getting killed in planes!'

Mary Halstead smilingly suggested: 'If none of us ever did anything dangerous, we'd have to give up a lot of things. Isn't the most dangerous thing to go to bed? So many people die in bed.'

Dave grunted and without invitation left the table and went to the sideboard and mixed a highball. Marcia protested: 'Davy, wait till after dinner.' He looked over his shoulder at her with hard eyes and then deliberately doubled the amount of whiskey in his glass, holding it up for her to see him do so. Mark had often wondered that Dave did not rebel at Marcia's constant solicitudes. Usually he submitted, good-naturedly enough, and Mark had heard him say: 'I think Marcia gets some sort of sensuous satisfaction out of coddling me.'

But clearly Dave was in revolt tonight. When Nell Ritchie rose presently, so did the others; but Dave kept his seat. Marcia urged: 'Come on, Dave. Into the other room.'

Dave's grin was dry. 'Shall we join the ladies?' he said mockingly, making no move to rise; and Bob looked at him and sat down at the table again.

'We'll come in presently, Nell,' he said.

So Mark and Ed and Tom also sat down. Dave had at first nothing to say, and the others talked at random. Landon had been nominated in Cleveland, Roosevelt in Philadelphia; and Bob, who never could believe in Roosevelt's continued popularity, thought Landon would be elected. The Seventy-Fourth Congress had spent nineteen million dollars; and Tom, always the banker, thought the country was on the road to bankruptcy. Farmers in the Dust Bowl were being put to work on WPA projects, and a year's moratorium had been declared on farm loans in the afflicted region. A Fascist rebellion, beginning in Morocco and headed by General Franco, had spread to Spain, and every capital in Europe was on the alert, France declaring its neutrality, England warning the rebels to mind their manners on the high seas and where British vessels were concerned, Germany and Italy watching the swift spread of revolt with a professional interest. Mark thought the great nations were like sheep, warily attentive to the movements of a wolf just outside their fold, at once fearful and yet fascinated; and he spoke of this sharp tension.

'It wouldn't need much to touch off an explosion over there,' he said.

Bob disagreed with him. 'Europe's not ready for a war, not yet,' he declared. He laughed. 'And in this Spanish business, none of them know which side they're on. Over here, we're always for rebels anywhere; but this is really a rebellion against a rebel government, against the crowd that kicked Alphonso out. At least that's the way I get it, not that I give a damn! I'm all through taking sides in Europe's quarrels.'

'We're still paying for the last one,' Dave drily reminded them, and that led to talk of the bonus, and Bob told them that he had had to persuade Mark to apply for his. They had all served in the last war, Ed Halstead in the Navy—he was still connected with the Naval Reserve —and the others in the land forces. Even Tom, after driving an ambulance for France, had gone to an officers' training camp and become a second lieutenant in the A.E.F. They agreed that Mark's attitude toward the bonus had been ridiculous. Their voices were loud enough so that they could be heard in the other room, but no one realized this till suddenly Emma Sheffield appeared in the doorway.

'What's this about the bonus?' she demanded.

Bob asked laughingly: 'Don't you read the papers?'

'Maybe the lady can't read,' Dave drawled.

But Emma ignored him. 'How much was it?' she insisted, and she challenged her husband. 'Tom, what did you do with yours?'

Tom looked wretchedly at Mark; and Dave watched him with one eyebrow cocked, grinning in mocking amusement, and Tom said evasively: 'A lot of men didn't apply for it, Emma. The feeling was all against it at the bank.'

Dave laughed shortly. 'What do they call that?' he muttered, as if to himself—'the lie circumspect?'

For a dreadful moment no one spoke. Then Emma said in brittle tones: 'Tom Sheffield, if you didn't apply, you're going to do it tomorrow, bank or no bank. Always preaching economy to me, and then not taking money that's rightfully yours!' Her eyes narrowed. 'I believe you did take it and then spent the money.'

Dave told her encouragingly: 'You're getting warm, Sister.'

Tom rose in a nervous haste, anxious to silence her, or to avoid letting these others hear the recriminations he foresaw. 'Come on, Emma,' he said pleadingly. 'Let's go home.'

'If you did get the money and spent it you'll be sorry,' she told him icily. 'And if you didn't get it, when you see my next month's bills you're going to wish you had!'

Tom for only answer gripped her arm, turned her almost forcibly toward the door. Mark met Bob's eyes, and then Ed's, and they rose to follow these two into the other room. Tom was already saying good night, Emma ominously silent. Marcia went to call Dave, to say they too must go; but Dave retorted: 'Not yet. I'm on a sit-down strike.'

French workmen had set that new style in labor warfare a few weeks before.

But Marcia insisted; and first Tom and Emma and then Dave and Marcia departed. The others, left behind together, stayed awhile in uncomfortable silence.

'Did Tom get his bonus?' Bob asked at last. 'Does anyone know?'

Mark told them the truth. They were all Tom's friends and could be trusted. They listened silently, till Nell said: 'Poor Tom. He's out of luck, all right.'

It was Ed who spoke of Dave. 'What happened to him tonight? I never saw him like that.'

Nell told them quietly: 'He was drunk. He'll be drunk for two or three weeks now. You know his nervous breakdowns. That's what they are, just long debauches. Marcia told me, last fall after Ruth's dance. He was drunk that night. He'll go along for months drinking nothing, but after a while he starts taking one cocktail, or two; and then some night, all of a sudden, something clicks, and he changes till he's the way he was tonight. He'll stay drunk for days now and Marcia has to take care of him.'

They were all shocked and surprised. Only Mark had half guessed the truth that night of Ruth's dance. When Ed and Mary presently went home, he stayed a little longer, and after Nell went upstairs, he said thoughtfully:

'You know, Bob, I used to think that all our lives, the lives of the people we know best, were as serene as on the surface they appear to be.'

Bob said in wry amusement: 'Emma wasn't very serene tonight.'

'I wonder,' Mark suggested, 'whether these blowups in the lives of people around us aren't really a symptom of some deeper, outside disturbance?'

'Partly, probably,' Bob agreed. 'A man's business goes sour, so he starts beating his wife.'

'It's not surprising,' Mark reflected. 'Were there ever so many things to upset a man as there are today? The world's haywire, and in our own country every business man is wondering where he stands, what Mr. Roosevelt will do next. Most men like you and me, men of reasonable means, feel that the Government is beginning to consider success a crime and to put a premium on mediocrity. Ambition and industry and thrift, the foundation of most successful careers, have become doubtful virtues.'

Bob nodded assentingly. 'We're on the defensive, Mark, men like us.'

And he said: 'I suppose nothing so quickly produces a reckless irrespon-
sibility in man as uncertainty, as not knowing what the future is likely
to bring.'

'We're all worried,' Mark agreed. 'And worry wears a man down. A
lot of men find themselves in the position of furnishing a livelihood
not only for their own families, but for their relations, their less successful friends, their servants. One of our clients told me the other day
that he has tallied up and finds his income and the salaries he pays are
the sole support of his family of five, his parents, his sister, two maiden
aunts, an invalid cousin, the widow and small children of an old college friend, his secretary and her mother, his chauffeur plus family and
parents, his cook and second maid—they are sisters—and their family
in Prince Edward Island, and his daughter's nurse who has been with
them a dozen years and is now an upstairs maid and who largely sup-
ports her dead brother's widow and baby. The total—outside his business—is thirty; thirty people dependent on him.' And he continued: 'You
know him, Dan Strawbridge. His family has always owned their mill
property and for a hundred years it's been the only industry in a town
of about a thousand people, employing two hundred men and women.
For three years his mill has operated at a loss. He has cut his personal expenditures seventy per cent and given up all contributions to
organized charity. If the mill loses money this year, he will have to shut
down, junk the machinery, throw two hundred people out of work;
and thereafter the shrinkage of his income will force him to discharge
household servants—all of them with dependents—who are all so old,
so long in his service, that they will have trouble in finding other places.
He has sleepless, harried nights, knowing that these people who depend on him will presently be deprived of their living.'

'Sure,' Bob assented. 'I could name a dozen like him. They're the ones
who are committing suicide, because they can't face all their direct and
indirect dependents and say: "Sorry, folks; I've failed you. You're on
your own now. I'm through."'

'It's happening all around us,' Mark said grimly. 'Some men like
Tom Sheffield, with demanding wives, are being driven to despera-
tion. Some, like Ed Halstead, with women like Mary to stand by their
sides, are all right. A man needs a fine wife, in times like these.' Bob
did not speak, and he added: 'I wonder about Dave—and Ruth. Ruth
I think has always set Dave high. What effect must it have on an intelligent, affectionate girl who proudly loves her father to discover that he
isn't as much of a man as she thought.'

Bob said loyally: 'It's not all Dave's fault. He's really a casualty of the last war. If you watch him you'll see that sometimes his nerves are all shot.'

'I know,' Mark agreed. 'Men never come out of war unmarked. And I sometimes think Marcia's no help to Dave. He's too gentle and considerate to rebel, but he must sometimes be fretted by her constant reminders—overcoat, rubbers, hat, all that sort of thing. She's refused to let him get well, has kept him sick.'

'Nell says he was pretty drunk and disagreeable at Ruth's dance,' Bob confessed. 'She says Ruth went all to pieces afterward.'

'It's a wonder Emma hasn't spread the story around, if she knows it.'

'Maybe she has, but she wouldn't talk to us.'

'I wonder if Ruth's all right now,' Mark said, half to himself. 'I hope Tony and I can make it for that week-end over the twenty-sixth. I want to see her.'

3

(August 1936)

Tony, when Mark spoke to him, welcomed the suggestion of a Cape week-end, since it would give him a chance to see Barbie; but the occasion was postponed. Marcia telephoned to say that Dave was having one of those nervous collapses to which he was subject and that she was keeping him quiet for a while. She suggested, instead, the week-end of August ninth, when she was sure Dave would be himself again; and that Friday afternoon Mark and Tony drove down. They managed an early start to arrive in time for dinner, and Dave, asleep on the couch on the wide veranda toward the sea, waked at the sound of their arrival and came to greet them. Mark saw that he was thinner, with an unhealthy pallor as though he had been too long indoors, and faint beads of perspiration—though the day was cool enough—across his brow. They shook hands, and Mark asked:

'Sure it's all right for us to come? Maybe you ought to be quiet for a while, Dave.'

Dave clapped him on the shoulder; he shook Tony's hand and said: 'Put the bags in your regular room, Tony.' When Tony had disappeared, he spoke straightforwardly to Mark: 'My nerves are just a loyal fiction which Marcia has invented, old man. My trouble this last month was that I tried to drink up all the liquor in eastern Massachusetts.'

He smiled as he spoke, but the pain and shame in his eyes was plain enough. Mark laughed reassuringly. 'That can happen to anyone, Dave —to take the one drink too many.'

Dave did not comment. 'Marcia's bridging at the club,' he said. 'Ought to be here any minute. Want a swim before dinner? Ruth's down on the beach somewhere—asleep in the sun, I suspect.'

Mark went to change and met Tony in brief swimming trunks coming down the stairs. Dave did not join them. 'I'm taking it easy,' he explained. 'Still pretty shaky.' Mark and Tony turned to the beach together. The white sands extended right and left in a smooth crescent, and there was no public access to the beach from the landward side so that it was never crowded. Just now there were only half a dozen figures visible in all its length; and they saw nothing of Ruth. Tony raced for the water and in, and Mark followed more quietly. They swam out beyond the breakers and floated there till Tony, looking shoreward, said: 'There's Ruth now.'

She had been reading, sitting on a shaded point two or three hundred yards away where a few stunted pines clustered, when she saw them plunge into the water; and she hurried toward them at once, and they made haste to meet her. She greeted them with an obvious delight, kissed Mark, shook Tony's hand, cried: 'Oh, I'm so glad you've come.'

'So am I!' Mark told her. 'I haven't seen you since your party.' She was, he thought, painfully thin. Above the top of her bathing suit he could trace the lines of her ribs across the arch of her chest.

She said again, clinging to Mark's hand: 'Oh, you just don't know how glad I am to see you!' Her voice caught as though it would break, and Mark looked at her in surprise and saw actual tears in her eyes; and she laughed at herself and said: 'It's just gladness, really. That's all!'

Tony watched her in a puzzled way, and Mark said: 'Remember the night we did wooden soldiers down here and your mother thought we were idiots?' They all laughed together, moving toward the house. Marcia was on the porch to greet them, with a highball for Mark after his swim and another for Dave. Ruth and Tony went to dress; and Dave, lifting his glass, told Mark: 'I'm down to one a day now.' He looked toward Marcia. 'I've told him,' he explained. She smiled in a quick, half-furtive way.

They were alone that evening. Mark, watching Ruth, sensing something tremulous and frightened in the girl, felt again that impulse to be tender toward her, to take her in his arms. It was clear that she had been terribly hurt, and the hurt had affected her profoundly, and even in physical ways. She was taller than most girls, and she had in the past carried herself well, but now she seemed to lean forward from the waist, to walk in a lurching, uncertain way as though she had no control over her legs. When they rose to leave the table, Marcia asked: 'Do you mind a quiet evening, Mark?'

'Just what I want,' he assured her.

Dave said: 'We'll go to the dance at the club tomorrow night,' and at the word, Ruth, just ahead of Mark, suddenly fell, crumpling on the floor in a ludicrous, reasonless fashion. Mark helped her up and she laughed breathlessly and he asked:

'Hurt yourself?'

She shook her head. 'No. My knee just gave way. It does that every once in a while. I don't know why.'

Marcia said in a brittle tone: 'You're at the awkward age, that's all.' Dave proposed that he and Mark serve Ruth as crutches, and she laughed and took their arms and went between them into the living room. Tony suggested that he and she drive over to see Barbie and Frank Parks—the Parks cottage was half an hour away—but she declined; so Tony drove off alone, and a little later Ruth went upstairs.

'She's going up to work,' Marcia explained, after the girl was gone. 'She makes costume jewelry, out of silver wire and semi-precious stones. She's really very clever at it,' and she added: 'I try to get her to see more of young people, but she doesn't seem to want to.'

Saturday afternoon, at Tony's suggestion, he and Mark went to the nearest airport to fly for an hour or so; and Ruth went with them, Dave and Marcia electing to stop at home. Ruth and Mark, while they watched Tony in the air, talked easily and happily; and Mark saw that in her interest in the flying she stood straight as she had used to do. It had seemed to him last night that she was as fond of Dave as she had always been; so clearly she did not blame her father. But her unhappiness at her own dance had made her self-conscious and shamed, had led her to avoid people of her own age. Mark knew something of the physical effects that may be produced by an emotional disturbance. He thought her slouching way of walking, her trick of dragging one foot a little, her falling down last night, might all have resulted from the same cause. She did not want to go to the dance at the club tonight, shrank from it instinctively; and that fall last evening might have been the subconscious preparation of a reason why she could not go, could not dance.

When he himself took the plane and rose, circling the field, he watched her and Tony on the ground; and he saw them presently separate. She went to stand by the hangars, while Tony stayed in talk with the pilot. After Mark landed, he suggested they all take a flight in the cabin plane housed at the field, and they did so, and once in the air the pilot yielded the controls to Tony and Mark in turn, and then at Mark's suggestion to Ruth. She kept the plane in level flight, made an easy turn or two, and her eyes were bright with pleasure.

He was not surprised when Ruth insisted that she could not go to the dance that night, but he overbore her protests; and while he and Tony were dressing, he enlisted Tony's help in what he proposed to do. 'I'll start it,' he said. 'You get Frank Parks and some of the others to help you and we'll give Ruth a whirl.'

Tony thought he might have difficulty in enlisting recruits. 'They'll all be afraid of getting stuck with her,' he explained.

'You can help me see that they don't,' Mark insisted. 'If we can get it started, Ruth's a fine dancer. They'll be fighting for the chance.'

So Tony agreed, and when the time came Ruth rode to the club with them, Dave and Marcia coming in their own car. Mark felt Ruth trembling with misgivings, and walking from the parking place to the clubhouse she almost fell down again; would have fallen if Mark had not held her. When he asked her to dance with him, she said: 'Oh, I can't, Uncle Mark. I'm sure to fall down.'

'Don't worry,' he insisted. 'I'll hold you up. Come along!'

At first she was stiff and uncertain, but Mark talked to her about flying till she forgot herself and then praised her dancing so extravagantly that she colored with pleasure. Then, as they had planned, Tony took her away from him, and then Frank cut in on Tony, and Mark himself claimed Ruth again and laughed and said: 'I have to fight for my turn with you, Ruth. Having a good time?' She nodded, her cheek against his; and Frank Parks cut back, and then a boy Mark did not know took her away from Frank, and Tony came to speak to his father.

'All right so far, Dad? Frank just did it as a favor to me at first, but he says she's a swell dancer, and he likes tall girls anyway.'

'Go take her away from that youngster who has her now,' Mark directed. 'Keep it going.'

So Ruth had that evening no chance to think about herself. Led by Tony and Frank Parks, half the boys there danced with her; and Mark, watching her as the evening progressed, taking his brief turn with her when he could, making sure always that she danced not long with any boy, saw the good change in her. To find herself courted and popular was the tonic she needed. She was flushed and happy and completely beautiful.

Mark thought he and Tony and Frank were the only ones in the secret, but later in the evening he and Dave went out on the veranda for a cigarette and stood a moment in silence; and then Dave said gratefully:

'Mark, you're a wise, good man. You've done Ruth a lot of good tonight, undone a lot of the harm I've done.'

'She's a grand girl,' Mark declared, faintly embarrassed by the other's word. 'Ruth and I always did get along.'

Dave touched his arm as though unconsciously. The simple gesture was eloquent. 'She and I have always been pretty close,' Dave said. 'It was a bitter cruel thing I did to her when I spoiled her party.'

Mark caught the sharp edge of tragedy in his tone, and he wished to reassure the other, but there was nothing he could say. Dave was a sensitive and gallant man; and he looked with honest eyes at himself and at the world.

4

(Winter 1936–1937)

For youth, a year is a long time; a tenth of a lifetime, or a twentieth; but as men grow older the years shrink and seem each one briefer than the last. For Mark, Tony's first year at Dartmouth passed quickly. When Tony left for Hanover, everyone was absorbed in the coming election. Bob was working for Landon, and Mark would vote for him, but he was not enthusiastic.

'I'll vote for him, sure,' he told Bob, in one of their many discussions. 'But he's not much. He's hedging, trimming his sails to catch every wind. I'd like to see him come out and say: "Mr. Roosevelt is wrong. The whole spending policy is wrong. Our honest course is to return to the gold standard, to reward industry rather than indolence, to demand that a man who is offered a job shall take it, to stop all these disguised doles, to give men freedom to work and a chance to achieve security by their own efforts, to refuse to pamper professional paupers."'

Bob smiled. 'If he said that, he'd be snowed under at the polls.'

'He'll be snowed under, anyway, but he'd go down with his flag flying. Bob, the future of the Republican Party depends on their taking a stand on these things which men like you and me believe.' He added thoughtfully: 'I sometimes think it might be best in the long run to let Mr. Roosevelt have his head, push his program to the limit. If it leads to an economic collapse in this country, then at least the people who vote for him will have learned that he led them into the quicksand. If his program does eventually lead to prosperity, to security, to free and happy lives for most of us—then he was right and we were wrong. But if he's wrong, if we who believe that you can't in the long run get something for nothing are right, then the lesson would be cheap at the price.'

Neither of them convinced the other. Maine elected a Republican Governor and Senator, and Bob jubilantly quoted the familiar phrase: 'As goes Maine, so goes the nation.' But Mark said: 'I'm not so sure. Maine men have a better idea of the value of money, and they came to their senses more quickly than the rest of the country; that's all! My father's a Landon man, but he says the Middle West will be solidly for Mr. Roosevelt. So will the South, of course; and so will New York and Pennsylvania.'

The last few weeks of the campaign were feverish. The Republicans predicted that if Mr. Roosevelt were elected ruin would follow. Frank Knox as the Republican candidate for Vice-President said that Mr. Roosevelt's policies left 'no insurance policy secure, no savings account safe.' Mark, remembering that Mr. Knox was a newspaper man, thought the publisher spoke in headlines; and yet he shared with the men he knew best a grave concern. World finance was shaky. France and Italy devalued their currency, and France, England, and the United States united to try to stabilize international exchange. The sit-down strikes in France had set a style, and labor troubles on that pattern spread across the United States.

Late in October, Mrs. Simpson won a divorce from her husband, and the gossip provoked by her long friendship with King Edward VIII took more concrete form. The election, the result of which had seemed for a while so important, came and went and was quickly forgotten; but not the derisive Democratic comment: 'As goes Maine, so goes Vermont!' Wallie Simpson left England, and Edward VIII abdicated, and millions of women, hanging over their radio, sighed with happy sympathy and sentimental sorrow when he gave up his throne for 'the woman I love.'

When Tony came home for Christmas, he and Mark went one warm day to fly; and Mark spoke to Hadden of the abdication. Hadden's eyes met his briefly. 'He was no more than a small part of a man,' he said, as one speaks, not too unkindly, of the dead.

During Tony's Christmas the house was full of young people, and Mark met the Dartmouth boys whom Tony knew best. Tony and Will Ritchie roomed together this first year at Hanover. Will was a powerful youngster, and he had played Freshman football, but he had not outgrown his awkwardness, and Tony told Mark he would never be good enough for the Varsity. They brought guests home for the holidays. Charlie Spring, with whom Tony had boxed at Hadley, roomed with Joe Hazen just across the corridor from these two. That old encounter with the gloves had founded a firm friendship between Tony and Charlie. Joe Hazen's home was in Pasadena, and he came home with Tony now while Charlie would stay with Will across the street. The four planned next year to share rooms in one of the houses in the village. Joe was the smallest of them, standing excessively erect, his head well back, his chest out, with the defensive swagger which little men so often put on to compensate for their lack of stature. Tony explained to his father: 'He's pretty unhappy. His father's a fine surgeon, and Joe wants to be one too; but he's so short he won't be able to operate without standing on a stool, and he's left-handed besides. It bothers him because he knows his father has always counted on it, and he's an only son.'

Mark, interested as he always was in the point of view of those he met, had much talk with Joe of politics and world affairs; but he thought the young man was so anxious to make a good impression that he talked more for effect than from conviction, repeating what he had heard his elders say rather than developing ideas of his own.

Charlie Spring had convictions enough, but they were his father's. His home was in Evanston, and his father and Frank Knox had been close friends, so Charlie's ideas matched the conservative Republican background against which his life had been lived. His father had died in September—Charlie wore a mourning band on his arm—and his mother had gone to spend the winter on the French Riviera, so he came home with Will.

To these four as a nucleus, others during Tony's holidays were added. Frank Parks, now a Freshman at Harvard, was staying in Cambridge for a part of his vacation. Mark gathered that he was working for a place on the *Crimson*; but Tony amplified this by saying that Frank did not get along with either his father or mother and preferred not to go home for the holidays.

Frank was full of opinions, but he seemed to Mark wrong about most things. The young man avowed himself a Communist and he had a high admiration for Russia.

'She's the only country in Europe with brains enough and courage enough to try to help beat Franco in Spain,' he said. The late summer and fall had seen steady rebel successes there, and every skirmish was followed by the execution of prisoners, sometimes by firing squads, more frequently by a simple pistol shot in the back of the head. In Madrid even priests were being butchered. Twelve hundred prisoners were shot after the capture of Badajoz; and at Bilbao, seven hundred rebel hostages were burned to death when the warehouse in which they were held prisoners was set afire by rebel shells. Death in Spain, multiplied a thousand times, administered in a thousand fantastic forms, ceased to have any reality to American minds; for where the death of an individual may be tragic or pitiful, the death of thousands—though each one was in fact an individual, loving and beloved—cannot be comprehended. Mark had found that to contemplate violent death in the headlines, day after day, was to acquire a certain tolerance for it, as men may acquire a tolerance for poisons. Perhaps that tolerance would be an armor by and by, if war spread across the world, against the horrors that might otherwise shatter the souls of man. Perhaps the chronicles of death in Spain, administered in homeopathic doses, were an immunization against the day when death would swarm everywhere.

Mark himself, instinctively trying to close his mind against these agonies which humanity yonder was enduring, had not given his sympathies to either side; but Frank, he found, was passionately against the rebels, against the Franco cause.

'They're a bunch of damned Fascists,' he said. 'That's why Italy and Germany are back of them. Hitler and Mussolini are using the war as a rehearsal for the war that's coming after this one. A dress rehearsal, complete with tanks and planes and everything. But they don't want to win too quickly, don't want the rehearsals to end till they've learned all they can; so they play along, and Russia alone has the heart and the courage to help oppose them, and England and France stand by and refuse to see what's going on.'

Rehearsal? The word stayed in Mark's mind disturbingly. Was this in fact a rehearsal, in Spain, for the tragedy that would one day sweep the world?

Frank spoke much, too, of Russia's Five-Year Plan. Mark had heard the phrase. 'But I've had my hands full trying to understand what was happening in my own country,' he confessed. 'I'm more or less ignorant about Russia, Frank.'

'No intelligent man can afford to admit that,' Frank said loftily.

Mark was amused, but he did not smile. 'I know one good thing about Russia,' he remarked. 'I met a year or two ago Colonel Hugh Cooper, who built the Dnieper Dam. I asked him what he thought of the Russians—he'd been over there off and on for years, you know—and he told me an interesting story. He said he dined one evening with the Russian who held a position corresponding to that of Chief Justice of our Supreme Court. This man had previously been a baker, and Colonel Cooper knew him well. After dinner, he said to him: "Mr. So-and-So, you're not an educated man, but you're intelligent and sensible. As a sensible man, do you consider yourself qualified to fill the position you hold?" '

Frank Parks made a scornful sound. 'Arrogant damned capitalist!'

Mark chuckled. 'Possibly!' he admitted. 'At any rate, the Russian handed him a book—just a book of ordinary size—and told him to examine it. It was in Russian, which Colonel Cooper could not read; but he saw that the book showed constant use, with sentences and paragraphs underlined, and notes in the margins. When he laid it down again, his Russian friend said: "I know that book from cover to cover, Colonel Cooper; and every law in force in Russia today is in that book. So—to answer your question—yes, I think I am competent to fill the office I hold." '

Frank Parks cried triumphantly: 'Of course! That's what Russia is doing; simplifying laws, simplifying life in every way.'

Mark smiled. 'If it could be done here, it would certainly simplify the work of us lawyers,' he agreed. 'But a lot of us would soon be out of jobs.'

'Laws are made by lawyers to make work for lawyers,' Frank said sententiously. 'That's one of the curses of our world today.' Mark, whenever he talked with Frank, envied youth its dogmatic certainties. Young men were so sure of so many things.

Dan Pride, Frank's roommate, usually came with him to the house; but he was a silent young man with little to say. These youngsters sometimes brought girls with them, and Dan's sister Lucy came once, and Mark thought her disturbingly attractive. She was only sixteen, but she seemed older, seemed to him to be one of those girls who the moment they appear focus every masculine eye, but who by the same token have few friends among their own sex. She was distractingly pretty, with fluttering, flattering ways; but Mark suspected that she was by no means the charming little idiot she seemed.

One evening a group of these youngsters gathered at the house. Barbie Parks, in Boston for two days during the holidays, was there; and Betty Ritchie, smoking an astonishing number of cigarettes, and escorted by a young man named Forbush or Frobush, from Harvard Business School, who looked as though he needed more sleep than he was getting. Someone spoke of Wallie Simpson and her royal conquest; and Barbie said:

'I thought his radio speech was wonderful.'

Lucy exclaimed: 'But he must be an awful drip to let her put it over on him!'

The others argued pro and con for a moment, till Frank Parks spoke like an oracle. 'You people never think for yourselves, do you? The whole thing was engineered by Stanley Baldwin, to get rid of the King. The Conservatives didn't like him because he was a friend of labor, wanted to improve conditions in the mines and the factories. So they rigged the whole show to dump him.' Someone expressed incredulity, and Frank retorted: 'Then why hadn't they had his coronation long ago? They'll crown the new King quick enough!'

Lucy cried admiringly: 'You're so cute, Frank!' The four-letter word became a long-drawn-out term of admiring endearment. 'You know just about everything, don't you! But I still say he was an awful meatball! He's been dating her for years and years, but he could have parked her somewhere till he was really King and then he could marry her or something and just tell the rest of them where to get off.' Her vocabulary always amused Mark. So far as he could judge, a droop and a drip and a wet smack and a meatball were all very much the same thing, masculine and unattractive. If she liked a boy, he was neat, or cute, or cunning.

Mark enjoyed these young people. When vacation was over and Tony went back to Hanover, the house seemed silent and empty and forlorn.

One incident of the later winter was to have for him a splendid sequel. A few days after Mr. Roosevelt's proposal to enlarge the Supreme Court, Mark attended a Bar Association dinner at which Professor Wearing of Harvard Law School was the principal speaker. He and Mark had formed even while Mark was in Law School a friendship which persisted. He was tall and a little stooped, with a thin, neglected mustache that drooped at each corner of his mouth. He had a dry wit—in which there was no malice—which endeared him to his classes; and tonight he had blistered Mr. Roosevelt with biting scorn and blasted the proposal to enlarge the court with a searing and logical precision which delighted his audience.

When Mark went to speak to him afterward, Professor Wearing said at once, chuckling, taking the other's hand:

'Well, young man, come to tell me that I didn't see Mr. Roosevelt's side of this question?' He had warned Mark long ago: 'You'll never make a good trial lawyer, because you always see the other fellow's side. A trial lawyer must be sure not only that his client's case can be won, but also that by all the laws of God and man his client deserves victory. You're too fair-minded for your own good. You ought to be on the bench, not in the bar enclosure.'

Mark remembered this now, and he smiled and said: 'No sir, for once I can only see one side.' He added: 'It's a relief to find a thing I'm sure about. On Mr. Roosevelt's social and economic legislation I blow this way, that way; but about the Court, at least, I'm sure he's wrong.'

Judge Sothern joined them. He was Mark's age, spare and youthful in appearance. Professor Wearing was saying: 'I've thought of you often, lately, Mark; thought that you must be perplexed in these times.' He spoke to Judge Sothern. 'Mr. Worth, here, Your Honor, is a man worth studying. He's a composite, an American. I'm New England for generations and so I expect are you.'

'New York and New England,' Judge Sothern agreed.

'Well, Worth here was born in Mississippi, brought up in Ohio.' Mark looked at the old man in surprise, and the Professor chuckled. 'Forgotten, have you? I cross-examined you thoroughly about your antecedents one day after your mental processes began to interest me.' He spoke to Judge Sothern again. 'Worth's ancestors on one side were New Englanders; on the other, two generations back, British. His mother was a Southern woman, with good rebel blood in her; his father an Ohio editor, son of a farmer.' He rested his hand on Mark's shoulder. 'So here in his head is something like a cross-section of the American mind; New England ancestry with the New Englander's interest in the seven seas and the far lands whose shores they touch; a Middle-West upbringing with the Middle-Westerner's certainty that if a wall ten feet high were built around the United States we'd still get along very well; an admixture of rebel blood so that he accepts nothing unquestioningly; and an editor father who gave him a balanced and judicial point of view. If you knew what Mark here was thinking at any time, you'd have a fair idea of what the United States—at least that part of it east of the Mississippi—is thinking.'

Mark said frankly: 'You'd have trouble deciding what I think. Half the time I don't know myself.'

Professor Wearing chuckled, and he told Judge Sothern: 'Worth here should be on the Bench, you know. He always sees both sides.'

The Judge smiled. 'When I decide to resign, I'll recommend him to the Governor,' he said.

It was undoubtedly as a result of this conversation that a few days Mark found himself appointed to sit as master in a particularly complicated piece of litigation. The task engaged most of his time and his thoughts for weeks to come; but in March there were rumors of war again. In April, college students in New York went on a peace strike, solemnly vowing never to support the United States Government in any war at all. Toward the end of the month, in reprisal for an aerial attack on their pocket battleship *Deutschland*, which killed and wounded more than a hundred German sailors, German naval vessels bombarded the port of Almeria, killing many noncombatants. There had been horrors enough in Spain, so that death had been robbed even of dignity; but at this massacre of the innocents under the *Deutschland's* guns, a shudder of anger shook the world, and Mark began to feel again the sense of a threatening cloud rising against the distant sky.

5

(June 4, 1937)

On the first Friday in June, Mark went back to his office at three o'clock to find a message requesting him to call Mr. Land, at the Governor's office. He did so, and Mr. Land said: 'Mr. Worth? The Governor would appreciate it if you could come up and see him any time before five o'clock.'

Mark was astonished. He had never met the Governor and had voted against him at the last election; but he asked no questions. 'I'll be glad to,' he agreed.

'Ask for me,' Mr. Land directed.

'I'll try to make it about four,' Mark promised. He hung up the receiver and sat staring at it for a moment, wondering what the Governor could want with him. If the state needed his legal services, the summons would presumably have come from the Attorney-General's office; yet no other explanation seemed possible. He remembered with a smile what Professor Wearing had said about him to Judge Sothern, a few weeks before, and he knew that there was a vacancy on the Superior Bench; but the Governor was a Democrat and Mark was a Republican. The appointment was not likely to come his way.

He shook his head at last. There was no profit in speculation. He could only wait and see. At five minutes after four he presented himself at Mr. Land's office.

'Sit down,' Mr. Land suggested. Mark did so, and the other tipped back in his chair. Land was a prematurely bald young man with a courteous manner and a mild eye. He looked, Mark thought, more like a school teacher than a politician. With the air of one making conversation, he said: 'Well, things are looking up. Business, I mean.'

'Why, apparently, yes,' Mark agreed.

'Another two years and we'll be back where we were in 1929,' Mr. Land predicted. 'Unless something happens.'

Mark said: 'If we are, I hope it will be on a sounder basis than 1929. This seems to me like an artificial prosperity.'

Land eyed him wisely. 'Probably you don't think much of Mr. Roosevelt,' he suggested.

'I disagree with almost everything he has done,' Mark assented, and then added smilingly: 'But so many others agree with him that I'm probably wrong.'

'He's all right,' Mr. Land declared. 'He's in the groove.' He added: 'Of course, no one man is ever going to make a lot of money in this country again—or if he does, he won't keep it—but a lot of men are going to make more than they ever did before.'

Mark, suspecting that this was in effect a cross-examination, said quietly: 'Well, of course, I believe in what we call the capitalistic system. Unless someone accumulates capital—and puts it into industry—there aren't enough jobs to go around.' He added smilingly: 'After all, our American civilization is at least in part the fruit of the capitalistic system. Our standard of living is the result of it, and our standard of living is so high that most of us are perfectly willing to believe that a man who can afford to drive an automobile may still be a worthy object of charity. If we had a dole, it wouldn't surprise anyone to see people drive up in their own cars to collect their money. That's the sort of country the capitalistic system has developed. I doubt whether any other system can do as well.'

Mr. Land looked at him thoughtfully. 'How do you stand on labor?' he asked in a toneless voice.

Mark answered readily enough. 'Why, I think it likely that in many lines capital still takes too high a share of the profits of industry. All my life, as long as I can remember, whenever labor has demanded a higher wage, capital has protested that it could not raise wages without facing ruin; yet each time capital has made some concessions—and has continued to operate profitably. I've seen wages go up from say a dollar a day to a dollar an hour—but capital seems still to make enough profit so that it stays in business.'

He paused, but Land only nodded, and Mark went on: 'That's been true so far, and as long as it is true that capital can pay higher wages and still operate at a profit sufficient to attract new capital into industry, I'm for higher wages. So far—except in our New England woolen mills and a few similar cases—capital has been able to meet labor's demands and still survive. But eventually labor will demand more than capital can pay. When that happens, capital will strike. When the manufacturer can no longer meet his employees' demands and still show a profit, he will junk his plant and throw his laborers out of a job.'

'The Government wouldn't let him junk his plant,' Mr. Land suggested.

'Perhaps not,' Mark agreed. 'But without a wise hand at the helm the plant will soon junk itself. The capacity for acquiring and managing money is not universal, you know. Some men have it; most of us do not. The breed of men who accumulate capital are a valuable national asset. It's a breed which should be encouraged and preserved.'

He added, before the other could speak: 'But I sometimes think the answer to the labor problem may lie in another direction. Labor, which produces goods, also buys them. Every man has two things to spend, time and money. A man working short hours will nearly aways spend more money—if he has it—than the man who works such long hours that at day's end he's too tired to do anything but eat and go to bed. Instead of raising wages, I'd like to see working hours reduced and wages maintained. I believe that would increase buying. I believe that to reduce hours without reducing pay is—if all manufacturers would do it—a good investment for industry as a whole.'

Land said triumphantly: 'Right, but we're reducing hours and raising wages too. That's better yet!'

Mark smiled. 'I doubt it. That means the destruction of capital—or a capital strike—sooner or later,' and he said: 'You know there's one thing to be said for large fortunes, from the Government's point of view. It makes it easier to collect taxes.'

Land smiled. 'Right again—and it tickles the rest of us to see the rich men get soaked.'

Mark said seriously: 'Of course the poor man gets soaked too. If a man earns a thousand dollars a year and spends it, he's paying about two hundred dollars a year in indirect taxes today—but he doesn't know it.'

'He's a damned sight happier not knowing it!' Land suggested.

'I sometimes think we'd have a better government if every voter knew how much taxes he was paying.'

The other chuckled. 'You'll never get Congress to go for that. Indirect taxation is the politicians' trick to keep the voter from finding out how much of his money they're spending.' And he said strongly: 'It's got to be so. We've spent ourselves out of a bad hole, this last four years. If the Government ever tries to stop spending, we'll have the damnedest panic this country ever saw.'

'There's no future to spending more than you earn except bankruptcy, for a man or a government.'

'We won't go bankrupt as long as we can borrow money,' Land insisted. 'And another thing, we made two billion dollars by reducing the gold content of the dollar. We can reduce it again any time we have to. It's easy enough for the Government to get money. No, we're going along all right. I still say we're sitting pretty—if we don't have a war.'

Mark said soberly: 'Well, we may have one. Hitler seems to mean trouble.'

'Sure, but the Neutrality Bill will keep us out,' Mr. Land predicted, and he rose. 'I'll see if the Governor's free.'

Mark spent ten minutes with the Governor, and he found himself at the other's words trembling in a deep excitement hard to control. The Governor rose, at last, smiling, his hand extended.

'Then that's settled,' he said. 'I'll send the nomination to the Council tomorrow. It will go through with no trouble. I'm glad to be the first to congratulate you, Judge Worth.'

Mark smiled with pleasure at that salutation. 'Thank you, Your Excellency,' he said. 'This is a great honor. I'll try to deserve it.'

6

(June 4, 1937)

Mark walked downtown to his office, full of an honest astonishment that the Governor should have selected him to fill that vacancy on the Superior Bench; but when he came to the office he did not go in. He was not yet ready to tell Bob Ritchie and the others what had happened. He turned to the garage and took his car and drove home. He came into the familiar hall and Elin emerged from the kitchen, a little surprised at this early appearance. She asked whether he wished an early dinner and he said:

'No, the usual time.'

He went upstairs and took a shower and on some whimsical impulse dressed for dinner. When he descended, Elin came in to speak to him, and looked at him in surprise. 'Are you going out?' she asked.

'No,' he said. 'No—I'm . . .' He hesitated, then laughed and told her frankly: 'I'm celebrating, Elin. I had good news today. The Governor's going to appoint me to be a judge.' No one except Tony would be as proud and as pleased as she.

She cried out in a quick delight; 'Oh, that's fine, that's wonderful, sir!' He saw her eyes shine with happy tears.

When she served his dinner, he ate slowly, wishing Tony were here to hear his news. His thoughts turned long to Nan, and it was these thoughts which led him, after dinner, to go up to her studio in the attic. More than in any other room in the house her memory persisted there. Her easel and her paintbox and her sketchbooks and some of her unfinished canvases were vivid reminders of her former presence.

He went directly to the table which had served her as desk and began to look through some of her sketchbooks. They were long familiar, yet he never tired of them. Three were filled with studies of Tony as a baby and as a youngster. Usually the faces were blank, but Nan had the trick of catching distinctive postures; and Mark thought that even with no faces drawn in he would always have recognized Tony. He chuckled over some of the sketches, and when at last he went downstairs again, he took paper and pen to write to his son.

Dear Tony—[he wrote] I feel like having a talk with you tonight, and since you're a hundred and fifty miles away this letter is the next best thing. I've just been up in the studio, looking through some of Mother's sketchbooks—the ones that are filled with you—and they made me remember so many things. There's the one she used the summer before you were born. It has some caricatures of herself. She used to say she looked like a little girl carrying a big bass drum, and there's a sketch of herself with a drum to prove it. I remember the day she drew it, about a month before you were born.

Then there's a series of sketches of you going to bed, all labelled, like one of Gluyas Williams's cartoons. It used to take you an hour to get undressed, sometimes, you found so many things to distract you. Sometimes Mother just let you take your time, and sketched everything you did.

I found some sketches of you pretending to be an automobile. Do you remember that? When you were four or five years old you would play automobile by the hour, making a noise like one, and steering with an imaginary steering wheel, getting out to crank the car the way we used to crank our first Ford, making a hissing noise as you primed the engine, going through the whole procedure. You always were what the advertising men would call car-conscious.

You can see that I've been thinking of Mother and of you even more than usual this evening; thinking of the night she died and how steady and brave you were, saying good night to me when I went to the hospital, and how much help you were when I came home in the morning to tell you she was gone. I thought a lot about you in the hospital that night. I planned our future, yours and mine; how we would go fishing together, and camping and touring. So far, we've done most of the things I planned, but I know that sometimes nowadays, with the clouds rising in Europe, the future seems troubled and confused to you. I'm sorry you could not have lived in the world as I knew it when I was a boy. Most people worked hard and lived decently and saved a little money and believed in the old virtues and lived by their beliefs. The automobile began to change that. Before there were automobiles good citizens didn't do things that were against the law. There are so many automobile laws now that no one can drive a car far without breaking a few of them. The people who made the laws went to such extremes that they converted us into a nation of law-breakers, just as telling a child he mustn't play with his new toys is bound to teach him disobedience. Any bad law has that effect. Unless a law is respected and obeyed by decent people, it ought to be repealed.

But those first automobile laws began to destroy our standards; and the war and what followed it finished the job. Germany perpetrated an international swindle by deliberately debasing her currency, and then repudiating it, and then England and France and the others refused to pay their debts to us, and then our own Government repudiated its gold bonds; and private morality began to disintegrate as governments showed the way. When I was a boy, people thought saving money was a virtue. Now the Government, by reducing the awards of capital, does everything possible to discourage saving even by private individuals.

So it's a changed—and a changing—world. Naturally young men like you are puzzled, groping for solid, sure things that they can hold on to. Well, there are such things, son, but you have to teach yourself to recognize them. We find out after a while that if we do the best we know how, from day to day, we can sleep well of nights, and we can be happy. That always has been true and always will be, because that's the way men are made. This doesn't mean you have to beat the other fellow. No one has to compete with anyone else. The only real competition is between what you do and what you're capable of doing. The nearer you come to doing your best, the happier you'll be.

But this letter didn't start out to be a sermon! It was just that I wanted to talk to you, because of course since Mother died you're closer to me than anyone. I wanted to tell you my good news. The Governor sent for me this afternoon. I've never been in politics, so I was surprised. He says he means to appoint me to the Superior Bench. He says he is doing so after consultation with some of the other judges,. particularly my friend Judge Sothern, and with leaders of the Bar in whose judgment he has confidence. Naturally I am much pleased, and I know you will be pleased with me. An appointment to the Massachusetts Bench is a sort of honorary degree, and it means a lot to me to have won it.

I had dinner with the Ritchies last night, and they all sent you their love. Nell had a Mrs. Merriman there as my dinner partner. I know Nell thinks I ought to marry again. She's forever dragging attractive widows out for me to inspect! Perhaps she's right, but though Mother's going left a big gap in my life, you and my love for you and my pride in you have filled it.

Remember me to Barbie when you write. Lots of love as always,

Dad.

P.S. The appointment will be sent in tomorrow, so it will be in the afternoon papers, but I wanted to brag a little to you!

Mark finished the letter and sealed it and addressed the envelope. It was almost midnight, but there was an early morning collection from the box at the corner, so he affixed a stamp and went to post the letter. The night was fine, with a full moon, and he walked slowly, pausing to fill his pipe and light it. He continued on around the block, strolling easily, thinking of Nan, thinking happily of his son. There was a dim light burning in the front hall in the Ritchie house, and he wondered whether Bob and Nell were still awake, and thought of dropping in to tell them his news. But for tonight, he decided, only he and Tony—he felt, having written, as though his letter was in Tony's hands—and of course Elin, whom he had already told, should know.

7

(June 4, 1937)

At about the time Mark began to write that letter, Tony and Barbie Parks were sitting in Tony's car beside the river a few miles from

Merryfield. Tony, with one examination out of the way that day, one still to come, and a week-end in which to prepare for it, had suddenly decided that he must see Barbie. Late in the afternoon he took his car from the barn below Hanover where he kept it in storage and, in no hurry once he was on the way, set out on the long drive to Merryfield. There had been rain that evening, and clouds were still heavy, but before he came to his destination the skies had cleared. He telephoned Barb, and when she heard his voice she protested delightedly:

'Babe? Where are you?'

'At the drugstore. I drove down to see you.'

'Oh, Tony, you shouldn't have come!'

'Maybe, but I couldn't help it! Barb, come for a ride!'

'Heavens, I can't! I'm studying for exams.'

'You can't study if I keep calling you to the telephone, and I will if you don't come riding!'

She laughingly declared that he was an idiot, and he admitted it; but he pleaded with her to come and be an idiot with him for a while. In the end, making him promise that it should be for no more than half an hour, she agreed.

They drove across the river, and turned at random along a country road, and he proposed that they walk through the meadow to the riverside; but she said it was too wet and he found a lane and drove down toward the river till they could watch the stars shine in the water sliding by. The night was warm and still.

'I like rivers,' she said, when, after a spate of talk, they had been silent for a while. 'They sort of keep tending to their own business, don't they?'

'They're so darned busy going somewhere, all the time,' he murmured. 'And they know where they're going.'

'They just keep running downhill!' she reminded him. 'It's the only way they can go.'

'That might be all right, at that,' he said in the same low tone. 'I mean, having just one way to go, not having to decide anything. Maybe we're all up against the same thing, only we don't know it. Maybe there's only one way we can go.'

'Do you really think that?'

'Oh, we make plans, and have ideas,' he admitted. 'But most of what happens to us is accident. I'll get through college and law school and go to work; but if a war comes along maybe I'll be in it, and even if I don't get killed, I'll not be good for much after that.'

She cried resentfully: 'Don't say that, Tony. You'll always be fine. You've been reading too much Hemingway!'

'Say, he's great, isn't he?'

'I don't think so!' she declared. 'He writes about a few people who didn't have enough courage and common sense to go back to work after the war, and he calls them a lost generation. But the generation was all right! Most of the men in the army came home and got jobs and married and raised their families like everyone else. They didn't all stay in Europe and make love and get drunk and go to bullfights, the way people do in his books. Most people are pretty decent, Tony!'

'I'm not afraid of having to go to war,' Tony said, half to himself, as though he had not heard her. 'I'm not even afraid of being killed. At least, I don't think I am. But the thing is—would I ever be good for anything afterward, even if I lived through it?'

She touched his hand. 'You'll be a lawyer, and a fine one, like your father, Babe.'

'Maybe,' he assented. 'But—the way it looks to me, the whole world's like a scrambled egg before you cook it! The old solid things are wrecked and the new ones are too soft to get your teeth into!'

She smiled in the darkness. 'You've been listening to too many professors, telling you what's wrong with the world instead of what's right with it. You won't have to settle things for the whole world, you know. You'll be kept busy taking care of yourself and your family!' And she laughed and said: 'Professors have too many theories! They live in a vacuum, just as if they were so many experiments in physics. You know, a falling object accelerates at the rate of thirty-two feet a second or whatever it is—in a vacuum. But the trouble is, things don't happen in vacuums.'

'Sure,' Tony assented. 'If a man falls out of an aeroplane, or jumps out, he falls faster and faster for a while; but then he reaches top speed and holds it. The air slows him down.'

'Of course. And so many of the things professors teach you are pure theory, not making allowances for—air, and the way people love their homes, and like to be decent and to live quiet, settled lives, and so on. Life is so full of exceptions; but teachers just give you the rules and you have to figure out the exceptions for yourself.'

Tony for a moment did not speak. Then he chuckled comfortably, looking up at the stars. 'Say, how did we get started on this, anyway? Who cares about professors on such a night!' And he finished the line: 'Leander swam the Hellespont.'

She met his new mood. 'Do you know anything about stars?'

'Not a thing—except to pick out the Big Dipper and the North Star. But who cares? I like to watch them.'

'I wonder if they watch us!'

'They wouldn't see much,' he said. 'When you're in the air, the towns and cities are just little scars on the face of the world. You hardly notice the towns, when you get up five or six thousand feet.'

'But you do notice the farmhouses, the farms,' she urged. 'They're a lot more interesting, set off each one by itself. Houses all huddled together don't mean anything. One family or one person is always more interesting than a crowd.'

'I know,' he assented almost drowsily. 'I can read in the papers about a million people starving to death in China, or something like that, and I don't feel half as bad as I did when a little girl drowned in the lake back of our house last summer, or when Jan Ritchie sprained her ankle and had to go on crutches.'

She asked thoughtfully: 'You and she have grown up together, haven't you?'

'Yes, sure. Jan's just a kid.' There was an affectionate mirth in his tones. 'She thinks I'm hung to the moon.'

'Does Betty feel the same way about you?'

'No, we've always fought.'

'Then probably she's the one you'll marry!'

He looked sidewise at her, and his voice suddenly was husky. 'I'm not going to marry either one of them, Barb,' he said.

'You can't tell.'

'I can tell!' he insisted. But it was not yet time to say the things he wished to say, not for years, not till he was through with college and probably with law school too. He opened the car door and turned sidewise so that his legs hung out, and he lay down with his head on her lap. 'Rub my head,' he said.

She laughed and ran her fingers through his hair. 'You're like a cat, always wanting to be rubbed.'

'I wish I could purr,' he spoke drowsily. 'I'm going to sleep. Wake me at daylight.'

They stayed talking quietly for long, and once she said: 'You think a lot about war, don't you, Tony.'

'You can't help it, if you're my age.'

'Father says what we need is a good war, to start business booming again and get rid of unemployment.'

'Damn his eyes!' His tone was jocose, and she laughed with him and said:

'He doesn't really mean it, of course. But Tony, I know a lot of fellows your age who worry about it.'

His head on her knee, her hand on his head, he was too comfortable for much concern; but he said: 'It isn't only fellows my age. Dad, for instance. I know him well enough to know he's thinking a lot about it, dreading what may happen to me if we do have a war.'

'Frank says if there is a war, he won't fight in it.'

Tony grinned. 'Sure, we all say that. But we will. Everybody will. You can't get out of it, and when the time comes, you don't really want to.' And he said: 'Forget it, Barb. I'd rather talk about lots of other things.'

'I don't want you to go and fight in some old war.' Her tone was at once amused and fiercely tender; and he said huskily:

'You'd better not start being too nice to me, or I won't be responsible! Go on and talk about something else!'

So she laughed, and they talked about other things, till at last she lifted his head off her knee. 'That's enough! Time to go, Tony!'

He sat up. 'I hate to,' he confessed. 'But I'd better, at that. I'm driving back tonight.'

'Oh, tonight? Do you have to?'

'I've a lot to do over the week-end, another exam Monday. I'll sleep late tomorrow and then get at it.'

Yet he drove slowly into town, reluctant to end this hour. Before they parted, standing in the shadows by the dormitory, he asked softly: 'Some fun?'

'Some fun!' she agreed. 'But we shouldn't have done it! I hate your driving so far tonight. Be careful. Keep awake.'

'Sure!'

'We were crazy, honestly. But I'm glad we were.'

'So am I.'

She said, 'Now you'd better start. Good night. And drive slow!'

'I can't do anything else! If I push this old car over fifty it shimmies right off the road. Well, good-bye—and thanks for coming out. You're a good sport!'

'Good night, Babe!'

He did not kiss her good night. Sometimes, when they had not seen each other for a while, and particularly if others were about when they met, they did kiss, in a brotherly-sisterly fashion; but never when they were alone.

8

(June 4, 1937)

Tony decided to fill up with gas, and he stopped at Holburn's garage. He pulled up behind a car that was being serviced and recognized Chad Frame, an old Hadley boy who was now at Dartmouth, holding the hose as the gas poured into the tank, spilling gas on the ground, arguing with the service man who tried to take the hose away from him.

Chad quite obviously had had too much to drink, but this was not unusual. His father and mother had been divorced during his first year at Hadley, and the proceedings had had sensational publicity. Mrs. Frame brought the suit, but Mr. Frame contested it, claiming collusion, asserting that he had agreed to give Mrs. Frame legal grounds for her proceedings, and had done so as agreed. Mrs. Frame denied any fore-knowledge of her husband's offense, and the court accepted her testi-mony; but there had been ugly sequels—which the newspapers cheer-fully reported. There was a Polish count whom Mrs. Frame would have married one winter at Palm Beach but for his belated discovery that her income would be cut in half after her remarriage; and as for Mr. Frame, he had thrice been haled into court by pretty ladies whose least damning charge against him was breach of promise to marry.

Chad when Tony first knew him was an attractive youngster, but the effect of this ill fame on him was devastating. So long as he was at Hadley, Mr. Carbrey's wise kindliness kept his life in precarious bal-ance; but he was not strong enough to stand alone in the greater freedom of college. His excesses arose not so much from any weakness in himself as from an instinct to defy the opinion of the world; to silence before they were uttered those half-pitying, half-scornful criticisms of his father and his mother which he read in every eye. He was a year older than Tony, a Sophomore at Hanover now, and his fame among his fellows there was unsavory. But Tony, with the loyalty which Hadley instils into its boys, had always felt for him more sympathy than reprobation, and when he recognized Chad now he went to speak to him and Chad caught his arm, insisting that Tony have a drink. Tony said he didn't need a drink, but Chad declared that after driving all the way from

Hanover on one of Jim Hedge's blind dates, liquor was the only thing that would console him.

'He told me she was a wooing little heifer, Tony,' he complained. 'But she was ter'ble, jus' ter'ble!' He produced a bottle, almost empty, and Tony said he had better save it till he got back to Hanover, but Chad said: 'Tha's all right. I got another one. See?'

He drew a bottle out of the car, still neatly wrapped and secured with strips of gummed paper. Tony decided that if Chad started for Hanover as drunk as he was, and with this bottle unopened, he would never get there; so he took it and laid it on the front seat of his car while Chad was drinking from the other. Then he accepted a sip of raw liquor out of the bottle Chad offered him, and Chad tossed the bottle aside and it broke; and the service man began to sweep up the broken glass and to swear at Chad, and they were still arguing and near blows when Tony, his own tank filled and the bottle on the seat beside him, drove away.

He drove out of town, at first slowly; but after he passed the last houses, his speed crept up. The night was fine. The wide valley was all good farming land, tobacco barns dotting the fertile fields; and the road ran straight and tempting, and the car sang sweetly.

It was past midnight; and he was sleepy, and he was thinking more of Barb than of his driving, when a barn suddenly rushed down the middle of the road to meet him. At the last moment, the road swerved sharply to the left and his brakes screamed as he negotiated the turn. The steering wheel shimmied violently, fighting to escape from his grip, and the car was so near to rolling over that he dared not risk the brakes again.

Another turn had still to be made, to the right, this time; and there was a narrow bridge which he must hit exactly or come to grief. He managed it, his left mudguard scraping the bridge parapet; but another car approached the bridge at the same time and from the opposite direction, and his speed had thrown Tony to the wrong side of the road, so that now he faced that other car head on, not ten feet away.

He tried to dodge it, but their fenders touched. His car swerved into the ditch and his head thumped hard against something and blackness settled down.

9

(June 5, 1937)

Mark had been asleep an hour or more when he was wakened by the persistent ringing of the telephone. He turned on the lights and went downstairs to answer, moving at first sleepily, and then, as he recognized the possible implications of this telephone call in the small hours of the morning, in a prickling fear. At the phone his own voice was strange to him.

'Hello?' he said.

'Hello! This Mr. Mark Worth?'

'Yes.'

'Well, this is the Chief of Police at Merryfield. You've got a son named Anthony?'

'Yes!' Mark asked uncontrollably: 'Is he hurt?'

'Hurt?' No, he's all right.' Mark waited breathlessly. 'But he's been in an accident. Side-swiped a New York car just outside of town here. Nobody hurt, but both cars are wrecked.'

'You're sure he's all right?'

'Just some scratches and bumps. He was too drunk to get hurt much. We've got him locked up. I thought you'd want to know.'

'Drunk?' Mark was perfectly sure that Tony had not been drunk.

'Yeah, plenty!'

There could be no virtue in arguing the point over the telephone. Mark steadied his voice. 'I'll be right up. Merryfield is near Hadley, isn't it?'

'Just a few miles.' The other man asked in a sudden interest: 'He go to Hadley, does he?'

'He did. He's in Dartmouth now. I'll start at once. I'll be there by six o'clock.'

'I thought you'd want to know,' the Chief repeated. 'I've got a boy myself.'

'Thanks,' Mark said. He dressed in haste and set out to drive a hundred miles to get Tony out of jail.

10

(June 5, 1937)

Mark had driven to Hadley so often that he needed to give no thought to the road. He circled past the Stadium and picked his way through Cambridge to the Concord Turnpike. The telephone had waked him at a little past one o'clock in the morning. Now it was almost two. Day would begin to break before he came to Hadley, for this was June and dawn came early. At intervals he saw headlights far away and they came toward him, increasing in size at first slowly and then with a rush, passing with a hissing roar. Now and then a radiance behind him warned him that a car was overtaking him; and presently it surged alongside and then pulled on ahead, the twin red tail lights receding in the distance. But for the most part he had the Turnpike to himself.

He had been half asleep when he answered the telephone, but he was wide awake now, his thoughts clear. The Chief had said Tony was drunk. That, Mark was sure, could not be true. He thought in a slow alarm that if Tony's manner were that of one intoxicated, the youngster must have suffered some head injury; and the thought turned him cold with fear and he wished to stop and telephone the Chief again, insisting that a doctor be called. But to do so meant delay, so he pressed on.

Once, almost casually, he remembered that he must telephone the Governor in the morning and warn the other not to nominate him for that judgeship. A man whose son was under arrest for drunken driving —even though Tony was surely innocent of the charge—was not a proper candidate for the Bench; and the Governor's political enemies would be quick to point this out. Mark accepted the necessity of withdrawing his name with no second thought. Tony's accident was his immediate concern.

Hadley Village and Hadley School lie a little off the highroad down the valley. When Mark passed the familiar fork in the road and pushed on toward Merryfield, the sun was just rising. Spring was flooding into early summer, the trees in full new leaf, the meadows green and beautiful; and as the sun rose higher, it touched the bright drops of dew and turned them into diamonds for a brief moment before they began to evaporate and disappear. Since daybreak, Mark had driven more rapidly. When he saw Tony safe and well, he would be himself again; but till he saw Tony, he would not be able fully to believe in his son's safety.

As the sun rose, early morning traffic began to move upon the road, trucks and farm carts and cars. Mark was only half conscious of the scene about him; the broad fields under cultivation, the tobacco barns, the river of which he caught an occasional distant glimpse. He passed through two villages and saw, still at some distance, the first houses on the outskirts of Merryfield; but before he reached them, he came to the spot where Tony's accident had occurred.

He recognized the scene because Tony's car lay in the field beside the road. It was upside down, its wheels pointing to the sky; and even before he alighted, Mark saw that the left-hand front wheel had been shattered, the mudguard crushed. It seemed impossible that anyone who had been in that car when it turned over could have escaped unhurt.

Mark braked to a stop and switched off his motor and alighted. Tony, according to the Chief of Police, had side-swiped another car; but there was no other car here now. Mark stepped off the road and went to where Tony's car lay and stooped to look inside. Both doors were jammed shut, but the windows were open. Tony must have crawled out through one of them. The dash locker was open, as though someone had rummaged there; and road maps and two or three sticks of chewing gum, and a pack of cigarettes and some monkey links for fixing broken tire chains, and a few other odds and ends had spilled out. Lying among them Mark saw what was obviously a bottle, wrapped in brown paper and sealed; but the paper was stained, suggesting that the bottle had been broken in the accident. The smell of whiskey in the car was sufficient proof of what the bottle had contained; but Mark picked it up and tore the paper gingerly away. The bottle was shattered; but the neck was sound and he saw that the seal was unbroken.

Mark examined the marks in the soft earth of the field, and in the ditch, till he was able to guess what had happened. The accident had occurred where the road coming north rounded the corner of a barn and then, making an S-turn, immediately crossed a bridge just wide enough for two cars to pass. Tony, by the way his car lay, had been coming north, up the valley, returning toward Hanover; and the corner of the barn would have obscured his view of the bridge and of the road beyond. He had been driving rapidly. So much was plain from the dark marks on the roadbed where when he set his brakes his tires had dragged and slewed. The other car, coming south, had applied its brakes —the marks were clear—and swerved to the right to give him as much room as possible; but when Tony's car struck it, it went off into the ditch just short of the bridge, turning on its side. It was gone now, had presumably been hauled out of the ditch and towed off to town.

The story was told by the marks in the dirt and the streaks in the road; but while Mark was still examining these indications, an informant appeared. He was an aged man in overalls and a blue shirt and a wide straw hat who emerged from the barn and came toward Mark and watched his investigations with an incurious eye. Mark said: 'Good morning.' The man grunted, and Mark said: 'Looks as though they had an accident here last night?'

'Yup,' the man agreed, in a complacent satisfaction. 'They have a lot of 'em. That barn of mine, it gets 'em every time. They pile into the side of it, or they hit the curve too fast, or they ram into the bridge or something. Guess't I've hauled more'n twenty cars out that had rammed into the side of my barn, in my time.' He added: 'Town's figuring to straighten the road soon's they can raise the money. There's been three people killed here in the last seven years, and more cars wrecked than you can shake a stick at.'

Mark saw that the old man took a sombre pride in his barn's grim record. He asked: 'Do you know what happened last night?'

'Yup. Kid full of liquor, coming north, driving like a bat out of Hell, swung too wide on the turn. Car coming the other way—a woman driving it—swung out as far as she could to give him all the room she could, but he hit her, knocked her into the ditch, turned a somersault hisself.'

'Anybody hurt?' Mark asked. No need of arguing with this man.

'Nope. The woman had slowed down enough so she just slid into the ditch and turned over on her side. The kid was too drunk to get hurt, I guess.' Mark colored with loyal anger, but he held his tongue. 'I was asleep abed, but it woke me.' The man pointed to the house by the barn. 'I run to the window and looked out and there they was, this one with its wheels in the air still a-spinning. I pulled my clothes on, and by the time I got downstairs, this woman come knocking at the door for help, wanting to use the telephone and all. Real handsome she was, too! Don't know as I ever see a handsomer! Police car come along while she was telephoning, and I went on out there. I judge she telephoned Charlie Holburn, because his wrecking car got here right away, and one of his taxis come to take her along to town. The cops had took the young feller. I stayed and watched them haul her car back on the road.'

'Was it badly smashed up?'

'Went off to town under its own power,' the old man said. 'Guess't could be fixed up all right.'

Mark asked stiffly: 'How do you know the boy was drunk?'

'They could smell it on him, a mile off; and he acted it, kind of dumb and stupid. I didn't see him myself, but that's what they say.'

'Where did the wrecking car come from?'

'Holburn's garage, in town.'

Mark nodded, thanked the old man, and drove on into Merryfield. He passed Holburn's garage and recognized the name; but Tony was his first concern. He went directly to the police station and introduced himself to the officer on duty. 'I'm Mr. Worth,' he said. 'The Chief telephoned me at one o'clock this morning about my son's accident. Anthony Worth. I think you have him here.'

The officer said at once: 'Why, no, Mr. Worth, he's gone. The Chief called Mr. Carbrey, after you said the young fellow went to Hadley, and Mr. Carbrey said he'd be responsible, so we let him go.'

'Where did he go?'

'Back to Hanover, he said.'

Mark asked: 'Did Mr. Carbrey put up bail?'

'No, no need. Everybody knows him around here.'

'When will you want Tony in court?'

'Tuesday. Mr. Carbrey said he'd be here.' The officer added: 'We're charging him with driving to endanger, and driving under the influence.'

Mark asked quietly: 'Are you sure he was drunk?'

'Sure. He sobered off some before he left here, but he smelled like a barroom.'

'Did you call a doctor to examine him?'

'No. No need of that. You could tell to look at him.'

Mark smiled faintly. This was a typical police assumption. He said reasonably: 'I'm sure the boy was not drunk. There was a whiskey bottle, broken, in the car. It hadn't been opened; but when it broke, some of it must have spilled on my son's clothes. It may have been that that you smelled. I'm sorry you didn't call a doctor. If he was drunk, he ought to be punished, of course; but I don't believe he was.'

'Well, that's up to the court.'

'I don't want you to think I'm trying to cover up for my son. No doubt he was driving too fast; and that's a dangerous corner. But I don't believe he had been drinking.'

The officer nodded. 'We get a lot of kids driving down to see their girls in the college,' he agreed. 'Like I said, the Chief goes easy on them.

He might throw a scare into your boy; but I'm guessing if the lady he run into doesn't make trouble the case will be placed on file.'

II

(June 5, 1937)

Mark, thus reminded that there had been another car in the accident, returned to Holburn's garage. Two men were at work straightening the fender of a club coupe with a New York number plate, and Mark spoke to them.

'Is either of you Mr. Holburn?'

The older of the two answered. 'I am, yes.'

'My name's Worth.' Mark explained. 'My son was driving one of the cars in that accident north of town last night. I suppose this is the other car?'

Mr. Holburn nodded. He was a well-fed, amiable man, large and fat and bald, with a grease smear on his cheek. 'We've got it just about ready to navigate,' he said. 'Nothing but a crumpled fender and running board. These cars can stand a lot of grief. I went out and got it, last night.'

'Did you see my son, out there?'

'No, the police had fetched him away before I got there.' Holburn added with a chuckle: 'But I see him just before he started out of town. He stopped here to gas up, and him and another fellow finished a bottle of whiskey before they drove off.'

Mark's cheek reddened in angry disbelief. 'There was someone with him?' he asked.

'No, the other fellow was in his own car.' Holburn added: 'They drained the bottle bottoms up and heaved it away. It broke all over the place. We was sweeping up glass for an hour after.'

Mark did not press the point. Argument would only make Holburn more stubborn and sure. 'About this other car,' he suggested: 'What will the repair bill be?'

Mr. Holburn scratched his bald head. 'Say fourteen dollars and a quarter,' he suggested. 'I'd ought to charge fifteen, but I like the sound of the odd cents.'

'I'll pay that.' Mark did so. 'Where is the owner?'

'She put up at the Inn, but she aimed to get an early start this morning. Guess't you'll find she's eating her breakfast about now.'

'Can you tell me her name?'

'Mis' Kerr.'

Mark produced his card, scribbled on it his address. 'If by any chance I don't find her, will you give her this?' he asked, and he explained: 'I'll try to catch her at the Inn.'

He drove to the Inn; but when he came into the lobby, he remembered that he must telephone the Governor and withdraw his name as a candidate for that appointment to the Bench. It was still early, nevertheless he put through the call.

'Sorry to disturb you, Governor,' he said when the connection had been made. 'But I wanted to be sure to catch you at home.' He explained the circumstances. 'So you must not send in my name,' he said.

The other hesitated. 'It might be awkward,' he admitted. 'With your son's accident in the papers, and a charge of drunken driving against him, it would be embarrassing for both you and me.'

'I'm sure he wasn't drunk,' Mark declared. 'But there will be some publicity, of course.'

'Thank you for letting me know,' the Governor said. 'But I hope there may be another later vacancy, Mr. Worth. We need men like you on the Bench.'

Mark, when he left the phone, went to the desk and asked for Miss Kerr. As he did so, a woman stopped beside him, and the clerk said to her: 'This gentleman was just asking for you, Mrs. Kerr.'

Mark turned, and he was suddenly a little breathless, facing thus without warning the most beautiful woman he had ever seen. Even in that moment he felt a faint disappointment because the clerk had called her Mrs. Kerr.

12

(June 5, 1937)

Robin Kerr was one of those women who are sometimes to a casual glance dull and lustreless, but who at other times, by an accident of light, or by the faint flush on their cheeks, or by the clear radiance of their eyes after a restful night, become startlingly and completely beautiful. She was thus beautiful this morning. Mark's first impression was that she was as tall as he, but this was not in fact the case. She was of no more than normal stature; but there was in the way she stood, in the slenderness of her waist and the firmness of her shoulders and the way her head was set on them, a flawless purity of line. Her heavy hair was worn long, and it was the color of gold, a tawny gold; and her eyes were deep and dark, and Mark could not be sure whether they were blue or brown. Her features were strong, and yet so proportioned as to seem delicate and fine; and there was, thus early in the morning, a freshness about her like that of a flower still bedewed. He noticed the pale clear blue tint of the whites of her eyes. She might have been any age from eighteen to forty; but whatever her years, she was young.

For a moment when he faced her now by the desk in the Inn, Mark forgot to speak, and she asked in a friendly tone: 'Were you inquiring for me?'

'Mrs. Kerr? Yes. Was it your car which was damaged in an accident last night?'

'Yes.'

'It was my son who ran into you. I'm Mr. Worth.'

'Oh, is he all right?' she asked quickly, and Mark found himself liking her for that instant solicitude. 'Did he get home safe? Is your home here?'

'No. We live in Boston. They called me on the phone and I drove up.' He added: 'He's all right, yes. He's gone back to Hanover, had gone before I arrived. I came to make sure that you were not hurt.'

She smiled. 'I'm perfectly all right—as you see. Have you had breakfast? I'm just going in—if you'd like to join me?'

'I will,' Mark agreed. When they were seated and had ordered, he said: 'I wanted to explain to you . . . I stopped at the garage, paid the repair bill on your car, and I left my card with Mr. Holburn if you wish to make any further claim.'

'I'm not sure it was altogether your son's fault,' she confessed. 'I was tired. I'd driven straight through from Montreal, and perhaps my reactions were slow. I saw he was out of control, and tried to give him room; but he couldn't quite clear me. That's a bad corner.'

'Did you talk it over with him afterward?'

'No, I didn't see him.' She hesitated, explained apologetically, 'I should have, of course; but I was a little shaken. I ran to the house to telephone for help. Then I had a chill, nerves or something; so I stayed in the house, and Mr. Holburn sent a car to take me to town. I suppose your son came in the police car.' She added: 'The police seemed sure it was his fault, but I blame myself too.'

The sun touched her cheek, and Mark saw the faintly pulsing color under the skin. There was an almost invisible scar at the corner of her mouth, a delicate white line. It was an old scar, but Mark thought how flying glass might have cut and gashed that flawless countenance. 'I should never have allowed him to have a car,' he said. 'I'm really the one to blame.'

'How old is he?'

'Seventeen, last September.'

She smiled. 'He is rather young, isn't he? But it's hard to deny them anything.'

Mark assented, and he explained. 'You see, his mother died seven years ago, and since then I've sort of wrapped up my world and put it in his hands. He's an only child.' She nodded, as though she had guessed this, and he went on: 'When he came away to school, I gave him an allowance large enough to pay all his bills and have a margin for saving. He has always been a little crazy about automobiles. The first word he ever said was "beel." He used to stand by the window for hours, watching the traffic go by, squealing with delight, even when he was just a baby.' She smiled, and he said with an apologetic grin: 'I don't know what started me off like this!'

'Go on. I like it. You gave him a big allowance?'

'And he saved all he could. When he wanted me to give him our old car, instead of turning it in, I tried to refuse, and he offered to buy it from me—with money out of his savings. I hadn't the heart to say no.'

'He must be a fine boy.'

'I think he is.' He added honestly, 'The police say he was drunk last night.'

'Oh! Do you think he was?' Her eyes were gentle.

'No, I don't. Tony was free to drink at home if he wanted to, a glass of wine or even a cocktail; but he never did. I can't imagine him getting drunk, but Mr. Holburn says he saw him drinking, just before he drove out of town, a few minutes before the accident; and the farmer up there and the police both say he was drunk.'

'You haven't seen him yourself?'

'No, he was gone before I got here.'

'I'm sure you're right—no matter what they say. Is his car badly damaged?'

Mark smiled faintly. 'Ruined, I expect. But it wasn't worth much at best.'

'I really ought to pay for repairing it. I was as much to blame as he.'

'I'm as well pleased it's out of commission.' He added: 'Tony may feel differently, but I'm letting him decide that. The car's still in the field over there, but Tony can see about it when he comes to court Tuesday.'

'Oh, are they prosecuting him?'

'Yes—charging him with driving to endanger, and while drunk.'

She protested: 'If I don't blame him, they shouldn't.' And she added smiling: 'They can't do much to him without witnesses, can they? I shan't be here to testify.' She looked suddenly at her watch. 'That reminds me, I ought to be on the road right now.' She rose.

He rose with her, regretful that thus quickly his moment with her was over. He offered to drive her to Holburn's garage, but she explained that Mr. Holburn was sending her car to the Inn. At the desk the clerk said her car had come; and she told him to send a boy up in five minutes to bring down her bags, and turned to say good-bye to Mark.

'If anything else goes wrong with the car,' he suggested, 'please advise me. Your home is in New York?'

'Yes. I'll give you my address. You must let me know if the boy is all right.'

He asked, almost diffidently: 'Mr. Kerr wasn't with you?'

She hesitated, said then simply: 'No.' Something in her tone and in her eyes made him wish to put a further question, but he did not. She produced a card and scribbled on it and gave it to him, and he read in block letters: 'Robin Kerr.' Below she had written her address, a New York apartment. He wondered why she was not 'Mrs. So-and-So Kerr.' She said, smiling: 'Tell your son I don't blame him. Good-bye.'

Mark took her hand and she turned at once away. He hesitated, reluctant to let her go, wishing to ask her more about Mr. Kerr. But she crossed to the elevator and disappeared. He went out to his car, and he wondered how Mrs. Kerr had come to be so wise in the ways of boys. Probably she had sons of her own; but if she had, they must be young. She herself could hardly be more than thirty. In the car he sat a moment, thinking about her, remembering the way she stood, the firm grasp of her hand, the intonations of her voice. He thought it would be pleasant to know her—and of course Mr. Kerr.

VI

Finns Pay Their Debts

(June 1937–Autumn 1937)

I

(June 1937)

MARK'S instinct, after Mrs. Kerr was gone, was to drive up to Hanover and make sure that Tony was all right; but to do so would be to suggest doubts and distrusts which he did not feel, so he decided to return direct to Boston. But at Hadley he stopped to thank the Head for his intercession.

Mr. Carbrey said reassuringly: 'Why, I was glad to do it. I'm sorry Chief Evans called you. He didn't know, till you told him, that Tony was a Hadley boy, or he'd have called me in the beginning.'

'I thought of going up to Hanover for the week-end,' Mark confessed, 'but I've decided to let Tony work this out. If he needs my help he'll ask for it.'

Mr. Carbrey nodded approvingly. 'Chief Evans is reasonable,' he said, 'and I know Judge Prior of the Merryfield court. He's a good man. You can go back to Boston with an easy mind, Mr. Worth, I'm sure.'

Driving slowly homeward, Mark found himself thinking more of Robin Kerr than of Tony. He remembered her hair, and the way her head was set upon her shoulders; and he remembered that tiny scar at the corner of her mouth, and he tried to remember whether her eyes were blue or brown. He drew out and examined again the card she had given him, with her name, simply: 'Robin Kerr.' Sometimes professional women or artists or the like, even though married, kept their maiden names; but the clerk had spoken of her as Mrs. Kerr. Yet Mark was sure she wore no wedding ring. He wondered if it were possible that Mr. Kerr was dead.

It was mid-afternoon when he came home. There was a telegram from Tony, a night letter filed at Merryfield at 3.05 A.M. The boy had wired:

I had a slight automobile accident but no one was hurt. Don't worry. Just starting for Hanover. Will write at once. Love.

Tony.

Mark asked Elin when the wire arrived.

'They telephoned, early,' she said. 'I didn't know where you were, so I told them to deliver it here.' The anxiety she had felt was plain in her eyes. 'I didn't know where you were,' she repeated. 'Is Tony all right?' Mark told her strongly: 'Yes, he's all right. He's fine.'

Tony's letter arrived that evening by special delivery. The boy had written in haste, and in straightforward contrition. He had driven down to see Barbie Parks—Mark as he read, felt an unreasonable resentment at the girl because she had been the innocent cause of what might have been a serious accident—and he and Barbie had a happy hour together. He described how the bottle of whiskey came to be in his car, and how, driving up the valley in haste, he forgot the S-curve at the barn till too late to negotiate it safely. He wrote:

I didn't really know much that was going on till they had me in the police station at Merryfield. They asked me if I wanted to telephone anybody, but I didn't want to wake you up in the middle of the night, so they said they'd have to lock me up.

He wrote of his subsequent release and explained:

I ran into a Dartmouth man just starting for Hanover [this was Chad Frame, somewhat sobered now, but Tony did not say so], and I came along up here with him, and now I'm writing this. There's not much I can say, except that I'm sorry; and I feel pretty rotten, because I know how you'll feel, but I don't want you to worry, and I don't want you to get me out of this mess. It's my job to straighten it out, or to do whatever I have to do. The thing that's hardest for me to take is knowing the way you'll feel. I never mean to make trouble for you or to make you unhappy; but I guess I've done it now, all right.

Your loving son,

Tony.

There was a postscript which Mark read thankfully. Tony wrote:

P.S. I have to go to court down there Tuesday, but I can handle that all right. I've decided to sell the car for junk. It will be time enough for me to have a car when I can keep out of trouble.

I have my last exam Monday. I'll express my trunk from here before I go down there, and come straight home from there.

So Mark was reassured, and glad that Tony would so soon come home. Tuesday morning Tony telephoned to say that his case had been placed on file; and Mark said: 'Fine. I know you weren't seriously to blame.'

'They tell me the Chief telephoned you and you came up here that morning.'

'Yes, but I decided you could handle the situation.'

Tony hesitated, and then he said quietly: 'You're pretty swell, Dad. I'll be home for dinner.'

'Right,' Mark agreed, and his throat astonishingly filled. 'See you tonight,' he said hurriedly. 'Good-bye.'

Tony was at the house when Mark arrived, and they dined together companionably, talking at first of the accident, and then of casual things; till at last Tony said:

'Dad, you wrote me a letter Friday evening. I didn't get it till after I wrote you. You said the Governor was going to appoint you a judge.'

'Yes,' Mark admitted. 'He sent for me that afternoon, as I wrote you.'

Tony asked soberly: 'Why didn't he do it?'

'I withdrew my name.'

'On account of me?'

Mark told him honestly: 'Well, yes, son. The news of your arrest was sure to be in the papers. If the Governor sent my name in for the Superior Bench, his political enemies would make capital of it. I wasn't of his party, anyway, so his political machine would have resented the appointment in any case; and there's a good deal of public sentiment, of course, against drunken driving.' He added, to take the sting out of his words. 'Even though I knew you weren't drunk.'

'I wasn't,' Tony assented. 'But—why didn't the Governor go through with it anyway? Didn't he have enough backbone to face criticism, if he knew you were the man for the job?'

Mark smiled. 'A man in politics has to be practical about such things. I realized his position. I wouldn't have allowed him to put in my name, even if he had wanted to.'

'You wanted that nomination.'

'Yes, of course.'

Tony for a moment did not speak. Then he said quietly: 'OK, Dad. I just wanted to get it straight. I know how many things you've done for me before, and how much more you've always been willing to do. I did you a pretty dirty trick, cheating you out of this.'

'It was an accident.'

'Sure,' Tony agreed. 'But you wanted the appointment, and I lost it for you. That's one I owe you. I'll make it up to you some day.' He asked: 'Did you see the woman in the other car, make sure she wasn't hurt?'

'Yes, she was all right, Tony.' Mark added: 'She said she was as much to blame as you.'

'What was her name?'

'Mrs. Kerr. I paid for the repairs to her car. She promised to write me if any further trouble developed, but I haven't heard from her.'

'I'll pay you back,' Tony promised. 'Have you her address?'

'Yes.'

'I want to write to her.'

Mark nodded. 'I'm sure she would appreciate that.' He was amused at himself because he wished that there were some good reason why he, too, should write to Robin Kerr.

2

(Summer 1937)

Late in June Tony and Mark went to fish for salmon on Anticosti Island, and they returned by way of the Gaspé, stopping to try for trout in likely waters, carrying camping gear and sleeping where they chose. They were almost a month away from Boston; and by the time they returned, the President's court-packing bill had been defeated, and Japan had begun an undeclared war on China. The newspapers all that summer would be filled with reports of the slaughter of helpless civilians by indiscriminate air bombardment of crowded cities, and readers, already sickened by the tales of death in Spain, turned the pages hurriedly, their refusal to read these horrors their only defense against the unendurable.

Most of Mark's friends were away for the summer. Nell Ritchie and the children were at Boothbay, where Bob joined them for week-ends. Ed and Mary Halstead had taken a beach cottage at Humarock, and twice, when Tony was away over Sunday, as he was apt to be, Mark drove down to spend the day with them.

He came that summer to know their children as individuals, with personalities of their own. Edwin, the oldest, was a quiet youngster of sixteen with an almost feminine sweetness in him, and a shy devotion to his father which shone in his eyes when they were together. Mark spoke of this once and Ed said, laughingly proud and pleased:

'You're right. It's a heck of a responsibility for me, too. He thinks everything I do is just about perfect, tries to imitate me if he can; so I have to be damned careful!'

Ann was twelve, a stringy, long-legged child with a mop of curly black hair and dark eyes that promised startling loveliness in a few years more. She showed musical talent, and her voice was promising. Mary herself sang well.

'I'm giving Ann lessons,' she explained. 'The piano's never in tune down here, but we work hard, just the same.'

Burt and Dan, the two little boys, were a riotous pair. On Sundays when Mark went down they all spent most of the day on the beach, the golden-brown bodies of the children gleaming and beautiful in the sun, while Mark and Ed and Mary, sprawling on the sand, watched and talked slow talk together.

Emma and Tom were in town this summer, but Mark seldom saw her. Once or twice he lunched with Tom, who said Emma was often away. She had spent a week with Nell Ritchie, another with Dave and Marcia Rollins on the Cape; and Tom told Mark that Dave had had another of his periodical aberrations just before Emma's visit, was sober but still weak and shaken while she was there.

'He's a fine fellow when he's normal,' Mark commented. 'This other —it's really a disease, Tom.'

'I know,' Tom hesitated. 'I've known other people like that. They can't help it, once they start.' Mark wondered whether he were thinking of Emma, whose steady drinking began to be remarked, justifying her in his thoughts.

'How's Ruth?' he asked.

'Emma said she seemed sort of sad,' Tom reported. 'I guess it's tough on her when Dave has one of his times.' And he said: 'I always liked Ruth.'

'I like her too,' Mark agreed. 'She's a grand girl.' He thought he might invite himself down for a week-end with them, found himself looking forward to seeing Ruth again.

3

(August 1937)

One day in late July, Mark was surprised—and deeply pleased—to receive a letter from Robin Kerr. She wrote:

Dear Mr. Worth—

I've had such a charming letter from your son. I hope to meet him some day under less abrupt circumstances. He wrote to thank me for not pressing the charges against him. I'm glad the police weren't too hard on him. Any boy may drive a little too fast on a warm June night. I've done it myself.

He was concerned as to any possible hurt I had suffered. I've written assuring him that I'm in my usual splendid health. Please don't either of you give the incident another thought.

Sincerely,

Robin Kerr.

Mark had known that Tony meant to write her, but since Tony had not mentioned doing so, he did not tell his son about this letter. There was no reason why he should have kept it, but he did, carrying it in his pocket for a week or two till he perceived the absurdity of this and gave it to his secretary to file.

He decided it required no answer, but when a week later business took him to New York, he told himself that he should show Mrs. Kerr some small courtesy, so he telephoned her apartment.

'I've been grateful for your attitude last summer,' he explained. 'I thought you and Mr. Kerr might dine with me this evening.'

She hesitated for what seemed to him a long time before she replied, but then she said: 'There is no Mr. Kerr, Mr. Worth. He died some years ago.'

Mark felt his heart pound with a sort of exultation. He had been sure that this was somehow true; but here was certainty. 'Oh, I'm sorry. Perhaps you and I, then?' he suggested.

'Yes, I think I'd like to,' she agreed.

They dined at the Starwick, a quiet apartment hotel where Mark always stayed when he was in New York, returning to it as to a refuge after each venture abroad. He had no liking for the great city, was fiercely—and perhaps defensively—scornful of the men and women, the men a little too sleekly dressed, the women with elaborately curled hair and fingernails like talons and pale faces with a slash of color where the mouth should have been, who seemed to be idle everywhere, drinking cocktails, their cheeks a little flushed, their voices shrill with empty laughter, their eyes weary and unsmiling. Sometimes he had walked for hours on end through the crowded streets, his ears alert for every passing word, trying to guess at the inner lives of those about him. Rich men, poor men, beggar men, and thieves seemed to him alike in one respect: their lives were cramped and compressed; but they thought their lives rich and expansive. They slept in caves, emerging belatedly into the daylight, toiling for a few hours, then diving into other caves full of lights and voices and music provided by famous orchestras or by nickel-in-the-slot machines, where they laboriously pleasured themselves till time to dive into their own small secret caves again.

He and Robin spoke of this feeling on his part when they were together. She had never been in the Starwick, and he explained that it was the nearest thing to home which he had been able to discover in New York.

'I know where things are, here,' he explained. 'I know the names of the men at the desk and of the waiters and even of the maid who takes care of my room; and they know my name.' He smiled. 'This has been a typical New York day for me. I had two appointments; one for lunch and the other at three o'clock. Except to keep these appointments I've stayed in my room.'

'Working?' she asked. 'Going over papers?'

'No, just reading, just killing time.'

She made an amused gesture. 'You don't like New York?'

'No, I don't,' he agreed. He chuckled. 'I discovered, one morning two or three years ago, the typical New Yorker. It was early, and I walked up through Central Park. There's a pond there, you know; muddy water in which float bits of old newspapers, and banana peels, and orange rinds, and cigar butts and cigarette stubs disintegrating, and crusts of bread. There were a few ducks in the pond that day, black ducks, the sort I've shot in Maine. I've seen them flying tirelessly, arrows darting across the deep blue of the sky, high in the sun, sweeping in great circles for the sheer joy of flying, able to choose their alighting place, master of say forty thousand square miles of wilderness and beauty at the cost of an hour's flight. Yet there they were, in that garbage pit—that pond up in Central Park. Those ducks are the typical New Yorker.'

She looked faintly puzzled. 'I don't see . . .'

'Paddling in dishwater,' he explained, 'and eating garbage, and gabbling happily—when between dawn and dark they could reach any spot within a thousand miles. They were free to go—but they preferred to stay. So does your typical New Yorker.'

She laughed delightedly. 'You do feel strongly, don't you.' Her eyes narrowed. 'I don't believe you have any friends in New York.'

'Oh, yes. Some good fellows too—and attractive wives. But I've found by experience that if I get in touch with them, hoping for an evening at their homes, they insist on my dining with them, and then going to a show, and perhaps a night club afterward. So I don't get in touch with them.'

'I promise you, New York is full of people who don't go to a theater —or a night club—once a year.'

'What do they do?'

'Read, think, talk; just what intelligent people do everywhere else.' She looked around. 'This is my first time of dining in public in a month—almost two months.'

'As often as not, I have my meals served in my rooms,' he confessed.

'We might have done that tonight.'

It had not occurred to him that he might suggest this, and for a moment he did not speak, thinking how pleasant that would have been. She asked how Tony was, and he told her of their fishing, and of their flying, and she wished to hear more, prompting him with questions, liking the way he spoke of his son, quick to understand the strong bond between these two; till he said at last, in smiling apology:

'I've talked long enough about myself and Tony.'

'Not much about yourself,' she suggested. 'I don't even know what your business is.'

'Oh, I'm a lawyer.'

She looked at him appraisingly. 'Really. Then I'm sure you don't do much trial work.'

'Why not?'

'You're not—aggressive. At least you don't seem to me to be. I think you probably tell business men what the law is, and draw contracts and things like that.' She smiled suddenly. 'I think you'd make a wonderful judge.'

He leaned back, laughing in an ironic amusement. 'My professors at Law School said the same thing,' he admitted. 'You must be a psychoanalyst, something like that.' And on impulse he told her about that appointment to the Bench which had been so nearly his, and how it had been lost.

'You called up the Governor and told him about Tony?' she asked, echoing his word.

'Yes.' He added, remembering: 'That was just before we had breakfast together in Merryfield.'

'Did Tony know about the appointment?'

'Yes. I'd written him the night before, after the Governor told me what he meant to do.'

She said thoughtfully: 'Tony would blame himself for your disappointment. That must have brought you two closer together than ever.' And she said: 'I want to know him some day. Does he ever come to New York?'

'He might be coming down to a football game. If there's a chance, I'll arrange for the three of us to get together.' He said: 'But see here; it's time to talk about you for a while.'

She hesitated for a moment. Mark had ordered dinner without waiting to consult her; a clear soup, a steak, a salad, and an ice. The salad was being served, and she did not speak till they were again alone. Then she said simply:

'Why—I'm a sort of artist, mostly watercolors, a few pastels, sometimes an oil.'

'Portraits?'

'Of children, mostly. I like them, and I do them better than I do grownups. Usually in watercolor.'

'Are you good?' he asked directly; and she answered as frankly as he had asked:

'Yes, fairly good. People like my work. I'm busier all the time.'

'Mrs. Worth used to do such things, a little,' he told her. 'She was clever with a pencil, but of course she was an amateur.'

'Davy was very good,' she said. 'I think he might have become great.' He understood that she was speaking of her husband. 'We met in Paris,' she explained. 'We were both studying there. Then when we were married we went travelling around the world, but he—died.' Her eyes met his. 'Our baby was born afterward,' she told him. 'He lived to be almost a year old.' He said nothing. There was nothing to be said, and she smiled at him, grateful for his silence. 'So I know how you feel about Tony,' she explained.

'Does your family live here?'

'No, my home was in Montreal. But Davy and I planned to live here, so I do.'

'I suppose you have a lot of friends.'

She said slowly: 'Yes, in a way. But I'm not—not much inclined to easy friendship. I've two or three good friends, of course; but this is the first time . . .' She smiled. 'The very first time I've dined with a man since—well, for four years.' And she added, as though by way of explanation: 'Davy was pretty grand.'

He said in a low tone: 'It's a lonely business, isn't it. My wife died seven years ago.'

'But you have Tony,' she reminded him. 'And of course I have my work.'

'Tell me,' he asked curiously. 'If you haven't done it before—why did you dine with me?'

'I wanted to,' she said honestly. 'I wanted to see you again.'

His eyes rested in hers a moment. When she smiled, the tiny scar at the corner of her mouth seemed to give her lips a faint wistfulness that made her appear helpless and appealing as a child. He said as honestly as she: 'I wanted to see you, too, although I knew you only as Mrs. Kerr.' A shadow touched her eyes, and he asked: 'Were you long in Paris?'

'Two years before I met Davy, and a few weeks afterward, and I've gone back every year since.'

'You like the French?'

'Yes. Yes, very much.'

Events this summer had revived in him a deep and anxious preoccupation with world affairs. Japan, following the conscienceless pattern set by Italy in Ethiopia, had undertaken the conquest of China; and in Spain that rehearsal for war of which Frank Parks had spoken still went on, Mussolini and Hitler using the conflict there to test the impact of planes and guns, of bombs and shells on human flesh. Hitler had requisitioned the entire German crop of wheat and rye 'To safeguard the nation's bread supply.' Mark saw that action as preparation to withstand a blockade, a hint that Germany expected war. He asked gravely: 'Why have the French let Hitler tear up the Versailles Treaty, reoccupy the Rhineland, rearm, without interfering?'

'Partly because England wouldn't cooperate,' she said, 'but also, because the French want peace, and to interfere would mean war.'

'It seems to me war is coming,' he suggested, 'whether France wants it or not.' And he explained apologetically: 'Perhaps I'm overly concerned, but—I fought in the last war, as well as I could, because I thought if we won, we would end war forever.'

'France won't fight again,' she said. 'Oh, the Government may lead the country into war, but Frenchmen won't fight.' And she explained: 'You see, the French, particularly the French peasant, the ordinary man, is the most logical, the least emotional person in the world. He remembers that although France won that war, won it completely, he was worse off afterward than he was before. He suffered terribly for four years—and more—and got nothing out of it.'

'No one wins any war,' Mark agreed. 'Everyone loses—and the loser often loses less than the winner.'

'The French—the ordinary Frenchman—knows that,' she assured him.

'I thought in 1919 that Germany won the last war,' Mark said thoughtfully. 'She lost nothing but men and money—and a little territory, some of which she has already regained. But France lost factories and fields and villages and cities—and men and money. After Versailles, Germans had nothing to lose except their lives; but France had everything to lose—and no strength left with which to defend it.' And he said: 'I've talked with men who travel much abroad. They say the Germans are astonished and delighted at the blind folly of the Allies. Versailles said Germany must not rearm—so for fifteen years she was free from the terrific cost of armaments, while the rest of the world poured out money for war materials and to maintain their armies. So Germany grew strong financially while France and England spent themselves to the verge of bankruptcy—bankruptcy for themselves and for the world. They drove themselves off gold, repudiated their debts, went morally bankrupt in the effort to maintain vast armaments which —if the war did end wars as they promised it would—will never be needed.'

She nodded. 'The French peasant knows that,' she assured him. 'He never pays a cent of taxes without grudging it and grumbling. And that mass feeling among farmers and workers has grown stronger all the time. They want to be let alone to prosecute their own affairs. They don't want another war.'

'Perhaps not,' he agreed. 'But when war comes, they'll fight as well as ever.' He looked at her with a grim face. 'Once war is begun, it is too late to think,' he said. 'I remember, as a boy, the Spanish-American War; and I was in England for a while a few years after the Boer War. Many people opposed those wars before they began; but once they were begun, everyone shouted "Remember the Maine" and cheered Dewey and Teddy and the rest; and our soldiers died from eating rotten beef, and from yellow fever, and dysentery, and the British soldiers died from other plagues, and in the World War there was the influenza. But everyone shouted: "Hurrah for the war!" Anyone who said the war was a bad one and that we should have kept out of it, and that we ought to make peace, was a traitor, and he might be mobbed—or sent to jail.'

'I know,' she agreed.

'Who was it said: "In time of peace, prepare for war"?' She did not know, and he smilingly confessed: 'Neither do I. A friend of mine quoted the phrase to me one day, and I tried to find it in Bartlett. Shakespeare spoke of "this weak piping time of peace," and Burton said a happy city "in time of peace thinks of war." Burke quoted Machiavelli as saying that the wise prince saw peace only as a breathing time, and Horace said much the same thing. Washington said to be prepared for war was a good way to preserve peace; and Publius Syrius agreed with Horace. I had the impression that someone said in so many words: "In time of peace, prepare for war," but I can't find the quotation.'

She said thoughtfully: 'Isn't it even more important to do just the opposite? I mean, in time of war prepare for peace? But no one ever does that. They go on fighting till suddenly the other fellow surrenders and they say: "Hello, we've won. Well, what will we do now?"'

Mark nodded. 'But maybe the best rule of all is, "In time of peace, prepare for peace." Why shouldn't the world go to work, now, planning for world peace, instead of stupidly accepting the inevitability of another war? After all, we've got to live in the same world with Germany. It doesn't help to start calling her names.'

They had forgotten their surroundings; but Robin said, in sudden realization: 'Mercy, we're keeping the waiters up, Mr. Worth. I think you'd better take me home.' She smiled, and he noticed the small scar on her lip, and she saw the direction of his eyes. 'That's from skiing,' she explained. 'I was lucky not to lose some teeth.'

'It's becoming to you.'

She laughed. 'Like the little black patches ladies used to wear to accentuate their fashionable pallor? But pallor's out of fashion now.'

When they parted—she did not invite him to come up to her studio —he said: 'I haven't had so pleasant an evening in a long time.'

'I've enjoyed it, too. Really.'

'I hope you'll let me see you again?'

'Do!' Their eyes held, and after a moment she said quietly: 'I think we may come to be pretty good friends, you and I.'

4

(September 1937)

Tony would be eighteen on the ninth of September, and a week beforehand Nell Ritchie told Mark that she was planning a surprise party to celebrate the occasion, and she enlisted his cooperation.

'It was Jan's idea,' she explained, and laughed and said: 'You know

Jan always did think that after Tony was made, the mold was broken.'

'She's a sweet kid,' Mark declared. Jan was sixteen, on the verge of that change which may come overnight, when a girl who was a child is suddenly a child no longer. She had been till this summer still a little awkward, but now, just as a machine with use acquires smoothness it did not at first possess, so all the parts of her seemed to be falling into place to make a harmonious and delightful whole. Mark thought her much more attractive than Betty, though it was Betty who had the beaux, who went to Yale and Princeton and Dartmouth for football games and carnivals and house parties. 'I hope Tony will wake up, some day,' Mark added. 'They don't come any nicer than Jan.'

'She's working out all the details,' Nell explained. 'I'm so busy I've no time.' Her energy seemed to have no limit—but relatively little of it went into the routine direction and management of her home.

So it was Jan, more than her mother, who planned this party for Tony. Jan and Elin arranged the details, and Mark's only duty was to see to it that on the appointed day Tony did not come home too soon.

That was easily arranged. Tony picked Mark up at his office at four —the day was fine—and they drove out to Norwood and flew for an hour apiece, so it was almost seven when they left the airport. Tony, as always after an hour in the air, was tremendously stimulated; but Mark already foresaw the probability that he himself would do less and less flying as time went on. He had long since ceased to have any qualms about the danger of an accident; and he was quietly sure that as long as the plane held together and did not catch fire he could land it somewhere and—as Mr. Hadden said—walk away. But he saw no likelihood that he would ever buy a plane, and he had gone as far as for simple pleasure flying he cared to go.

But Tony, of course, would continue to fly. Mark had long since accepted this in his own mind; and he accepted the hazard involved. In the back of his thought there was always the certainty that if war came, Tony would choose the air service. There was nothing Mark could do to avert that war, if it were coming; and if Tony must fight in a war, better the air service than any other. He would at least escape the slimy horror of the trenches, where half-rotted dead men and the gorged rats that fed on them were your companions, and your thought at each new dawning was: 'Perhaps tonight I too will lie there. Perhaps tonight the rats will be devouring me.'

And if Tony was to be a fighting pilot, his every hour of training now would be useful then. He did some flying at White River during his months in Hanover, and Mark made no objection. 'But I want you to attend to your college work too,' he said on the way home today. 'College is like a club, and you pay your dues by keeping up in your studies. I hope you'll always work hard enough so you'll never have to work too hard.'

When they turned into the garage, no cars were parked in sight of the house. Jan must have seen to that, making sure the surprise she planned should be a surprise in fact. Mark and Tony went in through the French doors to an empty living room, but Mark detected signs of preparation in the dining room; a stack of plates, silver laid ready, glasses and bottled beer on the sideboard. He hoped Tony would not notice them. They stepped into the hall to put away their hats; and then suddenly there was a stamp of many feet above their heads, and the crowd hidden upstairs began to sing the 'Happy Birthday' song and everyone came marching down.

Mary Halstead's children led the way, and the others followed, graded according to height from the smallest to the tallest. Danny Halstead was only four years old, but he led the procession, and Tommy Sheffield, well over six feet, came last of all; and everyone was singing except Betty Ritchie, to whom all this seemed faintly childish. They crowded around Tony in the hall, and everyone had a present for him, till his arms were heaped with bundles. While he was thus burdened —Mark saw Jan's management in this—Barbie Parks appeared alone, and paused on the stair till Tony looked up and saw her and grinned and dropped everything and sprang to meet her, crying:

'Gosh, Barb, this is swell!'

Mark saw Jan smiling happily, no shadow in her eyes; and he felt a warm affection for the girl.

After that first moment there was persisting confusion; cocktails for the grownups and tomato juice for the young, then spaghetti with meat cooked in it in a way Elin knew, salad, hot rolls and honey, milk, beer, and a huge cake with the proper number of candles to go with the ice cream. Everyone, large and small, was called on to make a speech. Jan had written for the smaller children little poems which they read, but the grownups were allowed to say what they chose.

Afterward they played what was mysteriously called John's game, which gave a person's name to every chair, and each player had to assume the name of that person so long as he or she sat in that chair, and to be ready when that name was called to answer with another name before the count of ten. If you failed, you went to the last chair, like the loser in a spelling match, and everyone else moved up. Ed Halstead worked his way to the head chair and held it, dodging every trap, and Mark saw the pride in Edwin's eyes at his father's victory. Then someone started the phonograph and the children rolled back the rugs in the hall and everyone danced till Ed Halstead was red as roast beef and dripping profusely, and Mark's breath came short. He had noticed several times lately a certain thumping in the region of his heart, and even thought of giving up cigarettes—he smoked seldom less than two packs a day—to see if the thumping would disappear. He felt it tonight and felt too a vague tingling in his left arm, as though it were about to go to sleep; so he stopped dancing and sat with Emma Sheffield, watching the others.

Emma said at once: 'Well, I see you still have that pretty Swedish girl living with you.'

Mark ignored the innuendo. 'I hope she'll stay on forever,' he assented cheerfully. 'But probably that's too much to expect.'

'I suppose she's so devoted to you she hasn't time for young men.'

'As a matter of fact,' Mark assured her, 'she's very much in love with a young Finnish boy. He's ambitious, trying to set himself up in the garage business; but he isn't doing so well. Otherwise I suppose they'd be married by now.'

'I doubt it,' Emma maliciously insisted. 'I don't think she'll ever leave you. I've been watching her tonight. If she isn't in love with you, she ought to wear dark glasses so people wouldn't see the look in her eyes.'

'You know,' Mark told her in a quiet resentment, 'sometimes I've been tempted to try to persuade her to marry me—just to give you something to talk about.'

Emma laughed. 'Marrying her's hardly necessary, is it?'

Mark was red with anger. 'Some day,' he said, 'you'll find yourself sued for slander.'

'Some day,' she countered, 'you'll find yourself sued for breach of promise!'

He rose, afraid of his own tongue. 'Have a highball?' he asked stiffly.

Emma nodded. 'I'm dry as dust!' She laughed teasingly. 'And don't be mad at me, Mark. Lord knows I don't blame you. No man can be expected to live quite alone. That's why I send the maids away when I leave Tom for a week-end, so they won't be alone in the apartment with him.'

Mark found a drink for her and saw her take half of it at a gulp as he turned away. Ed and Bob and Tom had escaped to the terrace, and he joined them there. Bob was arguing that what was happening in China and in Chinese waters—American merchant ships had been warned by the Government to keep away from Shanghai, where fighting centered —was not our business.

'We're too fond of meddling,' he declared. 'What happens in China doesn't hit us!'

'It might,' Ed pointed out. 'With things the way they are, a war could explode in our faces overnight.'

Mark said thoughtfully: 'Italy and Japan are cut off the same piece of goods. Japan started this new fashion of intentional brigandage in Manchuria. Italy copied it in Ethiopia, and now it's Japan's turn again.'

Ed nodded. 'Yes, and Germany will try her hand at it next,' he said. 'And nobody does anything but talk. I'd like to see England send her fleet over and blow Italy out of water. That would stop a lot of this nonsense.' He had kept up his work in the Naval Reserve.

'I'm not sure she could,' Mark confessed. 'Italy's planes and submarines could do a lot of damage. I don't believe England could transport troops through the Mediterranean if Italy wanted to stop her.'

'England can handle Italy any time,' Ed retorted. 'If she didn't go to war over Ethiopia, it was because it wasn't worth her while. That's all.' Edwin had joined them, and Mark saw the boy intent on his father's words.

They turned indoors presently, and the Halsteads were the first to leave, and a general exodus began. Barb was visiting Jan and Betty, but she did not depart with them, and she and Tony settled themselves before the fire on the hearth with such an obvious intention to stay awhile that Mark said good night and went upstairs. He heard their voices long after he was abed, and he remembered with a faint doubt Tony's quick delight when he saw Barbie on the stairs, and his long affection for the girl. Mark liked her well enough, but although there was a scant two years between them she seemed so much older than Tony. Tony's complete happiness with her was manifest, and she clearly liked him; but Mark thought it was on her part no more than this, no more than an elder-sisterly affection. One of these days she would meet an older man, and love him, and marry him. Mark hoped Tony would not be too grievously hurt when that happened. He was still awake when they went out, Tony taking Barbie across the street; but Tony did not at once return. Probably they had stayed talking in the shadows somewhere.

Mark, aside from Emma Sheffield's sharp tongue, had enjoyed the evening. Their best friends—except Dave and Marcia and Ruth, who were still at the Cape—had all been here. But while he lay awake listening for Tony to come home he thought how pleasant it would have been if Robin too could have been among the company.

5

(Autumn 1937)

Tony presently departed for Hanover, and that evening after Mark's solitary dinner, Elin came into the living room to speak to him. She said, a little breathlessly: 'Einar's here to see you, sir, for just a minute.'

'Of course,' he agreed. 'Bring him in.'

So she disappeared, and she returned a moment later with Einar, stiff in high collar and best suit. They stood side by side to face him and Mark said: 'Good evening, Einar,' and Einar said hurriedly:

'Yes sir.' His right hand was in his pocket. He drew it out, extended it to Mark. 'Here,' he said. 'Count it, please.'

Mark saw a tight fold of bills, fresh from the bank. He took it and counted the bills obediently, wondering what to do. It was all here, the money he had loaned Einar three years ago. He wanted to say: 'Take it, keep it. It's yours.' But that would not be fair to these two young people standing here before him, proud of having met their obligations. Finns paid their debts. Finland had never faltered in her payments to the United States, nor had Einar failed now. To give them the money would be to refuse them the high satisfaction they had earned.

He said: 'Why, that's fine. Sure you don't need it any longer? You're welcome, you know. There's no hurry.'

Einar said in his careful English. 'Thank you very much, no, I want to pay you back now.'

'Well, I'm glad you're making a go of the garage,' Mark said, and he saw Elin's quick glance flash to Einar, saw the young man redden; and Einar said with a wry grin:

'It is not what you call making a go. It is gone. I have to sell it. But I have saved this to pay you first, and the garage will bring enough when I sell it to pay the rest that I owe.'

Mark nodded. 'I see.' Probably it was just as well for Einar to be rid of the garage. He was not equipped for success as a man of business. 'I'm sorry. What will you do?'

'When I have sold the garage, I will be a chauffeur again.' Einar smiled, a quick, flashing smile; and he said: 'This time I spent the money to buy the garage first before I had it, and then I had to save up to pay for what I already had. Next time I know better. I will save first and spend afterward. I do not like it to be owing money.'

Mark gripped the other's hand, a quick emotion moving him. He had never seen Einar smile before, and there was something valiant and gay in that brief smile. 'You're all right,' he said. 'You'll get along fine. And—I'm always glad to help you in any way I can.'

When they turned away, Elin's hand rested on Einar's arm, her eyes turned up to him in a high pride. Mark thought the world would be better off if there were more such people in it.

He heard their voices for a while in the kitchen, heard Einar presently depart; and Elin went upstairs and he called a good night to her, but for a long time he sat with his neglected book on his lap, thinking about these two. Einar the Finn and Finland the nation had worked and sacrificed to keep alive in the world virtues that needed to be preserved; thrift, and honesty, and pride in their given word. He thought of Elin and Einar often during the days that followed, while British and French warships hunted 'pirate submarines' in the Mediterranean, and Japanese planes slaughtered the civilians packed in Chinese cities and Mussolini paid a state visit to Hitler and the two dictators vowed that they wanted only peace, and the League of Nations said Japan was wrong to bomb the Chinese cities. From thinking of these things, to turn to thinking of Elin and Einar was like stepping from a crowded, noisome, smoke-filled room into the clean winter air; and one day Mark asked Elin while she served his dinner:

'What's that young man of yours doing tonight?'

'He'll be coming to see me, as soon as he's off,' she said.

Mark hesitated, uncertain whether to tell Elin what was in his mind or to wait till she and Einar were here together. It was better perhaps to discuss it first with Elin. 'I want to talk to the two of you,' he said. 'But first to you. Elin, I think you and Einar should get married.'

Her eyes, to his astonishment, filled. 'Oh, so do I, Mr. Worth,' she agreed in quick, eager tones. 'But Einar sold the garage and it brought not so much as he hoped, so he still owes money he paid for tools and machines, and first we must get out of debt.'

'Where is he living now?'

'He's driving a car for Mr. Marshman, and he has a room over Freeman's grocery store.'

Mark nodded. 'Well, here's what I was thinking,' he explained. 'Tony's away all winter, except at Christmas and Easter. I never have guests, but if I did, they could sleep in his room. The guest room hasn't been used more than half a dozen times since Mrs. Worth died. Why don't you and Einar get married, and live here? You could have the guest room for a sitting room. We could move the bed to the attic, and if Tony ever brings home overflow guests, they could sleep up there. Your room and the guest room would make you a pleasant little apartment.' She started to speak, her eyes shining, smiling through tears; but he added quickly: 'It would save me money, because Einar could shovel snow and tend the furnace and I could let Mat go.' Mat Riley had attended to these household chores for years.

Elin was almost breathless with delight at this proposal. 'But Einar would not want to put Mat out of the job,' she confessed. 'Mat needs the work too.'

'Well, we'll keep Mat on, then,' Mark agreed. 'Einar has his own work to do, anyway. I really want this, Elin.' He smiled. 'I wish you'd do it to please me, to let me have the satisfaction of making you both happy.'

She looked at him for a long moment, thoughtfully. 'I think that is true,' she said then. 'It would really please you. I will talk about it to Einar tonight.' She added: 'I have to let him decide.'

'Of course,' Mark assented. 'But if he doesn't agree, let him come speak to me.'

She promised to do so, and an hour later she and Einar came smilingly into the living room. Einar was as grateful as Elin, and he and Mark talked together, Elin listening silently, her eyes on Einar all the while.

'We will find how to make it up to you,' he said gratefully.

'Good! Then it's settled!' Mark was more and more pleased with his plan; and he said: 'Now see here, Elin, I want you to let me give you your wedding. I want you to be married here. We'll ask your friends and Einar's, and my friends who know you. And—let's make it soon.'

He led them to agree; and on the day set—in mid-October—a score or so of scrubbed, stiffly dressed, shyly grinning friends of the two young people crowded into the house; and Dave and Marcia Rollins, and Ruth, and the Ritchies and the Halsteads and the Sheffields came; and Tony and Will Ritchie drove down from Hanover.

Mark had not seen Ruth for more than a year, and when she and her father and mother arrived she came to kiss him with a frank affection, and he saw that she was well, strong, and serenely happy. 'My, but you're a beauty,' he told her laughingly, and she kissed him again and said: 'I just love you, Uncle Mark.'

'College agrees with you.'

She nodded. 'Um-hmm! And I agree with college.' She said in shy pride: 'Everyone likes me, Uncle Mark. I like to be liked.'

'That's all right for you,' he told her smilingly, 'but it makes the competition awfully tough for me.'

'Nobody can ever compete with you.' She squeezed his arm. 'I've been in love with you since I was thirteen, you know.'

They laughed together and he looked at her with wise eyes, smiling a little. Her tone, frank and easy, was eloquent. She was no longer a child, but a woman—she must be twenty now, he reflected—and she was old enough to be amused at her own childish affection for him. Yet also her tone made him realize that from her point of view he was old, old enough not to misunderstand her. Dave joined them and Ruth went to speak to Tony, and Mark said: 'That's a mighty attractive young woman, that daughter of yours.'

Dave nodded, looking after her. 'I suppose you know how much you've done for her—and for me. No man ever did me a greater service, Mark.' He smiled. 'You can draw on me any time, for anything.'

'She'd have straightened out herself. I just happened to be there at the time.'

'You gave her back something I'd stolen from her.'

Mark hesitated, spoke quietly, 'You're all right, Dave.'

'If it would help Ruth,' the other said in a low tone, his eyes on his daughter, 'I'd start out any night to swim to Spain.'

Mark felt a cold breath of tragedy, but he said only: 'She's always loved you, Dave. You're everything to her.'

When the time came, Mark himself at Elin's request gave the bride away; and afterward there was merrymaking in which everyone joined. Elin's uncle had brought a curious three-cornered instrument like a wooden banjo, and one of Einar's friends had a fiddle, and Mary Halstead and Tom took turns at the piano and they danced till everyone was panting; and Elin made a strange drink with an unpronounceable name that sounded like 'Glug,' putting wine and spices in a pot over the open fire, with a huge molded loaf of sugar on top of it, over which she poured brandy till the brandy began to burn, and they drank it in coffee cups, and they sang Swedish songs and Einar danced a folk dance, with much stamping of his feet, while they all kept time with clapping hands.

Mark, to give these two a sort of honeymoon, had arranged to go to New York for three days, leaving on the midnight train; and Tony would spend the night at the Ritchies', so that Elin and Einar would have the house to themselves. When it was time for Tony to drive Mark to town, his friends said good night to Elin and to Einar and to him, departing at the same time; and Emma Sheffield, when he shook hands with her, leaned nearer to whisper maliciously in his ear:

'You're well out of that, Mark! Clever man! When does her baby come?'

VII

Lebensraum

(October 1937–September 1938)

I

(October 1937)

MARK saw Robin during his three days in New York. She dined with him, welcoming him with a quick pleasure in her eyes which he could not fail to recognize. She made him tell her all about Elin's wedding and he did so, and she laughed with him at his description of those happy, jolly hours. He did not mention Emma Sheffield's remark directly, but he did say:

'Some of my friends—my feminine friends—are relieved. Elin's really lovely, and they've thought it was scandalous for her to be in the house alone with me when Tony was away.'

She smiled. 'Women are that way,' she commented. 'Elin must be fond of you, of course; she's been with you so long.'

There was in her word the frank suggestion that no one could know him well without liking him; and Mark was deeply pleased. She asked about Tony, and he told her what there was to tell, and asked questions in his turn. She was about to sail for two or three weeks in Paris, would return direct to Montreal to spend Christmas with her family there; but she would be back in New York in January.

'You're not afraid of running into an explosion in Europe while you're there?' he asked. 'Things seem to be pretty tight, ready to snap. Italy and Germany and Russia are all in this Spanish business. It wouldn't need much to touch off a real war.'

She was sure France and England would refuse to become involved in Spain; and this led them to some talk of the disordered world, and Mark referred to Mr. Roosevelt's speech in Chicago two weeks before. The President, obviously with Japan in mind, had denounced the ruthless murder of civilians and of women and children by aerial bombardment; he had referred to German and Italian participation in the Spanish revolution; and he had insisted that the United States was menaced by 'the present reign of terror and international lawlessness' and suggested that the peace-loving nations quarantine the aggressors. He had been damned by the newspapers for this 'sudden burst of bellicose oratory'; and the stock market hit a new low for the year after the speech was delivered.

'I think he was wrong,' Mark told Robin. 'He seemed to me to be asking for trouble. I think we're talking bigger than our britches. We cuss out Japan for what she's doing in China, and we damn Germany— although Germany has been stepping softly for a long time now—but we're not prepared to back up our talk, except, perhaps, by sending more words after words.'

'I wondered why he said what he did,' she remarked. 'Certainly the United States will never again be stampeded into sending an army to Europe.'

'I don't know why he did it,' Mark admitted. 'Bob Ritchie thinks it's a red herring, that he's trying to distract our attention, make us forget his appointment of a Ku Klux man to the Supreme Court, make us forget the depression his wasteful spending hasn't cured. But whatever his reason, he did a dangerous thing. By all reports, the Japanese are a fanatic race, and this speech was aimed at them. It's likely to provoke some shameful outrages on American citizens in Japan or China. The Japs will feel they've "lost face" and that they can only regain their own self-respect by striking back somehow, abusing our citizens over there or something.'

'The editorial writers all blame him,' she agreed. 'They say he's trying to get us into another war. If he really thinks war is coming, he's spending so much money on WPA and all those things, why doesn't he spend it on munition plants and training camps and things we'll need?'

Mark smiled. 'Probably Congress would yell bloody murder if he tried it.'

'They'll let him do anything he wants, after last election. But I can't believe we'd ever go into another war, even if he wanted us to. Everybody's against that.'

Mark said slowly: 'He doesn't have to persuade anybody, of course. Congress has the sole power to declare war, but the President as Commander-in-Chief of our armed forces can easily enough force other nations to declare war on us.' He shook his head doubtfully, 'I don't know what I think,' he confessed. 'My mind is so full of questions,

much of the time, that there's no room in it for answers.' He added: 'I
can't even be sure I condemn Germany. Certainly—outside of her internal policies, her brutality to the Jews, her concentration camps, and
so on—she has done nothing thus far except to correct some of the
wrongs done her at Versailles. I can't help seeing her side.'

She touched his arm as though unconsciously, in an affectionate gesture. 'You always see both sides, don't you?'

He laughed. 'It's the Ohio in me,' he confessed. 'You know I've too
much Ohio and Mississippi in me ever to be a complete New Englander. The men I know in Boston damn Mr. Roosevelt; but I exchange
letters now and then with men in the little Mississippi town where I
was born and they think he's wonderful. My friends in Boston damn
the Germans; but my father in Ohio feels almost as strongly against the
British. He thinks I'm an Anglo-maniac, but my friends in Boston
probably think I'm pro-German—and suspect me of being a Roosevelt
man!'

'Of course,' she agreed. 'That's bound to be true, isn't it? To a partisan, a neutral is always an opponent. "He that is not with me is against
me." '

Their talk was not all of abstractions. They were happy together,
laughing easily, finding when they were in company humor in things
which would not have amused either of them alone; and when they
parted at last it was with mutual regret, even a little sadness.

'I hate saying good-bye,' he confessed, and smiled. 'Didn't someone
say that even a little parting is like death? I'll want to see you in January, to hear about your trip, to hear how things seem in France.'

'Do come over when you can,' she agreed. 'I'll want to see you, too.'

2

(Winter 1937)

Tony's letters that winter meant much to Mark. It was like seeing
his son to hold them in his hands. Tony was becoming increasingly
aware of international affairs, and he seemed to accept, though with a
hot resentment, the fact that when war came the United States must
eventually take a hand in it.

But his letters were more apt to be concerned with personal matters.

Often he spoke of Barbie Parks, and once, in reply to some word of his father's, he wrote:

> About Barb, I seem to tie for first place in her estimation with a fellow whom she describes as 'inclined to be morbid, devoid of any sense of humor, and the most pityful boy in the world.'

Mark was always tenderly amused at Tony's mistakes in spelling. They seemed to him reminders that despite the growing maturity of his son's letters, Tony was still very young. Tony went on:

> My hope is that her feeling for him is governed by her maternal and sympathetic instincts. She admits that she is thrilled when either of two other fellows looks at her; but I realize that she is sure to have an affair every now and then with someone beside myself.
>
> She has every characteristic to make her a popular girl, but the average run of fellows will give her up when they discover that she won't neck. As for myself, I'd rather have a smile from her than a kiss from Greta Garbo.

Mark did not smile as he read. He and Tony were so close to one another that such confidences did not surprise him. To one hope he clung above all others, that if Tony were ever in trouble he would turn for help first of all to his father; and to make this as certain as possible Mark had worked always for Tony's confidence, careful never to punish or even to chide the youngster for a fault confessed.

When Tony came home for Thanksgiving, they had good hours of talk together, much of it concerned with Tony's work; and sometimes Mark was faintly troubled. Once Tony, speaking of his course in Zoology, said:

'We've been dissecting clams till I doubt if I'll ever eat one again.' He added seriously: 'But if you're going to go on doing any sort of research, whether it's into the innards of a starfish or into the respective merits of Kantian and Utilitarian ethics, you've got to fortify yourself against the disillusionment and disgust which goes with increased knowledge and understanding.'

Mark took issue with him on that. 'You're wrong there, son,' he urged. 'If increased knowledge provokes you to disillusionment and disgust, there's something wrong with your professors.'

Tony said thoughtfully: 'I see what you mean. But we do get a lot of that, Dad. Of course I didn't mean it, about the insides of clams; but in most of our courses we hear a lot about mistaken ideas and policies.'

Mark spoke as strongly as he felt. 'Don't lose your balance, Tony. I've no sympathy with the muck-raking system of education, which puts emphasis on wrongs and errors, and fails to emphasize the fine things man has done. True education ought to teach you to seek out and to recognize that which is good. Maybe modern education is too much inclined to pounce on what was bad and throw stones at it. You ought to try to remember that there's more good than ill in the world—and look for that which is good and hold fast to it.'

'Well, I get a lot out of the courses, in spite of it,' Tony said, half to himself; and he added: 'For one thing, I'm beginning to understand my personal religious beliefs. Reading William James made me think I was a sort of agnostic, but then I decided that I believed in a harmonious universe, and in some kind of God.' He grinned. 'So I've sort of decided to let my religion grow up with me and see how it comes out.'

Mark smiled, deeply pleased. 'Don't worry about religion,' he advised. 'A man's religion, in the long run is that philosophic attitude which he acquires as he grows older, and which if it's sound enables him to be undisturbed by the small crises of life, and to keep his head high and his spirit strong through the big ones. When the time comes that you need a religion, you'll find that you have one.'

'I'm planning a theme about it for one of my English courses,' Tony explained. 'I expect to bring in Materialism, and Dualism, and Idealism, and to show that there is some being spiritually higher than any we know.' He laughed. 'Probably you don't see how I can prove the existence of a supernatural reality through a description of the assertions of Atomic Materialism, but that's the general idea.'

Mark chuckled. 'I'll have to confess that I don't feel completely sure what Materialism—even Atomic Materialism—and Dualism and Idealism are. You're over my head. But maybe those are just big words for simple things. Scholars have a way of complicating things. That habit traces back to the days when knowledge was a mystery, confined to the few, surrounded by a lot of mumbo-jumbo. If you do your job in the world as well as you can, recognize your responsibilities and accept them, love your neighbor, fear God and hate the Devil, you'll get along. As Kipling said, "You'll be a man, my son." '

Tony nodded slowly, and he grinned. 'You know, you're awfully good for me, Dad. Without meaning to, you sort of—put me in my place. I'm apt to think that when I decide something, I'd better tell the world, as if the world had been just thirsting for the answer till I came along.'

Mark found complete contentment in these interchanges with his son. It interested him to watch Tony's mind develop, to watch his reaction to a new line of thought. There were no reticences between these two. One evening during the Christmas holidays they sat late together, Tony full of eager talk, Mark glad to listen and respond; and Tony spoke of Chad Frame and how his life was wasting, and Mark asked whether Chad was in his dissipations unique among his fellows.

'Sort of,' Tony admitted. 'He's a lone wolf, goes off by himself to New York or Springfield or Montreal or somewhere, just sort of cold-bloodedly, to make a fool of himself. But of course a lot of the fellows have a time for themselves when they get a chance.' And he added, at first in shy embarrassment and then in a strong and earnest tone: 'I take a lot of kidding, because when they get to talking I say I plan to marry a virgin. The fellows claim that every girl who is at all good-looking loses her virginity long before she reaches the marrying age. They say that if I don't become an expert in sexual intercourse before I marry, I may easily wreck my marriage. I take quite a ride, but I claim that there are virgins left in the world if you look up instead of down.'

Mark spoke in quick agreement. 'Fine!' And he said approvingly: 'I like that phrase of yours. Look up instead of down when you come to choose a wife. Read *The Adams Family*. The men in that family regularly had the luck or the wit to marry girls better and wiser and stronger than themselves. Their wives made them great—and passed on a fine heritage to their children.' And he added: 'One reason for marrying—as people say—above you, or, as you say, for looking up instead of down, is that women mature earlier than men. Only the rare woman continues to grow and develop mentally all her life; but there are some men who do not reach their full powers till they are forty or even fifty. You're much more likely to grow up to your wife's stature than she is to grow up to yours. I've known many men who might have gone a long way if they had not been anchored to a wife unable to travel that long road with them.'

Tony said acutely: 'Like Mr. Sheffield?' Mark sometimes thought it was a commentary on his friends that Tony always spoke of Tom and Emma thus formally, while Ed and Mary, Bob and Nell, were always Uncle Ed, Uncle Bob, Aunt Nell, Aunt Mary.

'Tom would have gone a lot farther with the right wife,' he agreed. 'A wife a little above you can—if you have the stuff—help you climb up to stand with her, and to go forward side by side.'

Tony did not speak, and Mark added quietly: 'Of course I'm not talking about morals. They're your own affair. You know that if you're intimate with a girl there are at least two definite possibilities of trouble; that she may become pregnant, and that you may acquire an unpleasant disease. I think it is also true that if you're intimate with a girl, even if no tangible harm to either of you results, you'll regret it later; but that is for you to decide.'

Tony's eyes met his father's frankly. 'I know, yes sir,' he said. 'I feel the same way. Maybe I'm a sissy, but I sort of take pride in the fact that the only girl I've touched in Hanover was one I sat beside the other day at a basketball game. I lighted a cigarette for her, and when she held my hand I got a thrill that shook my shoes!' He grinned. 'We don't see many girls up there, so maybe we think too much about them; but I've learned that a few minutes with Barb or at home with some girl I know and I'm normal again.'

3
(January 1938)

Mark saw Robin Kerr again in January. He wrote her that he was coming to New York, and she wired that she would expect him. When his business was done and he telephoned to her, she insisted that he come to her studio apartment and dine with her there.

'I want to show you that New York isn't all night clubs,' she explained.

He did as she suggested. She cooked dinner herself, had it ready to serve when he arrived at the appointed hour; but there was time for cocktails before they sat down. He thought her more beautiful tonight than she had ever been; and he wondered how old she was. There were hours when she seemed as young as Elin or as Barbie Parks—and younger than Betty Ritchie, for instance, who always wore a remote composure beyond her years—and this was one of them. When she opened the door on his arrival, she was a little flushed from the heat in the kitchen, with a crisp blue-and-white bib apron over her gown, and her eyes were shining and there was a rich happiness in her voice which had the lift of youth, so that at first he felt by contrast older than he was. But they were presently laughing together. They laughed because they liked each other, and because they had looked forward to this occasion, and because it pleased her to be able to display her housewifely arts to him just as it pleased him to be served by her; and they laughed because there was in each one of them a fine excitement, a sense of anticipation, which they were not yet ready to avow. Their eyes met silently over the lifted cocktails, but their talk at dinner was gay and the business of washing dishes afterward was hilarious; and then they came back to the living room, and Mark forgot the passage of time and so did she. The night was stormy, snow beating against the window-panes; and there was a fire on the hearth between them, a small frugal New York fire. They sat facing each other, and Mark watched the play of the firelight on her cheek and in her hair, wondering how it happened that she wore her hair long, glad she did. For a moment after they were settled, neither of them spoke, their eyes meeting; and she smiled at him and her smile and their silence made his pulse quicken and he hurried to speak. She had spent Christmas in Montreal, and he asked: 'What do they think in Canada about the way things are going in Europe?' Since he last saw her Italy had joined Japan and Germany in their pact against Communism; and Japan had sunk the *Panay*, on the Yangtse River above Nanking.

'My father thinks Hitler is planning war soon,' she said, readily taking his cue. 'He's building the Siegfried line, trying to make himself secure against attack in the west; and Father thinks that sooner or later he will attack Russia.' She smiled a little. 'Father gets pretty hot about it, never calls Hitler anything milder than: "That damned devil!"'

Mark said thoughtfully: 'It doesn't help matters to call Germany and Italy outlaw nations. After all, we're at peace with them—and most of us want to continue to be.'

'I try to keep a level head,' she agreed. 'But I hate the concentration camps, the cruelties, the persecution of the Jews.'

'I hate those things too,' he assented. 'But—I don't wholly believe them. Perhaps that's because to a normal mind they seem incredible. Our newspapers and magazines make a bad case against Germany; but German newspapers probably make a bad case against the United States, playing up lynchings and strike riots and gangster killings and Southern chain gangs, and so on.' He asked: 'Did you go to Germany while you were there?'

'No. I spent most of my time in Paris.'

'How do the French feel?'

'They feel safe,' she told him. 'They think Germany can never break the Maginot line.' And after a moment she said with a little shiver: 'It scared me, somehow, to see how smugly safe they feel.'

'Perhaps they're right. It was pretty hard to break a strong defensive line in the last war.'

'Germany can always come through Belgium again.'

'She's promised not to,' Mark reminded her.

Robin nodded. 'And the French people want to believe she'll keep her word this time,' she said. 'They don't want war. That's the whole story.'

Mark reflected: 'I wonder why we Americans so easily feel that what Germany does inside Germany is our business. I suppose there are quite as many miserable Americans in New York as there are wretched Jews in Berlin.'

'Or as there are suffering children in Spain,' she assented.

He nodded. 'Yet my friends in Boston have excited themselves about Spain,' he remarked. 'While in Cleveland fifteen thousand people stood in line two days, here not long ago, to get the wretched charity of a bottle of milk and a loaf of bread.'

'The thing that scares me,' she confessed, 'is that there is in Germany a willingness to sacrifice and to serve. In France people all want to be let alone, to go their own way. The men in power, even in the army, are sure nothing is going to happen. And a lot of money that has been spent for planes and tanks and things has been wasted—or stolen. In Germany—if Lindbergh is right—they're making every move count.'

He spoke gravely. 'Yes, that's true—and not only in material ways. A whole generation, born during the last war or just afterward, has been taught to believe that Germany was betrayed, that she must make herself strong again. Here in our country—and I suppose in France and England too—boys have been taught that the last war ended wars, that we won't have another; and we've been told over and over that we were betrayed by our own friends, that we were suckers, left to hold the bag.' He said grimly: 'There's a will to fight in Germany. There isn't here.'

'Nor in France,' she assured him.

'Take this *Panay* business,' he suggested. 'Japanese soldiers sank one of our warships—I suppose to demonstrate their resentment at Mr. Roosevelt's Chicago speech—and we're not at all excited. Yet—remember the *Maine?* We fought Spain just on suspicion that Spain sank her. Remember the *Lusitania?* We fought Germany because her submarines sank English and American merchant vessels with Americans aboard. Now Japan deliberately and openly sinks one of our warships, and the average man doesn't give a hoot, thinks the *Panay* had no business being where she was. The American mind is made up to stay out of trouble, even if we have to accept insults and outrages.'

'Do you agree?' she asked. 'Or do you think we ought to declare war on Japan.'

'I don't know,' he confessed. 'I think we're in danger of becoming contemptible in the eyes of other nations, of "losing face" as the Japs themselves would say. They must be grinning over the fact that they can sink our warships and get away with it.' He added in an ironic tone: 'But certainly there's no indication that our outraged citizenry want to spring to arms over the *Panay*, not even in New England.' He smiled on a sudden thought. 'As for the Mid-west, I had a letter from my father the other day. He says we've no right to resent the *Panay*, says Standard Oil sent three vessels up the Yangtse into territory where fighting is going on, and the *Panay*, one of our warships, took those three vessels in tow. As he puts it, one of our Government vessels was helping Standard Oil do business with the Chinese; and he denies that it's the Navy's business to do that. I suspect his is the point of view of most people in the Middle West.'

She asked, watching him, seeing how these thoughts troubled him, thinking to lead him to speak of more personal and less disturbing matters, how old his father was. 'Seventy-one,' he admitted, but he clung to his thought. 'Yet it isn't only the older men who feel so. Borah said much the same thing, I mean about Standard Oil, at the time; and Maas of Minnesota said we should get out of the Orient, and Reynolds of North Carolina said we should stop trying to police the world. In the South and West most people feel that way.' He added: 'You know Tony's at Dartmouth, and undergraduate opinion there includes samples from most of the forty-eight states. Tony has a friend, Joe Hazen, from California; and another, Charlie Spring, from Evanston; and there are others from all over. Tony tells me they all hate the thought of war, say we were betrayed in the last war, swear they won't lend a hand to help in the next one unless they're made to. Of course some of that comes from their professors, but it reflects the opinion in their home states, too. Harvard and Yale are even stronger than Dartmouth in their feeling against war.

'And yet these boys are all certain that war is coming, and that we'll somehow be tricked into it, and that they'll have to go off and be killed. That's a bad frame of mind for youngsters; that feeling that they'll come out of college with no future but mutilation or death. They're apt to say: "What's the use of anything?"'

She was able then to lead him to talk about Tony, and about himself; and they sat for hours, in long talk together, of their work, of their thoughts, of their emotions and ambitions. Their voices were low in the quiet room. Now and then Robin added fuel to the fire, and save for a shaded lamp on the table, the flames were their only light. Mark, completely content and at peace, forgot the time till at last he glanced absently at his watch and rose in dismayed apology.

'For Heaven's sake, I'm sorry,' he exclaimed. 'I was too comfortable to notice how late it was.'

She smiled. 'So was I,' she agreed. 'I was comfortable too, and I don't mind late hours. We must do it soon again.'

They parted, but Mark's thoughts stayed with her, cleaving to her, longing for her. But he refused to let those thoughts take concrete form, for he would soon be fifty, and she was so young; scarce older than Ruth Rollins whom he had known since she was a child.

4

(February–March 1938)

In Boston, Mark found that the men he met began to forget the *Panay* in their renewed indignation at Mr. Roosevelt and his policies. In December the President had accused the newspapers of preaching a philosophy of fear, which was harmful to business; and a week later the Assistant Attorney-General of the United States, in a speech at Philadelphia, accused big business of going out on strike against the United States and deliberately organizing a business depression. Mr. Roosevelt at the Jackson Day Dinner said that a 'mere handful' of business men were wrecking business in an effort to 'retain autocratic control over the industry and the finances of the country.'

The effect was to produce in the men of Mark's acquaintance a choking fury, and Mark heard more than one man—men of weight and sense and self-respect—damn the President in unmeasured terms. Bob Ritchie put the case in his usual lucid fashion. 'Mr. Roosevelt has spent our money for five years,' he said, 'promising that by doing so he would put men back to work; but there are more men out of work than ever, and he has sense enough to know he's to blame, so he's trying to distract attention from his own mistakes.'

Mark found himself, as was apt to be the case, between one party and the other. 'There's no question that capital's going on strike,' he suggested. 'Mr. Roosevelt, by reducing the rewards which capital can expect to receive from business, has made sensible men put their funds into low-return, safe securities. People with capital will take three per cent, or one and a half, or they'll bury their money in a hole in the ground, rather than risk it in a venture where they've no chance for a real profit, and every chance to lose.

'So there is a capital strike, today, just as Mr. Roosevelt says; but on the other hand, it's a strike in self-defense, and Mr. Roosevelt is responsible!'

When in mid-January Owen D. Young, Thomas Lamont, and John L. Lewis called on Mr. Roosevelt to urge that he do something to steady the nerves of the business world, they had the backing of the overwhelming majority of business men, large and small, in the United States; and through February the country waited hopefully for any sign from Washington. Confidence, based on the feeling among business men that their cause was just, began to rise.

And then Richard Whitney went into bankruptcy, and confessed the embezzlement of funds which he held in trust. Mr. Whitney had been for the world of finance their knight in shining armor; he had been the leader of a forlorn hope that sought to palliate the first shock of the market crash eight years before; as President of the Stock Exchange he had fought hard and boldly for everything which the financial world held right and in the public interest. His personal background was in the finest tradition of American life.

His confession sent a sick shudder of disgust and dismay through every banking house and brokerage office in the country. Other financial leaders had been discredited; but none who stood in the public mind as high as he. It would be a long time before another broker could say proudly, secure from contradiction: 'We are a company of honorable men!' In the eyes of many, Mr. Roosevelt's case was by this one man's crime proved beyond immediate controversion; and any man who spoke in defense of men of finance was sure to hear the hecklers cry: 'Oh yeah! What about Dick Whitney?'

5

(Spring 1938)

The fact that Einar and Elin were married made astonishing little difference in Mark's routine. Einar was usually gone to work before Mark himself came downstairs, and he was away in the evening whenever Mr. and Mrs. Marshman required his services to take them to the theatre or the opera, or to dinner. Except that Elin wore a happy radiance, she was as she had always been. Mark tried not to let himself remember that this arrangement could not be permanent, that sooner or later she and Einar would want a family and a home of their own.

He had begun to correspond regularly with Robin. For the most part his letters, though they were sometimes long, because he found it pleasant to write to her, were completely impersonal. When in February Hitler assumed supreme command of the German armed forces, Mark had an uneasy feeling that this presaged some new step by Germany; and he wrote her: 'Remember your father thought Germany would attack Russia? I've been looking at the map. Austria stands in the way, and Poland, and Czecho-Slovakia. If your father is right, Hitler will have to find a way past them, or through them.'

She was not a ready correspondent, and it was some time before her answer came. German troops marched into Austria; and the word 'anschluss' took its place in American vocabularies. Robin's letter arrived a week later, telling Mark her recent activities, asking when he would be in New York again, assuring him that she wished to see him when he came and suggesting that he let her know beforehand so that she could plan her time accordingly. Only in the postscript she said: 'You see, Hitler has found his way to pass Austria—or to go through her. Perhaps Father was right.'

He replied, commenting on the flight of Jews from Austria. 'I've been puzzling over a curious thing,' he said. 'Call an Englishman an Englishman and he takes it as a compliment. Call a Frenchman a Frenchman, or call one of us a Yankee, and the result is the same. But if you call a Jew a Jew, he feels insulted. It's strange that a race with so noble a history, with so much of which to be proud, should be ashamed.'

She suggested: 'Perhaps it's because the Jews are a people, not a nation. The English, the French, the Americans are nations. In art, the theatre, books, sculpture, the Jews have done great things, and also of course in business; but they have done those things as individuals, not as a nation.'

He reminded her that Jews had no gift for politics, for getting along with their neighbors, and she retorted that some of her best friends were Jews. 'But what you say is quite true,' she admitted. 'They know it themselves. I've heard the elder Mr. Morgenthau quoted as saying that no Jew would ever hold a higher office in our Government than his son now holds.'

They wrote more and more frequently as winter gave way to spring; and in May he went to New York avowedly to see her, and with no business pretext. He had told no one, not even Tony, that they were become friends; so there was something clandestine about the relationship which pleased him.

He had looked forward so eagerly to being with her again that his own hunger half frightened him. They met for breakfast Sunday morning—he had come over on the midnight—and it was a fine sunned spring day, and when afterward they walked up the Avenue, people were going to church. Mark himself was not a churchgoer, but he thought she probably was. 'Maybe I'm keeping you from going,' he suggested.

She had felt the restraint in him, not fully understanding it, a little concerned. 'Let's both go,' she suggested.

So for an hour they sat side by side in a goodly company, and Mark was intensely conscious of her nearness, watching her pure profile with sidelong glances till she met his eyes and smiled, and he did not look at her again. When afterward he still was silent, thinking he must be troubled, wishing to distract him, she proposed that they find a hansom cab and drive around the Park. 'It's fun,' she said. 'A fine day like this.'

The close intimacy of the cab made his heart pound, and he began hurriedly to talk. He kept the conversation, as though defensively, on international affairs. She had been struck by Sir Anthony Eden's resignation from the British Cabinet in protest against Chamberlain's continued 'conversations' with Italy, Eden insisting that Italy should first withdraw her volunteers from Spain before any understanding could be reached.

'I like Mr. Eden,' she said, and smiled and confessed: 'Perhaps it's just because he's a handsome devil, and Mr. Chamberlain looks like an old fuddy dud.'

'Chamberlain's working for peace,' Mark reminded her. 'And the only chance for continued peace in Europe is for England and France and Germany and Italy to get together somehow. Of course France could impose peace by force. If she had moved when Germany marched her troops into the Rhineland, she could have ended Hitler then. Or even now, in this Austrian business.'

'Wasn't Italy the one to interfere with that?'

'The trouble is, Italy has no friends. She's alienated England and France, and she can't stand up to Germany alone.' He said soberly: 'England and France are obsessed with the desire to keep out of war, and France doesn't want to move without England's backing, I suppose. Did you see Hore-Belisha's statement that English infantry would never again be sent to fight on the Continent?' She had not, and he explained: 'He was introducing an army bill in the House of Commons. He said there would never be another expeditionary force of English infantry; that Englishmen would be kept at home to defend England;—except perhaps for a mechanized force—and that an Empire army drawn from Australia and New Zealand and India and Canada would do the Empire's fighting. I interpret that as a warning to France.'

The old horse which drew them jogged on clopping hooves. She said, weary of this war talk, watching him with a faint smile: 'You think a lot about European affairs, don't you?'

'I do, yes.' He hesitated. 'There seem to me so many signs of trouble coming.' He spoke slowly. 'I think sometimes that there is in the air, if we could hear it, the sound of a great bell far away, ringing an alarm. Remember that passage in a French novel—one of Victor Hugo's I think it is—which describes a distant church tower where the sky beyond the tower is revealed and then obscured as the bell swings. The sound itself cannot be heard, but those who look toward the tower know that the tocsin is ringing. I think it's like that in the world today.'

'I'm afraid I'm so busy with my own small affairs that I'm willing to let the world work out its own salvation,' she confessed, wishing he would speak of other things; but in an instinctive defensive gesture he stuck to his subject. The Archbishop of Canterbury had condemned Versailles. Poland had sent an ultimatum to Lithuania, forcing the smaller country into abject surrender at the sword's point. The insurgents seemed on the road to victory in Spain. Tokio, tongue in cheek, had paid damages for the *Panay*. Hitler had visited Mussolini in Rome and seen an impressive demonstration of Italian naval power. England and France were rearming; and even here in the United States Congress was passing a bill to spend a billion dollars on the expansion of the navy in the next ten years. He spoke of all these things, and at length.

'Mercy!' she protested at last in amused dismay, 'you sound like a news commentator!'

He hesitated, seeing himself for a moment clearly. 'I get a sort of talking jag on when I'm with you,' he confessed, laughing. 'Just being with you makes me want to talk and talk. I suppose I stick to world affairs because—well, for fear of what I might say if I didn't.'

She was silent, her eyes meeting his, her color rising; and then suddenly she nodded. 'You're right, Mark,' she said, in a tone almost sombre. 'It's much better for us to talk about—well, about my handsome friend, Mr. Eden!'

There was a deep exhilaration in him. It was as though she had confessed a feeling to match his; had admitted that they were passing beyond friendship into something warmer. He was intoxicated, and yet cautious too. He spoke hesitantly.

'You know this is the first time I've ever come to New York just to see you, with no business to bring me.'

She smiled. 'Really?' Her eyes were teasing. 'What would your friend Mrs. Sheffield say if she knew?'

He chuckled. 'By the way, she's in the hospital,' he told her.

'Oh, is she? Is it—dangerous?'

'A gall bladder,' he said. 'She's almost ready to go home. Tom's been worried about her, but I judge she's all right.'

'You've told me so much about these friends of yours that I seem to know them, but I've never even met Tony.'

He said quickly: 'I want you to meet him soon.' His deep thoughts were taking form. 'We must plan on it.'

There was a faint reserve in her tone, yet her words were open enough. 'Yes, of course,' she agreed. 'Probably it will happen naturally some day.'

The hansom pulled up at the curb, their perambulation done. He expected they would have the rest of this day together, till late afternoon when he would take the train for Boston; but there was some sudden change in her. When he had dismissed the cab driver, she said apologetically:

'I'm sorry I'm going to have to leave you, Mark. There's a Philadelphia woman in town just for the day, wants me to do her children, wants to see some of my things.'

He felt himself dismissed, and yet he was almost relieved by this dismissal. They had come so close together today that it would have been easy to come closer; and it was hard not to do so, hard to hold back the word he at once wished and dreaded to say. So they parted, and he tried to decide, after he had left her, just how much she understood of the things he had not said; tried to decide whether there was a promise in her tone.

6

(June 1938)

Wednesday evening after his return, Mark had dinner with the Ritchies', and Nell told him that Emma had gone home from the hospital. 'With a nurse,' she said. 'She's still playing invalid. I saw her today. She's even acquired an invalid's outfit, new dressing gown, satin bedjacket. Trust Emma! There's never anything wrong with her that new clothes won't cure. I don't know how Tom pays all the bills.'

Bob laughed. 'Maybe he's related to Roosevelt,' he suggested. 'There's the greatest family of moneymakers who ever got into the White House. Roosevelt sells his official papers to the magazines, and Eleanor writes "My Day," and lectures, and cashes in plenty, and their daughter and Elliott are on the Hearst payroll, and Jimmie made his pile in the insurance business here in Boston and retired on four or five years of profits. Being President is a great racket, the way they work it.'

Mark was silent, faintly uncomfortable, as he was apt to be when he heard such rancorous criticism of Mr. Roosevelt. What Bob said might be true enough. Certainly it was common report, in print and out; and yet—was it not also true that to ridicule and to belittle the President weakened the nation? The hour was coming when strong leadership would be needed. To undermine that leadership could serve no good end. But there was no profit in argument with Bob. He, like most of the men Mark knew, condemned the President and all his works. Mark said good night early, and went home. During the days that followed, he remembered what Nell had said, and felt some sympathetic concern for Tom, but he did not see the other for the rest of May. Another crisis came to a boil along the Czecho-Slovakian border, and then simmered down, and Cordell Hull in a speech at Nashville called isolation a 'bitter illusion,' and a day or two later Tom telephoned Mark to make an appointment.

When they met, Mark was shocked by his friend's appearance. Tom's reddened, weary eyes testified to sleepless nights, and he had lost weight, and there were drawn lines around his mouth. He sat down, and Mark asked for Emma, and Tom said she was fine, and Mark spoke of Tommy, who after being graduated from Harvard the year before had gone to work in Tom's department in the bank.

'He's doing fine,' Tom said. 'He's on the way up already.' He added—smiling a little: 'He's thinking of getting married, Mark, as soon as he gets his next raise.'

'Fine!' Mark exclaimed. 'He's a great boy. Who's the girl?'

'No one you know,' Tom said. 'She works in the bank, Mr. Newell's secretary. Her name's Mary Clancy.' He grinned. 'Tommy and I haven't told Emma yet. I don't know how she'll take it. But Mary's all right. She has a lot of ability, and a lot of common sense and character. Her father is a contractor in South Boston. She's pretty, and she's crazy about Tom, in a calm, motherly way. I'm all for her.'

'Fine,' Mark said again, but he wondered what Emma would think of this when she knew. He waited for Tom to come to the point of his visit.

And after a moment Tom did so. He produced an envelope, laid it on Mark's desk. Mark drew out of it what he saw at once was a bill, from Doctor Mann, one of the leaders of the profession in Boston. The bill was for seven hundred and fifty dollars.

He looked at it and then at Tom. 'This is for Emma's operation, I suppose?'

Tom nodded miserably. 'Mark, doesn't it strike you that's a hell of a lot of money for him to charge?' he asked. 'I don't know how in God's name I'm going to pay it. I had to borrow to pay the hospital bills. Emma was bound to have the best room, and day and night nurses; and of course the hospital had to be paid in advance.' He made a wry face. 'They don't take any chances, no matter how sick you are!'

Mark smoothed the bill between his fingers, and Tom added: 'The hospital and nurses cost me more than that. I thought maybe you could get some sort of settlement with him.'

Mark hesitated. 'Well, Tom,' he said, 'doctors' bills are elastic, of course. They usually make what they consider a fair charge, proportional to the patient's means. Did he discuss it with you at all?"

'No, just sent it along.'

'Did Emma need so many nurses?'

'Why, she thought she did. He said she could go on floor care, but she wouldn't.' He added: 'And she had a lot of new clothes delivered to the hospital. I suppose he thinks I'm rolling in money.'

'Why don't you go to him, explain your circumstances, see if he won't make some adjustment?'

Tom colored miserably. 'That's what I want you to do, Mark. If you will.'

Mark hesitated, and his lips set. 'Well—all right, Tom,' he agreed. 'But it's hardly a lawyer's job. Can't you do it yourself?'

'I suppose I could, but I'd hate it, Mark. I'd hate asking a man to reduce a bill he thought was fair. After all, he saved Emma's life. But I just simply can't pay it.' He added frankly: 'We're always in debt as it is, I get five hundred a month, but it's spent before I get it. We owe bills all over Boston, and—I borrowed from Dave Rollins to pay the hospital.'

'How's Dave?' Mark asked absently. 'When did you see him?'

'He's fine. Marcia says he's been all right for a long time. I saw them a couple of weeks ago.' He added: 'Ruth's engaged—to a young school teacher from Ohio. Marcia's wild, trying to break it up.'

'Engaged? They haven't announced it.'

'No, Marcia's fighting it tooth and nail.'

'What's wrong with the young fellow, aside from the fact that he comes from Ohio?' Mark's tone was dry.

'Dave and Marcia haven't met him,' Tom explained. 'Nothing wrong with him except that he's poor, as far as I know. Ruth met him in Florida last Christmas. He'd driven down there on his vacation.'

'How does Dave feel about it?'

'He says Ruth is the one to decide.' Tom came back to the point. 'Will you do this, Mark? Go see the doctor for me.'

Mark hesitated, thinking how Emma's extravagance had harried Tom so long, and he swung his chair to look out of the window, afraid the other would read the deep anger in his eyes. 'All right,' he said. 'I'll see him.'

He did as he had promised, and reported the result to Tom. 'I wish you had gone to him yourself, Tom,' he confessed, regretting what he had to say. He hesitated, but Tom did not speak, and Mark went on: 'He told me, what I already knew, of course, that his bills were normally adjusted to the patient's apparent capacity to pay.' He hesitated, and then, in a sudden wrath, knowing Tom must resent his word, yet welcoming a valid reason for saying it—the word had needed to be said for such a long time—he went on: 'He says Emma insisted on the best available room—at twenty-two dollars a day when there were rooms at seven dollars that would have been perfectly satisfactory. He says she kept three nurses throughout her stay, long after she needed not even one. He spoke of her expensive clothes, all those things.'

Tom nodded, looking down at his hands resting on his knees. 'Yes, I know. Emma has expensive tastes.'

Mark did not comment. He had heard that phrase so many times. 'He said if he were prescribing for Emma now he'd tell you to take her over your knee and give her a thorough paddling,' he said, and added: 'And he's sending you a corrected bill, for two hundred dollars. If that's too much, you need pay nothing. He figures that's billing you just for the cost of the operation, showing him no profit at all.'

Tom after a moment said slowly: 'Well, thanks, Mark.' He came to his feet. 'Emma's all right in a lot of ways,' he urged.

'Of course,' Mark agreed. Having gone so far, he might as well go farther. 'But she's not to be trusted about money, Tom. If you don't put

your foot down, you'll never keep your head above water.' He smiled.
'Maybe that's a mixed metaphor, but you know what I mean.'

Tom hesitated, but then he met Mark's eyes, smiling a little, speaking
with a loyal dignity. 'Thanks a lot, Mark,' he said and extended his
hand. Mark took it, gripping it hard, saying with that strong handclasp
what he could not put in words. He stood watching Tom go through
the door. Tom did not look back, and Mark thought unhappily that the
relationship between them could never after this day be the same. If you
criticized a man's wife, no matter how friendly your intention, there was
a barrier between you and him forevermore.

7

(June 1938)

Looking backward, remembering every moment of his last hour with
Robin, Mark began in these weeks to feel a deep misgiving. It seemed
to him in retrospect that at a certain instant there had arisen between
them a restraint which had not been there before; and he became increasingly sure that Robin had contrived a pretext for sending him away,
that for some reason she had been unwilling to be longer with him that
day. She who had always given so freely of her friendliness had suddenly drawn back, had raised a barrier between them. Recalling each
word they had spoken, he thought the change in her had been provoked
by what he said about bringing her and Tony together, as though to
meet his son had for her a significance which she was not ready to
accept.

The reluctance which he suspected in her affected him like a chal-
lenge. He had not yet consciously asked himself whether he loved
Robin, but it became important to him that she and Tony should meet.
He wrote her a letter which he made as casual as possible, concluding:

> I realized after I last saw you that you must sometimes be bored by my
> talk about the European mess. Of course it's much in my mind, as I sup-
> pose it must be much in the minds of all Americans today.
>
> But one reason I talk so much to you about these impersonal things is to
> conceal the excitement I always feel when I am with you. Possibly one rea-
> son for this is that—just why I don't know—I've never told anyone, not even
> Tony, that you and I have come to be friends. When I see you—especially
> when, as this last time, I went to New York just to see you—it's an adven-
> ture for me!

Next time I think I'll bring Tony along. After he comes home from Hanover we can easily run over. We'll suit your convenience as to time. You'll like each other, I know. He's developing finely and I'm very proud of him.

Yours sincerely,
Mark Worth.

He waited eagerly for her reply, but when it came, it was disappoint- ing. She assured him that she was never bored by his talk of world affairs, and she said she saw no reason why a man and a woman might not find each other mentally interesting, just as man and man might. She wrote at length, but there were so many things she did not say; and most conspicuously she said nothing at all about Mark's proposal to bring Tony to see her. Mark felt himself rebuffed, gently but definitely. It was as though she warned him that he and she might be friends, but they could be nothing more.

Her letter depressed him, and perhaps because of this he thought through that month of June that a cloud of danger shadowed all the world. There were reports of troop movements near the Czecho- Slovakian border, and the London *Times* urged the Czechs to grant a plebiscite in the Sudetenland. The crisis passed, but it was as though on the surface of a stream a sudden boiling surge had suggested the spasmodic movement of some great fish hidden in the depth. Now the surface was serene again, but the creature, whatever it was, which had caused that disturbance, was still there.

Then Tony came home from Hanover, and at dinner the first night, he said: 'Dad, I want to go to Europe this summer.'

Mark for a moment did not speak, struck with sudden fear. He said at last, carefully: 'I'd hate to have you in Europe if trouble started.'

'I know,' Tony agreed. 'Most of the fellows think war is surely com- ing, and when it comes Germany may smash every city in France—and England—with her planes. But I want to see those cities while they're still there.'

Mark asked curiously: 'You boys up at Hanover expect war, then?'

'Sure. And the United States will be roped in. Yes, we all know that.' Tony's young jaw set hard. 'But there's nothing we can do about it.'

'I suppose there's not much any individual can do.'

'Except to have a good time till it starts,' Tony said, and he cried passionately: 'Why can't this country learn to mind its own business? What difference does it make to us if Japan takes all of China, or if Italy grabs Ethiopia? I wouldn't see one of my classmates killed to save all the Chinamen and all the Ethiopians in the world! It makes me sick!'

'A nation is like a man,' Mark soberly suggested. 'In the long run a man is happier if he accepts his responsibilities and tries to meet them; and the same thing is true of a nation.'

'Yes, but we don't have to assume all the responsibilities in the world! There's enough poverty and misery and starvation and sickness right here in the United States to keep us busy. The Italians set out to civilize the Ethiopians, even if they had to kill them to do it, and England thinks maybe she'd better civilize the Italians, and Germany says England must let the Italians alone; and we say Germany must let the English alone, and there you are. We'd be a damned sight better off if we stopped worrying about people three or four thousand miles away and started worrying about people in our own slums, Americans like ourselves.'

'That's only partly true, son,' Mark objected. 'Anatole France says in one of his books that an altruist is often a great nuisance to his neighbors; but altruists do a lot of good, too.'

Tony said stubbornly: 'The trouble with people who are always busy helping others—they're apt to neglect their own families. Like some women always busy working for causes and clubs and things, and their husbands' socks need darning, and their children run wild.'

'I'm not sure as many children don't go wrong from too much mothering as from too little,' Mark suggested. 'There are not many things a parent can do for his children—and be sure he's right.'

'He can do his own job, tend to his own business, set them a good example, at least,' Tony insisted. 'I'll bet if everyone spent his time being as decent as he could himself, he'd do a lot more good in the world than trotting around telling other people what they ought to do.'

Mark chuckled. 'Robert Frost said in a talk I once heard him give that he prefers people who do things well to people who do people good,' he remarked. 'Christ said something like that, something about casting the beam out of your own eye before you start worrying about the mote in your neighbor's eye.' Then he asked: 'Have you made any definite plans for this trip this summer?'

So they turned to a discussion of what Tony wished to do. He and Joe Hazen and Charlie Spring would go together, and he had saved enough money out of his allowance, had made steamer reservations and all routine preparations. It was as though he presented his father with an accomplished fact. Mark could find no good grounds for opposing him, no reason except his own fears; and he stifled them. Tony sailed on the twenty-ninth of June.

8

(Summer 1938)

That was for Mark a lonely summer. The fact that Tony was away would have made this true; but also Nell Ritchie and the children went West, driving out to a dude ranch in Wyoming, where Bob joined them for a month in August, so the house across the way was closed and empty. When Einar had a fortnight's vacation, Mark let Elin go away with him to a boarding house in the mountains; and he himself lived at the club, where he had the company of bachelors and of other members like himself whose families were away. Once Dave Rollins wrote to invite him down for a week-end, saying Tom and Emma would be there, but Mark found a pretext to decline. He did go frequently to Sunday dinner with Ed and Mary Halstead at Humarock. They were always the same, always a source of peace and strength. He said so, one afternoon while in bathing suits the three of them sprawled on the beach and the children were in and out of the water.

'You don't change, you two,' he declared. 'It's a treat for me to come down here.'

Mary laughed. 'Nothing ever happens to us,' she agreed. 'It's pretty monotonous, probably, but we like it.'

'I dunno about that,' Ed drawled, lying on his back, his arm across his eyes. 'Sometimes I'm tempted to start something, just to relieve the . . .' He sat up, blowing and spitting out the handful of sand which Mary had poured in his mouth, and reached for her and she ran, and he ran after her. She raced for the water, slim as a girl, faster of foot than he; but he caught her in knee-deep shallows and they went down in a lusty grapple, and the children shouted gleefully and Mark sat up to watch, and Mary somehow got Ed's head between her legs and he came puffing to his feet with her on his shoulders and she clung there, her hands set in his hair till he waded deeper and dove and they both went under and after a moment drifted quietly to the surface, embracing, his lips on hers, till the children hooted and Mary slapped him and broke free and they came sedately ashore again. Mark, watching them, felt a deep loneliness in him, thinking of Robin, thinking of Nan, realizing that he thought not so often of Nan nowadays, and much of Robin.

He had not seen her since May. After Tony's departure he had proposed going to New York, but she said she would be away. Just now she was in Canada. It had begun to seem to him that she wished not to see him. Perhaps that letter of his had alarmed her, yet he knew now that it had said less than he meant; knew that his life without her would be empty and forlorn.

Ed and Mary came back and joined him again, dripping, sleek as seals; and Mary laughed and said: 'What was that remark about monotony?'

Mark smiled. 'Happy nations have no history,' he reminded her.

Ed said in a sober tone: 'Speaking of history, Mark, I see Mr. Roosevelt has promised that if England goes to war with Germany, and Germany attacks Canada, we'll take a hand.'

Mary spoke quickly, in a mock ferocity, sounding for a moment so like Bob Ritchie that they both laughed. 'Who does the guy think he is?' she demanded. 'Committing us to a European war?'

'That's just one implication of the Monroe Doctrine,' Mark reminded her.

'He can't declare war all by himself,' Mary insisted, but Mark saw her watching Ed in a still concern. 'Congress has to do that. I think Congress ought to stay in session all the time, just to keep him quiet.'

'He can get us into war any time, Congress or no Congress,' Ed pointed out. 'As Commander-in-Chief, he can send the Navy into action —and we'd have to back him up.'

'Bob Ritchie says he's capable of doing it, just to get a third term,' Mary declared. Mark felt sure that the precedent which forbade a third term was one which every American respected, and he said so, and Mary said: 'Well, I think the third-term rule is silly. If there's only one man in the country fit to be President, it's ridiculous to throw him out and put in someone else not so good.'

Mark asked in amused perplexity: 'Are you for Mr. Roosevelt or against him?'

Ed, sprawling on the sand, his head on her knee, said lazily: 'Don't ever argue with a woman, Mark. Arguing with Mary is like batting at butterflies. She never stays put.'

She laughed down at him. 'I've a notion to put some more sand in your craw!' she declared, and he threatened her with many pains and penalties and they abused each other happily. But Mark remembered the concern in her eyes awhile ago, when Ed spoke of the possibility of war, and he guessed the reason. If war came, Ed would go into the Navy; and dread of that must lie always in Mary's mind.

Early in August the Governor again sent for Mark, again offered him an appointment to the Superior Court; and this time there was no hitch. Mark was astonished by the number of letters and telegrams of congratulations which he received. The newspapers united in editorial approval, and Robin telegraphed from Montreal:

> So happy and delighted for you, Mark. How pleased Tony will be. Writing.

Her letter, when it came, was all gladness for his sake; but she said that her mother was ill. 'I'm afraid she's not going to get better,' she confessed. 'I'll stay here with her for a while. I don't yet know how long.'

9

(September 1938)

Mark had many letters from Tony that summer. Tony and his friends went from Paris to Venice, and thence to Munich, and for the last fortnight.of their stay abroad to England. Munich he enjoyed to the full, and he wrote:

> I like the feeling of the place, and the people you see on the streets. Everyone seems so happy, and they look so darned healthy. If I weren't a young American, I'd want to be a young German.

He wrote nothing at all of the possibility of war, and Mark thought it probable that the European peoples knew less than the people in the United States of the dangers that threatened them. When in August a crisis arose that for a day or two promised trouble, Mark was tempted to cable Tony to come home, but the tension eased. Mark wrote Robin:

> I've been wishing Tony were here, safely out of the way of trouble, but according to the papers the war is postponed till fall. I suspect we are reaching a point where the long suspense will become unbearable and we may even begin to wish for war—or for any certainty. It would perhaps be easier to endure it than to dread it.

Tony landed in New York early in September. Mark had hoped to be able to go over to meet him; but when the day came he was engaged in court and unable to get away. So Tony came home on the one o'clock train and Mark met him at the station, and that evening they talked for hours, Mark listening to the chronicle of the summer's journeying, thinking that Europe had made an astonishingly slight impression on Tony. He spoke little of things seen and heard, spoke much of friends whom he and Joe and Charlie had encountered in their travels; other Dartmouth men, and girls they knew. Once Mark said smilingly:

'It sounds to me as though you went to Europe principally to see something of your friends.'

Tony grinned, and said: 'Well, it was certainly a lot of fun, seeing people we knew. We ran into Lucy Pride and Alice Prentiss and May Stevens in Paris.'

Mark remembered Lucy Pride, but he did not know the other two.

'Where was Barbie this summer?' he asked. 'Was she over there?'

'No, she was down on the Cape,' Tony told him. 'I'm going down for the week-end.' Clearly his feeling for Barbie was as strong as ever. His eyes lighted when he spoke of her.

Mark was glad to have Tony safely out of Europe during the fortnight that followed, when war seemed a daily possibility. Three days after Tony's birthday—he was nineteen—with an effect of suddenness after the slumbering summer, the storm clouds began to rise. On September sixth, Hitler told his people that Germany had had a good harvest, that her food reserves were enormous, and that she need never again fear an economic blockade. A scant week later, speaking at Nuremburg, he denounced the Czechs, asserting that they were abusing three and a half million Germans in the Sudeten districts; and as though his speech were a cue, riots in the Sudetenland followed, and men were killed.

Tony had gone down to the Cape the day after his birthday, and he made a long week-end with Barbie there, but he came home that day, and he spoke of the news at dinner.

'I guess this is the beginning of it, Dad,' he said.

Mark shook his head. 'The beginning was at Versailles, when Czecho-Slovakia was set up as an independent state. Czecho-Slovakia and Yugo-Slavia!' There was an angry ring in his tones. 'The very names, hyphen-ated as they are, are a confession of the artificiality of these new nations. These states were fruits of Wilson's idea for the self-determination of small peoples; but that was manifestly unsound.' And he explained: 'I remember when I was a boy in Ohio, there was a predominance of Welshmen in the population of the southern part of the county. The Welsh language was taught in the Sunday schools; and the elders of the churches were for all practical purposes the governing body. But not even Mr. Wilson would suggest that those Welshmen had a right to self-determination—nor had the Indian in the West, nor the Mexican along the Texas border, nor for that matter the negroes in the South, where there are towns, cities, regions, and probably whole states, in which a negro population predominates.'

'It certainly sounds crazy,' Tony agreed.

'It is,' Mark assured him. 'If this theory of self-determination is valid, then the negroes have a right to set up a nation of their own in the South. Mr. Wilson's proposition was on its face absurd, but now that old absurdity may well plunge all Europe into war.' And he said: 'With the tremendous increase in the speed of travel and of communication, I sometimes suspect that the day of small states is ending. We have French and Germans and Italians and Russians and Spaniards in this country, but after a generation or two they all become Americans. Maybe we'll never see permanent peace in Europe till it, too, becomes a melting pot, and the various nations and peoples there merge and become one, a United States of Europe.'

Tony laughed. 'I guess it will be a long time before that happens,' he said, and Mark nodded.

'Yes,' he admitted. 'I'm afraid it will.'

During the days that followed, happenings in Europe drove everything else from the minds of men. The news that Chamberlain had flown to Berchtesgaden to see Hitler seemed to Mark to have a significance far beyond the simple fact. He told Tony: 'Mr. Chamberlain's journey has the effect of magnifying Hitler, of elevating him to a perfectly extraordinary eminence. Until today he was merely the truculent tyrant at the head of a warlike European state; but now Mr. Chamberlain by his action has told his own people and the world: "Here is a man to whom I must do a certain homage, at whose footstool I must present myself."'

'It's pretty grim, all right,' Tony agreed. 'As a matter of fact, Dad, you've got to give Hitler credit. I hate his guts, but he's quite a man.'

'I'm trying to read behind the news,' Mark confessed. 'Back of every event in history there is a fact. What is the fact here? Is it simply that Chamberlain is willing to forget the dignity of his position for the sake of peace, and because he is a peaceful man?'

'I think he's scared,' Tony declared. 'Germany can smash London overnight, and Chamberlain knows it.'

They were both absorbed in the news from day to day. Mr. Chamberlain returned to London for the week-end, and the British people packed the London streets to welcome him with an enthusiasm that was not dampened by reports that the Czechs had lost hope of avoiding war.

Russia and France had pledged themselves to help the Czechs resist any aggression, and the Czechs proposed to resist! From this confrontation, war seemed the only avenue.

But on Monday came the news that Britain and France had decided that the Czechs must yield to Hitler's demands. Mark found that hard to believe. It seemed to him that England had abased herself; but Tony said:

'I don't see it. The thing is, Hitler has a good case. Nobody wants a war just to save Czecho-Slovakia, anyway.'

'I've no great sympathy for them,' Mark agreed. 'They've not been blameless. They were the first nation to take arms against Versailles, against the very treaty which gave them a national existence. When Poland was at war with Russia in 1920, the Czechs took advantage of her preoccupation to seize Teschen, which Versailles had made a part of Poland. Now that chicken comes home to roost. Poland refuses to help the Czechs against Germany, or even to permit Russian troops to cross her territory to do so.'

'The newspapers are roasting Chamberlain for making the Czechs give in,' Tony commented.

Mark made it a point to read editorials from all across the country and he found them unanimous in damning England's surrender to Hitler. This was so even in the Middle West and in the South. The editors agreed that Mr. Chamberlain had only postponed the inevitable, and that, by doing so, England and France had suffered a tremendous loss of prestige. The *Washington Star* commented: 'No nation that scuttles a solemn mutual assistance pact as the French have welched on the Czech alliance can any longer aspire to the trust of other states, large or small'; and the *Richmond Times-Dispatch* said: 'The year 1938 will mark the beginning of the end of the British Empire, and the decline of France as a world power. Hitler's contempt for the great democracies has been justified.'

So what Tony said was true. 'I know,' Mark assented. 'I've read some of them.' But he did not wholly agree with the editors, and since it now appeared that war was at least postponed, he felt—for Tony's sake—an almost guilty gratitude to Mr. Chamberlain.

War would be the ultimate catastrophe, but the constant threat of war was almost as bad, clouding every mind. Tony could think of nothing else. The day he was to leave for Hanover to begin his Junior year—he would drive up with Will Ritchie—he and Mark sat long at breakfast together, and Mark said thoughtfully: 'You know, Tony, I believe you were right in saying Mr. Chamberlain was scared. England has almost no army and no real air force, and France, though she has a great army, has few modern planes.' And he added: 'I suspect that in any war against Germany, England might find the British Isles an untenable military position.'

'Well, anyway,' Tony said grimly, 'if they decide to have a war it's their business. They'll try to get us in, but there must be enough brains in this country to keep us out of it!'

'It's hard on boys your age,' Mark reflected. 'You face this thing much more directly than we older men. I wish you didn't have to. But the world's too small for us to stay out, son. Anything that happens over there is bound to affect us.'

'Well, we don't have to send an army over there!' Tony cried, his voice full of passion. 'I've grown up with this war coming nearer all the time, Dad! All the fellows have. And we hate it! We're not afraid to fight if we have to; but we'll not fight to settle Europe's squabbles.'

Mark said gravely: 'You can't dodge it, Tony. Nobody can dodge it. You might as well think straight.'

Tony laughed grimly. 'Think straight? I'm ready to go nuts, thinking about it.' And he said with a twisted frown: 'I know you're right, of course. I've heard the fellows talk about war for years. We kid ourselves by saying the United States will keep out, or that we'll refuse to fight or something; but we know that's not true.' His face set in hard lines. 'It's a hell of a thing to go through school and college knowing that you're due to go out and get killed before you can settle down to work and marry and live.' And he said: 'Our professors don't help much, telling us that the last war was a mess, built on lies and finished off with a rotten treaty.

'They keep telling us so, and everything we read says the same thing, and you fathers tell us the same thing, and yet we don't really believe it.' Mark watched his son with tender eyes, seeing the boy's perplexity, wishing to help. 'Inside, we're all right. I mean, fellows my age. If our country's going to fight, we really want to be in it. Our hearts do; but the trouble is, our heads keep saying our hearts are wrong! That's what keeps us so upset! That's why the psychiatrists are the busiest doctors in any college town. It's the fellows who think too much who crack up worst. The ones that don't think at all, but just go along wise-cracking about the lousy Germans, and Roosevelt, and Eleanor, and so on—they seem to be all right.'

Mark nodded. 'Thinking can be a torment,' he agreed. 'The happiest men today are probably the ones—there are lots of them—who believe everything Hitler does is wrong and everything England does is right. That simplifies the whole thing for them, settles all their problems. I can't do that. Sometimes I wish I could, but not often. Man is the rational animal, and also he is perhaps the only imaginative animal, with the capacity to put himself in the other fellow's place. So many things Hitler does are surely and hopelessly wrong—by our standards. But so are so many things the Eskimos do, or that the English do, for that matter. And I suppose there's no question that Hitler has improved the living conditions of eighty or ninety per cent of the German people.' He said gently: 'You sons aren't the only ones whose thoughts have been bad company these last years, Tony. About the time your mother died, I began to foresee the danger of another war.' He smiled in a strong affection. 'I think a lot of you, you know. It's been fairly tough for me to watch you grow up and to know what you might have to face.'

Tony grinned and came to lay his hand on his father's shoulder. 'I know. But—let's stop worrying. If there's a war, and we're in it, I'll be in it; but I can't do anything but wait, wait and do what I'm told. And —there's nothing you can do.'

'I wish there were,' Mark admitted. 'Not to save you from having to do your job when the time comes. Neither of us wants that. But if the job has to be done, I wish I could have a hand in it too.' He smiled slowly. 'The soldier's mind is at peace, at least, Tony. He doesn't have to make decisions, can leave all that to his superiors. That's not so bad.'

He was reluctant to say good-bye. When he left the house, Tony kissed him, clapped him on the shoulder. 'Don't worry more than you can help, Dad,' he urged. 'Whatever happens, it won't make any difference between you and me.'

10

(September 1938)

That afternoon a hurricane swept New England and there were trees down everywhere, and telephone lines were broken. The storm for a day or two almost crowded the European situation out of the papers; but Mark, once he had news that Tony was safe, was more concerned with the dispatches from abroad. When Britain laid Germany's peace terms before the Czechs, and the Czechs refused to agree to them, Mark damned them in his thoughts. He and Bob Ritchie met for lunch that day, and

Bob's matter-of-fact point of view was like a rock to which Mark could cling.

'Hitler's right, of course,' Bob declared. 'The Czechs are trying to hold on to something they never should have been given in the first place. You saw what Hitler said. "This Czech state began with one big lie and its father's name was Beneš." Now they're ready to commit national suicide, and throw the whole world into war to perpetuate that lie. But they're done for. Germany will take what she wants, and Poland will take back the territory around Teschen that the Czechs took from them twenty years ago, and Hungary will take a slice. There won't be enough left of Czecho-Slovakia to bait a mousetrap.'

Yet there were still days, running to almost a week, when Mark thought England might decide to fight after all. She agreed to back France and Russia in going to war if Hitler invaded Czecho-Slovakia —as he threatened to do unless his demands were met. President Roosevelt appealed to Hitler not to break off negotiations; Paris and London prepared to endure air raids; Mr. Roosevelt made another appeal. Hitler held his ground.

And then, when war within hours seemed sure, came the announcement that Hitler, Mussolini, Chamberlain, and Daladier would meet at Munich. On September thirtieth the headlines read: 'Peace Terms Signed.' The crisis at last was passed.

Saturday Mark drove Bob home from town. That day there was a Polish ultimatum to the Czechs, and Mark spoke of it. 'Poland's as bad as Hitler,' he commented.

'Worse,' Bob agreed. 'Hitler steals the pie and Poland trails along to pick up the crumbs.'

'The Czechs will have to give in.'

'There's no Czecho-Slovakia left,' Bob assured him. 'The meat's all gone. There's just a little gravy on the plate, and Hitler will mop that up whenever he's ready.'

Mark nodded. 'What do you think of this agreement between England and Germany?' he asked. 'Hitler and Chamberlain having a love feast, swearing that their two countries will never go to war with one another again, promising to use the consultation method to deal with any other questions that come up? If that means anything beyond a polite exchange of compliments, it means that they will hereafter settle all differences by negotiation rather than by war.'

'That's what it says,' Bob agreed. 'But it means more than that. It means that Hitler will now feel himself secure in the west. France can't attack him without England's help, and Chamberlain has promised to consult rather than to fight. So Hitler will think he can go ahead as he chooses in the east while he "consults" with England in the west.'

'It means that to me,' Mark assented. 'And yet I can't believe that England will actually give Hitler a free hand in the east.'

Bob grinned. 'Why, man,' he said derisively, 'what else can she do? Hitler told Chamberlain to put up or shut up, to fish or cut bait. England couldn't help the Czechs if she wanted to. If she's wise now, she'll get ready, not be caught with her pants down again.'

'Won't she feel bound by this promise of Chamberlain's?'

'No nation in the long run, is bound by anything but self-interest.'

Mark nodded regretfully. 'The London crowds gave Chamberlain a great reception,' he commented.

'Sure. Why wouldn't they? He saved their hides, and they knew it.'

'He says he brought them peace with honor.' Mark added quietly: 'But for the average man, the average man who pays the taxes and gets killed, there's no such thing as a dishonorable peace—or an honorable war.'

Bob nodded. 'Chamberlain says it's peace in our time,' he remarked in a weary scorn. 'The poor, flutter-witted, futile old man!'

VIII

Peace in Our Time

(October 1938–January 2, 1939)

I

(October 1938)

ON THE first anniversary of her marriage to Einar, Elin came to Mark, happy and proud, to tell him that in February she was to have a baby. Mark had known that some day this would happen, and he had half dreaded the disruption of his household which must result; but he forgot this now as he told her how glad he was.

'I am so glad, yes,' Elin agreed. 'But it is too bad, too.' She smiled apologetically. 'Because, you see, when it comes, Einar and I will want our own home.' She said in quick reassurance: 'Only I will bring my cousin here and show her everything how to take care of you and Tony. She is a good girl and a fine little cook and very neat and clean. Her name is Anna. It will be just the same as me.'

'No one can take your place,' Mark told her affectionately. 'But I'm as happy about this as you are. Happy for both of you.'

He congratulated Einar, too, and Einar grinned redly and declared that if the baby were a boy it should be named for Mark. Mark insisted that Elin engage a laundress and cleaning woman to take the heavier work off her hands during the months remaining. 'This baby is the first consideration now,' he reminded her. 'Nothing matters except to give him the best possible start in the world—and to make things comfortable for you.'

She protested, yet submitted to his insistence. He thought approaching motherhood became her. She wore a certain radiance as the days passed, and Einar seemed taller and stronger, he stood so straight and proud.

Mark, though he did not let Elin and Einar see how he dreaded her departure, felt the imminence of loneliness. He wished he might see Robin, but she was still in Montreal, where her mother's illness went its hopeless way. It was months since they had had an hour together. Mark had recognized for a while in her letters a definite reserve, as though she had been alarmed by the more personal tone which crept into his; but now when she wrote it was with an open affection, a frank friendliness. She wanted to see him soon again, she said, but it would not be possible until she came back to New York, and she could not do that while her mother lay desperately ill, while her father needed her so sadly.

Mark told her in one of his letters Elin's news. 'So my household will have to be reorganized,' he said. 'But Elin promises to bring a cousin in January and train her to fill Elin's place here.' Robin replied: 'I'm sorry for your sake, but glad for Elin's. I want to know her some day. She has always taken such good care of you.' Mark read into this word of hers a promise for the future which made him warmly happy. There was no longer any doubt in his mind that he loved Robin, that he wished to marry her.

But until she and Tony knew each other, he would not tell her so; for if by any chance Tony did not like her, then he must forget his dreams.

2

(November 1938)

During the month after Munich, Czech troops withdrew from the ceded territory, the Germans marched in, and Hitler said Christmas would be a festival of peace and began to negotiate with England for the limitation of armaments. He gave Lindbergh a decoration. Beneš resigned and fled to London. Poland and Hungary and Germany between them seized a third of Czecho-Slovakia, and a third of her people.

But these events, Mark reminded himself, were incidents. Back of Munich, back of all that had happened since, there was a fact; a fact which he sought to discover and to define. The fact he sought was the hidden reason for England's surrender. Fundamentally, he decided, England surrendered from necessity. The experts said over and over that, with Germany and presumably Italy on one side, and England, France, Czecho-Slovakia, and probably Russia on the other, Germany was sure to be beaten; but Mark did not agree, and neither, he was convinced, did Mr. Chamberlain. Not for the sake of peace alone would England have surrendered so completely.

For her surrender was complete. On November first, in the House of Commons, Mr. Chamberlain said that German must occupy the predominant position in central and southeastern Europe, and he declared that England had no wish to interfere. Mark thought Mr. Chamberlain's statement, coupled with the words of that document which he and Hitler had signed, meant that England was giving Hitler a free hand in the east; and he was confirmed in this feeling when Winston Churchill predicted that all the countries of central and eastern Europe would make the best terms they could with the Nazis.

His conviction that only Chamberlain's fear of England's defeat could explain his course at Munich led him into some discussions, heated on the other's side, with old Mr. Ritchie, Bob's father; and it brought about an open quarrel between him and Judge Sothern. A week after the November election, Professor Wearing invited Mark to dinner, and Judge Sothern and three other gentlemen were there. The Republicans had made modest gains in House and Senate, and those among the diners who disagreed with Mr. Roosevelt's internal policies thought this the beginning of a turn back to sane ways of life again; but after some discussion of political affairs the talk swung from Mr. Roosevelt's domestic program to his foreign policy. Early in October, the President had demanded that Japan respect the Open Door in China. Japan's reply was to warn the great powers of the world against continuing to send aid to China. The United States joined France and England in urging that the Yangtse River be reopened to commerce, but Japan flatly refused.

Professor Wearing thought Mr. Roosevelt was wrong to lay himself open to these rebuffs. 'There used to be a maxim in the days of our western frontier,' he reminded the others here, 'that you should never draw a gun on a man unless you were prepared to shoot. That's a cardinal principle in human affairs; never to threaten what you don't mean to try to perform. I suspect that our national prestige in the Far East is weakened by every protest Mr. Roosevelt makes—so long as his protests are not backed by action.'

Judge Sothern disagreed. 'The President is hampered by our national indifference,' he argued. 'We become hysterical on slight excuse——' He smiled. 'You remember the invasion from Mars two or three weeks ago and how the great radio audience reacted. We're easily excited about things near at hand, but we've no solid, intelligent national opinion in foreign affairs. As a nation, we don't really care what Japan does to China, or what Germany does to Czecho-Slovakia.'

Professor Wearing wagged his head. 'I'm afraid Mr. Roosevelt's too warlike for my taste,' he insisted. 'For a year now he's had us all on the edge of our chairs, wondering how soon we'll have to fight to back up his loose talk. Mr. Chamberlain chose a wiser course at Munich.'

Judge Sothern said warmly: 'War would have been the better choice there, better than that crime!'

Mark offered his opinion. 'I'm not so sure,' he suggested. 'It seems to me Mr. Chamberlain did the realistic thing. It's clear enough that his policy was based on a recognition of the fact that if war came, England might be beaten.'

Judge Sothern protested: 'England beaten! That's pure nonsense!'

Mark shook his head. 'I don't think so,' he insisted. 'And certainly Mr. Chamberlain doesn't think so. German submarines came within a whisper of starving England in the last war. Her subs and planes may do it in the next.'

'Aerial bombardment doesn't win wars,' the other retorted. 'That was proved in Spain!'

'I don't mean that,' Mark explained. 'I mean air attacks on freighters. With long-range bombers, Germany can fly a patrol around the British Isles, and a bomb doesn't have to score a direct hit on a freighter to sink her. England can be starved.'

Judge Sothern colored with anger, and he insisted so strenuously on England's strength that Mark was put on his mettle. He remained perfectly good-humored, but he was persistent too.

'If England goes to war,' he predicted, 'victory will be decided in the Atlantic. England is an island, not self-supporting. Her ships are her life line. If that life line can be cut, the day may come when she will have to surrender at discretion.'

He was so intent on making his point clear, referring to his own flying experiences, describing how easy it was for even a novice like himself to handle a plane, and how deadly that plane might be, that he did not realize Judge Sothern's temper was at the snapping point till the other said harshly:

'You'd better take a trip to Berlin, my friend, and claim your decoration, like Lindbergh! Hitler must count you a first-rate advocate.'

Mark was instantly silent, regretful that he had driven the other to make such a remark. Professor Wearing quickly took the conversation in hand, and when the others presently departed, he kept Mark behind, and he said in a tolerant tone:

'Don't take Judge Sothern too seriously, Mark. He's always a partisan

—even on the bench; and his mind has cooled and hardened in the mold, is no longer flexible.'

Mark smiled. 'He's not unique in that. Most of the men I know are so completely hostile to Germany that they can't even give her credit for fighting power; and they damn as pro-German anyone who concedes to Germany a certain martial capacity.'

'Some of them do it to avoid having to face facts,' the other suggested.

'It's war psychology,' Mark pointed out. 'Even Mr. Chamberlain is now being accused of being pro-German. I suppose any man who thinks Germany might be a dangerous enemy must keep his thoughts to himself —or risk offending his friends.'

He hoped the breach between him and Judge Sothern would be quickly healed; but it was not. When they next met in the Court House, the other passed Mark with a hostile glance. New German persecution of the Jews by that time had aroused American newspapers and periodicals to universal indignation, and Mr. Roosevelt condemned these fresh outrages and recalled the American ambassador to report upon conditions in Germany. Hitler retaliated in kind. There had been a time in the past when the recall of ambassadors was a prelude to war; and Mr. Roosevelt must have meant the gesture as another of those empty threats which Mark thought beneath the dignity of the United States.

He sought to find, for the sake of his own peace of mind, some formula; some statement of what he himself believed our foreign policy should be; and one evening a word from Bob Ritchie helped focus his thoughts. Bob had come in after dinner to sit awhile and talk of casual things; and Mark spoke of Judge Sothern's attitude. Bob laughed. 'Father's almost as bad,' he said.

'I know,' Mark agreed. 'I've learned not to argue with him.'

'He's more rabid than ever since Germany started after the Jews again,' Bob explained. 'But I don't much blame the Germans. In the inflation period, the Jews got hold of everything in Germany that was for sale. They didn't produce anything. They didn't work. They just traded, dickered, bought and sold. They still own half the real estate in Berlin, and they own a lot more than their share of all the capital wealth in Germany. So naturally the Germans hate them.'

'That doesn't excuse pogroms,' Mark pointed out.

'No, but it explains them.'

Mark abandoned the point. 'What I'm trying to figure out,' he confessed, 'is what I want to see done by the United States. Germany's

internal affairs are—as far as any active interference by us is concerned
—her own business. But Germany's external policies may lead to war, to
a general European war. What's our part then?'

'Stay out of it.' Bob was definite.

'Suppose we can't.'

'We can if we want to. We fell for the old palaver once, but we
won't again.'

'Suppose we do stay out and England is beaten?'

'Then she takes her licking, that's all.'

'I don't know.' Mark shook his head. 'I've no brief for England; but
I'd hate to see her licked.'

Bob laughed. 'Why?' he challenged.

'Well, we'll pass that. But—what should the United States do if she
sees England in trouble?'

'Why, stay out, mind her own business.'

'Mr. Roosevelt won't do that.'

'I know. He's bound to put his oar in! Hitler told him to keep out
of the Czech mess. That was good advice.' Bob said strongly. 'Why,
Mark, the next big war is going to knock hell out of every country that
gets into it. If we tend to our own troubles, we'll be all right; but if we
stick our nose in, we'll be busted higher than a kite.'

Mark was not satisfied. 'I don't believe in our interfering,' he admitted. 'But I do believe we ought to get ready to meet what's coming,
somehow. We ought to be working out in our minds now a peace program. Suppose you were a world dictator and wished to lay down conditions which would have some chance of leading to a permanent peace?'

Bob shook his head. 'I wouldn't take the job.'

'It's a job the United States may have to take on. Even if we don't
fight in the war that's coming, we'll be able to dictate the peace, simply
by our economic power. We ought to be deciding what our idea of a
world set-up is going to be.'

But he could not lead Bob into any discussion of such abstractions. 'I
say we tend to our knitting, tend to our own business, let them tend to
theirs,' Bob insisted. 'We had one try at reforming the world and made
a mess of it and damned near went broke in the process. That ought to
be enough.' And he said more strongly: 'Why, man, our foreign trade
isn't ten per cent of our national business. We could build a wall around
this country and keep the world out and still get along fine.'

Mark smiled. 'The Chinese tried that once.'

'They didn't make it stick. We could.'

'Suppose someone climbed the wall?'

'Who? How? Why? We'd toss them outside again.'

'With what? We've no real army.'

'We could get one damned soon.'

Mark said in faint irritation: 'You talk like Bryan. A nation can't spring to arms overnight unless there are arms to spring to.'

'Well, we might build up a big reserve of planes and submarines,' Bob conceded. 'That's all we'd need.'

Mark looked at him thoughtfully. 'You know,' he said, 'I've been thinking along the same lines. Maybe you've got something there! Maybe a tremendous program of preparedness is our best immediate policy.'

'Sure. Let's build our Chinese wall out of submarines and aeroplanes.'

Mark smiled at his own thought. 'I'd like to see you try to sell that idea in the Middle West, to my father, for instance. I mean, the idea of spending a lot of money on preparedness. But he'd be all for the Chinese wall angle.'

Bob said in matter-of-fact tones: 'Sure. Say we build enough stuff so that if anyone tried to play in our yard we can take them apart. So they don't try. So we don't get into any war. Let the rest of them fight it out, and then we'll pull our chair up to the peace table and say: "All right, boys! This was your war, but it's our peace. Here's what you'll do—or else!"'

'We'd need a program, need to know what that peace should be.'

'There's time enough,' Bob said confidently. 'The war isn't started yet, much less ended. But one thing sure, we ought to start right now to prepare, to get in training, so when the time comes we can speak our piece and make them listen. That's our ticket now.'

Mark did not agree with all Bob said; but he began thereafter to be increasingly sure that we should prepare for war.

3

(November 1938)

Tony came home for Thanksgiving, and Mark thought there was a change in him, even in these short weeks. A certain boyishness had vanished. His lips set in a firmer line. It was hard for Mark to remember that his son was only nineteen. When they talked together, the boy seemed as mature as he, as old and as wise.

And Tony was bitterly convinced that war was coming. 'All the fellows think so,' he said. 'It's the same old story. England will never let any European power get strong enough to challenge her, not if she can help it. In the last war she enlisted a lot of allies, let them do most of the fighting, and then grabbed for herself most of the loot. She'll do it again if she can.'

Mark said thoughtfully: 'I'm in a curious confusion, Tony. I don't like England. The time I spent over there as a boy is probably responsible for that. Everyone we met was friendly, nice to us, did pleasant things for us; but I hated the things I saw. Miserable poverty everywhere; the rich running the country, every man tipping his hat to his "superiors."' His tone was dry with scorn. 'And expecting his "inferiors" to pay him an equal courtesy. Most men can't even own real property—or couldn't then. They lease—a ninety-nine-year lease—from the big landowners; and they improve the land, perhaps build on it; and their sons do the same, and their grandsons—and when the lease expires, the landowner can take back the land with all they've done to it, and all their buildings. Then the ordinary man has one vote, where the rich man may have twenty. At least it was so at that time, though I think that's been modified. There were a thousand things that irritated Father and Mother—and of course me.'

'But damn it, Tony, bad as England is, I don't want to see her licked.'

'Oh, she won't be licked,' Tony sardonically assured him. 'She'll get France to fight for her, and Belgium, and Russia, and the United States —and then she'll take the gravy. After the last war, England got 2,400,000 square miles of territory. France got Alsace Lorraine—less than 6000 square miles—and some of Africa; and Italy got a little. But England took the cream, and all the United States got out of it was some promises to pay the money we'd lent them—and they broke those promises.' He added harshly: 'They got us into the war with lies—about German atrocities and all that; and they'll do it again. We'll lose a few billion dollars and a few million men—and be left again to hold the bag.'

'It's hard now to know what's coming,' Mark suggested. 'But one thing seems to me certain. If Chamberlain had thought England could win, he'd have gone to war in September.'

'I wish he had,' Tony declared, in a strange weariness. 'I'm getting tired of the waiting, Dad.'

Tony had come home the night before Thanksgiving, and at his suggestion they went next morning to the airport and Tony flew for an hour. Mr. Hadden rode once around the field with him for a check flight, then let him go alone.

'He's a flier, that lad,' he told Mark as they watched Tony take off. 'A fine light touch, a feeling for it.'

'He's kept it up,' Mark assented. 'Flies a little, right along.'

'You've not been flying yourself lately.'

'No.' Mark smiled. 'I've gone as far as I can without owning a plane.' He had not flown, in fact, since he began to be more and more frequently conscious of that heavy thumping in the region of his heart. He accepted it as a warning that there were some things he had better not do. He had sometimes considered seeing Doctor Hethering, but he postponed the day, assuring himself that his imagination was at least halfway responsible for the discomfort he sometimes felt. He and Hadden watched Tony in the air, and Mark said—remembering Hadden was an Englishman—that war for a while had seemed near.

Hadden nodded grimly. 'Yes,' he assented. 'They're working up to the big show again.'

'I remember you were in it last time.'

'Yes.' Hadden's tone was curt, and Mark looked at him sidewise and saw his lips set hard. Then the other spoke. 'I was in it,' he repeated. 'So were a million or two others, fine lads, a lot of them friends of mine. Most of them were dead before we saw the end of it. Not of their own fault, not even war's fault, but because some fat, comfortable staff man looked at his map and put a little pencil mark on it, at a place he'd never seen, and said: "Do so and so here at dawn tomorrow." I'll never get into another mess like that.'

Mark thought Hadden sounded astonishingly like Tony, and he wondered how old the other was. Forty, certainly. 'I was in the infantry,' he said quietly. 'The war was an impersonal thing for me. Only once or twice did I actually see any Germans except prisoners, and they were far away, out of small-arm range. I didn't fire a shot, except at targets. But men were killed all around me, just the same. I was wounded myself— by the misdirected fire of one of our own batteries.'

'I'll have no part in it another time,' Hadden repeated. 'No part.' There was an extraordinary emphasis in the simple words. Then Hadden added: 'I told you how near I came to a court. The same thing happened to my brother. He was an artillery officer. Staff sent him orders to move his battery to a position that was more exposed and at the same time less effective! He argued, but they insisted, so he obeyed orders, moved the guns—and the Germans spotted them and the guns were destroyed and most of his men were killed inside twenty-four hours. I've seen like things happen a hundred times. Half the men killed in any war are killed by the mistakes of their own officers. No, I'll have no part of it.'

Mark met the other's eyes, smiled in a friendly way. 'I wonder if you mean that,' he said.

Hadden after a moment grinned almost shamedly. 'I hope I do!' he declared. 'I hope to God I do.'

Tony when he landed urged Mark to take the plane up for a while, but Mark put him off, and they started for home. On the way, after a silence, Tony asked quietly: 'Dad, do you feel all right?'

'Of course. Why?'

'Well—you're not flying. And sometimes I have a hunch you don't feel so good.'

'I'm fine,' Mark insisted. That turbulence in the region of his heart was surely nothing. 'Don't worry about me.'

Tony affectionately touched his father's arm. 'Well, all right,' he said, 'But—take care of yourself. Sometimes when you're just sitting, thinking, or maybe reading, you look—sort of tired.'

'I am, sometimes,' Mark confessed. 'Probably I think too much about what's happening in Europe.'

'Worrying about my getting into it?'

Mark said quietly: 'I know you'll do your job, son, whatever it is.'

'I'll hate it, but I'll do it,' Tony assented. He laughed, shook his head. 'But quit worrying about it, Dad. It's not good for you. I don't want anything to happen to you.' His tone was light and he was still grinning. 'You and I have to stick together, you know.'

'We always have,' Mark cheerfully agreed. 'We're all right, son.'

For Thanksgiving dinner they went to the Ritchies'. Betty had not yet come downstairs when they arrived, but the others were there. Mark saw Jan as always with an affectionate pleasure. She was seventeen now, and prettier every day, with a pleasant play of color in her hair; and her freckles had disappeared. She linked her arm in his, and Tony told her about his flying that morning, and Will said he would have gone with them to the airport if he had known their plans, and dinner was announced, and Bob called upstairs to Betty. They were all seated before she came down to take the chair beside Mark, facing Tony. There was a smooth, hard perfection about her which always made Mark uncomfortable. While Bob was carving, she said to Tony:

'I saw Barb Parks at the dance the night before the Yale-Princeton game!' Her tone was maliciously amused. 'You've got a rival. She danced all evening with the same man!'

Tony grinned. 'Whoever he was, he knows how to pick them,' he said amiably. 'Barb's swell!'

'If you'd been there you'd have been wild. His name's Huston. If she elopes with him, or something, don't say I didn't warn you.'

Her intent to make Tony unhappy was so manifest that Jan said resentfully: 'Old silver tongue! What a two-spot you are, Betty!'

And Tony drawled: 'Don't worry, Bet.' She was always infuriated when anyone called her by this diminutive, and it was his revenge. 'Barb and I are O.K. She came up to the Cornell game.'

'She's swell, Tony,' Jan loyally declared. 'Betty's just trying to get a rise out of you.'

Mark, too, had resented Betty's gibe, and he was grateful for Jan's partisanship. After dinner he had a chance to tell her how well he liked her. There was a plan afoot to go skating on the pond. Betty had asked Frank Parks to join them, and they had scarce left the table when he arrived, with Lucy Pride and a boy named Sam something or other, whom Mark had never seen before, and Dan Pride, Lucy's brother. Mark thought it was characteristic of Lucy to have three boys in tow. She was almost extravagantly lovely, and when she came in now, her cheeks glowing, the tempo of the moment seemed to quicken excitingly. She was at once the focus of the scene, and after the first greetings she told them:

'We've been having the most wonderful discussion coming over. About talents!' She turned to Mark, came near him in the way she had of drawing close to any man to whom she spoke. 'Don't you think everyone has some particular talent, Judge Worth? Yours is law, of course, and so is Mr. Ritchie's, and Frank's going to be a Communist. Dan . . .' she made a face at her brother. 'Dan's only talent is to sit on sofas and smoke too many cigarettes, but Sam's going to be a doctor, and of course Tony will be a lawyer, and Will too.'

Will said, grinning: 'How about an aesthetic dancer?' His awkwardness still persisted, and defensively he now made a joke of it. They all smiled, and Lucy chattered on: 'And Betty, we decided that you'll be a great artist, a sculptress or something, and they all say I'll surely go on the stage! Of course it's just a game; but I think it's fun deciding what your talent is, don't you?'

Jan said in exaggerated despair: 'You've fitted out everyone but me,

Lucy! Can't I please have a talent too? Even if it's just for washing dishes?'

Everyone laughed, and Betty sent Will to find her skates, and in the flurry of preparation Mark spoke to Jan, his arm affectionately across her shoulders.

'I think I know your talent, Jan. I think you'll make some man a wonderful wife.'

The others were all talking at once, and no one had heard him. Jan looked up at him, her cheeks warm, her eyes shining. She said happily: 'I'd rather have that talent than any of the others.'

The pond was not a hundred yards away; and they went trooping out, laden with skates and hockey sticks. Jan was the last to go, and Nell called her back for a word of warning. 'Don't start a fight with Lucy, Jan. You always bristle when she's around.'

Jan said flatly: 'I know it. I hate her. She's a free neck! G'bye!' She whirled away.

Mark chuckled. 'Jan's a great kid, Nell.'

'She's crazy about Tony, of course,' Nell reminded him. 'Always has been.' And she said: 'His case on Barbara Parks has lasted a long time, hasn't it?'

'They seem to have a good time together,' Mark agreed. 'But it's an unsentimental affair, no foolishness on either . . .'

'What will you do when he gets married?'

He smiled. 'I needn't start worrying yet! Tony has college to finish, and law school.'

'If he wants to get married before that, you'll finance him,' she predicted. Mark knew this was true. He could afford to finance Tony's marriage, and he would want to do it. He believed in early marriages— if a boy were marrying the right girl. 'And then you'll be left flat alone,' Nell reminded him. 'Tony fills your life now, but it will be empty when he marries. You ought to get married again. You're a natural husband!' He smiled, and she exclaimed in a startled amusement: 'Heavens, Bob! He's blushing! I believe he's been looking around!'

Mark managed a disarming laugh. 'Time enough to think of that when Tony's . . .'

'Why wait?' she protested, interrupting him as she was apt to do. 'Tony's away at college all winter.'

'He'll live at home when he's in law school. I want to keep things comfortable for him.'

'A wife wouldn't make things less comfortable,' she insisted. 'And you can't wait forever. You're getting along, you know. Your hair's just a little thin in spots already.'

Mark for a moment did not speak, half minded to tell these old friends about Robin. There was no longer any question in his mind that if it were possible, he would persuade Robin to marry him. Perhaps it was his years, the fact that youth was behind him, that age was approaching, which had made him feel of late incomplete, as though he had still a function to fulfill. He had Tony, and Tony was fine; but a man was made to father many sons. Suppose war came, and Tony were lost; then when he himself died his line would end. He remembered reading somewhere that apple trees, if they thought themselves about to die, bore fruit. There was this deep instinct in all living things, to perpetuate themselves. Flowers, cut back in midsummer, were apt to hurry to a second blooming, as though, foreseeing their own ends, they feared their task of reproduction was not yet done. And it was so with men and women. When war's shadow lay across the world as it did now, lovers drew together; and marriages came in a rising flood. Everywhere men, facing the possibility of death, hastened to perpetuate the life in them.

He felt the urge to paternity strong in him now. He wanted Robin, and marriage. Yet what Nell said was true. His hair was a little thin in spots. He was forty-six years old. He had never asked Robin how old she was, but she was certainly years younger than he. So he must hurry, hurry, hurry. Perhaps it was already too late.

He laughed at Nell, and told her all women were matchmakers; but he decided to see Robin soon, as soon as possible. If she did not presently return to New York, he would go to Montreal.

He said good-bye and went home and at dusk Tony brought the young people in, and Elin gave them scrambled eggs and milk and cokes and they stayed awhile. Jan had not come with them, and Mark guessed that she had had her fill of Lucy. The others presently departed, and Tony yawned comfortably.

'I'm sleepy,' he confessed. 'Too much dinner, and then outdoors all afternoon.' Nevertheless, he sat awhile before going upstairs to bed, and Mark, his misgivings about Barbie revived by what Betty had said, wondering how much Tony would be hurt if Barb preferred another, asked: 'Are you and Barbie as good friends as ever?'

'Better,' Tony assured him. 'Better friends all the time, Dad.' He looked at his father in a quick, shy way. 'We have a mighty wholesome friendship,' he said. 'Nothing sentimental about it. You see, Dad, I know we can't be married for a long time, and if we go ahead too fast, we'd spoil it. I mean if we got engaged now, even with just the two of us knowing it, there'd be a long wait, and we'd be—well, it wouldn't work out.' He hesitated. 'But Barbie likes me better than she likes anyone else. I know that. If we still feel the same way by the time I'm in Law School, maybe we'll get engaged then.'

'She seems like a fine girl,' Mark said carefully. 'Of course I don't know her well.' He lighted a cigarette. 'She gets through college this year, doesn't she?'

'Yes, she's two years older than I am.' Tony smiled confidently. 'But I don't think that makes any difference. Do you?'

'It needn't,' Mark assured him. He said approvingly: 'You're taking a finely sensible point of view, Tony. I like the way you're keeping your head.'

'Oh, we're not going to make darned fools of ourselves,' Tony assured him. 'Barb's got a level head too.'

He went off to bed and Mark sat awhile alone; and he added a postscript to his letter to Robin. Her answer came a week later. She wrote that her mother had died the day before. 'I'll be back in New York next week,' she said. 'And oh, Mark, I do want to see you. It's been a long time. Come over soon.'

4

(December 1938)

Before he went to New York, made wary by his own eagerness, Mark warned himself to go slowly. Robin's last letter had filled him with a strong impatience, and with something like a certainty that this long separation had worked in her as it had in him, drawing them together. But—she and Tony had never met; and Mark meant that they should. Tony was in Hanover. To summon him to New York, or to take Robin to Hanover, was like a declaration of his hopes from which Mark shrank. Better if these two could meet somehow casually, so that if Tony did not like her, Mark himself would not have been committed. It was clear in his mind that he would never marry Robin without Tony's complete approval.

He took the Saturday night train to New York, waited till ten o'clock to telephone Robin, and asked then doubtfully:

'Did I wake you?'

'Heavens, no. I've been sitting on the phone for two hours! Where are you?' He told her and she said: 'I wish you could come here, but the place is in a mess. I haven't had time to straighten things up, so I'll come to you.' And she suggested: 'Meet me at the Plaza in half an hour and we'll walk up an appetite.'

He found himself smiling absurdly at the telephone, even after he had hung up the receiver. He was at the rendezvous before her. When she appeared, coming toward him with outstretched hands, he looked at her in a startled surprise, and for a moment could not speak. She asked:

'Am I late?'

He shook his head. He said: 'You've cut your hair!'

She smiled. 'Yes, of course.' And she challenged: 'Like it?'

'I don't know. Why did you do it?'

Incredibly, she blushed, her cheeks suffused, confusion in her eyes. 'I—just thought I would,' she said, and she insisted: 'Don't you like it?'

'It makes you look younger—like a child.'

'I hoped you'd like it.'

'I probably will, when I get used to it.' He laughed a little. 'I'm still—surprised,' he admitted. 'It's hard to tell. You're so different. I hardly know you!'

She laughed and touched that faint scar on her lip, lifting her face nearer his to let him see the better. 'You can tell me by this.'

He wished to take her in his arms, but he said carefully: 'You look well, not tired.'

'I'm not,' she assured him. 'Come along.'

They went out into the fine sun of a December day, crossing to the park, walking at first in silence. The pond was frozen over, and she said: 'See, your typical New Yorkers—the ducks, remember—have gone South for the winter.'

'How's your father?' He resented his own tone, unnaturally restrained; but seeing her again, more beautiful than he remembered, more surely youthful now, had filled him with a sense of the folly of his thoughts of her.

'He's well,' she said. 'It will be harder for him later. It was a long strain, you know. He hasn't quite realized Mother is gone.'

They walked on, silent, his strides lengthening in his abstraction so that she had difficulty in keeping pace with him, till she protested laughingly: 'Is there a fire?'

He chuckled and slowed his pace, and she asked: 'Have you been well?'

'Oh, yes.' He added: 'I've been pretty steamed up over Munich and the rest of it, of course. I see Daladier is having trouble with the labor problem in France. Something like martial law, forced labor. Remember what you once said about the Frenchman hating the thought of war?'

She asked in a mischievous amusement: 'Oh, are we going abroad again?'

He laughed and said he was sorry, and asked whether she had heard Anthony Eden speak here in New York a few days before, but she had been in Montreal at the time. Then she said he seemed to be more dignified than he had been, and then she cried: 'Oh, but I forgot, you're a judge now, aren't you? Will you let me see you sometime in all the grandeur of your robes?'

So they laughed together, and Mark, more at ease, forgot the new thing he sensed in her. After an hour they turned back, and she said she was starving. At table, since now they faced each other, he saw again how changed she was. He had not realized she was so young. He had known it, but knowledge and realization are not always the same. With her heavy hair braided and coiled, she had always seemed to him a woman, mature and poised and serene; but now she might have been eighteen, and he was made conscious of the gulf between them. Till now, he had been able to ignore it, but he could not ignore it now. He felt older than his years as she seemed younger than hers, and a sense of loss oppressed him. She saw this, said at last, laughing at him and yet with something rueful in her tone: 'Don't wear such a long face. You're looking at my hair, but I can let it grow again.' She made a little grimace. 'It's a joke on me. I was so sure you'd like it.'

'I think I will, give me time,' he promised.

She watched him for a moment in a grave, scrutinizing fashion, so that he knew her thoughts were far away; and then she said, as much to herself as to him: 'I really had it cut because being with Mother so long made me feel old, and when I got back here I wanted to be ever so young and gay again. It wasn't just to please you.' She smiled, said quickly, in a different tone: 'I don't know what Father will say to it when I go back up there next week.'

'Go back?'

'Yes, to be with him over Christmas.'

'Oh, of course.' He asked in quick concern: 'Will you stay on there, live there now?'

'No, no, I'll come back here after New Year's. He'll be all right then.'

He recognized, in her plan an opportunity to arrange for her and Tony to meet. 'See here,' he suggested. 'Why not come back by way of Boston, spend a few days there?'

Her eyes widened faintly, and after a moment she asked in a low, cautious tone: 'Why?'

'Well—you might have a "one-man show" at one of the galleries,' he suggested. 'Tony would enjoy seeing you again.'

'It's not "again," ' she reminded him, watching him smilingly, yet alertly too. 'I've never actually seen him, you know.' She laughed. "I've almost begun to think he's imaginary, doesn't exist at all!'

'You ought to show some of your things over there,' he urged, unwilling to confess his real purpose, half afraid to alarm her, sensing the vigilance in her. 'You'd build up a wider market.'

'I don't know about the show,' she decided, her eyes on him thoughtfully. 'But I might come home by way of Boston, stop long enough to let you and Tony take me to lunch.'

'Fine!' Mark agreed. 'It's a date. Let's set a day.'

'Well, I could plan to be in Boston the day after New Year's; but I ought to come on here on the five-o'clock.'

Mark chuckled in a great elation. Elaborately he made a memorandum in his notebook, speaking the words aloud. 'January 2. Robin, Tony, Lunch.' And he added with pretended gravity: 'Just so I won't forget.' They laughed together, yet there was a reticent uncertainty in her laughter too. He asked: 'Sure you can't stay over a few days?'

'I'm afraid not. I'm anxious to get back to work. I'm planning to do some work while I'm in Montreal, in fact; some watercolors, snow scenes and skiing and so on. I'll go to some ski place, wherever I can find the best snow.'

They lingered long, and afterward they walked down the Avenue together. Her cheeks were glowing in the crisp chill of coming dusk, and Mark's heart warmed at the sight of her. Yet he felt in her more and more clearly a reserve and a reluctance which disturbed him. Her letters in these last weeks had been full of eagerness to see him, and when they met she was bright with happiness; but little by little that radiance had faded, shadowed by some thought he could not read. He thought she might guess what he hoped from this Boston visit, might dread hurting him when the moment she foresaw should come. He knew her fondness for him, and yet it would not be surprising if she remembered sometimes that he was old, that she was young.

He was to take the five-o'clock, and they said good-bye at the entrance to her apartment. She asked him then, directly, watching him with grave, honest eyes:

'Mark, why do you want me to come to Boston? You didn't tell me, but—you did make rather a point of it!'

He dared not tell her the truth. 'Why—no particular reason,' he evaded. 'But Tony will enjoy meeting you.' He added almost sadly: 'With your hair short, you don't look any older than he.'

'You don't like my hair short, do you?' Her eyes were still and remote, her thoughts her own.

'It changes you so much it scares me,' he confessed, trying to laugh.

She stood uncertainly for a moment, but then as though in decision she said: 'Well, I'll see you in Boston, Mark. I'll wire you from Montreal.' She held out her hand, smiling again. 'And don't be scared,' she said. 'I kept the braids. I can pin them on, so I'll look the same.'

Then she was gone.

5

(December 1938)

Through the weeks till Christmas, Italy trumpeted her claims in Africa, and Chamberlain said England would fight to preserve the Mediterranean *status quo;* and in a new defense of his course at Munich he said that the alternative had been war with Germany, Italy, Japan, and possibly insurgent Spain. The Commons at his request appropriated a hundred million dollars to armor British homes against aerial bombardment. Mr. Ickes in a speech at Cleveland said German culture had reverted to the centuries when men were 'unlettered, benighted and bestial.' Germany demanded an apology and Assistant Secretary of State Welles retorted that Mr. Ickes had expressed American public opinion. The Atlantic squadron was put in readiness to defend the American coast, and a tremendous rebel drive began in Spain. War clouds everywhere darkened the sky.

Mark, looking forward to the holidays, had anticipated a rich fortnight with Tony, in which Robin should have a part; but Tony arrived with other plans already made.

'A bunch of us are going to Canada for some skiing, the day after Christmas,' he told his father during his first evening at home. 'I knew you wouldn't mind. Joe Hazen knows a slick place up there, an inn north of Montreal.'

'How long will you be gone?'

'Oh, just four or five days.' Tony had heard the doubts in his father's voice. 'Is that all right?'

'I want you here for New Year's,' Mark confessed.

'Anything special?'

Mark felt his cheek hot with embarrassment. He laughed, evading a reply. 'I like to have you here.'

'We'll be back, sure.' And Tony explained: 'Barb's going; she and Frank, and Lucy Pride and Dan, and Keith and Beth Warren.' They were a young married couple. 'And Mike Vernon—his father's a professor at Hanover—and Ingrid Sigurdson and Joe Hazen and me.'

'Who's Miss Sigurdson?' Hers was the only name which Mark found unfamiliar.

'Ingrid? Oh, haven't I told you about her? She's great! She's a Norwegian girl, a great skier. Mike Vernon met her over there when he lived in Switzerland, and she came to this country to ski this winter and came to Hanover to see him and she's been staying with the Vernons ever since.'

'Sounds as though she were engaged to Mike?'

'No, but he's been in Norway, knows her folks, and Mrs. Vernon likes her. She's the best woman on skis I ever saw. She's a swell girl! She's pretty, and husky, and she's been going off skiing with crowds of fellows all winter and I've never heard anyone make a dirty crack about her. That gives you an idea. She does a lot of things an American girl couldn't do and get away with it; but the way she does it, you never think anything about it.'

'It sounds like a grand party,' Mark assented. He was trying not to show his disappointment at the prospect of losing a week of Tony's vacation, but Tony caught the shadow in his tones.

'See here,' he urged, 'why don't you come along, Dad? There are good practice slopes, and you'd have a swell time. You need a rest, anyway.'

Mark had done some skiing. When he went to Hanover to see Tony, as he liked to do on an occasional winter week-end, he was apt to spend a few hours on the hills. Also, Robin was an enthusiast, and he had sometimes thought of trying to learn more about the sport in order to share her pleasure in it. He remembered that she had said she planned to do some skiing during her stay in Montreal, and it occurred to him that if he went with Tony he might see her. He might even suggest that she come to this same inn to which Tony planned to go. But the thought of going to Canada with Tony's group of youngsters, of introducing Robin to all of them, was alarming.

'I'm too busy,' he confessed. 'I want to come to Hanover for a weekend in February, over the twenty-second. We'll save it for then.'

He wished to tell Tony what he and Robin had planned, but he did not. There was time enough for that. To speak of it so far in advance would be to give that prospective luncheon an excessive importance in Tony's eyes. Mark wished this meeting upon which so much depended to be on the surface a casual affair.

Christmas morning was always for them both a lonely time. They missed Nan more then than on other days; but each of them, to hide this from the other, put on an extra cheerfulness of manner, an elaborately vocal gratitude for the gifts they mutually exchanged. The Ritchies came for Christmas dinner, and afterward they all went to call on those of their friends who kept open house; but Tony came home early to pack, and to assemble his skiing gear for his departure. Early Christmas evening Mark drove him to town to join the others of his party and to catch the Montreal train.

Mark stayed to see the train pull out. He had an astonishing sense of loss in that departure; and he thought it would seem long till Tony returned.

6

(December 1938)

The inn of which Tony had spoken was small, open only to old patrons and their friends, accessible only by automobile, and with accommodations for about twenty people. It stood on the crest of a steep hill with abrupt slopes on two sides and more gentle descents to the south and east. From it ski trails radiated in several directions. The longest, never worse than a fifteen per cent grade, descended for almost two miles paralleling the road; and a car shuttled back and forth, carrying skiers from the bottom to the top. There were three steeper trails, but except on the longest, you earned your downhill runs by an arduous climb.

The living room of the inn was two stories high, with balconies that admitted to the bedrooms on the second floor, in radiating wings. The big fireplace, big enough to take four-foot logs, dominated the room. There was a wide leather couch in front of it. Girls, sitting on this couch, were apt to curl up in a ball, their legs under them. Men, if they used it at all, sprawled at ease.

Tony's group, this first evening, after a long afternoon on the slopes, clustered upon the couch or threw cushions on the floor in front of it; and some of the younger guests joined them in an easy friendliness. Lucy Pride had a pleasant singing voice, warm and husky and true; and she sat on the bearskin rug before the fire and thrummed a guitar and sang, and the others joined sometimes in the choruses. The keeper of the inn, a fat old Frenchman with a bald head and a beaming smile, came to add a fresh log to the fire, and Lucy captured him and made him teach them to sing 'Allouette,' with all the wicked verses added; and they sang louder and louder, with much stamping of the feet and shouting. Then Joe Hazen opened the piano, badly out of tune, and someone began to dance, and Lucy sat on top of the piano and imitated Helen Morgan and sang 'Just My Bill' directly at Tony with such extravagant emotion in her tones that everyone laughed with delight and Tony blushed to his ears.

After a while they began to grow sleepy and to drift away, but Barbie did not go, so Tony too stayed; and the time came when they were the only ones remaining. The old Frenchman put another log on the fire and bade them good night. The fire seized the fresh fuel with a crackling gusto, and slowly a hush drew all about them, and they spoke in low tones, as though afraid of disturbing the sleepers everywhere near-by. Barbie was in a corner of the couch, her legs tucked under her, her eyes shining in the firelight. Tony sat in a deep chair beside her, content to watch her while they talked.

'I'm glad you didn't go to bed,' he said. 'Some fun, being here together?'

'Some fun,' she agreed, smiling sleepily.

'Old M'sieu Beaulieu is great, isn't he?' It was Monsieur Beaulieu who had taught them to sing 'Allouette.' Barbie did not answer, and Tony began to sing under his breath, and she laughed and said:

'Wrong key, Tony! You never could carry a tune.'

'People are too bigoted about tunes,' he said comfortably. 'Always singing 'em the same way! I like 'em different every time. I like 'em the way I sing 'em!'

She asked, watching the fire: 'Do you like Lucy's voice?'

'Sure.'

Her eyes touched his. 'Do you like Lucy?'

'I guess everybody does.' He chuckled. 'Except Jan Ritchie. The kid's hardly civil to her.'

'Oh, I saw Betty Ritchie at the Yale-Princeton dance. She's lovely, isn't she?'

'I guess so. I never thought so much of her looks.' He remembered what Betty had said about that dance, and about the man named Huston who had given Barb such a rush; and to avoid any appearance of curiosity he changed the subject, said thoughtfully: 'You know, I was talking before dinner with that fellow who's up here from Montreal, Mr. Green. Canadians aren't half so worked up about the war as we are.' He talked on, and she watched him with still eyes, till he said laughingly: 'You're not listening, but I don't blame you. This is too swell to spoil by worrying about wars.'

She said contritely: 'I didn't mean not to listen. I was thinking about something else.'

'That's what I like about being with you. It's so darned comfortable! We always could be quiet together and not talk at all and still have a good time.'

She met his eyes. 'We've been mighty good friends, haven't we, Babe?'

He nodded contentedly. 'Sure have!' Then he chuckled. 'You know, you're the only one who ever calls me that.'

'You were such a boy, the first time you came home with Frank! You seemed so much younger than the rest of us.'

'Less than two years younger than you!'

'That's a lot, Tony.'

'It is at our age, because girls grow up quicker than boys do.' He laughed confidently. 'But by the time I'm through law school, you'll seem like a mere child. A very nice child!' he added in affectionate reassurance.

She said gravely: 'You're about the sweetest boy I know.'

He grinned with pleasure, and then he realized uneasily that there was something in her tone he did not understand. 'Say!' he protested. 'What if I am? Don't take it so hard! You sound as if you were saying good-bye forever!'

'Oh, no!' she said quickly, a hint of panic in her tones.

'What's the matter?' he persisted. 'Anything wrong?'

'No, Tony. Only . . .'

He sat up straight, looking at her in a strong concern. 'Are you all right, Barbie?'

'Of course!'

But his suspicions now were certainty. 'Come clean, Barb,' he urged. 'What's on your mind?'

She hesitated, moving at last to lean toward him in a strong solicitude. 'Well—I did want to tell you something,' she confessed. 'That's why I stayed downstairs tonight.' Her tone became determinedly cheerful. 'I want you to be the first one to know.'

Tony stared at her, and he licked his lips that were suddenly dry. 'Know what?' he challenged hoarsely.

'I'm going to be married, Tony,' said Barbie Parks. He did not move nor speak, and she hurriedly explained: 'You don't know him. I met him at the Princeton-Yale game. His name's Charlie Huston and he's a broker in New York. He's been up to Merryfield to see me every weekend since. You'll like him, Tony.' She spoke almost desperately. 'Honestly you will. I'm going to go on and graduate, and we'll be married in June.'

She finished. She was waiting for him to say something. Tony looked up at the roof high above them. He had an absurd feeling that it was about to fall, that it was falling, crashing down upon his head. He looked at her again, echoing her last word.

'In June?'

'Yes.' She seemed to plead with him. 'He's wonderful, Tony, truly he is!'

Tony, moving slowly and cautiously, as though afraid of disturbing a precarious equilibrium, leaned back in his chair and gripped the arms of it. A strong current, a roaring river was plucking at him, trying to tear him away. He must hold fast to something. He said carefully:

'Why—that's fine. I guess you're pretty happy.'

'I am, just sort of crazy happy. But I haven't told anyone but you!'

Tony managed to grin. 'Thanks.' He forced himself to relax his grip on the chair. 'Go on, tell me about him,' he said. 'I know you enjoy talking about him.'

'You're sweet, Babe!' she cried in a soft gratitude. She was suddenly infinitely older than he, wise and gentle. 'I know, of course, that you're pretty crazy about me; and I am about you, too. But we've never been—sentimental. You're more like my brother. This is ever so different, Tony. You'll find out the difference yourself, when you meet the right girl.'

'Sure.' He asked, snatching at a straw: 'What do your folks think about him?'

'They don't know anything about it yet. No one does but you.'

'Pretty swell, is he?'

She said happily: 'Yes, he is. He's tall and strong-looking, and kind of ugly-beautiful, like Lincoln, if you know what I mean.'

'Sure, I know,' he drawled.

'And he's . . .' Her talk ran on, and Tony watched her, and he said the right things at the right time, but he was thinking: 'I guess I'll go home tomorrow. I can't keep this up for four or five days.' He felt empty, like an abandoned barn through which cold winds blow; and he was cold. Once he clenched his teeth to keep them from chattering. He encouraged her to talk, because she was so obviously happy in talking; but it was a relief when at last she rose.

'So now I've told you all about it,' she said, smiling up at him, appealing to him. 'And you're the first one I've told. You're glad for me, aren't you, Tony?'

'You know darned well I am!' He took tight hold on himself, defiantly bound not to let her see his hurt and his angry bewilderment.

'He's awfully anxious to meet you. I've told him so much about you!'

He grinned, teasing her. 'Wait till I tell him a few things about you!'

'I'm not worried!' she assured him, her eyes shining. She put her hands on his arms. 'Good night, Tony,' she said, and waited. He saw that she waited to be kissed.

For a moment he hated her, and wanted to hurt her. He took her fiercely in his arms, took the kiss she offered, so that his kiss was like a blow, till she turned her face away and whispered:

'Tony! Tony, don't!'

He released her then so suddenly that she was off balance, caught the arm of the chair to steady herself. He said grimly:

'There!'

She whispered: 'Please!'

'Sorry!' He brushed his lips with his hand. 'I'm all right now,' he said. 'Forget it.'

She hesitated, then turned and fled; but from the stairs she whispered appealingly: 'Good night, Tony.'

'Good night!' The word was harsh. He ached with youthful sorrow. He watched her climb the stairs. But from the balcony she looked down, her eyes beseeching him; and he relented, said in a low tone:

'Good luck, Barbie.'

'Oh, thank you, Tony dear,' she cried softly, and she smiled, radiant again.

When she was gone, he stood a moment, then switched off the standing lamp beside the couch and moved along the corridor toward his own door. He shared a room with Joe Hazen. Joe did not wake when he came in, and Tony undressed quietly and lay down.

But he did not sleep. He and Barbie had never been on the surface anything but friends, but he had been clear in his own mind that some day they would be more. He had known it must be years before they could be married, and he had been prepared to wait. Now all that dream was ended. He grinned bitterly in the darkness. Maybe that was the way women were, smiling, and saying you were sweet, and then sticking a knife into your heart and twisting it there. It would be a long time before he let another woman make a fool of him!

He could not sleep, and after a while he heard the fire in the living room crackle and spark, and a log broke with a faint sound. Maybe that spark had jumped out on a rug or something. He imagined the inn catching fire, imagined himself carrying Barbie through the flames to safety; but it would be easier to go make sure the fire was all right. He pulled on a wool bathrobe and warm sheepskin slippers and went to the living room again.

The fire gave now the only light. He came to the end of the couch before he saw it was occupied. A girl sat there, wrapped in a Hudson Bay blanket, curled up where Barbie had been sitting. Her bright hair caught the flames, her cheeks were golden in the firelight, her eyes were deep and dark. She looked up at him, and after a moment smiled.

'I couldn't sleep,' she said.

'Neither could I,' he admitted, wondering who she was. Certainly she was attractive. 'Say,' he protested, 'I didn't see you skiing this afternoon?'

'I didn't ski. I was doing a sketch; the slope, and the woods and mountains beyond. But I saw you.'

'I didn't see you in the dining room, either! Nor with the crowd here after dinner.' He was almost accusing.

'You were all having such a good time. But I went to my room early.'

'Did we keep you awake?'

'No, I liked it.' She smiled. 'That girl with the guitar has a lovely voice.'

'That was Lucy Pride.' Something stirred in him. He thought of Barbie, angrily. This girl was swell, and there was a defiant loneliness in him. His world was in ruins! Nothing mattered now! He said: 'Too bad to leave this fire to burn out, all by itself. Mind if I sit down?'

'Do,' she said. He sat beside her there. He was near enough to her now so that even in the firelight he could see a faint scar at the corner of her mouth, a delicate white line.

7

(December 1938)

Robin Kerr's birthday fell in January. In another fortnight now she would be twenty-nine; in another year she would be thirty. Since she had come to know Mark Worth, it seemed to her that the pace of time had steadily accelerated. Before that, grief and loneliness were her companions; but she liked Mark at their first encounter, and welcomed his friendship as she had not welcomed the friendship of any other, feeling the loneliness in him to match her own.

They became friends, and last spring she had realized that they were becoming more than friends, and had reminded herself that for good reason this must not happen; but during the long months of her mother's illness, when they did not see each other, her affection for him grew. Yet when he suggested that she come to Boston and meet Tony, and she understood what was in his mind, she was frightened, perplexed, uncertain what to do.

She came to Montreal to be with her father, and found him already accepting his solitary lot, and left him and brought her box of colors for a few days at the inn. Once when she and Davy were just returned from Paris, beginning that trip around the world which they had planned, they had come here together, to ski all day, to sit late before the big fire after everyone else had gone to bed. Tonight, when the youngsters had gone to their rooms, she slipped down to sit awhile alone before the fire, to think of Davy as he had been in those bright days.

The tall young man who came to join her looked like Davy in the firelight. If her son and Davy's had lived, he might by and by have grown up to be like this youngster; but at the same time this boy persisted in looking like Davy. She was deliciously sleepy after her day in the open air, completely relaxed and comfortable. When he sat down beside her she watched him with eyes half closed, seeing Davy in him. His head was set on his shoulders in the same way; the shape of his mouth was the same. She saw that his mouth had a little hurt twist, as though he were suffering some faint, persistent pain.

She curled in one corner of the couch. He was half sitting, half lying, his long legs extended, his head resting against the back of the couch, his weight partially supported on one elbow. He talked idly of the skiing, asking whether she enjoyed it; and she said she did, but that she must do her stint of sketches too; and he asked whether he might see some of them tomorrow, and she said of course he might. She liked the way his lips moved when he talked; and when he fell silent and stared brooding at the fire and began unconsciously to frown a little, she was troubled for him, sharing his trouble without knowing what it was. He was too young to be troubled. He was a part of the youth to which she must soon say good-bye, and she wished to comfort him. She said quietly, smiling as she watched him:

'You're not having as good a time as you expected, are you?'

His head turned so that he could look at her, 'Sure I am,' he protested. He grinned. 'Say, you're beautiful, with the fire flickering across your cheeks and in your hair.' He spoke not tenderly, but in a way that was almost bitter, that had recklessness in it. She thought: the young are reckless when they have been hurt. Someone has hurt this boy.

'Why are you disappointed?' she asked; and when he did not speak, she said: 'That was a lovely girl skiing with you, the dark-haired one.'

She saw him wince, but then he laughed. 'She's going to marry a Princeton guy,' he drawled. 'She told me tonight.' He spoke in an affected tone, as though in mimicry. 'She wanted me to be the first to know!'

Robin smiled to herself, but not for him to see. The story was so plain. She said, in a murmur like whispering: 'You know, I never saw you before, and you never saw me before, and I'll never see you again and you'll never see me again. But sometimes it helps to talk things out, like thinking to yourself. If you feel like talking, perhaps I won't even listen, but you'll feel better afterward.' There was so much tenderness in her; she did not wish to see his hurt without easing it. He might have been her Davy, or he might have been her son, as her son would have come to be a dozen years from now if he had lived.

'Oh, there's no reason why she shouldn't marry anyone she wants to!' he declared, too vigorously. He stared at the fire, seemed for a while to forget her presence there. 'We've known each other for years, since before I was sixteen. She's two years older than I am. She always called me Babe, making fun of me for being so young.'

Robin laughed softly. 'Did you have to learn in school that famous speech, Disraeli's reply to someone? It begins: "Whether youth can be imputed to any man as a reproach, I will not, sir, assume the province of determining."'

'It wasn't a reproach,' he assured her. 'It was just her way of teasing me. I've always been crazy about her. I've always had an idea that we'd go on the way we were till I was through college and everything, and then we'd be married.' He grinned. 'That shows you what kind of a general damned fool I was.'

'I don't think that was so very foolish.' She herself had been a year older than Davy when they were married.

This boy lay down on the couch. He lay with his head toward her, now and then looking up over his eyebrows at her. 'I don't think so, either,' he admitted. 'Maybe I was foolish not to—make love to her, marry her while I could. I think there've been times when she would have married me. We've really been mighty good friends.'

She said: 'You need a pillow! You don't look very comfortable!'

He sat up. 'I'm not. I never could figure how a girl can be comfortable on a couch like this. It's too wide to sit on, but they manage it, somehow. If I sit up, my feet stick out; and if I lie down, my neck gets cramped.' He asked: 'Are you here with a crowd?'

'No, just by myself.'

'I didn't let her see how I felt, tonight,' he said, staring at the fire. 'I mean, I tried not to. I said all the right things, said I was sure she'd be happy, and when would I get a chance to meet him, and so on.' He grinned in a wry way. 'She says he looks like Lincoln!' he confessed, in a ludicrous wrath, and they laughed together at that; and while they were still laughing, he moved toward her, looking up at her as though asking permission. Then he lay down again, putting his head on her knee for a pillow.

She was curiously touched and pleased. Davy had used to like to do that. She said casually, pretending not to notice:

'I hope he isn't as old as Lincoln!'

'I judge he's thirty or so.' Then he drawled, his voice full of self-scorn: 'She said I'm the sweetest boy she knows! That was what gave me the first idea that anything was wrong, the way she said that, as though she were old enough to be my mother.' He was looking sidewise at the fire, his cheek on her knee, his face turned away from her. 'So I told her she sounded as if she were saying good-bye forever, like Tosti or whoever it was, and I asked her if there was anything wrong. She said there wasn't; but she said she wanted to tell me something. She said that was why she stayed downstairs when the others went to bed. She said she wanted me to be the first to know!'

He hesitated for a moment, and Robin watched him, wishing he need not be hurt so.

'They're going to be married in June,' he said. 'He's a broker. She met him at the Princeton-Yale game.' He frowned. 'I don't know whether she said he was a Princeton man. I sort of got that impression. I was out on my feet.' He grinned up at her sheepishly. 'Punch drunk.'

Davy, when he lay with his head on her lap, had liked to have her run her fingers through his hair. She touched this boy's brow with her palm, lightly, brushing back his hair; and for a moment he did not speak. She asked: 'Do you mind that? Some people hate it.'

'No, I like to have my head rubbed. Even by a barber. I always have a shampoo and a head massage when I get a haircut.'

They laughed together, and she said: 'I had my hair cut, two weeks ago. I'd always worn it long.'

'Is that so? You don't see many girls with long hair nowadays.'

She realized that he thought of her as his own age, or possibly a little older; and this realization was unaccountably pleasant and reassuring. 'I began to feel conspicuous,' she confessed. His hair was crisp and wiry, almost like that of a fox terrier, pleasantly harsh on her fingers. 'You said all the right things to her,' she assured him. Better that they should talk of his affairs than of hers. If she weren't careful, she would be confiding in him, telling him about Mark.

He frowned a little at her word. 'Oh, yes, I told her she'd be mighty happy, and she said of course she knew that I was crazy about her, but she said we were really like brother and sister. She said this was different. She said I'd find that out for myself, when I met the right girl.'

Robin nodded understandingly. 'But there wasn't much comfort in that, was there? You might have been reading your lines out of a book, both of you, saying all the regular things.'

'I didn't know what I was saying, half the time. She said he was ugly-beautiful, whatever that means. That was when she said he looked like Lincoln. I felt cold, as though someone had left a door open somewhere and I was in a draft. I wanted to yell and beat my arms across my chest and run up and down. I was so cold my teeth tried to chatter.'

She pressed her hand firmly on his forehead, shook his head to and fro with a sort of quiet fierceness, full of tenderness for him. 'You'll be all right in the morning.' He was so like Davy that her eyes dimmed.

'Oh, sure. But I couldn't go to sleep. I heard a log break in the fire here, and came out to see if it was all right.' Neither of them spoke for a while. His eyes closed, and he said drowsily: 'I could go to sleep right here, though, with you rubbing my head that way. If I were a cat I'd purr.'

She laughed. 'You feel better, don't you.'

'It's tough all the same,' he assured her, in a different tone, laughing at himself now. 'To be disappointed in love and me so young!' She thought that already his hurts began to heal. He looked up at her. 'Ever been disappointed in love?' he challenged. 'Haven't you any troubles to confess? You've made me feel a lot better, listening to mine. I'd like to do the same for you, do my good deed for the day!'

There were so many things she might have told him, but she would not. She tipped her head against the back of the couch, looking at the fire. 'Do you ever see things in the flames?'

'I'd rather watch you.'

'I can see a lion,' she assured him. 'With a great red mane and everything, and black teeth.'

He looked toward the hearth. 'Where?'

'That knot on the log, the one that's pointed toward us, with flames coming out all around it, and fire showing through for his eyes.'

'I see it,' he agreed. 'And that stub on the back log, see that? That's Joan of Arc burning at the stake!'

'I don't think much of her figure!' They both laughed, and she said: 'And the little flames along the top of the log are an army marching, with bright banners.'

'And the hot coals are a pirate's hoard of diamonds and rubies and things.'

'I'd hate to wear them for a necklace!' she protested. After a moment she said: 'I like to lie on my back, in summer, on a hilltop somewhere, and see things in the clouds. I wonder if they aren't really there? They seem so real, sometimes. Don't you think if things are real to you, they're really real?'

He looked up at her again. 'I guess so. I think probably everybody makes pictures for themselves, pictures of things they hear about and never see. I remember when I was a kid, one of the neighbors had a baby and it died, and I remember someone saying her soul had departed, and I thought a soul was something like an old-fashioned spy-glass, all telescoped together, with wings.'

'I know where you got that,' she said, in a quick interest. 'We've an old family Bible at home, with a page for deaths and births and marriages and so on; and at the top of the page for deaths there's a scroll, rolled up tight, with wings on it. Probably you saw one like it somewhere. Maybe someone told you it was a scroll and you thought they said "soul."'

'My grandmother had an old Bible,' Tony agreed. 'But I don't remember anything like that in it.' He was watching her contentedly. 'I've always made pictures of things I've read, too; in my mind, I mean. I've always known just what the Lily Maid of Astolat looked like.'

'Very pale and slender, in a trailing grass-green gown?'

'Of course,' he assented. 'And the Blessed Damozel. You know: "The Blessed Damozel leaned out from the gold bar of Heaven." She looked just like you, looking down at me the way you are now.'

She laughed happily. 'That horrid girl—the one who is going to marry the Princeton man—she was right,' she said.

'About what?'

'Saying you're a sweet boy.'

'Hold on there!' he protested. 'Don't you start telling me you want me to be the first to know. I've had about all the disappointments I can stand, for one night.'

'I won't,' she promised laughingly; and then she said in a gentle tone: 'Terribly disappointed, aren't you?'

'Well, not so much as I was,' he admitted, smiling up at her. 'If she hadn't told me, you see, I'd have gone to bed and gone to sleep, and then I'd have missed coming out here and finding you.' They laughed together and he settled himself comfortably. 'Some fun?' he asked, and when she did not speak, he explained: 'You're supposed to answer: "Some fun"! It's a password.'

'Some fun!' she assented, looking down at him seriously. For a moment there was a breathless silence on them both, their eyes meeting. Then she looked at the fire. 'Will you be here tomorrow?'

'Sure!' He had thought of leaving, but not now. 'Can't you forget your sketches for a day? I'll bet you're good on skis.'

'It depends on the light, in the morning. If there's sun I want to catch it.'

'I hope it snows.'

'I've been here before,' she explained. 'There's a trail that runs north through the hills three or four miles, along a wonderful old wagon road that no one uses nowadays. I'll show it to you. They used to skid lumber on it.'

'Show it to me in the morning?'

'If it snows, yes,' she promised. 'Or even if it's cloudy. I want bright sunlight for the things I'm doing. I don't like to do gloomy days.'

On the hearth, the last log burned through and broke; and the flames quickened. 'I ought to put another log on,' he said, 'but I'm too comfortable.'

'No, don't! That will burn bright for a while, and I'm almost sleepy enough to go to bed.' She said: 'So many things are brighter at the very last, aren't they? Sunsets, and fires, flaring up as though they wanted one last fling.'

'If I were you,' he declared, 'I'd never have any other light in a room except firelight. I don't know what you'll look like in daylight, but it couldn't be better than this.'

'I think,' she said in a reflective tone, 'that that young woman is making a mistake. No Princeton man, no matter how much he looks like Lincoln, could possibly be as nice as you.'

'Ovid knew something,' he declared. 'He said a clever woman would always meet her lover in a subdued light.' He reached up suddenly to touch her cheek. She took his hand, drew it down, held it for a moment and then released it. 'I just wanted to see if your cheek would burn my fingers,' he said. 'It is hot, you know.'

'The fire's hot,' she assented, 'with the flames burning bright like that.' She stirred. 'I think it's safe to leave it now. It won't spark, or roll out on the hearth, or anything.'

'Do we have to go? This is too good to end.'

'It's late.' She was faintly uneasy, sorry he had touched her cheek. 'I'm sleepy.'

He sat up readily enough, and she rose and he stood facing her. "Hullo,' he said then, with a chuckle, 'I didn't realize you were so little.'

'I'm not, in high heels,' she assured him. 'It's my slippers.' She extended her hand. 'Good night.'

'Good night.' He took her hand, holding it a moment. 'See you in the morning?'

'If it snows.'

'If it snows,' he agreed. 'But even if it doesn't, I'll come and watch you work.'

She turned toward the stairs; but as she reached them he came beside her, touching her arm, turning her gently to face him, and he asked again huskily: 'Some fun?'

'Some fun!' she echoed.

He drew her toward him. For a moment she hestitated; but then she laughed a little, and as though explaining herself to herself she said: 'You really are a sweet boy, you know.' She met his quiet kiss, and freed herself and turned up the stairs. From their head she looked back. He was standing at the stair foot. 'Good night,' she said softly. He lifted his hand in a gay salute, and she turned away.

But in her room, she faced her mirror; and she stood for a long moment there without moving, her eyes grave and steady. She could always be honest with herself. That was a nice boy, down there, and he had been unhappy, and she had comforted him. But she had deceived him, too. He had thought her a girl his own age or a little older.

Tomorrow, in daylight, he would know better. Yet perhaps he would not care whether she were old or not. She thought he would turn to her, if only to show that other girl his independence. She did not want that to happen. She liked him too much. He had been hurt once. She did not want him to be hurt again.

But if he were to be hurt, it should be done quickly, before the hurt would leave too deep a wound. She nodded, her decision made.

She rose early and spoke to the amiable Frenchman who was their host. He promised not to tell anyone her name, nor where she could be found. Before the other guests came downstairs, she was gone.

8

(December 1938)

The week from Christmas to New Year's with Tony away seemed to Mark a long and weary time. Elin's baby was coming early in February, and she was training Anna, her cousin, who would take her place here. During his evenings at home, Mark could hear their brisk voices in the kitchen, but otherwise he was alone.

There was a tremendous excitement in him, as he looked forward to Tony's return and Robin's coming. If he went to bed and tried to sleep, he could hear in his ear pressed against the pillow the pounding of his heart, with an occasional hesitation and then a louder thump, as though his heart had gone to sleep for an instant and then suddenly awakened to its duty again. At first that thumping had alarmed him, till with long familiarity he came to accept it as a regular companion of his wakeful hours. He seldom felt it in the daytime, forgot it till he lay alone in darkness, waiting for sleep.

Wednesday evening he had callers. He was in the living room when the doorbell rang and he heard Anna go to the door and heard then Ruth's voice. 'Is Judge Worth at home?' He went into the hall to meet her, and a tall young man stood beside her, and Ruth came to Mark and kissed him happily and turned at once to her companion, saying:

'This is Stanley, Judge Worth. I wanted him to know you, because he and I are going to be married.'

Mark, knowing of her engagement, had already guessed this. He extended a cordial hand.

'Congratulations, Stanley,' he said. 'I've known Ruth a long time. I can give her first-rate references.'

'Stanley Mason,' the young man corrected, and Mark felt himself rebuffed for undue familiarity. There was something belligerently defensive in Mason's bearing, as though he expected criticism and intended to resent it; but Ruth obviously was brimming with proud delight in him.

'How do you do,' Mark returned in properly formal tones. 'Come in and sit down.'

They did so, and Ruth explained: 'We're to be married in June, Uncle Mark. Mother wants me to stay in college and graduate, and I think Stanley really agrees with her.' She looked at her young man with an affectionate grimace. 'But I don't want to wait, so we've compromised on June. Stanley's a college professor . . .'

'Instructor,' Stanley corrected. Mark thought this was a literal-minded youngster, who would permit no one to take liberties with the facts.

'In Ohio University,' Ruth continued, ignoring Stanley's protest with a smile of apology, 'We'll live there.' She told Stanley: 'Uncle Mark lived in Ohio when he was a boy.' Stanley seemed to find nothing worth comment in this; but Mark spoke of Ohio, asking kindly questions. Stanley had been a farmer's son, had worked his way through college; and Mark suspected that semi-poverty had embittered him, had taught him to wear this hard, defensive shell. Ruth said: 'Father's promised us a farm for a wedding present—Stanley knows one, just outside of

Athens—and we'll live on it. I've always wanted a farm, horses and dogs and things.'

'Don't forget the chickens and pigs to be fed, and the cows to be milked,' Stanley grimly reminded her. He told Mark: 'The farm's Ruth's idea. I grew up on one, and I could stand never seeing one again; but if that's what she wants . . .'

Mark thought with a faint amusement that the farm had left its traces on Ruth's young man. His hands were big and rough and capable, his arms and legs seemed somehow too long for his garments, his hair was wiry and disordered. Perhaps Ruth's fondness for him had originated in the fact that he was so completely different from the young men she knew. Certainly the difference was manifest. Stanley was so obviously awkward and ill at ease, bristling, looking for a slight in every word.

Yet there was also a quality of helplessness about him which might have attracted her. He was like a hurt child in need of comforting. The psychologists said that an inferiority complex might be a source of strength—in such men as Lincoln, for instance. But it could be a source of weakness, too; or—what was worse—it could provoke a man to a defensive rudeness, so that he habitually rebuffed the friendly decent folk who might have liked him. Mark thought Ruth's young man was so alert to take offense at every word or act or glance that his very vigilance was an offense in itself. Most people were uncritical, quite ready to like other people unless they had reason not to do so; but clearly Stanley did not know this.

They stayed for an hour; and Stanley's manner did not change, although Ruth tried prettily and tactfully to put him at his ease. When they were gone, Mark silenced his doubts. If Ruth loved this young man, then there must be in him more than appeared on the surface; and certainly Ruth would bring out his best qualities. Mark remembered Tony's remark that in choosing a wife, a wise young man looked up, not down. Certainly young Mason had done this. Ruth would do many fine things for him.

9

(New Year's Eve 1938)

Tony's train from Montreal reached Boston Saturday morning, and Mark planned to meet him; but when he went to the garage a tire was soft, and the delay made this impossible. He would have liked to wait till Tony reached the house, but business called him to town, and when he came home in the early afternoon Tony had gone out. They were to have dinner at the Ritchies'. Nell Ritchie's New Year's Eve parties were an institution, beginning toward eight o'clock, ending with scrambled eggs at four or five in the morning. Elin reported that she had reminded Tony, and that he planned to be home at six; but it was half-past seven and Mark was dressing before he heard the door bang and Tony came plunging up the stairs to greet him and then slide out of his clothes and into the shower. They talked back and forth between their rooms.

'Have a good trip?' Mark asked.

'Swell!' Tony assured him. 'The best ever.'

'How's Barbie?'

'Swell!' Mark was not conscious of the momentary hesitation, till Tony said casually: 'Oh, by the way, she's engaged. It isn't announced yet, so don't say anything about it.'

Mark looked quickly toward the door of his son's room, startled at this news, hearing over again the tone of Tony's voice, trying to decide how much of hurt and disappointment there was in it. He spoke carefully.

'Is she really? Who to?'

'A fellow named Huston,' Tony said. 'She met him at the Princeton-Yale game. He's a broker in New York. They're going to be married in June.'

'You've never met him?'

'No.' Tony added: 'I judge he's been out of college long enough so he's doing all right.'

'Well, that's fine, isn't it?' Mark said experimentally.

'Yes, great!' Tony agreed. He laughed so that Mark could hear him. 'Of course it was a shock to me, at first. I've always been crazy about Barb. I had a sort of an idea I might marry her myself some day but that was just kid stuff. She's so happy about it that it's fun to watch her.'

Mark was almost deceived; almost, but not quite. He knew Tony well enough to be sure that this must have been a sorry blow; but if Tony had already weathered it, so much the better. He himself was relieved, sure now that he had never liked Barb. For Tony's sake he had pretended a liking he did not feel; but since she had hurt Tony, Mark felt toward her a harsh anger, and he was glad Tony was rid of her.

'Just your crowd up there?' he asked casually.

'A few others,' Tony said. 'There was one swell girl, but she didn't stay long enough for us to get acquainted.' He came to his father's door, tying his tie, and Mark at his son's tone was suddenly attentive. Tony spoke almost tenderly. 'I wasn't sleepy one night, so I went out into the living room to read awhile. She was curled up on the couch, and we sat there and talked for an hour or so.'

'Who was she?' Mark watched the boy.

'I don't know. We didn't tell each other our names. She was about the prettiest thing I ever saw, in the firelight. We got along swell. She made a date to go skiing with me the next day; but when I got up in the morning, she was gone.'

There was an honest disappointment in the youngster's tone; and Mark said with a quick sympathetic understanding: 'You liked her pretty well, I judge.'

'She was great,' Tony agreed. 'I never met a girl I liked so much, not on such short notice, anyway.' He laughed a little at his own discomfiture. 'I practically searched the place, trying to find her. The old Frenchman who runs it wouldn't tell me who she was. I tried to bribe the help, but no luck.' And he said ruefully: 'I thought I was making a hit with her. She kissed me good night; but she stood me up, just the same!' He laughed again, said with pretended ferocity: 'But I'll find her again, and next time she won't get away so easily.'

His tone was amused, but Mark recognized sincerity in it, too. There could be no doubt that this nameless girl had attracted Tony strongly. Probably the circumstances of that chance encounter, just the two of them awake in the sleeping inn, the pleasant firelight that set the shadows dancing, their hushed voices murmuring, had contributed to create an atmosphere which charmed him; but there was no question of the effect on Tony. He would remember that girl, at least for a while.

'Well, let's hope you do find her,' Mark assented; and he smiled. 'I'm glad to have you home, son,' he said.

'Me too,' Tony agreed, and he went to finish his dressing; and Mark hoped Barbie had left no lasting wound, and he was grateful to that girl, whoever she was, who had so quickly helped Tony to a settled mind again.

They were the first to arrive at the Ritchies'; but Ed and Mary Halstead, and Edwin—he was eighteen now, and looked ridiculously like his father whom he so admired—were on their heels; and almost at once

Jan came downstairs. Mark had seldom seen her in an evening gown, and he said in smiling admiration:

'My, you've grown up, haven't you. Happy New Year, Jan!' He kissed her, held her while he inspected her nose with a judicial care. 'I can't see a single freckle!'

She laughed. 'I use the very best powder, and plenty of it. Happy New Year to you! And to you, Tony!'

Tony, too, kissed her, and Mark thought her gown conferred upon her a new poise and maturity. She was, at least for this evening, no longer a child; but it would always be as hard for him to think of Jan as a woman as to think of Tony as a man. He wondered whether any of her childish devotion to Tony persisted. Certainly there was nothing but straightforward friendliness in her manner now; and Tony himself had never seemed to guess that Jan set him high.

Will Ritchie came downstairs and then Betty and another girl whom Nell introduced as Ingrid Sigurdson. Tony's description had made Mark think of her as sturdy and athletic, so he was astonished to find her slim and lovely, with sun-warmed cheeks and hair like spun taffy. He remembered that she had been on this skiing trip from which Tony had just returned, she and Lucy Pride too; and he thought with a smiling amusement that with these two to console him, as well as that nameless girl, it was not surprising Tony should have accepted Barbie's engagement with an easy philosophy. Ingrid spoke, he found, with only the slightest accent, and he thought she might have had an English governess. Only an occasional unusual sentence structure reminded him that English was not her native tongue.

Dave and Marcia Rollins and Ruth and young Stanley Mason appeared, and Mark thought Mason was not at ease in evening clothes, and in this group where he was the only stranger. He stood awkwardly silent, speaking only when he was spoken to; and when cocktails were passed, he refused to take one with what seemed an excessive emphasis, as though he disapproved. Mark decided he was something of a prig.

Tom and Emma Sheffield arrived belatedly. Mark had scarce seen Tom for months, and he thought there was a progressive and disturbing deterioration in this old friend whom he had lost. Mark asked where Tommy was, and Tom said the boy had plans of his own for the evening. Mark remembered Mary Clancy, whose father was a contractor in South Boston, and guessed she might figure in those plans. Dave and Bob Ritchie joined them, Dave with a cocktail in his hand, sipping it slowly; and Mark said Stanley Mason and Ruth seemed happy, and Dave looked across at his daughter and smiled and said:

'I'd rather see Ruth as happy as she is now than have a million in the bank.'

Mark spoke to Bob Ritchie. 'Well, Bob, I see Mr. Roosevelt's following your advice, wants us to build a big fleet, and ten thousand planes, and train a hundred thousand pilots.'

'My advice?' Bob echoed.

'Preparedness,' Mark reminded him. 'That was your idea of our proper course of action.'

'He'd do a lot more good if he muzzled Ickes and Sumner Welles,' Bob declared. 'Roosevelt's out to pick a fight if he can. After what happened in the last election he knows he'll be thrown out on his ear in 1940 unless he can get us into a war.'

Mark smiled. 'You're hard to please! You wanted him to build submarines and planes and he's doing it, and you're not satisfied.'

'He's just talking big,' Bob retorted. Dave accepted another cocktail. 'He thinks talk is planes; but you can't fly a headline—and all we've got is headlines so far.'

Dave said thoughtfully: 'You know, it's easy to criticize Mr. Roosevelt, but I don't envy him his job. We're the richest, laziest nation in the world, and the world is full of burglars waiting to take a crack at us. He has to see that they don't.'

'He doesn't have to lean out of the window and call the burglars bad names,' Bob insisted. 'The first thing we know he'll get them mad enough to break down the front door and start something.'

'Maybe that's the only thing that will wake us up,' Dave suggested. 'We're a soft lot, you know. When I was a boy "The Full Dinner Pail" was a good enough campaign slogan. Then it was "A Chicken in Every Pot." But now it's "Two Cars in Every Garage" and a radio in every room, and if you have your picture taken in some gaudy night club you're a member of the American nobility.'

Bob winked at Mark. 'Didn't I see you and Marcia in Town and Country last week?'

Dave smiled. 'Yes, and I'll bet you were proud to know us. But I'm serious,' he added. 'We admire a lot of foolish things and we laugh at a lot of good things. Maybe we need some decent reverences. Maybe it isn't so good for us to tell funny stories about the President of the United States and his wife, to call them Franklin and Eleanor. I'm inclined to give Mr. Roosevelt credit for trying to do a job for us.' And he said: 'He's a pretty gallant man, you know, and a hard fighter. He's had to be, to lick the infantile, to get where he is.'

Mark thought this point of view, this habit of giving the other fellow credit where credit was due, was characteristic of Dave—when he was himself. Dave sipped his cocktail at first slowly, but when it was half down, he drained it at a gulp and filled his glass again.

Bob laughed. 'You'll be trying to tell us Franklin himself is the Forgotten Man,' he said. Then almost angrily: 'He makes me sick. He's always wrong! For instance, did you see the German reply to Welles? They protested that Ickes speech, and Welles said German newspapers had been blackguarding Roosevelt and Wilson, and the Germans said there was a difference between an irresponsible newspaper and a cabinet officer. That makes sense, if you ask me!'

Dave drawled insolently: 'Who asked you, Bob?' Mark looked at him in surprise and then in regretful understanding; for thus abruptly Dave had changed. A moment ago he had been his usual courteous self. Now his very tone was an insult. He drained his glass again and went to get a refill.

Bob, too, had seen the change. He moved toward Nell and spoke quietly to her and Nell said quickly: 'All right, everybody. Get your plates and find what you want.'

But Dave had drunk a fourth cocktail before they all turned toward the dining room. Some defensive instinct made Mark go near Ruth and stay near her, as though to protect her from what was to come. Dinner was eaten haphazardly, in the dining room, in the living room, on the stairs, or wherever one could find a seat and a chance to balance a plate. Mark and Ruth and Mary Halstead and Will Ritchie stayed in a group in the dining room; and Will, sitting on the floor at Ruth's feet, somehow managed to slide all the food off his plate, spilling it on Ruth's slipper, clumsily trying to clean it off with his knife while they all laughed at him and Ruth told him not to mind, and Nell said despairingly:

'Won't you ever learn not to drop things, Will? You're as bad as the farmer's daughter who couldn't milk a cow without breaking off it's horns!'

'That's all right, Mother,' Will said in cheerful self-defense. 'Maybe being clumsy is a good idea. People are so sorry for you.' He told about an experience of the day before. 'I started to run up the stairs at the Boylston Street subway and tripped and almost fell and butted a lady right in the behind. She was cold-roast Boston, coming home from

Symphony or something, with a funny hat and queer clothes. I knocked her five or six feet, and I fell down—she didn't, and that was lucky—but before I could apologize she said: "Now, young man, don't you say a word. I know exactly how you feel!"'

Ruth asked, over their laughter: 'What did you do?'

'I ran away,' Will confessed. 'But gosh, I hope I see her sometime again. She was swell.'

Mark thought that to Will, as to Tony, every good thing was swell. Stanley Mason was standing awkwardly near-by, and Ruth whispered to him some smiling suggestion, and he went to where Bob was serving the plates and carried two of them into the other room, moving carefully, obviously afraid of a mishap. He did not reappear. Tony and Jan and Ingrid and Edwin Halstead came to join them here in the dining room, and Bob, his serving done, took a heaped plate and went to be with the others.

After dinner Nell—she was one of those hostesses who plan their parties to the minutest detail—turned on the radio and there was dancing for a while, the rugs kicked back, Mark and Tony and Will taking turns with Ruth while Stanley, who apparently did not dance, watched unhappily. Then Nell called for silence.

'Now we'll play Boston,' she said. 'Tony, you and Will fix the chairs.'

They always played Boston at Nell's New Year's parties, and Tony explained the game to Ingrid now. 'One person, blindfolded, stands in the centre of the circle,' he told her. 'Everyone else has a chair, and each person has a number. Whoever's blindfolded calls two numbers, and the ones that have those numbers have to change places, and the one in the middle of the circle tries to catch them at it. If you touch anyone, they have to stand perfectly still while you find out who it is.'

'How do I find out?' she asked, puzzled. 'With my eyes blind?'

Tony laughed. 'Why, by feeling around! If it's a man, feel to see if he's bald-headed or has a mustache or curly hair, and how tall he is, and whether he's fat or thin, or anything. I always like to catch a girl. I'll be able to tell if I catch you, by the muscles in your legs.'

She nodded smilingly. 'I think that must be fun,' she declared. 'Who is let to be the first?'

Will Ritchie took the first turn, and caught Mark and identified him by his Phi Beta Kappa key; and Mark caught Jan and knew her as soon as he touched her hair, cut shorter than that of the others here; and Jan caught Will again and recognized him by the broken finger he had acquired in baseball. No one caught Ingrid for a while. She was dextrous to avoid their blind gropings, till she realized that to succeed too well was to miss a fair share of the hilarity; and then suddenly Betty caught her very easily. For a while Ingrid caught no one, but then her hand just touched Tony's sleeve. He stopped still, bending his knees to conceal his height, and Ingrid grasped his hand.

'It's Tony!' she said instantly, and whisked off her blindfold. Tony stared at his own hand, turning it over, inspecting it.

'Say, how did you know?' he demanded. 'Just by my hand? I haven't got warts or anything!'

'I just knew,' she said, and everyone laughed, and Ingrid, tying the bandage firmly over Tony's eyes, was crimson at their laughter. Mark watched her thoughtfully; and he heard a chuckle beside him; and Dave said with a grin: 'Tony's got something there.'

Mark smiled, hiding an uncomfortable resentment at Dave's tone. He saw Ruth watching her father as the game went on. Someone caught Nell, and she caught Ed Halstead, and he caught Dave and at first could not identify him. 'It's either Tom or Dave,' he said, still blind-folded, running his hands over Dave's body and arms. Then he felt the highball glass in Dave's hand. 'It's Dave!' he cried triumphantly.

Emma Sheffield laughed in a shrill amusement, and Dave stood still while Ed tied a handkerchief across his eyes. He began to call numbers, swinging his arms, darting this way and that as those whose numbers were called dodged past him.

But suddenly he stopped and reflected and then moved slowly around the circle. Mark suspected that he was able to see the floor by looking down under the blindfold. He posted himself squarely in front of Stan-ley Mason. 'One and two,' he called. 'Three and four.' 'Five and six.' But he made no move, waiting for Stanley to respond to one of the numbers.

Stanley's number was eleven. When Dave reached it, Stanley leaned forward in his chair and tried to dart under Dave's arms; but Dave caught him by the shoulder and held him. He leaned elaborately nearer, sniffing at Stanley's sleeve. 'I smell barnyard!' he cried then. 'It's Stanley Mason.'

And he stripped off his blindfold, grinning at them all.

For a moment there was, except for Emma's sharp giggle, a shocked and dreadful silence. Young Mason stood still, his face blazing. Mark looked at Ruth and saw her white and tense. Then Dave moved around behind Stanley to tie the handkerchief across the other's eyes; and then at last Nell recovered her wits and intervened.

'That's enough of that,' she cried. 'Now we'll play The Game! Bob, you and Mark choose sides. Will, get the pencils and paper. They're in my desk. Now . . .'

She succeeded in bringing out of that strained and wretched silence a pleasing confusion. Everyone talked at once, rearranging the chairs, preparing for what was to come; but under cover of the general movement young Mason went into the hall and Ruth slipped out after him. After a moment, Mark heard the front door open and close; and these two did not return.

They were all sobered by what had happened. Even Dave, sipping his highball, peered into his glass and avoided every eye; and he defiantly refused to take part in The Game. But Nell kept the others at it, individuals acting out in dumb show such familiar phrases as 'This is the forest primeval' or 'Whether it were nobler in the mind to suffer' or 'The jawbone of an ass' while the members of the actor's team tried to guess what was meant to be conveyed.

Dave sat at one side and drank steadily, and watched the door for Ruth's return, but she did not reappear; and after what seemed to Mark a long time it was midnight, and they clasped hands and sang 'Auld Lang Syne' together. Soon afterward Mark decided to say good night.

10

(January 1, 1939)

Mark and Tony crossed the street and came home, and indoors Mark asked: 'Going to bed?'

'Pretty soon,' Tony said, but he turned into the living room and they sat down together there; and after a moment, Tony said: 'That was pretty rough, wasn't it?'

'Pretty bad,' Mark agreed.

'Why the hell does Uncle Dave make such a fool of himself?'

'It's—a disease,' Mark said soberly. 'He's simply sick, Tony.'

'Can't he take the cure or something?'

'I don't know. I'm sorry for Ruth. I suppose she and Stanley went home.'

'She's all right,' Tony said strongly. 'I like her a lot. She was kind of queer a few years ago, but she's fine now.' He added: 'But I didn't go for Stanley.'

Mark was silent for a moment, wishing he could see Ruth and perhaps help her. Thinking of her and of this young man she loved and whom Dave had hurt so grievously led him to think of Robin whom he loved. And suddenly a strong impulse moved him. He had not meant to speak till Tony should have met Robin, but he forgot that now.

'Tony,' he said, 'I want to talk to you. I've something on my mind.' He felt his cheeks burn; and Tony said, in amused curiosity:

'Say, you look embarrassed! What's up, Dad?'

'I want to talk to you about it,' Mark repeated. He added: 'I haven't talked to—anyone else. I wanted to talk it over with you first.'

Tony grinned. He said, in a dry way: 'You sound like Barbie! She said she wanted me to be the first to know, before she told me she was engaged.' He looked at his father in a sudden strong attention. 'Say, is that what you're going to tell me?'

Mark laughed. 'No, I'm not engaged!' Then he said, more seriously: 'Not yet, anyway.'

Tony had been sitting sprawled in his chair, his legs extended; but now he sat up straight and faced his father. 'Go on, Dad,' he said. 'Out with it.' He grinned encouragingly. 'It only hurts for a minute!'

Mark nodded. 'I wanted to ask you,' he explained, 'what you would think if I said I were going to be married?'

Tony stared at him, white and still. Then he said gravely: 'Why if I liked the woman, I'd say it was fine, Dad.' And he added: 'I know how tough it's been for you since Mother died. You know, you're a . . . Well, you're a natural husband and father. You've been so darned good to me that I've always been sort of sorry for the children who might have had you for a father too.' He grinned affectionately. 'But there's no woman good enough for you. Are you serious about this?'

'Yes,' Mark said, 'I am. I haven't spoken to her. I wanted to talk it over with you, and I want you to know her first. I don't know whether she'll marry me; but I know I want her to.'

Tony asked: 'Is it anyone I know?'

Mark smiled. 'You—came in contact with her once.'

'When was that? Who is she?'

'Robin Kerr.' Tony showed no sign of recognition, and Mark added: 'She was driving that car you ran into, up in Merryfield, your first year at Hanover.'

'Oh, yes!' Tony nodded. 'I'd forgotten her name. I never saw her. I wrote her a letter afterward, to make sure she was all right; had a nice letter from her. She lives in New York, doesn't she?'

'Yes.'

Tony looked at his father curiously. 'Have you been seeing her ever since then?'

'Yes,' Mark confessed. 'Whenever I go to New York on business, I get in touch with her.'

'But she was married, wasn't she?' Tony remembered. 'She was Mrs. Kerr?'

'Her husband died, some years ago,' Mark explained. 'She's an artist, does landscapes; oils and watercolors, and so on.'

The boy's eyes narrowed at some thought of his own. 'Watercolors?'

'Yes.' Mark added: 'She's fine, Tony. She's going to be in town, Monday and we three will have lunch together. I hope you're going to like her as much as I do.'

Tony said heartily: 'I know darn well I will! She must be a peach if you like her.' He asked, in a quizzical amusement: 'Haven't you said anything to her at all?'

'No.' Mark smiled. 'I was waiting to find out whether it was all right with you.'

'Why, it's swell with me!'

'I know you'll like her.'

'It doesn't matter whether I like her or not, as long as you do. But I will! I'll like her because you do!'

'Of course,' Mark admitted, 'I may be counting my chickens before they're hatched. She's younger than I.'

Tony grinned. 'Well, after all, you're no centenarian!'

'I don't feel like one,' Mark agreed.

Tony stood up and crossed and shook his father's hand. 'Well, trot her out, Dad,' he said, smiling affectionately. 'I'll look her over, make sure she isn't one of those designing females; but I guess if she suits you, she suits me.' They stood facing each other, the man and his tall son, and Tony said: 'I've wondered, sometimes, whether you ever would marry again. I always hoped you would. You're too—nice to go on living alone.'

'I'm not alone, as long as I have you.'

'You don't have me, a lot of the time. That's the trouble! I've another year of college, after this one, so I'll be away all winter anyway; and then there'll be law school.' He clapped his father on the shoulder. 'Go ahead, Dad,' he said strongly. 'If you've found what you want, go after it. I think it's swell!'

11

(January 1, 1939)

Mark saw little of Tony on New Year's Day. He himself woke early, and rose and breakfasted alone; but he was too excited to sit still, so in mid-forenoon, with Tony still asleep, he went for a walk, and Jan Ritchie saw him start out and joined him. They walked at random for an hour or two, talking at first about nothing in particular, laughing at slight provocation or at none; and Mark liked to watch the color play in her cheeks and burn bright there as their brisk pace made her blood run faster.

For a long time neither of them mentioned the party of the night before, each a little reluctant to refer to what had happened; but at last Mark asked: 'Did Ruth and Mr. Mason come back after we left, last night?'

Jan shook her head. 'No. That was pretty grim, wasn't it?'

'Hard on both of them,' he assented.

'I never saw Uncle Dave say anything unkind to anyone before. He's always so darned nice.'

She spoke in a puzzled tone, and Mark tried to make her understand. 'Dave's one of those men who should never take a drink,' he said. 'He can go along for months taking one or two cocktails and then—maybe one cocktail will do it—he changes completely. It's as though he were walking along a pleasant woods trail and suddenly stepped into a hidden pit. He's lost before he knows it.'

'Does he have to drink?' Her tone was resentful, faintly intolerant as youth is apt to be toward the weaknesses of older people.

'You must think of him as a sick man, Jan,' Mark said, and he added: 'Not all the casualties of the last war were left on the battlefields. Once, only once in the years I've known him, has Dave told me anything about his war experiences. I had happened to say, in his hearing, that I never fired a shot during the war, never saw an enemy to shoot at. I saw him look at me strangely; and when we were alone, he asked me whether what I had said was literally true. I said it was, and he shuddered, and said under his breath: "God help me, I wish I could say the same!" And he told me that he was a machine-gunner in front of Arras, and that he fired in one forenoon several hundred rounds of ammunition at waves of advancing Germans who were sometimes so near him that he could almost see their faces. I remember he said: "I must have killed a hundred men." '

Jan looked up at him, shivering deeply. 'He must hate remembering that. He's naturally so gentle and kind.'

Mark nodded. 'That left a lasting wound in him, I'm sure. And of course he was gassed too—and probably shell-shocked. Not all war wounds show, you know. I suppose there are thousands of men his age and mine whose lives were forever distorted by the war.'

She asked, eyes straight ahead: 'Uncle Mark, do you think we're going to have another war?'

'I'm afraid so.'

Her eyes met his shyly. 'Will Tony be in it?'

'I'm afraid so,' he repeated.

They were homeward bound now, and for a while she did not speak. Then in a different tone she asked: 'Did Tony have a good time in Canada? I didn't have a chance to talk to him last night.'

'Fine!' he told her. 'He said the skiing was good, except that there was no tow.'

She asked, eyes straight ahead: 'Does he know about Barb?'

Mark was surprised, and for a moment he was uncertain what to say. Tony had warned him to secrecy about Barb's engagement, but apparently Jan already knew. He hesitated just long enough so that Jan looked up at him inquiringly. He said then: 'Oh, yes, she told him. But I thought it was still a secret?'

'Nobody's supposed to know it yet,' Jan assented. 'But Mr. Huston's sister is at Sarah Lawrence and she told Ann Hawkins, and Ann wrote to Betty about it, because of course she knows Tony's crazy about Barb.'

'Tony says Barb's very happy,' Mark said. 'Huston must be a fine man.' He added: 'And of course, Tony's glad for Barb's sake.'

She gave him one swift, searching glance, but that was all. They parted at his door. He and Tony had dinner together, and then Tony went to join Ingrid and the Ritchie young folk for skating at the club. 'We're doing open houses afterward,' he said. 'Probably I'll see you.'

After Tony was gone, a wire came from Robin. 'Arriving eight-five as planned. Must take five-o'clock. Love.' He smiled, remembering some-one's definition of 'love' as the tenth word in a telegram. He decided to meet her train. It might be more tactful to let her—as women put it—freshen up first; but his own eagerness drove him.

Yet she should have some warning, so he telegraphed her in Montreal.

12

(January 2, 1939)

Waiting next morning in the North Station for Robin's train to pull in, Mark tramped up and down, full of a restless energy, at once eager and uneasy, wondering what, when the time came, he would say to Robin. He amused himself by imagining stilted phrases. 'Madam, I have my son's permission to pay you my addresses.' Or he might say, more easily: 'Robin, I talked to Tony last night about my marrying again. He says it's all right, so—will you marry me?' He laughed at himself, but when the train slid slowly into the station, he felt his heart thumping in his throat, and he went through the gate to meet the stream of alighting passengers with such excitement in him that his lips were dry and his tongue seemed swollen in his mouth.

The light from the open end of the train shed was in his eyes, and the passengers coming toward him were dark silhouettes; but he recognized Robin, even in silhouette, while she was still two car lengths away. He knew her by the poise of her head, by the way she carried herself, by a dozen intangible signs. He went to meet her, brushing past the porter who carried her bags.

'Hello, Mark!' she said quickly. 'I'm glad you're here. I hate getting off a train with no one to meet me. Did you have to get up awfully early?'

He laughed, intoxicated with happiness. 'I've been awake since before daylight. I was anxious to see you as soon as I could.' He told the porter: 'I've a car outside, near the taxi entrance. I'll show you.' He said to Robin: 'I thought we might have breakfast together.' He had a momentary impulse to take her home, but Tony would still be asleep, might sleep till noon, so he drove to the Copley. On the way to the hotel, he asked empty questions. Was her father well? Had the trip been a pleasant one? He thought there was in her answers some faint restraint; and he wondered whether she guessed what was in his mind, whether she were planning how she might most kindly tell him what she must tell him when the time came.

At the hotel she said she would take a room, and he turned her over to a porter and went to park his car and returned to wait for her by the elevator. When she reappeared she was hatless, and the whites of her eyes were a clear blue, and she was radiant as she had been that first morning he saw her in the inn at Merryfield long ago.

'Now!' she said, smiling at him.

He led her to the small breakfast room. At other tables men with newspapers propped in front of them ate alone; and there were two women, breakfasting together, talking in low tones. The waiter came to their table.

'I always have the same thing,' Robin said. 'Orange juice, dry toast, a little jam, a pot of tea.' He gave his order, and the waiter turned away.

When they were alone, Mark's eyes met hers. 'You're looking well,' he said, meaning it.

'I've had a wonderful rest,' she agreed.

'You don't look any older than Jan Ritchie!'

'Is she the one who is so fond of Tony?'

'Yes.' And he added: 'I'd like you to know her. I'd like to take you out to the house today, like you to see our home.'

'Don't feel that you have me on your hands. I know you're busy, and I've two or three people to see this morning.'

'I'm busy for a while,' he admitted. 'We'll have to lunch late. Is one-fifteen all right?'

'Perfectly.'

They ate breakfast slowly. He offered her a cigarette and they smoked together. He was silent so long that she said at last: 'You've work on your mind, I think. You'd better run along.'

He shook his head. 'No, I needn't go yet. I'm not in court this morning.' He stubbed out his cigarette, his hand shaking a little. 'Robin,' he said, 'I want to talk to you.'

She sobered, her eyes for a moment not meeting his. She said then: 'Do you?'

'Do you remember the first time we had breakfast together?'

'That morning in Merryfield. You were so distressed about Tony, and so worried for fear I had—what do they call them—internal injuries, or something that would show up later.'

'We've seen a lot of each other since then.'

'Yes, Mark.'

'We've grown to be pretty good friends.'

'I knew we would,' she assented. 'Do you remember, I told you so, the first time you saw me in New York?'

He nodded, and he said bravely: 'I remember what a relief it was to me, even then, to know that—that Davy was dead.'

Her eyes were lowered, and for a long moment she did not speak. Then she said, turning her fork over and over in her fingers, watching it: 'Was it, Mark?'

'Yes. Even after seeing you only the once, I knew I would always remember you.'

She laid the fork carefully down and the waiter set finger-bowls. 'May I have another cigarette?' she suggested.

He held a match for her. 'I've tried to be—sensible about this,' he said. 'Robin, I'm forty-six years old, almost forty-seven.'

'I'm twenty-eight—twenty-nine on the sixth,' she told him, a smile deep in her eyes.

'That's eighteen years between us.' His tones were even and steady, but his fingers drummed on the table. 'It seems like more. You look like a girl of twenty, and—my hair's getting thin.' He added, half smiling: 'Of course—I don't feel old. Probably no one does, except sometimes when things go wrong, or when they're tired.'

'Sometimes I feel like an old woman.'

'I don't think you'll ever look like one. But when you're thirty, I'll be forty-eight, and when you're as old as I am now, I'll be past sixty.'

Her eyes were dancing. 'Probably you'll be crippled with rheumatism, and walking with a cane, and carrying an ear trumpet. I can just see you! Poor old man!'

'It won't be so funny then,' he warned her, but her tone filled him with a deep excitement. 'I mean—the difference between us seems a lot even now; but it will be more by and by.'

She looked around the dining room. Half a dozen tables still were occupied. She laughed a little. 'Will it, Mark?' she said, but her tones were grave.

'I'm trying as hard as I can to be sensible about this.'

'I wonder.' Her eyes were thoughtful. 'Sometimes I've wanted to do things, and seen the difficulties and the obstacles in the way, and given up the idea. But I've always been sorry afterward, wondering whether, if I'd tried, maybe it wouldn't have come out all right.' She added: 'Other times I've gone ahead anyway, and when I came to the obstacles, they were nothing at all.'

He spoke slowly. 'You had a happy marriage with Davy. You were young and gay and warm and tender. Both of you. I was happy with Nan. I don't suppose things like that can ever be recaptured. I mean— being young and in love.'

'I'm not so sure.' Her eyes were shadowed, but he saw her lips faintly smiling. 'I was sitting the other night before an open fire. It burned down, and the last log broke, and suddenly the flames were as bright and young and warm and beautiful as they had been when the fire first was lighted.'

'But after a moment they burned out!' he reminded her.

'The embers were still warm next morning,' she insisted. 'There were no flames to scorch you, but it was still warm and comfortable.'

He said: 'To be with you, near you, looking at you, makes me forget that I'm in my forties; but—I'll be fifty soon.' Her cigarette was done. She stubbed it out in the ash tray with a certain decision in the gesture. He said slowly: 'I'd have spoken to you—in this way—long ago, if it hadn't been for Tony.' She watched him, and he explained: 'You know what he means to me, and what I've tried to mean to him. I hadn't told him about you, not till New Year's Eve.' She did not speak, and he went on: 'I told him I was thinking of getting married again, if the woman I loved would marry me. I asked him what he thought.'

She asked in dull tones, as though not hearing her own words: 'What did he say?'

Mark smiled. 'He said that was swell. He seemed to think I was meant to be someone's husband. He said if I was suited, I should go ahead.' His voice fell. 'I want you to marry me, Robin, but I'm trying to see both sides of the question. I don't want to—persuade you, lead you to do something you'd regret.'

She looked across the room. 'Our waiter has the check sticking out of his pocket in an ostentatious way!' she suggested.

He signalled the man, paid the check. She rose. 'Come up to my room,' she said quietly. 'I—must tell you something. I can't tell you here.' And without waiting for his assent, she turned away.

Mark, his heart pounding with a shaken terror at her tone, followed her to the elevator. Riding up to her floor, their eyes met, but they did not speak. In the hall she said: 'This way,' and he went with her. She unlocked the door and closed it behind them. Then she faced him, and the tenderness in her eyes led him one quick step toward her, but she stopped him.

'No,' she said. 'No, please. You'd better sit down, Mark. Sit quietly and let me tell you.'

He obeyed her, and when he was seated, she crossed to the windows and stood for a moment looking out, her back toward him. That moment seemed long. Then she turned and remained half standing, half seated on the window ledge, her hands braced at her sides.

'Mark,' she said simply, 'I've lied to you.' He felt cold, as though a vagrant current of icy air touched his cheek. 'At first I thought it did not matter,' she told him. 'I thought we could be friends. There was no harm in that. Then last spring I knew that—there might be harm in that. I saw that you cared for me. So I tried not to see you. All summer. Remember? I kept it up as long as I could, Mark, not seeing you. But when I finally knew I was to see you, I forgot everything except gladness.' She smiled pitifully. 'You see, I knew by that time that I loved you, Mark. I wanted you to—find me beautiful. That's why I cut my hair.'

There was a note like the tolling of a bell in her slow, sad tones. He could not speak, and she said honestly: 'I should not have let you—put this into words, Mark. But—oh, I wanted to hear the words. I wanted to hear you say you loved me.'

'I do,' he told her.

'I know. I'm so glad you do. Because I love you too. But Mark—Davy is not dead.'

For a moment after she spoke, the silence was a clamor in his ears, the world a dissolving confusion. She had not moved, stood watching him with beseeching eyes; but since he was silent, she spoke again.

'I know what you are thinking, what you must be thinking. But truly, Mark, I tried never to see you again. When I began to be uneasy about the feeling between you and me, I dined with other men, danced with them. It was not the same. It was only when I was with you that I felt the warm, complete content you always bring me. So I knew I must give you up, and I tried.'

She smiled wretchedly. 'It was a lonely business, Mark, trying to forget you, trying to let you forget me. I wished sometimes that I had told you about Davy long ago; but after I saw that you loved me, it was too late. Don't you see? I couldn't go to you and say: "My dear, I see you are in love with me, so it's only fair to tell you that my husband is alive." Or at least I thought I could not. I imagined you retorting: "Interesting, to be sure. But why tell me? I'm not thinking of marrying you."

'Can you understand, Mark? I'm not sure that I can understand myself—but can you, please?'

And before he could speak she said quickly: 'I've been afraid, Mark. I've seen myself growing old. I'll soon be thirty, and—it scares me!' Her voice broke, tears filled her eyes. 'Oh, Mark, I want marriage, and babies. More than anything else in the world I want to be married to you.'

She said no more, waiting for his word like a culprit awaiting judgment. He rose and came to her, stood near her.

'I love you,' he said simply. 'I've known it for months. Even if you had told me all this in the beginning, it would still have been too late. Something changed in me, changed forever, that moment I first saw you in Merryfield. I don't blame you for anything, Robin. I never will. And certainly nothing you could ever have said would have prevented my loving you. It could only have prevented my telling you that I loved you.'

'I'm glad you told me.'

'I'm glad I told you,' he agreed. 'We'll always have that to remember. That much at least. For as long as we live.'

There was a finality in his tone which frightened her. She said in quick urgency: 'But we can be married some day, Mark. You see . . .' She hesitated, biting her lip, her eyes brimming. He did not speak, and she made a quick gesture. 'Sit down, my dear.' And she said: 'I must tell you about Davy.'

'Not unless you want to.'

'I want you to know everything about me.' He sat down, obeying her, and she said in still tones, speaking as though by rote: 'All the people I know—or almost all—think Davy is dead. Everyone except the doctors and nurses, and of course my father.' And she went on, in slow, explicit words: 'I've told you how Davy and I planned to travel everywhere, see the whole world. We were in Shanghai when the Japanese attacked the Chinese there, and a shell hit a building and the whole front of it fell.

'We had taken shelter in the doorway. I wasn't hurt, just this little cut here.' She touched her lip. 'I told you it came from skiing, but I always tell people that. It saves explaining. But Davy was hurt, terribly. They thought he would surely die. His forehead was broken in, and his hips were crushed. They had to remove part of his brain, and they took off both his legs, right at the body. He was unconscious for days, weeks; but he lived.' She made a fierce, terrible gesture. 'His heart continued to beat, his lungs to inhale and exhale, his body to function. At first he knew me, but he was like an animal, Mark, with nothing left of the Davy I knew. My Davy was sensitive and gentle and kind. This that lived was—just an organism, with hungers and thirsts and nothing else. They told me that the damaged part of his brain, the frontal lobe, was the part in which all our conventional inhibitions are lodged. It's the front of our brains that makes us different from the monkeys. Davy —the Davy that went on living—was just an animal.

'He became terribly strong. His arms. They had to make a harness of light chains to control him, to restrain him. They found at once that they could not let him see me. They thought he might pluck me apart as a great ape might pluck a sparrow into bits.'

He asked, in a choking horror: 'Where is he?'

'When he was as well as he would ever be, I brought him home, to an institution. At first, except that he could not be trusted and tried to seize anything he wanted, he was—sentient. He could no longer talk, even incoherently, yet he was alive, with a tremendous vitality and strength.

'Then—this was just before I met you—there came some paralysis of the nerves that control his digestion. I don't know much about it, but they told me he would die.

'But he didn't. He recovered. A year ago, the same thing happened. They operated on him and kept him alive, but they said he would not live much longer. Twice since they have had to operate again.' Her voice shuddered. 'Oh, Mark, he's just like a piece of machinery that is shaped a little like a man. Each time they make repairs, he seems well for a while, and each time—the last was in November just before Mother died—the trouble returns. They say he should have died years ago.' There was a weary amusement in her tones. 'The doctors find him very interesting, Mark.'

He said in a harsh anger at the world: 'I've seen men torn and broken on the battlefield, men with no arms and legs—they called them basket cases—and men holding their entrails in with their hands, and men burned and screaming. Shells and bombs and bullets have slight respect for human flesh. War treats men badly.' His voice tightened. 'And always it is not only the man himself who suffers, but the women —and the men—who love him.' Robin's Davy was one of the casual fruits of war, even though his hurts came in a war in which he had no part. Yet perhaps Mr. Roosevelt was right. Perhaps there could never be a war, no matter how far away, which left us unconcerned.

'He's in a Veteran's Hospital,' she explained. 'They know how to handle such cases there. There are others almost as bad, from the World War.'

'I know,' he assented; and he asked in a sort of wonder: 'Why have you clung to him?'

'For Davy's sake,' she said. 'He's not Davy; but—I've clung to him for
Davy's sake. I always will, as long as he lives, Mark.'

He rose and with a sudden movement that was almost fierce caught
her in his arms. She clung to him, sobbing helplessly, clinging tight
and tighter, her lips, wet with tears, hungry for his. He held her long
in silent reassurance while she wept as though she would never be done
with weeping.

Presently she released herself and went to bathe her eyes, and when
she returned he was astonished to see her steady and serene again. He
spoke of this in tender wonder, and she said: 'I've lived with it a long
time, you know. I can go on living with it now, since you know.'

She sent him away at last, promising to meet him at a quarter-past
one in the corridor by the elevators. 'I'm looking forward to seeing
Tony,' she reminded him. He had almost forgotten that luncheon pre-
arranged. She kissed him and sent him away.

Mark, forgetting his car, walked down town to his office, and a storm
beat in him; a storm of tenderness and sympathy for Robin, and of
pity for the man who was no longer a man, and a hard revolt against
the rule deep planted in every human heart that life, no matter how
useless and hopeless, must be preserved at any cost. Why need the
wretched thing which had been Davy be kept alive, to remind the living
that he once had been a man? Was life, in fact, so precious? Over in
Europe they were preparing death for millions; death hideous and purposeless. Great nations would muster all their resources of money, brains,
muscle, and science to kill, kill, kill; yet at the same time, to preserve
this one pale flicker of distorted life, wreckage of another war, wise doctors labored tirelessly—and Robin suffered a living crucifixion.

It was true, of course, that the law would if she chose set her free; yet
he knew well enough that she would not thus choose. So long as the
dead thing lived, so long would she be loyal; and knowing this, Mark
loved her more and more.

13

(January 2, 1939)

Mark had planned to be at the rendezvous ahead of time; but Robin
was even more impatient than he. She came down from her room at
one o'clock. Mark had not yet arrived, and she walked through the
lobby to look for him and returned and sat waiting, wearily content. It

was as though, having given him her burden to share, she was rid of it altogether. Now and then she looked at her watch, astonished to see how slowly the minutes passed, winding the watch to be sure it had not stopped, eager for Mark's coming.

She watched the revolving doors through which men and women were constantly arriving. She watched other people, waiting here like herself, rise to greet newcomers and then move into the big dining room. Presently a tall young man came through the spinning doors and stopped to check his coat and hat; and she saw him with a sense of familiarity and then in sudden recognition.

He was the young man of the inn! She had liked this boy that night, and she knew he had liked her. It was to protect him from the hurt of liking her better that she had taken, next morning, an early departure. But she forgot that now in her pleasure at seeing him again, and she stood up quickly and he recognized her.

'Hello there!' he cried delightedly, and caught her hand. 'I knew I'd find you again, some day.' And he demanded: 'Say, why did you run out on me?'

'Did I?' She was smiling.

'Sure you did!' He turned with her to sit down, and in so doing faced the door; and he said suddenly: 'Oh, here's my father! I'm meeting him for lunch. I want you to know him.'

So Robin looked that way, and she saw that it was Mark who came swiftly toward them, happy at finding them together. But even then, she did not fully understand that the boy here beside her was Tony until Mark spoke.

'Hullo!' he exclaimed. 'You two recognized each other? Say, that's fine!'

IX

God Save the King

(January–June 1939)

(January 2, 1939)

R OBIN, as long as she lived, would always remember that luncheon with Tony and Mark as one remembers a nightmare, in dreadful fragments, recalling words and phrases which when they were spoken had bruised like a blow. She herself had no least sense of guilt for that evening with Tony at the inn. She had enjoyed it at the time and in retrospect, and to discover now that the boy whom she had found so attractive was Mark's son only confirmed her pleasure in their earlier encounter. When Mark, seeing them together, thought they had recognized each other, she began to say in frank delight:

'Oh, we've already met! We . . .'

But Tony interrupted her. 'Sure, we've met before.' He added quickly: 'Don't you remember, Dad? Mrs. Kerr and I ran into each other . . .' He laughed, as though at the double meaning in his own words. 'Or at least our cars did—up in Merryfield, a year ago last June!'

Robin looked at him in astonishment. Clearly he wished to conceal the truth, and this implied on his part a feeling that the truth was something his father must not know. She resented this; yet, even if it were true, concealment could only lend the incident more importance than it deserved. The harmless moment, if they spoke of it openly, was nothing; but if they made a secret of it, it would become a shadow to darken the future. She tried once more to speak, but Mark said, in a surprised tone:

'I didn't know you saw each other that night?'

'Oh, yes,' Tony assured him. 'I caught a glimpse of her in the glare of my headlights the minute before we bumped, and when I saw her here just now, I knew who she was. Besides, you'd told me she'd be here.'

'Well, that's fine!' Mark assented, turning toward the dining room. 'Hungry, Robin? Shall we go in?'

'I'm starved!' she assented; but as she followed the head waiter toward their table, Tony and Mark close behind her, she tried to understand Tony's attitude. It was true that she had kissed him good night at the foot of the stairs; but that was because he was young, and because he was the sort of boy her own son might one day have grown to be, and because he had been hurt by some girl and was lonely. Mark, she was sure—almost sure—would understand.

So when they were seated, her instinct was still to say: 'Nonsense, Tony. You know where we met! Tell him!' But she did not do so. She must go carefully. The bond between these two was so close, and Tony meant so much to Mark that she was unwilling to begin by opposing the boy.

The waiter came to take their orders, and when he was gone, Tony took command of the conversation, referring again to that automobile accident outside Merryfield. 'If I hadn't run into you that night, Mrs. Kerr, we wouldn't be here today,' he pointed out. 'So it was lucky that happened, after all.'

She nodded, and Mark said with a chuckle: 'That old car really brought us three together.' Robin met his eyes, smiling with him, but Tony said in haste, as though unwilling to let her speak:

'I was a Freshman, then, Mrs. Kerr. I wasn't supposed to use the car in Hanover. I kept it in storage, about a mile below town, in a farmer's barn.' He was talking fast, afraid of any silence. 'The farmer was an old fellow, drunk about half the time.' He added: 'You know, I had a bottle in the car the night I ran into you.'

'But you hadn't drunk any of it,' Mark loyally reminded him.

'I didn't need anything to drink that night,' Tony said. 'I'd been down to Merryfield seeing a girl I was crazy about.' Robin thought he was trying to tell her something, behind this screen of hurried words. 'Her name was Barbara Parks. I thought I was in love with her until here a week ago. Then she told me she was engaged to a Princeton guy. I took it big, at first; noble despair and all that! I was all ready to run away to sea, or do something reckless. But that didn't last. Lucy Pride kidded me out of it!'

Robin, trying to understand him, thought that perhaps he was seeking to reassure her, to make plain that that night at the inn had, so far as he was concerned, left no wound. Yet she sensed anger in him, too, and she listened warily, while Mark echoed Tony's word in some amusement.

'Lucy Pride? Jan says she's a "free neck."'

Tony grinned. 'When a girl says that about another girl, it just means the other girl is popular with boys,' he said, and he added, with a glance at Robin: 'Of course, if a man says it, that's not so good!'

Mark nodded. 'I think Lucy's the sort of girl who will have very few girl friends.'

'That's right,' Tony agreed, and he laughed again, his repeated laughter beginning to seem to Robin meaningless and strained. 'But, anyway, she saved my life up there. She caught me on the rebound! I'd have gone for any girl, after I knew about Barbie.' He met Robin's eye, and she felt her color rise, and he said: 'I asked Lucy up to Carnival, Dad, and she's coming. She'll be a hit at Hanover!'

'I'm sure of that,' Mark assented. Then, willing to dismiss Lucy, he asked Robin: 'Did you do any skiing in Canada? Tony went up to a place in Quebec for a few days with some friends of his.'

It was her first chance to tell him the truth, but since Tony had concealed their former meeting, so must she. 'Really?' she echoed. 'Where did you go, Tony?' He named the inn, as though reluctantly, and she said: 'Oh, I've been there.' She saw sudden alarm in his eyes and added reassuringly: 'Years ago.' Then, thinking she might thus justify herself to Tony, she told Mark: 'Davy and I went there once.'

Tony demanded: 'Who's Davy?'

'My husband.' Robin hesitated, and then—looking at Mark as though for his permission to continue this fiction—she added: 'He died the year after we were there.' She went on quickly: 'He and I used to sit up late at night in front of the fire and talk for hours.'

She was looking at Tony appealingly, wishing he would speak. It would have been so simple to tell the truth in the beginning. To do so now would be difficult; to do so was in fact already almost impossible. Yet anything was better than this deception.

Tony said unrelentingly: 'You sat on the big couch, I'll bet! I sat there for a while one night with a girl.' He spoke to his father, laughing. 'I told you about her, Dad. I'd gone to bed, but I heard a log roll out of the fire, and I put on my dressing gown and came out to fix it. She was curled up in the corner of the couch with a blanket wrapped around her, over her pyjamas, so I sat down and we got along fine. I thought she was swell, thought it was the beginning of a beautiful friendship! She gave me a great line, kissed me good night—but next morning the old Frenchman who runs the inn told me she'd gone.'

Mark was uncomfortable, beginning to sense the antagonism between these two; and Robin, herself faintly angry now at this hurt, angry boy, suggested quietly: 'Maybe there was some reason why she thought it best to go.'

'Oh, sure!' Tony agreed. 'I guess a girl can always think of a reason for anything she wants to do!'

Robin nodded, but she began to believe she understood Tony's attitude. He was warning her in so many words that he had told Mark about that girl at the inn; and he was assuming that his father would resent that incident, would blame her. Perhaps, she thought in an amused gratefulness, Tony was protecting her. Or, more probably, he was thinking that a young woman who would spend a casual hour with a strange young man as she had done was not good enough to marry his father. She felt Mark's eyes upon them both. He could not be deaf to the rancor in Tony's tones, and he said gravely:

'You're too young to begin to be bitter, Tony.'

Tony laughed. 'Oh, I'm not bitter.' His voice was suddenly harsh. 'But fellows my age, who have grown up in this man's world, aren't apt to be apostles of sweetness and light, you know, Dad! When you were a boy, you knew that if you worked hard and behaved yourself, you'd get along all right. But we know that whatever we do, we're due to stop a bullet—some of us, anyway. A lot of us won't ever have a chance to get a job and go to work, and get married and all that. And we know it. We're not bitter about it. We just don't give a damn!'

'That's a childish frame of mind for any man,' Mark said almost sternly. 'For any man, old or young.'

'Sure. Of course it is. It didn't really get hold of me till lately; but this fall, with Hitler bullying all of Europe, and making England and France say "uncle!" it's got under my skin. The dam is going to bust, pretty soon.' Tony added grimly: 'When you were my age you could plan your life, but what the hell! You can't plan when you know that some German is going to be potting at you with a machine gun pretty soon.'

Mark said quietly: 'Well, we stepped into a war too, Tony—when I was your age. And don't forget that if another war does hit us, there'll still be more fine people in the world than the other kind, after Hitler's gone.' Robin thought Tony's words were twisting her heart. This was what war did to boys—even a war that might never come. The dread of it robbed them of their dreams. Yet, just as a tree or a flower yearns upward toward the sun, so youth must always live in the future, must live aspiringly, if it is to grow straight and clean. 'That's crooked thinking, son,' Mark went on. 'Just because Hitler's setting Europe—and the world—by the ears, is no reason for throwing your own standards overboard.'

Tony laughed, touched his father's arm. 'I'm not as bad as I sound,' he said reassuringly, but when he looked at Robin his eyes were hard. 'That girl at the inn, for instance, I'm not blaming her! She gave me a good time. I was kidding myself, thinking she'd fallen for me, but I guess she was just what Jan would call a free neck, that's all!'

So Robin knew starkly that Tony despised her; and certainly no woman who was what he called a 'free neck' was a fit wife for his father! She urged: 'Aren't you assuming a great deal?'

'Maybe,' he agreed in a sardonic tone. 'Maybe she was just swept off her feet by my overpowering charm.' Then he said cheerfully: 'But I'll get over it. Bumps never bother me very long. I always come up smiling.'

Robin's nerves were jangling under the strain of this double-edged conversation. 'I've had bumps too,' she said, and then, to lend the phrase some meaning, and to get on less dangerous ground, she told him smilingly: 'For one thing, I do a lot of skiing. Do you ski at Hanover?'

He said shortly: 'Yes, of course.'

'I've never been there,' Robin confessed. 'Not in winter, when there's snow. I'd like to come, sometime. Are there good slopes?' She was talking with the surface of her mind, thinking that unless she could appease Tony she might cause a rift between these two. She fought to keep the conversation on this harmless topic, asking interminable questions about Hanover and the skiing there, and Tony answered grudgingly, and she strove to win him. For Mark's sake—and for her own—she must make Tony like her.

But he would go back to Hanover, and she to New York, and unless she went to him it might be months before they met again. 'Hanover sounds fine,' she said at last. 'I think I'll come up there, do some watercolors. Should I wait and come for Carnival?'

'Probably you couldn't get a room at the Inn,' Tony warned her. 'Every room in town is taken for Carnival week-end, long ago.'

'I'll come right away, then,' she decided. 'I want to stay two or three weeks. Perhaps I can persuade you to show me some of the trails.'

Mark suggested: 'I'm going up over February twenty-second. Wait till then. I couldn't keep up with you on skis; but when you're working, I can hang around.'

Robin, watching Tony, saw his faint frown, and she guessed that he would not want her and Mark to be staying at the Inn at the same time, to be exploring the surrounding hills together. She said quickly: 'I can't be up there then, Mark. I'll have to go right away, if I'm going at all.' The ordeal of this luncheon began to seem to her interminable. She looked at her watch, and with a sudden exclamation rose. 'Oh! I didn't realize how late it was!' she cried. 'I have an appointment at two-thirty.' Mark and Tony came to their feet. 'Will you excuse me if I run?'

Mark said in quiet disappointment: 'Of course.' Robin was drawing on her gloves. 'Can I see you later this afternoon?' he asked.

She hesitated, dreading the questions he might put, and which she must evade. 'I'm going to be busy, right up to train time. I must take the five-o'clock.' But then, relenting, she said: 'You might pick me up here and put me on my train.'

'I will,' he promised.

She spoke to Tony. 'I hope I'll see you in Hanover,' she said. 'Shall I get in touch with you if I come up?'

'If you don't, I won't know you're there.' His tone was grudging.

'Then I will, of course.' She shook hands with him. 'It's been nice to meet you when you're not driving an automobile!' she assured him with an attempted smile. 'Good-bye. Mark, I'll see you for a minute before I take the train.'

She left them at the table, picking her way toward the door. She wished to look back, wondering whether Tony were already telling his father why he disliked her. She hoped he would not. If he did, Mark would defend her, and he and Tony would quarrel, and the fault would be hers! That was a burden she did not wish to bear.

2

(January 2, 1939)

When Mark and Tony were left alone, they were both uneasy. Mark paid the check and they came out to get their hats and coats, and Tony was eager to escape. There was a strong sense of guilt in him. When he first saw Robin that night at the inn, she had seemed to him no older than Barbie, and in his hurt and anger he turned to her recklessly; but almost at once her gentle friendliness made him like her, and their hour together was so delightful that before they said good night he was completely happy in this newborn friendship. His affection for Barbie, he had always assumed, was vastly important in his life; but it was in fact no more than a habit. He was at the age when young men are strongly drawn to girls a little their elders; and he went to bed that night excited about Robin, looking forward to seeing her the next day. When he rose to find she was gone, he was at first disappointed and then half flattered, thinking that she had fled because she was attracted to him as he was to her.

So she had stayed in his thoughts, and when he saw her in the hotel corridor awhile ago, gladness surged up in him because he had found her again; and then the instant shock of realization that she was the woman his father wished to marry staggered him and woke in him a jealous desire to hurt her. But he did not recognize this feeling. He remembered how proud and happy his father had been, telling him about Robin; remembered his own word. 'If she suits you,' he had said, 'she suits me.' But that, he angrily assured himself now, was not true. This woman might suit his father all right, but she did not suit him! A girl who would start a casual flirtation in a hotel lobby with a fellow she had never seen before was not good enough to marry his father!

But he could not simply say to Mark: 'You can't marry this dame, because she's the one who flirted with me that night at the inn in Quebec.' Yet certainly, as far as marrying his father was concerned, this Mrs. Kerr would not do! He told himself that she had fooled his father, but she could not fool him; and he watched her with a hostile eye, and edged his tongue to wound her—while every blow he struck at her hurt him too. While they faced each other across the luncheon table, he had tried to decide how old she was. It was obvious that she was not so young as he had thought, yet he knew a lot of girls his own age who looked as old as she. Girls even in their teens wore so much lipstick nowadays, and adorned themselves in so many artificial ways, that sometimes they looked thirty.

But whatever her age she certainly was a lovely thing! When she was gone, leaving him alone with Mark, he knew a sudden keen regret for his own harshness toward her; but he fought that down, unwilling to admit even to himself that he had been wrong. For release from his own thoughts he turned to Lucy Pride. He had used her name awhile ago defensively, to prove to Robin that he had found it easy to forget her; but he had told Robin and his father that Lucy was coming up to

Carnival, and he must make that true. He would telephone Lucy this afternoon, at once, before someone else asked her.

While he and his father put on their coats, Mark was waiting for his son to speak, to offer some good opinion of Robin; but Tony did not, and the older man asked, suddenly almost shy:

'What are you doing the rest of the afternoon, Tony?'

'I'm meeting Lucy Pride.' He had to take the chance that she would be free. 'We're having tea at the Ritz.'

'Will you be home for dinner?'

'I'm not sure yet.' Tony dreaded being with his father alone.

Mark hesitated, then forced himself to ask: 'Well, did you like Robin?'

'She seemed very nice,' Tony assented, colorlessly.

Mark was hurt and disappointed, but he clapped his son's shoulder, laughed a little. 'We'll talk her over tonight,' he said. 'You'll like her better every time you see her. At least, that's the way it's been with me. You must show her a good time in Hanover; show her all the trails.'

'Sure,' Tony agreed. He looked at his watch. 'I'm meeting Lucy right away,' he said apologetically, and escaped.

3

(January 2, 1939)

When Tony was gone, Mark's eyes were sober with pain. He thought back with a sort of wonder to that hour this morning when he had waited for Robin in the station. Then all the world was full of a fine promise. He had confided in Tony, and he had his son's blessing, and he was full of a sure certainty that between Tony and Robin all would be well. Talking to her at the breakfast table, watching her eyes, listening to the tones of her voice, he knew that he and she were one.

And then came her confession that Davy was alive, alive and yet dead, a corpse that hung around her neck like the albatross around the neck of the Ancient Mariner. That stark revelation was at first too dreadful for belief. He heard her words almost without comprehension, full of tenderness for her, and when he left her, walking rapidly, the cold winter air burned out of his memory what she had said. He came back to meet her and Tony already assuring himself that since he and she loved each other, the future was secure. True, they must wait awhile—he knew that he would never urge her against her will to free herself of that incubus which once had been her Davy—but waiting could be borne when the end was sure.

He came back to her in rising spirits, and found Tony with her, and Robin's tears had washed her eyes till they shone, and her cheeks were clear, and her warm voice had a quality that pleased his ear as lovely color charms the eye. He was content to watch her for a while, till slowly he perceived that Tony did not like her; and he felt at that discovery a heavy sense of loss and hopelessness. Not even to win Robin would Mark lose his son.

After they both were gone, he filled somehow the hours till he returned to the hotel. He called her room, but she was out, and she returned with only minutes to spare. She met him smilingly, and said: 'My bags are at the porter's desk.' She picked up her transportation, showed the porter her space, checked out; and Mark had no moment for a word with her till they were walking the short distance to the station.

Even then it was she who took command of the conversation, telling him that she was considering moving her studio to Boston. 'I spent the afternoon with a friend of mine,' she explained. 'She moved over from New York two years ago, says she gets more work done here.'

Mark said smilingly: 'The top floor of our house is really a studio, with a good skylight,' he slipped his hand through her arm. 'You'd better look it over,' he suggested. 'If it suits, I'll let you have it—on the easiest terms!'

She smiled up at him in a warm affection, and his hand tightened on her arm and his throat filled. They turned into the station, and following the porter down the stairs he asked hopefully:

'Like Tony, did you?'

'He's a sweet boy,' she said, with no least reserve apparent in her tones. 'You're right to be proud of him.' They passed out to the platform. 'And to love him, Mark,' she added.

'I thought there was some strain between you two at lunch?' he confessed.

'I suppose he was surprised to see what I looked like,' she suggested, not daring to speak seriously. 'You may not realize it, but I'm a handsome young woman, Mark. He probably expected your intended would be someone more—mature. Children always think of their parents—even of their prospective step-parents—as old.' The train was pulling in, and they followed the porter toward her car. 'Probably it never occurred to him that the woman you were bringing him to meet today—object matrimony—would be a dazzling damsel in her twenties!'

Her tone made him laugh, and her good-bye kiss, generous and unstinting, made him forget all else. Then before he could speak she was climbing the steps. He followed along the side of the car, watching her take her seat. She looked out and met his eyes.

She did not smile, nor did he. Their eyes held in a long glance like an embrace, and then the train began to move and she was gone.

4

(January 1939)

Mark wished to tell Tony about Davy, but that was Robin's secret, to be shared with no one. He would have been glad for the outlet of long talk with his son, even though there was nothing that could be said; but till Tony returned to Hanover they had little time together. This was Tony's doing. To avoid being alone with his father, he stayed abed till Mark had gone to town; and he spent his evenings with Lucy Pride, or with others of his friends.

When Tony went back to college, Mark settled again into his solitary ways; but a day or two after his son's departure, Ruth came to his office. He saw at once a change in her. She was a woman now, quietly strong; yet there was trouble in her too. She spoke to him frankly, and the thing she told was hard to hear.

When she and Stanley left Nell's that night, she said, Stanley was almost hysterically angry. 'Like a woman, Uncle Mark,' she explained. 'Angry at Father, I mean. I couldn't blame him, but I tried to make him understand about Father.' Stanley had walked to the station, she said, and she went with him, pleading with him. They caught a train to Boston, and a late train to Lincoln, and despite her urgencies, he took a taxi to their home and packed his bags. 'He wanted me to go away with him that night,' she said in a wondering voice. 'But I couldn't leave Father. He needs to be loved, Uncle Mark.' Yet she had ridden back to Boston with Stanley, trying vainly to placate him. 'But it was no good,' she said. 'He told me at last he would never see me again.'

After he left her, she had sat in the lobby of a hotel till morning, then caught the first train for home. When she reached the house, her father was drunk as she had seen him many times before; but he was alone.

Her mother was not there. She put Dave to bed and gave him a sedative as she had seen her mother do.

'Mother has left him,' she told Mark quietly. 'She says they started home from the Ritchies' that night, and when they were in Waltham he insisted on driving and when she wouldn't let him he struck her and pushed her out of the car and drove away. She says she'll never go back to him.'

She spoke slowly, in a monotonous voice; and Mark listened in silence, interrupting her not at all.

'I'm taking care of Father,' she explained. 'He drank a great deal at first, but today he was almost himself, and he called Mother on the telephone and asked her to come home, and she hung up, and he began to drink again. I don't know what to do, Uncle Mark. I don't know how to help him.' Her voice broke. 'You're the only one I could come to,' she said, and waited, and it was as though something were gone out of her, she sat so small and weary in her chair.

Mark watched her for a moment, his thoughts drifting. Probably Ruth was well rid of young Mason, yet she would wear for a while a grievous wound. 'Is Dave alone at home?' he asked.

'Just the servants, and the nurse Mother always got to help her take care of him. We gave him the pills again, so he's asleep.'

'Dave's a fine man, Ruth, most of the time,' he said gently.

'I know. It's just that every few months he's—like this for a while, a week or two or three. But this is the worst time. Mother could always get him—straightened out again. But I don't know how.'

'Where is your mother?' Ruth told him, and Mark said: 'I'll see her. Perhaps I can persuade her to—change her mind.'

'He's never struck her before,' Ruth explained. 'Her mouth was cut and swollen.'

Nevertheless, Mark did see Marcia that day, hoping to win her to some relenting; but he failed. 'I can't forgive him,' she said. 'I've forgiven him so often. And—I'm afraid of him, Mark. For three or four years now, whenever he was this way, he has seemed to hate me. This time he threatened to kill me.' Mark spent an hour with her, but it was a fruitless one. 'No, no, no,' she insisted at last, in a sort of passion. 'I've done all I can, Mark.'

'He can't pull himself out of this without your help,' he urged.

'Then I'm through with him. Unless he can help himself, I'm done.'

That was her unshakable word. He took that word to Dave himself, on Saturday morning, making sure first by a telephone call to Ruth that Dave had been asleep since the day before, that he would be relatively sober when he woke. Mark found Dave in fact—save that he was weak and shaken and bathed in perspiration—almost normal; and Dave was glad to see him.

'I've really torn it this time, Mark,' he said, with a shamed smile. 'Marcia's left me and she won't come back.'

Mark, uncertain how to attack this problem, asked: 'Do you blame her?'

'I'd not have blamed her any time this twenty years,' Dave said steadily. 'She's been an angel to me, Mark.' He added simply: 'But if she doesn't come back to me, I'm lost.'

'I've talked with her.' Dave watched him with haggard eyes, and Mark said: 'She says you must take hold of yourself, Dave; straighten out and stay straight.'

'Will she come back if I do?'

'If you prove you're all right.'

Dave asked helplessly: 'Will I ever be all right?'

'I think you need help,' Mark admitted. 'You know, Dave, you're a sick man. This is a disease in you. If I were you, I'd put myself in a doctor's hands.'

He found Dave ready enough to agree to this, or to anything; and the result was that Mark sent for Doctor Hethering. The old doctor listened to the story—Mark talked to him while Dave sat silent—and he said at last: 'Well, Mr. Rollins, we can get the poison out of you, but we can't keep it out—not unless you want to do your share of the job.'

'God knows I do,' Dave said humbly. 'I want my wife back again, Doctor.'

'That's not enough,' Doctor Hethering told him simply. 'You must want yourself back again.'

'I do.'

The result was that Mark and Ruth drove Dave to the hospital that evening. Dave would stay there under Doctor Hethering's wise care for an uncertain time. Mark saw him settled, and afterward he took Ruth back to Lincoln. She would be able to see her father every day. Mark said good night to her, and he saw the gratitude in her, and saw that she was near collapse. 'You'll want a day or two in bed yourself,' he told her affectionately. 'You'll need to be rested and strong before he comes home.'

He thought when he left her that he, too, was very tired, with a heavy dragging weariness. When he was halfway home the car began to fight the steering wheel, swerving uncertainly, and he felt something like despair; but the tire had to be changed and there was no help near. He made a long business of it. The night was cold, and a raw wind blew, and he ached with fatigue before he was done. He drove home and Elin gave him hot chocolate and he went slowly upstairs to bed.

He woke at first dawn—or rather he was waked—by a discomfort in his left arm. It was as though the arm were asleep, yet in an unusually unpleasant fashion, the sensation seeming to centre in his elbow. He got out of bed, thinking that a change of position might relieve him, and swung his arm to and fro till the distress passed. The bedroom, with windows wide, was cold; so he was surprised to find that he was wet with perspiration. When his arm felt normal again, he went back to bed.

But he did not sleep, and within half an hour the pain returned; a sickening, deep-seated ache that pricked through his whole arm and made itself felt, though faintly, in his shoulder. There was a third attack and then a fourth, and the fourth time—he was by then up and dressed for the day—he saw in the mirror that his countenance had a pale greenish cast; and he was sweating profusely. He telephoned Doctor Hethering.

Mark spent the next week at home, not always actually in bed, but staying on the second floor. After Tony went back to college, Elin had brought her cousin, a stolid girl named Anna, to learn her duties here in preparation for Elin's imminent departure; and the two took care of Mark, Elin preparing his meals while Anna carried them up and down stairs. Einar and Elin had located a small apartment, for which now Elin was making curtains. During Mark's week abed he sometimes persuaded Elin to bring her sewing into his room and sit with him and they talked quietly together. The baby would soon be here, and Mark liked to watch her happiness, and the soft smile she wore as she sat with her head bowed over her needlework. Sometimes in the evening, if there were no callers, Einar too came in and sat with Mark.

Rest was Doctor Hethering's prescription for Mark, but he left a small vial of nitroglycerin tablets to relieve the occasional pain, and when the attacks ceased, and Mark could move about, the Doctor made an extended study of his condition and its possible causes. He took X-rays to look for any spinal distortion; he made Mark stand before a fluoroscope and swallow quantities of chalky white mush so that he could observe Mark's internal workings; and in the end he explained and instructed.

'The trouble was circulatory,' he said. 'The blood supply of the lower left side of your heart—never mind technical terms—fell a little below normal. You've had what's in effect a very mild warning to slow down.'

Mark smiled. 'I'm a pretty sedentary person, Doctor. If I slow down I'll become practically motionless.'

'Good. But I meant particularly that you must slow down mentally. Don't do anything that involves worry. Particularly, don't do anything that involves combined mental and physical exertion. Don't do anything which is physically hard to do. Don't change any more tires. Don't walk in a high wind.'

Mark suggested quizzically: 'Suppose I have a flat tire on a deserted road on a cold, windy day miles from the nearest garage?'

'Stay there,' Doctor Hethering advised him, 'till a rescuer comes along.'

'A Saint Bernard dog with brandy tied to his collar?' Mark suggested, smiling. 'How about alcohol, by the way.'

'Drink all you want. But don't smoke too much. And don't drink more than a glass of liquid at a time. Better not drink more than one glass an hour. But most of all, don't worry.'

'I've no particular worries,' Mark said thoughtfully. 'Unless you count Hitler, and the danger of war.' He asked: 'Is worry a real factor in such things?'

Doctor Hethering nodded gravely. 'Yes. You must have noticed in the last ten years a great many deaths from heart trouble among men about your age. Those deaths came from hypertension, from worry. Men suffer more than women, because to a great extent they keep their worries to themselves, have no outlet. I saw the other day some actuarial figures, showing the causes of deaths among policy-holders over the last twenty years. There's a suggestion of correspondence between the years when suicides rise and the years when deaths from heart troubles rise—allowing for the fact that if worry drives a man to suicide it kills him quicker than by breaking down his heart. We had a suicide peak, for instance, from 1929 through 1935. The figures dropped to normal again in 1936 and 1937.

'And on deaths from diseases of the circulatory system—that is, in many cases, from worry—a similar result appeared. In 1930, after the crash, such deaths went up about four per cent and they climbed steadily through 1936. Nineteen-thirty-seven was better; but in my practice there was a big increase last year, 1938. Of course part of this percentage increase has resulted from our new knowledge of how to handle other diseases; but most of it, I'm satisfied, arose from the mental strain of the depression.

'I expect the increase will continue. I believe a lot of men will literally worry themselves to death about European affairs and the danger of war.'

Mark said soberly: 'I suspect you're right. Not all war's casualties occur in the battlefield.' And he said: 'My friend Mr. Rollins is one of them, for instance.' He smiled: 'And perhaps, if you're right about me, I'm another to be listed among the wounded, at least. Certainly world events have been much in my mind—as my boy grows up.'

Doctor Hethering nodded. 'If war's to come,' he said, 'I hope it comes quickly. Suspense is worse than certainty. Worrying about what may happen kills more men than contemplating the fact after it has come to pass. For a state of national hypertension'—he smiled at his own words— 'I'd be inclined to prescribe the release of a good rousing war.'

5

(January 1939)

Mark did not tell either Tony or Robin, in his letters to them, about his illness; and he concealed the whole truth even from Bob and Nell. He wondered whether—if Doctor Hethering were right—his own concern over Dave Rollins had precipitated this attack; but he admitted to himself that he had another worry too. He could not blind himself to the fact that Tony had not liked Robin, so one of Tony's letters after his return to college was a welcome reassurance. Tony, after a page or two about his own affairs, wrote:

> I guess I didn't act very well to Mrs. Kerr, but I couldn't help it. I was in a pretty rotten mood. You thought I was bitter, and maybe you thought my tragic love life and Barb and everything had made a cynic out of me. I talked as if I expected dirty work from every female! That was foolish, of course, and I knew it at the time, but I couldn't seem to stop.
>
> But don't worry about me and Barb. I took it big at first, but that girl I told you about, the one at the inn, showed me that there are other girls in the world who are attractive and that there really is some chance that I've not yet met the girl who will be my wife. It sounds like something I should have realized long ago; but I didn't, not till I realized how much I liked it when she kissed me.
>
> I'll probably never see that girl again, or if I do she won't seem the same; but I'll see other girls. Lucy Pride, for instance. She's mighty good fun. So don't think of me as nursing a broken heart, Dad. I can dance at Barb's wedding and mean it. I knew that, even before I came back to Boston. It's just that the feeling in the air that the world's about to end makes me

nervous and upset and sore all the time. I'm sorry I took it out on you and Mrs. Kerr.

This was not complete, but it was something, and Mark read and re-read these paragraphs, and read into them more than they said. Then a few days later Tony wrote: 'Mrs. Kerr is at the Inn. We've a date to go skiing tomorrow.' Mark was glad of that, sure that these two would quickly come to be fast friends.

6

(January 1939)

Tony had no car, but Robin said she liked cross-country work; so for their first afternoon together they went up past the Tower and then took the trail down the Vale to the foot of the ski jump, and so to Oak Hill. He led her toward the foot of the ski tow there, setting a pace calculated to test her to the uttermost; but she kept on his heels. Perhaps, she thought, if she could convince him she was at home on skis, it would make him like her better!

At Oak Hill they rode the tow, ran the hill, experimented with the slalom; and they came home through the still cold just after sunset, when purple dusk was settling in the Vale. There had been moments when he seemed to forget how much he disliked her, but she would not hurry him. 'You needn't come clear back to the Inn with me,' she suggested. 'I can find the way.' But he did so, and at the Inn punctiliously put away her skis. She thanked him. 'And you mustn't feel that you have me on your hands from now on,' she said. 'I know you have plenty to do—and now that you've showed me my way around, I know where to go.'

'Well, if you want any dope, get in touch with me.'

'I will if I may. But I'll try not to bother you.' She wanted to invite him to dine with her; but she knew he would make some excuse, and she was unwilling to compel him to any evasion.

She went alone next day to Oak Hill with her pad and pencil—the day was too cold for watercolors—and made a series of sketches of figures in motion, catching the distinctive posture of this boy and that one. Tony was there, and once when he swung near her, he waved his hand in reluctant greeting and she responded; but when he checked his down-hill run as though he would have come to speak to her, she pretended to be busy with her pad again, and he hesitated, then went on. Later she heard the hiss of skis behind her and knew it was he who had stopped there to look at her work, but she did not turn her head till he spoke.

'Say, you're good!' he exclaimed.

She looked over her shoulder. 'Oh, hello, Tony. These are just to get line and pattern,' she explained. 'I'll make a composition afterward, working in my room, and put the color in.'

He stayed awhile, but she worked steadily, making no conversation; and he presently departed. When he came back again, she was finishing a sketch of a slender boy, gracefully poised in a tempo turn, and he recognized it.

'That's Mike Vernon,' he exclaimed.

'How did you know him? I haven't put the face in.'

'Oh, you've caught him exactly. It's Mike, all right. It couldn't be anyone else.'

'Of course, none of these things are right without color,' she confessed. 'But you can't use watercolor when your brushes freeze.'

'There's one thing we get up here sometimes,' he said with a quiet enthusiasm. 'I wish you could see it. It would make a great picture, if you could catch the color right. It comes when there's a crust, and a fine sleety snow falling, and the sun shining through the sleet.'

'Like a morning after an ice storm,' she suggested, gratefully recognizing the unwilling friendliness in him, careful not to alarm him. 'After the sun comes out and before it melts the ice off the twigs?'

'Only better,' he declared. 'There's a sort of golden gray light that's pretty wonderful. I've seen it twice.' Certainly for this moment at least he had forgotten to dislike her; but when she turned to look at him and he met her eyes, as though at a sudden memory he colored and said: 'Well, I'll be seeing you.' He set his poles and glided away, and she smiled at her work, thinking that healing time would set all right between them.

After dinner that evening she went across to the early show at the Nugget, and he appeared with three or four others and they bought tickets just behind her. She spoke to him and he grudgingly introduced her to his companions.

'This is Mrs. Kerr,' he told them. He added, like a warning: 'She's a friend of my father's.'

One of the youngsters grinned with open admiration. 'So's your old man!' he said. 'Sit with us, Mrs. Kerr. Any friend of Tony's father is a friend of mine!'

So she went in with them, and this boy was on her right, Tony on her left. The picture was a poor one, and the audience jeered openly; and someone behind her parroted the lines aloud in derisive mimicry. She turned to look at him, and the boy beside her warned:

'Don't look around. You'll get hit in the eye with a peanut! They throw them when the picture's lousy!' He added, seizing the chance to talk with her: 'I saw you skiing with Tony, day before yesterday. You're good!'

'I like it,' she agreed. Tony, on her other side, stirred uneasily, and she thought in faint amusement that he was probably criticizing her for being friendly with this boy, so she paid attention to the picture. Afterward, when someone suggested she go to the Wigwam with them for a can of beer, she looked at Tony and saw disapproval in his eyes and so declined.

On the slopes at Oak Hill next afternoon, she saw him skiing with a lovely girl, skimming down the slope side by side, swinging in matching turns that suggested a dance measure. The girl was expert, and Robin's busy pencil caught her in half a dozen postures. She was glad when the girl and Tony came to speak with her.

'This is Ingrid Sigurdson, Mrs. Kerr,' Tony said, and he told Ingrid: 'Mrs. Kerr knows Father.'

'Oh, I know him, too,' the girl declared. 'I like him very much.'

The sun was fine that day, and Ingrid, bareheaded, her cheeks glowing, was a picture to charm the eye. Robin said: 'Miss Sigurdson, will you do me a favor? Stand there by that small spruce for five minutes. I want to catch you.'

Ingrid agreeably took position, leaning lightly on her poles; and Robin's pencil flew while Tony watched over her shoulder. She laid in the figure quickly, indicating colors by pencilled notes. Then on another sheet she made a sure and perfect likeness, the face alone.

'Oh, that's swell!' Tony cried.

'I'll combine them later,' Robin explained. 'Do something in water-color.'

Ingrid glided toward her to see the sketches. 'You are very good,' she said judicially. 'I have seen others, some great ones, do that in Switzerland, and in Norway, too; but you are good, too, and so quick!'

'Would you like to see it when it's done?'

'Very much,' Ingrid confessed. She said eagerly: 'You must show it to Tony, too, when it is finished.'

Robin looked at her, caught by something in her tone; and Ingrid under that glance turned hastily away, but Robin called her back again. 'Have you time to pose for me tomorrow morning, in my room at the Inn? I can do so much better if I can watch you while I'm using colors. Can you?'

Ingrid hesitated, looking at Tony. 'If it is fine like today . . .' She asked him directly: 'Are you coming out tomorrow morning, Tony?'

'No, I've two classes.' He laughed. 'I have to work sometime, you know.'

'Then I will come, Mrs. Kerr,' Ingrid declared. 'But just in the morning. I want to ski with Tony tomorrow afternoon.'

She was so frank that Robin looked at Tony, and he grinned redly. 'Do come,' she told Ingrid. 'I'll be waiting in the lobby about nine.'

Next morning's mail brought Robin a letter from Mark and she read it at the breakfast table. 'Tony told me you were up there,' he wrote, 'and I'm glad you and he are having a chance to get acquainted. I wish I could be there with you, but I could never keep up with you two on skis.' There was more about Tony, and as she read, she could hear Mark say the words, hear the tones he always used when he spoke of his son. Afterward at the desk in the writing room she wrote him a happy letter. From where she sat she could watch for Ingrid, and when the girl appeared, in white windbreaker and blue gaberdine trousers, Robin called to her, asked her to wait a moment till the letter was done.

After it was posted, they went upstairs together; but Robin's room, though it was on a corner, with windows on two sides, was inadequate as a studio. She phoned the desk to ask whether there was any place better suited to her purpose, and since the Inn was not crowded, she was allowed to use one of the larger rooms in the old part of the structure. Ingrid had not brought her skis, so they sent downstairs for skis and poles.

'But you must change them afterward to be like mine,' Ingrid said smilingly. 'Mine are better than these.'

'I noticed yours yesterday,' Robin assured her. 'I'll put them in as they should be, and the snow, and the hillside, all the background.'

She experimented with various poses and positions, Ingrid cooperating like a lay figure in a complete docility, till Robin, studying the girl's fine color, the warm shadows in her hair, the deep hue of her cheeks, the friendliness of her eyes, decided what she wanted. She set up the easel full size, fixed on it a tremendous sheet of paper, and with pencil and gum set to work.

She was surprised, when she began to lay in Ingrid's figure in detail, to find how feminine it was. The girl seemed to the casual eye almost boyish, sturdy and strong; yet actually she was astonishingly slim. 'You're really quite small,' Robin said, eyes flashing from Ingrid to her paper and back again. 'I'll have to put something in the background to suggest that, or you'll look like an Amazon, a Viking woman.'

'I am little, yes,' Ingrid agreed. 'But I am strong.'

'When you're tired, say so and we'll rest.'

'I will not be tired.'

'How long have you been in this country?' Robin wished to lead Ingrid to talk. Then it would be easier to catch the play of changing expressions in the girl's face, to catch that something below the surface which had been yesterday so clear in Ingrid's tones.

'Since last summer. You see, when Mike Vernon was in Switzerland, he came to Norway and visited my father and mother, and he said I must come and see him sometime, when I could, so I came, and Mrs. Vernon likes me very much.' She spoke entirely without affectation. 'I have stayed a long time, but when I said I was staying too long, Mrs. Vernon said that was not true.'

'Will you stay on in this country?'

'No, I must go back soon, I think.'

There was something wistful in the girl's tone and her eyes were shadowed. Robin wondered whether her guess were a true one. 'You've made a lot of friends who will miss you,' she suggested. 'I know Tony is fond of you.'

'Yes,' Ingrid agreed. 'We have liked each other. I like him very much, better than Mike Vernon or anybody.'

'He skis well, doesn't he?'

Ingrid smiled. 'Oh, yes, but he tries too much. Skiing is doing everything the easy way.' She said, seeking to make this clear: 'It is like Tony tells me about flying. He goes down to White River to fly, sometimes when it is not good snow for skiing, and I go with him. I fly, too, sometimes, but not good. They say I over-control. It is the same with Tony when he is on skis. He flies well, but when he skis he controls too much. It is like he fights the skis all the time, the same way I fight the aeroplane. Skiing is to let yourself go, just a little this and a little that, so you go where you want to go.'

'Will you come back to this country?'

'Maybe, yes. I want to come back, sometimes, and sometimes no.'

'Here to Hanover?'

'I think so. If Tony is here.'

Robin smiled faintly. The girl's straightforward frankness pleased her and touched her too. 'Tired?' she asked at last.

'No.' After a moment more Ingrid said: 'Do you know Miss Parks?'

'A friend of Tony's?'

'Yes, that is the one.'

'No, I never met her. Tony tells me that she's engaged.'

'Engaged?' Ingrid's eyes widened in a sharp surprise. 'So!' There was curious excitement in the word. 'I did not know that!' The girl was silent for a moment, said then thoughtfully: 'He has invited Lucy Pride up to Carnival. Maybe that is why?'

'You know her?'

'Yes, I know her. I was surprised when he invited her, because I did not know about Miss Parks; but if she is going to marry someone else, Tony is unhappy about that, so he would invite another girl quickly.'

Robin nodded abstractedly. She was working in silence now, no longer conscious of the girl in front of her except as something elusive and beautiful which must be captured and fixed on her paper here. Ingrid did not speak again, but suddenly Robin looked up at her with a new intentness, then at her paper again and back at Ingrid; and she smiled in quick apology.

'You're tired,' she said. 'Your color's fading. We'll rest awhile.'

Ingrid laughed in relief. 'I am tired, yes,' she said. 'All of me is tired, aching from being so still.' She moved about the room, swinging her arms, stretching them. She lifted one leg and, holding it straight out in front of her, bent the other knee, squatting till she was sitting on her own heel. She came erect and went down again, effortlessly, over and over. She changed, shifting her weight to the other leg; and Robin said admiringly:

'That's wonderful! I can't do it more than two or three times, to save me.'

'Yes, my legs are good,' Ingrid assented. 'That's why I am good with skis.'

Robin spoke on sudden impulse. 'Ingrid, you're fond of Tony, aren't you?'

The girl did not hesitate. 'Oh, I like him very much, yes.'

'I mean—you'd like to marry him?'

The girl seemed gravely to consider this. 'Maybe yes,' she said then. 'I think yes.' She added honestly, 'But that is not going to happen to me. I know it.'

'Is that why you're going back to Norway?'

Ingrid looked at her, smiling frankly. 'I would not go anywhere except where Tony is, if he wanted to marry me.'

'Does he know how you feel?'

The girl shook her head. 'No. He does not think anything about it. I am fun for him to ski with, or to listen while he tells me about Miss Parks, or to make fun of me because I cannot fly a plane easy the way he does.' She hesitated, and her cheeks suddenly were crimson. 'This is how I am sure he does not know. One day last fall we played tennis, and then we played what he calls Indian wrestling, holding hands, and you try to pull the other one off balance; and I pulled him, and he fell against me, and then he tried to throw me down and it was like puppies fighting, and everyone was laughing at us, rolling on the grass; and I am strong as he is, but I was not strong then, because it was Tony holding me. I was all weak and not strong at all, because it was him. But for him, I was just someone he was pretending to fight with, for fun, like a boy. So I know he does not think anything about me at all.' She laughed at herself suddenly. 'It is all just "Barbie Parks, Barbie Parks" with him!' she cried, in a derisive mimicry.

But Robin saw the hurt beneath Ingrid's laughter, and she wished to take this lovely girl in her arms. 'Why don't you stay?' she urged. 'He might—find out?'

Ingrid shook her head. 'No. Besides, there is the immigration law. Already I have had my permit changed so I could stay till now. Better I go.' She moved to take the pose again. 'Now you can be finished pretty soon,' she said.

Before lunch, the work was done in rough. 'I can do the rest without you,' Robin said. 'So you can have your afternoon with Tony. Thanks, mightily, Ingrid.'

The girl looked at what Robin had done, her head on one side. 'Yes, it is me,' she said. 'Prettier than me, maybe. But anyone would know it was me. I think Tony will like to look at it when I am gone.'

7

(January 1939)

Robin stayed on in Hanover a few days longer, but she saw not so much as she wished to see of Tony. A January thaw with days of warm rain put a period to the skiing, so her path and his did not cross; yet she thought it surprising that he never came into the Inn. So many of the other boys did so. Her acquaintance among them, begun that night at the Nugget, had widened till she knew a dozen or so; and if she was in the lobby when any of them appeared, they were apt to stay in pleasant, laughing talk awhile.

But Tony was never one of them, and the time came for her to return to New York. She could not go without trying to reach some better understanding with Mark's son, so she telephoned him and asked him to dine with her the night before her departure. He at first made excuses; but she insisted.

'I want to talk to you,' she said frankly. 'We've things to talk over, Tony.'

So, reluctantly, he agreed to come. It was true that after that first day or two he had avoided her. This was because when he was with her he liked her more and more, feeling in her the desire to be liked by him and responding to it; and because he enjoyed being with her, he blamed himself, taking his own affection for her more seriously than it deserved. Tony was not yet twenty years old. His years of close companionship with his father, who never treated him like a child, and the fact that as a result of a certain readiness at study he was a year or two younger than most men in his class, had made him seem to himself more mature than his years; but he was still young enough to exaggerate the importance of his feeling for Robin. It was to him tragic and terrible that he should feel so toward her whom his father would one day marry; and he thought in youthful despair of going far away, of leaving them to forget him and to be happy together.

He agreed to dine with her, he told himself, only because she insisted; yet because he was excited and shaken at the thought of seeing her again, he put on a severe dignity. She was waiting in the lobby when he appeared. When they were seated and had ordered, they were a moment silent, and she was amused at her own timidity in the face of this grave boy who watched her so sternly. She spoke of the sketches she had done. 'The one of Ingrid is the best, of course,' she said. 'But I've worked up some others. Come tomorrow morning and I'll show them all to you. They need to be looked at by daylight.'

'I'd like to see them,' he agreed politely. He was so persistently polite! She mustered courage.

'We need to be better acquainted, Tony,' she said. 'I know your father told you that he and I—love each other.'

'Sure,' he agreed, reddening miserably.

'He told you even before he told me,' she reminded him. 'You've al-ways meant more to him than I can ever mean.'

'We always got along all right.' There was a hard reserve in his tone.

'He's fine, isn't he?'

'He's swell.'

She said, in an instinctive feminine effort to put him on the defen-sive: 'You know, the first time I met him, he was pretty distressed about you and your accident.'

He looked at her, grinning almost amiably. 'Do we have to talk about that some more?' he protested. 'We talked that business dry at lunch in Boston.'

She smiled with him; and this mutual amusement made her bold. 'Tony,' she challenged, 'you don't want me to marry your father, do you?'

'Sure, go ahead.' His lips were white.

'You don't mind his marrying again?'

'No, he'll be a lot happier.'

'But you don't want him to marry me?' she insisted. 'Isn't that true, honestly?'

He hesitated. 'I want him to marry whoever he wants to,' he declared. 'He's the one to be satisfied, not me.'

She shook her head. 'No. I want you to be satisfied too.' Then she added strongly: 'I love him too much to be willing to make any differ-ence, any slightest break between you two.'

'You can't!' he said, almost sharply. 'Dad and I understand each other.'

Robin hesitated, suddenly wondering that she could talk thus simply of marrying Mark when that must be, for as long as Davy lived, impos-sible. But then in a complete lucidity she understood herself. Davy was alive, it was true; but she knew fully and completely her love for Mark and his for her, and the fact that Davy was alive was no barrier to that love. True, Davy's being alive made their marriage impossible; and yet in deep ways they were already one, their vows exchanged, their hearts sure. Davy, though life still clung jealously to his broken body, was no barrier between her and Mark except in formal ways.

But this boy here, with the unrelenting sternness of youth in him, was a barrier. She looked at him again and asked steadily: 'Why didn't you want him to know about our being together that evening at the inn?'

It was Tony's turn to hesitate. 'Why, I'd already told him about that,' he said awkwardly. 'After what I had said—I didn't want him to know you were that girl. Not with him feeling about you the way he did.'

'What had you told him?' Her tone was still.

For a moment he did not answer her, remembering what he had told his father, remembering his happy certainty that he would find that girl some day again. He said uneasily, in a grim scorn: 'Oh, just what I told him at lunch that day, that you kissed me good night, and made a date for the next day and then stood me up.'

She asked quietly: 'That I flirted with you?' He did not meet her eyes, and she said in an even tone: 'You thought of me, perhaps, as a girl your own age. But you know—I'm ten years older than you, Tony. You seemed like a boy to me—a boy in trouble. I liked you and wanted to help you.'

'Sure,' he agreed, scorning himself. 'And I cried on your shoulder about Barbie!'

'You didn't cry on my shoulder,' she protested, trying to make him understand her own mood that night. 'You were fine. But I could see you were hurt. And I liked you, Tony. You see, you reminded me of Davy, and perhaps without my knowing it you reminded me of your father, too. You do look alike, though I didn't think of it that night. But after we said good night—forgive me—I thought you liked me, and might come to like me a lot, and I didn't want you to be hurt again. That's why I left, Tony.' He did not speak, and she asked gently: 'Why are you blaming me? For running away—or for liking you?'

'I don't blame you for anything,' he told her, heroically assuring himself that since she and his father loved each other, she should never know the truth. 'Forget it!' He tried to smile. 'Go ahead and marry Dad. If you make him happy, it will be all right with me. I'll be all for you.'

She urged, almost pleadingly: 'If you blame me for that night, I wish you'd bring it out into the open so we can talk it over.'

'There's nothing to talk over,' he retorted, and he added, in a noble resignation: 'Talking never does any good, anyway.'

'I think you're wrong about that.' She smiled, appealing to him. 'Didn't it do you good that night to talk to me about Barbie, to blow off steam?'

'I suppose it did.'

'Then it might do some good if we talked freely now.' He stirred restlessly, uneasy under her insistence, half angry. 'Is it because you think I flirted with you?' she asked straightforwardly. 'Is that it? I can understand your feeling that way.' She smiled a little. 'But—can you understand that a woman of thirty—almost thirty—might be happy for an hour with a nice boy—even if she's never going to see that boy again? She might feel young again, as young as he.' He did not speak, and she said: 'I suppose you can't understand that, so you—think ill of me. Is that it? Tell me the truth, Tony.'

Think ill of her? That she should so misunderstand seemed to him not to be endured. Surely, even though he must go out of her life forever, it was his right that she should know the truth. He looked at her steadily for a long moment, and his lips were white, his cheeks hard and tight. 'The truth?' he challenged. 'Is that what you want?'

'Yes.' His tone was so intense that she wished to smile; but it was wrong to be amused by the intensities of youth. She realized for the first time how young he was, despite his outward maturity; and she felt herself infinitely older than he. 'Yes,' she said; and then, half guessing what he was about to say, she added a reservation. 'Yes, if you want to tell me.'

But he heard only her affirmative. She wanted the truth. Well, she should hear it. He leaned a little toward her. 'All right,' he said, in a low, defiant voice. 'You asked for it. Here it is. I don't want you to marry Dad because I'm in love with you, myself. More, every time I see you!'

She leaned sharply back in her chair, her hands pressed against the table, and sat staring at him, shocked and silenced. After a moment he rose in harsh defiance. 'There! Take the change out of that!' he said, and strode away. His head was high, he felt himself a giant; he marched back across the campus toward the dormitory with heels pounding like a conqueror.

Robin, thus abruptly abandoned, watched him go with troubled eyes; and she no longer wished to smile. She half rose to follow him, but that could do no good. She did not see him again before she left Hanover, returning to New York to the safe harbor of her work once more.

8

(February 4, 1939)

Mark's affection for Elin had led him to suggest that her baby be born here at home. Nell Ritchie was frank in her disapproval of this arrangement. 'You can imagine what Emma Sheffield will say about it,' she declared. But Mark stuck to his guns.

'I don't value Emma's opinion,' he told Nell. 'As for this baby of

Elin's, she and Einar are fine, self-respecting young people; but they have to count every penny. I could pay Elin's hospital bill, but then they would feel indebted to me, and—Finns pay their debts, you know. This will save them money. One of Elin's cousins is a graduate nurse, and she will come and help, and Doctor Hethering won't charge them much. So that's the way it's going to be.'

The baby was born in the early morning of the fourth of February. Einar woke Mark soon after midnight, and Mark called Doctor Hethering. Elin's cousin, the nurse, was already in the house, sharing Tony's room with Anna. Doctor Hethering came at once, but there was waiting, and he and Mark sat in long talk in the living room downstairs, the older man going up occasionally to see how Elin did.

They talked of Dave Rollins, who was still in the hospital. 'He's an unhappy man,' Doctor Hethering said. 'There is the root of his trouble. He thinks of nothing but winning his wife to come back to him again. I don't know her?' His word was a question.

'I doubt whether they ever will be reconciled,' Mark admitted. 'She's gone through a lot with him in the past, till perhaps her love for him has just worn itself out.' He had sometimes blamed Marcia's coddling for Dave's weakness, but there was no need of saying so. 'His daughter is a fine young woman.' Ruth had come half a dozen times to see him during his own illness. She was tempered now and strong.

'Yes, she is,' Doctor Hethering agreed. 'And she means much to him, but it's his wife he wants. If he ever gives up hope of her, it will go hard with him.'

They talked, too, through those long hours, of other things. The Spanish war was all but ended. Barcelona had fallen. Loyalists by the scores of thousands had fled from Spain into France; and Mark hoped that with the end of the Spanish bloodshed there was a better chance of settled peace in Europe. In the Far East, Japanese bombs were still slaughtering Chinese civilians, and the United States had begun to send supplies to the Chinese forces through Rangoon and overland by the Burma Road.

'Probably Japan doesn't like that,' Mark commented.

'The United States, considering how weak we are in a military way, shows a singular eagerness to make enemies,' Doctor Hethering agreed. 'We're selling war planes to France now, and Hitler calls Mr. Roosevelt a warmonger.'

'I suppose Mr. Roosevelt's statement that our eastern frontier lies on the Rhine was his retort to that.'

'He denies having said it,' the Doctor pointed out. 'Although I suspect he's lying.'

Mark said reasonably: 'When a maid tells a caller that her mistress is not at home, that is a convention, not a lie. Certainly Mr. Roosevelt could not admit having made such a statement.'

'It sounds like something he might have said,' Doctor Hethering insisted. 'I don't suppose there's any doubt that he thinks we will eventually have to fight Germany—and wants us to. And as I said to you a few weeks ago, if we're to have a war, let's have it soon. If it's coming, then "'twere well it were done quickly."' He chuckled. 'Like having babies,' he said, and went up the stairs to Elin.

Elin's baby was born a little before daylight, and Einar brought it, wrapped warmly, for Mark to see. Mark thought Einar had grown inches taller overnight. 'But he is a girl,' Einar said apologetically. 'So she will be named Anna, because now we cannot name it after you.'

The baby squalled raspingly, and Mark shook Einar's hand and remembered that night, now almost twenty years ago, when Tony was born. Einar bore the baby away upstairs again, and Doctor Hethering came down to say that Elin was all right. 'Now I'm going home to bed,' he said. 'And I prescribe the same for you.'

But Mark did not at once go to bed. He sat thinking, wrapped in a sense of well-being. As long as babies went on being born, humanity could always make a fresh start, and all would in the end be well with the world. He had a sudden thought which amused and pleased him. To him, and to most men, what was happening in Europe seemed to be a matter of vital and permanent consequence. Yet it was perfectly possible, was even probable, that from the point of view of men living fifty years hence, the most important event of this year 1939 would seem to have been the birth of some baby like Elin's. Hitler must be about fifty years old. Then the most important event of the year 1889, from the point of view of the world of today, had been the birth of a baby whom she named Adolf to a poor woman somewhere in Austria. How different the world of today might be if that baby had never been born, or if it had fallen victim to some childish ill!

Some day the world would remember certain years as the years when great men had been born. Was Christ born in the year one, or in the year zero? Mark was sufficiently interested in his own fanciful thought to turn to the Encyclopedia and check a few great names. Shakespeare was born in 1564, George Washington in 1732, Napoleon in 1769,

Abraham Lincoln in 1809, Christopher Columbus in 1446—or some said, 1451. These were important dates in the history of mankind.

But no one appreciated the importance of those births at the time. A great man, like a great work of art, might go unrecognized for fifty years. People—everyone except the mothers and fathers most closely concerned—took babies as a matter of course, forgetting their potentialities. Mark remembered a remark attributed to Ben Franklin when the great philosopher had watched a balloon ascension. Someone challenged: 'Yes, but what use is it?' and Franklin countered: 'What use is a baby?'

Thinking of Elin's baby and of all the babies born in this decade, who among them would make the world of fifty years hence, Mark had that sense of personal unimportance which may come from looking at the distant stars. His own life, and the lives of most men his age, were already lived, their importance in the scheme of things determined; but any baby born today might grow to be the greatest man or the greatest woman the world had ever known.

Or the worst! If the world blessed 1446, or 1564, or 1732, or 1809, because in those years Columbus, Shakespeare, Washington, Lincoln, had been born, so might millions come to curse the year of Hitler's birth. His deeds in Europe bulked large today, but from the point of view of the world of 1989, the most important event of this year 1939 might well seem to have been, not the travail of Europe, giving birth to another war, but the travail of some obscure and humble woman, giving birth to a son who would one day shake or save the world.

9

(February 1939)

Tony had asked Lucy Pride to Carnival more to impress his father and Robin than to please himself. But after Lucy accepted, and after that day at the Inn when he had told Robin he loved her, he hoped Lucy would not come. He wanted to be alone, and he wrote Lucy and warned her that she probably would not have a very good time at Carnival; but she blithely replied that of course she would! He thought in grim resentment that he might have to conjure up a broken leg or an attack of influenza to keep her away, but he did nothing.

He was by that time able to look back at his last hour with Robin with honest eyes, feeling that he had been a little ridiculous, or worse;

and a few days before Carnival he wrote to tell her so, saying straight-forwardly:

Dear Mrs. Kerr:

I've made a damned fool of myself, made you unhappy by saying what I did that night here, and made Dad unhappy, too, by the way I acted that day in Boston. This is just to tell you that I know it, and to ask you to for-give me and to forget what I said. I'm still young as Hell in lots of ways. I'll grow up after a while, but when you were up here, I was just a spoiled kid crying for the moon!

I'm not even going to say I'll get over it, because there's nothing to get over. I think you're swell, and I've acted like a heel, trying to make you un-happy, that's all.

When are you and Dad going to get married? Can't you make it during my spring vacation? Don't keep him waiting too long. He's the best there is and you're the next best. Make it as soon as you can.

Sincerely yours,

Tony.

He mailed that letter, and looked forward to Robin's reply for reassur-ance and forgiveness; but the Carnival week-end arrived and he had had no word from her, and he was worried when he met Lucy at the train.

She was radiant with excited anticipation, and when they reached the house, she quickly became the centre of the group there. She had brought her guitar, and after dinner she was made to sing for a long time in the big living room with no light except from the open fire; and she sat cross-legged on the floor, leaning back against Tony's knees, and sang till she was tired. Then she and Tony walked around the campus to see the ice statuary, and he brought her back to dress for the dancing that would last till dawn. He hoped there would be a letter from Robin in the late mail, but there was not; and when they met again, Lucy saw his abstraction and teased him about it with many questions, demanding that he tell her what was wrong.

'There's nothing wrong,' he assured her. 'Just your imagination.'

'You can't fool me, Tony,' she urged. 'When a boy dances with me as if I were something clammy, I know he's worried about something! Aren't you going to tell me?'

'There's nothing to tell.'

To punish him for his reticence, she devoted herself to Joe Hazen, disappearing for more than an hour; but Tony was rather relieved than irritated by this, and when she returned he made no attempt to recap-ture her, till in the end she sought him.

'You haven't come near me for hours, Tony,' she said. 'Aren't you going to dance with me again at all?'

'I thought you were doing all right for yourself.'

'I'm never all right when you're mad at me,' she told him sweetly, and he laughed and took her in his arms. She had the trick of making any man feel himself expert, and Tony danced well enough. It was as though she lay close to him, her cheek pressed against his; and she said nothing, nor did he, till the music paused. Then she looked up at him, her cheek flushed, the soft hair on her brow pressed moistly down where his cheek had rested. His blood was racing, too, his sullen anger vanished now.

'I guess you didn't think you were dancing with a clammy something that time!' she whispered breathlessly.

'Some fun?' he challenged.

'Some fun!' She touched his arm. 'Take me somewhere, Tony,' she said in a husky voice. 'I want to be just with you.'

His throat was full. He found someone's fur coat in the hall, and high overshoes, and bundled her into them; found his own things, and they went out-of-doors. 'Let's get a car and drive,' she said. There was someone's car in front of the house with the key in the lock, and they took the Lime road, turning off across the golf course to the ski jump. The night was cold and clear, the stars bright. When he stopped and turned off the headlights, she said contritely:

'I was mean to you tonight.'

'No, you weren't.'

'I meant to be!' she insisted. He laughed.

'You don't know how to be mean to a man.'

'Well, not to you, maybe, Tony. But—I wanted you to tell me things, and you wouldn't, and I was furious with you. But I don't care now. I don't want you to tell me anything now—except how much you like me.'

He chuckled, recklessly glad to forget his own thoughts. 'There isn't time for that. That would take years!'

She pressed against him, said in pretty cajolery: 'Of course, if you happened to want to tell me why you acted so glum at first——' He put her off for a while, insisting that she was imagining things which did not exist, stubbornly bent on holding his tongue; but they were alone and the night was still and she was sweet in his arms. He said at last:

'Why, Lucy, it's nothing, really. Only—you know how Dad and I are.'

'No, I don't.' She looked up at him in the darkness, mirth in her tones. 'How are you?'

He laughed. 'Why—I mean we always get along pretty well. But he told me at New Year's that he's going to get married again, and I'm still trying to get used to the idea, that's all.'

'Married?' She was instantly excited. 'Is she nice? Do I know her?'

'I don't think so. She's an artist.' Then he said, in sudden recollection: 'But maybe you do, at that! She was at the inn up in Canada where we all went after Christmas. She was doing sketches, out on the slopes, the day we got there?'

'Oh, I saw her, of course. She's awfully clever. I looked over her shoulder.'

'Well, I met her up there,' he explained. 'After we all went to bed that night, a log rolled out of the fire and I went to fix it, and she was there, and we sat and talked awhile.' He had an uncomfortable feeling that this confidence was dangerous, but it was easy to talk in the darkness where they sat together here, with Lucy close beside him; and he needed the balm of speech. 'But I didn't know who she was,' he confessed, 'until I got back to Boston and Dad introduced us. We all had lunch at the Copley.'

'But she's young! She's our age!' Lucy protested.

'She's older than she looks, I guess,' he explained. 'And Dad's not so damned old.' He added: 'She and I talked for a long time that night.'

Caught by his tone, she twisted in his arms to look at him in sharp attention, cried in shrewd conjecture: 'And you liked her yourself!'

'Sure, she's great,' he said heartily, hoping thus to content her; but Lucy tugged at his arm, shook him fiercely.

'Oh, not that! You know what I mean.' Her voice rose with excitement. 'I think that's awfully dramatic, Tony. I mean your falling in love with her and then your father telling you he was going to marry her. I think that's perfectly thrilling!'

'Hey,' he protested, trying to laugh away her guesses. 'Don't go getting so many ideas!'

'But it is, Tony!' she cried. 'Both of you in love with the same girl!'

'Don't be a damned fool!'

'I'm not a damned fool! I'm a lot smarter than you think.' She held his hand in both hers. 'Poor Tony!' she whispered, laughing at him. 'Is his heart broken?'

'Nuts!' His cheek was hot in the darkness.

'Well, I know you're desperately in love with someone!' she insisted. 'How do you know so much?'

'I can tell by the way you've been treating me!'

He chuckled. 'Oh, is that so?' He took her in his arms, and she tried to put his arms aside; but he cupped her chin in his hand and turned up her face and kissed her. 'There!' he challenged. 'Does that feel as if I were in love with someone?'

'M-hm!' she said in happy assent.

'Who?'

'Me!'

'Now, you're talking sense!' There was suddenly a riot in his blood, and her cheek was hot against his own. He would have clipped her close again, but she drew away.

'No, Tony,' she protested. 'I think we'd better talk about your father some more. When are they going to be married?'

'I don't know. They haven't decided.' And in sudden concern he urged: 'Say, don't tell anybody what I told you, will you? I didn't even tell Dad that I'd met her up there.'

'Why not?' She was instantly alert again. 'Tony Worth, did you make love to her?'

'Like this, you mean?' He sought to illustrate.

'Don't!' she insisted: 'Did you, Tony?'

'You want to know a lot, don't you?'

'Well,' she retorted, 'you want to kiss a lot. I'll trade with you! You tell me every single thing that happened and I'll kiss you.'

'How many times?' he bargained.

'Well—some! Did you make love to her?'

'No, I didn't!' There was a stubborn caution in him still. 'We just talked, but it was swell!' He leaned toward her, here in the circle of his arm. 'Now!'

But she fought away. 'No, no. You haven't told me anything yet! Didn't you kiss her even once?'

'No!'

'I'll bet you did. If you didn't, why didn't you tell your father about knowing her?'

'No reason,' he insisted.

'Hasn't she told him?'

'No. I didn't tell him, so she thinks I don't want him to know, and she doesn't want to make trouble between us.'

'But why should it make trouble between you—if you didn't do anything?'

He said harshly: 'Damn it, I've told you all there is to tell!'

'I'll bet you kissed her!' She pleaded prettily: 'Didn't you even kiss her once, Tony? Just a teeny-teeny little one. Just when you said good night!'

'I already said "No."'

'Tell me the truth, Tony! Please!'

He grinned. 'Oh, all right, yes,' he admitted. 'I kissed her good night. So what?'

'So now we're getting somewhere,' she sighed contentedly, settling back in the seat beside him. 'Oh, I think it's just marvellously exciting; both of you in love with the same girl.'

'Don't be that way! I'm not in love with her!'

'Then—are you in love with Barbie?'

'Hell, no. We're just good friends.'

'All the same,' she reminded him, 'after she told you she was engaged, you were just miserable! Only you tried to hide it!'

He laughed. 'I've grown up since then.' He spoke half bitterly. 'I'm growing up fast,' he said.

She touched his brow in teasing mirth. 'Poor boy, his hair turned gray in a night! But Tony—' Her voice was husky, cajoling. 'If you're not in love with Barbie, or with the other one—aren't you in love with anybody at all?'

He chuckled. 'Maybe I'm in love with you.'

'Then tell me!' she demanded.

'O.K., then, I am in love with you!'

'Tell me another way!' she urged softly. Her lips were upturned; and after a moment, greedily, she whispered: 'Now another way!' And again: 'Now another way!'

Her lips, laughing under his, inspired him to infinite invention; and he surrendered to the magic she knew how to weave. But he was at the same time almost abstracted, thinking more of his father and of Robin than of this teasing, electric, laughing girl beside him; wishing Robin's letter would come to give him absolution.

When Lucy departed Sunday afternoon, she made him promise to come to Boston soon. He said at first that he could not; but she protested in mock warning: 'You'd better, Tony! Remember, now I know your guilty secret—and your father's—I've got you in my power!'

He laughed: 'Blackmail, eh?'

'You bet!' Then she laughed and told him softly, her eyes warm: 'You might like it, though!' She could be so stingingly sweet! 'If you come, we'll get a car and drive out to some more ski jumps!' she promised. This was at the train, just before she went aboard.

'Well, I'll try and make it,' he told her. When he kissed her good-bye, her lips moved against his.

'Please do come soon, Tony,' she pleaded, and freed herself and climbed aboard the train. Safe on the top step she said maddeningly: 'I want you to tell me that in another way!' He would have sprung up the steps to meet this challenge, but the train began to move, and she fled. Tony rubbed his hand across his mouth. His pulse was thumping in his throat. She waved to him from the window as the train pulled away.

10

(March 1939)

Mark had wished to see Robin immediately after her return from Hanover to New York, and he wrote to suggest this; but Robin, remembering in her every waking hour what Tony had said, dreaded seeing Tony's father. It seemed to her that she could not be with him for long without betraying Tony, and the thought was intolerable. Of course, Tony's word had been no more than a boy's madness; but she was sure Tony thought that word true.

So she dared not see Mark, and to escape him she conjured up a hurried trip to Southern Pines. 'It's to paint pictures of horses, of all things, darling!' she wrote him. 'But I'm a business woman and I have to go. I'm leaving tomorrow. I'll be back in a week or two, wanting terribly to see you.'

Her week at Southern Pines extended itself. Tony's letter, delayed in forwarding from New York, reached her there, and when she read it her eyes filled with grateful tears. Certainly Tony could do no more than he had done to reassure her. She wrote him with a brief sincerity, and then she was afraid he might find her answer curt, and she tore up that letter and wrote another, full of understanding and affection. Tony had urged that she and Mark be married at once, and she replied:

> We'll be married soon, I hope. I know that's what you want, and it's what we want, too.

She hesitated, tempted to tell him about Davy; but that was a secret she had kept so long; so she said only:

> But there are a number of things, commissions I must finish first. I'm a business woman, you know. I'm down here on business, and I've orders for a long time ahead. I want to get them all out of the way beforehand, be-

cause some of them mean travelling, down here and to other places, and I won't want to be so much away from home after we're married.

She added a few paragraphs about Hanover, and Ingrid, and quoted a passage from one of Mark's recent letters, and said she wished Mark did not worry so much about what was happening in Europe, and that she and Tony must conspire together to give him other things to think about. But when the letter was done, it did not satisfy her. She was sure of Tony's fondness for her, and would not have had it less; but there was no way to say that without saying more than she intended. Tony was a boy, young enough so that he would surely change and yet old enough so that he must be taken seriously. And certainly that night at Hanover he had thought he meant exactly what he said.

She stayed longer than she had expected in Southern Pines, but early in March she wrote Mark that she was returning to New York, and he wired that he would fly over Monday afternoon to dine with her and take the midnight back to Boston. She bade him come to her apartment, and she waited his coming with a great gladness, and when she opened the door to him she went happily into his arms.

'Oh, I don't like separations, Mark!' she cried. 'Not such long ones!'

He held her strongly. 'Nor I, Robin.' She clung to him, and he touched her hair with his hand. 'I wish this was the last one, that we never need be separated again.'

She freed herself and borrowed his handkerchief to dry her streaming eyes, laughing up at him. 'I always cry if I'm too happy to bear,' she said. 'Some fun?'

'Some fun!' he agreed; and then he said in quick, amused recognition: 'That's one of Tony's catchwords. Did you learn it from him at Hanover?'

She remembered instantly that she had learned it from Tony that evening in Canada, and she wished terribly to tell Mark the truth; but to tell him now meant so many explanations. 'Yes, of course,' she said. 'Have you seen him lately?'

'I was in Hanover over the twenty-second.'

'How was he?' she asked carefully.

'Fine,' he assured her. 'We talked a lot about you—naturally. You won him completely, you know.'

Won him? Her heart was shaken. Perhaps she had won him too completely.

'He's ever so nice,' she said easily, and led the way to her small kitchen where there was a steak to broil, and for a while they worked happily together there. She was reminded of Elin and asked for her and for the baby.

'They're gone now,' Mark said. 'Einar found a small apartment in an old house near where Mr. Marshman lives, so he can go home for lunch and in between times. It was a ramshackle place, but Elin's already doing wonders with it. I gave them some of their furniture for a wedding present.' He smiled. 'I think Elin's homesick sometimes, though. She comes to the house when she can, brings the baby, and bosses Anna around.'

'How's Anna working out?'

'She's all right, a good cook, and a good worker; but she lacks something.' He laughed. 'Lacks flavor, perhaps,' he said. 'The things she cooks always need a little more salt—and so does she.'

'Heavens! I don't think I salted this steak,' she exclaimed, and did so. 'I hope you don't miss Elin too much. There, now we can sit down.'

At table, he spoke of Tony again. 'I'm glad you could see him in Hanover,' he said. 'He wasn't at his best, that day we had lunch together.'

'Don't blame him,' she urged. 'I don't think we realize, you and I, what a hard time boys his age are having with themselves. I talked to some of them in Hanover, Tony and others too. They're worried about politics, and they wonder what the country's coming to.'

Mark nodded. 'I know. There's not much stability in the world today, and these youngsters in college miss it, are lost without it.'

'You're the stable foundation of Tony's life, Mark. That's something he must never lose.'

'When we're married, he'll have both of us.'

She said smilingly: 'He won't have as much of you as he has now. I'm greedy, Mark. I'm even a little jealous of him.'

He touched her hand, smiling with her. 'I'm glad he's not a little older. He might want to marry you himself!'

She said quickly, laughingly: 'If he ever did, I might have a time deciding between you!' On this point safety must always lie in jest.

'I wouldn't blame you,' he confessed.

'All the same,' she said, more seriously, 'I'm glad, really, that you and I must wait awhile, Mark. It will give Tony time to get used to the idea of losing you.' She added with a smile: 'Remember, he's just lost Miss Parks.'

'He's already recovered from that,' he told her. 'I don't know whether you remember, he spoke about a girl at the inn in Canada?'

She held her tone steady. 'Yes, I remember.'

'That girl really made a deep impression on him,' he said thoughtfully. Robin could not face him and she hurriedly rose to clear away, and he to help her, and while they moved from table to kitchen and back again, he added: 'He told me about her the night after he came home. He liked her a lot.'

'Shall I make coffee?' She could not bear to listen.

'Not for me, thanks. And he hasn't forgotten her. After he went back to Hanover, he wrote me that he liked that other girl so well that he realized Barb wasn't the only girl in the world for him.' He added: 'Perhaps he'll find her again. I hope he does. It's good for a boy to be in love.'

'I'm not sure he cares for that other girl,' she suggested, a little desperately. 'He called her a "free neck." Remember?'

Mark smiled. 'That was just to get even with her for running away from him.'

Robin forced herself to speak lightly. 'There's a Norwegian girl at Hanover, Ingrid Sigurdson, who thinks he's pretty wonderful,' she said. 'I did watercolors of her and we became good friends. She told me—as good as told me—that she was in love with Tony.'

'I've met her, at the Ritchies',' Mark assented. 'I remember I had an impression she was fond of him.' He added: 'I've always hoped Tony might wind up by marrying Jan Ritchie.'

'He'll find someone!'

He said thoughtfully: 'He's taken a fancy just now to Lucy Pride, had her up for Carnival. I'm not sure I like that. She radiates excitement, gives it off just as a cat gives off sparks after it's been lying under a stove. Her husband will have to be extremely understanding, or he'll have an unhappy time.' And he asked, for his thoughts were easily turned that way: 'Did you talk with Miss Sigurdson at all about what's happening in Europe?'

'No.' Tonight she seized on this impersonal topic, since it meant they would not talk about Tony any more. 'Do you still think war is coming?'

He nodded gravely. 'Yes. I'm afraid Chamberlain has persuaded himself that he really achieved a permanent peace at Munich, and I'm sure he's deluding himself. He went off to Rome to see Mussolini, here last month, and came home to England beaming and flattered. But I think England at Munich lost something she'll have to fight to regain.'

'Will we get into it? Now that I know Tony, I dread it as much as you do.'

'Well, a lot of Americans have the appeasement point of view,' he reminded her. 'Congress refused to fortify Guam, here ten days ago. The Japanese had said they didn't object; and the idea was just to dredge the harbor, put up some barracks. But the Republicans said that to fortify Guam would be a threat against Japan, and they virtuously object to pressure diplomacy, and enough Democrats joined with them to kill the measure.'

'Perhaps they're right.'

'Perhaps they are,' he assented. 'I sometimes think we'd be better off if we let the Philippines go, made Hawaii our western frontier.' He added: 'But of course all this is a sideshow. Japan will never attack us. Europe is the problem.'

She nodded, but she asked another question, clinging to talk of Europe's affairs as an escape from talk of Tony; and she persisted till Mark, remembering how he in the past had talked to her of a thousand things so that he might not say that which was foremost in his thoughts, half suspected the truth. When he had to leave at last to catch his Boston train, he said in gentle amusement:

'I've a feeling you've been making conversation, Robin, as if we dared not be silent together.'

She came close to him, laughing, pressing her fingertips against his lips. 'My dear, my dear,' she protested; and she said tenderly: 'I wish you didn't have to go.'

'I'll come again, soon, for a longer time.'

'Do, Mark, do!' she whispered. She smiled up at him. 'Do you know that once a woman has admitted she loves a man, her surrender is complete, my dear. I want to be with you always.'

He said huskily: 'I'll be praying every day for that time too.'

II

(March 1939)

Their longing to be together grew with every hour of separation. Robin had almost daily letters from Mark, and she treasured them, reading in them his need for her till she was heartsick because she could not yet be completely his. She was distressed, too, by his steady preoccupation with events in Europe. She herself, absorbed in her love for him, could forget all else; but Mark never wrote without some reference to what was passing overseas. In mid-March, Hitler's troops occupied Bohemia and Moravia. After Munich, France and England had guaranteed what was left of Czecho-Slovakia against 'unprovoked aggression'; but now, because under threat of invasion the Czechs had 'invited' this incursion, Mr. Chamberlain at first insisted that since there had been no unprovoked aggression the guarantee did not operate; and when in Parliament there were cries that Hitler had broken his promises, Chamberlain refused to associate himself with this charge.

Mark's letters to Robin were hot in denouncing this evasion, and he wrote once: 'The newspapers say England is "slightly bored" with the Czechs, that she "resolutely looked the other way," that her "apathy is overpowering." If she's ever to take a stand, it must be now. Hitler for the first time is seizing territory without even the pretense that the inhabitants are German, and the Italian papers are saying scornfully: "England and France stood even that!" '

When a week later, Chamberlain changed front, charging in his Birmingham speech that Hitler had violated his treaty pledges, Mark wrote exultantly: 'So there's some backbone in him after all. Perhaps the English people refused to let him make cowards of them. Or perhaps he finally realized that Germany has seized enough Czech planes and material to equip forty divisions of troops.'

In that same letter he urged her to come to Boston for a week-end during Tony's spring vacation. Sure of his need for her, she agreed to do so. She wrote too:

> I think Czecho-Slovakia was doomed, Mark. Versailles set her up as a nation, but she was really just a scarecrow designed to hold Germany in check. But Germany doesn't scare easily. The only way to destroy those sixty or seventy million energetic, ambitious, fecund people is to kill all of them.
>
> Germany has grown strong in adversity, but France has gone soft. Parisian politicians are too busy cultivating the good will of labor and defending their own prerogatives to remember the good of France. Employers and labor alike are playing treasure hunt, looking for profits, insisting on the individual's right to do as well as he can for himself, but forgetting that he has also duties.
>
> But, my darling, I wish you needn't distress yourself so much about all that. Why not be happy in planning our life together? It worries me to see you so disturbed by all these other things.

He replied, forgetting Europe—as she had hoped—in his delight that she would come to Boston. He wished her to stay at the house, but she pointed out that if she did so, his friends would guess the truth.

'And after all, my dear,' she reminded him ruefully, 'I'm still a married woman, and you're a judge—and you must avoid even the appearance of evil. No, I'll stay at the Copley. I've other friends in Boston, you know. It will seem natural enough.'

He agreed; but he confessed that he had told Bob and Nell Ritchie something about her. 'Not everything, of course. Nell wanted me for dinner Saturday evening, and I said I was considering having you do my portrait. Would you like to tackle that job, my dear? I hope the sittings will be many and long.'

She smiled at that, wired him her arrival hour, and—since she was to meet some of his friends—she spent a day in the shops by way of preparation.

12

(March 1939)

Tony came home for his Easter vacation the day before Robin would arrive, to find Mark in a rare excitement at the prospect; and Tony laughed affectionately. 'You're as nervous as a bridegroom, Dad,' he declared.

'I feel like one,' Mark admitted. 'It's a sort of landmark, son; Robin's first introduction to our friends.'

She would reach Boston at five Saturday afternoon, and Nell's dinner was at seven. Mark had planned to meet her train, come home to dress, and then go to fetch her out to dinner, and he calculated there would be time enough; but Tony said: 'That's going to hurry you. Why don't you stay a few minutes with her when her train gets in, and then come on home, and I'll go in and bring her out?' He added: 'I've a date with Lucy tonight, but I'll show up in time so you can have the car to take Mrs. Kerr back to town afterward.' Mark welcomed this suggestion, and it was settled so.

Tony, driving to town on that errand to fetch Robin, wondered whether she would be as he remembered her. When she joined him, he could not bear to look at her, because she was even more lovely than his memories; but almost at once he said, his eyes on the traffic: 'Mrs. Kerr, I want you to know I was talking through my hat, that day in Hanover. I was sore—God knows why—and I wanted to make it tough for you. I didn't mean it. Forget it, will you?'

'I knew you didn't mean it,' she assured him; but this was not completely true, and her word now did not convince him. He laughed a little, said in an amused tone:

'I see you don't believe me. I suppose a woman is always a lot quicker to believe a man when he says he loves her than when he says he doesn't!' This was so true that she could not speak. 'You think I'm just making a noble gesture, but I'm not broken-hearted, honestly.' He grinned at her. 'What do I have to do to convince you? Marry someone else?'

She laughed with him. 'Don't be absurd, Tony!'

'I might, at that,' he assured her. 'I'll do anything you say.'

She was silent beside him, sorely troubled. His words were fair enough, and she knew he meant them; yet she felt in him that emotion which he would never again willingly confess. She was sure of his loyalty, doubtful only of his strength. 'Don't worry,' she said quietly. 'Everything will be all right.'

'You're swell,' he said. 'You're perfect for Dad. I mean it, honestly.'

'You think a lot of him, don't you?'

'Of course.'

She touched his arm. 'So do I, Tony. I mean to make him happy in every way I can.'

They turned into the driveway. 'All right,' he said. 'I'll leave it to you two. Just as long as you know that I—that I'm not standing in the way. The sooner you're married, the better I'll like it.'

She made for a moment no move to alight, tempted again to tell him about Davy, to give him all her confidence; and she might have done so, but Mark had heard the car, and before she could speak, he opened the French doors and came out on the terrace to meet them. Tony called cheerfully to his father: 'Here she is, Dad, safe and sound! I'll be back in time so you can have the car.' Mark assured him he need not hurry, and Tony backed out of the driveway and departed as Robin met Mark and stepped with him into the living room.

She stood a moment, looking all around, then turned to him with a smile. 'I know it's a—commonplace remark, my dear; but—so this is where you live!'

'I've looked forward to your first time here.'

She came to him and kissed him. 'It's such a nice, comfortable, ordinary house, Mark. You're such a nice, comfortable, ordinary man.'

He laughed in a deep exhilaration, bowed elaborately. 'I'd never thought of myself in that way,' he confessed. 'Probably we all secretly think of ourselves as rather remarkable individuals.'

'I'm glad you're not one. Remarkable individuals must be terribly trying to live with.'

'I'd like to show you everything here, every book I've read, every picture and chair. I'm like a boy, wanting to show off his possessions.'

'I want to see everything, too. I want to know everything about you, your whole life. I want to see pictures of you when you were a little boy. I told you I was greedy, Mark. I'll never have enough of you, never have as much as I want.'

He laughed richly, his voice full of happiness. 'But there's no time for sight-seeing now. We're due at Nell's,' he said.

There were ten at Nell's dinner table that evening; Bob and Nell, Ed and Mary Halstead, Mark and Robin, Bob's father and mother, and a Mr. and Mrs. Merryman. Mr. Merryman was a Detroit man, a banker with the easy friendliness of the Mid-Westerner. He had come to Boston for a fortnight that would combine business and pleasure. Bob Ritchie was acting as Mr. Merryman's counsel, and Nell's dinner was in their honor. When Mark and Robin went across the street, they found the others, except Ed and Mary Halstead, already gathered; and Mark introduced Robin to Nell with such complete pride in his eyes that Nell could not fail to see it. Robin was slim and fair in something smooth and white, snug to the waist, flaring a little below; and her cheeks and throat and shoulders were as warm as new ivory. He watched the other men, saw their admiration, saw how easily she met them; and then Nell pinched his arm and whispered:

'Mark! You're beaming like a proud father! Why didn't you tell me?'

He laughed in frank delight. 'Isn't she wonderful?'

'Of course she is! But unless you want everyone to know all about it, for Heaven's sake, behave! Just wait till I get you to myself!'

So Mark tried to mend his ways; but at dinner he watched Robin so constantly that he forgot his own responsibilities till Mary Halstead at his elbow said mischievously: 'I'm Mrs. Halstead, Judge Worth. Ed's wife. Remember me?'

Mark laughed and turned to her, and Mary eyed him in smiling amusement while he asked how the children were; and he laboriously devoted himself to her till she said: 'There, I don't mean to be unreasonable, Mark! You can look at her once in a while!'

Robin, when his eyes turned that way, was laughing at a story Bob's father was telling, one of the current anecdotes about the indolence of WPA workers; and Bob countered with another; and Mr. Merryman had an anecdote which was new to these Bostonians; and Bob's father asked some question about labor problems in Detroit, and everyone listened to Mr. Merryman's answer. Then Mark asked curiously:

'How do Detroit people feel about Hitler, Mr. Merryman?'

The banker hesitated. 'Well,' he confessed with a deprecating smile, 'I'm afraid we take a view that's unpopular in the East. We think he's a pretty able man. His absorption of Czecho-Slovakia seems to us a superb example of power politics.'

Old Mr. Ritchie snorted. 'He had to do something!' he declared. 'Germany's economic situation was desperate, and German morale was sagging. He had to do something!'

'Aren't you in danger of believing that just to reassure youself?' Mr. Merryman suggested. 'You people in the East—I gather—expect us to fight Germany, so you welcome any report of her weakness.' He cleared his throat like a man about to make a speech. 'We're farther from the seaboard—and a lot farther from Europe—than you,' the Detroit man reminded them. 'That gives us a better perspective. England for this last two weeks has been playing her regular game, trying to get Poland and Russia and the others to do her fighting for her. The Polish Corridor is the next thing on Hitler's list, and he certainly has right on his side on that question. If the United States had lost a war with Canada, and had been forced to give Canada the state of New Hampshire, including Portsmouth and leaving Maine cut off from the rest of the country, we'd never rest till we won it back again. Will we fight to prevent Germany's doing just that?' The question was obviously rhetorical; and he said: 'England's "Peace Front" is a failure. Not even Poland will cooperate. Nor Russia.'

Mark thought old Mr. Ritchie was near an explosion. He was one of those fortunate people who were tormented by no doubts. For him, Hitler and Germany were always altogether in the wrong in every way. He had till recently abhorred Mr. Roosevelt, but now the President's foreign policy began to win him. His opinions were so violent that not even Bob ever ventured to discuss the war with his father; and Mr. Merryman's opinions and his dogmatic way of stating them had clearly brought him to the boiling point. His cheeks were red, his eyes blazing; and Nell, foreseeing a blast that would wreck her dinner, said quickly: 'Has anyone noticed how many new words we're getting out of this war talk? "Peace Front" and "Appeasement" and "Anschluss" and "Drang nach Osten" and "Lebensraum." No one ever heard of any of them till lately.'

'Words have an astonishing power over our minds,' Mark suggested, following her lead. 'We human beings are the only animals who talk. Perhaps that's why we're so easily influenced by words.' And he added smilingly: 'I wonder if Hitler's party wouldn't have won more sympathy over here if we hadn't learned to call his followers Nazis. I suppose to our ears there's hardly any combination of sounds more unattractive.'

'Of course,' Nell cried delightedly. 'Mark, that judicial mind of yours makes everything so simple. Nazis are nasty—naturally. With a name like that, they're simply bound to be.'

'The German language is an awful load for any nation to have to carry,' Bob declared, lending a hand while his father fumed in silence. 'It's always either ugly or funny. Take "Blitzkrieg," for instance. That sounds like some sort of fee-fie-foe-fum out of a Mother Goose rhyme; like a little boy trying to scare his nurse! And "Ersatz" sort of connotes "cheap" and "shoddy." Our "synthetic" means the same thing, but it sounds scientific and dignified.'

Mary Halstead helped them along. 'I should be completely terrified if a man ever told me he was a member of the Gestapo,' she declared. 'It's almost as bad as Ogpu. Nazis with their Gestapos under their arms would never be welcomed in our home—but I think Lebensraum is beautiful. It would make a lovely song title.'

'"Anschluss" is the worst of all, for my taste,' Nell declared. 'It's like talking with your mouth full! And a Nazi Anschluss! Phooey! You almost have to hold your nose to say it!'

Mr. Ritchie had begun to cool, and no one ventured on dangerous ground thereafter, and Nell had not again to interfere to keep the peace, and presently dinner was done. When the ladies left the room, Mark saw Nell whisper to Bob, guessed she had warned him to keep his father and Mr. Merryman from coming to blows; but these two and Ed began to talk together amiably and Bob asked Mark for news of Dave Rollins; and Mark was able to tell him that Dave was at home now, that Ruth was with him.

'I saw Ruth Wednesday,' he said. 'She's badly worried. Dave thinks of nothing but Marcia, talks of nothing else. He calls her on the telephone every night.'

'Where is Marcia?'

'In Florida. Ruth says her mother insists Dave must get along without her for at least a year.'

'Think he can do it?'

'I don't know.'

'I'll have to get out to see him.'

'I drive out once or twice a week,' Mark agreed.

He was glad when they rejoined the ladies, glad to draw near Robin, glad when at last Mr. and Mrs. Merryman said good night. Then Bob's father and mother departed, and he and Robin went across the street together.

'I'm afraid I was pretty transparent tonight,' he confessed, when they were alone. 'Nell said the way I looked at you gave me away. She and Mary are probably talking us over now, as fast as their tongues can wag.'

'I like your being transparent,' she assured him; and she added: 'I like your friends, too. Mrs. Halstead's sweet; and Mrs. Ritchie's clever. Did you see her stop the war? Old Mr. Ritchie was just about to start shooting.' She smiled. 'I wish Mrs. Ritchie could be given a chance to handle Chamberlain and Hitler. She'd make them come to terms.'

They were awhile together, sitting before the fire Mark lighted, till Tony presently returned. Then Mark drove her to town; and she came to spend most of Sunday at the house. She and Mark inspected the studio in the attic, and planned that she should come in June to do his portrait there. Other work, already arranged, would engage her through April and May. Mark put her on her train late Sunday afternoon. Driving home alone thereafter, he smiled to himself, thinking of Nell's many questions which he must answer now.

13

(May 1939)

One early morning in May, a telegram from Hardiston warned Mark that his father was being rushed to the hospital in Columbus for an operation for appendicitis. Mark was able quickly to arrange a few days' absence; and he flew West, arriving in Columbus early that afternoon. The operation had by that time been performed, and successfully. Dan Worth had always been a completely healthy man, and Mark found him rather proud of himself—and his affliction.

'The doctors tell me,' he explained, 'that it's almost unheard of for a man my age to have an appendix.'

Mark smiled affectionately. 'You're a very remarkable fellow,' he agreed. 'How do you feel?'

'Never better!'

'You'll soon be all right,' Mark promised. He stayed not long that first day, for the older man was still weak, and tired easily; but on the third day they had a long hour together.

Mark had spent the intervening time reading files of the Ohio papers, and he had talked with many Columbus men, appraising their point of view. Germany was pressing for a solution of the question of the Polish Corridor, and England had promised Poland that if she were attacked, and elected to resist, England would fight on her side. Mark spoke of this to his father, and he said:

'People out here seem to think that promise was a crime.'

The older man nodded. 'Worse than a crime, a mistake,' he corrected. 'Who was it said that? Napoleon? Some Frenchman.' And he said: 'England's put the lives of millions of young Englishmen and Canadians and Australians at the disposal of a handful of hot-headed Poles.'

'It at least simplifies the issue,' Mark suggested. 'If Germany invades Poland, there will be war. If she doesn't, there won't. So the decision— and the responsibility—is squarely up to Germany.'

'It leaves the fate of England in Poland's hands,' his father insisted. 'And the fate of the United States, too, because Roosevelt is determined to back England. There'll be no war unless and until the United States promises the Allies our support, but Roosevelt has certainly given England that promise; so he's delegating to England—and England is delegating to Poland—the decision as to whether the United States will go to war.'

Mark half smiled. His father had the trick of simplifying the most complicated issue, reducing it to a phrase; but oversimplification was always a danger. Yet he did not wish to argue with the older man. 'How did people feel out here about the Italian seizure of Albania?' he asked.

'That was to be expected,' Dan Worth said. 'England was trying to encircle Germany, to enlist the Balkan States on her side; and Italy is Germany's ally—so naturally she seized Albania and locked the door on the Balkans. That's just common sense.' And he added strongly: 'Germany and Italy have no illusions, Mark. That gives them a great advantage. England can never persuade herself to do anything without alleging some highly ethical reason, but the Axis doesn't bother with such nonsense. England was trying to line up the Balkans with talk of non-aggression pacts and peace fronts and all that; and the Axis stopped her with an army, that's all.'

Mark in their long afternoons together found his father strongly against Mr. Roosevelt's course in foreign affairs. They spoke one day of the President's farewell to the people at Warm Springs, his remark: 'I'll be back in the fall if we don't have a war.'

'He's bound to lead us along that road,' Dan Worth said. 'The will for peace in this country was never stronger than today, but he'll get us in.' And he added: 'You know this notion that if there's a fight anywhere we have to get into it is a new thing, new in my lifetime and in yours, Mark. Along about 1900 we began to talk imperialism. The munitions men financed the Navy League, and the Navy League worked on public opinion till people began to say we ought to go out and grab a share in world trade, not by making better goods and selling them cheaper than anyone else, but by gathering in a few colonies. The Spanish War gave them a start. Teddy brandished the Big Stick and impudently stuck his nose into the conference at Algeciras; and then Wilson came along and announced that it was our province to remake and reform the world.'

'And he only succeeded in creating Hitler,' Mark suggested.

'In a left-handed way,' the older man agreed. 'Wilson married us to Europe at Versailles, and the Senate gave us a divorce; but Hitler's the son of that brief, mistaken marriage.

'But even after the divorce, the game went on. Now Roosevelt, having failed to cure our domestic ailments, is using Europe as a counterirritant. His policy reminds me of a doctor I knew down in Mississippi when you were a baby. A big darky had his hand badly cut in a sawmill. The doctor set out to trim off a few fingers and thumbs; but he had no anaesthetic. To keep the negro from feeling the pain, he put hot irons against the soles of his feet. Then he fixed up the hand all right, but the darky's feet were so badly burned that he couldn't walk for six weeks. If Roosevelt tricks us into another war as a counter-irritant to his domestic failures, it will take us longer than six weeks to recover.' He added shrewdly: 'You Bostonians don't feel that way, I know. You're sold on imperialism.'

'Not quite,' Mark assured him. 'Most of the people I know hate Hitler, but no one wants war.' He added smilingly: 'Of course there's a lot of feeling that England ought to fight him.'

'England won't fight till she's sure we'll help,' Dan Worth declared, and he said strongly: 'Even Canada has more sense than we have. She's said she wouldn't send troops abroad to help England. You saw what Prime Minister Mackenzie King said, that the idea that Canada should feel called on to save Europe every twenty years was a nightmare and sheer madness.' He chuckled. 'That's why the King and Queen are coming over; to remind Canadians of their loyalty.'

Mark asked: 'What did you think of Roosevelt's note asking Hitler to promise not to invade any more countries for ten years?'

The older man said scornfully: 'That was just a trick question, like the other one: "Are you going to stop beating your wife? Answer yes or no." If Germany gave the assurance, she'd be admitting she was the aggressor. If she refused, she'd be self-convicted. But I thought Hitler's answer a masterpiece.'

Mark nodded reluctantly. 'If I were a German I'd think it a wonder-ful speech,' he agreed.

The older man smiled in a warm affection: 'You always, even as a boy, saw both sides,' he remembered. 'If other boys got down on one boy, you took his part; but if one boy tried to run the crowd, he had to fight you.' He added quizzically: 'You're a natural-born neutral, Mark; but that just means that when the shooting starts, you'll be between two fires.'

'It seems to me the shooting will start soon,' Mark confessed. 'I read recently where some Polish statesman said that if Germany attacked Poland, there would be Polish troops in Berlin within three weeks. He said Poland could handle Germany easily and alone. That sort of boasting doesn't help things.'

The older man said soberly: 'I saw an editorial in the *Detroit Free Press* the other day. It said: "If outside amateurs who imagine that they are world statesmen can be persuaded to keep out of affairs that are none of their business, the peace of the world may yet be preserved."' Mark remembered Mr. Merryman. Probably he read the *Free Press*. Dan Worth added: 'And John McCutcheon, in a *Tribune* cartoon the other day, had Uncle Sam say: "I don't believe there will be a major war in Europe until Britain and France have my promise I'll come in with them, and I don't intend to go in. Once was enough!" That's the whole story, Mark. They won't fight unless they're sure we'll help them finish it.'

Mark nodded; but he saw that the older man seemed to be tired, so he changed the subject. 'By the way, Father, I've some news for you.' He told the other about Robin, and Dan Worth was delighted.

'That's fine, son,' he said. 'I've always hoped you'd marry again. Your Tony's a fine boy—but one grandson isn't enough to satisfy me. When will you be married?'

So Mark spoke of Davy. 'Of course, she could have her freedom,' he said. 'But she doesn't want to do that. There's a blind loyalty in her which I can't help respecting. But she doesn't think he will live long.'

His father nodded understandingly. 'I'll have to come on soon to meet her,' he said. 'It's a long time since I've been East.' Mark came to Ohio when he could, usually running out for a few days at least once a year, but his father preferred to stay close at home in Hardiston. The older man added: 'I want to give you both the paternal blessing. What does Tony think of her?'

That was a question to which Mark was not sure he knew the answer. The discord between them, of which he had been conscious that first day at luncheon, seemed to have disappeared; but he remembered it, wondered sometimes whether it had had any tangible cause.

Yet there was no need of telling his father his faint doubts. 'Oh, Tony thinks she's perfect,' he assured the older man. 'She's only a few years older than he, you know. He likes her a lot!'

He stayed in Columbus till he was sure that his father would soon be himself again, could presently go home to Hardiston.

14

(June 1939)

When Mark returned to Boston, Anna told him that Miss Rollins had been trying to reach him on the telephone. Mark called Ruth at once, and she said: 'Father's—sick again, Uncle Mark. The nurse is here, but he won't let me leave him, and he won't let me send for Doctor Hethering. Could you possibly come out? He'd like to see you, I know.'

Mark drove at once to Lincoln. He dreaded seeing Dave, remembering that insolent truculence which was apt to characterize the other when he was drunk; but tonight he found a different man. Dave —sitting with a decanter and a glass beside him, gulping raw liquor— was profoundly depressed; but he spoke with that gentleness which had always been his sober habit. Ruth took Mark to him, and they were all three together for a while, talking of everything except that which was in all their minds. Mark had seen Dave drunk before, but he had never seen Dave when he was drunk speak gently, as he did now. There had always been courage in him, truculent and abrupt if he were drunk, gallant and steady if he were sober; but tonight he spoke humbly, like a beaten man.

Yet it was Dave who had the will to come to the point. He said to Ruth:

'Will you leave us alone, dear? I want to talk over some things I'd rather you didn't hear.'

Ruth departed without objection, and Dave said: 'Highball, Mark? There's ice and soda on the table.'

Mark after a moment's hesitation served himself and sat down. Dave said simply then:

'Well, you see, I'm lost, Mark.'

Mark hesitated. 'I see,' he agreed, wondering what to do for this old friend. 'What happened, Dave?'

'I got tired,' Dave told him. 'Just—deadly tired. You know we men—or at least weaklings like me—need a wife. We draw strength from them. Ruth is loyal and strong; but she's young, and I always know that she feels youth's intolerance for my weakness, even when she's sweet as Heaven to me.' And he said: 'You see, I've no very high opinion of myself. Marcia always took care of me. Maybe she babied me. I felt she didn't blame me, and that helped me—hold up my head.' His voice changed, steadied, had a certain lost and desperate ring in it. 'But she won't come back to me, Mark. And I don't think—I'm speaking fact, not just a figure of speech—I don't think I can live without her.'

Mark, after a moment, watching the other, hoping he might be able to find a way to help, asked in plain words: 'You mean you'll kill yourself?'

Dave's eyes met his directly. There was no drama in his utterance, nothing but simple truth. 'Yes,' he said.

But after a moment his eyes fell. He tumbled a little liquor into his glass and drank it. Mark sat quietly, seeking how best to speak to this befuddled man. Marcia in the past would have given him a sedative, nursed him, loved him. But—Marcia had never really helped him. Was it not possible that the opposite procedure would have better results? Was it not possible that the spur of scorn, of strong masculine contempt, might better serve?

He forced himself to try it. 'You poor snivelling rat,' he said, as harshly as he could. 'You whining coward!' Dave's eyes met his steadily, and Mark wished to cry out that he had not meant those words, wished to offer the other any comfort he could find. Yet the remedy, if it were to be effective, must be driven home. He rose. 'I'll call Doctor Hethering,' he said scornfully. 'He'll get you patched up again, but it won't do you any good!'

He rose and crossed to the telephone, his back to Dave, waiting in desperate hope for some word from the other. What made him turn was no word. It was the sound of metal hitting wood. What he saw when he turned was Dave leaning far forward to pick up a small automatic pistol from the floor at his feet. Even while Mark leaped that way, he thought Dave must have had the pistol in the pocket of his dressing gown, must have snatched it out with fumbling and uncertain fingers and somehow, mercifully, dropped it.

As Dave straightened up with the pistol in his hand, and before he could raise it to his head, Mark struck him in the face with all his strength; and Dave collapsed, stunned and helpless, in the chair. The weapon dropped to the floor again and Mark picked it up; and then Ruth opened the door and saw Dave, blood trickling from his mouth and nose; and she came quickly to Mark's side, staring at her father and then at Mark. She saw the pistol and caught her breath in terror.

Mark touched her arm. 'It's all right,' he said. 'I got to him in time. I had to hit him, Ruth.' He looked at the chunky little pistol, put it in his pocket. 'I'll call Doctor Hethering,' he said, and went to the phone again while Ruth began gently to clean the fresh blood off Dave's cheek and lips and chin.

After a moment, Mark heard her say: 'There, there,' as one speaks to a hurt child. He spoke to the doctor and turned from the telephone to them. Dave was conscious, watching him, his hand over his bruised mouth, saying nothing.

Mark stood above him. 'You really are just a plain, spineless coward,' he said evenly.

Ruth, kneeling by her father, came to her feet to face Mark, and her eyes were blazing with anger at him for that brutal word; but before she could speak, Dave said: 'Easy, dear.' He smiled at Mark with swollen lips. 'Thanks, Mark,' he said, and he nodded thoughtfully, and Mark realized with a quick, wondering gratefulness that already Dave's voice had a different timbre. There was strength in it, and clearly Dave was sober now as death itself. 'You're quite right,' he said. 'I can see it plainly enough, once it's put in words. But Mark, now that I see it, I can change it.'

He asked Mark to stay with them for a day or two. 'I'll want to think this through,' he said. 'Decide what to do.' So Mark did so, going to town every day, but coming out to Lincoln in time for dinner; and

night after night he and Dave sat in talk together, Ruth silent with
them. In mid-May, England's King and Queen had landed in Canada,
to meet warm-hearted welcomes everywhere on their progress westward
across the Dominion day by day. Early in June they came into the
United States. The newspapers reported their every movement and
public word; and their pictures appeared again and again. They went
direct to Washington to a tremendous and affectionate reception, and
Dave said that night:

'You know, Mark, I sometimes think the finest thing about England
is her love for her King. The late abdication and the circumstances
which surrounded it were a shock to the Englishman's sense of decorum,
but this fine young fellow and his sweet wife have wiped out that
memory. They've conducted themselves so winningly that they've
charmed us. There are some people whom you instinctively like, even
at first sight. These two fall into that category.'

Mark agreed with him. 'The reverent loyalty which an Englishman
pays to "The King, God Bless Him," is a good thing,' he assented.

Dave asked: 'Remember what Drinkwater said?' And he quoted:

> ' "When the high heart we magnify,
>   And the brave spirit celebrate,
>   And honor greatness passing by,
>   Then 'tis ourselves we elevate." '

And he reflected: 'Intangibles are more important than tangibles,
Mark—just as circumstantial evidence is more reliable than direct
testimony.'

Mark smiled. 'I spent a year or so in Cardiff as a boy,' he said. 'And I
didn't like Englishmen. I used to despise what seemed to me their truck-
ling as debasing. Now I'm inclined to think a proud humility is a
source of strength. I'm amused at myself—and yet I can say quite
honestly: "God Save the King." ' He chuckled. 'I like the guy,' he said,
and he reflected: 'I still think of "My Country, 'tis of Thee," as our
national anthem. Plato or Aristotle or one of the old Greeks once said:
"He who writes a nation's songs rules that nation"—or something like
that. When the English and ourselves sang the same tune, it created a
bond between us. I'm sorry we changed to this other thing which no
one can sing.'

'Their visit will win a lot of friends for England here—and in
Canada,' Dave predicted. 'Probably that's why they came. If that was
the reason, it was a wise one.'

Mark heard another point of view on the royal visit when in mid-June—Dave was himself again so that Mark was no longer needed in Lincoln—Tony came home and brought Joe Hazen with him. Barbie Parks was to be married on the seventeenth, and these two would be ushers, spending only the one night here on their way to New York. Frank Parks, Barbie's brother, just finishing his third year at Harvard, would drive them over, and he came to dinner that evening. Someone spoke of the royal visit, and Frank—Mark remembered his old fondness for Russia—said it was pure propaganda.

'Engineered by our capitalist rulers,' he declared. 'To dazzle the proletariat. England's preparing to plunge the world into war, but she doesn't dare do it till she's sure Canada and the United States will back her—so she sends her trained seals over here to put on their act.'

'Well, I'll say they put on a good one,' Tony declared. 'The Queen strikes me as pretty swell—and the King's all right too.'

Joe Hazen laughed cheerfully at Frank's point of view. 'Why don't Mr. and Mrs. Stalin—if there is a Mrs.—come over and convert us to Communism, if it's so easy?' he challenged.

'We appeal to the minds of men, not to their love of fairy tales,' Frank said loftily; and the three young men plunged into an argument to which Mark listened with a lively interest. Joe's home was in California; and when they spoke of Hitler's avowed hatred of all things Russian—Frank said that hatred was based on fear, and that when the time came Russia would smash Germany—Mark asked Joe how California felt about Hitler.

'Oh, we hate his guts,' Joe said casually. 'He's almost as bad as the Japs.'

Mark nodded. 'The west coast has always disliked the Japanese, of course.'

'Sure,' Joe agreed. 'I wish we'd come down on them hard when they started after China. Instead of that, we go on selling munitions to Japan. Maybe some of that scrap iron we're shipping them will make bombs to be dropped on San Francisco, some day.' He added drily: 'But I suppose it's good for business to keep selling to them.'

'It's hard for us in the East to imagine fighting Japan,' Mark confessed. 'We've nothing to gain by a war in the Pacific.'

'We've nothing to gain by a war anywhere,' Tony reminded him.

'All the same, I'd like to see us wipe Japan off the map,' Joe declared. 'We can do it any time we want to.'

Mark remembered that conversation a day or two later. Tony and

Joe were still in New York when the newspapers reported that the
British and the Japanese were at odds in Tientsin. There had been
trouble at the British concession there, and British women had been
struck by Japanese soldiers, and even stripped and searched. That evening, Dave Rollins and Ruth came to see Mark; and they spoke of this
deliberate outrage. Dave said quietly:

'It's much more than a shameful affront, Mark. White men have
been able to dominate the Far East for many years by impressing upon
the native mind a conviction of their superiority. There are thousands
of places where the unsupported authority of one white man rules a
horde of unquestioning and submissive people—in India and Java and
the Malay Peninsula, in China and Burma. I think the Japs are setting
out by these insults—which go unpunished—to demonstrate to the
natives that the legend of white supremacy is ended.'

'That supremacy rests in the last analysis on force,' Mark suggested.
'The natives know that behind every solitary white man there are
armies and navies ready to punish any offense against his authority.'

'Possibly,' Dave agreed. 'But the basic thing is white prestige, however acquired. They don't like us, out there. A white man is, quite
literally, an offense to the Oriental nostrils, you know. Now the Japs
are demonstrating that we are not only physically offensive, but also
helpless and contemptible. The whole structure of white supremacy in
the East can be brought down by enough such incidents as this.'

Mark saw some truth in what the other said. 'But England's more
concerned about trouble on the high seas,' he suggested. 'She's demanding that Japan stop halting and searching her ships.'

'Yes, and Japan retorts that England must stop helping Chiang Kai-
shek. England won't risk war out there as long as things in Europe
go on as they're going.'

They talked awhile longer, Ruth sitting silently, her eyes on her
father, till Dave caught her glance and said at last: 'Well, Mark, this
isn't just a casual call. We came to tell you our plans.'

'You look well,' Mark told him.

'I'm on the mend,' Dave assented, and he said: 'You did me a good
turn, Mark. You'd have made a good psychiatrist. Ruth and I both
have reason to know that. We've discussed how you helped her
straighten herself out when she needed it. I believe—I hope—you've
done me some good, too.'

And since Mark did not speak, he went on: 'At least, you've made
me realize that I'm my own problem; and that I'm the only one who

can solve it. Ruth is going to stick with me while I try to do it. We're taking the schooner, Mark, heading to Labrador. We'll fish for salmon, get a lot of exercise. I've always coddled myself.' Mark thought it was rather Marcia who had coddled Dave; and Dave knew this as well as he. Perhaps it was typical of the change in him that he did not say so. 'I'm going to stop that,' Dave said. 'We'll fish, and maybe hunt, and carry packs, and camp out, and I'll help handle the schooner.' He added slowly: 'And I'm taking twenty cases of whiskey, Mark, and we'll keep a decanter in the cabin all the time.' His voice steadied. 'But I'm laying odds I won't take a drink while we're gone.'

They stayed discussing this project for an hour, Ruth saying little, watching her father with a high pride. While they were here, Mark applauded Dave's intention; but after they were gone, he had his doubts. He knew to what extremes of daily and persisting torment Dave was committing himself; and he realized suddenly that the other man was surprisingly frail and small, not even as tall as Ruth. Fired by the zeal of his new resolution, Dave seemed to glow; but that might so easily prove a fitful flame. Mark thought ruefully what Ruth's hard part would be if her father's resolution failed while they were far away.

15

(June 1939)

Robin came to Boston on the twentieth, to do Mark's portrait. She stayed at the Copley, and each day when he was free, Mark picked her up and brought her out to the house and he posed for an hour or two, while she took full advantage of the long June afternoons.

In the hours together while he sat relaxed and easy, her eyes flashing from him to the canvas, they were sometimes silent; but also they talked much, drawing together in many small ways, each learning every day some new thing about the other; and all they learned strengthened the bond between them.

'You're a balanced man,' she told him once. 'Mentally, I mean. You're not bigoted about anything, always seem able to see another side.'

'I've often been told that,' he agreed. 'But it's not a habit of mind which makes for peace, Robin. I sometimes envy people who can be sure of things; sure that Roosevelt is a great man, or that he isn't; sure that Hitler is a devil, and that the Germans are a race of fiends who ought to be exterminated; sure that Willkie is the hope of the country; sure that bankers are crooks at heart—or that they're altruists, devoting their lives to the service of their depositors; sure that labor is right, or that labor is wrong. Except for a few simple questions of ethics—and except that I know I love you—I'm not really sure of anything!' He chuckled. 'Maybe it's partly my age. Tony's sure of most things, but his certainties are apt to be destructive. He thinks—speaking broadly—that whatever is, is wrong.'

She smiled and suggested that that was true of most undergraduates. 'It's the influence of their professors, isn't it?' she hazarded. 'It's no longer the fashion to teach boys and girls that God's in His heaven, all's right with the world. The professor likes to be known as a challenging personality; and he challenges all the old conceptions.'

He thought this was true, and he said in a troubled tone: 'I sometimes suspect that our educational system is unsound. Boys in their teens, their minds still as pliable as soft concrete, come under the influence of some magnetic, arresting professor who insists that they form opinions of their own on questions to which the world has been seeking answers—without finding them—for thousands of years. The result, in the case of a thoughtful boy, is too apt to be a profound mental disturbance. They tell me the psychiatrists are kept busy in college towns; and of course the occasional waves of student suicides are damning proof that something is wrong! Youth has a right to be optimistic, confident—overconfident, perhaps—bold and eager and sure. Too many of Tony's friends are sure only that the world is in a mess.'

Robin nodded. 'So they're scornful of the old standards, of decent ambition and fine aspirations.'

'The individual professor loves to knock down idols,' Mark commented. 'But he's not sufficiently careful to raise others in their places. Everyone—and particularly every boy—needs someone or something to worship. He needs something of which he can always say to himself: "This at least is fine and true and eternal. This at least is good and has endured and will endure."' He added strongly: 'But too often he has only a fund of half-baked opinions—which have been presented to him as dogma, as truth.'

'Haven't you any opinions?' She was smiling at his heat. 'Full-baked ones, maybe overdone?'

'None that I can't change in twenty minutes,' he assured her, and smiled and said again: 'Except that I love you.'

She said in a quiet solicitude: 'I wish you didn't worry so about Hitler and things.'

He nodded, laughing a little, apologetically. 'I know I should forget all that, but it's really Tony I'm thinking about. For years, while I've watched him grow up, I've thought of Hitler, way off there in Germany, as engineering a gigantic plot to get Tony killed some day. I've read all that happened over there in terms of Tony. I welcomed Munich because I thought it might save Tony. I've welcomed England's stronger attitude because I thought that might stop Hitler and save Tony. I've damned Roosevelt because he seems to be leading us toward war, and so I see him, too, as a threat to Tony. From my point of view, Hitler and Roosevelt are conspiring to get my son killed! That's colossal egotism for you!' And he added grimly: 'And the queer part of it is that I'm sorry when Tony speaks out his hatred for the thought of war; yet if war comes, he'll want to be in it, and I'll want him to be in it.' He said in a wry mirth: 'So here are Hitler and Roosevelt and I, all of us in this murderous conspiracy to get Tony killed!'

They spoke only once in these days of her Davy. Mark had asked no question, but she said one afternoon: 'Davy is better, Mark. They think it marvellous that he should be alive at all; but they say every day he lives, every crisis he survives, increases his chances for longer life.'

She was working as she spoke, concentrating upon the texture of his cheek as she tried to lay her paint justly on the canvas. Her eyes did not meet his, so that she seemed not to speak to him at all, as though the sense of her words came to him from her without any physical communication. He did not answer her. It was impossible that they should wish for Davy to die; but it was equally intolerable that he should continue to live. There was no word Mark could say.

Tony was at home now; and Mark saw happily that he and Robin were easily friendly. One afternoon when, driving out from town with Robin, he approached the house, they saw a group of youngsters on the Ritchie tennis court and pulled up to watch. Tony came to the backstop to call:

'Hi, Dad! Hello, Mrs. Kerr! We'll make this the last set. Stay and root for us!'

Mark looked inquiringly at Robin, and she said: 'Yes, let's. The light's bad today, anyway.' So Mark nodded and Tony returned to the court. Tony's partner was Ingrid Sigurdson, here for a week's visit with Betty Ritchie. Their opponents were Will and Betty, and Mrs. Ritchie and Jan were watching the match. Mark could still be a little startled by the scant garb of athletic youth. Tony himself wore shorts, socks and sneakers; and Ingrid, except for a bandanna handkerchief knotted between her shoulder blades, wore no more than he. Will, too, was in shorts, Betty in a white sharkskin tennis dress that ended well above her knees. Tony and Ingrid were as brown as though they had spent months on a sunned beach; and Mark wondered how they had managed that, so early in the summer. He watched Ingrid curiously. Her legs were astonishingly muscular, and she was obviously an athlete in top condition; but tennis seemed new to her. Her strokes were awkward, yet they were surprisingly effective, and she hit the ball as hard, if not as accurately, as the others.

At Mark's suggestion, Robin went to join Nell and Jan while he put the car away. When he returned, the tennis was over and the young people were standing with the others. Mark joined them, and when the players trooped off to the house for cokes and showers, Nell saw his expression and laughed and said:

'You look a little dazed, Mark!'

He smiled. 'I'm old-fashioned,' he confessed. 'What happens if that handkerchief comes untied?'

'She'd get Tony to tie it again, probably!' Nell assured him; and Jan said indignantly: 'The trouble with grown-ups, they're always imagining things. I think Ingrid's swell!'

'Where did she and Tony get so brown, this early in the summer?' Mark inquired.

'Tuckerman's, on the snow,' Jan assured him. 'And Ingrid says they've been going down to the river at Hanover every afternoon, a crowd of them, swimming and sun-bathing.' She saw the amusement in his eyes and flushed and said loyally: 'Well, why not?'

Mark appeased her. 'I like it, Jan. It's a lot better than the way we did these things when I was Tony's age. I think pretty well of this younger generation of yours, you know.'

Robin said: 'I thought Miss Sigurdson would be gone home to Norway before now, Jan. She told me last winter she expected to go soon.'

Mark thought there was for a moment a shadow in Jan's eyes. 'I guess she doesn't really want to,' she confessed. 'I guess she likes it here.'

When Mark and Robin turned away, Robin asked: 'Jan's the one who's always been so fond of Tony, isn't she?'

'Yes.'

'She's a thoroughbred,' she said.

16

(June 1939)

Before the end of June, the portrait was done. Mark had been grateful during Robin's stay in Boston for the tactful attitude of his friends. After that evening when he took Robin to dine at the Ritchies', Nell had asked him a thousand questions. He told her how he had met Robin, told her they were good friends, told her he hoped they might some day be more than that. Nell—and Mary too—were delighted at the prospect, and Nell said urgently:

'And for Heaven's sake, hurry it up, Mark. Anyone can see she's fond of you.'

'We'll have to work it out, Nell,' he warned her. 'It could be spoiled pretty easily.' And he said frankly: 'Mrs. Kerr and I are adults, you know. We've—well, we've discussed it.'

'Sweep her off her feet,' she advised. 'She's ready for it.'

He laughed her urgencies aside, and when it was settled that Robin should come to do his portrait, he hoped Nell would not speak in the same way to her; but Nell—and the others—were during her stay here discretion itself, never betraying by word or smile that Robin was anything but what on the surface she appeared to be, an artist executing a commission.

When the portrait was finished and their comments were invited, Nell was delighted with it, and said Robin must do one of Bob. 'You can come and stay with us,' she urged, but Robin put her off, said work already planned must keep her busy till well into the fall.

Robin would take the portrait back to New York with her. She had worked in oils, and she said the finished product should have time to age before it was varnished. 'Then I'll have it framed—with glass at first—and I'm going to keep it, Mark, till I can bring it here to you.'

The day she was to leave, Mark brought her out to the house in the afternoon to supervise the proper packing of the canvas, and she saw something wrong with the mouth and remedied that and went to remove the paint smears from her hands. Needing cold cream, she looked in the bathroom cabinet, and a label on a small dark bottle on the shelf there caught her eye.

```
┌─────────────────────────────────┐
│          Moulded                │
│          TRITURATE              │
│                                 │
│            100                  │
│                                 │
│        NITROGLYCERIN            │
│                                 │
│           Trinitrin             │
│                                 │
│          1/100 grain            │
└─────────────────────────────────┘
```

She picked up the bottle and stared at it, with a sudden contraction in her throat. She had seen such a bottle before, on her father's bureau in their home in Montreal, and its significance was terrifying. She put it slowly back in its place, looking at it fixedly as though it had been a serpent. She closed the cabinet, and came quietly down the stairs. Mark was waiting for her in the hall, and when he saw her he exclaimed in startled tones:

'What's the matter?'

'Matter?'

He laughed. 'You look as though you'd seen a ghost.'

She tried to smile, shook her head. 'Do I? I'm quite all right.'

'You're better now,' he agreed. 'Your color's coming back.'

'It must have been the light,' she suggested.

They went out together to the car, in which her bags and the canvas were already stowed. For a moment after they were under way, she did not speak; but she must know the truth.

'Mark,' she asked quietly, 'are you well?'

'Well?' He looked at her in surprise. 'I'm well as a horse.'

'Tell me, Mark,' she insisted.

He asked, still smiling: 'What's bothering you, Robin? What is it?'

She said slowly: 'I saw a bottle of nitroglycerin tablets in your bathroom.'

For a moment he did not speak, watching the road while she watched him. Then, as though making up his mind, he nodded. 'It's nothing,' he assured her. 'It's just that here awhile back I had a sort of pain in my arm, as though it were going to sleep; so I went to Doctor Hethering. He checked me over, said I'd been working too hard—and he gave me those tablets to relieve the pain. I haven't used them for months, meant to throw them away.'

She said gravely: 'My father keeps nitroglycerin near him. He has had an attack of angina.'

Mark hesitated. 'That's just a word, Robin,' he reminded her. 'It just means "pain."'

'Tell me, Mark,' she insisted.

'I'm quoting Doctor Hethering,' he assured her. 'He said it's just a word, not to be frightened.'

'I know. I've talked with the doctor about Father. But what do you have to do about it?'

'Not work too hard,' he said. 'Not worry. Not drive too long at a time.' He chuckled. 'Never change a tire. Take things easy. It suits me fine, Robin; gives me an excuse not to do any of the things I don't want to do.'

'Not work too hard. And—not worry,' she repeated; and after a moment she asked: 'Is it hard on you, being a judge?'

'No.'

'But you do worry—about Tony, about war, about me. Uncertainty is bad for you, my dear. I want to help you.'

'You do help me, every hour I'm with you.'

She asked earnestly: 'I haven't made things any different between you and Tony, have I?'

'Of course not!'

'About the war,' she said, half to herself. 'You'll have to find something to bring you peace of mind, Mark. You think too much about it. You'll have to find something you're sure of, some settled conviction, some opinion you won't have to change. You'll have to make up your mind.'

He said in sober assent: 'I'd like to. Sometimes I wish war would come—if it's coming. Once you're at war, there's no more uncertainty. I was in the last war, and sometimes it seems to me those were the most serene months of my life. I had only to do what I was told.' She did not speak, her own thoughts absorbing her, and he repeated: 'Yes—if war's coming, I wish it would come. Then there'll be no more uncertainty, no more questioning. We'll all just do what we're told. There's peace and certainty in that, Robin.'

'Certainty,' she echoed, half to herself. 'Certainty. You mustn't have any more uncertainty, my dear.'

He chuckled. 'I might cable Hitler to fish or cut bait,' he suggested.

'I want to help you, darling.' Her eyes, too, were now straight ahead. 'I can't help you about Hitler, and all that. But you mustn't have any uncertainty about me.'

'I haven't, Robin. I know we love each other.'

She was silent, thinking of Davy. 'It's the waiting, Mark,' she said, after a moment. 'The not knowing when we will be free, the long waiting when we want each other so.' She hazarded: 'I could divorce poor Davy, I suppose.'

'No.' His tone was stern. 'Neither of us wants that.'

There were silent moments then, till they pulled up at the station. A porter came to carry her bags. She told the man her space on the train and he departed. She and Mark followed him, more slowly. They descended to the lower platform, and for minutes more they did not speak. He wished to, but her silence bound him, too.

Till at last she turned to him with tender eyes. 'Mark, my dear,' she said, 'I've decided what we'll do. Listen to me. Don't say anything. In a minute, kiss me good-bye and go. But listen now.'

He waited, wondering; and her cheeks burned warm, but her eyes were steady and serene.

'I won't have you worried and longing,' she said. 'We can't be married while Davy lives; but I want you to know I'm yours. Come to me soon, Mark. Come soon. For when you come—I'm going to make you certain of me.'

He stood utterly still, and she rose on tiptoe to kiss him softly. 'Now go, my dear,' she said. "Good-bye, till you come to me.'

X

The Danzig Herring

(July–August 1939)

I

(July 1939)

MARK drove home slowly, unconscious of his surroundings, his thoughts tumbling like dry leaves before the wind. He tried to bring them into some order and adjustment; but to seize one was to lose the last. It was impossible that Robin had meant what she had seemed to mean; and yet it was equally impossible that she had meant anything else. To be sure of that, he had only to remember her eyes, warm with a lavish tenderness.

When he came to the house, Tony had telephoned that he would not be home for dinner, so Mark dined alone. Afterward he went out on the terrace in the warm twilight, and then walked down to the little summer house by the lake where he and Nan had sometimes served cocktails before dinner on pleasant evenings; and he sat there quietly, smoking many cigarettes, flipping the butts through a briefly gleaming arc into the water below.

After an hour or two Tony came out on the terrace, calling: 'Dad!' Mark answered, and Tony came to him through the shadows. 'What are you doing out here?' Tony asked. 'Aren't the mosquitoes eating you up?'

'Just—enjoying the evening,' Mark told him. 'No, they're not bad. Where were you? Movies?'

'No, I flew for an hour,' Tony told him. 'And Mr. Hadden and I got to talking afterward and he took me home to dinner. His wife is swell, and his boy's a great kid. Mr. Hadden sent his best to you.' He asked: 'Why did you quit flying, Dad?'

'I'm getting a little old for it, Tony. I'm forty-seven.'

'Shucks, you're not old,' Tony protested. 'Does Mrs. Kerr want you not to fly?'

'She's never said so.'

Tony hesitated, lighting a cigarette of his own before he asked: 'When are you and she going to be married?'

Mark did not at once reply; and when he did it was almost curtly. 'We don't know yet, Tony.' He wished he could tell his son about Davy; but he knew what the boy's advice would be—to persuade Robin to seek a divorce. To Tony's generation that would seem the natural, straightforward thing, but to Mark it was not so simple. Robin's loyalty would make her reluctant to take such a step, and certainly he would never urge her to do so.

Tony felt the finality in his father's tone, and he did not push the question, sitting in troubled silence for a while; and he was sorrowfully sure that it was the thought of him which kept these two apart. Robin would not readily forget his word that day in Hanover. Yet somehow for his father's sake—and for hers—she must be made to forget it. Perhaps if he devoted himself to Lucy, then Robin would be reassured. And certainly—he smiled in the darkness—it would be no hardship to devote himself to Lucy. He had seen her often in the months since Carnival, when he came home for week-ends, or for spring vacation, and since college closed in June; and always she welcomed him charmingly. But he was sure he would never want to marry her. She had an incandescent beauty which when he was with her drove every thought except of her out of his head, and she knew a thousand bewitching ways; yet she enchanted others as well as him, and delighted in doing so. There was no one who was prettier or more delightful company than Lucy could be when she chose.

He rose at last to toss his cigarette into the water. 'I'm ready for bed,' he decided. 'Coming in?'

'I think I'll sit awhile longer,' Mark told him; but then, before Tony could move away, he asked: 'Son, how would you like to go off salmon fishing with me. I'm taking a vacation—most of July. I thought we might go—unless you've other plans.'

'I've none I can't change,' Tony assured him; and he added in a shy tone: 'In fact, I sort of wanted to be with you as much as I could this summer. It may be our last summer together, if you're going to be married.'

Mark did not trust himself to speak. He lighted a cigarette, inhaled deeply. 'Good!' he agreed. 'I thought we'd go to Anticosti again—and maybe the Restigouche open water, too.'

'Say-y, swell!'

'I'll see if we can get water,' Mark said.

They stayed a little longer, discussing plans, before Tony went to bed. Mark after a further time came indoors and sent telegrams of inquiry about Anticosti water, and about the Restigouche; but he was still too wide awake to sleep; and at last he turned to his desk, sat for long minutes, and so began a letter to Robin.

My Darling—I never loved you as much as I do tonight, never realized so completely what a richly wonderful woman you are. The trust and love you have given me mean more to me than anything I have ever won or hoped to win. This in spite of the fact that I know it is beyond anything I deserve.

You will deny this; but that is because you do not know me as well as I know myself. May I tell you something about myself? I know your answer to that question—so:

My Southern grandmother was a completely devout church woman, a deaconess or something of the sort. My grandfather's brother was a Bishop of the Methodist Church. I never knew the Bishop, but for at least a month or two every year till I was about ten years old, we visited my grandmother in Mississippi; and she made a great impression on me. My father's father and mother were equally religious—family prayers night and morning, church twice on Sundays, Sunday School, and so on. Father and Mother were churchly people too. Father was once superintendent of Sunday School— I remember that he, as Superintendent, expelled me for putting chewing gum in an unpleasant little girl's back hair—and till we went to Wales, I attended Sunday School and church and Christian Endeavor and so on with complete regularity. I signed the total abstinence pledge—twice, I think— before I was ten years old. I was taught that the first drink of alcoholic beverages was the first step to an inevitable drunkard's grave. I remember wondering why, if this were true, they served wine—which I liked very much—at communion. Playing cards was wrong, and dancing was wrong, and the theatre was wrong.

Father and Mother presently became more tolerant of these peccadilloes. We played cards at home, and we went to the theatre, and I learned to dance. But fundamentally they were not changed. I remember when I was in college Mother was shocked because I wore a bathing suit with no sleeves —just as I was shocked the other day here at Tony's tennis costume, and at Miss Sigurdson's.

I tell you these things because I suspect you will—at least in your own thoughts—presently accuse me of being a prig; and to that I'm entering a plea of what might be called 'Confession and avoidance.'

I don't know tonight whether I'm deliriously happy, or reverently proud of your love and trust—or just plain scared! Perhaps more than anything else I'm scared! But in spite of being more frightened than I have ever been in my life, I love you more deeply and more proudly than ever before. If I start telling you how wonderful you are, I'll never be done.

You said: 'Come to me soon.' I want to. But Robin—perhaps it's just because I am scared—I'm not coming soon. You were, possibly, moved by a wonderful and generous impulse which you will later regret. I'm sorry you saw that little bottle in my bathroom cabinet. Usually I keep it put away, so that Tony will not see it, because he doesn't know why I have it; but he has been away all spring, and I have so nearly forgotten all that business about my health that I did not remember to hide the bottle before he returned.

Don't be worried about it, Robin. Doctor Hethering assures me I am normal now, and that there is no reason why I should ever be troubled again.

I said I was sorry you saw it. I am not, actually, because seeing it led you to let me know you completely, to appreciate you completely for the first time. If I saw you tonight, loving you as I do tonight, there would be no barrier between us.

But I think we need time to be sure what we want to do. Tony and I are going away for a month, more or less, to fish for salmon. May I come to you in August, as soon as we return? I think not coming to you tonight is the bravest thing I've ever done.

Or perhaps it's just because I'm scared! Be patient with a badly frightened man, my love. God bless you.

Mark.

He re-read what he had written, and felt it inadequate, but she would understand all the things he could not put in words.

He mailed the letter that night. At the earliest possible moment her telegram reached him.

Come when you will, dear coward. I'm yours always. Love.

Robin.

He chuckled. There it was again; the tenth word in a telegram.

2

(July 1939)

Mark and Tony drove north from Boston, in no hurry, with three days to reach Kedgwick for a week on the Restigouche. They stopped the first night at Belfast and spent the evening with John Harmon, who had been one of Mark's teachers at the Allen School more than thirty years before. Mark, though at long intervals they exchanged letters, had not seen John for years. He told Tony, on the way north, something about the older man.

'He and I always got along,' he said, 'even when I was a boy in school. He taught mathematics, algebra, and so on. He never could persuade me that A to the zero power was equal to 1, and we used to argue the point interminably. It was he who recommended Bob Preble to me—to tutor you. Preble was a Belfast boy, by the way.'

'How old is Mr. Harmon?' Tony asked, and Mark said: 'I don't know. I suppose he's in his seventies somewhere.'

He asked the same question of John Harmon that evening. 'Because, except that you've lost a little hair, you look no older than you did at the Allen School,' he said.

'I'm seventy-seven,' the other told him; and Mark laughed in quick satisfaction.

'Then you were forty-seven in the Allen School,' he exclaimed. 'I'm forty-seven now—and I'd begun to feel old.' His own years had seemed like a tangible burden which he bore, in these days since he last saw Robin, who was so richly young. 'But—you don't seem to me any older than I. If you're any criterion, I've thirty good years ahead of me. But maybe you've a secret process?'

The older man chuckled. 'No, no secret. Although I suppose part of it is working hard so that you keep interested, and part of it's knowing how to loaf. But most of it's just not worrying. Someone told me once about an old negro who was asked how he kept his youth and he said: "I wears life like a loose garment!" '

Mark nodded, remembering Doctor Hethering's advice; and he suggested that the old negro's prescription was not so easy in these days when the lava flood of war might soon erupt across the world. John Harmon, he found, did not expect war.

'And if it comes,' the older man said, 'we needn't be in it. England's navy will strangle Germany, just as it did before.'

'I know a lot of people agree with you,' Mark assented. 'I saw a statement the other day by Sir John Reith of the British Overseas Airways. He sees no danger of war. And Watson, President of International Business Machines, says the same thing, and there've been others. But I'm pretty sure it's coming, all the same.'

'I hope not,' the older man declared. 'Because we'd be so dead set on getting into it! Reminds me of an old friend of mine. We were in college together at Orono. Every so often there'd be a fight in town between the townies and some of us; but we didn't have telephones or radio to bring us the news, so sometimes we didn't hear about these fights till after they were over. I remember one night somebody came back from town and said a big fight was just starting. This boy—Ed Hamilton, his name was, and he loved a fight—set out for town as hard as he could run. It was a couple of miles. By the time he got there the fight was over and everyone had gone home and Ed sat right down on the curbstone and cried because he hadn't got there in time to take a hand.' Mark and Tony laughed with him; and he added: 'We're the same way in this country. Seems as if we couldn't see an argument start anywhere in the world without wanting to take a hand in it. But if this ruckus starts in Europe and we keep out, England can handle it.'

Tony asked challengingly: 'What about Germany's airplanes?'

'You talk like Bob Preble,' John Harmon admitted. 'He was here last week. He says Germany's planes can destroy every city in England. He says Lindbergh and Al Williams, the old army flier, say the same thing.'

'What's Preble doing now?' Mark asked. 'Still working on airplane engines?'

'Not engines, no,' Harmon told them. 'He and Bert Stevens—Bert's a Belfast boy, you know, the one who made the stratosphere flights— got together here a couple of years ago and started talking aerial photography; and now Bob's doing research work on night photography, using infra-red rays or light filters or something. It's all Greek to me, but Bob says what he's trying to do is work out a way to let the human eye see as much as the camera can see, even at night.'

'Gosh!' Tony exclaimed in a lively interest, 'that would be something, for night flying—and for night bombing. A pilot with some rig like that could blow hell out of everything on the ground.'

Harmon nodded, said cheerfully: 'That's what Bob thinks. But I've lived a long time, seen a couple of wars; and it's been my experience that whenever one fellow produces a new weapon, the other fellow finds some way to meet it.'

'Tony has the flier's point of view,' Mark explained. 'He and I have done some flying—and he still does. He thinks the plane is the great offensive weapon today.'

'The experts seem to think the defensive has a three-to-one advantage,' Harmon suggested.

Tony said quickly: 'All right. Then, if there's a war in Poland, even if France and England go in, Germany will just go on the defensive in the west, and England can't help Poland.'

'Poland seems to think she can help herself,' Mark pointed out; and Tony said scornfully:

'She can't. She hasn't any planes fit to fight at all. She'll be smashed in three months.'

Mark stirred restlessly. 'Let's forget Europe, Tony. We're on vaca-

tion,' he urged; and the easy talk ran on other matters till the evening
was done. Mark said when he and Tony were alone: 'I'm glad to have
seen John again. I was beginning to feel old; but he's lived a lifetime
since he was my age.'

'You'll never be old, Dad,' Tony said. 'Not inside yourself. You're
too interested in things. You're about the youngest person I know.'

They made a short run next day, stopped the night at Presque Isle,
came to the Restigouche in good season Sunday afternoon, and had a
fine week on the great river there. The salmon took well. Tony's twenty-
six-pounder was the record for the week; but they killed between them
twenty-one salmon that averaged sixteen pounds. Leaving there, they
drove leisurely around the Gaspé, stopping to try for trout in an occasional brook, stopping for the night where they chose, spending two
nights at Percé; and Europe and her concerns seemed far away. Mark
refused to look at newspapers, they had no radio in the car, and they
avoided casual conversation with other Americans they encountered on
the way.

They spent a day on the Madeleine and killed three salmon; and at
Quai Rimouski they waited for the plodding little steamer which would
take them down to Anticosti. They went aboard her at midnight and
she sailed at dawn. All that long day the Gaspé shore which they had
followed in their car marched with them to the southward.

Their river was the Jupiter. In the Lord Grey pool, great fish lay
in their hundreds, but they were reluctant to take the fly. Mark fished,
and slept, and rested; and Robin was always near him in his thoughts,
smiling by his side, happy in his pleasuring.

The steamer would pick them up, but when the day came, a high
sea ran, making small-boat landings on the shingle beach impossible;
and they waited two days till the seas abated. On the steamer they came
abruptly back into the world again. There were a dozen or more Americans aboard; a group from New York, another from Texas, a third from
Chicago; and they had radios and their talk was of Japanese hatred of
England, and of the debate in Congress over the neutrality law, and
of the Irish bombing outrages in London, and of the United States'
renunciation of the 1911 treaty with Japan. Mark found that without
exception these men damned Mr. Roosevelt; but also they were sure
there would be no war, quoting Sir William Wiseman and Lord
Beaverbrook and Percy Strauss, and a dozen others. Mark told Tony:

'We're entering the phase where we try to prove things by saying
that someone said thus and so. The same thing happened in the last

war. Keep your head, son. Don't believe anything you hear. Don't believe anything unless your common sense tells you it's true. No one
knows whether there'll be war or not—except perhaps Hitler. So no
one's opinion is worth a hoot!' He added: 'We don't accept hearsay
evidence in the courts, Tony; but in wartime, or when there's a war
cloud in the air, people believe—and eagerly repeat—every bit of hearsay that comes to their ears.'

Tony nodded. 'I think it's up to the United States,' he said. 'Hitler
has the army and the planes to go ahead if he wants to. Nobody can
stop him. England knows that, and she won't even try, unless she's sure
we'll help her on the long pull. So it's up to us.'

'She's promised Poland she'd fight,' Mark reminded him.

'Sure, and she promised to guarantee what was left of Czecho-
Slovakia too,' Tony scornfully retorted. 'But what's a promise between
friends.'

They landed at Quai Rimouski before dawn, and drove along the
lovely shore to Rivière du Loup and turned southward, homeward. July
was almost gone.

Mark was much silent on the last day's drive, thinking of Robin,
thinking he would see her soon.

3

(August 1939)

Mark and Tony reached Boston on the first of August, driving that
day from Bangor; and in Portland when they stopped for lunch Mark
bought the *Boston Herald*. It was almost a month since he had read a
paper. At first glance the chance of war seemed to have been forgotten.
There was no reference to European conditions on the front page except a small paragraph reporting that a London barrage balloon had
been struck by lightning and that another had fallen in someone's garden. But on page 13 there was some foreign news. The Poles had
ordered that all Nazis committing crimes should be tried by court martial instead of in the civil courts. England and Russia were having staff
talks, discussing land, sea, and air strategy. England and Japan were
about to iron out their recent difficulties. But these dispatches were
brief and inconspicuous, and the effect of reading the paper was treacherously soothing, as though the European danger could be averted by
ignoring it.

When they came home, Elin was at the house to make sure that Anna had all in good order; and she had brought the baby to be admired. Watching her happy pride, Mark found it easy to hold on to the relaxed and rested mind which this month had given him. After all, babies and young mothers and fathers were the really important things in the world—and no baby was ever better off because a war was fought.

He spent the evening with his mail. There were three letters from Robin, brimming with a frank and unstinted affection. She was in Montreal, and she wrote that her father was ill, said straightforwardly: 'He has had a heart attack, Mark. You know that filled me with a double terror, dear. The doctors have put him to bed, but he is better every day. I must stay with him for a week or two, that is all.' He had written her, at least a few lines every day, during his absence, although at Anticosti there had been almost two weeks when he could not mail a letter. She referred to the fact that she had not heard from him, and he wired her: 'Letter mailed from Quai Rimouski to New York, and I am writing tonight.'

Next morning's papers were jubilant over the fact that the House of Representatives had killed Mr. Roosevelt's 'Spend-Lend' bill; and Mark smiled at a paragraph about a boy who had eaten some goldfish, remembering the folly of last winter when hardly a day passed that some college youngster did not set a new record in this novel field. He spoke of it to Tony at the breakfast table; and Tony said defensively: 'Sure, they tried it at Hanover too. It's crazy, of course; but you can't realize, Dad, how strung up all the fellows are about the war. They're apt to do any fool thing; and at least this goldfish business gives them something else to think about.'

Mark smiled. 'Will Ritchie claims a goldfish record,' he said. 'He swallowed one, and stopped at that. He says he can take them or leave them alone.'

He found on the back page a dispatch reporting that Danzig had protested to Poland because Poland was refusing to import from Danzig margarine and herrings. College boys who ate goldfish were surely no more absurd than nations which quarrelled over a Danzig herring.

Friday after their return Ruth Rollins telephoned, asking Mark and Tony to come for the week-end; and even over the phone Mark sensed the happiness in her voice. They drove down to the Cape after lunch on Saturday. Clearly that trip to Labrador had been a success, for Dave was lean and brown, and so was Ruth. Yet they were both heavier than they had been.

'And it's all muscle,' Dave assured them, and he told tales of pack trips into the interior, carrying all their food and gear, fishing streams no white man had ever fished before, or stalking caribou with a camera.

'That damned camera weighed a ton, after you'd packed it all day,' Dave declared. 'But we got some fine pictures. I'll show them to you tonight.'

'But we didn't get any pictures of the mosquitoes and the black flies,' Ruth smilingly reminded him. 'They were magnificent! If six of them had laid hold of me at once, they could have carried me away.'

Mark saw pride in her clear eyes and in her quick smile. She and Tony disappeared together Sunday morning, departing in bathing suits for a sail; and Dave and Mark stayed at ease on the veranda. Inevitably, they spoke of European affairs. 'I saw an interview with Patterson, the publisher,' Dave remarked. 'Giving odds against war this year. Think he's right?'

'Things seem to have quieted down,' Mark commented. 'They're just talking, now.'

'But it's chip-on-the-shoulder talk,' Dave pointed out. 'Chamberlain says England is ready for any emergency, and Churchill says this crisis is worse than Munich, and Forster, that Nazi in Danzig, says they'll soon scrap the last ten per cent of Versailles, and Goering says the German army is ready to strike with "lightning-like rapidity and un-dreamed-of impact."'

'I can't believe they'll go to war over a Danzig herring,' Mark insisted smilingly; and Dave said with a chuckle:

'Yes, I saw that too.' He asked: 'Mark, how about Japan? Chamberlain told Commons it made his blood boil to hear what the Japs were doing to Englishmen out there—and he even threatened to send the fleet out.'

'That's bluff, I should say.'

'Probably,' Dave assented. 'But you know, I think bluffing is bad business. Chamberlain says that about the fleet without meaning it. I wonder if he means what he says about backing Poland.' He added: 'If Germany thinks he's bluffing, she may grab Danzig and the Corridor.'

'She may, anyway!'

'I doubt it. Norman Crump, the financial editor of the London *Times,* says Germany couldn't stand the strain of a war that lasted more than three or four months.'

Mark smiled. 'You know, Dave, I said to Tony awhile ago, we're reaching the stage in our national thinking when we try to prove things by quoting what someone said—without asking whether he knows what he is talking about. We believe things we want to believe—just because someone said them.'

Dave nodded, and he said thoughtfully: 'If anything does start over there, I think I'll try to get back into the service, in some capacity. I want a job to do, something to keep me busy.' There was for a moment a hint of terror in his eyes. 'I don't do so well, just sitting around,' he confessed.

'You look fine.'

'I am fine,' Dave assented. 'I've no real craving for liquor. No physical craving. It's just that I get so damned bored.' He rose restlessly. 'Swim?' he suggested; and afterward, while they lay on the sand he said: 'Or I may go to work, go into business of some sort. That will keep me from thinking about Marcia. I do, you know. Maybe it's just habit, but she and I have been married a long time.' Mark asked no questions, but Dave confessed: 'She doesn't write to me, Mark. I write to her, of course, long letters—just telling her what we're doing, how we're getting along.'

'Where is she?' Mark asked.

'She's in Honolulu this summer. She writes to Ruth sometimes, sends messages to me.'

Mark felt a strong anger at Marcia, and an almost tender affection for this valiant man.

He talked with Ruth awhile that evening, and she spoke proudly of her father. 'He's whipped it, Uncle Mark,' she said. 'It was terrible for him. I didn't know a man could suffer so. There was always a decanter of whiskey on the table in the cabin; and at first just seeing it would make him shiver and perspire, and sometimes his face was gray with pain. But he never tasted it. I've been so proud of him.'

'He's a fine man, Ruth.'

'I wrote Mother all about it, but she says he's done the same thing before, so often. She won't believe he's different now, Uncle Mark.'

'She will in time.'

'He'd be all right if she were here.'

Mark said gently: 'She's tried that, Ruth, tried to help him by being with him. Perhaps now she's trying this other way. I'm not sure it isn't as hard for her as it is for him.'

'I wish you could talk to her.' She touched his arm in a quick affection. 'You seem to understand people. Me, and Father, anyway.' And when presently they rose to go indoors—Tony and Dave were playing backgammon—she kissed him. 'Father and I both love you a lot, you know,' she said.

4

(August 13, 1939)

Everywhere in Europe there were mock battles, the clank of tank treads and the stamping feet of marching men. Bulgaria and Hungary demanded slices of Rumanian territory. The Italian army suddenly halted its maneuvers; and Paris commented in a sly glee that this halt was ordered because the maneuvers proved blitzkrieg tactics were unsound against well-organized defense. Congress had adjourned, and the House of Commons went home, to come together again in October. Southeastern England had a practice blackout; and Poland threatened to meet force with force in Danzig. German papers retorted that if she did so, Poland would be crushed. The foreign news crept back to the front pages; but Mark half forgot this when Robin wrote from Montreal that she would return to New York before the end of August.

'I hope you can come over to see me soon,' she said. 'I'll let you know the day I'll be there.'

Nell Ritchie with Jan and Will were at Boothbay—Betty and Ingrid had elected to drive to the coast this summer, would not return till September—and Nell had taken the servants; so Bob was apt to come across the street and breakfast with Mark and Tony. Usually he went to Boothbay for week-ends, but in mid-August business kept him in town Saturday, so he stayed in Boston and Mark invited him for Sunday dinner. Bob came, and when he appeared, he said:

'I'm supposed to go to Father's.' Mr. and Mrs. Ritchie spent their summers at Scituate. 'But I'm not going. He's so haired up about the war that he can't talk about anything else, and we usually end in a row.'

'You talk as if there were war already,' Mark commented.

'So does Father,' Bob retorted. 'Personally I think if there's a war, England will start it.'

'Yes, and Germany will finish it,' Tony predicted.

Bob chuckled. 'Got it all figured, have you?'

'Yes,' Tony told him soberly. 'I think there'll be a war and that Germany will win it—quick. England and France are on the down grade. Germany will rule Europe, and Japan will rule Asia, and we'll rule the Americas—after about a ten-year war with Germany.'

'There'll be no war, for my money,' Bob insisted.

'Mr. Roosevelt seems to expect it,' Mark reminded him. 'At least he says Congress made it impossible for him to prevent war, when they refused to repeal the arms embargo.'

'That loose-mouthed blatherskite gives me the pip,' Bob declared. 'If he'd keep his mouth shut, there'd be no war. He's just egging them on.'

'I'm inclined to be more hopeful since Forster's last speech in Danzig,' Mark said. 'At least he didn't wave the bloody shirt. And Ciano's probably trying to cool down von Ribbentrop.'

'One damned sure thing,' Bob declared, 'they won't get us into it this time. Outside of my father—and Franklin—I don't know anyone who's for it.'

'We're all against it,' Mark agreed. 'But we haven't any real voice, you know. Mr. Roosevelt can take us in.' He smiled. 'He'll follow Hitler's rule, take one little step at a time—like the Irishman cutting off the dog's tail an inch at a time so it wouldn't hurt so much.'

Bob said in a harsh tone: 'We've bragged so much about how good we are that we think we can run the world. I wonder if we are so damned good. Take this *Squalus* business.' The tedious process of raising the sunken submarine with the bodies of twenty-six of her crew still aboard was reported in the papers every day. 'We keep bragging about what a job we're doing to raise her, and forget all about the fact that we let her sink! We're always having submarine disasters, but I don't remember the Germans losing any submarines in peace times!'

After dinner, Tony went off to fly, and when he returned, Mark saw at once that something out of the ordinary had happened. 'Well, how did it go?' he asked.

'All right,' Tony told him in an abstracted tone. 'I was practising loops and spins.'

'I never went that far. Power stalls and wing-overs were my limit.' Tony did not comment, and Mark asked, groping for the reason for the other's manner: 'How's Mr. Hadden?'

'He's going back to England!'

'Going home?' Mark was surprised. 'Why?'

'He thinks he might do some good, training pilots over there,' Tony explained; and after a moment he said in a puzzled tone: 'You know how he's always talked, Dad, about no more war for him, and all that; but he's going now! He acts kind of embarrassed about it, but he's going.'

Mark nodded. 'No matter how you feel beforehand, there's only one thing to do when war comes.' He thought this news of Hadden's decision was proof enough that war was sure.

5

(August 20, 1939)

In mid-August, since they had taken the cottage for only six weeks, the Ritchies returned from Boothbay, and Ed and Mary Halstead suggested a Sunday clambake at Humarock. The day proved dull and foggy, and Mark, waking before dawn, heard rain falling; but he knew Ed and Mary well enough to be sure this would not discourage them. He saw the Ritchie car drive off just before he and Tony went out to the garage.

They found Dave and Ruth at Humarock before them. 'And I asked Tom and Emma Sheffield,' Mary explained. 'I haven't seen them for so long, and I thought we could get the old crowd together. But Emma said they couldn't come.'

'I never see them,' Mark admitted. 'I miss Tom.'

Mary nodded. 'Emma's going downhill,' she said in a low tone to him alone. 'I had lunch with Ed at the Copley last week, celebrating his birthday, and she was there with another woman, drinking cocktails. She didn't recognize me. She'd been drinking quite a lot, I think.'

They picnicked among the dunes east of the cottage, disregarding the evil weather—the rain persisted and fog hid the sea—baking lobsters and clams and sweet corn in a sheet-iron cylinder stuffed with seaweed. Ed was cook, but after the fire was lighted and a supply of wood on hand, the others swam. Mark and Jan came out of the water together, and Mark said they were all here but Betty—still in the West with Ingrid—and Jan said: 'She wouldn't have come even if she were at home. She hates picnics unless there are boys, hates sand in her food, and she hates rain like a cat.'

Mark smiled. 'Boys?' he echoed. 'Edwin's a nice youngster—but I suppose he's too young to interest Betty.' Edwin Halstead was eighteen, would go to Bowdoin in the fall. 'Or what's the matter with Tony?'

'Edwin's sweet,' Jan agreed. 'Isn't it cute the way he adores his father! Just like you and Tony—only Edwin shows it more.' Mark saw her eyes go toward where Tony lay flat on the sand, with the Halstead youngsters—Burt was nine, and Dan a chubby six-year-old, bundled in absurdly voluminous oilskins against the light rain—bouncing up and down on him, while Ann, who was fourteen now, watched them smilingly. 'Ann's crazy about Tony,' Jan said. 'Just the way I was at her age.'

Then Ed shouted: 'Soup's on! Come aboard and have a hake!' Tony dumped the two little boys, and everyone trooped to the fire, and the smoke, veering in the uncertain airs, annoyed them all impartially, and rain hissed on the hot iron cylinder while they devoured the feast and praised Ed's cooking. Afterward Mary said:

'Now it's women's work to clean up. Go along, the rest of you. You can go sit on the veranda out of the rain.'

So Mark and Dave and Bob and Ed moved toward the house, and Tony and Edwin, after they had helped clean away the rubbish of the picnic, joined them. Rain fell harder, and the others, their task done, went indoors. Rain and fog blotted out all but the nearer sea, and Ed puffed his pipe and said slowly:

'Can't see much out there. Anything might be happening in the fog.'

'Or on the other side of it,' Dave suggested. 'I suppose the smashup is surely coming.'

Mark said: 'All over a few Danzig herrings.' Ed looked at him curiously, and he explained: 'That was the detonator, you know. Poland refused to buy Danzig herrings, and Danzig said that in that case she'd return to the Reich, and the Polish ambassador in Washington says if she tries that, Poland will act at once—and that England and France will have to come in.'

Ed nodded. 'Everyone seems to agree that Danzig should plausibly be German—but if Poland yields on that, Germany will grab the rest, just as she did in Czecho-Slovakia.'

'I wonder,' Mark reflected, 'whether if England and France had stood firm on their Munich guarantee of Czecho-Slovakia, we'd have this new crisis now?'

'Poland's asking for it,' Bob said vigorously. 'And she'll get it!' Mark thought that even Bob showed the strain of this long suspense. There was a harsh anger in his tones.

'I'm not so sure,' Ed commented. 'The experts claim Poland has one of the best armies in the world.' Mark saw Edwin watching his father with wide eyes.

Dave Rollins disagreed. 'Poland certainly hasn't might on her side,' he said. 'And I'm not even sure she has right.'

Bob spoke strongly. 'Germany's a highwayman, but Poland's a sneak thief,' he declared. 'She stole some scraps from the Czechs while the Germans were making their grab there. But the whole mess comes from England's damned stupidity. Did you see that London was "stunned" by the Russian pact with Germany?'

Mark, puzzled by his own mind, said: 'I don't understand myself. England's muddling infuriates me, but the queer part is that whatever she does, I hope she wins. Why should I feel that way? There's no sense to it!'

'There's no sense to any of it,' Dave agreed; and he said in a low tone: 'In the ears of the whole world, the martial rumble of the distant drums.'

Tony had been sitting silent on the veranda rail, but with a strong motion like a bound he came now to his feet. 'Excuse me while I explode,' he said hotly. 'I've got to boil over. The unspeakable greed of your generation—oh, I don't mean you four men, but I do mean all the men your age and older—is only equalled by its stupidity. England and France and the rest of them carved up Germany in 1918—and expected her to take it lying down. You couldn't even end the last war right, and now we go into this mess with you still running the show.'

Bob said amiably: 'Hold on there, son. We weren't running it twenty years ago. We just did the fighting.'

'Well, you're running it now,' Tony insisted. 'And yet you haven't enough brains to see that the airplane is the answer. Planes sank battleships—the *Ostfriesland,* and the *Alabama*—in bombing tests years ago, and there are better planes and better bombers now. But the Navy's still being run by a lot of Admirals who want to have battleships for their private yachts, because they're more comfortable than destroyers and cruisers.'

Ed chuckled. 'Inconsistent, aren't you, Tony? If planes can sink battleships—then the battleships aren't going to be so damned comfortable.' Edwin grinned with him.

'The Admirals won't admit planes can do it!' Tony reminded them. He hesitated, a little abashed by his own violence, but he insisted: 'You can't win a war without planes any more than you can win a war without infantry.'

Dave asked gently: 'What do you think Germany's planes can do, Tony?'

'The first thing they'll do will be to smash every airport and hangar and airplane factory they can reach. Once they command the air, they can do anything they want to, sink ships, smash cities. Europe will take a nose dive right back into barbarism!'

Bob Ritchie said: 'Right! That's why I say, stay out of it. I'm for peace.'

'Peace?' Tony cried. 'There'll be no peace till Hitler and his breed have been wiped out.'

'How will you do that?' Bob asked drily.

'Planes!' Tony insisted. 'Planes and more planes!'

Mary came out of the house. 'For Heaven's sake,' she protested laughingly. 'What's all the shooting for? Come on inside. Nell wants us to play some games.'

But Mark stayed where he was. Tony's outburst had filled him with regret, because the boy—like all boys his age—was forced to face the vast confusion of the blundering world. He thought of a stanza in the Rubáiyat, remembered only its sense; that men did thus and so and went here and there and came out by the same door where in they went. That was what the minds of men were doing today, churning and wheeling and making false starts and recoiling only to start again. These friends of his held each an individual point of view. Ed was ready to believe that the German threat was overrated, that it could be met. Ed had served in the Navy in the last war, as second in command on a destroyer; and he still made a hobby of navigation. Mark once had borrowed from him and read with a layman's interest Lecky's Wrinkles and he was enough the mathematician to enjoy many of its chapters. Ed even had a sextant, with which Mark had tried to 'shoot the sun,' and he had been astonished to find how easy it was to detect the exact moment when the sun reached its zenith and began its downward course.

Thus Ed's was to some extent the professional's point of view, the point of view of the naval man. From that point of view, war against Germany would be a grim business, but it could have only one outcome; and Ed, Mark suspected, would wish to do his share, if war came.

Bob, on the other hand, believed that Europe's wars need not concern us; that we could keep clear, and should keep clear. This, Mark thought, was the natural point of view for a man of Bob's unsentimental, completely logical and thoroughly practical mind. The United States could gain nothing by a European war—and win or lose, such a war would cost her heavily. Therefore, we should stay out. That was Bob's position.

And Dave? Dave saw the rising danger, not in terms of military and naval strength as Ed did, and not in terms of self-interest as Bob did, but rather as an epic tragedy that threatened to overwhelm all the peoples of the world. There was something of the poet in Dave; a keen sensitivity, a capacity for understanding the feelings of others. Mark had seen Dave's sympathetic eye on Tony when the younger man was driven into violent speech awhile ago. In terms of human suffering, Ed could as a naval man on blockade duty participate in starving German women and children, and while he would not relish the task he would do it, for what seemed to him the greater good. Bob would be able to view the sufferings of both sides with a certain grim complacency as long as the United States kept clear. Dave would feel a compassion as keen toward suffering enemies as toward allies and friends.

Most Americans—certainly most Americans away from the seaboard —would probably agree with Bob that Europe's madness was no affair of ours. A smaller number, men who were either in the armed services or close to them, would range from Ed's quiet readiness for duty to a gleeful zeal at the prospect of playing the bloody game for which they had been trained. A less numerous group, like Dave, would be torn by an almost feminine sympathy for all the millions who would suffer on each side in any war that came.

And Tony? Tony represented all the young men, rebellious at the thought of being dragooned into battle and intolerant of what seemed to them the follies of their elders, even while they were driven irresistibly by something within themselves to go forward, to fight, perhaps to live, perhaps to die.

Mark thought that in watching these friends of his, and in watching Tony and Edwin, he was seeing a picture of the whole composite mind of America, as it waited now, helpless to interfere, for other nations to make a world-destroying war.

He did not attempt to define his own convictions. He was all men in one, his mind the arena in which every opinion met to contest supremacy; and the long years in which he had watched the nearing tragedy had wearied him sorely. Frequently of late he had felt that thumping of his heart again. He was tired, tired, tired. He thought of Robin as of a healing spring.

6

(August 20, 1939)

Driving home with his son that afternoon Mark said in a quiet sympathy: 'You're taking this business in Europe pretty hard, Tony.'

Tony nodded. 'It's all such a terrible mess, Dad! I can't make head nor tail of it. And I change my mind half a dozen times a day. I can't see any way out. No matter where I look, it's a long bloody fight back to peace and decency again.' And he added after a moment in a sombre tone: 'I pray to God that we stupid Americans will realize that airplanes are the Yes and No in a modern war. Start building airplanes and training pilots. We'll need every one of them. Give us airplanes and more airplanes. With our air definitely our own, give us battleships if you can't get enough easy-chairs for the Admirals any other way; but first and mostly, give us airplanes.'

Mark said wearily: 'I suppose we have to let the experts decide what we need.'

'Experts, my eye!' Tony exploded. 'Just because a man has gone to West Point or to Annapolis for four years, we call him an expert. Some of them are all right, sure; but most of them are just technicians, knowing how things have been done before, and sure the same things must be done in the same way again. If you live long enough, and don't break the rules, you're bound to get to be an admiral or a general; but being old doesn't qualify a man for figuring out how to win a war.'

Mark nodded thoughtfully. 'The great generals were usually young men,' he agreed. 'Even Napoleon made his reputation, won his greatest victories, as a youngster.' He smiled. 'I remember something Colonel Cooper, the man who dammed the Mississippi and the Nile and the Dnieper, told me. He said he was no engineer; that he could hire all the engineering talent he wanted at thirty dollars a week. He said he was a dreamer; he dreamed vast dreams, and persuaded other men to make them come true.' And he laughed at a sudden memory. 'Mark Twain, I think it was, wrote a piece once about a man who went to Heaven and told Saint Peter he wanted to see the great generals of history. Saint Peter showed him a thousand of them, with Alexander and Napoleon and Frederick the Great at the top of the heap; but in a chair all alone, sitting over them, there was one man. The newcomer to Heaven asked who he was, and Saint Peter said: "He's the greatest general who ever lived; but there was no war during his lifetime, so he spent his days as a cobbler in a little town in Illinois."'

'Right,' Tony agreed. 'But if we get into a war, the old generals and admirals will go right on making their mistakes. The cobblers won't have a chance.'

'There's something in the Bible along this line,' Mark remembered. 'The old men dream dreams, and the young men see visions—or maybe it's the other way around. But the point is, in either case, young men imagine themselves achieving the impossible, while old men are content to remember the past. The trouble with being experienced, in war or in anything else, Tony, is that when an action is proposed, old men foresee all the difficulties and the obstacles in the way and are beaten before they begin. But young men, knowing nothing of the difficulties, ignore them—and sometimes they win through.'

They drove then in silence for a while, and Mark thought that the world was committing a crime against mankind by subjecting millions of boys like Tony to the intolerable tension of these days. There had been a reckless violence in Tony today which no young man should ever come to feel.

While his thoughts were of Tony, so were his son's of him. On their fishing trip together, Tony had seen lines drawn in his father's countenance and a shadow in his eyes. He asked suddenly: 'Dad, are you all right?'

Mark was surprised. 'Why, yes, of course,' he said.

'Where's Mrs. Kerr? Still in Montreal?'

'Yes.'

'Why don't you go up and see her? It would do you good.'

'She'll be back in New York in a few days.' Mark was grateful for Tony's solicitude. The boy asked:

'When are you two going to get married? What are you waiting for?' He saw Mark smile disarmingly, and he urged: 'You ought to go ahead. It's what you need, to take your mind off things.'

Mark felt bound not to tell him about Davy, certainly not without Robin's permission. 'Robin's the one to decide that,' he said.

Tony was silenced, thinking his own thoughts. He was sure their delay was not Mark's doing; therefore it was hers. And if she delayed —was not he to blame? He said abruptly: 'Dad, I'm meeting Lucy tonight. She's been visiting in Bar Harbor, driving home today, and we're having dinner at the Ritz. Mind?'

'No, of course not.'

'She wants me to go on down to their place on the Cape tomorrow,' Tony explained. 'Tomorrow afternoon. I thought I might, if it's all right with you.'

'It's all right, of course,' Mark assented. He commented: 'You're fond of Lucy, aren't you.'

Tony hesitated. 'I sure am,' he said then strongly. 'Of course I hate to go and leave you at home alone, but you're tied up all day—and I'm

all steamed up, too steamed up for my own good! Lucy will take my
mind off the war—I hope.'

Mark nodded. He hoped so, too.

He himself had supper with the Ritchies, explaining why Tony did
not come with him. 'He had a date with Lucy Pride,' he said, and he
spoke of Tony's projected visit on the Cape. Will and Jan were with
them, but afterward Nell called Jan into the hall and spoke to her,
and Jan presently summoned Will, leaving the three older people together. Mark thought this seemed to have been planned, and wondered why; but when they were alone, Nell came quickly to the point.

'Mark,' she said, 'I've got to talk to you about Tony and Lucy Pride.
He's seeing a lot of her, isn't he?'

Mark nodded, and he said smilingly: 'If I had been as openly devoted to any girl as Tony is to Lucy, my father would have felt I was
compromising her, and her father would have been wanting to know
whether my intentions were honorable. But of course things are different now.'

Nell asked, after a moment—and her hesitation was so unusual that
he noticed it: 'Do you know Mr. and Mrs. Pride?'

'I've met him somewhere,' Mark assented. 'He's an architect, isn't he?'

'Yes,' Nell agreed. 'Do you know Mrs. Pride?'

'No. But he seemed a nice chap.'

Nell said: 'He is!' She spoke sharply to her husband. 'Bob, quit fidget-
ing! I'm going to tell him. It's time he knew.'

'It's libel,' Bob reminded her gravely.

'Well, Mark's not going to broadcast it.' Nell turned to Mark again.
'I'm not just gossiping, Mark,' she assured him seriously. 'I've known
this for years—and so have a lot of other people. But everyone's so fond
of Ted Pride that no one talks about it.'

Mark smiled faintly. 'Come to the point, Nell. I'm all ears,' he assured her. Despite his casual tone, he was uneasy. Nell had a lively
tongue, but her gossip was usually harmless enough, repeated more for
the sake of telling a good story than to do harm.

'Well, I will,' she said resolutely. 'Here it is. I used to know Ted Pride,
before Bob and I were married. They had a place on the Cape near
ours. Ted was a sweet boy. He was years older than I was, of course;
but I liked Ted just the way Jan likes Tony.' She smiled. 'Only it was
even more hopeless, because he was ten years older than I, at the very
least.'

And she went on: 'Dinny—her name was Dinah, but everyone called her Dinny—was the prettiest thing you ever saw. Her father and mother were divorced, and she was gay and lots of fun, and every boy in sight fell in love with her. Ted was through college and he'd been in Paris for a year, studying, so when he came down to the Cape for a month he had a sort of foreign glamour—and Dinny picked him! They'd only known each other two weeks when they were married.'

She paused, but Mark only nodded, and she went on: 'Dan was born right away, in less than a year. I used to see them summers down there, and then, when Bob·and I were first married, we saw them some.' She said seriously: 'I'm not telling you hearsay, Mark. I'm telling you things I know.'

Mark looked at Bob. Bob said reluctantly: 'It's all straight enough, Mark; but damn it, it wasn't Lucy's fault! She always struck me as a sweet girl.'

Nell quickly agreed. 'She is! I could say some malicious things about the way she always plays up to men—and that men the age of you and Bob always fall for her—but I won't. I'm not just being malicious now. I'm telling you something you ought to know.'

Mark smiled. 'You mean you're going to.'

'All right,' she said. 'I'll give it to you in words of one syllable. About a year after Dan was born, Dinny Pride ran away from home with a man named Fardel. They went on his yacht. Ted told everyone she had just gone on a cruise, and that he was so busy he couldn't go. About two months later he had a nervous breakdown, and he was in the Waverley Hospital eight months. Then a month after Ted came out of Waverley, Dinny came home.' She added briefly: 'Mrs. Pride—Ted's mother—told Mother she begged Ted not to take Dinny back, but Ted did. Dinny was—she had no money, and she said she was sick, and Ted took her in. Mrs. Pride tried to stick it out, but she died soon after Dinny came home, died from an overdose of a sleeping draught. I think she killed herself, when she knew what was going to happen; but no one knows that for sure.

'But I do know—and so does everyone—that Dinny had a baby five months after she came home. The baby was Lucy.'

She was silent, watching Mark. For a moment he waited to steady his tone. 'It seems hard to believe that Mr. Pride would take her back, if that were true,' he protested then.

'It is hard to believe, but it's true,' she said earnestly. 'Bob knows it's true. You see, Ted is really a Christlike man.'

Mark looked at Bob, and Bob nodded. 'It's true, yes, Mark,' he said.

'But I don't see any reason to drag it up. It certainly wasn't Lucy's fault.'

'Of course it wasn't,' Nell agreed. 'But Mrs. Pride is no good. There've been things since. I could give you names and dates. The crowd they go with now is used to Dinny—and Ted acts as if he thought no one knew the facts of life.'

Mark asked, hardly knowing what he said: 'Is Mr. Pride down at their summer place now?'

'I suppose so. He plays the game. They have a daughter a year or so younger than Lucy, you know, so there's no question that Ted forgave Dinny completely.'

Mark said, after a moment, smiling ruefully: 'Nell, I remember an argument you and I had, one evening a few years ago. I'd been reading some book in which adultery played a part, and I said such books were remote from reality; that the people I knew all seemed to lead normal, healthy, happy lives.'

'And I told you you were wrong!'

'Yes, you did. Yet even now I don't know at all well anyone who has been divorced.'

'You may, soon,' she told him. 'I had a letter from Marcia . . .'

But Bob said quickly: 'Pipe down, Nell! That's enough of that.'

Mark said grimly: 'Such things as this can happen then, and lives go on.' He was thinking as much of Ruth—who would be so crushed if what Nell hinted were true—as of Lucy's mother.

'Of course.'

He rose, in a stark need to be alone. 'I'm glad you told me, Nell,' he said. 'Of course I agree with Bob that Lucy's not to blame, but—well, I don't know just what can be done. I'll have to find some way to tell Tony, I suppose. Certainly he ought to know.'

At home he thought he might wait till Tony came home, talk to his son tonight; but he shrank from doing so. There was time enough. Certainly Tony, with a year of college still ahead of him, would not yet involve himself with Lucy. Mark decided to wait for wisdom and the useful word.

7

(August 1939)

Mark met Tony at breakfast and asked how Lucy was, and Tony said she was swell. 'She's shopping this morning,' he explained, 'and we're meeting for lunch and starting right after.'

'How long do you plan to stay?'

'I don't know. Over the week-end, maybe. Of course I'll come back any time you say.'

Mark's doubts were in his voice. 'I suppose there'll be a crowd of young people around.'

'Oh, sure, there always is, around Lucy.'

It was impossible to ask questions, but Mark said: 'I think I met Mr. Pride once. I don't know Mrs. Pride.'

'She's a darned fool,' Tony told him. 'One of these kittenish women. Mr. Pride's all right; not much to him, but he's jolly and friendly. I guess he's a pretty good architect.'

Mark made his tone casual. 'If you and Lucy ever get serious about each other, I'll want to meet her family.'

'Oh, sure!' Tony seemed to guess his father's concern, for he said re-assuringly: 'I think a lot of your opinion, you know, Dad. When the time comes that I'm considering asking some girl to marry me, you'll know before she does.'

Mark smiled. 'I hope she won't mind that.'

Tony laughed. 'Let her mind. But she won't, if she knows you.'

Mark said: 'Of course you know I'll welcome—and love—anyone you love and who loves you. But I believe it's perfectly possible to let your head work with your heart in marriage, Tony. I remember a discussion we had a year or two ago about the importance of marrying a girl a little better than you were; of looking up, not down, when you come to choose a wife.'

'Sure, I remember. Don't worry. The first time I feel a proposal coming on, I'll talk to you.' And Tony added smilingly: 'Just as you talked to me, about Mrs. Kerr. Remember?'

Mark smiled gratefully. 'I'll always remember that, Tony.'

'When does she come back to New York?'

'Any day now.'

Tony said in a curious, breathless fashion. 'When she does, go over and see her.' He laughed and gripped Mark's shoulder. 'Those are orders, Dad. I'll stay down at Lucy's till you do!'

'Sounds like an ultimatum!'

'Well, ultimatums are the fashion nowadays.'

They said good-bye, and when Mark came home that evening the house seemed empty. He read the evening paper, but as the sands of this month ran out the newspapers were ugly company. After dinner he wrote Robin, still in Montreal, a letter in which he raged at the stupidity of statesmen; and her reply a day or two later was full of passionate tenderness. During the days that followed he tried not to look at the newspapers, since whenever he did so a blind anger filled him. He was angry at the fatuous editors who fed their readers reassuring nonsense instead of what seemed to Mark the bald and terrible truth. Under a picture of some British planes one day the caption ran:

> Wellington bombers, which, according to British, can fly from Britain to Poland over Germany, dropping explosives on the way, then reload and refuel in Poland and repeat performance.

Under another picture of German artillery, the caption declared that Germany, by rushing her war equipment to the Polish border, showed her respect for the Poles as fighters. An editor announced that a million and a half Poles were under arms—and quoted 'military experts' as saying that one man on defense was worth three on offense. Therefore, said the editor, the Poles could stand off—the mathematics were simple —four and a half million Germans. Mark's eyes blurred with rage as he tossed the paper aside.

On the twenty-fifth of August, Mr. Roosevelt sent a note to Hitler urging discussion, arbitration, conciliation. Mark thought the procedure as futile as throwing dead leaves at a hurricane. The same day a letter came from Tony.

> Dear Dad:
> Lucy and I almost didn't go to bed last night, listening to the news. We took her portable radio down to the beach, and after every commentator had had his say, we had a swim to cool off! Lucy didn't want to go to bed and neither did I. There seemed a good chance that London would be bombed before morning; and that bombardment might have been the beginning of all sorts of things. It might have made last night the most important night in the history of the world! And tonight may be just as important as last night could have been. But tonight there seemed to be little change since last night. Or rather, this morning things are about as they were last night—as nearly as can be told by reading the papers. And already we are beginning to get used to and comparatively indifferent to the tension which last night had the whole world by the ears.
> The only hope of avoiding war, apparently, is to let Hitler have his way with Poland and all of Europe, and I think that is the best thing to do. No loss could be as great as the losses that would come with war. And Hitler is mortal. We act as though he were a Devil. We are willing to send the world to war to stop one man. But Hitler will die, and when he does, the radicals and the conservatives will start fighting.
> It all boils down to one fact—none of us know what's going on. And to another fact—war will be worse than slavery for men my age. It will be death.

The bank teller in Czecho-Slovakia may not be quite as well off now as he was a year ago—but he's still alive.

I've got to stop now. Lucy's just come downstairs.

Lots of love,

Tony.

Mark, reading this letter, thought Tony was like a man blinded by a dazzling light, who stumbles forward into any pit that lies in his path. He was at once sorry and glad that his son was not with him, sorry because in Tony's distress they could not be together, glad because he recognized the fact that there was no reassurance he could give. Whatever was to come could not be averted. They were helpless as chips in a whirlpool, their own puny strength useless against the current which swept them on. He himself could not think clearly. In these last days of August he succumbed to a sort of apathy, stunned by the actual impact of these events so long foreseen. He remembered the opening days of the last war; the crashing German invasion of Belgium, the rout of the French, the pitiful losses of the gallant little English army, the long weeks when headlines blared every morsel of hopeful news while the maps told their relentless story of German victories. And then the German tide reached its peak and rose no higher, and then came the race for the Channel, and trenches and machine guns took command, and the world began that process of bleeding to death which was to last so dreadfully long.

Tony wrote again, this time briefly:

Hitler has made me practically inarticulate. I'm between ghastly pessimism and glorious optimism; for I see in these amazing days promise of all the heaven and hell within mankind's reach. Certainly I'm ready to grab any piece of heaven I can find—before hell reaches out for me.

'Any piece of heaven!' The phrase rang in Mark's mind. He envied Tony the solace of Lucy's affectionate companionship, and he wished terribly to see Robin; and thinking of her, he saw a Montreal paper on a newsstand and bought it and found in it an editorial headed:

Why Don't You Speak for Yourself, John Alden?

The editorial suggested that the United States, instead of urging England and France to stop Hitler, might better commit herself to that enterprise. This editorial was just the beginning, Mark thought. If war came, there would inevitably follow a dogged campaign—lecturers, speeches, books—to bring in the United States on England's side.

Sunday morning Tony telephoned—with an embarrassed apology in his tones—to ask whether he might stay another week. 'Lucy wants me to,' he explained. 'I hate leaving you alone, but she says . . .'

Then Lucy took the telephone away from Tony and pleaded prettily, and Mark laughed and said of course Tony could stay. 'Give him a good time, Lucy,' he told her. 'Take his mind off the war.'

'I will,' she promised. 'You just leave that to me!'

Afterward Mark was sorry for himself, but within the hour a special-delivery letter came from Robin. She would reach New York Monday morning, and she wrote: 'If you don't come to me soon, my darling, I shall come to you.'

Mark could not go at once; but against all obstacles, he arranged to be a few days away, and Wednesday afternoon he boarded a New York plane. He was thinking of Tony's phrase: 'to grab any piece of Heaven I can find.' To be with Robin would be Heaven for him too.

8

(August 1939)

Mark had wired Robin his arrival time, and she met his plane, came into his arms in an ardent rapture, clung to him, held him at arm's length to look at him with searching eyes, and then came close to him again. 'It's been so long, so long,' she whispered, smiling up at him through her tears. 'You're all right, aren't you, darling? You're all right. You're just fine.'

He laughed in a rich happiness. 'I'm fine,' he told her. 'Never finer than now.' He said: 'You're tired, aren't you?'

'Not now, not now!' she cried, and tugged at his arm. 'Come along, Mark. We mustn't stand here, scandalizing everyone. Wasn't I silly to cry? I didn't know I was going to. Oh, I've worried so about you.'

In the taxicab, he told the driver to go to his hotel; but she said: 'No, to my apartment.' She gave the man the address. 'I've moved, Mark; yesterday and today. I'm very grand now. I want you to see it.'

'I'd better leave my bag on the way. Then we can have dinner somewhere.'

'No,' she insisted. 'Dinner and everything's all planned, Mark. I've a surprise for you, my dear.' And she added: 'How's Tony? Is he at home?'

'He's still with Lucy.'

'Are they engaged?'

'Oh, no,' he assured her, and he said soberly: 'I hope they never will be.' She asked him why; and he told her about Lucy's mother. 'Nell Ritchie—Nell and Bob—told me,' he explained. 'I don't know Mr. and Mrs. Pride myself. I've met Mr. Pride, that's all.'

She said gravely, her hand through his arm: 'It's not a very good inheritance for Lucy, is it?'

'Shall I tell Tony?' he asked.

Robin considered. 'They're very young, of course. And Tony won't become engaged to her without discussing it first with you.'

'Or Lucy may turn to someone else,' Mark assented. 'She's a fairly giddy young woman, I gather.'

'Perhaps that's just because she's never met the right man.' Her hand pressed his arm. 'Someone like you—or your son.'

He smiled with pleasure, and then his eyes shadowed again. 'Robin,' he said, 'Tony keeps asking why you and I don't get married. Will you let me tell him about Davy, so he'll understand?'

'Of course,' she cried at once. 'I don't want to make you have secrets from him. I think of him as just another part of you.'

'You're good for me,' he said gratefully. 'You're a powerful—something or other.' He laughed. 'I haven't thought of Hitler since I met you.'

'Millions of people all over the world will go right on loving each other, whatever Hitler does,' she smilingly agreed. 'But please, no war talk today. We've more important things.'

They came to her new home, in a building near the East River with studio apartments high above the street. The doorman on duty carried Mark's bag to the automatic elevator and Robin pressed a button. She was suddenly quiet, silent here beside him. When the elevator stopped and the door opened, she led the way, producing her key.

'There, isn't this nicer?' she asked, looking up at him in a shy pride. The studio with north windows held the familiar litter that went with her work. Her easel and a model-stand were near the windows, and tubes of paint and boxes of crayon and watercolors lay on the table in neat array, not yet disordered by use. There was a fireplace, and beside it, comfortable chairs. 'I've been making curtains madly for two days,' she told him. 'Only just finished hanging them in time to go meet you. Like it?'

'It's perfect.'

'You might as well see it all at once.' She led him, almost hurriedly, through a door into a narrow hallway. 'Here's the kitchenette,' she said. 'Our steak is in the refrigerator.' Beyond, toward the river, two doors stood open and she turned that way and he was suddenly conscious of the shy, tremulous excitement in her. 'And two bedrooms,' she said, and without looking at him she added quietly: 'That's why I didn't want you to go to the hotel, Mark. I want you to stay here with me. This is your room.'

They stood in the doorway, he at her shoulder; and they were silent for a moment. He surveyed the pleasant room, and he looked down at her and dropped his arm around her waist. She turned then to meet his eyes, and came into his arms, and he kissed her gently, whispering to her, hearing her whispering responses, wordless sounds that were all tenderness. His arms tightened around her and they stood close-clasped, her eyes holding his while he said what he had made up his mind to say and while she listened. He found an eloquence he had not known he owned, trying to make her understand.

'But I knew I must not see you too soon,' he said at last. 'Not till I had thought it through. But I have, Robin. My mind is clear.' He laughed in a husky way, apologetically. 'It's my bringing up, I suppose! Can you understand?'

She nodded strongly, smiling up at him, touching his cheek, looking at his eyes and lips and brow; and she said: 'I can always understand you, my dear. Because I love you.'

'The world's rocking on its foundations—so we have to try to stand firm on ours.'

'I know.' She nodded in full reassurance.

'Are you blaming me?'

'Are you blaming me?' she countered, smiling still. 'Do you think I'm a hussy?'

'You're the most gracious and generous and noble person I have ever known.'

She said earnestly: 'But Mark, I want you to know that I really mean it. I want you to be sure I'm yours.' She smiled a little. 'Whenever and forever, dear.'

'I do know. I am sure.'

She held his shoulders with her hands, looking into his eyes; and after a moment she said: 'I think I knew always what you'd say, when the time came.'

He laughed, shaken with happiness in her, teasing her. 'What if I'd surprised you?'

She kissed him. 'I love you, my dear. Nothing could change that. But

—I'm glad you're the way you are.' She challenged, her eyes dancing: 'Shall we have a cocktail? Do you think we could, and still be so discreet?'

They were merry together at dinner, and afterward they sat long, assuaged and contented by their complete understanding. It was late when Mark said good night. He promised to come for breakfast, and he did so, with the morning papers, and she made him read them at the breakfast table.

'Like an old married couple,' she declared. 'Go ahead. Don't pay any attention to me!'

But Mark read aloud to her what news there was. The port authorities had held the *Bremen* for a few days, but she would sail today. There was no surface change in Europe. One editor wrote that Germany could not conceivably choose war; and he said: 'It appears that England and France have saved Poland and civilization.'

But Mark was not persuaded. 'I don't believe it,' he told her. 'This is the jumping-off place. Tomorrow or the next day or the next it will begin.'

He read that Germany was on a war basis, that Poland had two and a half million men under arms. 'That's enough to hold seven and a half million Germans, if the experts are right in giving the defense a three to one advantage,' he commented. 'But they're probably wrong.' A Warsaw dispatch said, absurdly, 'The Polish Government's patience is nearly exhausted,' and they found a sardonic humor in the bombastic words. Military experts—'neutral military observers and Polish officers,' in the newspaper phrase—predicted that Poland would keep at least half the German forces busy for six months or more, and one said of Poland: 'Her army, highly mobile, familiar with the ground it is fighting on, and of high morale, is always dangerous, and doubly so to a highly motorized force. The Germans will be lucky to have control of Poland in a year's time.'

Mark and Robin spent the long day together, and although she tried to lead him to talk of other things, he continually reverted to the European crisis, till she urged at last: 'You can't go on like this, darling, wondering and worrying. You must find some formula that will straighten you out. Worry's bad for you, remember?' And she said: 'Let's talk, talk and talk, see if we can't settle on some things you're sure of, that you can hold to.'

'I suppose all over the United States millions of men are as confused as I am,' Mark reflected. 'But it's damnable that the whole world should go to war over the Polish Corridor.' He laughed harshly. 'Over a Danzig herring.'

She did not know what he meant, and he told her, and she laughed with him; but she asked then: 'Mark, wouldn't it help if, instead of worrying about England and Germany and Poland, you just held on to the fact that we're Americans, and decided what you think the United States ought to do?'

'It's hard to do that,' he reminded her. 'And when war comes, it will be harder all the time. England and France and Germany will each be doing everything they can to enlist our sympathies.'

She knew he needed not tenderness nor any feminine consolation nor any pretty cajoleries, but sober man-talk; needed an anvil on which he could hammer into shape his own convictions. So, as though she were a man, instead of a woman who loved him, she challenged:

'Do you think we ought to declare war ourselves, or tell Germany we'll be against her?'

'If we could speak with any authority, that might do some good,' he reflected. 'If Germany knew that we had an army equal to hers, ready to throw into Europe, she'd think twice about going to war. But we haven't—except perhaps potentially—so anything we say now is completely futile.'

'Does it have to be?'

'Yes, until we make ourselves strong enough so that we'll be listened to. Germany can ignore us and our opinions now as completely as she ignores—Portugal. More completely, in fact. Portugal might be for her a useful ally, with harbors for her submarines; so she'll keep on good terms with Portugal.'

'How can we make ourselves respected?' she asked. 'Do you mean we ought to become a big military power?'

He nodded, his eyes hard. 'Yes,' he said firmly. 'We ought to start right now—we ought to have started two years ago—to build an Atlantic Navy as strong as England's and a Pacific Navy as strong as Japan's.' He remembered Bob Ritchie's word. 'We ought to build planes and tanks enough to equip a big army—and train at least skeleton crews to handle them.'

'But then that's one thing you can be sure of,' she said triumphantly. 'You believe we ought to prepare tremendously, so whatever we do that tends toward preparedness, you approve, and anything that hinders preparedness, you oppose.'

'Yes, of course.' His eyes lighted, and he added more slowly: 'And another thing.' He smiled at his own inconsistency. 'I've noticed over and over the past year that no matter how much I criticize England, I don't want to see her beaten. I don't believe we'll ever stand idly by and see England lose.'

'Why not?' she protested, opposing him because by so doing she could best stimulate his thinking. 'You've no love for England. Are you afraid if she were beaten, Germany might attack us?'

'No,' he said. 'My feeling's not based on fear, or greed, or anything so tangible. It's—sentiment, maybe. If England's beaten, forced to sue for peace, forced to surrender her navy and her merchant fleet and to dismantle her shipyards, she'll be reduced to the status of a helpless little island off the coast of Europe, dependent on others for the very bread she eats. I don't want that to happen.'

'Why not?' she insisted. 'Why don't you?'

'Well,' he reminded her, 'so many of our roots are in England. Our laws, our literature, our traditions are all based on England's. If anything happened to her, these foundations would be shaken—and so would our lives.' And he went on: 'Some Englishman said the other day that the England which would be left after even a winning war would be a country in which he did not wish to live. I don't go that far, but if the England we know were destroyed, something fundamental in our national life would be gone forever. I don't want that to happen.' He added slowly: 'And I think fundamentally all Americans—or most of us —feel the same way. I don't believe we'll ever let England be beaten if we can help it.'

'A lot of people would disagree with you. I mean when you say we won't let England lose.'

He nodded, remembering Judge Sothern. 'A lot of people even resent the suggestion that England might lose. But I'm sure that's a possibility. And I'm sure we won't let it happen if we can help it. But we may not realize we feel that way until England is clearly in danger. It may need some English disasters to wake us up.'

She still questioned his every word, forcing him to answer her and in so doing to crystallize his own ideas. 'So many Americans dislike England. I can't believe you're right.'

'So many children dislike their parents,' he reminded her. 'But no matter how much a boy hates his father, if another man attacks his father, he'll take his father's side.' And he said in a sudden contentment: 'No, Robin, I'm sure I'm right—and that gives me a platform. I can set it up like a proposition in logic. I think England may be beaten. But

I'm sure we will never stand by and see that happen. Therefore, we ought to prepare tremendously.' He laughed in a strong satisfaction. 'Mr. Wilson had his fourteen points. Well, three points are enough for me! Besides, his didn't hang together, and mine do. They're program enough for any American.'

There was a firm contentment in his tones, so that she knew she had given him what he needed; yet she persisted still in opposition, wisely understanding that in seeking to convince her he would convince himself. Till at last she saw his mind was settled, and in a profound gratefulness she repeated after him:

'I think I see. England may be beaten. But we won't let that happen. So we must make ourselves strong.' She came close to him, urging: 'Will you hold fast to your three points, Mark darling? Please! For my sake! I can't have you troubled as you have been.'

'If I can hold on to them it will help,' he confessed. 'But all the same, I'll be glad when the waiting ends. If war's coming, let it come quickly.'

Next day, war came.

XI

Blitzkrieg

(September–October 1939)

I

(September 1, 1939)

THE news that Germany had invaded Poland came to Mark as a welcome release from long uncertainties. His spirit at once was easier; and when he arrived at Robin's apartment for breakfast, he told her so. 'There's a grim sort of contentment in knowing that at last the thing is settled,' he said. 'There's no longer any doubt whether it is coming. It has come.' And he confessed: 'I remember much the same feeling the morning Nan died. During her illness the strain had been unbearable. As hope grew less and less, and she suffered so, I was ready to accept her death as a release for her—and even for me—from the burden of those days. I was drained empty of all emotion long before she died. There was left nothing but thoughts racing like squirrels in one of these whirling cages, treadmills, which we used to have for them. It's been the same way with me—in increasing degree—for years now about Hitler and his plans. Now at least we know.'

'We don't know the future,' she reminded him. She was this morning not so philosophical as he. There had always been in her a blindly optimistic faith that in the end the worst would somehow not come to pass.

'No, that's true,' he agreed. 'We only know that the past now is a closed book; that the world in which we have lived is forever ended. And the future is a book of which the leaves are uncut, which we must read a day at a time.'

He had planned to return to Boston this morning, in order that this afternoon and tomorrow he could clear his desk and be ready to go on with his routine Monday. She wished he might stay, but he held to his original intention. 'I told Tony I'd be home for the week-end,' he explained. 'I suspect he'll be as anxious to be with me, right now, as I am to be with him.'

'I'll hate being so far away from you,' she confessed. 'And I'll hate having you so far away from me.' At the end she clung to him passionately, whispering: 'Oh, my darling, my darling, it isn't fair. We shouldn't ever have to be apart.'

She wished to go with him to the airport, but he dissuaded her and they said good-bye at her door.

2

(September 1, 1939)

On the plane Mark read the morning papers through, and as he did so the magnitude of these events so long foreseen and now beginning slowly came home to him, not in any certain terms but in an overpowering confusion. He was like an aviator who has been flying high above the South American jungles, scanning them from the air, awed by their vastnesses, and yet secure and remote from the terrors and the dangers which they held, but who suddenly is compelled to abandon his plane and trust his parachute, and so finds himself precipitated into their green and tangled depths. His instinct, like that of any man lost in the wilderness, was to run wildly, headlong, anywhere; and although there were other passengers around him here, he felt himself alone in an empty world. He had had a like feeling, twenty-odd years before, on a battlefield in France, when he and his fellows were advancing against deadly machine-gun fire and came into that thicket of little evergreens through which bullets clipped like fast-flying birds, the trees growing so close together that it was impossible to see the men nearest you, impossible in the battle's steady din even to hear their progress.

He remembered Senator Borah, who had been so sure there would be no war this year. Other Mid-Western Congressmen had agreed with Borah. Probably now they would say that it was only on the promise of eventual American help that Poland had precipitated this conflict. Mark himself blamed Poland. Germany's final peace proposals—the return of Danzig, a plebiscite in the Polish Corridor, the shifting of some populations, and demobilization—had seemed to him surprisingly reasonable. But Poland would not yield, and now war was begun, and an anonymous English journalist named Augur exulted in the morning papers because Germany, by waiting these eight days before she struck, had given France time to mobilize. There was a leering glee in that dispatch, a suggestion that France had tricked Germany and was now ready to strike her a powerful blow.

Mark wondered whether any nation could pay the costs of modern war, and he thought: 'To us, even after these years of Mr. Roosevelt, a billion dollars is a lot of money. But before this is done, if we prepare as we should, we'll be spending fifty billions a year, whether we fight or not.' Billions of dollars and hundreds of thousands of lives would be consumed in this conflagration just begun. He came back to his certainty that England was in danger, and that England must not lose. There was a solidity in the English way of life which he did not wish to see destroyed. He half smiled in sudden realization of what Jerry Crocker would say to that sentiment, imagined Jerry's very words. 'Solidity, my eye! There's a solidity in English skulls if you like!' And he thought of something his father had once said, remembered the sense if not the words. 'England became an empire when she opened a drawing account in India at the point of a gun. She mastered the world by sheer weight of gold bullion, plus a complete and unscrupulous readiness to cut the throat—or to persuade assorted allies to cut the throat—of any nation that threatened to achieve an equality of power. She built up the Dutch Republic to weaken Spain; she built up Prussia and Spain to beat Napoleon; she built up Germany to beat France in 1870, and then she built up France to smash Germany in 1918. Since then she has built up Germany against Russia, but she overdid it, so now she wants us to help whittle Germany down to size again.'

And Dan Worth in that same conversation had said: 'If the rest of the world sank into the ocean, we'd still manage to get along; but for fifty years we've been told so often that our job is to rule the world that we're beginning to believe it—God help us! There was some sense to the Monroe Doctrine, but now we've got the Stimson Doctrine, that we won't stand for conquests anywhere in the world!'

Mark thought it was perhaps fortunate for us that no one took the Stimson Doctrine seriously. Japan in Manchukuo, Italy in Ethiopia and Albania, Germany in Czecho-Slovakia and now in Poland, had all ignored our empty preachments.

The experts in the morning papers predicted that Poland would hold out for months; and they were sure the French army was the best in the world, and that General Gamelin was a great commander. Mark had read many newspaper and magazine eulogies of General Gamelin. It was said of him that he knew every detail of Napoleon's campaigns;

but if this were his chief qualification, then mentally he was a hundred and fifty years old! The French relied upon the Maginot line, upon the defense; but the Germans were trained for the attack, and Mark was sure that only attacks win wars.

What should the United States do? Why, prepare, certainly. As for our national policy in international affairs, the test should never be: 'Does Germany want us to do this?' or: 'Does England want us to do this?' The only test that should ever have any weight with us was: 'Does it help the United States?' But Mark foresaw that the debate would come on a question of definition. Who was to decide whether a stated policy would help the United States?

Well, the future would decide. The verdict of history would decide. And yet would even the verdict of history give the true answer? For history was written by human beings, and human beings have each their own opinion. Suppose the Revolution had failed and England had written its history, would that verdict be the true one?

Probably our course would lead us somehow into war. The decision would be made in the long run, not by Mr. Roosevelt, nor by Congress, but by all of us. If democracy was sound, then so would that decision be, because it would be reached by the composite American mind. That decision might be a manufactured one. He remembered a book by Christopher Morley in which Morley remarked that the most amazing achievement of modern society had been to teach millions of people to think they believed certain things which they did not believe at all. Morley said in that same paragraph another thing which had impressed Mark at the time and which he remembered now. He had said that the war of the future would be within the mind, a war between what we really think and what we think we think. Mark smiled grimly, thinking to himself: 'That is surely true. My mind has been a battlefield for years.'

He roused from long abstraction as the plane glided toward the airport. The harbor was bright beneath them. The motors hushed and stilled, the great wheels touched the ground.

3

(September 1939)

Tony came home late Sunday night. Till then Mark had been alone, while in Poland the bombers were busy, and France and England declared war upon Germany, and in the United States men tried to adjust their minds to this new disordered world. One editor wrote: 'After a fortnight of crises, the outbreak of war was almost a relief.' Another emphasized as basic in American sentiment two things: the hope that Hitler would be beaten and Germany humiliated, and the 'unshakeable determination of the people that this country shall not be forced into war or cajoled into it by considerations of sympathy, economics, ideology, or kinship.'

Tony drove up from the Cape with Dave and Ruth Rollins. Mark was abed but not asleep when he arrived, and Tony came to him for a few minutes, but the boy was abstracted, quiet, something almost like guilt in his demeanor; and almost at once he took himself to bed. Mark thought the war had hit him hard.

The morning's news was that the *Athenia* had been sunk, with some three hundred Americans aboard. No one believed Germany's denial that a German submarine had sunk her; but Mark, remembering the day of the sinking of the *Lusitania,* was struck by the difference in the public reaction now. Monday evening he wrote Robin:

> Certainly there is no real popular indignation at this *Athenia* sinking, no demand that to avenge it we plunge into the war. We seem to feel that American citizens on the *Athenia* should have been at home out of harm's way. It's already clear that our attitude toward this war is going to be very different from our attitude in the last. I suppose the burnt child dreads the fire. Certainly nothing but the conviction that England may be beaten will ever bring us into it. You see I'm back to our three points again!

Tony slept late that morning, so Mark did not see him at breakfast, and when he came home that evening, Anna had a message that Tony would not be home for dinner. Mark dined alone and went early to bed. He was still asleep Tuesday morning when the telephone's insistent ring woke him. His watch told him that it was half-past seven, and he expected this might be a night letter, perhaps from Robin; but when he reached the telephone he recognized at once Ruth's voice.

'Uncle Mark?' she cried. He said: 'Yes. Good morning, Ruth.' And she said, in a desperate and shaken whisper: 'Can you come out here, Uncle Mark? Father's dead.' He uttered some startled word, and she said: 'He died in his sleep. I just found him.'

'Have you called Doctor Hethering?'

'No, oh no, he's dead. He's—cold, Uncle Mark. I touched him.' Her tone shuddered pitifully.

'I'll come right along,' he promised. He waked Tony to go with him. Tony had questions, but there was no more than the bare fact to tell him; and beyond that Mark said only: 'I think you might stay with Ruth today. There will be things to be done. I have to be in court this morning.'

'Of course, Dad,' Tony assured him. 'I'll stay as long as Ruth wants me.'

When they came to the big old house in Lincoln, Ruth was composed enough. Mark thought that her cheeks wore a transparent purity, not pallor, but rather a warm whiteness, as though they were freshly scrubbed and clean, scoured perhaps by tears; but her eyes were clear and her voice was steady. 'I've saved breakfast for you,' she said. 'I knew you wouldn't stop for that. Tony, I'm glad you came, too.' And she added: 'I did telephone Doctor Hethering, Uncle Mark, but he had a baby case somewhere. He hasn't come yet. I told him there wasn't any hurry.'

She drank a cup of coffee with them, and she talked quietly and simply of what had happened. 'He was fine yesterday,' she said. 'We took a long ride in the afternoon. The horses hadn't had much exercise and they were frisky and he loved it. We laughed a great deal. It was just about the best day we ever had together. Then after dinner we played picquet for a while and went to bed early. I always took him hot water and orange juice in the morning; and when I went in, he seemed to be asleep; but he didn't wake up, and I thought he was just pretending, to tease me. Till I touched his arm, pulled at him. I turned him over and saw his face, and then I felt his cheek and it was cold.'

Doctor Hethering came while they were still at breakfast, and Mark went with him to see Dave. 'He's been dead several hours,' the old doctor decided.

'I never knew he had any—heart trouble.'

'There were some indications. I told him. Probably he never mentioned it.' He added, looking down at Dave: 'This was a brave man, Judge Worth. He knew that complete abstention from alcohol would put a heavy burden on his heart which had been so long used to it. He said, when I told him: "Nevertheless, Doctor, I'll not touch it again. I'd rather have alcohol kill me indirectly than directly."'

'I suppose you gave him some other stimulant.'

'Yes, but I doubt whether he used it. He said he was tired of being an invalid, that this was a private fight between him and alcohol, and he wouldn't enlist any allies.'

'I think he won,' Mark said quietly. 'Death was not defeat for him, but victory.'

Ruth, although Mark suggested she do so, preferred not to summon Nell Ritchie, or Mary Halstead. 'I'm perfectly all right now,' she said. 'I was lonely at first, but now he's with me more than ever.'

Mark said Tony would stay, and she agreed: 'I'd like that.' Mark himself came back late that afternoon and found them playing Badminton, both dripping and exhausted.

'I suggested we might stay here tonight, Dad,' Tony explained, 'and Ruth wants us to. So we drove over home and got your things and mine.'

At dinner Mark asked Ruth: 'Have you heard from your mother?'

'Yes. She's coming home.' Marcia was in Honolulu. 'But she hates to fly, so it will be two weeks or so.' Ruth added: 'And there aren't any other relatives to—notify. None that matter.'

Mark and Tony stayed with her till after Dave's funeral. Mark saw Tom and Emma Sheffield among those who came to do Dave honor, and Emma caught his eye and smiled—something malicious in her smile. Ruth urged all Dave's old friends to return to the house from the cemetery, and Ed and Mary and their children, big and little, did so, and the Ritchies, and Ingrid came with them. Ruth's quiet composure put them all at ease. Ingrid and Betty had to tell about their experiences on their drive to the coast and back—they had returned only the day before—and Ingrid said she was about to go home to Norway.

'There is a cable from my father that I must come now,' she explained. 'One of his ships is in Boston next week, so I will go on that.'

Bob Ritchie said teasingly: 'The submarines'll get you if you don't watch out.'

But Ingrid laughed. 'Oh, no. Germany is a good friend to Norway,' she declared.

Mary Halstead wanted Ruth to go home with them. 'We'll be at Humarock through September,' she explained. 'And we have loads of room.' Ruth decided to stay here tonight to see the house in order, promised to drive down next day. Mark and Tony offered to spend another night here, but she said there was no need, and in the end they all departed.

On the way home, Mark said: 'Ruth's a fine woman, Tony.'

Tony nodded. 'But have you noticed the way she speaks of her mother?' he asked. 'I don't believe they'll ever get along.'

They saw Ruth again next morning. They were at breakfast—this was

apt to be a leisurely meal, since Mark did not leave the house till nine
o'clock or so, and Tony's days were free—when she appeared; and Mark
thought the girl wore a sort of radiance. She said at once:

'I hurried, wanting to catch you, Uncle Mark. Something wonderful
happened to me last night, something you'll understand.' And she explained: 'You see, all my life since I can remember I've had a night
light, have never slept in the dark. I couldn't without terrible dreams.

'But last night when I was ready for bed, I went into Father's room.
It was like saying good-bye to him. I threw myself down on his bed,
where he died, and cried quietly for a long time. I could feel the hollow
in the mattress where he had always lain, and I cried and cried; and at
first it was bad, and then it began to be a calm, happy sadness.

'And at last I was sleepy, and a little cold. I turned down the covers
and drew them over me. There was a light on the bedside table and I
turned it out, so the room was dark.

'And I felt a strange deep peace and happiness fill me. I went to sleep,
and slept all night, with no dreams, nothing but rest and content, in
that dark room alone.' She looked at Mark for a long moment, and she
smiled at last. 'I expect that doesn't sound like much to you.'

'It sounds like a great deal to me.'

'I'll never be afraid in the dark again.'

Mark said quietly: 'You're fine, Ruth. You'll never be afraid of anything.'

4

(September 1939)

This week since war began had been for Mark a crowded one; and
Dave's death and his own concern for Ruth filled his thoughts even
while he was on the bench, so that he was forced sometimes to force his
attention back to the case on trial before him. He read the papers, but
not attentively. The editorials seemed to him nonsensical. One writer
said blithely that if England could destroy Helgoland and Wilhelms-
haven she could command the Baltic; and Mark wondered by what
strange chance a man capable of such futile wishful thinking had come
to be an accredited editorial writer on a great newspaper. The same
editorial suggested that England and France would demand that Italy
join them or face invasion. Mark thought it would be hard—if Italy
preferred to remain neutral—to make her neutrality a pretext for a holy

war against her. Yet in such times as these, ethical principles lost their meaning. What was profitable would be accepted as right—by those who did it. War was self-defense, and in self-defense anything was permissible.

The day after Dave died, Mark saw headlines:

FRENCH ATTACK SIEGFRIED LINE
BRITISH BOMB WARSHIPS AT KIEL

And below in smaller type, he read:

Poles Report Slashing Cavalry
Drive to German Soil

So, clearly, the Germans were not having things all their own way! This Polish invasion of Germany made Mark's blood tingle. He had no time to read the paper thoroughly; but apparently the experts had been right who said that Poland would give a good account of herself. If she could hold on—the war was only five days old, of course; but she seemed to be holding her own—the French and English in another day or two would be smashing toward the Rhine.

But the next day, for almost the first time since the war began, he was able to give the morning paper more than a casual glance. The headlines were tremendous and heartening.

FRENCH BATTLE WAY INTO REICH
BRITAIN RUSHES TROOPS, PLANES

Poles Fight Like Fiends;
Hold Foe Back Near Warsaw

That smaller headline awakened Mark to the truth. Warsaw was deep in the heart of Poland. He turned the pages of the paper and found, hidden away on the eleventh page, a map showing the battle lines; and he made a rapid rough measurement of distances.

The Germans had driven into Poland in some places as much as two hundred miles!

But if that were true, then, despite the soothing headlines, Poland was already beaten! The Blitzkrieg, that German tactic at the threat of which the world for so long had smiled, was a success!

He recaptured the papers for the preceding days to discover exactly what had happened. The tally was a grim one. On the first of September, German troops attacked Poland from the north and west, and from

Slovakia. By nightfall of the third, her armies from East Prussia and from the Reich had joined forces, isolating the Corridor. At the same time her armies had thrust deep into Poland southwest of Warsaw. On September fifth the army from East Prussia was within thirty miles of the Polish capital. Next day Cracow was captured, and it was clear to Mark that the Polish lines had everywhere been smashed; that her armies were being rolled back as a housekeeper rolls back a rug.

So Poland was beaten. Yet the headlines next day were again encouraging.

NAZIS RUSH TROOPS TO WEST

If that meant anything, it meant that the French attack was bearing fruit, that the pressure on the Poles had been relieved. The dispatches emphasized that the Poles still held Warsaw, but when they added that the 'Polish army is still intact,' the word strained Mark's hopeful credulity. Intact? That meant 'untouched.' Yet certainly no army could retreat two hundred miles in seven days without major losses. The headlines could be ignored. The maps told the story. No army surrendered a foot of its own soil unless it must. Regardless of the encouraging dispatches—which he wished to believe—Mark accepted what he knew now must be the truth. Poland, the Poland that was to have held out for six months or a year, was already beaten—in seven days!

He and Tony that day had dinner together. It was the first time since the war began that they had been alone with no distractions. After Dave's death and his funeral, there had been among the young people a succession of festivities to fill Ingrid's last week before she sailed for home; but now she was gone, and Tony would soon be returning to Hanover, and Mark was grateful for this hour with him. He had felt since Tony returned from the Cape a deep unhappiness in the boy. This might be the result of the outbreak of war; but if it were not, if there were any cause more personal, Tony would surely tell him.

He asked no questions, but Tony did. 'You haven't told me about Mrs. Kerr,' he reminded his father. 'How is she? Have you and she set the day yet?'

Mark gratefully seized the opportunity to speak of Davy. 'We can't be married, Tony; not now,' he said. 'I didn't tell you before, because it was her secret, but—she wants you to know. You see her husband is still alive. But he's hopelessly crippled and hopelessly insane.'

He went into detail, while Tony listened with a still intentness; and when Mark finished, Tony said in a hushed voice:

'Gosh, Dad, that's awful. Can't she get a divorce?'

'She's a pretty loyal person, Tony. She doesn't want to do that. As long as he lives, she will still be his wife.'

'She's swell,' Tony said in a low tone. 'That's a pretty grim thing, isn't it?'

'Yes.'

'Are you going to—just wait?'

Mark said wearily: 'Yes, son.'

Tony rose and came to his father's side and touched Mark's shoulder. 'Gosh, that's tough,' he said. He spoke half to himself. 'I wish I'd known it before.'

Something in his tone, some accent of despair, made Mark look at him quickly. 'Why?'

Tony spoke hurriedly, returning to his chair again. 'Oh, nothing. Only I've been afraid it was on account of me, because she thought I wouldn't like it. I mean, the reason you didn't get married.'

'Why, you've been urging us to go ahead.'

'I've meant it, too,' Tony assured him. 'But she had an idea I didn't like her. You know, a woman gets ideas!'

His tone was light, but there was a shadow in his eyes. Mark said tentatively: 'I've thought you were—bothered about something, this last week or so.'

Tony hesitated, then laughed. 'Bothered? I'll say so. The way the war's going has got me. The Poles were supposed to be good, but the Germans are going through them like a finger through wet paper. They must be a lot stronger than anyone guessed.'

'Either that or the Poles are a lot weaker.'

'I think it's airplanes,' Tony declared. 'But whatever it is, you've got to hand it to the Germans. They're hot stuff. But Dad, why hasn't Germany launched her Blitzkrieg against France and England? Is she planning to smash Poland and then offer peace?' Mark watched his son, sure that it was not the war alone which troubled the boy. 'Why is Russia mobilizing?' Tony asked.

'Probably just a precaution.'

'Is Poland really licked? Or is she just falling back, waiting her time?'

'I think she's beaten beyond hope,' Mark admitted. Perhaps Tony talked about the war to avoid any more personal word, but Mark would follow his lead.

Tony made a harsh gesture. 'You know what I wish would happen?

I wish the papers would run a series of articles about the facts of the last war: the British guns, made in England, sold to Germany for killing British soldiers; the American troopship that was torpedoed off the coast of New Jersey, with the loss of five thousand soldiers; the American force that quit the front lines and marched back to rest billets, leaving their line for the artillery to hold; the rent we paid France for the land our soldiers used. Let's show up this business of war for what it is! Have every newspaper in the country run a false front page every once in a while—have them run one of the front pages they used during the last war. The ones with the biggest lies on them.'

Mark said gravely: 'Don't be too ready to believe all you hear, son. No American transport was lost during the last war. Germany very possibly had some British guns. There was international trade in war material, still is. And I believe we did pay rent to France—though I don't know about that. But we'll be fed lies—or half truths—by both sides from now on.'

'How can you tell them apart—and tell truth from lies?'

Mark smiled. 'Well, I'm inclined to distrust anything I want to believe,' he confessed. 'I think if I were Hitler, I'd instruct all my propaganda men to try to persuade this country that England can't be beaten, that Germany's sure to lose in the end. Every man who tells us that lulls us to sleep, persuades us there's nothing to worry about.' He added: 'If I were England, on the other hand, I'd start yelling for help right now. I'd tell the world—and the United States especially—that England is doomed.'

Tony said sympathetically: 'This is going to be a tough war for you, Dad. You'll be wanting to give advice to me—and there's not a man in the world who can say anything about this war without guessing!'

'Those of us who remember the last war have that much advantage over men your age, son.'

'I'm wondering about that. I'm wondering about comparisons with the last war, just where the comparisons are valid, where not. How much better informed are we now than during the last one? We all talk about propaganda and censorship. We all know the radio and the newspapers are dishing out lies because they are given lies to dish out. But are we mentally and psychologically more conscious of the follies and fallacies of war?'

'There's a great difference,' Mark assured him. 'When the *Lusitania* was sunk, everyone was fighting mad. But when the *Athenia* was sunk the other day, no one got excited.'

'Yes, but you'd been educated up to the *Lusitania.*'

'It will take some pretty outrageous and concrete acts to make us want to go to war against Germany this time,' Mark predicted. 'Unless, of course, we realize all of a sudden that England may be beaten. Then I think we'd be ready to go into it.'

'It might be too late,' Tony suggested; and Mark nodded.

'That's why, if I were in charge of English propaganda, I'd start yelling for help right now.'

During the rest of that brief campaign in Poland, Mark's resentment at the newspapers grew. The headlines overemphasized every grain of hopeful news, and gave small display to the tremendous dreadful truth. When the Germans entered Warsaw, the newspapers shouted that the Germans in France were in retreat. They played up the splendid story of Warsaw's valorous but vain resistance and played down the fact that Poland itself was lost. Poland lay prostrate under the feet of the German armies, but the headline writers trumpeted: 'French Launch New Offensive'; or, 'Allies Smash to Key Nazi City.'

Even Tony protested. 'Why the hell don't they play up the big news, Dad?'

'Because the big news is all bad,' Mark told him. 'We'll get the same thing as long as the war goes on; overemphasis on every hopeful rumor and the soft pedal for deadly facts. You could read the headlines for the last ten days without suspecting that the conquest of Poland is over.'

When Russia invaded Poland, the truth was plain to every mind, but to Mark the event had a graver significance. 'England promised to help Poland against any enemy who threatened her independence,' he reminded Tony. 'But she'll not declare war on Russia.'

'She has troubles enough without that! She's apt to get hell licked out of her as it is.'

Mark agreed. 'I saw an editorial today about the fact that young Americans aren't rushing to England to enlist against Germany. It said boys your age have the same point of view as your "cautious elders." But Tony, as soon as we realize England is in danger, that will change.'

'She's in danger all right.'

'The big news in the paper today,' Mark told him, 'was a London dispatch hidden away on an inside page. An under-Secretary of the Admiralty told Parliament that the Navy could hold the seas, but that it could not guarantee to keep England's supply lines open. That was worth a front-page headline, if only to wake us up to the fact that

England may lose.' And he said gravely: 'Once we realize that possibility, here in the United States, we'll know our own minds.'

5

(October 1939)

Tony went back to Hanover to begin his Senior year. There had been
since early in September a sort of shamed recklessness in the boy which
puzzled Mark, yet he thought he could understand it. Tony, like all
Americans, hated war; but no young man could view these great events
yonder without a secret impulse to take somehow a part in them.

Even older men felt this impulse. Mark himself remembered with
regret that uncertain heart of his which made it out of the question for
him to do anything at all. When at the end of September, Ed Halstead
went back into the Navy—even though Ed's would only be a desk job
in the Navy Yard—Mark secretly envied him. But if Ed, a man almost
fifty years old, felt himself bound to offer his services to the expanding
armed forces of his country, it was not surprising that Tony, and young
men everywhere, should feel the same compulsion—even though like
Tony they resented this feeling in themselves.

Ed himslf disclaimed any high motive. 'I met Emma Sheffield in the
Copley yesterday,' he told Mark one day. 'She said she hadn't realized
my business was in as bad shape as all that!' He laughed. 'I didn't admit
it, but that's the answer, Mark. A Lieutenant Commander's pay isn't to
be sneezed at, not these days. If we ever get into this war you'll see a lot
of men my age—and younger too—jumping at the chance to get easy
commissions in noncombatant work at a lot more pay than they could
earn in civil life. I'm getting in on the ground floor, that's all.'

Mark smiled affectionately. 'You can't fool me—or yourself, Ed. As a
matter of fact, I envy you—and so do the rest of us.'

'Not Bob,' Ed assured him. 'He says I'm a damned fool.'

'Bob's illusion is that he has no illusions,' Mark commented. 'He likes
to quote the polls of public opinion, to point out that only thirty-seven
per cent of us want to help beat Germany. From my point of view that's
an astonishingly high percentage.'

'What gave Lindbergh the idea that he's qualified to tell us what to
do?' Ed wondered.

'A lot of people feel as he does,' Mark suggested. 'When Russia took a hand in carving up Poland and England did nothing about it, it hurt her case with us. Right there and then this stopped being a holy war.'

'It never was,' Ed agreed. 'Germany's out to conquer the world, and England—and we, too—will have to give in or fight. That's the whole story. It's self-defense—if you want to call that holy. It's holy enough for me.'

'How's Emma?' Mark asked. 'I haven't seen her or Tom—except at Dave's funeral—for a long time.'

Ed said Emma was just the same. 'Dressed like a million dollars,' he said. 'Tom must be doing all right for himself.' And he added: 'Tommy's gone to France to drive an ambulance.'

Mark was completely surprised. 'Has he really? But—when did he go?'

'I don't know,' Ed admitted. 'Emma just told me he's gone.'

Thus quickly, then, Mark thought, the war that had seemed so far away began to draw young men toward the vortex. Even Tony might wish to do as Tommy had done. Scores, perhaps hundreds, of young Americans had taken part in the war in Spain, and some of them gave their lives there for a cause that was not their own. Or perhaps they had made it their own, as young men will; or perhaps, more nearly right than their elders who, like the statesmen in England and France, decided that the conflict there could not concern us, they had seen that the issue in Spain was a world issue, had chosen their side and died for it.

Yet still he was surprised that Tommy Sheffield had gone to France. He had never known Tommy well, except as a pleasant youngster who played a strong game of Badminton, and whom Tom said showed promise at the bank. He remembered another thing Tom had said; that his son was in love with a girl in the bank, a girl named Mary Clancy, of whom Emma disapproved. He wondered why she and Tommy had never married. For no real reason, except that from Tom's brief description she sounded like a young woman who would know what she wanted and get it, Mark was surprised that they had not married long ago. He began to find something puzzling in this fact that Tommy had left a girl he loved and a good position to go and drive an ambulance in France. There was a suggestion of hidden drama in the incident, and during the next day or two he found himself wishing he might see Tommy's father again. They had so long been friends. Were it not for Emma they would be friends today.

He made no move to see Tom, but Sunday night Bob Ritchie came across the street to sit with him awhile. They spoke of the war. Now that Poland was done, except for occasional submarine activity there was little fighting anywhere. Hitler had said he was ready for peace, but England said she would make no peace with Hitler. Mr. Roosevelt had asked Congress to repeal the arms embargo, and he said a submarine had been sighted off the New England coast. Bob was sure that was a lie. 'Or at best a wild rumor that he had no right to pass on,' he amended. Russia had compelled Estonia to sign a 'mutual assistance pact' which was in effect a surrender of national sovereignty, and she forced Latvia to follow Estonia's example.

But while he and Bob spoke of these things, Mark became increasingly sure that the other had come for something besides casual conversation; and at last, smiling a little, he asked:

'What's on your mind, Bob?'

Bob hesitated. 'Shows as plain as that, does it?'

'I judge there's something.'

The other nodded. 'Tom Sheffield came to me day before yesterday,' he explained. 'He wants to divorce Emma.'

Mark after a moment said: 'I didn't suppose Tom would ever come to that. What grounds?'

' "Gross and confirmed habits of intoxication," ' Bob quoted grimly. 'Those are the grounds—and Tom can prove them, all right. But that's not the real reason. I'll tell you the whole story.' Mark did not speak, and the other explained: 'Some of this I got from Tom, and some from the people at the bank, and some from Dave Rollins. We handled Dave's business, you know. I drew a new will for him in June, before he and Ruth went to Labrador. I'm executor. There's a clause in the will instructing me to tear up certain notes for moneys owed him by Tom. Tom owed him thirty-four hundred dollars.'

'I knew Dave had lent Tom money,' Mark assented, and he asked: 'By the way, is Marcia here?'

'She's gone now,' Bob said. 'She and Ruth are in Charleston. Outside of Marcia's statutory rights, Dave left everything to Ruth.' He came back to Tom Sheffield. 'But here's the point about Emma, Mark. When the first of the month came around, the bank found that Tommy Sheffield was a thousand dollars short. This was after he'd sailed for France. He worked in the securities department. There was a Government bond for which he'd signed, one of a lot of ten, which was missing.'

'Did he take it?'

'No,' Bob said strongly. 'Mark, Emma stole that bond, as sure as shooting. But Tommy left a signed confession that he'd taken it, in the packet with the other bonds.'

'Emma? How did she get hold of it?'

'She came to see Tommy at the bank one day. She was sitting at his desk when this packet of bonds was delivered to him. He signed for them. There's a young woman named Clancy in the bank who's in love with him. She happened to see Emma lift her handbag as though to take something out of it, and spill things all over the bonds. The bonds were loose, not fastened together. Emma stuffed everything back into her bag and left the bank, and a minute or two later Miss Clancy saw Tommy hurry out after her. He was gone over an hour and came back looking like hell; and next day, without even saying good-bye to Miss Clancy, he disappeared. Later she had a letter saying he'd gone to France.'

'Tom told me about Miss Clancy,' Mark commented. 'Why weren't she and Tommy married long ago?'

'Miss Clancy says he couldn't afford it because he had to help support his mother. She says Emma not only begged money from him but borrowed—and didn't pay—right along. And Emma had been to the loan sharks, too. The last money Tom borrowed from Dave was to settle with one of them.'

'Does she admit taking the bond?'

'No, and there's no proof except Miss Clancy's evidence. Tom thinks she sold the bond and spent the money. She had a new fur coat last week.' He added: 'And Tom says he's through with her. He's always been a humble, meek sort of man; but you know what can happen when a man like that finally gets mad. Tom's living with his mother now—and he wants to divorce Emma.'

Mark urged: 'The important thing is to clear Tommy.'

'That's why I came to you,' Bob agreed. 'Tom has made up the loss to the bank—his mother gave him the money—and his mother will settle something on Emma in return for a confession, and the bank will agree not to prosecute her. They like Tom down there, and Tommy too.'

'Why did you come to me?'

'You know Emma. I thought you might be willing to tackle her.' Bob added grimly: 'I couldn't talk to her without wanting to wring her neck.'

Mark said in a weary sadness: 'Emma was a mighty nice young woman in a lot of ways, twenty years ago.'

'Maybe,' Bob admitted. 'I suppose if she'd married someone with some firmness to him, she'd have been all right; but she found she could bully Tom—and she did. Then during prohibition she started to drink. A lot of people started it then, just because they were told they shouldn't. Tom says she'd get lousy drunk at home, all alone, even then. But she was always careful, if any of us were around, till a few years ago.'

Mark nodded. 'The war brought prohibition,' he commented. 'And the nineteen-twenties were just a hangover from the war. A lot of us made fools of ourselves then. Most of us got over it, but Emma—and Tom too—are casualties of that war, Bob. Just as Dave was.' He thought of Robin and of her Davy, casualty of another war. 'Any big war leaves its mark on the lives of every one of us,' he said. 'The scars don't always show, but they're there, just the same.'

Bob nodded. 'And now we're in for another war,' he commented.

'I've been dreading this one for ten years,' Mark confessed. 'Dreading what it will do to Tony—and to your Will, and to Edwin Halstead, and to Tommy, and to boys like them everywhere.'

Bob said soberly: 'Sometimes I think the lucky ones are the ones who got killed. This is going to be a hell of a world from now on, Mark.'

'Unless they make a quick peace.'

'I wonder if we'll ever see peace again.'

Mark spoke in some surprise. 'I thought you believed we could stay out.'

'I believe we ought to,' Bob corrected. 'But I don't believe we will. Not if it goes on.' And he asked: 'Will you talk to Emma?'

Mark shook his head. 'I can't, Bob. Even off the bench, I'm still a judge.'

'That's so, of course.' Bob rose, yielding without argument or persuasion. 'I was afraid you'd feel that way. You're right, I suppose. I'll have to get my father to handle her.'

Mark went with him to the door. Afterward, when he was alone he sat awhile, thinking of what Bob had said. It occurred to him that Bob seemed to be losing weight, that he did not look well; but this was presumably imagination. He put the thought aside, and as he was apt to do when he was troubled, he wrote to Robin, told her the ugly tale Bob had told him.

'Tommy had the chivalric point of view of youth,' he commented. 'I wish he had stood his ground, but of course he couldn't accuse his own mother.' And he asked: 'Am I wrong to think this, too, can be traced to the last war? Perhaps my hatred of wars and of what they bring has become an obsession. I see the scars of the old war on men and women everywhere.'

6

(October 1939)

It was astonishing, Mark thought, to find how quickly the war dropped out of public interest. Dan Worth wrote from Ohio, early in October:

> Well, the excitement seems to be over. Not that there ever was any real excitement in this country—except in the headlines. The city papers . . .

Mark smiled at that scornful phrase. His father had always said: 'If you want to know what folks are really thinking, read the weeklies. When I write an editorial that folks don't like, they come in and stop their subscription, so I know pretty well what my subscribers think without taking a poll—and so does every other editor like me.'

Mark read on:

> . . . The city papers tried to stir up some excitement over the *Athenia,* and Mr. Roosevelt tried to scare us with his talk about submarines up your way, but folks just plain wouldn't excite.
> I see Hitler's ready to talk peace, now that he's got what he wanted. But England's got to hang on. Her stock's pretty low right now. When Russia took a cut at Poland, and England didn't do anything about it, that told the whole story. England didn't go to war to save Poland. If she had, she'd be fighting Russia now. But she will never let any one country be the boss in Europe if she can help it. I don't blame her. She can't afford to. You know, the only thing I like about England is that she's always working for England. We could afford to be more like her, that way.
> It's safe to say that England thought Poland would put up a better show than she did. I wouldn't wonder if Chamberlain isn't lying awake nights, right now. He's got a bear by the tail and he don't know how to let go.

Mark found among the men he met from day to day a general feeling that Hitler's peace moves were an admission of weakness. Ed Halstead was confident that England's Navy would throttle Germany in the end. 'Hitler never really believed England would fight,' he declared. 'He knows now that a quick peace is his only hope.' This seemed in fact the general view. Germany was isolated, penned in behind the Maginot line and the British Navy, with Russia always ready to nibble at her eastern frontier. She was trapped behind a wall of neutral and enemy nations, and there was for her no escape at all.

Mark himself wished to believe this. If the war he had dreaded so long could indeed thus be isolated and contained, perhaps the world might still survive. Perhaps the Blitzkrieg was folly after all, successful enough against a Poland which the experts now agreed had been a weak and defenseless nation; but the French were another story. He read enthusiastic articles about the capacities of General Gamelin, and of General Gort. Legends grew up of which they were the heroes, and noble tales were told of them.

Mark felt some slight uneasiness over Russia, now quietly absorbing the small Baltic states. With no great expenditure of men and munitions Stalin had added to his empire an area larger by some ten thousand square miles than all of New England. Was it not wholly possible that Russia might emerge as the dominant European power? Remembering the days of the Russian Revolution, the bestial cruelty with which Russian women had slaughtered helpless prisoners, Mark thought that of the two he would prefer Germany.

In mid-October, Russia's ponderous expansion struck close home. Since Elin after her baby was born left his house and put Anna in her place, Mark had been comfortable enough; but Anna was not Elin. Elin had intelligence and charm, and her presence in the house made it a more pleasant place in which to live; but Anna was a stodgy lump of a girl, doing what needed to be done rather as a duty than as a pleasure. So when one evening Elin came to see him, Mark was delighted.

'This is fine, Elin,' he said, shaking her hand. 'Is Einar with you? Did you bring the baby?'

She said, smiling with pleasure at his greeting, that she was alone; and he made her sit down and told her how well she looked, and told her the most recent news of Tony, till she spoke at last of her errand here tonight.

'I want to come back to work for you,' she said; and without waiting for his question she explained: 'You see, Einar has gone home to Finland. They think Finland must fight with Russia and she will need every man.'

Mark had noticed—with no particular attention—a Washington dispatch on the twelfth, reporting that after the Swedish and Finnish ambassadors had called at the State Department, the United States had asked that Russia's demands on Finland be moderated. But Finland was far away, and Russia would do as she chose, and Mark had not even remembered, when he read this dispatch, that Einar was a Finn.

'Has he indeed?' he echoed. 'Did they send for him?' Einar was not yet a naturalized American.

'No, sir,' Elin said proudly. 'But he heard from his home that there will be war, so he has gone.' And she continued smilingly: 'So I will want to work. The baby will live with my uncle. I thought I would like to come back here, and I have found another place for Anna, a very good place, so she will let me come here if it is all right with you.'

'It's fine with me,' Mark assured her. 'Anna's good, but I've missed you, Elin. I'm glad you're coming back.' He said gently: 'You must be proud of Einar.'

'Yes, I am proud,' she said. Her eyes filled, but she repeated, almost fiercely, 'I am very proud.' She had no need to tell him her secret terrors; but when she turned away, it was swiftly, as though to hide her tears from him. The door closed behind her, and Mark said under his breath: 'Damn the Russians, anyway.'

He thought that Finland could not hope to resist that overwhelming power, and it seemed to him unlikely that resistance would even be attempted. There might be glory in a struggle where defeat was fore-ordained, but there could be no hope of victory.

Yet with hope or not, Einar was gone, and Mark was proud of him, sharing Elin's brave pride.

XII

Sitzkrieg

(October 1939–April 1940)

I

(October 1939)

MARK wrote Robin of Einar's going, of Elin's return. 'So I am in good hands again,' he told her. 'For Elin knows all my ways—and Anna never quite learned them.' Almost every night he posted a letter, walking down to the mailbox on the corner before going to bed; and Robin's letters came to him, rich and unstinted. In their thoughts they were constantly together; and because their physical separation was of their own choice and election, they found it bearable. 'Sometimes I'm surprised,' Mark wrote her once, 'at my own willingness to live apart from you, but the mere knowing that we can be together whenever I choose makes it easier. Perhaps I'm like the child who keeps its piece of cake as long as possible, relishing the joys of anticipation. The only difficulty is Nell Ritchie. She blames me for not "sweeping you off your feet." Mary Halstead is more tactful. Ed, by the way, has gone into the Navy. He and Mary have such a fine, straightforward, loving life together. Bob and Nell are equally devoted, in their way, of course; but Nell's so efficient and so businesslike, and Bob's so completely logical, that it's hard to imagine any demonstration of affection between them. I've been worried lately about Bob. He doesn't look well.'

One Sunday in late October Mark crossed the street after dinner to sit awhile with Bob and found Bob's father and mother there; and Nell took Mrs. Ritchie away upstairs, leaving the three men together. Mark when he was elevated to the bench had withdrawn from private practice, so he seldom saw old Mr. Ritchie now, and he spoke of this. 'That's one of the drawbacks to the job,' he confessed. 'I'm like a baseball umpire, have to walk alone.'

'We miss you in the office,' the older man told him cordially. 'But I can see it agrees with you. How's that boy of yours?'

Mark told him Tony was well. 'But he takes the war pretty hard,' he confessed.

Bob, as though to change the subject, said his father had brought Emma Sheffield to time; and Mark asked:

'Have any trouble, sir?'

Bob's father snorted. 'Trouble! No, why should I? I cut the ground from under her, put a detective to work and found where she sold the bond, and found the man who bought it. Then I sent for her, told her she'd either sign a confession—which only the bank would see—and receive a lump-sum payment from old Mrs. Sheffield, or face prosecution. She said the confession wasn't true, but she said she'd sacrifice herself to clear Tommy's name; and I told her she could dramatize it in any way she chose, as long as she signed. And she signed.'

Mark asked: 'Is Tom still bent on divorce?'

Bob answered him. 'Yes, but he's letting her get it. She's gone to Reno. There'll be no trouble.'

'Any divorce is a damned outrage,' old Mr. Ritchie said strongly. 'Children or no children, a divorce breaks up a home. That's the trouble with this country. If more people had homes and lived in them, generation after generation, we'd have some national stability, instead of blowing to and fro like a lot of human tumbleweeds.'

Mark said thoughtfully: 'They're shifting whole populations in Europe, Poles to Siberia, and Germans from the Baltic states to Poland, and Germans out of the Austrian Tyrol. That will make for instability over there. And in England the children are being moved out of London into the country. That's likely to change the whole English social picture.'

Bob was about to speak, but his father said: 'You're right, Mark. But that change may be for the better.'

Bob laughed. 'I read a letter from an English woman the other day,' he said. 'You both know Ed Nathan. It was from one of his sister's friends. She said her lot—six boys from five to nine years old—were not only filthy with lice so that she had to have their heads shaved, but they weren't even house-broken—and didn't seem to want to be!'

'And yet,' his father suggested, 'I'll warrant she was beginning to love them, in a heart-broken sort of way.'

'She didn't say so!' Bob declared, and he laughed. 'She said they were like so many little pigs.'

'Children are mighty attractive animals,' Mark reflected. 'I've often thought that you seldom see a really vicious-looking youngster. Probably one of the strongest indictments of our civilization is that it takes all these chubby, healthy, lovable little creatures and turns them into the twisted, maimed, warped, miserable men and women so many of them become.'

'We're doing better than we used to,' Bob suggested. 'A hundred years ago, about one baby out of every three died before it was two years old.'

'We keep them alive,' his father retorted. 'But some of the things life does to them are worse than killing them. Yet there's no question that England's due to be changed by what's happening over there. The woman who wrote that letter isn't likely to forget, as long as she lives, what sort of children are turned out by a London slum; and she won't be able to help feeling responsible.'

'We've our slums, too,' Mark reminded him. 'And—you've noticed the troubles with the relief set-up in Ohio cities recently. They call the distribution of money and food "riot insurance" out there.'

'It's a hellish commentary on this country that we're always bragging about,' Mr. Ritchie said. 'We raise more food than we can eat and let a lot of it rot in the ground—and in our cities people are starving, right along.'

Bob filled his pipe. 'And they'll be starving in Europe if this war goes on,' he said grimly.

'If the war goes on, it's our fault,' Mr. Ritchie said with a sober passion. 'The issue is plain enough. If President Roosevelt had the courage of his convictions, he's ask for a declaration of war tomorrow.'

'He can't get one, sir,' Mark suggested. 'He'll never be able to rouse this country until we see that England's in danger.'

'England?' The older man's voice rose. 'What's England got to do with it? The issue's clearly drawn. When there's a mad dog loose in your neighborhood, you go out and help destroy him. You don't wait till he bites your mother!'

Bob, knowing how unshakeable his father was, said nothing; but Mark asked gravely: 'Do you mean Hitler? Or Germany?'

'What difference does that make? Hitler is Germany, today! I tell you, the man has hydrophobia—and he's bitten the whole German people. They're all mad!'

'I remember mad-dog scares when I was a boy in Hardiston,' Mark reflected. 'But sometimes it turned out that the dog wasn't mad at all, just parched for a drink of water, or having a fit because of improper diet.' And he said: 'I've just read Oswald Garrison Villard's autobiography. He was in Germany during the peace negotiations, after the armistice. Villard had money, and he could buy whatever food was available; but he lost fifteen pounds during his short stay in Germany. You can imagine what was happening to people who had no money. German people were starving then, and I judge England and France expect to win this war by starving Germany again.'

'A damned good thing, too!' the old man declared.

'Starvation will be Germany's weapon, too,' Bob reminded them. 'She came within six weeks of starving England last time.'

'We'll smash her flat before she can start that,' Mr. Ritchie persisted. 'We've pulled our merchant ships out of the war area, told our citizens to stay at home, played the coward so far; but that won't last. We're already secretly ashamed of ourselves.' And he said in level, hard tones: 'Hitler's a liar, a treaty-breaker, an international gangster of the worst sort. The sooner we admit that and turn out a lynching party to deal with him, the better.'

'And yet,' Mark admitted, 'I can't help seeing the German point of view. Danzig and East Prussia were certainly German. The Polish Corridor was an outrage against common sense and against German national pride.'

'Pride!' the older man exploded. 'What cause for pride has Germany? For two thousand years the Germans have been trying to bully their neighbors. Sooner or later they always get licked, but as soon as Germany gets on her feet, she tries again. Now she's out to conquer the world, admits it, announces it—and you say you can see her side!' He leaned forward, driving home his indictment. 'Hitler's a green-goods man, a plain swindler. He swindled himself into power with the Reichstag fire, and once in power he turned butcher, set up his concentration camps, beat men to death with rubber clubs, chopped off heads, shot his own fellow gangsters, robbed and beat the Jews; and now he's set out to treat the world the same way. He's a liar and a thief and a murderer, and the sooner we turn to and help put a rope around his neck, the better for us and for the world!'

Mrs. Ritchie appeared in the doorway, came smilingly to his side, Nell on her heels. 'There, my dear, you're shouting again,' she protested. 'Disturbing the neighborhood. I shall take you home.'

Still frowning, he submitted; but he had a last word. 'Trouble with you, Mark,' he said, 'you can't forget you're a judge. But the time for impartiality is past. From now on, a man's either against Germany or he's for her!'

Mrs. Ritchie silenced him. 'Hush!' she protested. 'You're talking nonsense and you know it. Mark isn't on Germany's side. Nobody is. Now come along home and have your nap and you'll feel better.' She kissed Bob good-bye, said gently: 'And remember, take better care of yourself, son.'

'Don't worry, Mother, I'll see that he does,' Nell assured her, and went out with them to their car. But Mark was reminded by Mrs. Ritchie's word of his own misgivings.

'Bob—are you all right?' he asked. 'You've lost weight lately.'

'I've been a little off color,' Bob admitted. 'But I'm all right now.'

'What's wrong?' Mark's tone was full of a strong solicitude.

'Why, I had some trouble years ago,' Bob explained. 'I sprained my back, helping get a truck out of the mud when I was in the R.O.T.C.' Bob and Nell had been married in 1917 before the United States declared war, and Bob went to an officers' training camp soon after Betty was born, a year later; but he never reached France. 'It didn't do one of my kidneys any good,' he told Mark now. 'I had some albumen for a while, and they kept me in hospital. It hasn't bothered me since, except that every few years I have a lame back. I had one here ten days ago.'

'All over it now?'

'Oh, sure.'

Mark nodded, a little embarrassed by his own concern for his friend, just as Bob had been embarrassed by Mark's anxiety; and for a moment they were both silent. Mark asked: 'Want a highball?' and Bob said: 'No, thanks, I'm on the wagon for a while.' And he said apologetically: 'Father gets pretty worked up, doesn't he?'

'So do I, when I start thinking about the war.'

'Compared to the last one, it's a poor imitation, so far.'

'It was the real thing for Poland,' Mark reminded him. 'But now Germany's still hoping for peace in the west, I suppose. She won't start anything as long as that hope lives.'

'If there was enough brains in Europe to bait a lobster pot they'd get together, make peace somehow, while they can.'

'Nations—and men—become obsessed with ideas,' Mark reflected. 'I remember an article by Bertrand Russell during the last war. He pointed out that Russia had gone to war with Turkey—I've forgotten how often —to try to achieve the freedom of the Dardanelles; but she had the freedom of the Dardanelles in peace time. The only time she didn't have it

was when she went to war to get it. It's ideas—most of them as foolish as
that one—that make wars, Bob.'

'Ideas—and stupid old men,' Bob amended.

Mark nodded. 'The old men make them and the young men fight
them,' he agreed.

2

(November 1939)

By the first of November it began to seem as though there was no
war. What had happened in Poland was over and done with, and peace
rumors filled the papers day by day. But another war was brewing.
Premier Molotov of Russia said Germany's colonial ambitions had provoked England to war; that the fear of losing world supremacy was
England's motive in fighting—and he warned the United States not to
interfere between Russia and Finland. Elin had a letter from Einar. He
was safe at home, and he said everyone thought Finland would soon be
attacked. Hitler narrowly escaped death in the bombing of the Munich
beer hall which was a Nazi party shrine, and Germany said English
secret-service men had contrived that attempted assassination. There
were rumors of atrocities in Poland, and Tony wrote:

> The same old thing is beginning again, the stuff this country was fed in
> 1914; the stories that Germans are murderers, killing, raping, and looting. To
> me it looks as though Germany since the last war had been working like hell,
> trying to get back on her feet, while the rest of the world has been loafing
> on the job. Now Chamberlain and Daladier and a lot of old men have got a
> war started. It's a game for them, like playing chess, with wooden pieces. No
> one is going to shoot them. It's the young men who will be sent off to get
> shot. The old men will strut around in uniforms and give orders and look
> wise and have a real good time for themselves; but it's no pink tea for fellows
> my age—over there or over here. The young men are the ones who must die.

The words stayed in Mark's thoughts. 'The young men must die.'
The phrase had an inexorable and a terrible ring. The old men had
made themselves a war. Well, by the eternal gods, why could not they
as easily make themselves a peace? Surely there was enough justice on
each side—and enough simple sense and decency—to find some common
meeting ground. He wrote Robin: 'Peace by consultation seems simple
enough, and yet of course the idea is fantastic! Peace treaties are written

not in a conference room but on the battlefield. In any peace negotiation there is always a victor and a vanquished; and when they disagree, the victor casts the deciding vote. Perhaps if victors were less anxious to reward themselves and more anxious to assuage the vanquished, there would be fewer wars; but now the war is joined, and—as Tony says—the young men must die.'

Tony's letters since he returned to Hanover had not been as many nor as long as usual, and Mark looked forward to Thanksgiving, when he and his son could be together; but a day or two beforehand Tony wrote to say that Charlie Spring, whose home was in Evanston, was coming to spend the vacation week-end with him, and the day they were to arrive Elin received a telegram saying there would be four other extras for dinner. She told Mark: 'We'd better have the turkey tonight, so there'll be plenty.'

Tony and Charlie Spring and Chuck Little and Joe Hazen presently appeared together. Charlie and Joe, Mark already knew. Chuck Little's father was one of the executives in an airplane plant in Hartford.

'He and Joe are driving on to Hartford after dinner,' Tony told his father. They had come down from Hanover in Chuck's car. 'And I asked Frank Parks and Dan Pride to come to dinner, Dad. We want to see if the fellows at Harvard feel the same way we do about the war.'

The four young men went upstairs to remove the marks of their journey and Tony was the first to come down, so that he and Mark had a few minutes alone together. Mark again was conscious of a disturbing restraint in his son. Tony asked for news of Robin, and Mark said Robin was as always. 'I'm going over to see her in a week or so,' he added.

'Is her husband—is there any change in him?'

Mark shook his head. Tony said. 'Oh, I had a long letter from Ingrid last week.'

Mark was interested. 'How did she find things at home? Do they feel about the Germans as we do here?'

'Not about the Germans, no; but they hate the war. Ingrid's father is in the shipping business, you know. All he wants is a chance to send his ships out and see them come safely back.'

'Does he blame the Germans for starting it?'

'No,' Tony said. 'Ingrid says they know so many nice German people. The Germans come to Norway for their vacations, to ski, or just to visit. She has a lot of German friends. There are two German boys visiting her brother now, and they say Germany didn't start the war. They say

England had agreed to negotiate on everything, but that when Germany wanted to negotiate about Poland and Danzig, England declared war on her. According to Ingrid—only of course she's just saying what the Germans say—it was England who broke her promise not to fight. She says that's what her father thinks, too.'

'Does he want Germany to win?'

'He just wants the war to be over, so he won't lose his ships and his captains and his men.'

'But it's the German submarines which sink his ships.'

'Germany sinks them, but England seizes them, too,' Tony retorted. 'Ingrid says he has some ships carrying iron ore from Norway to Germany, and England grabs them every chance she gets.'

Mark nodded. Probably most men in the world, most of the small, simple men, were like Ingrid's father, wanting only to be let alone in their own pleasantly profitable pursuits. Certainly that was true in England and in France—and in the United States. Only in Germany was there any general willingness to serve the nation at no matter what cost to self. The newspapers, the magazines, everyone assured you that the German people were slaves, forced to serve against their will; but that assertion collapsed in the face of simple common sense. There could be no honest question that in Germany a great and controlling mass of the people were devoting their lives and their energies unswervingly to a cause they held high. He remembered Doctor Spear's phrase, at Tony's graduation from Hadley: 'to devote their energies to some cause outside of and greater than themselves.' How many young men in England or France—or in the United States—were ready to do that? Hitler had somehow been able to persuade the Germans that devotion and self-denial and self-sacrifice and service were virtues.

Well, were they not? Mark himself had always believed so; but there was something horrifying in the thought that Hitler had harnessed these virtues to serve his own dark ends.

At dinner that evening, Mark listened more than he spoke. Once or twice the youngsters sought his opinion. Chuck Little asked what he thought of the Cash-and-Carry Bill, and Mark said: 'I was for it. I believe we ought to prepare tremendously in this country; and if we make war material for England and France, we will be expanding our own productive capacity, increasing our ability to manufacture the things we need for ourselves.'

Charlie Spring said courteously: 'You're one of the honest supporters of the bill, Judge Worth; but most of its backers had selfish motives.

Some of them wanted to help the Allies, and of course the munitions makers were for it because they saw a chance to make a fat profit out of killing men.'

Chuck Little said hotly: 'I suppose you'd put my father in that class, as long as we make airplane engines.'

Frank Parks commented: 'It's safe to say he was for the bill. Did you read *Dynasty of Death?* The arms-makers have always fomented wars.'

Chuck retorted: 'Oh, so? Well, what do you think of your friend Stalin now, hooking up with Hitler—and ready to start a war with Finland?'

Frank colored hotly, but he said: 'Russia's acting only in self-defense. The Finnish border is near enough Leningrad so that the Finns could bombard the city. All Russia wants is to see the Finnish forts moved back out of range, and the Finn naval bases near Leningrad in safer hands. That's just common sense.'

Mark asked, thinking of Tommy, 'Have many Dartmouth boys gone into the ambulance corps, or into the show in any other way?'

Tony laughed. 'No one but Chad Frame,' he said. 'You don't know him, Dad. He used to go up to Montreal every so often, to the cat-houses there; and here a couple of weeks ago he went up there and enlisted in the RCAF. He used to fly some; but I guess he was drunk when he enlisted.'

Their talk went on. Joe Hazen—his home was in California—was much more concerned with the chance of war in the Pacific than with European affairs. He and Chuck Little were the only belligerent minds in the group. Charlie Spring and Tony agreed that we should let Europe work out its own damnation; and Dan Pride said drily:

'There's nothing for us to get steamed up about. It's their war. As far as I'm concerned, they can have it!'

Mark watched Dan with a thoughtful interest. He was Lucy's older brother, and he seemed—except for a youthful tendency to look on European affairs with a lofty indifference—an attractive young fellow. Mark wondered whether Dan knew the truth about his mother; and he remembered guiltily that he had not yet told Tony. Perhaps there would be no need. Tony had scarce mentioned Lucy since his return from last summer's visit to her home.

The six young men talked freely enough during that leisurely dinner. 'We're drifting toward war,' Charlie Spring insisted. 'Professor Smead says our definition of neutrality is anything that helps England, and that already we're calling the real neutrals bad names.'

Tony said: 'Dad, the *Dartmouth's* been printing a sort of "deadly parallel" between the things that happened in Hanover in 1914 and 1915 and what's happening now; but we're a lot nearer war today, because we already hate Germany.'

'That doesn't mean we have to fight her,' Dan Pride argued. 'We fought one war to end war, and look at the damned thing now! You can't keep sober by drinking liquor—and you can't keep the peace by fighting.'

'We hate Germany all right,' Charlie Spring assented. 'But we've got to remember what happened when we went on our last hating spree.'

'I wouldn't give a damn for a man that won't fight for what he thinks is right,' Chuck Little declared.

'If you ask me,' Dan Pride commented, 'it's sacrilege to keep talking about "right" and "wrong" in a war for political supremacy in Europe.'

Mark asked them: 'What do your professors have to say?'

'Most of them are making fighting talk,' Tony admitted. 'But we Seniors can all remember when they were saying that only the innocent and the naïve went to war for their ideals. They always said the last war was a mistake, but now they say we ought to go and get killed to correct that mistake.'

Charlie Spring supplemented that answer. 'You see, Judge Worth, our generation has been through a wave of post-war literature about the generation that lost itself in the last war. We've sat in classrooms and listened to men tell how that war shattered their hopes and their ideals. Now, because we believe what they then said, they call us weaklings and cowards and pro-Nazis. It's shocking to them to see us; but it's even more shocking to us, who listened to them and believed them, to see them now disavow all they once said.'

Mark nodded, asking no more questions, listening as the talk went on. Much of it was a retracing of old ground, but Frank Parks said something—he said in fact a great deal—which impressed Mark.

'Maybe what this country needs is a good war,' Frank declared. 'To shake us out of this rotten world we've made. Did you ever stop to think that the United States is a tough place for a poor man to live in? Every paper and magazine he picks up is full of pictures of beautiful, expensive things—cars, and yachts, and clothes, and gadgets, everything under the sun—things he can never possibly buy. We've glorified an expensive way of life, expensive and sensuous and depraved. Pictures of girls are our favorite ads. We buy toothpaste, or shaving soap, or a special kind of car, because some pretty girl likes to kiss men who use that toothpaste or that soap or who drive that car. We want to spend our winters at Palm Beach or Miami or somewhere because according to the ads they're full of beautiful nymphs in bathing suits, waiting to flirt with us. Our idea of heaven is to spend every evening in a café where men and girls sing smutty songs to us and the head waiter knows our name, and to spend every day lounging on a sunny beach drinking zombis or something expensive with a glamour girl. A lot of magazines print nothing except stories about the way actual people with too much money spend it! You read the same names in those magazines month after month; how someone spent ten thousand dollars to throw a party for some eighteen-year-old kid with plucked eyebrows and red paint on her fingernails; and how much Glamour Girl Number One spends for shoes, and Number Two for lingerie. They're all numbered like public enemies; and in a way they are, putting expensive ideas into our heads. We devour gossip columns about women who spend enough on hair waves every year to support a workman's family! The national bill for lipstick and beauty aids and perfumes is probably bigger than the national bill for bread! We buy a new car every year or every other year and practically give away our old one when it's just well broken in. We discard things, not because they're worn out, but because we're tired of them, and because we like the feeling and the look of something new. We pay a hundred and fifty dollars for a suit when we could buy one just as good for forty, and ten dollars for a shirt, and five dollars for a necktie—and what our sisters spend for gowns they'll wear once or twice and then start calling an old rag is nobody's business! We're suckers for smart salesmen, who sell us things we don't want or need, and our national heroes and heroines are the men and girls who work twenty-four hours a day at the job of spending money, and we sneer at anyone who has money and doesn't spend it. Ever since I can remember, we've been pouring money down the sewers—or envying the people who do it!'

His very passion silenced the others, and he went strongly on:

'England glorifies the Man of Property. Read Galsworthy. But at least there's some dignity attaching to the ownership of land and houses. Over here we glorify, not the Man of Property, but the Man of Money! Our idea of success is to make money—no matter how; and especially if you spend it. Our idea of a home is an architect's nightmare queer enough to be photographed for *Vogue* or *Town and Country*. They print the pictures and we lap them up. New York is the epitome of the whole thing; the New York of the night clubs, Broadway. The rest of the country sits around biting its nails, waiting for New York—and Hollywood—to decide how women shall cut their hair, and what plays we shall see, and what books we shall read, and what we shall think about, and what we shall think about it. We're a bunch of sheep waiting for New York to blow a whistle and drive us anywhere it decides for us to go. Did any of you ever read one of Upton Sinclair's novels? No, because New York sneers at them. But the rest of the world reads them. We call ourselves a literate country. Well, there are a hundred and thirty million of us, but if ten thousand people buy a certain book, that's a pretty good sale, and if a hundred thousand buy it, that's marvellous! Literate, my eye! Instead of reading, we look at pictures, or listen to the radio. If we can read enough to decipher the captions under the pictures, and puzzle out the radio programs, we're satisfied.

'New York has taught us all that spending money for foolishness is the most charming thing we can do; and the real tragedy of this war for a lot of dimwits is that they can't conveniently winter on the Riviera or at the Lido. If a novel comes along that glorifies the Christian virtues, New York tells us it's trite, so we don't read it; but a nice piece of dirt about some rich wench whose husband doesn't understand her is great art! Women take husbands instead of lovers, nowadays. The only difference is that they go through a mock marriage. Women make a profession of divorce and brag about it. I heard one woman say she wouldn't divorce her husband till she had lined up someone better.

'Oh, maybe most of us are sound; but all the same, the stories we like to read, the way of life that interests us, the fodder that makes successful magazines and plays and books today is the sort of stuff that used to be published in paper covers and used to be read by little boys out behind the barn. Money, money, money; women, women, women; Palm Beach and Palm Springs; Miami and Hollywood; who divorced who and who did she marry then and will it last a year? That's the sort of stuff we want to read about.

'Yes sir, maybe what we need is a good war. The women will put on uniforms, and the more expensive the uniform, the prouder they'll be; but at least the men who have to do the fighting and pay the taxes will find out that there are other ways to be happy besides spending money and being photographed at night clubs!'

He stopped and there was a long moment's silence; and then Joe Hazen drawled: 'Jeremiah is the name!' They all chuckled, and even Frank smiled, and Mark was interested by Joe's comment and by their reaction. Did this new generation read the Bible, then? Young men and young women had so many virtues which they preferred to conceal.

The talk broke out afresh, but Mark had ceased to listen. Frank's words had set him thinking. If the United States did indeed go to war, total war that would tax our every resource, that would reduce our standard of living to a subsistence basis, letting us have only food and clothing and shelter, would a new and better, a simpler and kindlier world perhaps emerge?

3

(December 1939)

Russia attacked Finland, and the 'experts'—Mark had begun to grin with a dry and mirthless scorn whenever in the newspapers he encountered the word—set the limit of Finland's possible resistance at two weeks. The Finns appealed for aid from the democracies, and Mark, sampling the opinion of the men around him, found everywhere a strong respect and sympathy for that small nation which alone in all the world had honored its obligations to us. For his part, not only his sympathy but his passions were aroused. Here was a conflict in which there could be only one side. Finland had made of itself the model of what a nation—large or small—might be; a nation in which neighbors cooperated for the general good, and in which the individual was still the individual even while he subordinated his personal interests to the interests of his fellows and of his country. The Finns had known how best to combine liberty and law; how to give freedom to the parts without weakening the whole. Now that half-savage monster which was Russia would overrun the thrifty farms, the busy little towns, the beautiful small cities, murdering and wrecking and befouling everything she touched.

In his disturbed mind he turned to Robin, going to New York for a week-end with her; and when she met his plane she was distressed, thinking he looked badly, looked tired.

'I am tired,' he confessed. 'I've been lying awake nights thinking about Finland.' They were in the taxi, on the way to her apartment.

'Darling, darling,' she protested. 'Thinking does no good, just wears you out.'

'I know,' he assented. 'And I've been surprised at my own—anger. Probably knowing Elin and Einar sharpens my feeling. I had no special sympathy for Poland and the little Baltic states and Czecho-Slovakia. The people there were simple "foreigners"; but I don't think of the Finns as foreigners at all. They're our kind of people; and as a nation they've achieved a way of life worth our admiration.'

'We're helping Finland,' she reminded him. 'We've loaned them ten million dollars.'

He said drily: 'That's typical of us, to think that money will help; and besides, since they must spend the money here, it's good for business! But lending money doesn't give them guns. And England and France are holding back. The London dispatches say they're afraid of stumbling into war with Russia!' He laughed grimly. 'What price England, the very perfect gentle knight, defending small nations against the aggressor now?'

'England has to think first of defending herself.'

'Oh, I know,' Mark agreed. 'But the stage-setting of this war in Finland gives it a particular horror for me. That fighting in the darkness of the Arctic night, in the snow and the bitterness of cold, where a wounded man freezes to death before his hurts can be tended, is beyond imagining. I suppose it's even worse than Napoleon's retreat from Moscow.'

Robin said, almost desperately: 'You must learn to shut your mind to it, darling. For your own sake.'

'I could if it weren't for Einar,' he admitted. 'Elin carries a high head, of course; and she has a sublime faith that he will come through. She says he's in one of the ski regiments, fighting in the north, and that he's such a good skier no one can hurt him. I think she really believes it— as if a man on skis could outrun a bullet!'

'If to believe this comforts her, isn't she wise?'

'Anyone's wise to hold fast to any comfort,' he assented, and he said gratefully: 'You're my comfort. That's why I turn to you—and I feel a lot better already.'

They came to her apartment, and in the elevator she said: 'I wish you'd stay here, Mark. Stay here with me. I so want to take care of you.' He kissed her, and the elevator came to her floor, and when her door was closed behind them and she was in his arms she urged: 'You could, you know. That's what my extra room is for, for you, darling.' She told him mischievously: 'I'm not afraid of being compromised.'

He laughed. 'But think of my reputation, Robin!'

They went together to the kitchen to prepare dinner. There was a thick steak rubbed with lemon juice and garlic, larded and well peppered and salted, to be oven-broiled. 'I always give you steak,' she said, 'because you always order one when we dine out.'

'You and Elin are the only women I know who accept the fact that if a man likes a thing he likes it, never gets tired of it.'

'Why should he? If men got tired of the same fare, day after day, what would become of marriage?' And she asked: 'How's Tony?'

His eyes shadowed. 'I've been worried about him, this winter. He's changed since the war began. We're not as close to one another as we used to be.' And he said: 'Of course the war has confused him. He thinks about it as constantly as I do; thinks one thing one day and another the next. I've a letter from him here.' He produced it, read it to her while she was busy with the salad.

> Dear Dad—
> There's no talk here but of the war. Naziism can only thrive in a nation of men and women who have suffered as the Germans did during and after the World War. We must not let the world suffer that way again. And we must not let this smouldering war burst into flames, because it may be a consuming fire that will leave us a battered people ready to accept doctrines as brutal as those of the Nazis.
>
> There seems to be only one thing we can be sure of. Britain has proved that she will lie and cheat as freely as Hitler or Stalin; but with all her faults, there seems to be a fairly consistent thread of humanity in Britain's national mind, and so we must support her. I'm like you. I don't want to see England licked.
>
> There's another sure thing, at that. The world will never be the same again. Everyone is saying we must discard old ideas, old military tactics, old books, old thinkers, old morals, old standards; and everyone is pretty well right—but we're apt to think that because one standard has been wrong all standards are equally vile. We cannot discard the civilization we are supposed to be fighting to save, but neither must we seek desperately to hold on to all our old world, because there is no question that much of it cannot serve in the new.
>
> What comes next? I can't help feeling that England is more worried than she confesses. This long lull, when everyone knows that Germany has tremendous weapons not yet used, must be a terrific strain on the men in command of the English and French forces, and particularly of England. It's as certain as anything can be that before England wins the war by starvation, as she hopes to do, Germany will have tried every weapon at her command.
>
> But talking doesn't help, except to blow off steam. I hope you go to see Mrs. Kerr soon. Give her my love.
>
> Tony.

He finished, and Robin said: 'Well, that's not particularly effusive, but it seems to me a sensible letter. I don't think you need worry about him.'

'It's so darned—impersonal,' he assented. 'Of course, a lot of what he says is true.'

'Yes—but no one can say those things openly without being criticized,' she suggested. 'Oh, I forgot the cocktails. You know where the ice is. Everything else is on the table.' He went to do her bidding and came back with the shaker and the glasses, and she said the steak was almost done, turning flushed and beautiful to take the glass he filled for her, and their eyes met as they drank, and she smiled at him and set her half-empty glass on the end of the stove while she lifted out the steak for him to carve and served their plates with wild rice and grilled mushrooms. Only when they were at table she added, as though there had been no interruption, 'At least you can't say them here in New York. Most of the people I know are already mentally at war with Germany.' She smiled. 'There's more fighting—with words—in New York drawing rooms this winter than there is with arms in Europe.'

'Except in Finland,' he reminded her. 'There's fighting enough there!'

But she led him to talk of himself, and of Tony, so that he forgot Finland for a while. The portrait which she had made of him hung on her wall, and she said she liked it better every day. 'I think I did a good job on you,' she said proudly. 'I was almost a great painter then.' And once she rose from the table to find the watercolor of Ingrid which she had made in Hanover, and to show it to him; and he told her Tony had had a letter from Ingrid.

'She's a lovely girl,' Robin said. 'And she'd have married Tony at the drop of a hat.' She asked whether Tony was still interested in Lucy Pride; and Mark said gratefully:

'I think that's wearing itself out. He's hardly mentioned her since last summer.'

'Perhaps he's turning to Jan Ritchie. You always thought he might.'

'If he is, he hasn't said so. Jan's a Freshman at Merryfield this year, by the way.'

They talked of themselves for a while, and dinner was done and the dishes to be washed. Afterward she left him alone a moment, and rummaging among her sketches he found one or two of Tony, on skis.

'I'd know him anywhere,' he told her when she returned. 'Even though you don't show his face. See here, Robin, why don't you do a portrait of him for me, during the Christmas holidays? You could stay at the house.' He smiled. 'We'd have him for a chaperon!'

She laughed. 'You're such a cautious man!'

'Well, when you're as lovely as you are this evening I have to be cautious!' And he said, in laughing challenge: 'You probably couldn't do a very good job on him, of course, but I wouldn't mind, as long as we had you over there.'

Her eager desire to be with Mark led her to agree. Before he said good night the thing was settled. She would go to Montreal, to her father for Christmas Day; but the rest of Tony's vacation she would spend with them. Mark returned to Boston filled with rich anticipation.

At home, Bob Ritchie told him that Tommy Sheffield had gone from France—where there was no present need for ambulances—to Finland, where there was dreadful need. Mark told Elin this, thinking it would be fine if Tommy and Einar should somehow come to know each other there.

4

(December 1939)

That Christmas season was for Mark richly contenting. To face Robin across the breakfast table, to have her good-bye kiss before he left for town—Elin, who was accustomed to help him with his hat and coat, tactfully disappeared into the kitchen at these times—to have her greeting when he came home, and to see her presiding at dinner, and to sit with her before the fire through the long evenings meant for him a happiness beyond measure. When she went away to Montreal, he had an absurd fear that she might never return; when she did, his world was full again. He would not let himself think that soon she must go back to New York, and they never spoke of this. She denied him nothing of herself which he wished to claim, and he knew she would not. He knew that if he so elected she would free herself from poor Davy to come to him; yet that was a loyalty to which they clung, not to be discarded now.

The world seemed to conspire to permit them this happy interval; for—except in Finland—there was peace talk in the air, and hope in the minds of men. Holland and Belgium and the other neutrals had proposed a peace move weeks ago. Churchill retorted that there could be no peace with Hitler; and he warned the little neutrals that their national existence depended in the end on English victory; but Mr. Roosevelt and the Pope were in correspondence, seeking some hopeful formula. Hostilities, except for the forays of German planes and submarines which forced England to stop using Scapa Flow as a naval base, were at a standstill. A poll of public opinion showed that the number of those who wished to aid the Allies in concrete ways was smaller than it had been when the war began; and Mark thought there was at least a chance that the war might smoulder and die. Only in Finland men battling in the frozen dark found death in strange and icy shapes. Elsewhere there was hope across the world.

Tony spent much time at the house during these holidays. For two or three hours each day when the light served he posed for Robin in the attic studio, and they talked while she worked. Mark had told her that Tony knew about Davy; and she thought it might be because of this that she found in Tony a sort of humble gentleness.

'He makes me feel, sometimes, that he needs me,' she told Mark once. 'He has so many troubled thoughts, so many perplexities. He speaks positively, but he has so little real confidence in himself.'

'His world is turned upside down,' Mark agreed; and he spoke of that evening when Tony and his fellows dined here. 'The tragic thing for them,' he said, 'is that their instructors, the men to whom for four years they have turned to find the roots of all wisdom, are now eating their own words—and blaming the boys for believing what they have been taught.'

'Tony's rather frighteningly at loose ends,' she assented. 'I wish he were in love with someone. That would at least distract his attention from himself. He's taking himself and his own thoughts much too seriously now.'

'Has he mentioned Lucy?'

'I asked him how she was,' Robin told him. 'He saw her at a dance the other night, but that was the first time he'd seen her since last summer.'

Mark smiled. 'Curious to see how such things burn themselves out, or just die of—non-support.'

'I suspect he's simply being sensible about it,' she suggested. 'He knows he can't well be married now, not till he's through college at least; and he's too intelligent to involve himself in what might be years of waiting. I think he's very fond of Lucy, might if he let himself go fall in love with her. I think he's making himself stay away from her.'

Mark said reflectively: 'I wonder if by any chance Nell Ritchie took it on herself to tell him about Lucy's mother.' He had told Robin that story months before. 'Nell's perfectly capable of it.'

'Possibly,' Robin admitted. 'If he knows about that he might be keeping away from Lucy—just as he is.'

She herself saw little of Nell or of Mary Halstead during her stay here. Nell was fanatically engrossed in the cause of Bundles for Britain, giving it all her energies; and although they foregathered for Christmas, Robin was at the time in Montreal. Betty had had a letter from Ingrid, which she read to them; and Mark remembered one passage:

> We are in very troubled thinking here, because in Finland we have so many friends. I know many boys there, and all that country where they are fighting the Russians in the north, I have been there. It is terrible fighting in the snow in the long dark nights, and many men freeze to death quickly if they are wounded. It is most hard for the Russians. Some of them do not even have mittens. But it is very bad for the Finnish people too.

He quoted that to Robin when she returned from Montreal, and she asked: 'Does Elin still speak of Einar to you?'

'Sometimes. But when she does, her eyes fill, so I never ask her questions.'

'She's a wonderful girl. I've grown so fond of her. She brought her baby to see me the other day.' To speak of Elin's baby made her remember Emma Sheffield's acid comment at the time of Elin's wedding, so she asked: 'Has Mrs. Sheffield her divorce yet?'

'Not yet.'

'I wonder if she'll ever come back here to live.'

'I don't think so.' He smiled grimly. 'I believe that was included in the bargain.'

They talked in these days together very little about the war; but once he read her a letter just come from his father. The older man wrote:

> The fire-eaters in your Eastern papers seem to have quieted down. Nowadays I never read an editorial on foreign affairs in which the editor doesn't take care to emphasize America's fixed determination not to be drawn into the conflict. There's quite a contrast between their tone now and before Poland. Then they were shouting that England and France must go on and stop Hitler, but now they're finely judicial and disinterested and talking about possible peace. If American opinion had been as cool-headed last summer as it is today, there might never have been a war.

She said, nodding gravely: 'Yes, that's true. In Montreal they're wondering why we don't do something to help, after all our big talk.'

'Father and I don't always agree,' he confessed, 'but he has some good ideas.' He read another paragraph from the letter

> The editor of a daily is at a disadvantage. He is forced to make snap judgments, to appraise events the moment they occur. But editors like me, who need bring out a paper only once a week, have time to achieve some

perspective, to see what has happened in its relation to other incidents before and since. The daily oracles have no time for meditation, no time to set their thoughts aside to cool. Or—to reverse the figure—no time to give their opinions a proper baking. So their biscuits come out of the oven half-baked, with burned black headlines on top, with a weak undercrust—and a soggy middle. If you want to find out what people who have time to think are thinking, read the country weeklies, not the city dailies. Consider the effrontery of a man like Walter Lippmann, for instance, who for twenty years or more has emitted every day or so the last and definitive and positive word on the most important world event of the preceding twenty-four hours. If you want a liberal education, go back even two years and read what the editors and the experts had to say—and see how wrong they often were.'

'Mercy!' Robin laughed. 'I wonder what he thinks of Dorothy Thompson.'

'The trouble,' Mark reflected, 'is not so much with the editors and the commentators as with their readers. We readers are too apt to think anything we read is true. We think we can prove a point by saying that someone said so in print. I met old Mr. Ritchie, Bob's father, the other day; and I expressed some opinion or other and he snorted and told me to read—Rauschning, is it? That book about a *Revolution in Nihilism*.'

'Did you do it?'

'No. I'd rather rely on a conclusion I've thought out for myself than on what someone says someone said.'

She asked: 'Is Mr. Ritchie well? Bob, I mean. It seems to me he has changed since I last saw him.'

'He had a little upset awhile ago,' Mark told her. 'But Nell's not worried.' He smiled. 'She's so busy with her war work she doesn't have time to worry about Bob.'

5

(February 1, 1940)

In Europe the armies seemed to slumber as the Sitzkrieg, the phony war, droned on; but now and then a line in the papers suggested an increasing tension yonder. In England and in France food began to be rationed. Some twenty-one hundred people had been killed in blackout accidents in London, a figure only two or three hundred below the total loss of life in the English Navy and air force. Only fourteen English soldiers had been killed in battle up to the first of February.

But in Finland thousands were dying from shot and shell and from bombings and from the deadly cold. Einar was killed late in January, and a cablegram brought Elin the news. Mark was late for dinner that night. He had met Professor Wearing in the Court House and they stopped at the club for a cocktail together and joined a group which was discussing the current debate in Congress over the proposed appropriation of a billion dollars or so for naval construction. The phrase, 'Two-ocean Navy,' began to be heard; the proposal was to build a Pacific fleet able to beat Japan, and also an Atlantic fleet strong enough to make us secure even if England's strength failed. Mark was struck by the fact that no one seemed disturbed at the amount of the proposed expenditure. To him, even after these years of the New Deal, a billion dollars still seemed like a great deal of money; and the proposed appropriation was only a beginning. Could even the United States support—without a complete change in the individual way of life—the expense of full-scale modern war?

He was still thinking about this when he came home, so that he did not at first notice any difference in Elin; but when he sat down at dinner table he heard a familiar sound in the kitchen, the formless 'Wah! Wah! Wah!' of a happy baby bouncing up and down on someone's knee; and when Elin brought his soup, he said smilingly:

'Sounds like your young daughter out there.'

As he spoke he looked up at her; and when he saw her face he came quickly to his feet. She was not crying. She held the plate of soup steadily in both hands, and her countenance was serene; but it was drained of all color and her eyes were wide and blank.

She put the plate down and rubbed her hands together, and said in a low voice: 'Yes, she is there.' Her eyes met his. 'I wanted her, so my cousin brought her out.' Mark could not speak, and after a moment she said: 'Einar is dead.'

Mark took her in his arms. She looked up at him and he kissed her—thinking even as he did so how strange it was that he had never kissed her before, despite his long fondness, despite the fact that she had for years been so close to him. When he kissed her, tears gushed from her eyes, and she was small in his arms, her face pressed against his coat, sobbing helplessly.

'There,' he murmured. 'There, Elin. There, my dear girl.'

She clung to him, her hands tight on the lapels of his coat; and he held her, touching her smooth hair. 'Cry it out, my dear,' he said. 'Cry all you will.' His own eyes were wet. They stood a long time so, till she was eased; and at last she looked up at him, and her eyes were proud.

'But he was ready to die,' she said eagerly, nodding as though anxious to persuade herself that what she said was true. 'He was willing to die.'

'Little Anna's a part of him you'll always have!'

'I'll always have all of him.' Her low tones were fierce with passion. 'I'll always have Einar! Always! Always! They can't take him away from me.' Her eyes pleaded with him to understand. 'Don't you see? If he had come back, he might have changed, might not have liked me any more, might have grown old. But now he's dead, so he can't change, so I'll always have him this way, the way he is now, loving me more than anything except Finland.'

Mark remembered that morning years ago when he had come home from the hospital after Nan died, when Elin met him at the door, and he saw the tender sorrow in her eyes, and felt the comforting warmth of her almost maternal fondness. Theirs had been a strange relationship, at once so close, living for the most part alone together and under the same roof, seeing each other daily, feeling a mutual affection—and yet their lives were so completely separate. He wished now to take her in his arms like a hurt child, and hold her till the terrible aching grief which racked her should have passed. He said slowly: 'You're a grand woman, Elin. I'm proud that I know you.'

For a moment she did not speak. Then with a faint shivering movement she came back to the comforting small familiar things that made up her life of service. 'Oh!' she cried: 'Your soup is cold.'

'No matter,' he protested; but she whisked it away to warm it for him again; and he heard the baby crow with delight when she came into the kitchen.

Thereafter, she served Mark's dinner without interruptions, and Mark did not speak to her. But when he was done, he said: 'Bring the baby in to see me, Elin. Will you?'

So he and she, with small Anna busy on the floor at their feet, were together for a while. She knew of Einar's end only that he was dead, the bare fact, nothing more. Mark thought she might like to be with her uncle's family for a week or two, but she said:

'Oh, no. It will be much better if I am busy here.'

'Then why doesn't little Anna come and live here with you?' he proposed. 'Unless it would be too much work for you. I'd like having her here.'

To his satisfaction, she welcomed that suggestion. They discussed

ways and means, and because he saw it somehow comforted her to plan
domestic arrangements, he asked many questions, objected to this detail
and that, led her into long talk of where the baby should sleep, and
what the routine of her life should be. There were problems that
would need solving and he spoke of them, making many unnecessary
difficulties, so that she must decide how they might be met; and slowly,
before his eyes, she became her familiar self again.

When she picked up the baby to take her back to the kitchen, she
turned to face him, smiling gratefully. 'You're a good man, Judge
Worth,' she said. 'And a wise man, I think. You made me talk about
all this because it is good for me to think of work and planning. I'm
all right now. Thank you for knowing the way to help me most.'

He said simply: 'I think a lot of you, Elin.'

She smiled, nodding in a brisk little way. 'I think a lot of you,' she
agreed.

6

(February 1940)

In mid-February, Bob Ritchie had an acute recurrence of that illness
which had made its onset a few weeks before; pains in his back, a high
fever, vomiting. Mark was in New York for the week-end, and knew
nothing of it till his return. Then at breakfast—he had come home on
the midnight—Elin told him, and Mark went at once across the street
to see how Bob was.

'He's in bed, feeling very sorry for himself,' Nell cheerfully explained.
'There's nothing in the world the matter with him except that he ate
too much, or ate the wrong thing; but you know what babies men are.'

'What does the doctor say?'

She laughed, yet Mark saw that there was real concern under her
apparent amusement. 'He's put Bob permanently on the wagon,' she
said.

Mark, on impulse, kissed her. 'He'll be all right.' Her arm tightened
around his neck, thin and strong, in a silent eloquence. 'Can I see
him?' he asked.

'Yes, of course. Go on up.' He turned toward the stair, but she
caught his arm, added in a low tone: 'His face is swollen, Mark. Don't
say anything about that. I don't think he knows it. Just tell him he
looks well.'

He recognized the anguished terror in her. Nell was on the surface always so briskly matter-of-fact that it was easy to forget this might be only surface. She and Bob had never been—as Ed and Mary Halstead were—openly affectionate toward each other, making no secret of their love. Mark thought it was easy to judge people by externals, to assume that they were what they seemed to be. No one would have expected Nell to be thus shaken with fear now. But, characteristically, she would go on with the normal routine of her life, just as Elin since Einar's death found comfort in small, familiar daily tasks.

He promised to mind his tongue, but when he came into Bob's room, he was glad she had forewarned him. Bob—there could be no question—looked like a sick man; and Mark felt a quick thrust of concern. But he said cheerfully enough: 'Well, they've got you in bed, have they?'

'For a few days,' Bob assented. 'But I'm all right.' He grinned. 'They claim I've been working too hard. No one ever accused me of that before.' And he said: 'Sit down. Nell says you've been in New York.' Mark nodded, and Bob asked smilingly: 'Why don't you marry the gal?' He said: 'She did a swell job on that portrait of Tony, Mark. And of course, on yours, too. She's good, isn't she?'

Mark saw that there was in the other man a hunger for talk. It was still early enough so that he need not at once start for town, so he stayed awhile and Bob asked what New York people were thinking about the phony war.

'Well,' Mark told him, obediently following Bob's lead, 'I heard some talk about the fact that we're financing Russia against Finland, and Japan against China, by buying their gold at thirty-five dollars.' Actually he had talked with no one except Robin in New York, but Bob need not know that.

'We're financing the whole war—what there is of it,' Bob agreed. 'Pretty soon we'll have all the gold in the world—and the rest of the world will have all our money. Probably Franklin will fix it so he can pay a hundred dollars an ounce before he's through—and send a check to everyone who has already sold gold to us to make up the difference. Big-hearted Otis, that guy! With our money!'

'I don't mind the gold so much,' Mark suggested. 'But we're selling munitions to Russia and Japan: scrap iron, and oil, and such things.'

'That's business,' Bob said in a sardonic tone. 'That's like a doctor setting up as an undertaker too.' He asked: 'When does New York think the fighting will start?'

'The idea seems to be that Hitler will have to start soon. They claim

German superiority in the air is passing and the experts all agree that she hasn't gasoline and oil for a long war.'

Nell came to say good-bye to Bob. 'I simply have to go to town,' she explained. 'And you're all right.' She told Mark: 'If I stay with him, he barks at me. When he's sick abed, he's not fit to live with. If you want anything, Bob, just shout and one of the girls will hear you. 'Bye,' she rushed away; and Bob grinned and shouted after her:

'Bundles for Britain! Hooray! Hooray!' He watched the door through which she had disappeared, and after a moment Nell called from the lower hall: 'Good-bye, Bob.'

'Good-bye, old girl!'

The door closed behind her, and Bob grinned at Mark. 'Nell tickles me,' he declared. 'You'd think she was winning the war.'

Mark said smilingly: 'You and she don't fool anybody, you know.'

'Oh, we get along,' Bob agreed, awkward and uncomfortable. He came back to impersonalities. 'You know, Mark—speaking of the war, this *Altmark* business made me gag. How about you?'

Mark had read the story, in the Sunday papers. 'There's something obscure about it,' he suggested. 'On the face of the dispatches, the British destroyer just ran alongside an unarmed vessel with British prisoners locked up in her hold, boarded her, shot a dozen of her German crew and released the prisoners. There were five Germans killed and seven wounded, but I can't find any evidence—not even any assertion—that the Germans made any resistance. One Britisher was wounded by what they call a "trap," apparently a sort of set-gun down in the cabin. That just simply isn't credible to me. No one—not even a German—would be likely to fix up a set-gun in his own cabin. There'd be no sense or purpose in it. The German captain claims his men did not resist. Even the British report says most of the Germans—or some of them—jumped overboard onto the ice alongside and tried to get ashore. It sounds to me as though the British were unnecessarily rough in handling an unresisting crew who had trusted to the Norwegian Government to protect them in neutral waters.'

'You're damned right!' Bob agreed. 'But look at the headlines: "British Exult at Bold Rescue!" And did you read all the guff about recalling the days of Nelson and Drake, and the best traditions of the dear old British Navy? I don't blame the British for entering Norwegian waters, or for shooting a few Germans—whether the Germans fought back or not—or for releasing the British prisoners. But when they talk about it as if they'd done something wonderful—you'd think the

Altmark had been a German battleship—by God, it makes me want to vomit!'

Mark thought it wiser not to excite the other. 'There've been some grand sea tales come out of this war,' he suggested. 'That farce comedy mixup over the *City of Flint,* and the great fight the *Rawalpindi* put up, and the grim business of the *Athenia*——'

'Do you think the Germans sank her?'

'I think so, yes. I suspect it was done by an individual commander who exceeded his instructions, and that the Germans at first denied it for fear of what the United States reaction would be—and then had to stick to their denial.'

'That's what I figure,' Bob agreed; and he added: 'But the *Graf Spee* business was the one I liked. The British used their heads on that one! They did a swell job.'

The two friends sat in talk for an hour or more, discussing the universal human interest in tales of adventure at sea, even on the part of those who had never smelled the salt; and they speculated about what Mr. Roosevelt expected to accomplish by sending Sumner Welles to Europe, and about the chances for a third term for the President. Bob pointed out that although in the latest polls of public opinion sixty-four per cent approved Mr. Roosevelt's conduct as President, fifty-four per cent would vote against a third term.

'That's not conclusive,' Mark suggested. 'It's how people vote at the ballot box that counts. And for another thing, November is still nine months away. A lot can happen in the meantime.'

'I think Dewey can beat Roosevelt even if he runs,' Bob declared. 'Dewey's a vote-getter.'

'Willkie sounds to me like a good man.'

'He can't be nominated. The politicians won't have him.'

'They don't like Dewey, either. If they can swing it they'll put up Taft.'

'I'd vote for anyone against Franklin,' Bob declared.

When Mark eventually had to leave, his solicitude crept into his tones. 'Take care of yourself, old man,' he said. 'I'll see you every day, tell you what's going on.'

'Oh, I'll be back on the job in a few days,' Bob declared. 'Don't worry about me.'

7

(March 1940)

Before the end of February, it became clear that Finland was being
slowly ground into the dust. When on the seventh of March, armistice
negotiations began, the question of how aid could best be sent to the
Finns was still being debated—while nothing was done. On the
eleventh, Chamberlain told the Commons that the Allies would proceed
to give Finland all possible help as soon as Finland asked for it. Mark
and Elin had talked much about this remote and terrible war which
had struck across thousands of miles to wound them both; and Elin
read Mr. Chamberlain's speech and said indignantly:

'The Finns asked for help in December. It's a fine time for him to
be talking now!'

Mark nodded. 'But he has his own perplexities,' he reminded her.
'England can't risk getting into a war with Russia. It might mean the
end of her empire.'

'Neither could Einar risk it!' she retorted. 'It did mean the end of
him!' She added wretchedly: 'Oh, Judge Worth, the thing that's hard
for me is not knowing what happened to him, not having any word
or message except the last letter, the one he wrote in January.'

He decided that without telling her his hopes, he would try to get
from the Finnish Government some details of Einar's death, and he
wrote a letter to that end; but a day or two after the Russo-Finnish
peace was signed, Tom Sheffield called Mark on the phone. Mark
thought there was a difference in the other's voice. Tom sounded
younger, and there was no weariness in his tones.

'I've a letter from Tommy that you'll want to see, Mark,' he said.
'He's been in Finland, and he met a young Finn, the one who married
your Elin.'

'Einar?' Mark felt a quick excitement.

'Yes. They were together——' Tom hesitated. 'I suppose she has been
notified about her husband.'

'Yes, she heard of his death.'

'Well, he and Tommy were together that day. Tommy says . . .'

But Mark preferred to read Tommy's letter for himself. He interrupted: 'See here, Tom. Have lunch with me. I want to see you. Bring
the letter along.'

Tom readily agreed. 'I want to see you, too,' he said affectionately; and when they met, even though months had passed since their last talk together, there was no restraint between them. Mark saw at once that Tom was his own man again. They sat down and ordered; and then Tom said:

'Here's Tommy's letter.' He added definitely: 'You can read the whole of it.'

It was a long letter, scrawled in pencil on rough paper. Mark read it through while Tom watched him silently. Tommy had heard of his own exoneration, and of the fact that his mother and father were parted; and he spoke of that affair at the bank, describing how he discovered that the bond was missing, and thought Emma had taken it by accident, and tried to find her. But when he did find her, she had already disposed of the bond, and she protested that she simply had to have the money and bade Tommy get funds from his father to make restitution. 'Probably I was a damned fool,' Tommy wrote in this letter. 'But I couldn't tell the bank my own mother was a thief. So I did the first thing I could think of.'

He came at last to Einar. Mark read slowly, and when he finished, he said:

'See here, Tom, may I take this home? Elin will want to hear the part about Einar.' He added: 'I'll see it safe back to you.'

Tom assented, and Mark put the letter in his pocket and they talked for a while about Einar's death as Tommy had described it. They had a fine hour together, and when they parted Mark said: 'Tom, I've missed you. Come out and have dinner with me. How about Sunday?'

'Mother likes to keep me with her on Sunday,' Tom confessed. 'She's not very well, and the doctors make her go to bed at six every night, so Sunday's the only day we can be together all day. But I'll come any evening, if you make it seven o'clock. She usually goes right off to sleep, and I can leave her.'

So they agreed upon a day, and parted; and Mark thought he had recaptured something long lost.

Tommy's letter would bring Elin some happiness and peace; but he decided to wait till after her dinner work was done before reading it to her. When at last he heard her about to go upstairs, he called and she came in; and he said:

'Elin, sit down awhile. I've a letter you'll want to hear.' She obeyed him, watching him with wide eyes; and he told her gently: 'It's a letter from Tommy Sheffield, Elin. About Einar.'

Her hand rose with a quick motion to touch her throat; but she did not speak. He said, sorting through the pages of Tommy's letter: 'This isn't all about Einar. I'll have the part about him copied so you can keep it. Shall I read it to you?' She nodded dumbly, and he read:

Here's something you will want to tell Uncle Mark, and he can pass it on to Elin. I met her husband over here. It was along the middle of January. I went to one of the front dressing stations to get wounded for the hospital in Viborg, and after I got loaded up inside, I took a couple of men who could walk all right on the front seat with me, and one of them—they knew I was an American, of course—said he had been in the United States, and I said I came from Boston, and he said he had worked there and that his wife and baby were still there. He said she had worked for Judge Worth and of course I knew Elin, so after that we had a lot to talk about.

He told me all about her. He loved to talk about her, and I told him how swell I thought she was, so we hit it off in great shape.

He had been hit in the right shoulder by a shell fragment, but he said it was nothing, only the foolish doctors sent him to the hospital till it could get well. I got him there all right, and I kept track of him. His shoulder was smashed up, and badly torn, but he said—I saw him every time I could—that it didn't hurt him. He was a damned liar about that, but you get so used to human bravery and to a man's ability to stand pain that you forget it. They had him in a traction splint for a while and then in a cast, and the doctors told me he might be as well as ever in a month.

After he could move around, he used to help the orderlies, and he was always on hand when an ambulance came in, to help with the stretchers. His left arm was all right, and he teamed up with another boy whose right arm was o.k. and they would take one end of a stretcher, and of course a lot of things he could do with one hand. Whenever I had a chance we'd get together and talk about Elin and their baby. She'd have been mighty happy to hear the things he said. He had her picture, and the baby's; kept them in his pocket. He said whenever he'd been fighting and got hungry and no supplies came up he could just look at those pictures and it was as good as a full meal.

I was there on the 29th when the Russians came over and bombed the hospital. That wasn't an accident. They went for it and they got it. Some fires started, and we were carrying wounded out of the burning wing, and Einar and his buddy had hold of one end of a stretcher and I had hold of the other when three planes came over low and machine-gunned the hospital yard where we were all hard at it, and stretchers everywhere. I wanted to duck for cover, but Einar and the other boy kept on, so I had to stick till Einar went down. The bullet got him through the head.

I knew him better than I knew any other individual among the Finns, and maybe that's the reason I was particularly sore at the Russian pilots for that business. They'd done the same sort of thing in other places, and I'd even seen it, but it was all in the game till that day. Einar's buddy was sore, too. When he was well enough—his left arm had had to be taken off—he used to go along on ambulances as an inside orderly, riding with the wounded; but three times when they were bringing in wounded Russians, the Russians were dead when they got to the hospital, shot through the head. He reported that they had committed suicide, and the authorities decided he could work off steam more easily if he went back to the front, so he's at it now, with one arm.

But I just thought you might tell Judge Worth to tell Elin. Maybe she'll not feel so bad, knowing just what happened, and knowing how he felt about her.

Mark finished, and put the letter back into the envelope. 'I'll have that part copied for you,' he repeated gently.

She rose, not looking at him; and after a moment she folded her arms across her body in a curious way and turned and went out of the room and up the stairs. Mark thought it was as though she carried a baby in her arms, pressed against her heart, forever sheltered there.

8

(March 1940)

A day or two before Tony's spring vacation was to begin, Mark had word from him that he and three of his friends proposed to go to Florida for a part of the holiday, driving direct from Hanover. Mark found this letter waiting for him when he came home at the day's end, and restraining his impulse to warn Tony and the others against the dangers of such a long, hard drive, he telegraphed: 'Go ahead, have a fine time.' But he was deeply disappointed. Tony had not come to Boston since Christmas, and his letters had been short and unsatisfactory. Mark had looked forward to the coming holiday, to long hours with Tony during which he might recapture something it seemed to him he had lost. At dinner he told Elin that Tony would not be here for the vacation, told her Tony's plan; and she said: 'I think he will have a fine time in Florida.' But her tone, full of understanding, assured him that she knew his disappointment.

He was alone an hour after dinner when the doorbell rang and Ruth Rollins came in, stripping off her gloves, calling: 'Hello, Uncle Mark.' He met her in the hall, tremendously pleased to see her—she had gone away with her mother soon after Dave died—and he hugged her hard, kissed her, cried delightedly:

'Hello, Ruth! I thought you were at Palm Beach or somewhere. My! but I'm glad to see you. When did you get back?'

'I'm not back yet,' she confessed. Elin took her coat away. 'I'm still on my way. I came in by the Worcester Turnpike and just decided I wanted to see you the first thing.'

'You drove North?'

'Yes.' She sat down, put her arms up over her head and stretched luxuriously, pulled off her hat and loosened her hair. 'I've driven from Baltimore today and I'm stiff as a board.'

'Have you had dinner? Elin can give you something.'

'A bowl of soup? I'd love that.' He went to tell Elin, and Ruth asked: 'May I go upstairs and clean up?'

She came down almost at once, and Elin brought her a tray in the living room, and Mark said: 'You're a sight for sore eyes! We've missed you, Ruth.'

'I've missed you,' she assured him. 'The truth is, Mother and I don't enjoy the same sort of thing. I tried, Uncle Mark. Honestly. I wouldn't let myself blame her for not sticking with Father; but she didn't even want me to talk to her about him.'

'Perhaps she was blaming herself—or felt you were blaming her.'

She considered that. 'Maybe so,' she admitted. 'I can see that might be it. But—I want to live somewhere, Uncle Mark.' She emphasized the word. 'Really live, have a home. But she just wants to go from one resort to another. I hope she'll get married again, but the sort of men who can spend all winter in Florida—well, I didn't see any I'd want to marry. She's going to Honolulu this summer—she's gone to Palm Springs now— and I decided to come back to Boston. I feel at home here. I like the people I know here.' She looked at him honestly. 'I like you better than anyone I know, as a matter of fact,' she said smilingly.

'I like you, too. You're a grand girl, Ruth.'

'If I am, you get the credit. You straightened me out when I needed it.'

'You straightened yourself out.'

She shook her head. 'No. I know. So do you.' She said: 'Whenever I'm in trouble, I find myself wishing I could be with you. I've driven like mad today, just because I was going to see you tonight.' She laughed, looked at him with her head on one side, her eyes dancing. 'I don't suppose you'd consider marrying me, would you?' Her tone was light, yet her words were not altogether jest. For a long time, since before her father's death, other men had suffered in her eyes by comparison with Mark.

He chuckled. 'Well, I can't do that,' he said, keeping his tone casual, although he knew as well as she that she was half serious. She was no longer a child, but a tempered woman now, supple and strong in spirit as a steel blade is strong. 'But I'll be a father to you. Will that do?'

She sighed elaborately. 'I suppose it will have to. I'm probably not in love with you, but you're certainly the nicest man I know.' She added, laughing: 'The trouble is, I suspect I've a rival. Tony told me about Mrs. Kerr. She sounds swell.'

'I want you to meet her soon.' He kept his tone steady, astonishingly touched by this moment that had passed, seeing in Ruth the unrest, the uncertainty, which time would find a way to cure. 'You will if you stay in Boston. She'll be coming over soon, I hope.'

'Oh, I'll stay,' she assured him. 'That's why I came back. I came to stay.'

'Have you any plans?' She was, he remembered, an extremely wealthy young woman.

She nodded. 'Yes, several.' And she said, frankly teasing now: 'I decided that if you refused me I'd study stenography, get a job, settle down to be an old maid. Or perhaps you'll let me be your secretary?'

They laughed together. 'I'm afraid you'd be a distraction, destroy the properly judicial mood I try to cultivate. But wait till you've learned your trade and we'll see.'

He enjoyed the long hour they spent together. She planned to take an apartment. The Lincoln house was too big for her alone, and too far from town. 'I may sell it,' she confessed, her eyes shadowed. 'I'd not want to live there.' When at last she said goodnight, he sat awhile in thought, glad that she had broken away from Marcia, sure that now she would build her own life sound and strong.

9

(March 1940)

Before time for Tony to come back from the South, Mark went to New York to see Robin. He told her about Ruth's return to Boston, about their evening together. 'I think she half meant what she said about marrying me,' he admitted.

She smiled. 'You men! You're a credulous lot.' But then she said quietly: 'As a matter of fact, I suspect she did, Mark. She sounds like a fine girl—not the sort to say a thing like that just for a joke. And you've been pretty close to her.'

'I think a lot of her.'

She said in a tender amusement: 'You're her Pygmalion, in a way. I wonder if Pygmalion was as embarrassed as you are when Galatea announced that she loved him?'

'I wasn't embarrassed,' he admitted. 'I was touched—flattered, too, perhaps—but chiefly I was touched, and—full of sympathy. She's at loose ends, quite alone, needing someone.'

'You can do a lot for her.'

He said: 'I wish she and Tony might hit it off. Of course she's two or three years older than he.'

'Have you heard from him? I know you miss him.'

'I do,' he agreed. 'No, I've had no letter, just a telegram saying they got through safely.' And he said: 'Robin, I have a disturbing feeling that he and I are growing apart. All this winter he has halfway avoided me, or he's made sure that others were with us when we were together.'

She asked after a moment: 'Have you set your heart on his going to Law School?'

'Why, no,' he told her, surprised at the question. 'We've always planned that he would, that's all.' He said thoughtfully: 'We used to speak of it, but I don't think we've talked about it lately.'

'I talked with him a lot at Christmas,' she reminded him. 'He didn't say so, not in so many words; but I don't think he wants to go to Law School—and I think he dreads telling you so. He thinks you're counting on it, of course. But he feels that we're surely going to get into the war, and that he'd not have time to finish Law School. I know that's in his mind.'

'He's coming home for a day—or a night, at least—before he goes back to college,' Mark reflected. 'I'll talk it over with him then.' He added ruefully: 'I've always thought that if Tony was worried about anything, he'd come to me.'

'Probably he'd have talked to you at Christmas if I hadn't been there.' She smiled. 'He could never get you to himself with me under foot all the time.'

He returned to Boston feeling enriched and refreshed as he always did after seeing Robin. Tony arrived a day or two later, and Mark, remembering what Robin had suggested, raised the question of Law School. He approached it indirectly.

'Well, son,' he said after dinner, 'in less than three months now you'll be through college.'

'It seems as if I'd been in Hanover a lot longer than four years,' Tony confessed; and he said: 'College seems like sort of wasting time, somehow. I'm anxious to get through and—get started.'

'You're still pretty young,' Mark commented. 'A year or two younger than most men in your class. I was twenty-two when I graduated. You won't be twenty-one till next September, and you'll be through Law School two years ahead of me.'

'Law School looks like a long pull, from this end,' Tony admitted. 'Maybe that's just because I'm sick of college, or I've got spring fever or something.'

Mark said casually: 'Well, if you still feel the same way about it next fall, maybe you'll want to change your plans. You're the one to decide, you know.'

'Sure!' Tony laughed. 'I guess I'm just sort of bored at the idea of plugging up for my comprehensives, or scared, or something.' He said: 'We had such a swell time in Florida that it's hard to think of going back to work. Tennis till you were hot and then swim till you were cooled off, and loafing around in the sun.'

'Was there a young crowd? Or were you a crowd by yourselves, the four of you?'

'Oh, there was a gang. Barbie and her husband were at her father's place. Mr. Parks owns an island, a house as big as the Stadium. And the Prides were at the hotel, and some girls from Philadelphia we met the year I went abroad.'

'How's Lucy?'

'Same as ever. We get along.'

Mark looked thoughtfully at his son. 'You haven't seen much of her this winter.'

Tony hesitated. 'We decided we were beginning to like each other too well,' he said at last, lighting a cigarette, tossing the match on the hearth. 'We couldn't be engaged, not till I go to work or something; so we decided to take a vacation from each other—till next summer, anyway.'

Mark nodded, asked no questions. If he did so, and if Tony said he and Lucy might presently wish to become engaged, then Mark would have to tell Tony that stale story about Lucy's mother, and he dreaded the necessity.

But that night before he slept he thought of what Tony had said about Lucy. In his daily work upon the bench he listened to many witnesses, weighing their words, watching their expressions, forming an opinion as to their veracity. Tony, he was sure, had not lied; he had told at least a half truth.

But also Mark was sure there was something hidden still. Tony had told him either too little or too much.

10

(April 1940)

Mark saw his father at least once a year. Usually he went to Ohio for a few days with the older man in Hardiston, but sometimes Dan Worth came on to Boston; and he did so in April of this year, arriving just after Tony had gone back to Hanover. Mark had sometimes urged him to sell his paper, to let a younger man take over that routine; and now he had done so, and he came to spend a few days with Mark by way of celebration.

'And I want to read your Boston papers,' he told Mark, the evening he arrived. 'And to spend some time in the Library. No Bostonian ever goes to Ohio to find out what the other half thinks, but it might be a good thing if they did.'

'Boston is just as determined to keep out of war as Ohio,' Mark assured him. 'The only thing likely to change our feeling here is the realization, if it ever comes, that England is not sure to win.'

'We're already committed to going in,' Dan Worth insisted. 'Didn't you read the German White Paper?' Mark had seen only newspaper reports of its contents, and the older man said: 'They claim that Bullitt told the Polish ambassador that if Poland went to war with Germany, we'd come in on the Allied side.'

Mark objected: 'Mr. Roosevelt says the whole thing is propaganda, and Cordell Hull says he doesn't believe a word of it.'

'I know,' his father agreed, 'but you remember I told you a year or two ago that there'd be no war unless England and France knew we'd back them. Maybe the documents are faked, or doctored; but I believe Bullitt said something like that.'

'Even if Bullitt did say it, it was only his opinion. He had no power to give a guarantee, a binding promise.'

'We're committed,' his father insisted. 'Wait and see.' And he asked: 'Have you been following the talk about England's stiffening the blockade?'

'I saw something about it.'

'There's a murmur in the air, Mark, like the whisper of rain across a distant hill.' The older man spoke half to himself. 'A hint of great events impending. Churchill warns the little neutrals that the Allies will hereafter "follow the war wherever it leads us," regardless of neutral rights. Apparently from now on a country's neutrality is only as durable as its ability to defend it. And Chamberlain tells Parliament that "certain practical steps" will be taken to stop Germany's getting iron ore from Norway. What steps?' Mark did not offer any answer, and the other insisted: 'Will England blockade Norwegian ports? Or invade Norway?'

Mark smiled. 'Ask Mr. Chamberlain,' he suggested. He was too well pleased at having his father here to risk an argument with the older man.

'I'm afraid Chamberlain's feeling his oats,' Dan Worth said soberly. 'Did you read that speech of his where he said England is now strong enough to take care of herself, and that Hitler missed the bus?'

'I saw that, yes.'

'That's a plain confession that Germany might have whipped England last fall.'

'It's also an assertion that she can't do it now.'

'I hope Chamberlain knocked on wood when he said it. He talks too much, unless he's ready to do something.'

Mark did not wholly agree. If to blockade Germany would beat her, England need do no more than that. It was Germany which could not afford to sit idle under the blockade. But the morning papers reported that England had taken the aggressive, had laid a mine field in Norwegian waters, to force ore vessels from a port named Narvik in northern Norway to use the outside route on their way to Germany. But for them to do so would be to risk capture by the British fleet.

Dan Worth was, it seemed to Mark, surprisingly impressed by this news, sure that Germany would somehow retaliate. Mark did not agree. After all, England had command of the seas; so Germany was helpless. Norway would make a formal protest, but there was nothing she could do.

But when next morning he came down to breakfast, the paper lay beside his plate and Germany's answer blazed there in black headlines:

NAZIS INVADE DENMARK, NORWAY
COPENHAGEN AND OSLO SEIZED

So the Sitzkrieg, the phony war, was done.

XIII

The Battle of Europe

(April 1940–June 1940)

I

(April 15, 1940)

THE abrupt revival of martial activity in Europe came upon Mark with an impact which surprised him. Unconsciously he had accepted the Sitzkrieg—the derisive term pleased the general mind, eager to mock at Germany's passivity which looked like helplessness—as a permanent condition. But now all that was over, and there was instantly, in the minds of the men Mark met, something new; an intense absorption in the tremendous panorama which each day's dispatches unfolded, a violence of opinion and a readiness for argument. There were prophets on every street corner. For the first three days Mark's father spent his time among the crowds which watched every newspaper bulletin board, setting down in the notebook he always carried dozens of overheard remarks which seemed to him striking and significant.

'They're all alike in one respect,' he told Mark. 'It hasn't yet occurred to them that what is happening matters to them as individuals. They're children watching an eruption of Vesuvius, awed and fascinated and even delighted by the wonder of the spectacle without in the least realizing that they are themselves in the path of the lava flow.'

Mark assented. 'That's true,' he agreed. 'And it's curious, when you come to analyze it. A year ago, everyone here was damning Hitler, saying he must be stopped. I heard a dozen men say: "If I were Chamberlain, I'd do so and so." We felt an almost personal humiliation after Munich, and an almost personal pride when England's attitude stiffened. But once the war started, it tended to become an abstraction. Some men still felt hotly about it, but not many. We're like spectators at a football game today.'

On Saturday of that first week, Dan Worth went home to Hardiston. Although he had sold the paper, he would still write its editorials when he chose. 'I've that to do,' he explained. 'And also I want to get farther away, get all this into perspective. Another week here and I might begin to think like you New Englanders.' He chuckled, 'God forbid!' But he promised to come to Hanover for Tony's Commencement, now two months away.

Monday evening, Mark and Bob and Ed and Tom Sheffield dined together at the Union Club. This was at Bob's suggestion. 'We four haven't been getting together as we used to, not for a long time,' he reminded Mark. 'I've missed seeing Tom, and Ed's so tied up with his Navy work that even when he's with us he's thinking about his job.' He went on: 'I'd like to start a new custom, Mark. Let the four of us meet once a month, say; just have an evening when we can talk, or play a little bridge, or maybe do nothing but eat together. Was it Doctor Johnson who said a man's proper business in life should be to keep his friendships in repair?'

Mark thought Bob was changed in these weeks since his illness. This suggestion for the revival of old friendships, for the renewal of ties that had worn thin, was completely unlike anything the other might have proposed a year ago. Mark approved the idea, and Bob got in touch with Tom and with Ed, and they met at the appointed time, all of them at first a little ill at ease, a little embarrassed by this outwardly purposeless reunion. When they ordered cocktails, Bob said cheerfully:

'None for me. The doctors say never again.'

Ed laughed. 'Never's a long time, Bob!'

'Not always,' Bob corrected, in a lower tone; and Mark knew what he was thinking. He saw Ed look at Bob, start to speak, then hold his tongue. Tom alone among them knew less than the truth, and he laughed and said:

'It just seems long, maybe, when you're on the wagon.' Tom was happy to be with these old friends again, his eyes shining, a chuckle in his tones.

'I wish Dave were here, too,' Bob remarked.

'Have you seen Ruth?' Mark asked. Bob nodded, and Mark said: 'Tom, I think she wants to sell the Lincoln house, if you're interested.'

Tom looked at him with a quick attention. 'I certainly am,' he declared. 'Mother and I could be together there, and Tommy's coming home soon. I'll talk it over with her.'

Bob asked: 'Is Tommy going into the bank again?'

'No, he says he's planning to enlist. He thinks the war has just begun.'

Ed said confidently: 'The war's as good as over. Germany's licked herself, by going into Norway.'

'That's what Mr. Churchill says,' Tom eagerly agreed. 'He said Germany has stuck her neck out, laid her head on the block. He said Hitler's invading Norway was as bad a mistake as Napoleon's invading Spain.'

'He's right,' Ed assented. 'England's Navy can force the Skaggerak, cut Germany's supply lines. The Germans in Norway today are gone goslings.' He added strongly: 'Germany's gone, for that matter. This is her last shot. She can't get at France. She can't break the Maginot line; and there's an article in the new *Atlantic* by Lieutenant Colonel Requette of the War College in Brussels. He says a rapid crossing of Belgium to make a surprise attack on France is no longer possible.'

'Professors have been mistaken,' Mark warned him.

Tom urged: 'Germany's getting a licking in Norway already. The British have recaptured Narvik, and they've landed troops, and they've smashed the German fleet, what there was of it.'

Mark spoke quietly. 'Tom, you're an optimist. You've been reading the headlines and believing the dispatches from Stockholm. Our papers snatch at every favorable rumor. The *New York Times* headlines Thursday said the Germans had been driven out of Bergen and Trondheim, and that the British Navy had forced its way up to Oslo and "ordered the Germans out," whatever that means. But none of those things were true then, and they're not true today.' He said: 'Mr. Roosevelt remarked the other day that what's happening in Norway will wake us up in this country, make us start thinking about what this war may lead to. He's right—I hope. It's certainly time to stop believing headlines, and the flood of rumors from Stockholm.'

Bob said: 'The war's certainly come closer to us. That Norwegian girl, the one who used to visit Betty, Ingrid Sigurdson, her home was in Trondheim. I wonder if she's there now.'

For Mark, remembering Ingrid seemed to bring the headlines to life. He saw her as vividly as though she stood before him. There were German soldiers in Trondheim. Some of them perhaps were boys she had known, boys who had visited her brothers in the past. Probably no harm would come to her, unless by the dark chance of stray bullet or bomb or shell; yet remembering her he thought for a moment he heard the thunder of guns, the crackle of rifle fire.

'The war in Poland never was completely real to me,' he commented. 'It might as well have been in Africa. I don't know any Poles—except

Paderewski; but Elin's home is in Sweden, and Ingrid's Norwegian, and Elin's husband was killed in Finland. Scandinavia seems nearer to us than France.'

'The British Navy will force Trondheim Fiord,' Ed predicted. Mark thought the Navy was Ed's God, and men trusted the gods they had made for themselves. 'This invasion of Norway has given England a chance to do something. Remember they had fifty thousand men all ready to throw into Finland. They'll probably shoot that lot right over to Norway.'

The talk turned from the war to politics. Dewey had beaten Vandenberg again in Nebraska, but Bob now thought Willkie would make a better candidate. 'Dewey's a front runner,' he said. 'He'll weaken in the stretch.'

They all agreed in liking Willkie, agreed in opposing a third term. 'Give a man a third term,' Bob predicted, 'and he'll begin to think like that French King—Louis Fourteenth, was it—who said: "I am the state." He'll get delusions of grandeur, think that anyone who disagrees with him is a public enemy.' He laughed. 'Mr. Roosevelt has already reached that stage, even on two terms.'

Mark said reasonably: 'After all, our theory of government is that the people—the majority—make the decision. If they want Mr. Roosevelt, they should have him.'

'If we're in the war, they'll want him,' Ed predicted.

'He's not fit to run a war!' Bob said hotly. 'He hates to admit that any of his appointees is a failure. Of course that's because he hates to admit having made a mistake. But if we do get into the damned war, any man not up to his job ought to be kicked out, whether he's one of the New Deal dreamers or not. And that's something Franklin would never have the guts to do!'

They were all made uncomfortable by the violence of Bob's words, glad to speak of other things. After dinner they played three rubbers of bridge before breaking up. The evening had been a success and they planned to repeat it.

'I'll get in touch with you all,' Bob promised. 'Along toward the middle of May.'

He and Mark drove home together, and Mark commented on their varying attitudes toward the war. 'I suppose we four represent cross-sections of American public opinion,' he reflected. 'Ed's attitude is: "I hate the Germans, but they can't hurt us." Tom says in a wistful way: "They're terrible, but we're beating them—aren't we?" You're like Jerry

Crocker. He has no brief for either side. "They're all a bunch of bastards. Show me one that ain't." And as for me . . .' He hesitated. 'Well, Bob, I'm not as neutral-minded as I was. I've never completely believed the horror tales about concentration camps and all that. I could see that the Germans might feel justified in persecuting the Jews. I could even accept Czecho-Slovakia; and certainly Poland deserved no sympathy. But Norway—well, somehow, Ingrid personifies Norway for me. I've always liked the Scandinavians, anyway. Elin may have something to do with that. Germany's stroke at Norway seems to me quite as evil as Russia's at Finland. Germany can't even plead self-defense. This is an attempt at out-and-out conquest.' And he concluded in a sombre tone: 'No, I'm not as neutral as I was.'

Bob asked challengingly: 'Would you be willing to see Tony go to war to save Norway?'

'I'm not sure about Tony,' Mark admitted. 'But certainly there are some things I'd be willing to die myself to try to save.'

Bob laughed. 'Such as England,' he assented in amused derision. 'I know. But you'll not find many Americans who feel that way.'

'I suspect a lot of us do feel just that way,' Mark declared. 'But we may have to see England in real danger before we realize how we feel.'

Before they parted there was a moment when they both were silent; and then Bob said, almost shyly: 'I think this was a good idea of mine, this dinner, don't you?'

'Grand,' Mark agreed. 'I hope we can make it a regular thing, every month or so.'

'Right,' Bob assented; and he chuckled and added: 'From now on.' They were reminded of the darky who had just been sentenced to life imprisonment, and who asked the court in puzzled tones: 'Does y'all mean f'm now on?' Mark wondered how many of these monthly dinners he and Bob would both attend. When they said good night, on a common impulse, they gripped hands.

2

(April 1940)

The following Saturday, Tony came to Boston. He came without advance notice, taking advantage of an opportunity to ride down with Bill Stanley, who lived in Salem, and coming on to Boston by train.

It was late afternoon when he reached the house. He threw open the front door and called: 'Hi, Dad,' and Mark answered from the living room, quick to meet him in the hall. Tony kissed his father as he had used to do before he went away to college; and Mark saw at once that there was a fine excitement in his son, an eagerness and zest which all this winter had been submerged. It was as though Tony had taken a dose of some powerful and pleasantly stimulating drug. His eyes were shining, and there was a sharper tone in his voice, and brighter color in his cheeks. Mark had seen small boys thus excited and—as the phrase goes—'above themselves' in the presence of an attractive little girl. Tony looked as though he wanted to run up and down and shout and leap and stand on his head and do a thousand hilarious and ridiculous things which his dignity would not permit; and this was in such contrast with his almost sombre reserve all winter that Mark thought perhaps spring, the first warm days, were in his blood. But he had at once a more concrete explanation; for even before Tony tossed aside his hat and coat, he was asking:

'Going to use the car tonight, Dad?' Mark said he was not, said Tony could take it, and Tony explained: 'Lucy and I are driving out to the Wayside Inn for dinner. It's a long time since we've seen each other, except down South. I got a chance to ride down from Hanover and called her up, and she broke a date to go with me. Is it all right with you?'

'Of course,' Mark assured him, realizing that it was the prospect of seeing Lucy which had made this change in Tony, wondering whether it was longing to see her which had made the boy for months so different from his old self. If that were true, then there was a real bond between these two.

Tony went up to change his clothes, and Mark to sit with him while he did so; and Tony talked steadily. 'I saw Mike Hennessy in town today, in the station while I was waiting for my train,' he said. Mike was Tony's old boxing teacher, to whom when he was in Boston he still sometimes went for a friendly round. He laughed. 'I said something about how England was giving the Germans hell now.' The newspapers all this week had reported the activities of the British expeditionary force in Norway, exulting over the successes which Stockholm dispatches chronicled, agreeing that Germany had committed a gross and perhaps a fatal blunder, a blunder that had already cost her a third of her fleet, and that was likely to cost her all the troops in Norway. 'He damned near took a crack at me,' Tony said gleefully. 'Mike always

hated England, you remember. Now he's red-eyed because England
hung a couple of Irishmen for a bomb outrage in Coventry. I hadn't
seen anything about it in the papers. He said it happened last February,
and he said the British just murdered them, because they were members
of the Irish Republican Army, according to Mike, so they were prisoners of war. Do all the Irish hate England as much as Mike does?'

'Hardly all of them,' Mark hazarded. 'And those bombings have been
going on in England for months. They had to be stopped.'

'I never realized till Mike told me that Ireland hadn't declared war
on Germany in this war.'

'No.'

'There are a lot of Irish people in Boston, aren't there?'

'Yes. More than fifty per cent,' Mark said, and he added: 'You can't
blame any Irishman for feeling the way he does, Tony. That Black and
Tan business in Ireland was pretty rough. Ireland was actually in revolt, claimed belligerent rights; but the Black and Tans burned and
looted and murdered right and left. They killed Mike's father and his
brother, you know; just stood them up against a wall. And they burned
his home, turned his mother out. The whole thing left scars in Ireland, in Irish hearts, that may never heal. But of course from England's
point of view the men they were fighting were rebels and criminals, and
they acted on that theory.'

'I know you think most Americans would rather fight Germany than
see England beaten,' Tony reflected. 'But do you think the Irish feel
that way?'

'I think they will if the pinch ever comes. But I may be wrong.'

The talk was interrupted when Tony went to the shower, began
again when he came back still busy with the towel; and Mark while he
talked watched his son, sensing the strong excitement in the younger
man, thinking of Lucy whom Tony was eager now to see. Tonight
these two young people—if Lucy was as eager as Tony—would be
equally intoxicated by their reunion. Mark thought this was perhaps
the hour when he should tell Tony that old tale about Lucy's mother;
but it was good to see the boy thus happy again. He could not bear to
mar that happiness. So he assured himself that what Lucy's mother
was or had been was no discredit to Lucy, and because he could not
bring himself to hurt or distress Tony, he persuaded himself that he
must not injure Lucy.

Tony presently raced away, and though Mark read till late, he was
asleep when the other returned. In the morning Tony did not rouse till

Elin went to wake him, a little after noon, so that he came downstairs just in time for midday dinner with Mark.

Mark met him in the hall and Tony yawned and said: 'Say, I had a real sleep.' They went into the dining room together, and Tony asked: 'Any news today?'

'Well, there's a Stockholm story that fifty thousand French and British troops, equipped with tanks and everything they need, are attacking the Germans in Norway,' Mark told him. 'But practically nothing true has come out of Stockholm yet.' Tony was eating his soup, bending over it; and when he met his father's eyes his own were blank, so that Mark saw the younger man was absorbed in his own thoughts. The exuberance of yesterday was gone. In its place there was—gravity? Determination? Mark found no apt word. Whatever this new change in Tony, his evening with Lucy must have been responsible; and Mark asked, trying to speak casually: 'How's Lucy?'

'Swell,' Tony said, and finished his soup, carefully capturing the last drop.

'I haven't been out to the Wayside Inn for years.'

'It's great. They gave us dinner in the old kitchen. I fixed that, because Lucy likes it. Then we just sat there in front of the fire.'

'I didn't hear you come in.'

'We had a lot of lost time to make up for.' Elin brought the roast and Mark began to carve, and after a moment Tony asked: 'Dad, how's Mrs. Kerr's husband?'

Mark, wondering why Tony asked, said slowly: 'He's alive. We never speak of him, practically never.'

'That's a damned shame. I mean, his living so long. Tough on both of you.' Tony urged: 'Why don't you make her divorce him?' And he said harshly: 'With the world going to pieces around us, anyone who waits for anything is a damned fool.' Mark did not speak, understanding that this was no more than a preamble; and Tony said, facing his father squarely: 'Dad, here's what I'm getting at. Lucy and I want to be engaged.' Mark served their plates, and after a moment Tony said uneasily: 'I guess you're surprised!'

Mark found himself looking up at Elin, who was passing the vegetable dishes, as though he sought for help from her. He said in a thoughtful tone: 'Why, yes, I suppose I am.'

'Of course, with law school ahead of me, I ought not to think about getting married for a long time yet,' Tony admitted.

'Lucy's charming,' Mark said carefully.

'She sure is!'

'It must have been particularly sweet, seeing her again after so long, finding her as glad to see you as you were to see her.'

'It was,' Tony agreed, almost curtly, 'for both of us.'

Mark knew with a sudden clarity that it was too late now to tell Tony that shameful story about Lucy's mother. Tony loved Lucy—or thought he did; and to put any obstacle in the way would only be to provoke the boy to stubborn insistence. Tony loved Lucy and wished to marry her, and Mark could only accept her and love her too; for Tony's loyalty would—rightly—be to Lucy now.

Yet Mark thought he could work for delay; or he might by indirection achieve his end. 'She's so generously affectionate,' he said. 'I think Lucy likes most people.'

'Sure,' Tony grinned. 'She can't help being nice to every fellow she sees, but that's just friendliness!'

Mark spoke carefully. 'Yes, she's a mighty sweet girl. Of course, she won't change.' He chuckled disarmingly. 'Her husband will never be able to afford the luxury of being jealous.'

'Oh, she'll forget all that after we're married.'

'Probably,' Mark agreed. 'Being in love and being married are different in a lot of ways. Being in love is exciting; but being married is quiet and gentle and calm. She'll always like dancing and parties and things.'

'Sure,' Tony assented. 'So will I, at first. But you outgrow that when you settle down!'

Mark did not think Lucy would ever outgrow it, but that was not a thing he could say to Tony, and certainly not now. 'What do Mr. and Mrs. Pride think about it?' he asked.

'We haven't told them yet,' Tony explained. 'I wanted to tell you first, see what you thought.' He looked at his father with a doubtful grin. 'I guess I'm taking it for granted you'll say it's O.K. I mean for us to be engaged.'

Mark hesitated. 'I'm not sure I think well of long engagements.'

Tony for a moment stared at his plate. Then he met his father's eyes. 'Dad, do you still think I ought to go to Law School?'

Mark waited a moment. 'I've always expected you would want to be a lawyer,' he admitted.

'It means three more years' studying.'

'You're still young enough so that you can afford the time.'

Tony cried in a sudden resentment at the world: 'There isn't any time, except today, Dad! Nobody knows where we'll be tomorrow.' He repeated: 'There isn't any time! The world's apt to come tumbling down around our heads.' And he said: 'I'll go to Law School if you say so, but Lucy and I have figured it out. You've always given me a good allowance, and I've saved a lot. I've over a thousand dollars in the bank, besides my insurance. We could live on my allowance. I know we could if we lived at home.'

Mark smiled reassuringly. 'That needn't be necessary. If you lived at home, I don't think you'd work so well, for one thing; and for another, I think the contacts you'd make through living over in Cambridge would be worth your while later on.' He said: 'I can increase your allowance, if you haven't enough.'

'I guess you think I'm crazy, but some fellows do marry even before they finish college, and it seems to work out all right. What do you think?'

Mark had to fight against something like panic. 'Of course, you won't be able to spend much time and energy going to parties and so on,' he suggested. 'Does Lucy understand that?'

'Yes. Sure.'

'What will Mr. and Mrs. Pride say, when you tell them?'

Tony said confidently, grinning at his own words: 'They'll be keen for it. Mrs. Pride told me once she'd sleep better nights after Lucy was married and settled down.'

Mark had a moment's insight into Mrs. Pride's mind. He was able in this instant to comprehend what her life had been, to understand that it had needed courage for her to go on living, seeing every day people who knew her story, facing them with a high, defiant head. And yet she must love Lucy, and to discover in the girl those same qualities of quick affection and of laughing ardor which had brought her to shame must indeed have given her sleepless nights. Marriage, settling down, had not anchored Mrs. Pride in a haven of respectability; yet she could hope and pray they might better serve Lucy and make her safe against herself.

And perhaps she was right! Perhaps Tony was right. Lucy was still young, and if she were affectionate, eager to like and to be liked, why, these traits were not faults in themselves. If she loved Tony, then for her to marry Tony might be the good answer to Mrs. Pride's wistful prayers. How often Lucy's mother must have whispered in her heart: 'Oh, dear God, Lucy's so sweet. Don't let her be the way I am, please, dear God.'

He felt a deep surge of sympathy for this woman whom he had never seen. As much for her sake as for Tony's he said: 'Well, you're the one to decide, son; but I wish you'd wait till after Commencement. That's only two months. You and Lucy can take that long, to be completely sure.'

They agreed upon this. The engagement would be announced—unless some obstacle arose—in June; Tony and Lucy would be married during the summer or early fall. With this much, Tony was content and grateful; but Mark still hoped that what could not otherwise be helped, time might cure.

3

(May 2, 1940)

Tommy Sheffield and Mary Clancy were married on the second of May; and all Tom's old friends were invited to the wedding. Mark saw Bob and Nell and Ed and Mary Halstead and Ruth Rollins there. Tony and Will and Jan were at Hanover or at Merryfield, and Edwin Halstead was at Bowdoin. Fifteen-year-old Ann came with Ed and Mary, and Mark thought she had become almost a young woman since he last saw her. The younger boys Mary left at home. 'They think weddings are silly,' she explained. 'Burt's at that age, and Dan was too young to come.'

Betty Ritchie stayed away. 'Because it's a Catholic wedding,' Bob told Mark resentfully. 'I wish I'd used a hairbrush more often on Betty when she was a kid.' Tom Sheffield had explained to Mark a day or two before:

'Tommy became a Catholic last year. Miss Clancy's a grand girl and I'm mighty fond of her; but I was disturbed by that.' He added: 'But Mother highly approves, so I guess it's all right.'

Mark said thoughtfully: 'I'm not a church-goer myself—although I was brought up to be. It has often seemed to me that if I ever felt the need of a formal religion I would become a Catholic. Certainly no other church has such a hold upon the minds and hearts of its people. I suppose that's because it has a permanence, an eternal quality, a tradition of long service and loyalty, which most Protestant churches lack. It's endured through a good many centuries, itself largely unchanged in the midst of constant change. Young men nowadays need something stable to which they can cling. I'm glad Tommy's found it.'

After the ceremony there was a reception—at a social hall which Mary's father had engaged for the occasion—where what seemed to Mark to be hundreds of people gathered. When Tommy, standing proudly beside his bride, had greeted them all, he sought out Mark to give him Einar's worn old pocketbook, with Elin's and little Anna's picture in it.

'He didn't ask me to bring them to her,' Tommy said. 'Because he never thought he might be killed. Even after he was dead, even when I knelt beside him, I couldn't believe it. He was so damned much alive a minute before.' He said: 'I took this out of his pocket right then. Probably I could have sent it, but I liked having it in my pocket, and I knew by that time that Finland would soon be beaten, that I'd be coming home.'

Mark thanked him. 'Elin will probably write to you herself,' he said; and he suggested: 'I expect you've been wishing you were in Norway during the fighting there.' The Norwegian campaign was over. The ten days past had seen a succession of optimistic dispatches from Stockholm. A fast-swinging British and French expeditionary force, hammering away with a battering ram of tanks, was battling the Germans along a line from just above Trondheim to the Swedish border north of Oslo—or so said Stockholm; and the headlines shouted: 'British Foil Nazi Attack.' 'Allies Wage Decisive Battles.' 'Nazis' Lightning Drive Stopped.' But now Chamberlain was facing an angry Parliament and it was clear that Norway was lost.

'No,' Tommy said. 'Finland proved to me that sooner or later we'd have to fight Germany and Russia, and I want to get ready to help. I knew Norway had no chance.'

'Didn't you believe all the good news from Stockholm?'

'I don't believe any good news,' Tommy assured him. 'The worst thing that can happen to us in this country is to believe good news, to begin to think things are going our way. This war has just begun.'

Then someone else claimed Tommy, and big Matt Clancy, Mary's father, took Mark's arm. 'Come along with me, Your Honor,' he said cordially. 'Into the other room away from this. There's one there wants to pay her compliments to you.' Mark had shaken Matt's hard hand in the reception line, had felt even in that moment an emanation of strong and lusty friendliness in the big man, which immediately attracted him. Matt Clancy was American born, the youngest son of one of the many Irishmen who came to Boston in the years before the War Between the States. His father had been a laborer, and Matt himself at twelve years old went to work as water boy on a construction job. He had a quality of merry wit, and a trick of singing haunting Irish songs that brought tears to Irish eyes; and when he grew old enough for heavier work, he early evidenced a capacity for finding short cuts which made it possible to finish a task in less time. 'It was no more than laziness in me,' he liked to say, with that great booming laugh of his. 'But it's laziness—finding easier ways to do things—that makes a man get ahead.' At nineteen he was a foreman, at twenty-two he took his first contract—for a piece of excavation. 'Digging the cellar and foundation trenches for a great mansion twenty foot one way and twelve the other,' he used to say, recounting the familiar tale. 'And a proud man I was when I had the papers signed, and prouder the night I met my first payroll, to the men I'd hired.' For ten or fifteen years he worked with his hands, side by side with his men, on ever more important undertakings. 'And I can do the work of two men today,' he might boast. 'And I've done it, whenever there was need.' But for twenty years past his interests had been so wide and so varied that most of his time was given to the business rather than to the construction end of his work.

He led Mark proudly to where a little old woman in shining black, with a fine lace collar and cuffs and a lace cap on her soft white hair, sat in a high carved chair with her feet upon a stool. The men and women clustering around her fell back and the big man thrust Mark proudly forward. 'Here he is, Mother,' he said. 'His Honor himself, and many's the time you've heard of him from Tommy and from Charley Land.'

Mark took her old small hand, bones in a loose wrinkled skin, and bowed before her, and her black eyes sparkled and she said: 'Aye, I have so. His father's best friend, Tommy says you are.'

She still held Mark's hand, and Mark said smilingly: 'I think a lot of Tommy, too.'

She tugged at him, drew him nearer, nodded as though to say: 'Lean down to me, I've a word for your private ear.' Mark obeyed that gesture and she said in a sharp whisper: 'Then why did you not rid them both of that harpy that's preyed on them so long?' Mark did not find an answer and she laughed at him and tossed her head. 'My Mary gave her what was due her, and a good thing, too.'

'If Mary takes after her grandmother, Tommy's the lucky one,' Mark told her, smiling; and she released his hand, seemed to push him away, cried:

'Go along with you. I'm too old a cat to be caught with butter.' She caught her son's eye. 'Take him into the back room, Matt. Give him a drop to warm him there.'

Over their fiery drams, taken straight and all standing, Matt Clancy said: 'Eh, but it's a pity, one way, that you're on the bench, Your Honor. It's a grand politician you'd make. If you ever wanted to, you could be Governor any time.'

Mark laughed quietly. 'I'm afraid you don't know me very well.'

'I do, and who does not,' Matt Clancy assured him. His eyes were shrewd. 'D'ye think there's a judge on the bench I don't know all there is to be known about him, me that never has less than a dozen cases in the courts any time? It's my business to know them, Your Honor: the ones that are a little slow of wit, so that I'll send a clever lawyer to beguile them; and the ones that are puffed with dignity, so I must tell my lawyer to put on his cutaway and his striped pants to face them; and the ones that are kind, so I can send a young blundering man and the judge will be sorry for him and help him make his case; and the ones . . .'

Mark chuckled. 'I didn't know that side of the law. I thought it was the juries you tried to win.'

'Sure and juries are easy—unless they can see the judge is down on you. Let a jury see the judge look at you with a kind eye and your case is half won.'

'I've never seen you in court, have I?'

Matt winked. 'Not I. Say I was to show myself and there was a man on the jury had ever worked for me. The case would be thrown out of court. I keep my friends, Your Honor. No, I've no need to watch a judge in action to know what manner of man he is. The Governor said to me: "Matt, what would you think of Mark Worth for the Superior Bench?" I said to him: "I'll take them as they come and find a way to make them think well of me." So the next I heard, he'd spoke to you—and you'd withdrawn your name because your boy got into a bit of trouble with the police.' His tone was almost resentful. 'Man, man, if you'd only come to me, knowing me or not, I'd have fixed that up for you in the wink of an eyelash. But all the same, after that, said I to the Governor: "Next time, he's your man." ' He chuckled and clapped Mark on the shoulder. 'Did you ever hear what Charley Land said about you—and how could you, to be sure?'

'Who is he?'

'It was him put you through the sieve that day the Governor sent for you the first time.'

'Of course, I remember.' Mark had guessed on that occasion that he was under scrutiny.

'Charley told the Governor to appoint you. "Get him on the bench as quick as you can," he said. "Because if you don't and he ever goes into politics, the Republicans will have the state in their pocket as long as he lives. For I never saw a man," says Charley, "that can say as many things you don't believe and make you like him for saying them, to match that one."'

Mark laughed. 'I'm not a Republican,' he objected.

'Nor a Democrat, to be sure,' Matt Clancy agreed. 'You're your own man. That's what Charley said. He said any man you talked to would always think you were on the other side from him—and want to cross over to your side. Another drop of this, now.' He picked up Mark's small glass. 'A one-legged man walks lame.'

Mark was warmed as much by the big man's generous words as by the liquor. Some of Matt's friends joined them, and someone brought in Tom and Ed Halstead, till this small room was crowded, and another bottle was opened and another; and tongues were loosened, and the talk turned to the war, and Matt and his friends alternately damned England for her failure in Norway and exulted in the defeats she had suffered there.

Mark and Ed presently moved into the other room together, and Ed said in dry amusement: 'Well, Mark, there was mighty little love for England in that crowd.'

'They're glad to see her get her bumps,' Mark admitted. 'As long as the bumps aren't serious. Just as a mother, if a disobedient child falls down and bruises itself, might say: "There, you see, it serves you right." But I think that's a superficial feeling. They'll not stand by and see England lose.'

'Ireland has kept out of it so far.'

'Wait till the pinch comes,' Mark insisted; yet he admitted to himself that it was true that very few men of Irish birth or ancestry felt any loyalty to England. The Black and Tans had killed that, once for all. It was even possible that an unfriendly Ireland was the Achilles' heel which would defeat England in this war. Certainly if England could base her fleet on Ireland it would be infinitely easier for her to police the sea lanes through which her life blood flowed. Ed spoke of this now, as though he had read Mark's thoughts.

'Probably England will have to take the Irish ports before she's done,' he said. 'In northern Ireland, anyway.'

'German planes from Norway can make it hot for her there.'

Ed laughed. 'You and your planes! You're still barking up that tree. Why, man, the Germans dropped a thousand-pound bomb fairly on the *Rodney* without doing any serious damage.'

'I read that, yes,' Mark agreed. 'And I'm sorry it happened. It will convince you Navy men that planes needn't worry you—and you'll go on, trustingly, till German planes sink a few battleships for you.' He said more strongly: 'Why, man, don't you realize that planes drove the British Navy out of Norwegian waters? They protected German transports, and they made it impossible for England to reinforce her troops in Norway. Planes won this Norwegian campaign.'

Bob Ritchie and Nell and Mary joined them, and Bob said: 'Come on, let's get out of here. I've just been trying to sell Willkie to Mr. Clancy and I'm hoarse.' He had heard Ed's prediction, and he added: 'You and your Navy! You're always spoiling for a fight. Did you see where Admiral Taussig said we were going to have to fight Japan?'

Ed grinned. 'That would be like shooting fish,' he declared. 'We'd clean them up in a month.'

'Don't be too sure of that,' Bob warned him. 'They're apt to do what they did to the Russians at Port Arthur, block the Panama Canal, or sink half our battleships without bothering to declare war.'

Ed laughed at him. 'You can't get around sea power,' he declared, and Mark half smiled. Ed was a Navy man, so he believed that battleships could win a war, just as generals put their trust in an army, and fliers in the air forces; and business men wanted a business man like Willkie for President, and lawyers never quite trusted anyone except other lawyers. Was there anywhere a composite man able to allocate to each element in the great problem its proper and proportionate importance?

As though in answer to the question in his mind, he caught sight of Jerry Crocker looking lost and unhappy in the crowd and moved toward him and said smilingly at his shoulder: 'Hullo, what are you doing here?' They had not seen each other since Mark cleared the title to Jerry's house.

At Mark's word, Jerry wheeled around sharply; but when he recognized Mark he relaxed. 'Oh, I've known Matt Clancy for years,' he said. 'I just got here. Where is he?'

'In the back room. I'll show you.'

Jerry grinned. 'Right. Let's see what the boys in the back room are having. A mob like this gets me down.'

Mark led the way, but the crowd in the hall blocked them and they stayed in talk there. 'I've been thinking of you lately,' Mark confessed. 'Wishing I'd run into you—or someone like you, with an honest and informed and balanced point of view. I'm pretty sick of the wishful-thinking we're being fed by the newspapers—and Chamberlain and Churchill—in this Norwegian business.'

Jerry nodded. 'They're all a bunch of bastards . . .'

'I know,' Mark smiled. 'But—do you include our own newspaper editors? Haven't we a right to expect a little common sense from those upon whom we depend for information? Instead of a lot of fatuous optimism.'

'We're a nation of optimists,' Jerry reminded him. 'Optimists and blovalating blowhards.'

'That's not altogether our fault,' Mark suggested. 'We've lived for generations in a land where if one opportunity were wasted, there was always another waiting to be seized; and if we were wasteful, why, our resources were—or appeared to be—inexhaustible.'

'Those days are just about over,' Jerry declared. 'Optimism is as dangerous today as a stupefying drug.' And he said in a harsh anger: 'Before Poland we were told that the Polish army would raise hell with the Germans. After Poland flopped, instead of admitting that Germany had the stuff, the same people told us that Poland was a hollow shell. When Germany went into Norway, Churchill told us Hitler had made a fatal mistake, and the military attaché of the British Embassy in Washington said there would be two hundred thousand English troops in Norway by midsummer; but now England's pulling out of Norway, leaving the Norwegians to take the rap!' He added grimly: 'Probably Belgium and France will come next.'

Mark asked in grave concern: 'Really? You look for that?'

'Certain!' Jerry said precisely: 'Beginning with Czecho-Slovakia, Germany has been fighting the Battle of Europe. I believe she'll conquer the whole continent—and possibly England, too—within the next year.' Ruth Rollins, catching Mark's eye, came toward them through the crowd as Jerry went on: 'France and England have been fed on the same soothing syrup we're lapping up. They've thought they could sit tight behind the Maginot line while England's Navy starved Germany to death.' Then Ruth greeted Mark, and Jerry saw her and gulped down his last word and turned to escape, but Mark touched his arm, made introductions.

'Jerry comes nearer knowing the truth about European affairs than any man I know,' he told Ruth; and Jerry colored miserably. He was a bachelor, not from any dislike for womankind, but from a deep-rooted fear of them which was a part of his fear of being swayed by any sentimental consideration. Ruth saw this instantly, with the fine and tender understanding which some women possess; and to avoid increasing his distress she said at once:

'I didn't mean to interrupt you, Uncle Mark.'

She would have left them, but Mark made her stay, his hand through her arm; and he said to Jerry: 'I wish you were editing our newspapers, or doing a radio comment or something. Why don't you write a book?'

'I'm working on one,' Jerry admitted.

'I'd like to read it.'

'No one will ever publish it.'

'About the war?'

Ruth stood quietly, and every author likes to talk about his work. Jerry began to forget her. ' "Cold Truth About the War," ' he assented. 'I've a stack of manuscript at home this high.' He measured off six inches between his hands. Then he grinned: 'The trouble is no one can read my handwriting.'

'You need a secretary.' Mark thought of Ruth here beside him, and the idea pleased him.

'She'd have to be able to puzzle out my turkey tracks,' Jerry said. 'And I can't even do that myself.'

Ruth saw how uncomfortable he was in her presence and freed her arm from Mark's touch. 'I want to say hello to Uncle Ed and Aunt Mary,' she explained, and moved away, and Mark after a moment suggested:

'There's a girl who could do that job for you, Jerry.' He added, remembering that under the other's violent hatred of sham and hypocrisy and ignorance there was always a quality of compassion: 'Her father's dead, and she's been taking a secretarial course and—she needs a job.' There was no reason to tell Jerry that that need was not financial; that Ruth needed not so much a job as friends. Let him sympathize with her if he would.

Jerry looked after her. 'She's a nice-looking girl,' he said. 'And she doesn't talk all the time.'

'I've known her since she was a child. She's had a hard row to hoe. I'd like to see her get a break.'

'I'd like to finish this book,' Jerry admitted. His voice rasped with anger at his own thoughts. 'Damn it, Judge, it's time someone spoke

out in meeting. We still think of England as omnipotent, but Germany
has her scared. England didn't dare risk battleships in Norway. She
sent a few soldiers with not enough tanks and guns, and the German
planes butchered them. We talk a lot about the Fifth Column as a sort
of apology for German success; and in our indignation at German
treachery we discount German victories. But the German success—however it was won—is what matters.'

Mark nodded, smiling a little. 'The lawyer tells his client: "They
can't put you in jail for that." But the poor devil is in a cell all the
same.'

'Right,' Jerry agreed. 'It's high time we stopped saying: "The Germans didn't play fair" and remember that fair or foul, they're winning,
and that in war the winner makes the rules.'

'I'd like to read that book of yours. Take Miss Rollins, give her a try.'

Jerry turned to look around the crowded room, but Ruth was not in
sight. 'A girl as nice as she is won't have any trouble getting a job,' he
said evasively.

'You'll have trouble finding anyone as intelligent as she,' Mark assured him. 'Let me give you her address. Then if you decide to try
her . . .'

'Hell, man, I couldn't work with a woman.'

Mark laughed. 'Pshaw! When I'm dictating to my girl, I forget she's
there. Besides, this would be just copying. You don't need to be with
her. Just mail her your manuscript, let her do the work at her apartment.'

In the end Jerry noted down the address Mark gave him, and driving homeward presently Mark hoped the other would get in touch
with Ruth. It seemed to him that they were in different ways the two
loneliest people he knew.

4

(May 11, 1940)

The British withdrew from Norway, and Chamberlain fatuously
boasted that the retreat had been accomplished without the loss of a
man; but Churchill, more honest, admitted defeat and accepted the
blame for it. He admitted that England had been able to land only
twelve thousand ill-equipped troops in Norway to face ten times that

many Germans; and he admitted that he himself had refused to risk major fleet units in an effort to do more. The swift days sped, and Germany attacked Holland and Belgium, and although he had half expected this, Mark felt the world tremble under his feet at the shock of that colossal impact.

One result was that on Saturday morning he went down to see Bob at his office. He had decided—since the world seemed to be coming to an end, since his own health was uncertain, since Tony in another month would graduate from college, since Tony would be twenty-one in the fall, and since quite possibly Tony and Lucy would be married this summer—to rearrange his will, made after Nan died. The possibility of his own death at any time had been for a year or two now always in the back of his mind. An occasional thumping in his chest, an occasional faint sensation of stifling kept him reminded that his heart was not completely sound.

After their talk together, he and Bob decided to lunch in town. When the Germans struck in the Lowlands, Chamberlain had resigned and Churchill took his place; and Mark thought well of Churchill.

'At least he doesn't sugar-coat bad news,' he reminded Bob. 'Day before yesterday—even before the Germans attacked—he said England was in greater danger than at any time during the last war.'

Bob nodded. 'I wish the newspapers would imitate him. You saw the morning paper headlines: "Dutch and Belgians stop the Germans: Allies Pour Men Over Borders." "Dutch Leader Lauds Troops; Says Blitzkrieg Has Failed." It makes me sick!'

Mark asked after a moment: 'Bob—are you scared? I'm beginning to be. These Germans are good.'

'They're good fighters,' Bob agreed. 'But I'm not scared, because it's none of our business. The Germans won't do anything to get us down on them, and the Allied propaganda won't work this time, Mark. We'll not get into this war.'

'All the same, I'm scared,' Mark repeated, though smilingly. 'You know we only have about half a million men in our army—and they're not equipped. It would take eighteen months to give them what they need—even if we don't enlarge the army. Suppose Germany occupies the Channel ports. She can bomb England to death.' He added: 'I'm scared, and I'm mad too. Norway, and now Holland, and Belgium. This man Hitler has to be stopped—and we may have to do it.'

Bob laughed. 'Keep your shirt on, old man. England's been warning the neutrals that she might have to ignore their rights. If she'd been smart, she'd have occupied the Low Countries herself. Maybe she was planning to, but Germany got there first, that's all.'

'That's a cold-blooded point of view.'

Bob said grimly: 'Wake up, Mark. War's a cold-blooded business, and Hitler's playing for keeps. He hasn't any scruples. He'll do anything to win. Well, it's up to England and France to be just as tough as he is.' And he said in a sharp anger: 'Why, damn it, man, which would be better, for England to occupy Holland and Belgium—conquer them if necessary—or for her to let Hitler lick her?'

Mark hesitated. 'Damned if I know,' he admitted. 'Ethical principles are so firmly planted in us—and in the English—that we can't just say: "To hell with decency and honor. I'm going to do this anyway." We have to . . .' He smiled. 'Well, we have to persuade ourselves first that what we're doing is the decent and honorable thing to do.'

'Like a woman.' Bob laughed. 'She can always kid herself into thinking that she ought to do what she wants to do.'

'I suppose it's a form of—intellectual dishonesty,' Mark assented. 'Like telling ourselves today—I read an editorial this evening—that the Blitzkrieg is a failure because the Germans aren't in Paris yet.'

'Sure, I read that too,' Bob agreed. 'But the point was farther down, where it said the U.S. was completely unified in its insistence that we're not going to be dragged into this war.'

'I'm beginning to lose my mental balance,' Mark confessed. 'To let myself be tricked into believing what I hope. I tell myself that when Germany beat Poland she was just picking on a cripple, but that now she's up against the big league. Everybody seems to agree that the French army is the best in the world.'

'Well, if it is or it isn't, it's no skin off our onion,' Bob declared. 'Let them have their fun.' He added: 'I see the famine in China's so bad they're eating each other. The Japs arrested some Chinese shopkeepers in Swatow the other day for selling human flesh. They'll be starving in Europe, too, if this keeps on.'

They drove home together. On the way Bob told Mark that Tom Sheffield had bought back from Ruth the Lincoln house. 'Passed the papers this morning,' he said. 'Ruth's a great girl.'

Mark put the car into the garage and they parted. When Mark came into the house, Elin appeared to greet him, and she had news. 'Tony came home from college,' she said. 'He went right out again, and he won't be here for dinner, but he said he'd be back early.'

Mark was surprised, yet vaguely apprehensive, too. Something in Elin's tone disturbed him. Tony had undoubtedly come to Boston to see Lucy. He asked: 'How is he, all right?'

She hesitated. 'He looked bad,' she admitted. 'Sort of worried, and tired.'

5

(May 11, 1940)

It was only a little after ten that night when Tony appeared, and Mark was still downstairs, writing to Robin at his desk in the living room. He heard a car stop outside the house, guessed that Lucy had brought Tony home; and he thought she might come in and hoped she would not, unwilling to see her, doubting his own ability to put on toward her a cordiality he did not feel, and which he must feel toward the girl Tony was to marry. The car stood there for a considerable time, and then Mark heard one of its doors slam, and the starter grind, and the car moved away as Tony opened the front door.

Mark called: 'Hi, son,' and went to meet Tony in the hall. 'Well, glad to see you. I didn't know you were coming down.'

Tony laughed. 'I didn't know myself, but I had a letter from Lucy and she—it made me want to see her.' They came in to the living room together.

'How is she?'

'O.K.' Tony sat down, lighting a cigarette, flipping the match toward the hearth; and Mark realized that the boy was troubled, had some word he wished to say. To let Tony take his own time he remarked:

'Well, this is the real thing in Europe now.'

Tony nodded. 'It's easier to take, in some ways,' he commented. 'The waiting's over. You feel that your future is being decided for you over there and you don't have to worry about anything; just go with the current.' He added: 'This war will be over, soon—because we're not ready to take a hand.'

'You think the Germans will beat England and France, then?'

'Either beat them or come so near it they'll be glad to make peace. Then we'll have the collapse of Europe, economic confusion, panic, mass starvation. More people will die from starvation than the war will kill.'

'The last war started in much the same way,' Mark suggested. 'With

German successes. After all, Germany hasn't got far yet—and even if she does, she may be stopped when her first momentum is lost.'

'You can't judge by the last war,' Tony urged. 'Things will happen faster, this time. You didn't have parachute troops capturing cities last time, for instance.'

'Rotterdam seems to be holding out.'

Tony sat staring at the fire, and he spoke in a low tone so that Mark thought it was as though, listening, he heard the dreams of youth. The young men dream dreams, dreams of a fine brave world. Tony was saying: 'I think maybe out of this war will come a good and permanent peace. The only hope for that is an incredibly wise, thoroughly just group of peacemakers who know their responsibility and are capable of doing what may be the greatest good ever done to mankind. I can see some hope of a good peace in an Allied victory, very little hope for one in a German victory. I believe the Germans must be beaten, either by the Allies or by us, and with them the gangster elements in Russia and Japan, and possibly Italy. But there is hope even in a German victory. There are Germans who may come to power with more wisdom, more justice, more intelligence, more foresight, and less vindictiveness than any men the Allies or we can choose to name the conditions of peace. Men like Otto Strasser might make a better peace than men like Churchill. And men like Strasser might be able to help the suffering of all the have-nots, particularly Russia and Japan. We can't be done with war until we are just toward everyone.'

Mark did not speak, and Tony went on: 'Perhaps it is youth, perhaps it is foolishness, but I believe we can build a better world on the ashes of the one we are losing. I believe we need not destroy all of this one. And I believe this better world can be built by Germany. I believe it is more likely to be built by the Allies—but I believe German victory will not necessarily condemn us all to decades of world-wide suffering. Lippmann says if Germany wins we won't see peace in our time. I think he's wrong.'

Mark, listening, was less attentive to what Tony said than to Tony himself. He thought that Tony was no longer a boy. There was a new maturity in the young man tonight, as though he were working out for himself a firm philosophy. Mark said in a low tone, almost tenderly: 'You're a grown man, Tony. You've passed from boyhood to manhood this winter.'

Tony turned his head slowly to look at his father, and he spoke half to himself with a faint bitterness. 'It's about time,' he said. For a moment he was silent, and then he rose, stood by the hearth, his hands clasped behind him, facing the older man. 'Dad,' he said strongly, 'Lucy and I want to be married right away.'

Mark waited, feeling an odd tremor in his breast as though his heart had leaped into a furious beat. 'Right away?' he repeated emptily.

'As soon as I graduate,' Tony said. He hesitated, and his eyes met his father's squarely, and his voice was a man's voice. 'Or maybe, before. I don't know which would be the best. You see, Dad—Lucy's going to have a baby.'

For a long time—a short instant that seemed interminable—there was silence then between them. Mark's first thought was: 'Mea culpa. Mine the guilt.' If he had told Tony long ago Lucy's heritage, he might have saved his son. But there was no time now for weak self-condemnation. Now, more than ever before, Tony needed him; needed him completely. That tall young man standing there by the hearth was in fact not a man but a bewildered boy, not knowing what to do, needing his father's steady, strengthening, and guiding hand.

He wished to speak, yet it was Tony who first found words, and Mark recognized at once the truth of what his son said. 'You're blaming Lucy,' Tony hazarded. 'You're bound to do that, because you love me. But don't, Dad, because she's going to be my wife.' He smiled appealingly. 'And you're going to love her for my sake.' And he said: 'It's my fault, and hers, too, of course. She says it's all her fault.' He hesitated, went bravely on: 'Her mother's a sort of fool, Dad. She made a fool of herself years ago. Lucy told me about it, last summer.' His cheeks reddened in a shamed way. 'I was almost crazy, when the war started. I was down there with her, and nothing seemed to matter. The world was going to hell in a week, and I didn't see any sense in holding on to anything. I was ready to do anything to forget the war, and Lucy wanted to— reassure me, be sweet to me. She loves me, you know, Dad. Really. I told her there was nothing left in the world to hold on to, and she said I could be sure of her always.'

Mark heard again Robin's words, offering him comfort. 'I'm going to make you sure of me.'

'And when I felt rotten about it,' Tony went on, 'she said it was her fault, not mine; and she said she was just naturally bad—and she told me about her mother.' He spoke in a flat tone. 'Mr. Pride isn't Lucy's real father, Dad.'

So Lucy had told Tony that story. How long had Lucy herself known it? Her mother must have told her, in some moment of dreadful terror

provoked by Lucy's generous fondness for the boys she knew. Probably
Mrs. Pride had sought to warn Lucy to be on guard against this weakness in herself. He imagined her saying: 'I've been wicked, wicked,
wicked, darling; and you're like me. But please don't be, please don't be
like me.' He felt a sudden deep pity for this woman whom he had never
seen, and who for all her light and heedless follies had had the courage
to tell her daughter the shameful truth.

He said at last: 'I'm sorry, Tony, of course. But you know—I don't
blame either you or Lucy, not as much as you think. When a great war
begins, something stirs in young people everywhere. The human race
has a persistent habit of multiplying. War, threatening to kill human
beings by the millions, has a profound psychological effect on all of us.
The number of marriages increases, the birth rate rises. You and Lucy
were in the grip of something much bigger than your mutual attraction
for each other.'

Tony said soberly: 'Maybe. But we didn't—make excuses to ourselves.
We decided not to see each other till next summer, but this spring I
wanted to see her, terribly. We'd waited long enough to be sure of
ourselves. We'd only been writing once a month, but we felt just the
same. So I came home in April to see her, and when I did, it was so
wonderful. We sort of went crazy, I guess.'

Mark nodded. 'I saw how much happier you were, that night you
came home,' he agreed in strong reassurance. 'You'd been so obviously
unhappy and at loose ends all winter.' He said: 'Sit down, Tony. Let's
make some plans.'

The next hour was for Mark in many ways a happy one. He forgot
everything except his pride that Tony, needing help and counsel, had
come to him; and he found a keen, contenting pleasure in being able
to help Tony now, to discuss what should be done. They would be
married immediately after Tony's graduation, announcing the engagement at once. Then they would take an apartment in Cambridge, as
though Tony still planned to go to Law School in the fall; but toward
the summer's end they could announce a change of plans, and Tony
would go instead to—say—the University of Virginia, and they would
live quietly there, and make some excuse not to come home at Christmas,
so that there need be no fuel for wagging tongues, no counting off of
months. 'We can work it all out when the time comes,' Mark promised.
'You and Lucy and I between us.' And he asked: 'Will Lucy tell her
father and mother?'

'No, no,' Tony said quickly. 'Not if we can manage so they needn't know. Mrs. Pride's anxious for Lucy to be married. She'll get a great kick out of arranging things in such a hurry. She's awfully good-hearted, Dad, even if she is a fool.'

And when at last he said good night—Mark would finish his letter to Robin before going to bed—Tony said gratefully: 'You're pretty wonderful, Dad. I've always known that, of course, but never so much as now. It's almost been worth—getting into this mess—to see how you've acted about it.'

'It's almost been worth it to me,' Mark acknowledged honestly, 'to have a chance to—help you, and to have you come to me for help.'

He sat down at his desk again, after Tony was gone upstairs; but he did not at once begin to write, reluctant to tell Robin the truth. She would blame neither Tony nor Lucy, yet something still restrained him. In the end he told her only that Tony wished to marry Lucy in June, that he had agreed.

'We're to see her and Mrs. Pride tomorrow,' he explained. 'Have a family conclave.' And he added: 'From what Tony tells me, Mrs. Pride has been a pretty good mother to Lucy, the best mother she knew how to be. I think Lucy and Tony are going to be fine. Already this has brought me and Tony closer together than we ever were before. You know how that pleases me.'

6

(May 12, 1940)

Sunday afternoon, Mark and Tony called in due form on Mr. and Mrs. Pride. Tony had paved the way, going to see Lucy's father and mother that morning; and he reported at dinner that Mrs. Pride was as delighted as he had known she would be.

When they arrived at the Pride home, Lucy and Tony almost at once disappeared together; and Mark, a little terrified at the prospect, was left alone with the older people. Mark had met Mr. Pride long ago, but he had no clear recollection of the other. He found him a gentle little man with an eager friendliness which made Mark like him at once. To like people—as Mr. Pride so clearly did—was the surest road to being liked yourself. They said the things parents always say on such occasions. Mr. Pride told Mark: 'We're mighty happy about this, Judge Worth. Mrs. Pride and I long ago agreed that we liked Tony immensely. He's a splendid young man.'

'I'm fond of Lucy too,' Mark told him. 'I've not seen her as often as I'd have liked, but no one who ever saw her could easily forget her.'

'We're very proud of her,' Mr. Pride assented. Mark had been uncomfortably afraid that the other might think himself bound to tell the truth about Lucy's paternity, but Mr. Pride had long ago accepted Lucy as his own daughter, and in that acceptance there was no reservation and no apology. Mark was relieved when he saw that this was true. He had expected to feel toward this man that faint scorn which is the accepted portion of the betrayed husband; but clearly, when Mr. Pride took his wife back into his life, it had been like a renewal, for better or for worse, of the sacrament of marriage, which blotted out even from his memory whatever had gone before. Thus now he respected Mrs. Pride and he respected himself, and it was impossible to condescend to such a man.

Mark found Mrs. Pride to be superficially a pretty, giddy, light-witted, laughing woman who perhaps exaggerated her happy pleasure in the discussion of plans for the announcement of the engagement, for the June wedding. But behind this mask Mark felt a profound and reverent thankfulness that Lucy, the fruit of her own waywardness, was presently to be married to a nice boy, with whom she would presumably live loyally and happily forever after. For years, watching Lucy grow into an ardent and seductive girlhood, Mrs. Pride had lived a life of secret terror, of humble prayer; and not content with empty prayers she had with a rare courage confessed her own fault, hoping thus to warn Lucy against the pitfalls inherent in her heritage. Now that long fight, that fight to save Lucy, was over, and she was full of triumphant happiness.

Mark thought she must never know the truth. To know it, to know that she had failed after all, might be more than this tormented woman could endure.

She told Mark frankly: 'No one will ever know, Judge Worth, how much it means to me to have Lucy safely married.' He wondered whether she guessed—since she knew Nell Ritchie, knew how close he and Nell were—that Nell must have told him the truth. Her tone suggested this, as though she said humbly: 'You know what I've done. But I've loved Lucy so. Thank you for letting your splendid son marry her.' Mark, to his own astonishment, found himself liking and respecting Mr. Pride, found himself almost admiring Mrs. Pride, before he and Tony said good-bye.

Tony and Lucy reappeared only when Mark rose at last, and Mrs.

Pride called: 'Lucy dear, Judge Worth's going now.' When the two young people came into the room, Lucy was flushed and radiant, her eyes soft, her whole countenance somehow shining as though illumined from within. She came straight to Mark, threw her arms around his neck, kissed him; and there were grateful tears in her eyes and the faint salt taste of tears upon her lips, and she held him tight and whispered:

'You're so wonderful! I love you so. Thank you! Oh, thank you. I promise to be the best wife for Tony. I promise truly.'

His arms around her shoulders, he felt the extraordinary tingling sweetness in her. 'I know you will,' he said gently, bound to love her for Tony's sake. 'You're a grand girl, Lucy. I know you will.'

She kissed him again, laughing up at him, and linked her arm through his, going with him and Tony to the car; and Tony shook hands with Mr. Pride, and kissed Mrs. Pride, and kissed Lucy last of all. Driving homeward together, Tony said at last: 'You were swell, Dad.'

'Did you tell Lucy—that I knew?'

'Yes. She thinks you're grand.'

'She's pretty fine herself,' Mark said reassuringly, feeling in Tony the doubts and the hopeless regrets which could never be admitted. 'I like her; and I like Mr. and Mrs. Pride.'

But Tony only repeated: 'You were swell!'

7

(May 1940)

Mark told Bob and Nell Monday morning that Tony's engagement was to be announced at once. To tell them was necessary, yet he dreaded doing so; but they seemed not at all surprised, and—since what was done could not be mended—they made no reference to Mrs. Pride. Bob said: 'I think he's smart; Lucy's a charming girl.' And Nell exclaimed: 'There, I knew it was bound to happen soon. The war gives people ideas. I'm surprised Betty hasn't got herself engaged long ago.' Then, as though anxious to get away from dangerous ground, she asked: 'But what about you, Mark? That will leave you alone. Isn't it about time you and Robin . . .'

Bob, to Mark's relief, interrupted, asking: 'Will Tony go on with Law School just the same?'

'Oh, yes,' Mark told them. 'But possibly not at Harvard. Lucy has so many friends here, they'd never be left alone. They're going to take an apartment in Cambridge for the summer, see how it works; but if they find they're too popular, Tony may go to Michigan, or perhaps Virginia, somewhere where they won't know so many people.' Bob agreed that this might be wise.

Mark was at dinner that evening when Jan Ritchie came hurrying in, and kissed him and made him sit down again. 'I've only got a minute,' she explained. 'I came down for Peg Merritt's dance tonight—going back in time for my first class in the morning—but I had to run over and tell you how happy we all are about Tony. Lucy's a peach, so pretty, and so —charming.'

'You're quite a picture yourself,' he said approvingly. Jan was dressed for the dance. She had grown into a lovely young woman and her gown, snug bodice of pale silvery brocade with a bouffant skirt that was a soft cloud of tulle, became her perfectly. 'Do dances start as early as this?'

'I'm going to a dinner first, in Scituate. Billy Hill is picking me up at eight o'clock. But I wanted to see you first. Aren't you happy about Lucy?'

'Yes, indeed,' he assured her, wondering whether Jan still had any trace of that old devotion to Tony. He could not resist saying gently: 'Though I might not have picked her for him. Perhaps I'm prejudiced.'

She laughed with no apparent restraint. 'I know, you were always on my side. But that never would have worked, Uncle Mark. Tony and I have known each other too long. There has to be some—mystery, you know.' She said: 'And don't worry about Lucy. She's sweet. I know how you feel, but lots of times that kind of girl turns out to be wonderful! I mean, after they're married and everything.'

'I know,' he assented. 'Nan was just as gay and lovely and popular as Lucy.'

'I wish I were!' Jan confessed. 'Of course I'm nice, and everybody seems to like me all right, but——' She laughed. 'Well, when Lucy looks at boys, they just fall down in rows!'

Mark smiled. 'You're fine, Jan. You'll do to take along!'

'Maybe I'm too—too meek, or something,' she confessed. 'I know one thing. I know just exactly the kind of man I want to marry; and when I grow up, and see one that suits, if he hasn't any—strings on him, I'm going to go out and get him!'

'You sound pretty fierce!' he said, tenderly amused.

'I feel pretty fierce,' she assured him, her eyes twinkling. 'I've been meek and mild too long!'

'You suit me, Jan. You always did.'

She rose, laughing at him. 'Yes, but you're going to marry Mrs. Kerr. All the nice men are always going to marry somebody! Somebody else!' Her cheeks suddenly were burning. 'Good-bye,' she said hurriedly, and from the door she called back breathlessly: 'Give Tony my love, won't you?'

Mark said he would, but—writing to Tony that evening—he did not mention Jan. To do so might wake in his son regrets for which Mark did not wish to be responsible.

He went to New York to spend the next week-end with Robin, driven by a hungry need for the solace of her tenderness and understanding. The week had been a stirring one. Churchill in his first parliamentary speech as Prime Minister had told his people: 'I have nothing to offer but blood, toil, sweat, and tears,' and, defining England's policy, he said it was to 'wage war by land, sea, and air; war with all our might and with all the strength God has given us, against a monstrous tyranny never surpassed in the dark and lamentable catalogue of human crime.' The brave and steadfast and yet humble words electrified the world. The armies of Holland surrendered; and the Germans broke the French line at Sedan and came racing toward the Channel. They captured Brussels; and General Gamelin bade his soldiers die in their tracks rather than retreat. But the Germans took Antwerp, and in France they reached the Aisne. Holland was gone, Belgium was staggering, France was desperate.

Mark saw for the first time the beginnings, in the minds of the men about him, of a perception of the fact that Germany might win. Washington, according to one dispatch, was 'somewhat alarmed' and Mr. Roosevelt had asked Congress to appropriate a billion dollars for arms and material to supply our ill-equipped skeleton army. He proposed that we prepare to build fifty thousand planes a year. The figures, a billion dollars, fifty thousand planes, startled the national imagination; and Mark thought men felt a complacent pride in the words, as though the planes were already in the air. But to him the proposed appropriation seemed grotesquely small. To build fifty thousand planes would cost surely as much as ten billion dollars; to train men to man them would cost at least a billion more. Mr. Roosevelt—Mark gave him full credit—had been proved a true prophet; he had foreseen and predicted, at least in general terms, all that had happened. Yet though he had seen and presumably now saw what the future might hold, it was obvious that he did not comprehend it, that he had no real conception of the magnitude of the task that must be done. It was as though a man, foreseeing the collapse of a tremendous dam, proposed to dig a drainage ditch to handle the flood. Since the United States must prepare for war on the scale on which Germany waged war, a hundred billion dollars would only begin to meet the cost.

Perhaps Mr. Roosevelt, like the rest of us, was drugged by the persistent journalistic practice of giving every piece of bad news the rosiest possible tint. Major Eliot remarked in his daily comment on the great battle that 'For the moment, the Germans have attained none of their objectives,' and the editors chose to feature this faintly hopeful line on the front page, and on the editorial page commented: 'We mean to help the Allies in every way humanly and nationally possible short of taking up arms ourselves.'

Yet these things, whether they suggested the dawning perception of the truth in the public mind, or demonstrated the complete failure in Washington to measure the forces now let loose upon the world, or evidenced the pathetic journalistic hope-complex which fed to readers every crumb of comfort and ignored the fat loaves of black disaster, could no longer move Mark to the sombre wrath they had once provoked. Tony was more important to him than England and all of Europe rolled into one.

He told Robin, as soon as they reached her apartment, the truth about Tony and Lucy; and she listened without interruption, except that she came to sit on the arm of his chair, her arm across his shoulders, her hand stroking his cheek. When he was done, thinking only of him, she asked quickly: 'Are you distressed, Mark? You mustn't be. They'll work out a good life for themselves.'

'I'm not, as a matter of fact,' he said. 'It meant a lot to me to have Tony come to me honestly, as he did; and to find that when he needed me, I could help him.'

'At least,' she said gratefully, 'it's taken your mind off the war.'

He nodded, then smiled. 'But not Tony's,' he said. 'I had a letter from him this morning.' He took it out and read a passage.

> The United States will soon be in it. We'll have to be! If the Germans can get Belgium, they'll flank the Maginot line, smash France too. And they're grabbing the Channel coast. Once they get that, they can hit France or England, either one; and we've got to save England.
>
> We talk about building fifty thousand planes, but what we need more than planes or guns or brains or anything else is courage and faith: courage to think and act without hysteria, faith in our past, and our present and future. My favorite hymn has the line 'faith of our fathers, living still.' We must not let cynicism destroy that faith.

Around me here in Hanover, and in other colleges, there's a lot of cynicism and damned little faith. The fellows are sure that what's happening in Europe is none of our business and that we ought to keep out of it. Some of them got up a petition this week asking President Roosevelt to keep us out of war. Over a thousand—out of about twenty-five hundred in college— signed it and they sent it to Washington. They wanted me to sign it, but I wouldn't. I used to think the same way—but when a thing as big as this comes along, we're all in it, whether we want to be or not.

Men your age have a great job ahead of you. You must do everything to help men my age keep our faith. I wish you were President. You'd find a way to help us see things straight, and get ourselves out of the mess we're in—just as you knew how to give me what I needed at home the other night.

'Is that all he says about—you?' she asked, faintly critical.

Mark laughed. 'It's a lot from Tony. And it means a lot to me.'

She leaned down to kiss him, hugging him tightly. 'I think he ought to just jump up and down and shout how wonderful you are,' she declared. 'But maybe I'm prejudiced.' And she said; her hand gripping his: 'Mark—don't ever blame Tony or Lucy. I know so well how they felt. You don't blame them, do you?'

'I'm—sorry, of course,' he admitted. 'But I can understand, too. Tony's been—troubled and unhappy for years, like most boys his age, growing up to face this war that's on us now. I remember his writing me when he was with Lucy last summer that he was ready to grab any piece of heaven while he could.' He added: 'And Lucy loves him, and she knew how unhappy he was. I can understand how forces outside of themselves thrust them together.'

She kissed him gently again. 'You're a good man, my dear,' she said, and smiled mischievously. 'Sometimes I wish . . .'

She hesitated, and he asked, his heart suddenly pounding: 'Wish what, Robin?'

Her smile passed in tender gravity. 'I wish I could always be as steady and strong—and as patient—as you,' she told him, and she said: 'That's why you must never blame Lucy, Mark. She loves Tony as I love you. We're both women in love, desiring above all else to be everything to our troubled, beloved men.'

'We're lucky, Tony and I,' he said. 'Probably if I didn't know you, I might blindly condemn her. But I can understand her, knowing you.'

'The only difference between them and us,' she told him quietly, 'is that Tony's still a boy, and you're a strong man.'

They had on Sunday a long and completely happy day together, driving far up the Hudson through the burgeoning beauty of the May countryside, dining at a quiet inn they found, returning in the late afternoon to her apartment to sit for hours before the chuckling little fire till it was time for him to go to take his train. Completely forgetful of herself, she tried in every way to content him and give him peace and rest and strength; and it was only at the end that she clung to him in a tender despair because he must go, and she whispered: 'Oh, it's so long, Mark. It's so dreadfully long.'

'I'm never complete except when I'm with you.' He was as moved as she.

'Are you well, my dear?' she asked, leaning away from him in his arms, looking at him challengingly. 'Do you ever have those—feelings any more? If you do—I can't bear it, Mark. I can't let you go.'

'I'm fine,' he assured her. The faint discomfort he occasionally felt she need not know. 'I'm better every day, Robin. Don't be afraid for me.'

She let him go at last, reassured and yet desperate because needing her he nevertheless must go alone; and she lay hours sleepless that night.

And so Robin came at last to a decision long contemplated. It had become intolerable that she and Mark should continue to be parted. There was no fairness and no rightness in remaining Davy's wife when he himself did not know it, when she could mean nothing to him, and when she could mean everything to Mark. If she freed herself from Davy, she could—and would—still do as much for him as she did today. That she would remain his wife as long as he lived was a loyalty to which she had clung with a blind tenacity; but—alone tonight after Mark was gone, she knew she had been wrong.

Yet she knew, too, that if she now proposed to divorce Davy, or to have that marriage annulled—she had never inquired into the legal aspects of her situation—Mark would protest, would wish her to cling to that ideal devotion which had been so long the foundation of her life. Whatever she did she must do without his knowledge. She went next day to see a lawyer, told him the facts.

'I don't know whether there's anything I can do, here in New York, or not,' she confessed. 'But I'll go to Reno, or anywhere that's necessary.'

He said reassuringly: 'You needn't go anywhere.'

'I've always understood there was only one ground for divorce in New York.'

'For divorce, yes,' he agreed. 'But since your husband has been a hope-less mental case for over five years, an annulment petition is in order.'

He explained the procedure, and she instructed him to do whatever was necessary. She would not tell Mark; not till she could go to him and say: 'My darling, I can marry you today.' That would be soon, her lawyer promised; a matter of a few weeks, no more.

8

(June 1940)

The Belgian army surrendered and the Germans reached the Channel, and Bob Ritchie told Mark: 'They're pouring through a lane not a dozen miles wide, with most of the French army on one side, and the rest of the French plus the British on the other. If the French don't cut that lane, then either their whole army's rotten or they're betraying England.'

Mark did not dissent. His father wrote a day or two later, saying much the same thing, and he added:

> I see the Allies—all except Churchill, who keeps his head when, as Kipling said, all around him are losing theirs and blaming it on him—say Belgium betrayed them by her surrender. But everyone who follows the news intelligently knows how terribly the Belgian army was being battered; and after the Germans reached the Channel, the armies in Flanders were doomed. If Belgium had fought on, she would have been a rear guard, thrown to the wolves. The British seem to have done a grand piece of work in pulling their army out of Dunkirk. Fog helped keep off the German planes, of course; nevertheless, it was as splendid an exploit as a forced retreat can be. Fog may turn out to be the most powerful single weapon in this war, since it can minimize air activity. Maybe some day ships will surround themselves with artificial fog as a defense against planes.
>
> Now France is left to face Germany alone. I see some military men think the French can hold them. But the Gamelin myth is already exploded, and the myth of the invincible French army won't last much longer. A month will see the end of France.

Mark did not agree with this prediction. Like most men who had served in France, he believed in the French army; or he wished to believe in it. He could not be sure, even in his own mind, whether it was hope or faith which prompted him; but he could not accept as a foregone conclusion the fall of France. The fragmentary reports from Dunkirk made his blood tingle; and he read with a spine-prickling exultation Churchill's splendid words: 'We shall defend our island, whatever the case may be. We shall fight on beaches, on landing grounds, in fields, in streets, and on the hills. We shall never surrender, and even if—which I do not for a moment believe—this island or a large part of it were subjugated and starving, then our empire beyond the seas, armed and guarded by the British fleet, will carry on the struggle until in God's good time the New World, with all its power and might, sets forth to the liberation and rescue of the Old.'

A day or two after that grand speech was reported in the papers, Tony came home during an interval between his examinations, and Mark invited Lucy and Mr. and Mrs. Pride to dinner. The German armies had turned on France, and Mark thought—made himself think—that General Weygand's 'accordion' defense must surely succeed. There had been since it began no official reports of the progress of the battle, but the unofficial dispatches were hopeful. Mr. Pride, Mark found, had a simple faith that the German drive would presently collapse.

'It's impossible that evil can succeed in the long run,' he declared. 'That isn't the way the world is made.'

'I'd hate to trust intangible moral factors to defeat the Germans,' Mark declared. 'They've done vicious and wicked and damnable things, yes. But perhaps it's just as vicious and wicked and damnable for us to sit smugly back and say: "They'll get their come-uppance, because they're naughty, naughty people."' He smiled to take the sting out of his words. 'The wicked have a way of prospering,' he suggested, 'until the good get up enough energy to do something about it.'

But Mrs. Pride would not tolerate long talk about anything except the plans for Lucy's wedding. 'I'm busy from daylight to dark,' she told Mark joyously. 'Trying to crowd into five or six weeks what needs six months to plan and do just right. But I think sometimes it's as easy to do things and get them over with as to drag them out. It's terribly short notice, but Tony and Lucy are so impatient. I think young people in love are charming, don't you, Judge Worth?' She was completely happy, her fears for Lucy all forgotten now.

Lucy, too, was radiant. Mark thought she was like a child which, having committed some small misdemeanor and finding itself forgiven, is troubled by no conscience pangs. Her father and mother, knowing nothing of the truth, were as happy as she. Only in Tony's eyes Mark saw some shadow; but he saw, too, Tony's gentleness toward Lucy, and his tender, affectionate solicitude. Tony might have regrets, might contemplate with dismay the pit which he had digged for himself; but he would never let Lucy see that, nor confess it to anyone at all. Mark, knowing Tony, knew how his son must be cringing at this shabby, tarnished business that should have been so clean and brave and beautiful; and for Tony's sake, to try to heal his son's shamed regret, Mark

played his part to the uttermost, affectionate toward Lucy, laughing
with Mrs. Pride, talking easily and graciously with Mr. Pride. Outwardly these five people were like any other happy lovers and their
proud, fond parents.

Tony went back to Hanover Sunday afternoon. He and Mark had
not mentioned that which was foremost in both their minds, but when
Tony said good-bye, Mark clapped him hearteningly on the shoulder,
and Tony suddenly turned and gripped his hand hard before he hurried
away.

Mark during the days that followed scarce looked at the papers. Italy,
a jackal on the lion's heels, declared war. When Mr. Roosevelt said:
'The hand that held the dagger has struck it into the back of its neigh-
bor,' he spoke the thought of every honest man anywhere in the world.
Paris heard the German guns. Reynaud made a last appeal for clouds of
American planes to beat back the Germans.

But there were no planes to send, and France was lost.

9

(June 14, 1940)

When Mark set out to drive to Hanover for Tony's Commencement,
Lucy was beside him. At her insistence, they turned back the car's top,
and the wind caught her hair, and burnished her cheeks, and she
laughed easily. They passed through Cambridge on the way and she
asked:

'Did Tony tell you we've picked out our apartment?'

'He said he'd left it to you to do that.'

'He did really,' she assented. 'There were three apartments I liked,
and I wanted him to see them, but he said for me to decide, and I've
decided.' Her eyes were shining. 'It's Nell Damon's,' she said. 'She and
Bill have lived there for three years and they've loved it. Of course it's
small, just one bedroom; but the living room's big enough for a party,
and the dining room's sweet.'

'You won't be having many parties,' Mark suggested. 'Tony's going to
need to study hard, you know.' Apparently Tony had not told Lucy the
apartment was only temporary. It was like her, Mark thought, to be for
the present serenely unconscious of the practical difficulties in the way
of a winter in Boston.

'Oh, of course!' she agreed. 'Don't worry, Judge Worth. I'm going to settle down and be the best wife Tony ever had!' She linked her hand in his arm. 'The Damons are moving out as soon as Bill's exams are over,' she said. 'Going to Cleveland. Then, when they're gone, the man who owns the apartment is going to have it all done over; new wallpaper, and paint the woodwork, and do the floors and things. I've been picking out paper and choosing paint all this week, till I'm dizzy! Mother is going to get the furniture in and get us all settled while Tony and I are away.' She and Tony proposed to take an automobile trip around the Gaspé, in the car which would be Mark's wedding present to them. 'So when we come back, everything will be all ready for us to move in, except curtains. I'm going to make them myself.'

'Won't it be hot there this summer?' It was necessary to keep the conversation alive. Silence between them would be unbearable. His own thoughts might appear in his countenance, and that must not happen. She was to be Tony's wife, and at whatever cost he must maintain at least a surface affection between them. So now he asked the empty question, to keep her talking. 'Won't it be hot there?'

'Oh, we'll be running down to the Cape and places!' Lucy assured him. 'Mother and Father are letting us have their cottage for August. But we'll be all settled before Law School opens.'

'I'm glad it's not going to be a big wedding,' he said emptily. 'Tony's been afraid you'd want a church affair.'

Lucy laughed. 'I know. He worried himself sick! But Mother and Father were married down at our summer place—it was Grandfather's then—and I want to be. We'll be married in the garden if it doesn't rain. Of course, there'll be a tent in case it does.'

She talked on happily about their plans; but Mark, driving automatically, only half listened, answering at random as the miles slipped by, till she fell silent too.

'Sleepy?' she asked at last. They were approaching Nashua. 'Want me to drive awhile? Your eyes are fairly glassy!'

He welcomed the suggestion, gave up the wheel to her. Driving after an hour or so was apt to tire him, to produce a disturbing numb dizziness; and Doctor Hethering had warned him against persisting when he felt this. Beside her he relaxed, closing his eyes, and presently he slept. When he woke they were in Concord, and the afternoon was waning. They had been delayed in leaving Boston and it was now almost five, and an hour and a half or a little more to Hanover. Tony would be waiting for them at the Inn. He would expect them about six, and they would be later than that; but they need not hurry.

She saw that he was awake and looked at him laughingly. 'You've slept over an hour,' she said.

'Want me to take it? You must be tired?'

'Oh, I love to drive,' she declared.

Yet she drove faster than he liked. Her speed ranged from a dangerous forty in the villages to a headlong pace in the open country. Mark saw that she handled the car surely and well, but he watched the speedometer and he watched the road, till she looked at him with a flashing glance.

'Too fast?' she asked.

'No, you're driving.'

'I'm in a hurry to get there,' she said. 'I want to see Tony!' He watched her with a dispassionate eye. Everything about her was warming and exhilarating. After a moment she looked at him again. 'Am I all right?' she asked. 'I can feel you looking at me.'

'You're well worth looking at.'

She smiled at him gratefully. 'Aren't you nice! It always makes me feel as though I want to be so wonderful when you say nice things to me.'

'This next turn is sharper than it looks,' he suggested; and the brakes bit and they slowed, the tires hiccoughing.

'I was going too fast, wasn't I?' she confessed. 'I was paying more attention to you than I was to the road.' She straightened out beyond the curve and stepped on the throttle again. 'It's your fault, turning a poor girl's head!'

'I have an idea you've a pretty level head,' he said quietly. 'I don't believe you're half so—so——'

'Giddy?' she suggested, laughing up at him.

'Well—yes,' he agreed. 'You're not half so gay as you pretend.'

'I'm not,' she assured him. 'I'm really awfully serious underneath. That's why I like Tony.' She added: 'Because sometimes he's pretty sober.'

'I'm afraid he gets that from me.'

His tone, without any intention on his part, mirroring his thoughts, was grave and stern; and she looked at him sharply, but his eyes were on the road. Lucy since she was a baby had wanted people to like her, had been happy when this was the case, unhappy and resentful under any chiding. She read into his tone a reproach he had not meant. His tone echoed his deep grief over the circumstances of Tony's coming marriage; but for what happened he had refused to let himself blame either her or Tony. So he had no thought of damning her now, yet— always sensitive to the people around her—she thought he had; and she resented this, and wished to strike back, to hurt him. She knew his love for Tony, knew by that keen instinct which was a part of her, that he accepted her only for Tony's sake; and she wished to prove to him that his wonderful Tony was not perfect after all.

And she remembered suddenly that she held a weapon in her hand. 'Sober as a judge?' she rejoined smilingly, and looked at him again, and they met a car in a dip in the road that hid it till it was just upon them, so that she had to swerve sharply to give it room. She said teasingly: 'I'll bet you're not sober when you're with Mrs. Kerr!' She asked, eyes carefully on the road now: 'When are you and she going to be married?'

That was a question he had had to evade so many times. 'You'd better ask her,' he said. 'She's coming up for Tony's Commencement, coming by train tomorrow morning.' And, feeling that his tone and words had been unfriendly, he added: 'Will Ritchie's graduating, too, you know. Jan's coming up from Merryfield, and Bob and Nell are driving up today. Betty's away somewhere.' His father had planned to come on from Ohio, but a heavy summer cold had sent him to bed, made this impossible.

Lucy persisted, bent on wounding him: 'Tony says Mrs. Kerr's grand. He's told me all about the first time they met, at the inn up in Canada, the time we were all up there skiing.'

Mark heard her with a sharp shock of surprise. 'In Canada?' he echoed.

Her eyes turned toward him in a pretty pretense of consternation. 'Oh, I wasn't supposed to tell you! Tony will give me fits.' His thoughts were blank confusion, and Lucy, as though anxious to mend the harm she had done, said hastily: 'But really, that was perfectly all right, you know.' She spoke as though he needed reassurance. 'Tony didn't realize how old she was, that was all!'

'She's very young-looking, of course,' Mark carefully assented, waiting, nerving himself to hear whatever Lucy might be about to say. He realized, even then, that her word had been no accident. She had meant to betray this secret, whatever it was.

'And he didn't know her from Eve, of course, when he found her sitting there by the fire!' Lucy declared. Mark in sharp comprehension remembered vividly all Tony had said about that girl whom he met in the firelight at the inn; and Lucy laughed and went on: 'Of course, he thought she was flirting with him; but sitting there in front of the fire that way, they were bound to get just a little sentimental. You see that was the night he was so broken up about Barbie. I teased him about it the next morning, but I really fell in love with him then, he was so pathetically brave. So I know just how Mrs. Kerr felt, wanting to comfort him.'

Mark said, at random, seizing any pretext to protect Robin: 'Oh, she knew who he was. I'd shown her his picture. She thought it would be fun not to tell him till afterward.'

Lucy looked at him shrewdly. 'Really? He never knew that!' Then, laughing in quick triumph, 'I don't believe it. Why did she leave so early next morning?'

He spoke in sharp warning. 'Look out!' She caught the car just in time as, while her eyes were on him, it edged toward the side of the road. 'She had already planned to leave early,' he explained, and he said harshly: 'You'd better let me drive, Lucy.' Then he tried to laugh, to take the sting out of his words. 'My nerves will stand about so much! You almost hit the ditch that time!'

'I'm sorry. I'll be good,' she promised, and made no move to yield the wheel; but she slowed to a ridiculously leisurely pace, and a car overtook them and Mark saw Bob and Nell Ritchie, and Bob pulled up, and they stopped to speak to him.

'Say,' Bob called, 'look out for her, Mark. Lucy, I drive pretty fast myself, but you've given me some thrills the last few miles.'

Lucy laughed. 'You must have been going as fast as we did, to keep us in sight!'

Mark said: 'We'll trail you from now on.'

'No, we're stopping for gas at the next town,' Bob warned him. 'Pass us any time you want.'

He pulled on, and at first Lucy stayed behind them; but after three or four miles they stopped at a gas pump, and Lucy waved as she sped by.

She drove more rapidly again, but Mark hardly noticed, considering what she had said awhile ago, assuring himself that if there were in that first encounter between Robin and Tony anything that he should know, Robin would have told him long ago, or Tony would have told him. He was certain of this, and yet there rose in him a muttering storm of unhappy doubt. If what Lucy said were true—and he did not question it, found plentiful confirmation in his own memories—why, then Robin and Tony, the two people who were his whole world, had conspired to keep from him—some secret or other. But why? He could not believe that there had been anything which required to be concealed. Yet if not, then why the concealment?

And—why had Lucy told him? He was sure she had done it deliberately. Was she actuated merely by a feminine love for gossip? Or by purposeless malice, by a sadistic desire to cause him pain? He knew in this moment that—Tony's wife or not—he could never either trust or like her.

She was quiet beside him, intent upon the road. The steady pace of the car had a soporific quality. The sun was low enough so that the road lay sometimes in the shadow of the western hills; and across the meadows and the intervales long shadows reached like lances from every tall elm. Mark always enjoyed the last few miles of this drive to Hanover. The countryside was beautiful, the shabby little towns alone marring the scene. But today he was in haste to be rid of Lucy. He remembered that there was a short cut past Lebanon, and he decided they would take it, thought with a sudden yearning that in a few minutes now he would see Tony.

But at the same time he knew he could never ask either Tony or Robin to read this riddle Lucy had set to torment him; and a week from now Tony would be married to this girl, and after that, Mark knew, there would be a gulf between him and his son. There would be some things Tony would never tell him, and there would be some things about which he could not offer Tony any word or sign. He looked at Lucy again. In her small person she held so many potentialities of happiness or misery—happiness or misery for Tony.

She met his stern glance, and he directed her to take the cutoff and with no word she obeyed him. They crossed the river by the narrow covered bridge, and turned right beyond the lumberyard. She drove swiftly again; and he said: 'There's a bad corner ahead where we cross the main road. I'll tell you in time.'

She looked at him with a flashing, angry smile, hating him. 'You're awfully careful, aren't you?' she drawled. 'Such a careful man!'

He said warningly: 'There's the stop sign. Better slow down.'

But she had an impish desire to oppose him, to show him that he could not command her. She held her pace. The crossroad ahead seemed clear of any traffic. She raced toward the intersection at a reckless speed.

10

(June 14, 1940)

Jim Smiley was on his way to Lebanon with a truckload of junk, odds and ends salvaged from a dump where automobiles past their useful days had been left to rust away. There were a dozen engines or parts of engines, two or three frames, fenders, radiators, a disorderly miscellany. Jim's truck was a big one, but it was as old and worn out as the load it bore; and Jim himself was a worn-out man. He and Mrs. Smiley lived on a starved farm which insufficiently provided for themselves and their six children, the oldest not yet twelve years old; and Jim all his life—a life completely devoid of alternatives—had been harried into frenzied efforts to earn just a little more money. This morning he and Mrs. Smiley had had one of their almost daily quarrels, arising out of his worry and perplexity and out of her weariness, an aching fatigue which for as long as she could remember had never ceased. The quarrel, its beginning quickly forgotten, had flowered like flames in oil-soaked waste, and at the end, leaving her, Jim had pushed her aside with a gesture that was almost a blow.

Knowing himself in the wrong, shamed and sorry, loving her in a fashion completely inarticulate, he was in haste to come home to her now again. A dreadful terror drove him, for she had threatened this morning to kill herself; and though Jim had heard the threat a thousand times, and always laughed at it, his laugh was never genuine, while his fears were real. He was not sufficiently vocal to say to himself, like a prayer: 'I wish I could take better care of Mom and the kids. I wish I could be good to them, and earn a little more money and give them things.' Yet this was what he meant when he said to himself: 'God damn her to Hell, always after me, spending every cent I earn.' He had bought this truck for twenty-five dollars and tinkered it into running order, with high hopes that it might pay its way. The load of junk now aboard it he had purchased as a speculation, thinking the profit might pay a little more than the cost of hauling. He did not expect it to pay for his time. His time was worthless.

But in his haste to come home to Mom, he had driven a poor bargain, and he knew the load might show him a loss. That, for some reason obscure even to Jim, was somehow Mom's fault. When he came home

to her now, she would accuse him of having been off all day loafing
somewhere, and he would tell her to shut her mouth before he shut it
for her; but each in some strange way would know that these were their
mutual apologies, were a sort of endearment; and tonight in their sleep
they would be close together, each warmed by the other, in their sleep
clumsily offering the awkward caresses which awake they were ashamed
to bestow.

So Jim was in a hurry to come home, and he drove faster than his
brakes justified. He knew that dangerous intersection, but he forgot it.
When he came over the rise which had till the last moment hidden it
from his view, he saw a sport coupé with the top down and a man and a
girl in it, moving fast, about to dart out in his very path not a hundred
feet away.

The road from him to them pitched downward at a fair grade; and
his brakes failed even to check his speed. He tried to swing to the right
to clear the other car. He saw the girl who was driving twitch the coupé
to the left, trying to give him room to pass; and he heard her terrible
scream. Jim himself, standing on the useless brakes, cried: 'Oh, Christ
Almighty!'

Then the truck hit the little car a glancing blow. The truck with its
load may have weighed five or six tons. It was travelling at a full fifty
miles an hour, and the coupé was going as fast. The light car was thrown
aside as a bow wave is thrown by a fast-travelling motorboat.

Jim saw the girl come up out of the car as though off a springboard,
flying headlong through the air in a looping arc. He did not see what
happened to the man.

II

(June 14, 1940)

Hanover on a fine June afternoon has a peculiar beauty of its own.
When Tony came across toward the Inn to wait there for his father and
Lucy, there was a game of soft ball in progress on the campus, with
many shouts and much laughter; and along the fence, girls come for
Commencement perched with their escorts, watching the game and
cheering. Tony stayed to watch awhile, as attentive to the stream of cars
arriving at the Inn as he was to the game. He saw Joe Hazen and Chuck
Little standing together and joined them; and Charlie Spring came
along a moment later. Tony and Joe and Charlie had been in Paris

together two years before; and today the Germans had marched into Paris, tanks, motorized divisions, and infantry pouring along the Champs Élysées between thin lines of silent, sullen onlookers.

'I guess it wasn't much like that when we were there, Joe,' Tony said, speaking of this; and Joe laughed.

'The Germans can have Paris, for all of me. I didn't like the way it smelled.'

Chuck Little said strongly: 'If the French had some decent planes, they could still hold them. It's planes that have won this whole battle of Europe. I wish we could have sent over about five thousand good pursuits when Reynaud asked for them, or before that.'

Charlie laughed. 'War-monger,' he said derisively. 'It's guys like you that start wars to kill off the likes of us, Chuck—while you do some essential defense job in your dad's factory.'

Charlie Spring had been Tony's closest friend in Hanover, and Charlie would be best man at the approaching wedding; but Tony began increasingly to resent the other's opinion—mirroring the general sentiment in Charlie's Mid-Western home—that the United States, resting secure behind our ocean barriers, should let the war burn itself out. Before Chuck could speak, he said:

'That sort of talk doesn't get anywhere, Charlie! This thing is so damned big we're bound to be pulled in.'

'Not if we keep our heads.'

'If we keep our heads too well, we'll get them knocked off.'

Charlie laughed. 'Say, even if the war ended today, it would take Germany ten years to absorb and organize her new empire. She'll have enough rebellions and insurrections and sabotage to handle to keep her busy for a while. She has to digest what she's got before she swallows any more.'

'Yes, and after she's digested Europe, our turn will come.'

Joe Hazen said: 'If Europe's like China, Germany never can get things quieted down over there. The Japs have been doing what they damned well pleased in China for a long time, but they're not getting anywhere.'

Chuck Little took up the argument with Charlie, and the clock in the Library tower struck six, and Tony decided it was about time for his father to arrive, so he left them and crossed to the Inn. He went to the desk and inquired to be sure Mark and Lucy were not already here, then came out and sat on the veranda rail to wait for them. He greeted occasional passing friends with a cheerful word, but his eyes were shadowed. More and more often nowadays he and Charlie came to the verge of an angry argument about the war. What was beginning to seem to Tony the other's blind and selfish stupidity irritated him. He resented Charlie's belief that isolation was the answer to the great puzzle of the day much more keenly than he resented the same position in men to whom he was not so close. His fondness for Charlie in some obscure way aggravated his disappointment at the other's obduracy; and he realized this, and thought he was like a devoted father, more distressed by the misdoing of a beloved son than if the error had been committed by another.

His own father, Tony remembered, must have been thus terribly hurt and grieved by what he himself had done; and Tony was sick with shamed regret and at the same time warm with gratefulness for Mark's understanding and for the fact that there had been no word of reproach, and for his father's unreserved readiness to help in every way. Tony had never loved his father so much as now, never so deeply vowed to remember and by a lifetime of good work and decent living and loyal devotion to repay the older man. He thought of Lucy, too, and with a protective tenderness, telling himself that only by a life well lived at her side could he pay his score to her. His first rebellious reluctance he had long since put aside. It was too late for that now. Now and in the future his concern must be to retrieve the errors of the past.

He saw Jan Ritchie coming toward the Inn from the corner by the Commons, and slid off the rail to go to meet her and to shake hands and to say warmly:

'Hi, Jan! Glad to see you! Your folks here yet?'

'No, they're driving up,' she told him. 'Mother and Father, that is. Will's over at the House. He says Father and Mother won't get here for another hour, anyway; but I'm anxious to see them, so I thought I'd come and be on hand in case.'

'Dad said he'd be here about six,' Tony explained, and they sat side by side, watching the moving figures which, traversing the campus paths, wove an intricate pattern of movement across the green.

'Is Lucy coming up with him?' Jan asked.

'Yes.'

'I'll bet you're pretty excited!'

'Sure!' And he grinned and said: 'But not as excited as Lucy. She picked out our apartment in Cambridge, and the landlord's doing it over for us. I had a long letter from her this morning, all full of what color paint she was going to use, and wallpaper, and so on.' He chuckled.

'She's planning to make the window curtains herself, this winter, in the evenings while I'm working. I can't imagine Lucy sewing, can you?'

'I think she'll surprise you,' Jan loyally assured him. 'I think she can do anything she wants to do.'

'She sure can!' Tony agreed. He hesitated, then said half to himself: 'We'll have our ups and downs, but I'm going to be awfully good to her.'

'I'm so glad you can be married right away.'

'So am I.' His eyes were clouded. 'I feel as if I wanted to hurry about everything, as though the world might come to an end around my head.' He added: 'I've been feeling that way for a year, now.'

'The war?' she suggested, and he nodded, and she asked: 'How do the boys here feel about it?'

'All of them think it's rotten, and a lot of them think we ought to stay out. That's what we've been taught all our lives, of course; that the Allies made suckers of us in the last war.' He hesitated. 'I think remembering Ingrid has swung me around more than anything else. She thought the Germans were all right, not too bad, anyway; and look what they did to Norway. She lived in Trondheim, you know. I keep thinking what may have happened to her. I used to try to see their side of it—but I can't see that they have any side now.

'But they're winning. I guess England will be next—and then us.'

'I don't suppose we really know the truth at all,' she said. 'I mean, about what's happening.'

He laughed harshly. 'Plenty of awful things are happening,' he assured her. 'We're selling arms to Russia, and we're selling oil and scrap iron to Japan, and as like as not they'll both be fighting against us before this is through. Because we may have to fight. We've got to teach the Nazis a lesson—but we can't do it by beating them in a war. They're more sure of their faith than we are, more willing to die for it. We can learn from them as much as we can teach them. I hope we'll win—but when we do, I hope we'll lift up the defeated Germany to share the world with us. We've got to prove—by our actions—that we and they really want the same things for the world; I mean for the individual. What we all want is a world where a young man may know that he can work and save and live a straight, decent life and get along.'

She nodded. 'I see what you mean.'

'Maybe the real trouble now,' he said, 'is that we—I mean fellows my age—can't help admiring what young men in Germany are doing. They're serving an ideal, fighting for it, sacrificing, dying. Most of us here are just looking forward to earning a lot of money; but in the back of our minds we know we're wrong, and we're sort of ashamed of ourselves, and reckless; and we're restless, in a hurry, unhappy as Hell.'

'You're surely not unhappy, Tony,' she said smilingly.

'You mean Lucy?'

'Yes.'

He said grimly: 'Our getting married is the sort of thing I mean. We wouldn't be doing it if the war hadn't knocked us both off our foundations.'

'I think people who want to get married, and are ready to get married, ought to get married,' Jan assured him. 'War or no war.'

He looked at his watch. 'Half-past,' he said. 'They ought to be getting here pretty soon. What time are your folks due?'

'They said six o'clock, but they never get anywhere on time. They plan to start promptly at two o'clock, or whatever it is, and then at the last moment Mother has to go back and do something or other, and the first thing they know they're an hour late getting away from the house!'

'Dad was pretty sure he'd get here between six and half-past,' Tony commented, faintly uneasy. For a while they did not speak. Other cars were arriving, turning in under the porte-cochère, passing just in front of them. Across the campus, as the sun drew nearer the horizon, the shadows lengthened. The ball game broke up, and by twos and threes and fours the players and spectators drifted away. 'I'm going to miss this place,' he said thoughtfully. 'I like it here.' He looked at his watch again. 'I wonder if Dad had a flat tire?'

'It's just barely half-past six,' she said reassuringly.

'I'm in a hurry to see them,' he admitted, and grinned and said: 'If it was Lucy driving, I'd be worried. I don't dare ride with her. But Dad is a good driver.'

'Maybe they met my folks, on the road, and stopped for tea or something.'

'I don't think Dad would stop,' Tony declared. 'I think he's as anxious to get here as I am to see him.' He looked at his watch again. 'I wish they'd hurry, at that.'

'There was probably heavy traffic,' she suggested.

'That wouldn't make any difference, the other side of Concord; and from Concord here, everybody keeps moving.'

'They keep moving too fast!' she commented. 'You Dartmouth men have a lot of accidents every year.'

'Sure,' he agreed. 'But that's fellows racing to get to Boston or to get back here. Dad takes his time. He may be late, but he'll get here.' He stared at the Library clock across the campus. 'But it's quarter of seven!' he said in a doubtful tone.

She laughed at him, touching his arm reassuringly. 'Don't be so jittery, Tony!'

'Well, I wish they'd hurry up and get here,' he declared.

12

(June 14, 1940)

After that stop for gas, Bob Ritchie sought to make speed; but on a winding stretch of road he overtook a line of slow-moving cars blocked by a farmer's hay cart in front so that each car had to wait for a sufficiently long straight reach of road before it dared pass. That delayed him for miles. Then, not so familiar as Mark with the road to Hanover, he missed the cut-off that would have led him past Lebanon, so he came through the town itself.

As he approached the corner where the cut-off intersected the main road, they saw cars massed ahead, and people standing; and Nell said:

'Look, Bob. There's been an accident!'

Bob nodded inattentively, slowing to take the left-hand turn, but Nell caught his arm. 'Bob!' she cried, in a shocked astonishment, 'isn't that Mark's car?'

Through a rift which suddenly had opened in the thickening crowd ahead, Bob saw a coupé, its top folded back, its right side battered in, lying in the ditch beside the road. The color was the same as that of Mark's car. He jammed on his brakes.

'It looks like it,' he said sharply. 'I'll go see.'

He slid out from under the wheel and came around the rear end of his own car, and Nell joined him and they raced toward the wrecked coupé, Bob elbowing a way for them both. They passed a truck which, with its right front wheel in the ditch and its left front mudguard crumpled, stood at a drunken angle beside the way. They went directly toward the wrecked car, and as Bob got his first fair look at the number plate he said, over his shoulder, in a hushed tone:

'It's Mark's, all right, Nell!'

She was breathless. Beyond the coupé, where there was a bit of turf beside the road, a circle of people stood silently, and Bob passed through this circle and then stopped, with Nell on his heels. At one side, a robe borrowed from one of the cars had been spread over something which lay eloquently still and small. Six feet away, Mark lay on the ground with a state policeman and two or three other men standing by him.

They came to his side. Mark was unconscious, his face a smear of blood. There was a swollen lump above his ear, from which blood oozed through the hair. His right arm was hideously twisted, and his leg too. She looked up at Bob, and he spoke to the officer.

'He's a friend of mine,' he said thickly. 'Is he dead?'

'No. Not yet, anyway.'

'Have you sent for a doctor?'

'Yes, the ambulance is on the way.'

Bob pointed toward where Lucy lay with the robe drawn over her. He could not put the question, but the officer answered it without being asked.

'She's dead, all right,' he said, and he explained: 'They came racing out of the intersection, right in front of that truck over there. The truck had a heavy load and it was coming downhill, and its brakes let go. It couldn't stop in time. They tried to dodge, but the truck piled right into them.'

Nell was shaking with nervous, dry sobs. Bob put his arm around her. 'Steady, girl,' he said. He spoke to the officer again. 'Where's the nearest hospital?'

'We'll send him to Hanover. You say you know him? What's his name? And what's the girl's?'

Bob gave names and addresses. He hesitated, looked at Nell, said in sober resolution: 'I'll go telephone Lucy's father.'

'There's a phone over in the gas station,' the policeman told him.

'I'll be right back,' he promised. 'Nell, you stay here. Maybe Mark will come to, and it will help, seeing someone he knows.'

So Nell, steadier now, stayed where she was. Another state trooper was unsnarling the congested traffic at the intersection. The ambulance arrived, and two white-coated men made a hurried examination of Mark. They cut away his sleeve, and Nell at what she saw turned her head sharply aside. Then one of them went to lift the robe that covered Lucy and looked at her and quickly replaced the robe again. He came back to where Mark lay.

'We'll take him to Hanover,' he said.

Bob returned, reporting to Nell: 'I got Mr. Pride on the phone. He's a brave little man, Nell. But that's a job I don't want to have to do again. He's flying up.'

The men were lifting Mark's limp body into the ambulance. Nell said in a low tone: 'Tony is probably waiting for them at the Inn.'

Bob nodded, his lips set. 'We'll pick him up as we go by, take him on to the hospital.'

They trailed the ambulance to Hanover, but they left it at the Athletic Field to go up through the centre of town to the Inn. When they pulled in under the porte-cochère, Tony and Jan leaped down off the porch railing; and Jan whipped the door open and Tony, behind her, asked quickly over her shoulder:

'Did you folks see anything of Dad and Lucy?'

Nell tried to speak and could not, and looked beseechingly at Bob; and he said, after an interval that seemed long:

'Your father's hurt, Tony. He had an accident. They've taken him to the hospital.'

Tony gripped the side of the car; and Nell, as though she were a remote, disinterested spectator, found herself looking at his hand, watching how the knuckles turned white as the blood drained out of them. Tony spoke carefully, in a hollow tone.

'Badly hurt?' Then he asked sharply: 'Is he dead?'

'No. But he's badly hurt, yes. They don't know how badly.'

Jan quickly opened the rear door of the car. 'Get in, Tony,' she said.

Tony obeyed her as though he had no will of his own, climbing carefully into the rear seat. She took her place beside him, and the car leaped ahead. They left the campus behind, passed the Library, came in sight of the hospital before Tony asked: 'Where's Lucy?'

Nell turned, reaching to grip his hand, saying wretchedly: 'She's dead, Tony.'

He nodded almost inattentively, as though he were not listening, as though this were something he had already known.

13

(June 14, 1940)

When they reached the hospital, Nell Ritchie decided to stay in the car. She was shaken and trembling in the reaction from the shock of the accident; so the other three went in together, Tony moving stiffly, his eyes glazed, his feet uncertain. Bob made inquiries and returned to report.

'He's in the operating room, Tony,' he said. 'Doctor Forbes will come and tell us just what the situation is, as soon as he can.'

Tony, still unable to speak, turned and walked to the nearest chair and sat down. Jan and her father for a moment hesitated, and Bob said to her: 'Maybe you ought to go and stay with Mother, Jan.'

She shook her head, looked at Tony, 'I want to stay here.' Tony might need her. She yearned to comfort him.

'I'd better stay, too,' her father agreed. 'There may be something to decide, or to arrange.' He was not surprised that she wished to stay with Tony, did not question her decision.

Tony, for the first time since they left the Inn, began to be conscious of his surroundings. He drew his hand across his eyes, and some color came back into his lips. He tried to speak, but at the first attempt only a meaningless sound emerged. He wetted his lips and tried again.

'What happened?' he asked. 'Does anybody know?'

Jan looked at her father, and Bob said after a moment: 'Why, it was at a corner this side of Lebanon. We saw the crowd ahead, and Nell recognized your father's car.' He hesitated, then explained: 'A truck hit them. It was loaded with scrap iron, and the brakes didn't work.' He spoke with a grim precision, added now: 'I telephoned Mr. Pride—he's flying up—and then we came on to find you.'

A nurse passed through the waiting room on some errand and Tony's eyes followed her, but she did not glance in his direction, and he relaxed in his chair again, his hands gripping the arms.

'How badly is Dad hurt?'

'It looked to me as if his leg were broken,' Bob admitted, 'and his arm certainly was; and he had a big bump on the side of his head, and a cut and a lot of blood on his face.'

Tony nodded, watching the door, and for a while they said no more; but at length Doctor Forbes came into the waiting room and turned toward them and they rose, and Tony took a quick step forward. Bob and Jan stood at his elbow.

Doctor Forbes was a man in his late thirties, stocky, with black hair, and a firm mouth and chin and a surprisingly gentle voice which was at the same time full of strength and reassurance. He spoke directly and without evasion.

'I feel sure Judge Worth will recover,' he said. 'The chances are four out of five in his favor.'

Tony wiped his mouth with his hand and his shoulders lifted. 'How badly is he hurt?' he asked.

Doctor Forbes answered explicitly: 'He has a fracture of his right leg below the knee, both bones, not compound. We have reduced that. His left arm is broken, just above the wrist; a compound fracture, but that should give no serious trouble. The X-ray shows two broken ribs on the left side; but so far as we can determine, there are no internal injuries, beyond the obvious shock of the blow.' He hesitated, and added then: 'He has, however, a severe concussion. He received a heavy blow on the left temple. There seems to be no fracture, but I'm not yet satisfied on that point.'

Tony asked in a low tone: 'Is he conscious? Can he talk to anyone?'

'No. He's unconscious, and even if he revives, he ought not to see anyone for several days.'

Tony turned to Jan, his shoulders straightening. 'Then he doesn't need me,' he said. 'I'll go down and meet Mr. Pride.'

'I'll go with you,' she suggested. 'I'll drive you down.'

Tony hesitated. He had the hurt dog's instinct to be alone, but also he dreaded seeing Lucy's father, dreaded the anguish he must find in the older man's eyes; and he wished to escape, too, from his own thoughts—which if he were alone would keep him accusing company. So in a reluctant gratitude he consented. 'I wish you would,' he said.

The ordeal was not as bad as Tony had feared. They were at the airport when Mr. Pride's plane landed. Lucy's father had a quiet strength in him now, and under his example Tony was steady, too. They drove him to Lebanon and had some brief talk on the way, and Mr. Pride arranged the sober business there. Tony offered to go back to Boston with him, but the other said quickly:

'Oh, no, Tony. Lucy wouldn't want you to miss your Commencement.' In this tragic moment Mr. Pride was completely master of himself.

'None of that matters now.'

Mr. Pride shook his head. 'It all matters,' he said. 'You have to go on with your life. It's not ended.' He hesitated, speaking half to himself. 'I think I always knew Lucy would—die young,' he said. 'She lived like a leaping flame, and—bright fires burn themselves out so quickly.'

Tony could not speak; but Jan said quietly beside him: 'Everyone loved her, Mr. Pride.'

'She was a happy child, a happy young woman,' Mr. Pride agreed. 'And happiest of all these last few weeks, Tony.' He smiled. 'Not all of us are lucky enough to die at our peak of happiness.'

When they left him—he would start at once for Boston—they took

the Hanover road at first in silence, Jan still driving, Tony sitting with
blank eyes beside her. She said at last:

'He's a good man, Tony. You can feel goodness in him. He was thinking a lot more of you than of himself just now.'

It was late when they came back to Hanover. At Jan's insistence they
stopped at the Wigwam for a sandwich and a milk shake, before going
to the hospital. Jan's father was still there. Concerning Mark, he said,
there was no new word; but a telegram had come for him. Tony opened
it.

> Sorry I can't come as planned. I must go to Mercersville tonight, for two
> or three days. But Mark, they think it will be for the last time. Tell Tony
> I'm sorry to miss his Commencement. I love you always.
>
> Robin.

'It's from Mrs. Kerr,' he explained. He did not understand the reference to Mercersville, so he only said: 'She's been delayed. She was
coming on the morning train.' He added, looking at the telegram: 'I
ought to wire her about Dad—but I don't know where she is. I'll tell
Dad's secretary to send a wire to her New York address.'

Bob Ritchie said: 'There's nothing she could do here, Tony. Or you
either. You'd better get some sleep.'

'I'm wide awake,' Tony assured him. 'I think I'll take a walk.'

Jan asked: 'Do you want someone to come along?'

Tony looked at her thoughtfully. 'I may walk fast,' he said. 'I may
walk far.'

'I'll tag along if you like,' she offered.

Tony, after a moment, nodded: 'I'd like having you,' he decided.
'Come along.'

14

(June 14-15, 1940)

They left Bob outside the hospital, turning toward the golf links;
and they walked slowly, saying nothing for a while. They passed the
club house and went on across the velvet fairways. The moon would
not rise till late, but there were stars, and they could see their way well
enough. The night was warm as milk, serene and kind. They heard the
murmur of voices and of laughter on the bridge across the Vale as they
approached it, and met two couples as they crossed, passing in silence

and in darkness so that they went unrecognized. Beyond, they climbed the gentle slope and followed the border of the pines toward where the ski jump towered above the trees ahead. Someone was up there on top of the steel framework that supported the runway. Voices came down to them.

'And probably there's someone up in the Tower too,' Tony said. 'People like to get up high.'

'"I will lift up mine eyes unto the hills,"' Jan reminded him, '"whence cometh my strength."'

He looked up at the thin skeleton of the ski jump. 'I've got to get away from here,' he said hastily. 'Lucy and I came out here one night. Let's—go up on Balch. Is that too far for you?'

'No. Nowhere's too far!'

So they crossed the road, and went on in silence for a while across the open fields, Tony helping her to climb the fences. 'Lucky you haven't high heels on,' he said. 'You couldn't make it.'

'I'm all right. Don't worry about me.'

A pine wood lies at the foot of Balch. They threaded it, following the old ski trail there; and it was dark among the pines so that they went slowly, and once or twice Tony struck a flame on his cigarette lighter to show her the way. They emerged from the belt of woods and ascended the steep open slopes, moving in no haste, pausing now and then to look back across the plain below them to the College and the town.

'I've had a good time in Hanover,' Tony said. 'In spite of the war. I'll have a lot of things to remember.'

'That's the fun of being young,' she suggested. 'You accumulate a lot of memories and you always have them to turn back to happily.'

'I've got some that I won't want to remember.'

'I know, Tony.'

He said harshly: 'You don't know the half of it, Jan.' There was an irritation in his words, a hunger for confession in his heart, but she did not question him.

They moved on, came to the bald summit. Tony sat down, then lay down, looking up at the stars. 'They're not worried,' he said. 'Those stars up there! They're so damned calm and unconcerned. Or maybe they're bored, seeing the same things happen to people over and over.'

She sat down beside him. There was a ledge, and a moss-grown bowl beside it. It was a comfortable spot, the ledge, still warm from the day's sun, protecting them against the light breeze that drew across the hill-top. 'Maybe it's just that they're old and wise,' she said. 'Like grownups when children cry, sure that the children will forget their grief in a little while.' She looked down at him, seeing his eyes reflect the stars at which he stared.

'I wonder if Dad was driving,' he said at last. 'Probably he was talking to Lucy, not paying attention.'

Jan did not know, but she said quickly: 'Even if he was, you mustn't blame him. If you start blaming him, you'll lose him, even if you never let him know what you're thinking.'

'Oh, I'll never blame him.'

'You've got to go further than that,' she urged. 'You see, he's going to blame himself! You mustn't let him. You'll have to make him see that it wasn't his fault at all; and before you can do that, you'll have to make yourself see it.'

He said in a grim amusement: 'How did you get to be so wise?'

'It's just—understanding you both, knowing how close you and he are. If anything ever happened to spoil things between you two, you'd neither of you ever be the same again.'

He said after a moment: 'Jan, if Lucy hadn't been going to marry me, she wouldn't have been with Dad, wouldn't be dead now. So it's my fault, really.'

'You couldn't help loving her.'

For a long while he did not speak. 'My head feels as big as a barrel,' he said at last.

'Aches?'

'Yes, sure.'

'Want me to rub it? I cure Mother's that way, sometimes.'

'Go ahead.' He turned on his side, his cheek on her knee; and her strong fingers probed the congested muscles in his neck, loosening them.

'You're all tied up in knots,' she said. 'Relax, Tony.'

Under her hand he did so. There was a magnetic healing in her touch, and his eyes closed. 'Makes me sleepy already,' he said. 'I like having my head rubbed; always did.'

She did not speak. After a little he said: 'I met a girl once with hands like yours.' He hesitated, then went on in an ironic mirth: 'It was at an inn up in Quebec, the night Barbie told me she was engaged. On the couch in front of the fire. This girl rubbed my head, the way you're doing right now. I fell in love with her, but in the morning she was gone. Then I came back to Boston and Dad invited me to have lunch with him and Mrs. Kerr. He had told me he wanted to marry her, and when I met her, she was the same girl I had met at the inn!'

Jan made an astonished sound, warm with sympathy, and he laughed grimly. 'Joke on me, wasn't it?'

She did not speak at once. 'Does your father know?' she asked then.

'No,' Tony hesitated. 'I acted like a heel about it,' he said. 'I wouldn't let her tell him we already knew each other—and—I told her I was in love with her myself. But I got wise to myself afterward. I couldn't mess things up for her and Dad. That's why I started running around with Lucy, to get her out of my mind. I knew she wouldn't marry Dad till I did.'

When Jan spoke, it was after a long interval, and very quietly. 'I never thought you were really in love with Lucy. I know you weren't.'

He did not move, but after a moment he spoke, trying to laugh at her. 'How do you know so much?'

'Well, for one thing, you didn't think of her, at first, when you knew about the accident. You didn't even ask about her for a long time. You just thought of your father.'

He said carefully: 'That doesn't prove anything.' She did not insist, and for long minutes neither of them spoke, her hands firm on his head, his eyes closed, the stars bright and close, the soft wind deflected by the ledge just above them. The moon had risen. From the direction of the College came a faint far murmur of music; a dance at some fraternity house was now in the small morning hours in full tide. Then she felt a movement under her hand; and he said huskily:

'You're a queer kid, Jan. You're right, partly. I wasn't really in love with Lucy. I was crazy about her, but I wasn't in love with her. Just her hand touching mine was—well, it was something, Jan! And with the war and everything, I was reckless, anyway.' He stirred restlessly, his voice suddenly strained and empty. 'You're so damned fine and decent yourself you can't understand, of course.'

She said slowly: 'I understand lots of things. I'm not—' she hesitated. 'Not a child, you know.'

He spoke harshly: 'We lost our heads, Jan. It was my fault, of course. It always is, isn't it.' He lay very still, his head upon her knee. 'Jan,' he said, 'I've got to tell someone. Dad knew—but now maybe he's going to die. Jan—Lucy was going to have a baby. That's why we were getting married in such a hurry.'

She did not speak, nor did her hands cease their firm touch upon his head, but a blinding flash of agony thrust at her heart like a lightning stroke, stopping her pulse, filling her whole body and heart and soul with unbearable, scalding pain. He looked up at her, but she made no sound nor movement, and her eyes were fixed on the far dark shadows of the hills.

'Now she's dead,' he said, and he whispered, half to himself: 'There never was anyone more alive than Lucy. I've never seen her tired, or sleepy, or anything like that. She could dance all night and go to breakfast at sunrise and go home and change and go on all day. Sometimes I was ready to pass out, and she'd be as fresh as ever. And now she's dead.' He stirred, repeated slowly: 'Dead, dead, dead!'

She leaned against the ledge at their backs, looking down at him. Her arm was tired, aching with fatigue; and strength seemed to flow out of her through her fingers into him. She changed hands, shifting her position a little, and he asked: 'Tired?' She shook her head, not daring to try to speak, and he urged: 'Cold? Want to go back?' She shook her head again.

He said almost drowsily: 'You're a good kid, Jan. You've always been swell to me.'

But she still said no word, and he slept at last. When she knew he was asleep, she drew his coat collar snugly around his throat. Her mother, she thought remotely, might wonder where she was; but her father would understand. Probably they were both asleep long ago, and Will was dancing somewhere, and at dawn the dances would break up and everyone would troop away for early breakfast.

But she would stay here, gladly, if by so doing she could put strength and peace into Tony. She had loved him so truly and so long; but her love for him was all giving, not demanding. What he had told her had gripped her in a vise of pain, of pain and of bewilderment too; pain as though some physical part of her had been wrenched away, and bewilderment because, although she was informed and instructed in the physical mysteries, they were mysteries to her still. Lucy she had since she was a child distrusted, feeling in the other some quality which she found abhorrent. But Tony she had always set so high that, although she could know what his words meant, she could not comprehend them. So though she had never suffered as she suffered in this moment, she did not blame him for her hurt.

She did not even blame Lucy, for Lucy was dead. Lucy alive had worn always a something flaunting in her eyes, a challenge and a promise which every man could read, and which Jan had sensed and hated; but Lucy in death had found a sort of sanctuary. Jan was mature beyond her nineteen years, endowed with that innate and gracious understanding which is the birthright of some women, a sort of blindness which consists in being unable to see ugliness in those well loved, which accepts a man whole, in all his parts, for what he is, with neither praise nor blame, but just with love. Whatever Tony had done or might do, he dwelt in her heart. She could even understand that by confessing the truth to her, he had found a sort of absolution; that by hurting her he had eased himself; and that if she did not blame him, he would not torment himself with futile blame.

So she would never blame him, and for his sake she would hide and forget her own deep wound, telling herself that what Lucy had had from Tony was no part of the Tony she herself had always loved. Yet— since now he was asleep, and could not see her tears, her eyes filled. She wept not for herself but for him. She leaned her head back, letting it rest on the ledge behind her; and she watched the stars awhile through blurred eyes, and then her eyes closed.

Tony slept as soundly as a baby, without moving, his head heavy on her knee; and her foot went to sleep, till she cautiously straightened her leg, careful not to disturb him, and wriggled her toes till life came into them again. Then she herself must have slept, for when she began to be cold and opened her eyes, there was light in the eastern sky. Her leg was asleep, prickling and tingling, and this time when she moved it, Tony roused and sat up and stared at her stupidly. Then she saw his eyes clear as he remembered.

'Gosh, it's almost morning!' he exclaimed. He stood up and helped her to her feet, and she groaned and smiled.

'I'm so stiff I creak!' she confessed.

'Why didn't you wake me?'

'I was asleep myself.'

He hesitated. Then he said: 'Poor kid! Come on. Let's get back to town.'

They descended the open hillside, went through the woods and came to the road, and the pearl-gray dawn light was cool and quiet among the trees on either side. Once more he spoke to her, said in an awkward voice, not looking at her: 'Thanks, Jan. For letting me talk, I mean. That did me a lot of good.' She did not speak and he said: 'I hope you didn't catch cold.'

'No, I'm all right,' she said.

15

(June 1940)

Robin returned from Mercersville to New York on Tuesday, at once saddened and deeply and gratefully happy; for Davy at last was dead and she could go freely to Mark, without the necessity of carrying through the annulment proceedings she had dreaded. She had left in New York no forwarding address, so there was one of Mark's letters waiting for her and half a dozen others—from her father, friends, persons with whom she was negotiating for portrait commissions—and two telegrams. The first she opened was from Mrs. Wethered, an old client, in Pittsburgh, asking whether she could come at once to do a series of watercolor sketches of Gladys Wethered's prospective wedding. Robin smiled and said aloud: 'Sorry, my dear, but I've a wedding of my own to attend to now.' She tore open the other telegram.

This, forwarded by Mark's secretary in Boston, was from Tony. He had wired:

> Father injured in auto accident, still unconscious, but they say he will recover. He is in Hospital here.
>
> Tony.

Robin stared for a moment at the dreadful words, and then with a low cry she ran to the telephone. The telegram came from Hanover, so she called Tony there. When the Hanover operator said Tony's room was presumably vacated, Robin bade her try the hospital. Tony was not there, but Robin asked for the doctor in charge of Judge Worth, and Doctor Forbes presently came on the phone.

She told him who she was, and the Doctor said: 'Oh, yes, Mrs. Kerr. Judge Worth's son said you might call. Judge Worth is doing very well. I'm sure he will be all right.'

'Was he badly hurt?'

He recited Mark's lesser injuries. 'And there was a slight skull fracture,' he concluded. 'An operation seemed advisable, but it was completely successful. There's no'—he chose a layman's words—'no injury to the brain. A week or two of quiet will see Judge Worth as well as ever, I'm sure.'

Robin shivered uncontrollably. Davy's skull had been cracked and shattered, too. She asked in a choking voice where Tony was, and Doctor Forbes said he had gone to Boston. 'Miss Pride, the young lady with Judge Worth, was killed in the accident,' he explained. 'Tony went to Boston to her funeral, but he'll be back here this afternoon.'

Robin cried out in quick sympathy, and tears filled her eyes as much for Tony's grief as for his father's hurt. She asked Doctor Forbes to tell Tony when he returned that she would come to Hanover at once.

She reached Hanover that afternoon, flying from New York to Boston, from Boston to White River Junction. The flights were short, but they seemed to her interminable. When she could not endure her own thoughts—Suppose Doctor Forbes were wrong? Suppose Mark never recovered? Suppose Mark were to become a thing like poor Davy?—she read, the travel folders, the airways time-tables, the magazines and newspapers which the stewardess gave her. Reynaud in France had given way to old Marshal Pétain, and Pétain had asked for an armistice. France, which even a month ago had seemed to the world invulnerable, was conquered.

But to Robin all this was nothing, and only her eyes, not her thoughts, focussed on the words she read. A dreadful haste beset her; yet even after she came to Hanover, and met Tony, and heard all he could tell her, there were to be days of waiting till Mark could speak to her. During those days, in an historic railroad car in Compiègne Forest, France came humbly to her knees and Germany and then Italy dictated terms.

That, too, was nothing to Robin—nor to Tony, waiting on Mark's slow recovery. When at last they were permitted to see him, he smiled in a drowsy content at sight of them, and without questions fell gently asleep and slept the day away.

After that, whenever he waked, one or the other of them was by his bed. Robin had a cot in his room, sharing the duties of his night nurse; and Tony took over the vigil by day. As Mark presently began to wish to know what had happened, they told him at first less than the truth; but on the third day, alone with Tony, he asked quietly:

'Son, was Lucy killed?'

Tony tried to lie. 'No, she's all right, Dad.'

Mark shook his head in sober understanding. 'If she were hurt, you'd be with her. If she were all right, you'd bring her to see me. So she's dead.' Tony could not speak, and Mark closed his eyes. 'I'm sorry, son,' he said.

'You couldn't help it.'

'I should have been driving. She had driven all the way from Nashua. I should have relieved her.'

Tony held hard to his father's hand. 'It happened, Dad,' he said. 'All we can do is forget it and—well, forget it.'

Mark looked at his son for a long moment. 'I wish it had been me instead of Lucy,' he said.

Tony said sternly: 'Stop it! You're weak and hurt and sick, and you're not talking sense. Stop it, Dad. Stop it—and forget it. It's the only thing to do.'

Mark nodded quietly. 'Yes,' he agreed. 'The only thing to do.' He asked: 'Where's Robin?'

'I made her go for a walk. She stays here all night with you.'

Mark met his son's eyes, and he remembered what Lucy had told him, while they were driving up from Boston, about Robin and Tony and their first encounter. Yet remembering, he put a seal upon his lips. Robin and Tony need never guess that he knew there was a mystery.

But suddenly, in rushing, contrite words, Tony was telling him that story. 'I acted like a kid,' he said. 'Not telling you right away was the worst. Mrs. Kerr started to, but I interrupted her; and she couldn't tell you then without making a liar out of me. So she kept still. You see, Dad,' he finished honestly, 'I thought she was my age; but to her I was just a kid in trouble, so she was nice to me.'

Mark's eyes had closed with gratefulness. He might have said: 'Yes, I know. Lucy told me.' But if he did so, Tony would blame Lucy. There was no need of that.

'It's all right, Tony,' he said. 'I understand.'

He was asleep when Robin returned and took Tony's place beside him; and when he woke again, he was visibly stronger. He was even interested in events outside their own lives. 'There's one question I've dreaded to ask,' he confessed. 'France must be beaten by now.'

'Yes,' she assented. 'France surrendered. The armistice was signed day before yesterday.'

His eyes searched her face. 'Does Germany get the French fleet?'

She said: 'No one really knows. The armistice says the fleet will be demobilized and interned by Germany and Italy, except some vessels in colonial waters. On the face of it, Germany can't use the ships against England. But if she wants to, France can't stop her, and Germany's promises don't mean much.'

'If Germany gets those ships to add to hers and to Italy's navy, she can challenge England on the sea.'

Robin smiled. 'Hush, my dear! Whatever happens, you can't prevent it. Your job is to get well, quickly.' She leaned toward him, wishing to tell him now about Davy; but that might for the present be unwise. So she made him rest, and she stayed quietly with him till the doctor made his rounds. Afterward she went out into the corridor with the physician. Doctor Forbes said at once:

'He's making rapid progress now, Mrs. Kerr. He'll be as well as ever in a month.'

She asked: 'Is he strong enough to hear some news?'

He looked at her with a faint twinkle in his eyes. 'Good news?'

She colored deeply. 'Yes, the best,' she said. 'For him and for me.'

'By all means,' he assured her. 'Tell him. It's just what he needs.'

She nodded, and went back into Mark's room and sat beside him. After a little his nurse left them together. She leaned toward Mark, then, smiling; and he saw something new in her eyes.

'What is it, Robin?' he asked. 'You're suddenly radiant, shining.'

She clasped his hand, leaned gently to kiss him. 'My darling, my darling,' she whispered. 'Get well quickly. I can be all yours now.' His eyes widened in quick question, and she nodded happily, with streaming tears. 'Yes, Mark,' she said gently. 'Yes, my dear. Poor Davy is dead.'

XIV

Luftwaffe

(July 1940–June 1941)

(July 1940)

MARK and Robin were married on a fine sunny afternoon early in July. Mark was still abed, but the nurses trundled him out on the hospital veranda and propped him up with pillows, and Robin stood radiant beside him. Her own father was not well enough to travel; but Dan Worth, recovered from the cold which had made him miss Tony's Commencement, had come on from Hardiston, and Robin insisted that he give the bride away.

The Halsteads and the Ritchies drove up from Boston for the day, and afterward, Mary Halstead said they must go and let Mark rest; but Robin happily insisted that they stay awhile, so chairs were brought and they grouped around Mark's bed, and he asked the news in Boston, and Mary said, looking toward Ed beside her, reaching to clasp his hand:

'Well, of course, the big news for Ed and me is that Edwin has gone into the RCAF.'

Tony, frankly envious, cried: 'Gosh, that's great! I wish I were with him.' Then Robin caught his eyes in quick warning, as though begging him not to worry Mark, and Tony, understanding, added quickly, to reassure his father: 'But I guess England has more pilots than she has planes, right now.'

'We didn't want him to do it, of course,' Mary told them. 'But with Ed in the Navy, we couldn't say no!'

'I told him he was in too much of a hurry, that England didn't need men,' Ed explained; but Mark saw that behind their anxiety lay a high pride in this son of theirs. 'I told him if he really wanted to help, he'd better get a job in a factory.' He grinned. 'But he said that was too much like work! He wanted some excitement.'

Mark remembered how Edwin had always loved and respected his father, and he thought it was not surprising that with Ed in the Navy, Edwin, too, should have wished to serve. Tony asked: 'When did he go?' His own longing was only half concealed, and Mark watched him soberly.

'Ten days ago,' Ed said. 'He thought he might have trouble getting in, but they grabbed him.' Mary was near him, and Mark seemed suddenly to see Edwin standing here between these two; a tall, quiet boy with a girl's sweetness in his eyes. It was hard to imagine that tender lad coursing the skies to kill—or himself to die. Yet thousands of boys just like him, beardless, their cheeks as smooth as a woman's, their clear eyes untaught by fear, were at this Devil's business today at the command and direction of old withered sapless men who had forgotten youth's illusions long ago and were now enslaved by senseless, greedy ideologies. There was a bad taste in Mark's mouth at the thought.

He lay, Robin's hand in his, and listened to their talk. Ed spoke of the glory of Dunkirk; and Mark's father, with that individual point of view which Robin even in their short acquaintance had come to expect in him, said thoughtfully:

'I wonder if the Germans really tried to capture that British army.' Everyone looked at him in surprise, and he cleared his throat—Robin smiled, recognizing how it pleased him to seize thus the general attention—and went on: 'They tried to kill them, of course. But to capture them? I'm not so sure. That would have meant three hundred and fifty thousand more mouths for Germany to feed. As it is, England's just a concentration camp. The English army is a prisoner in England, and the threat of invasion will keep them there. If the Germans are as clever as they seem, they may have deliberately let the English get away.'

The suggestion startled them all into a lively discussion of what would come next. When Tony predicted that the Luftwaffe would before winter bomb England into submission, Dan Worth dissented.

'That will never happen,' he said certainly. 'The English are sufficiently brave—or stupid, if you prefer—never to know when they're licked. Bombing doesn't capture cities. Remember Madrid.' He chuckled. 'The English have endured that climate of theirs so long that bombing will be almost a relief. Anything to take the climate off their minds.'

Everyone smiled, and he added: 'The Germans may try it, of course; but it won't work. No, I suspect Germany will be content simply to pin the English army in England under a threat of invasion, and go ahead with the organization of a German Europe. She's won all she hopes to win. She'll be satisfied to consolidate her gains.'

Talk of the war went on. Robin and Nell and Mary left the men for a while together, and Ed exulted over the British action in smashing the French fleet at Oran; and Mark's father suggested that while the action may have been practical, it was not particularly glorious. 'The French couldn't fight back,' he pointed out.

Ed laughed and said good-humoredly: 'The trouble with you Middle-Westerners, Mr. Worth, you're all pro-Germans.'

Mark felt a sharp resentment, thinking that Ed's mind had narrowed since he went back into the service; yet perhaps an inelastic single-mindedness was a necessary part of the makeup of a good army or navy man. But Dan Worth only smiled and said tolerantly:

'To you pro-English, we pro-Americans seem like pro-Germans, I suppose. If war feeling continues to grow, it will soon be considered shameful in this country to stand up for purely American interests.'

That led them to speak of politics. Bob was jubilant at Willkie's triumphant nomination; but Dan Worth said:

'I'm afraid he's losing ground already. He hit his peak at the Convention. Up till then, he had been paying his own way, and saying what he believed; and people liked him for it. But now—no individual can finance a national campaign with his own funds—he'll have to play ball with the party leaders. They'll tell him what to say in every speech he makes. If he talks to farmers, he'll talk crops and subsidies, promise them whatever they want. If he talks to labor he'll say "Hurray for the CIO," or for the AFL as the case may be. Every word he says from now on will be dictated by politicians, inspired not by his own convictions but by his desire to win votes.' He added wisely: 'And he'll probably make the mistake of attacking Mr. Roosevelt—for that is a mistake. Those who dislike Mr. Roosevelt will vote for Willkie, anyway, but he's got to win the votes of a lot of men who like Mr. Roosevelt, and every time he attacks the President, he'll lose votes in that category.'

Bob did not agree, sure that a crusade against Mr. Roosevelt and all his works was what the country needed; and Ed took issue with him. 'Of course England's bound to win this war in the long run,' he said. 'But it will be a long run. Mr. Roosevelt has seen what was coming better than the rest of us. We'd better let him carry on.'

Mark, lying quietly, took no part in their discussion; but he thought that Dunkirk had made even Ed recognize England's danger; and as this realization swept the country, our national willingness to help England would increase day by day. Always in his thoughts he fell back on his deep conviction that in the end American sentiment would be overwhelmingly on England's side. Union Now as a formal political relationship was out of the question; but when their interests and their ideals and their aspirations ran together, the United States and England would stand associated in a free and equal partnership, pooling their resources in a common cause.

Even though he said little, he was beginning to be wearied by this talk and by the thoughts it provoked before Robin presently returned with Nell and Mary, and Mary said it was time to start the long drive back to Boston.

'I shouldn't have come at all,' she confessed. 'We've just taken in two little English refugees to live with us, and there's no telling what my crowd of barbarians has done to them by now.'

'Heavens!' Nell exclaimed. 'Didn't you have enough to do without that? They say a lot of the English children coming over are awful little brats.'

'Well, probably my young ones would seem like brats to some women in England,' Mary said cheerfully; and Ed suggested that England and the United States would be drawn close together when these children who had learned to know American ways grew up; and there was a stir in readiness for departure. But Dan Worth had the last word before the others left.

'You spoke of drawing this country and England together, Mr. Halstead,' he suggested. 'Dunkirk did that. Remember Kipling's story about the tree called the Monkey-Puzzler. The moral was that England and her colonies—and now it's equally true of England and the United States—are drawn together by the bonds of common funk!'

2

(Summer 1940)

They stayed in Hanover through July, waiting until Mark could travel comfortably; and when they were not with him, Robin and Tony were much together, and confidence and understanding grew between them. 'I can talk to you about things that I can't even discuss with Dad,' Tony said once. 'Because if I talked to him he'd worry.'

One of these things was his strong desire to imitate Edwin Halstead, to go into the Canadian Air Force. 'Or to do something!' he amended. 'Almost anything! It's not that I have any passionate conviction that it's my duty to fight Hitler; but I'm tired of thinking. I want to do something that will keep me too busy to think.'

Anxious for Mark's sake to dissuade Tony from any such move, she reminded him that Mr. Roosevelt had said in a message to Congress a few days before—a message asking for five billions more in defense appropriations—that 'we will not send our men to take part in European wars.' And she suggested: 'I think any American can stay in line with his country's foreign policy and still feel he's doing his full duty.'

'I'm sort of tired of hearing people say we're going to stay out,' he confessed. 'When you come right down to it, it's contemptible. Churchill says England's fighting alone, but that she's not fighting for herself alone, and that's about right.'

Robin tried in every way—short of open opposition—to persuade Tony to give up this idea; and she was successful for the time. He did nothing. Mr. Roosevelt was nominated and the Democratic platform swore that: 'We will not participate in foreign wars, and we will not send our Army, Navy, or Air Force to fight in foreign lands, outside of the Americas, except in case of attack.' The Republican platform and Mr. Willkie had taken much the same position; so the war was not formally an issue in the campaign just getting under way. There was even—after the end of the Battle of Europe—a lull in military action. Hitler offered England peace, and England refused it; and a few bombs fell on England and on Germany, but for a while that was all. After the first shock of the fall of France, the minds of men presently returned to their own affairs. Mr. Roosevelt, who in May had thought a billion-dollar appropriation sufficient to meet immediate defense needs, before the end of July had increased that figure by ten billions more. Mark said to Robin one day:

'Congress is giving him whatever he asks. I believe the American mind is ahead of Mr. Roosevelt in willingness to meet this situation honestly. The trouble is, he has no conception of the task ahead, no conception of its magnitude. To raise this country to a military status that can compare with Germany's will cost a hundred billion or more, and every day's delay—we should have started two years ago—makes the task so much more difficult and more costly. We need a man in the White House with sufficient vision to see what's coming and to see it in concrete terms—terms of men and planes and ships. Mr. Roosevelt's doing too little, and what little he's doing should have been done long ago.'

Doctor Forbes insisted on keeping Mark quietly in bed longer than seemed to any of them necessary. 'After all, Doctor,' Mark urged smilingly, 'this is no way to spend a honeymoon.' When he began to be permitted to stand up, to use his crutches, Doctor Forbes agreed that in a few days he might move to the Inn for the next stage of his convalescence. Robin elected to go to New York in the meantime, to close her apartment, see to the packing of her things, arrange for their shipment to her new home.

'And I've days of shopping to do,' she reminded them. 'What's a bride without a trousseau!'

The afternoon before her departure, she and Tony, after they left Mark at the hospital, went for a walk together, and they climbed Balch Hill and sat awhile there, watching cloud shadows sweep across the valley and the Vermont hills, and the blue crests of tumbled mountain masses against the blue sky far away. Tony said it was a great day for flying, and he spoke again of Edwin Halstead. 'If Dad weren't laid up, I think I'd be in Canada now,' he admitted. 'But if I did go, he'd think it was because of Lucy and blame himself. I don't want to worry him.' He looked at her smilingly. 'I keep forgetting he has you to take care of him now. It doesn't seem as though you and he were really married yet.'

'He'll need us both for a while,' she urged. 'I'm glad you're standing by.'

'I'm restless as the devil,' he admitted. 'I want to do something. The idea of settling down to Law School—with the world in the mess it's in—just makes me gag.' And he added: 'Maybe if they put through the draft they'll take me. That will let me off Law School, anyway.'

'Tony, why don't you tell your father how you feel about Law School?' she suggested. 'He'd advise you to give it up, if he knew.'

'Maybe I will.' He sat hugging his knees, his eyes afar. 'I always get a kick out of coming up here on Balch,' he said. 'Jan Ritchie and I came up here the night Dad was hurt. We stayed all night, till daylight; sat and talked for hours, till I went to sleep. I was worn out. But I felt a lot better for it. We did a lot of talking.' She looked at him, and he met her eyes, smiling. 'I'm glad you and Dad are married,' he said.

'So am I.'

'I told him about that night at the inn, about the first time I saw you.'

'Did you? I'm glad you did, Tony. I don't like secrets from him; but you were the one to tell him.'

'I wanted to straighten things out as well as I could.' He added, his eyes shadowed: 'But there are a lot of things I can't straighten out, ever.'

She said simply, after a moment: 'You're thinking of Lucy.' She added: 'Your father told me about—you and her, Tony.'

He looked at her miserably. 'Then you know how I must be feeling.' He made a wretched gesture. 'This is a hell of a world, isn't it.' He laughed shortly at his own words, went on: 'So much all poured in together, the things that are happening in Europe, and Lucy and me, and now she's dead. Maybe you think I ought to be kicked, or shot, or something. I think so myself, sometimes. But—I'm not trying to alibi myself, just trying to show you how it was—this last year has been tough on fellows my age. There've been so many things threatening to happen to us that it seemed to sharpen our perceptions, and make us feel, every time we did anything that was—sweet and thrilling and beautiful—that perhaps we were doing it for the last time. So we did it all the harder.'

'I know,' she assented. 'I'm young enough to feel the same thing. There's a war psychology that affects women even more strongly than men. It makes us want to give our men—everything—while we can.' She hesitated, then said quietly: 'You know, Tony, I was ready, since we couldn't be married, to—to love your father as Lucy loved you. Only his strength kept me from doing so.' She smiled. 'So you see I'll never blame you and Lucy, Tony.'

'Gosh!' he whispered. Then he said slowly: 'I think we'll all be better, or happier somehow, after this war. There's a sort of spiritual rejuvenation in tragedy, isn't there?'

'The old Greeks used to say so.'

'I've seen the war working on some of my classmates that way, making them better and finer. The best of them are beginning to get steadied down to this new world. I think a lot of fellows my age have accepted the fact that this is really a world revolution, and they want to do their share to work out a better world than the old one. Even if all they can do is to go to war and be killed.'

'You sound like your father.'

His eyes shone. 'He's great, isn't he. I'm just beginning to appreciate him. You know, he's worked out a personal philosophy that the world needs pretty desperately right now. I can remember things he's said to me ever since I was a baby, and they all fit into a pattern: doing your job as well as you can; doing the job that's within reach and that you can do, instead of worrying about things you can't help; competing not with others but with yourself; trying to make sure you do as well as you can, without worrying about whether you do as well as somebody else.' And he said thoughtfully: 'The thing that bothers him is, he always sees both sides. He sees some good in Germany, for instance, and some bad in England. I'm the same way, sort of. I can't help admiring the way Germany does what she sets out to do. Every time England does some damned bungling job and gets a black eye out of it, I'm sort of glad. But all the same, I don't want to see her licked.'

She nodded. 'The happy people are probably the ones who can just decide they hate Hitler and all his works.'

'Sure. Like being a soldier and just doing what you're told and not thinking about rights and wrongs at all. That's all right after you're in a war. You have to be that way. But till you're in, everybody has a right to think for himself.'

She smiled. 'It's a difference of opinion that makes horse races—and wars,' she suggested.

'Yes, and politics, too,' he reminded her. 'I'll be old enough to vote, this fall.'

'Are you for Mr. Willkie?'

'Sure. But Roosevelt will be re-elected. Even if he has to get us in the war to do it.' He added grimly: 'Or maybe he'll just do what Wilson did, brag that he's kept us out of war, promise to go on keeping us out, and then, as soon as he's elected, take us into it.'

'Do you think we ought to go into it?'

'Maybe I've caught it from Dad,' he said, 'but I think we ought to do whatever we have to do to kept England from getting licked.' He added grimly: 'Maybe we're too late already. Most of the English army got home from Dunkirk—but they left their guns behind. If Germany could land a couple of Panzer divisions in England today—now that France has given up—Good night!' And he said: 'Even without that, German planes can smash London.'

'You believe in planes, don't you?'

'They've won every campaign in this war,' he reminded her. 'The Luftwaffe is the most powerful weapon any nation ever forged.' He spoke in a fashion almost abstracted. 'It's the greatest air force in the world, and until England builds up her strength to meet it, the Luftwaffe can smash any country in the world today.'

Robin shivered faintly. 'I know so little about it,' she confessed. 'Planes can destroy buildings and cities, and they can kill. But Tony, can they ever smash the souls of men?'

He looked at her in quick gratefulness. 'You're swell,' he said. 'Women are swell, anyway. I've always been sort of in love with someone, Barbie Parks, and you—I love you as much as Dad does, you know.' His tone was completely frank and unconstrained. 'In a different way, of course; because he's a man and I'm still a boy. You don't ever need to worry about my feeling for you.' He added: 'And I loved Lucy.' He frowned at his own thoughts. 'There's been war—or the threat of it—in the world ever since I can remember, and I've worried and stewed about it, except when Barbie or you or Lucy or someone made me forget it. You women all have a way of bringing life down to simple things, love, and tenderness, and—well, what you just said about the souls of men. If I could look at things your way, the war wouldn't matter.'

'Men do so many things that seem foolish to women,' she confessed. 'And war's the most foolish of them all.'

They rose at last, at peace together, moving slowly down toward the pines and across to the golf links and so to the Hospital. Tony left her with his father, going on alone to the Inn.

3

(August–September 1940)

They came back to Boston—Tony went before them to pick out a new car and returned to Hanover to drive them home—and Mark's friends greeted him and made Robin welcome. Ruth Rollins called one evening, and she reported that she was working for Jerry Crocker, doing the typing on his book.

'He wrote to me, a week or so after Tommy's wedding,' she told Mark. 'He said you gave him my address.'

'I did,' he assented. 'I thought you'd find the work interesting.'

She laughed at her own thoughts. 'I do,' she agreed. 'His idea at first was that I'd just copy his manuscript, working at my apartment; but his handwriting's terrible and there were words on almost every line I couldn't read—he hates using the typewriter, always preferred to write his articles in longhand and then copy them himself, pecking them out a word at a time—and I said we could save time if I worked with him, near him, so I could ask him about the parts I couldn't read. So now I work at his home.'

'I cleared his title to that place,' Mark remembered. 'But I've never seen it.'

'I know,' she assented. 'It's a lovely old house, but he doesn't want people dropping in. He's awfully shy.'

'You and he get along all right, do you?'

'Oh, yes, he's really sweet. At first I was scared of him, till I realized that the reason he barks so is because he's scared of me!'

Mark smiled. 'But when he's interested in what's being said, he gets over being scared.'

She laughed in a pleasant content. 'Oh, he's all over it now!' she agreed.

Robin looked at her wisely, and after she was gone, Mark said: 'I'm glad she and Jerry are working together. They'll make a good team.'

'I like her,' Robin agreed. 'How old is she?'

'Twenty-two or three. But—she's mature for her age.'

'I've not met Mr. Crocker. He must be older than she is.'

'He's younger than I,' he assured her. 'I'm glad Ruth likes him.'

She laughed at his unspoken thought. 'Men are worse match-makers than women,' she declared, and he laughed with her, acknowledging the corn.

Elin had decided, in making the house ready for Robin, that her baby could no longer stay here; had taken little Anna to her uncle's. Robin would have had her come back, but Elin knew her own mind. 'It was all right with Tony away and Judge Worth in town all day,' she said. 'But not now.'

She and Robin from the first were friends. 'You know him so much better than I do,' Robin told her. 'You'll have to help me keep him happy.'

'All he needs for that is having you here,' Elin declared. 'He's a different man.'

Mark did not resume his duties on the bench until September; and they had their honeymoon at home. Tony, so that they might be alone, took a room in Cambridge in anticipation of Law School in the fall, but he came always for Sundays and often for dinner. Mark, now richly content, read the war news calmly. Mr. Roosevelt traded American destroyers for permission to build bases on English territory in the

Atlantic, and the nation accepted this as calmly as they accepted the draft. Mark thought these were the normal first steps toward our eventual participation in the war. The future, it seemed to him, was already decided for them all.

One day in September he had occasion to put his thoughts about that future in order—and in words. Ed and Mary Halstead—although Ed could only be there for week-ends—stayed at Humarock through that month. Saturday the twenty-first was a sultry day, and Mary telephoned Robin to urge them to come for a clambake on Sunday. Tony drove them down. For a month, Goering's Luftwaffe had been pounding England; and England's dogged acceptance of inescapable death and ruin, and the valor with which her fighter planes had stood off five or six times their number of attackers, had wakened American hearts to a proud sense of kinship long forgotten. Even Tony admitted that the Luftwaffe did not seem to be getting anywhere.

'I believe they're beaten,' Mark assented. He smiled. 'There used to be a story at Harvard about an advanced student who turned in a thesis attacking the philosophy of Plato. The professor wrote across the top: "When you strike at a King, you must kill him." The German bombings haven't beaten England, but they've tempered the English soul—and England's endurance of the raids has won American sympathies completely. So Germany's the loser.'

'Why do you suppose they haven't used gas?' Tony wondered.

'Probably for fear of reprisals. And England's pretty well prepared against gas attacks. Everyone seems to have gas masks.'

'What about mustard gas? Masks are no good against that!' Tony urged. 'It burns right through your clothes, burns you to the bone.' And he said: 'It's a cinch Germany will try gas any time she thinks it will win for her.'

Robin, sitting with Mark in the rear seat, shivered. 'How can men talk so cold-bloodedly about such things!' she protested. So they spoke of other matters for a while.

They reached the Humarock cottage just behind Bob and Nell. Will had come with his father and mother; but Jan was gone back to Merryfield, and Betty as usual had preferred her own devices. Sunday was almost as warm as Saturday had been, and Ann Halstead—she was a black-eyed, black-haired, tempestuously beautiful child of fifteen— begged Tony and Will to come for a swim with her and ten-year-old Burt. Danny, the youngest of the Halstead brood, had already departed to look for starfish and shells for the faintly odorous collection which he kept in a packing box under the veranda. Will went to swim with Ann and Burt, but Tony asked the latest news from Edwin, and Ed produced for him all of Edwin's letters, into which Tony plunged. Mary and Robin and Nell made themselves busy in the kitchen, and Mark and Bob and Ed walked out to the dunes above the beach to sit watching the swimmers, far enough from the house to avoid being called to help with the preliminary chores. Mark spoke of England's fine defense against the attacking German planes, and Ed agreed:

'They've done a good job, sure. But this air fighting is just a skirmish. The Germans can't hurt England as long as England's Navy's intact. And Hitler can't win without beating England. That's the ABC of the situation. England will starve her out in time.'

Bob protested: 'Ed, you're overlooking one thing. Germany has conquered Europe, so she holds a hundred million hostages against starvation. And Germany's ruthlessly practical. There's no sentiment in her. Every Norwegian and Hollander and Belgian and Frenchman will have starved to death before the Germans really begin to suffer.'

'You're crazy!' Ed retorted. 'If Hitler tries that, the starving people will rise against him.'

'There's no fight in starving men,' Bob said, grimly practical. 'There's only a dreadful, submissive apathy. They'll just lie down and die—unless we feed them.'

'Let Germany feed them!'

'Why should she?' Bob urged. 'They're her enemies. Why should she starve herself to feed her enemies? She'll never do it.' And he said: 'In total war like this, I don't think food is properly contraband. As things stand, it's England which is starving France and the others, not Germany.'

'The Germans took their food away from them!' Ed was red and angry.

'From the German point of view, that was only common sense,' Bob quietly insisted. 'But it's the English who won't let them buy more, won't even let us give them more. I think England's mistaken in that policy. The people of the conquered nations would have a lot more strength for revolt if they were well fed.'

Ed said hotly: "Why, damn it, man . . .' But before he could continue, Mary halloed to them from the house. 'Time to start the fi-i-ire!' So the three men set to work at this, and Will and Tony came up from the beach to lend a hand; and Will undertook to light the fire and made hard going of it. In his hands even a piece of driftwood seemed to acquire a maddening perversity, refusing to fit anywhere; and the matches he tried to strike broke, or sputtered and went out. They laughed at his failures, and called him thumb-handed, and Will grinned under their derision; but he nursed a small flame at last doggedly to life, and got a good blaze going.

After the clams were baked and devoured, while Ed helped Mary and Nell and Robin clean up the débris, burning paper cups and napkins, calling Tony and Will and the younger children to carry things back to the house, Mark and Bob sat on a drift log above the beach; and their talk ranged idly. The State Department had embargoed oil and gas to Japan and the Japanese protest had been filed; and the Japanese, having made a treaty with defeated France, were preparing to occupy Indo-China.

'If we didn't have this German mess on our hands, we'd be talking war with Japan,' Bob declared. 'But we're headed in the other direction. Churchill's going to hook us if he can.'

'I don't blame him,' Mark declared. 'He's doing a fine job for England. I wish we had as good a man in charge here.'

'Willkie'll be in, soon,' Bob predicted.

'I'm disappointed in Willkie,' Mark confessed.

Bob exclaimed in a frank surprise: 'Good Lord, why? You don't mean to say you'd vote for Roosevelt!'

Mark shook his head, smiling: 'Oh, no, I'll vote for Willkie, but as matters stand today I'll be voting not for him but against Mr. Roosevelt.'

Bob laughed. 'That's a damned poor reason, but it's better than none. There're certainly reasons enough to vote against Franklin.'

'I think so,' Mark assented. 'But Willkie has done just what my father predicted, last June. I thought him a brave man and an able one; but he's made his campaign on a basis of trying to say to each audience the thing that audience wanted to hear, and he's wasted time and talk on peanut politics. The United States, whether it wants to or not, is entering upon a period of universal military service, of tremendous taxation, of tremendous and continued armament. Yet Mr. Willkie talks about the Hatch Bill, and campaign expenditures, and Mr. Roosevelt's commercialization of the office of President.' He made a scornful sound. 'If Mr. Roosevelt neglected his duties to accept Willkie's challenge for a joint debate, he'd deserve to be impeached. There's nothing to debate. What we must do in the future has been settled for us. It was settled in Poland, if we'd had eyes to see.'

'Willkie has to play politics in the campaign,' Bob insisted. 'That's his only chance. What the devil do you want him to say?'

'I want him to say what I know he really thinks. I want to hear him say to us all: "The easy times are over. We have interpreted democracy as the right to serve our own selfish interests, but we can no longer do that. From now on, for as long as man can foresee, democracy demands from every man all he can give. Young men must learn to be soldiers. Business must yield the major portion of its profits to support an armament program. Labor must forget its rights and remember its duties. An unselfish devotion to the national good must be the first rule in every man's life. Social gains and personal advantages of every kind must go into the melting pot."' He had spoken strongly, but now he smiled at his own heat and concluded: 'That's what I'd like to hear Willkie—or someone say.'

'Suppose Franklin said those things,' Bob challenged. 'Would you vote for him?'

'No,' Mark confessed. 'It's too late for Mr. Roosevelt to say these things. If he promised to curtail labor's gains, for instance, his sincerity would be in question. But Mr. Willkie can say them, and mean them. I believe they are the articles of his personal faith.'

'If he said them, he wouldn't have a chance.'

'No chance of winning the election, perhaps! But if he said them and were beaten, he'd be a sure winner four years from now—because inside the year we'll all know he was right, know that those things are true.' And Mark added soberly: 'You know—as far as it's going to affect the life of the ordinary man and the lives of his children—this war is over. It has already settled our way of life for a generation—maybe two or three generations—to come.'

Bob looked at him thoughtfully. 'Won't who wins the war make a difference?'

'A difference of degree, not of kind. That's what Mr. Willkie should be saying. We face a future enormously complicated, demanding economy and good business judgment in every aspect of government. If Willkie pointed out—the obvious truth—that he is better fitted than Mr. Roosevelt to organize such a future, he'd lose the election—but he'd win the future.'

'He'll win this election, anyway!' Bob said doggedly.

'I doubt it,' Mark declared. 'I don't like Mr. Roosevelt any better than you do—but maybe I'm wrong. Maybe he's right. Certainly he's been right in his foreign policy. He told us in 1935 that there was trouble coming. In 1937 he made that Chicago speech. I thought him wrong then, and I still think he was wrong to talk when he couldn't back up his talk, but his talk was true talk. Then in 1939 he tried to start a peace conference. He tried to put through a repeal of the arms embargo, because if England and Germany went to war the embargo would hurt England, would help Germany. If we had repealed the embargo, it's just possible that there might have been no war. Borah killed that repeal, killed it by insisting that he knew better than Mr. Roosevelt whether war was coming. Roosevelt thought it was coming in 1939; Borah said it wasn't. Most of us thought—or hoped—Borah was right. But Roosevelt was right and the rest of us were wrong.'

Bob said: 'Borah represented the Middle West. They're still isolationists out there.'

Mark nodded. 'I've tried for years now,' he said, 'to read the composite American mind about European affairs. We in New England think one thing, and New York thinks probably about the same. The South will go along with Mr. Roosevelt. The West—or the Middle West, anyway—thinks the war's none of our business. In any group of say ten people, picked from the whole country, possibly one man wants to see Germany beat England, and wants us to stand aside and let it happen. Probably six or seven of the ten men want to see England beat Germany, and they're willing for us to help her as long as we don't have to fight to do it. And the other two or three men want us to go in right away on England's side.'

Bob nodded slowly. 'It's certainly true that the country hasn't made up its mind, not yet. And one thing's sure, Congress will never declare war.'

'Probably not,' Mark agreed. 'But Mr. Roosevelt may be able to goad Hitler into declaring war on us. I'm sometimes surprised Hitler hasn't done so already. I don't think Mr. Roosevelt will ever ask Congress to declare war—except as a last resort. He'll make Hitler start it.'

'If he's re-elected,' Bob amended.

'He will be, no doubt of that.'

Robin and Mary and Nell joined them, and Mark asked where Ed was. Mary said: 'Oh, he and Tony and Will are reading Edwin's letters and arguing about whether planes can sink battleships.' She laughed. 'They're fairly shouting at each other, as though any of them knew anything about it. Ed and Edwin argue even in their letters.' She added, looking at Mark: 'Tony's plane-crazy, isn't he? He'd like to be with Edwin.'

Mark smiled and looked at Robin, but she saw the shadow in his eyes; and Bob said, returning to their discussion: 'See here, Mark. I don't get what you mean by saying the war is over.'

'It's over so far as it affects the future way of life of the average man,' Mark explained. 'It was over a year ago. The conquest of Poland closed the old book. Germany's demonstration that an army of machines can beat an army of men means that from now on a major portion of our energies must be devoted to maintaining and manning, in self-defense, an army of machines.'

'England can beat Germany—and smash her machines—in time,' Bob argued.

Mark said drily: 'That's our national attitude today. We want to let England do it.'

'We're raising an army, drafting boys like Tony and Will,' Bob protested. 'And besides,' he added, 'we're already giving England what she needs. This war isn't costing so many lives, but it's destroying things. One bomb may wreck a factory. The men killed by that bomb can be replaced; but to replace the factory requires the labor of many men, and the capital accumulated by many other men. If we furnish the replacements of material loss, we'll be doing our share.'

Mary said strongly: 'Besides, Mark, you keep forgetting that the war will end sometime.'

'It will end, yes,' Mark agreed. 'But what then? It will end in victory, or in defeat, or in a stalemate. Suppose it's victory. That is, Germany sues for peace, and England and the United States and perhaps other nations collaborate in imposing terms. What—at a guess—would be the terms of such a peace?'

Mary laughed. 'I'll bite,' she assented. 'What would they be?'

'Well,' Mark hazarded, 'probably we'd begin by freeing France, Belgium, Holland, Denmark, Norway, Poland, Czecho-Slovakia. Poland would be difficult, because so many Poles are dead, or they've been transported to Siberia where they can never be found and brought back to Poland again. And maybe we'd send Hitler to Saint Helena. We might levy an indemnity, or dismember Germany.'

Bob nodded in agreement, and Mark went on:

'Such a victory may be achieved in three years, or four, or five. Say victory is won in 1945. Now what will the world be like after that victory?'

No one spoke, and he went on to answer his own question. 'Why, we'll have a prostrate Germany, surrounded by states from which she will have extracted every movable ounce of capital goods; and she will have expended those goods in her war effort. We'll have an impoverished and bankrupt Europe and a bankrupt England, her public debt colossal, much of her material capital destroyed by bombs, her people worn out by the long ordeal. We'll have here in the United States a public debt of, say, a hundred and fifty billion dollars. Our industrial plant—busy making munitions—will close down overnight. There will be say twenty million men either discharged from their jobs or demobilized from the army. We'll face a moral obligation to rebuild England, and to help rebuild those nations in Europe which Germany will have ruined; and for the sake of our own economy, we will have to rebuild Germany, too. Another fifty billion dollars to do it? Perhaps.'

He looked from eye to eye and said grimly: 'There's your victory! How do you like it?'

Bob laughed. 'Swell!' he drawled. 'You make it sound mighty attractive.'

Mary, too, smiled, and she said cheerfully: 'It's lucky Ed isn't here! You'd have a fine argument on your hands.' She looked toward the house. 'I guess he and the boys are still hard at it.'

But Nell asked Mark in a startled tone, 'If that's going to happen if Germany's beaten, what if she isn't?'

'The same thing, only worse and more of it,' Mark declared. 'Suppose England is forced to surrender. We must save England to win this war. We may not win the war even if we save England. We may get only a stalemate. But certainly if we lose England we lose the war.

'Suppose England has to surrender. Long before that becomes inevitable, the British Navy will be in Canadian and Australian and possibly in American hands. But Germany will dismantle—or seize and use—every British shipyard. She will destroy the British Isles as a military and naval station.

'But even if England surrenders, that would not mean peace; for the United States and Canada will never make peace with a victorious Germany. But there may be a truce, and a race by Germany's Europe on one side and by us on the other to build greater and greater fleets— of ships and planes—till we achieve mastery of the seas and of the air. And then another war to prove our mastery. There's your measure of defeat.'

They had listened in a close attention; and Mark, putting into words the thought which had so long absorbed him, forgot his listeners. With no prompting from them he went on:

'The other possibility is stalemate. Twice every day two opposing forces arrive at a stalemate on that beach below us here, on every beach that fronts the ocean. For six hours the rising tides conquer more and more of the land. Then for six hours the lands fight free of the receding seas. The process is repeated endlessly.

'Thus far in this war the German tides have been advancing. Probably Germany would make peace today on a basis of the *status quo,* plus perhaps the destruction of fortifications at Gibraltar and at Suez. She might even agree to release the western European nations and restore them to their former condition.

'But England would refuse such a peace, because some day the German tide will cease to rise. It will begin to ebb. Time enough then to talk of peace. That would be the English view.

'Suppose the ebb tide sets in. England and the United States achieve air superiority.'

Nell protested: 'But Mark, you keep talking as though we were already in the war.'

'We are, of course,' Mark agreed. 'It's true we're not yet fighting, but we're committed—committed so deeply that if England cannot win without us, we must join her, if only in self-defense.' And he went on: 'But about this stalemate, suppose England and the United States achieve air superiority. We gain footholds on the Continent, in Belgium and Holland and France; perhaps in Greece and Italy. Our advancing armies add daily to their gains.

'But the German defense, contracting, grows stronger every day, till at last England and the United States find themselves unable to advance farther.

'Then they might conceivably offer peace; but then Germany would not accept. She would hope to see the German tide once more begin to rise. Then a stalemate would be in sight. That might come in five years, or in ten. And stalemate, like defeat, would mean a tremendous armament race, and by and by another war.

'So, no matter how the war ends, so far as we in the United States are concerned—and we're already in it, inescapably—the result will differ only in degree. Hitler has forced us to meet his challenge, has forced us and the world today to meet him on his own terms. Victory will be bad enough, but stalemate or defeat will be infinitely worse. The world is like a city attacked by a great conflagration, when whole blocks of buildings must be dynamited to save the rest of the city from the fire.' And he concluded: 'So for us, for the average man in this country, in so far as it is to affect his life for the next two or three generations, the war is over. It was over a year ago, in mid-September, 1939. Victory is infinitely better than stalemate or defeat, but it is only a question of degree. Our way of life for years to come was settled when Poland fell.'

For a moment no one spoke. Nell shivered uncontrollably, and then Bob said in a serious tone: 'You make it sound pretty rough for the next generation, Mark. When will the damned thing end?'

'The last war isn't ended,' Mark reminded him. 'A lot of us still bear its scars and its unhealed wounds.' Bob himself was one of the belated casualties of the last war, and Mark remembered this as he went on. 'Perhaps you and I will never see peace again. Hitler has imposed his idea on us all, and we must live by it from now on.' He saw Ed coming toward them from the cottage, and Ed seemed to stumble, as though he were walking with his eyes closed. Mark watched the other in some puzzlement as he continued: 'We're entering an era of tremendous taxes, of a simpler way of life. Maybe we'll be better off, happier, in that new world, where because we have less we will be free from the tyranny of our possessions, from the tyranny of things. I think we will be. I suspect . . .'

And then abruptly he fell silent, for Ed was near, near enough so that Mark could see his face, white and drained and empty. Mark watched the other man, and Mary, following his eyes, looked around and saw Ed; and she scrambled to her feet and ran and clung to him and cried desperately: 'Ed! Ed! Ed!'

Ed held her in his arms, and over her shoulder he met their eyes. 'Just had a telegram,' he said thickly. 'From Ottawa. Edwin crashed. He's dead.'

4

(December 1940)

Robin saw more clearly than Mark the change in Tony after Edwin's death. Perhaps Mark refused to see what he did not wish to see; but Robin, since women are less apt to shut their eyes to tragic truth than men, watched Tony with open eyes. She watched him for Mark's sake, wishing she might somehow—for Mark's sake—avert what she foresaw.

There were occasions when she and Tony spoke together, skirting the fringes of the thought in both their minds. Tony might talk to her about Edwin. He said one day: 'He was a swell kid, the sort you always liked. You never got sore at him, even when we were all young ones, without being a little ashamed of yourself, because you knew it was your own fault.' He confessed that Law School bored him, that he did not want to be a lawyer. 'All lawyers do is talk. I'm sick of talking—and of thinking too.' She knew what it was he wished to do.

Edwin's death had had its effect upon all of them. Upon Mary, his mother, this was perhaps least apparent; but Robin knew why this was so, for she and Mary were much together. 'I can't let go, because of Ed,' Mary said. 'You see, he went back into the Navy because he thought he ought to, but he believes Edwin wouldn't have done any-thing—not so soon, anyway—if he hadn't done that, so he half blames himself. Then, besides, Ed thinks the Navy men are all overconfident and pretty stupid about a lot of things; but out of loyalty or something he pretends to be just like them, saying the same things, and he's really fighting himself all the time. So I have to do everything I can to keep him—well, to get him back into the groove; and so I can't think much about myself, or about Edwin.'

They were all in small ways changed by what had happened. Mark had fears he hid from Robin; and at the monthly dinners which he and his friends kept up, he saw a kindred taint of terror in Tom—Tommy was in the regular army—and in Bob, for Will's sake. Will had drawn an early number in the draft and would presumably be called when he finished his Law School year in June. Ed, too, was changed, no longer so dogmatically sure that Germany would be beaten; but he was even more determined that she should be. None of them now doubted that the United States would eventually be actively involved. Mr. Roosevelt before his re-election defined his policy as including hemisphere defense, aid to Britain, and no appeasement of the dictators; and the election was a mandate to him to proceed. After election, the army had turned over Flying Fortresses to Britain, and there were lesser steps on the sure road to war.

Mark and Robin decided to spend Christmas with her father in Montreal. Mark wished they might be in their own home for their first Christmas; but when Robin proposed Montreal—'I always go home for Christmas,' she explained. 'I never fail him'—he did not even suggest his own preference.

Tony when he heard their plans decided to go to Canada for some skiing, to join them on Christmas Eve. His more intimate friends at

Hanover were in Cambridge and Boston this winter—either for law or medicine or at the Business School—and they made up a party to go to one of the ski resorts north of Montreal. Tony brought Joe Hazen and Chuck Little to dinner the evening they were to take the train. He had during the fall often done this. Robin—and Elin in the kitchen —made them equally welcome. Mark enjoyed listening to their talk, watching the slow and almost imperceptible change in their opinions about the war; and they were all cheerfully in love with Robin. Sometimes, to see her with them, seeming not much older than they, made Mark feel his years; but more often it had the opposite effect, and he enjoyed the long discussions with these flexible young minds.

Charlie Spring, who had been Tony's most intimate friend at Hanover, was at Business School; but he was not among those who came often to the house; and Mark spoke of him tonight. Tony said, almost abashed: 'I haven't seen much of Charlie lately.' He asked the others: 'Have you?'

Chuck Little said: 'No. He always rode me pretty hard.' He grinned. 'Called me a war-monger, and a munitions magnate, and all that. We never got along.'

Tony explained: 'He and I got so we had an awful lot of arguments, Dad. He thinks Lindbergh is about the greatest man in the United States, you know. I guess most people in Chicago do. Charlie and I just don't get together much, any more.'

Mark was reminded of the rift between him and Judge Sothern, which had arisen when he suggested, that night at Professor Wearing's long ago, that England might lose the war. But that rift was healed now. Judge Sothern had come to him after Dunkirk with a frank apology. 'You saw more clearly than I did,' he said, and smiled and amended this. 'Or perhaps I saw the truth, too, and hated it, and therefore resented your putting it into words.' Since then they had been on the best of terms.

Listening to the talk at his own table here tonight, among these young men for whom death was already reaching out a tentative hand, Mark saw that these youngsters felt no fear, but only a sort of exhilaration, almost like gladness. Their clear tones rang. Chuck Little was saying:

'The Luftwaffe took a beating. There's no question of that. The English shot down thousands of their planes, made them stop the big daylight raids.'

Tony asked: 'Oh, by the way, Dad, did you ever meet Chad Frame?'

'I remember the name,' Mark assented. 'Wasn't he the fellow who gave you the whiskey that night in Merryfield?'

'Yes. He was a pretty heavy drinker in college, and he used to go to New York or come to Boston or go to Montreal for week-ends, run around with a hard lot of girls.' He looked at Robin apologetically, and went on: 'He got drunk in Montreal and enlisted in the RCAF, and Ed Spencer told me the other day that he's been flying a Spitfire in England and has shot down nine German planes, and he's been decorated and everything.'

Mark said, 'That's fine!' War had sometimes this compensation, bringing hours of glory into lives that must otherwise have been fore-doomed to end in vice and shame. If Chad survived the war, he would presumably be as ready for debauchery as in the past; but if he died in some valorous encounter in the skies, those who knew him would remember only his great deeds.

Tony and Chuck began to discuss the question whether it was possible to stop such night bombing as the raid which had smashed Coventry; and Mark saw Robin watching them, listening to their eager voices, and he thought with her that war in the long run was sure to exert upon the masculine mind an invincible fascination. The eyes of these boys were shining, their cheeks were bright. Joe Hazen presently reminded the others that Germany was not the only enemy.

'Japan has signed up with them,' he pointed out. 'She's promised to get into it if we go to war with Germany; and she's grabbing Indo-China in the meantime, getting into a spot where she can jump Singapore if she wants to. The Government knows it. They've advised Americans to pull out of China, and a lot of them are coming home.'

Tony said: 'Uncle Ed says the Navy can handle Japan any time.'

'Well, there are hundreds of thousands of Japs on the west coast, and in Honolulu,' Joe reminded them. 'The Navy can't handle them, because they're on shore. And if the Jap fleet stays at home, the Navy'll have trouble operating so far away.' He added: 'The trouble with us, we think we're good, and we think everybody else admits it. We do a lot of talking; but Germany's signed up Japan, and she's consolidating the Balkans—getting them to agree to be on her side. England's the only friend we've got.'

Tony cried: 'Well, O.K. I'm satisfied. I don't know any friend I'd rather have than England!'

Mark and Robin drove them to the train. Jan and Betty Ritchie and Will joined them there, and Will was carrying a burden of skis and

poles which were constantly out of control, the ends jabbing in all
directions while he strove to master them again and the others abused
him for his clumsiness and he laughed with them. There were a dozen
in the party, all laden with skis and poles and knapsacks and mis-
cellaneous gear. When he said good-bye, Tony promised to come to
Mark and Robin in Montreal for Christmas Eve and Christmas Day.
Then he was gone, and they drove home together in a quiet peace and
content; but Robin, remembering how Tony's eyes shone when he
spoke of Chad Frame's exploits, remembering the ring in his tones,
felt deep within herself a concern she dared not voice, a concern which
she hoped Mark need never share.

5

(December 1940)

Mark found Robin's father wise and thoughtful and well informed;
a tremendous man whose clothes and whose very skin were much too
big for him as a result of the fact that in recent years diet had reduced
his bulk. When he discussed the dietary régime which plagued him,
he spoke with a cheerful and amusing violence; but when he and Mark
talked about the war there was a calm firmness in his tones, a quiet
resolution and a complete acceptance of the fact of England's peril.

Through him Mark met other Montreal men, and to each one of
them he put the same question: 'Do you Canadians want us in the
war?' Their replies were uniform, and Robin's father spoke for all of
them when he said:

'No. As long as you can stay neutral, do so. You're helping us a lot
more now than you could if you were a belligerent. We need the things
you can supply us, and if you were in, a lot of that war material would
have to be kept at home.'

Mark was not sure whether this was in fact their opinion or whether
it represented merely their polite reluctance to attempt to influence the
thinking of even one American; but so far as he could judge, they
spoke what they thought. He found, too, that toward Mr. Roosevelt
they held a profound and grateful admiration. There was here none
of that criticism of the President which Mark was accustomed to hear
at home.

While they were there, Tony joined them for two days, and Robin
instantly perceived that some great and moving thing had happened

to him. Sometimes when he was directly addressed, he answered in a tone unnaturally loud, or with a movement of surprise, as though he had been waked from sleep. She wondered that Mark did not see this too; but if he did, he made no sign.

Yet he was not so unseeing as she thought, for when Tony had left them and she and Mark took the train for Boston, he spoke of it. She had said how well Tony looked, how happy he seemed.

Mark nodded. 'But he has something on his mind,' he told her.

'Did he talk to you?'

'No, but I could see.'

She smiled affectionately. 'I saw it too,' she admitted. 'But I didn't know you noticed. I should have known better. You've always been so close to him. What do you think it is?'

'He'll tell us when he's ready.' One of the things for which she loved Mark was that when he spoke of Tony, he never excluded her. Thus now he did not say: 'He'll tell me when he's ready.' He had from the first included her completely in that union between him and Tony which had been so long the biggest thing in his life.

He was proved right in his prediction; for the day Tony came home, he called them together, saying: 'I want to talk to you.'

He told them he had met Ingrid Sigurdson in Canada. 'She was up there skiing for two days, over the Sunday,' he said. 'She's working as a mechanic in an airplane factory in Ottawa. She told me about Norway.'

And he recited for them the story. Ingrid was at her home in Trondheim when the Germans struck. A young German whom they had known for years was visiting her brother. One morning early, Ingrid heard a sound in the hall outside her room, and when she opened her door, she saw him going down the stairs. He was in uniform, carrying a short rifle that must have been packed in his baggage. She tried to question him, and her brother heard their voices and came out into the hall, and the young German told them that Germany was coming into Norway to protect them against the English. Ingrid's brother protested, but they heard some scattering shots from the direction of the waterfront, and the young German turned and ran out of the house to do his appointed part.

Ingrid and her brother dressed hurriedly and went to see what was happening, and they saw German troops in control along the wharves, and more German soldiers and guns and tanks coming ashore from freighters there. They met some of their friends, as furious and as helpless as they; but then they met a young man who, although he was not in uniform, was an officer in the Norwegian army, and he told them all the Norwegian soldiers in Trondheim were slipping away to meet in the forests southeasterly. Ingrid and her brother hurried home and took two of her father's sporting rifles and all the ammunition there was in the house and made their way out of the city to join them.

During the next three days they met soldiers and others and formed a guerrilla band, and thereafter Ingrid fought with them, hiding on the mountainsides to fire at German troops on the roads below, setting fire to bridges, hindering the enemy in every way. Her brother was shot through the knee, and Ingrid helped cut off his leg—there was no doctor, and they had no anaesthetic and no instruments except sheath knives, a housewife's scissors and needles and thread, and a wood-worker's saw—and they dressed him in a uniform taken from a dead soldier in their band, so that if the Germans found him he would be treated not as a guerrilla but as a prisoner of war, and left him in a farmhouse when they had to retreat farther into the mountains.

Ingrid stayed with the band for almost three weeks. There were other girls at first, but they became exhausted or they were hurt or killed, till she was the only one. Eventually they joined the English operating out of Namsos, and then the English retreat began, and the embarkation. The Norwegian soldiers went aboard the English ships, but there was a difficulty where Ingrid was concerned.

'She says there was some rule against women on the ship,' Tony explained, 'or against foreign women, or something of the sort. She was terribly tired, half dead for sleep, and she doesn't remember exactly; but somehow it was decided that if she could marry an Englishman it would be all right. So a young officer, a midshipman or a lieutenant or something—she says he was just a boy, younger than she—offered to marry her and then let her divorce him in England, and the captain married them.

'But he was killed when the ship was machine-gunned by a plane, in the North Sea next day. She didn't know it till after she was landed in England, because she'd been put in the ship's hospital or sick bay or whatever they call it, and she slept all the way. Then afterward she decided to come to Canada, and she did—and I met her up there. I saw her coming down the hill toward us and recognized her half a mile away just by the way she handled herself or something.' He looked at Robin. 'You remember how good she was on skis.'

Robin did remember; she remembered many things about Ingrid, and with an extraordinary clarity. 'Yes,' she said quietly.

'We sat up and talked most of the night,' Tony said. 'The others knew her, too, of course; the fellows from Hanover, and Jan, and Betty. She told us some of the damnedest, most terrible things.' Mark nodded understandingly. It was thinking of Ingrid in Trondheim which more than anything else had brought the war alive for him He watched Tony now, half guessing what was in his son's mind even before Tony went on. 'It made me sure of one thing, Dad,' he said. 'We've got to lick those Germans. Somebody's got to do it, and England can't do it without us to help her.'

Mark felt the muscles in his cheeks stiffen into a mask, guessing what Tony was about to say. He sought to avert the inevitable, to fight for time.

'I think we'll be in it soon,' he said mildly, trying not to let his voice echo the desperate pleading in his heart; and he added, as calmly as possible: 'We're already under a war routine in one way; we just do what we're told. You young men who registered in the draft have done your part. They'll call you when they need you.' His heart was crying: 'Wait, wait, wait, my son! Wait till you must go.'

But Tony shook his head. 'They say they'll not draft anyone in college or in Law School till June,' he told them. 'That's six months. I can learn a lot in six months.' His jaw set and his cheek was white. 'Dad, I want to go into the air force, right now.'

Robin, watching Mark's face, came quickly to her feet and crossed and stood beside him, her hand on his shoulder. She saw Tony look at her in resentful protest, and she smiled, shook her head reassuringly. 'I'm not against you, Tony,' she said. 'We're not uniting against you. I—just wanted to be near your father. You know how he must be feeling.'

'Of course I do!' Tony assured her almost harshly. Because this was true, because he knew how sharp the impact of his words must have been, because he knew the sickening fears which moved Mark in this moment, he was angry at himself for causing that hurt, those fears; and this anger at himself translated itself into a surface anger at them. He said defiantly: 'But Dad has always been able to see my side of things, too!'

Robin did not speak; and after a moment Mark asked: 'You mean the Canadian Air Force, Tony?'

'No, no,' Tony said quickly. 'No, our own. No, I want to be with our own crowd.'

'I'm glad you feel that way,' Mark assented simply, and he smiled. 'We Americans must stick together.' Robin's hand tightened on his shoulder and he raised his and pressed hers. 'Have you found out what steps to take, how you can go about doing what you want to do?'

'I did that months ago,' Tony confessed. He grinned sheepishly. 'Last summer, when I came down to get the new car, I went in and talked it over. But I decided to wait till you were all right, and then I kept putting it off. But—well, I don't want to wait any longer, that's all.'

Robin suggested: 'I expect seeing Ingrid, hearing her story, knowing she'd been in it, made it a lot more real to you.'

'It sure did,' Tony admitted, his young face grim; and he added: 'Ingrid's changed. She used to be more like a boy than a girl, and you'd think fighting and going through all that would have made her even more that way, hard and—sort of grim. But she's a lot more—feminine.' He was not looking at them, absorbed in his own thoughts. Robin wondered whether Mark read Tony's mind as she did.

Father and son had long talk of Tony's plans, talk that was like an anodyne, blurring with many words the hard and naked facts; but Robin did not listen, having thoughts of her own. Very late that night, hours after they had gone to bed, knowing he was sleepless beside her, she rose without turning on the light and came into Mark's bed and took his head on her shoulder.

'There, my dear,' she whispered. 'There, sleep now!'

'Have you, too, been awake?'

'Of course, my darling. I knew you weren't asleep.'

'There's no sleep in me.'

'I know. But sleep now.'

He lay quietly for a moment, but then he turned on his back. In the narrow bed they were close together, her arm under his neck, her hand on his shoulder. 'I've been thinking,' he said softly. 'Thinking of what I've done and of what I haven't done to make this happen. The boy is going to fly, and fight; and I would die tonight to keep him safe and secure; and it is too late for that. If I had not come East to college, or even to school; if I had grown up in Hardiston, perhaps he would feel now as my father does, that the war is not our affair. But I came East to school and then to college and then to Law School; yet I need have done none of these things. My father and mother would not have made me do so. But I did, and I met Bob in college, and

I went into his father's office, and I met Nan and married her, and I became a judge, and Boston was my home, and England was a neighbor, and our friends here knew more about England than they knew about Hardiston—and so now my son is going to learn to fly and fight and kill and perhaps die.'

'He would have wanted to just as quickly in Ohio,' she urged. 'Or if not as quickly, then in a little while. We are all one country, Mark.' She kissed his hand, pressing it against her cheek.

'What ever Tony is, I have made him,' Mark insisted. 'This wish in him to do his share—perhaps I do not want him otherwise, perhaps that is why I am sending him off to this now. For if I told him not to go, he would stay at home. Should I tell him not to go?'

'He's a man, darling. A fine young man, in your very image. I love him for being so like you.'

'So many small decisions, each unimportant in itself, have led to this. Is that the way lives are made and lost?'

'My dear, my dear, it will all seem so different to you in the morning.'

'You didn't know Edwin Halstead, had scarcely seen him. He was a sweet boy. Sweet is the word I mean. He had all Mary's sweetness. No one ever called him Ed, or Eddie, but always Edwin, like a caress. He's dead now.'

'I know him through Mary,' said Robin by his side. 'I've seen a lot of her since you and I were married. She likes to talk to me about him.' She hesitated, said then: 'Mark, Mary is to have a baby in June or July. She is sure it will be a boy, and she means to name it Edwin. To please Ed.'

He spoke after a moment with a warm affection in his tones. 'I might have guessed that. She and Ed have always loved each other in such a perfect way.' He chuckled. 'I might have know they'd have another baby, now. They used to laugh at themselves, because always, when they were troubled, they hurried and had a baby.'

His tone was lighter, and she thought him at peace, but after a long moment when neither of them spoke, he stirred in a fitful way.

'I'll be glad when day comes,' he confessed; and then: 'Robin, keep me from letting Tony see how afraid I am.'

She said, lying quietly beside him in the night stillness, her voice low and clear: 'I had not meant to tell you, Mark; not till I was sure. But I am sure tonight, and you need to know. You see, you and I are going to have a baby, too.' She laughed softly, proudly. 'Mary's not the only one! You and I, too, my dear!'

6

(Winter and Spring 1941)

Early in January, Tony left them. For a day or two he was busy getting together the necessary documents; his birth certificate, and letters from Bob and Tom and Ed attesting his good character. Then he reported to the Army Base for his examination, and came jubilantly home; and thereafter, with a breathless haste, he was off to East St. Louis to begin the seven months' training routine which would lead to a commission.

When he was gone, Robin and Mark found that he was in some ways more completely with them than he had been while he was living in Cambridge, coming often for dinner or to spend Saturday night and Sunday. His letters from the first were many, and they were long and full of a deep exhilaration, of a keen delight in all he did and an enthusiastic certainty that they would wish to hear every detail of his days. 'The first night we were hazed in good shape and are still well taken care of,' he wrote in an early letter. 'We have air raids in the barracks. Some of us are supposed to be pursuit ships and run around, arms out, banking and making a noise like an airplane engine. Then we have parachute jumps. One man is the propeller, another the engine, and the man who is going to jump sits on top of a chair. We start the plane up and then when they think we are high enough, the man is told to bail out. First he sees which way the wind is blowing by wetting his thumb, then jumps, gathers in his chute, etc.' Each letter was full of a chucking hilarity which infected them as they read. Mark had copies made, so that the originals could be preserved; and to Bob and Nell, to Jan when she came home at Easter, to anyone who would listen, he read passages aloud.

'We're like proud parents showing everyone the snapshots of our baby,' Robin said, laughing at herself and at him. 'But I think people are interested, don't you?'

In one of his early letters Tony said:

> There's one thing, we're so busy we don't have much time to think about the war. I'm happier than I've been for years, I guess. It reminds me of something I heard Professor Wearing say one night last fall. A bunch of us had gone to his house in the evening, and we were talking about when peace was going to come, and what it would be like when it came, and I said

it didn't look to me as though we'd ever see real peace in our lifetime, and Professor Wearing said: 'The only real peace is to be at peace with yourself.' And then he said: 'I suspect that those boys in the Spitfires and the Hurricanes who are fighting the Germans over England are the only men in the world completely at peace with themselves today.'

I didn't know what he meant then, but I sort of do now. The war doesn't bother me any more! As far as I'm concerned, it can wait till I'm ready to attend to it. I'll get around to it by and by.

He spoke in that letter, and in most of his letters, of Ingrid. He and she were writing to each other, and he sometimes quoted things she had said. It was obvious that she and his work excluded everything else from his mind; but Mark was not so fortunate. Even though Tony was always in his thoughts, yet he read the papers; and at Robin's suggestion they acquired a radio. Tony had had in college a portable set, and Elin had a small one in her room, but Mark had prided himself on his immunity.

'One trouble with the world,' he told Robin when she proposed the purchase, 'is that our communications are too speedy. When anything happens anywhere, the news comes to us instantly, without any seasoning, without time to mellow and mature, overmagnified by its immediacy, out of proportion to its real importance.' But she said he needn't listen to the news broadcasts, that he would enjoy the Philharmonic and Information Please and a dozen other programs; and the radio took its place in their living room. Since it was there, Mark was apt to tune in for a news broadcast every evening. He expected great things from the British offensive in Libya, which had started early in December and which furnished the stuff of many jubilant headlines; but when in March, in a campaign of nineteen days, the Germans recaptured all the territory British troops had won in an arduous two months of fighting, the newspapers played the story down, and hid it away on inside pages, minimizing its importance, and Mark, as always, resented this wishful journalism.

'They're just encouraging us to play ostrich,' he told Robin. 'To hide our heads in the sand and refuse to see danger, or to recognize unpleasant things.'

Robin went often to spend an afternoon with Mary Halstead. Between these two a warm affection had developed. Robin and Nell saw each other not so often, since Nell was absorbed in many activities, seldom at home during the day. But early in February Bob again fell ill, and spent ten days in bed and a long fortnight at home; and Nell gave up everything to be with him. Mark and Robin, when Bob was well enough, were apt to go across the street after dinner; and Mark might sit awhile with Bob, Robin and Nell usually leaving them alone. Bob never talked about his own condition, and he and Mark clung to impersonal matters. Bob was rebelliously opposed to the Lend-Lease Bill; but he accepted the fact that it would pass, that the country wanted it.

'And once it passes,' he predicted, 'it's just a question of time till we're in the war.' And he said with a bitter vehemence: 'The hell of it is, Mark, we're such God-awful amateurs! And Roosevelt has got us hypnotized. We're not even holding back, now; we're just resigned, like a lot of sheep, going dumbly along even though we can see the slaughter house ahead.'

'Roosevelt's copying Hitler's technique,' Mark suggested. 'Hitler for a long time just took a little at each grab, took what he could take without starting a fight. Roosevelt's clever. Think back a year or two, to the days when we were all sure we'd never again lend money to England.' He laughed briefly. 'I was talking to Mat Riley the other day.' Mat was the neighborhood choreman, tending furnaces, mowing lawns, shovelling snow. 'He asked what I thought about the war, and I said it seemed to me wise to help England, and he nodded; but he said doubtfully: "Just the same, I wish they'd paid what they owed us."'

'A lot of us feel that way.'

'Yes. And yet Mr. Roosevelt—give him credit—has led us to the point where we're prepared to lend-lease anything they want, and not even ask for a promise to pay.'

'He and Churchill between them.'

Mark nodded. '"Give us the tools and we will finish the job,"' he quoted. 'Churchill is a master of splendid words. They—he and Mr. Roosevelt—keep assuring us that we'll never need to send an army to Europe; and as long as we can believe that promise, we're ready to accept anything else, any other sacrifice at all.'

'We've sent troops of Newfoundland!'

'That's the opening wedge,' Mark agreed. 'Newfoundland, and Bermuda; and then perhaps it will be Greenland and Iceland, and then maybe Ireland.'

'Roosevelt ought to be impeached!'

Mark said thoughtfully: 'I don't agree, Bob. I've been reading Sandburg's Lincoln, reading how Lincoln had to do much the same thing, gradually and patiently leading national opinion toward the final goal. I've never liked Mr. Roosevelt, but I do respect and admire the way he has guided and directed our national thinking. He's persuaded us—most of us, now—that we ought to help England by every means short of war.'

'Yes, damn him!'

Mark smiled. 'All right, but I've about concluded that he's a great man. We who have disagreed with him, maybe we're wrong.'

Bob grunted. 'Arsenal of Democracy!' He parroted the words with scorn. 'We're going to make everybody in the world free whether they want to be or not, and it's cost us thirty-five billions already and more to come. Suppose some country doesn't want to be a democracy? Are we going to stuff it down their throats? We'll be as bad as the conquistadores, converting the Mayas and the Incas to Christianity even if they had to kill them to do it.'

Sometimes he became so angry that Nell, hearing his raised voice, came upstairs to interfere, to lead them to talk of other things; of Tony, or of Will and Jan and Betty. She did so tonight. Betty had gone to Hanover for the Carnival week-end, and they spoke of this.

'She's always at some carnival or house party or off skiing or something,' Bob said wrathfully. 'She's getting to be what they used to call a college widow.'

'She has a wonderful time,' Nell reminded him.

'Yes, and you let her!' Bob said harshly. His tone toward Nell was apt to be curt and wrathful in these days, masking the love he could not confess without risking the weakness of tears. Nell, seeing that to quarrel with her somehow eased him, played her part, bickering and arguing while her heart ached with terror and with longing to hold him in her arms. To neither of them did tenderness come easily; but their half-angry recriminations were a language each somehow understood. Alone, they could be quietly together, talking commonplaces and content; but when others were about they seemed always to be at odds.

Mark spoke of this once to Robin. 'They don't mean anything by it,' he said, wishing her to understand these old friends. 'It's just their way, their way of loving each other.'

'I know,' Robin assured him. 'I've been with Nell a lot, while you're with him, you know. She's just a poor, grieving, frightened wife, Mark.'

Mark read Tony's letters to Bob. Tony appeared to be making fine progress. He had soloed quickly; passed his first P check in less than a month; was made a one-stripe corporal. He wrote of slow rolls, snap rolls, loops, Immelmans. Early in March he wired exultantly that he had passed his last check and would be home for leave before going on to Randolph Field for advanced training.

That leave was indescribably sweet, and terribly short. Tony talked endlessly of flying, and he spoke often of Ingrid in a way that made Robin watch Mark to see whether he guessed what even Tony perhaps did not yet understand. Not till after Tony was gone did Mark speak of this.

'He thinks a lot of Ingrid, doesn't he,' he said.

'I think she's always loved him,' Robin assented. 'She told me so, long ago, one day in Hanover. She's a sweet girl, Mark.'

Tony wrote from Randolph Field, describing his routine there. He began to resent drill and inspection, and the hazing which at first had amused him was an irritation now. There was a new seriousness in his tone, and a suggestion of nervous tension which they were quick to notice; but at the end of two weeks in his new surroundings, they read between the lines that he was himself again.

Bob's illness had worked a change in him. It had shortened his temper, and there was a harsh violence in his opinions and an increased and unreasoning condemnation of every move Mr. Roosevelt made. He was apt to contest any statement made in his hearing. The first time the four friends dined together after he was on his feet again, Ed told them that the Navy more than half expected war with Japan. 'Japan's grabbing Indo-China is due to make trouble,' he declared. 'Captain Markham is at the Yard now, just back from Honolulu, and he says the Navy has been warned by Washington to look out for a surprise attack on Pearl Harbor. They're on the job out there.' And he added: 'We could smash Japan in two months, and the sooner we do it the better.'

Bob hooted at him. 'That's what you say!' His tone was so scornful that Ed colored with surprise, and Mark said, like a peacemaker:

'I think it might be wise to keep on good terms with Japan till we settle Germany's case.'

'Fat chance,' Bob commented. 'Franklin won't be happy till he has a few wars on his hands.'

Ed stuck to his opinion. 'We can punch Japan's clock for her any time she starts anything,' he declared; and Bob took issue with him till Mark and Tom intervened to end the argument. Bob had never been so truculent before. Mark was reminded of how while he was ill he growled at Nell. Perhaps his harsh tone to these his friends now was like his attitude toward Nell, reflecting in a strange reverse way the fondness toward them which he would not admit even to himself.

Japan was for a while in men's minds. The British reinforced Singapore, and Congress voted at last to fortify Guam. But then Japan was forgotten in the rush of nearer events. The British landed sixty thousand troops in Greece to meet a possible German attack, and German submarines were reported operating south of Greenland, and Congress voted seven billion dollars for lend-lease, and German and Italian ships in American harbors were seized by the Government, and a new wave of strikes swept through munition plants, and Germany attacked Yugo-Slavia and Greece, driving southward toward the Mediterranean.

The evening of the day Salonika fell—Mark and Robin were reading in the living room—the doorbell rang and Elin answered it, and Jerry Crocker and Ruth appeared. Once or twice this winter Ruth had dropped in to talk about her work with Jerry, but Mark had not seen Jerry since Tommy Sheffield's wedding, months ago.

Mark and Robin made these two welcome, and Mark felt some surprise that they should come thus together, and wondered what their errand was; but they seemed to have no errand. Ruth said spring was almost here, and Robin said crocuses were in bloom, and Ruth looked at Jerry and for some reason laughed and asked what news they had from Tony, and Mark said Tony was now at Randolph Field and doing well and enthusiastic about his work; and he read a part of Tony's last letter. '. . . For the last two week-ends three of us have gone to the Gallagher Ranch, twenty miles outside of San Antonio. It's a beautiful place, and I'm going to spend the rest of the week-ends there. I've been doing night flying, started Wednesday with thirty minutes dual and then solo landings by flood lights, and since then solo landings by wing lights and on a dark field. I find night flying easier than day flying. The air is soft, and landing easier . . .' And since Ruth and Jerry—Ruth in particular, Jerry beginning to seem faintly uncomfortable—were enthusiastic over this, Mark read another passage. '. . . cross country. I was lost in every sense of the word. Finally when the ceiling dropped to about a thousand feet at ten minutes of six and a drizzle started, I decided it was time to come down. I spotted a good-sized field with some cattle on it, dragged the field at about thirty feet to scare the cattle and look for obstructions, and then in I came. Because of the cattle, I had to land well up the field, so I rolled over a small ditch, hit a fence, and rolled up a few feet of barbed wire. I called Randolph, spent the night at a ranch house. A flat tail wheel was the only damage. The next morning the Flight Commander came after me with a mechanic. He flew my plane out and I flew his.'

Ruth would have had Mark read other letters, knowing how it pleased him to do so; but Robin saw Jerry's uneasiness and asked how the book was going.

'Oh, it's all written,' Jerry said. 'In fact, we've rewritten most of it a couple of times. There's so darned much I want to say, and more keeps happening all the time, so there's no end to the job.'

Mark smiled. 'Pick a lull, sometime, and call it done,' he suggested.

'There aren't any lulls.'

'I'm not so sure,' Mark reflected. 'From Dunkirk till the German move in the Balkans here a day or two ago, nothing really happened except that England did not fall.'

'The thing I'm afraid of,' Jerry declared, 'is that Hitler will declare war on us. It would damned soon put a stop to our helping England. We'd send her no more planes until our own coasts were safe.'

Mark smiled. 'I suspect you underrate us, Jerry,' he suggested. 'I think if Hitler declared war we'd be a lot more anxious to beat him than to save Boston, for instance, from being bombed.' He added: 'You know I've been thinking that England is the Verdun of this war. Verdun was a hard position to defend, with only one small road to transport supplies; but Germany wore herself out attacking Verdun. England's a salient, equally hard to hold, and equally well worth holding. As long as England stands, Germany can't win the war.'

'Right,' Jerry agreed. 'I wouldn't be surprised if ten years from now we all see that the Battle of England this winter was the Gettysburg of this war, was Hitler's high-water mark. He came just so far—and no farther. The Luftwaffe, crashing by the hundreds day after day over England, were like Pickett's men at Gettysburg. And the Luftwaffe will never be the same again.' He added: 'Oh, Hitler will still do his stuff for a while; but he'll never again come as near real victory as he did last summer.'

'I hope you're right,' Mark said. 'But England's not out of danger yet.' He added soberly: 'If the time ever comes when England seems to us to be safe, you'll see our enthusiasm slacken. We're willing to do what we're told, now, fundamentally because we think we're helping England.'

Ruth and Robin had listened to them for a while, then with a meeting of eyes left the two men together and went upstairs; but now they came down again, and Robin brought a tray with decanter, glasses, ice and soda, from the pantry, and a plate of crackers, and built high-balls for them all. Jerry, watching these proceedings, was saying: 'The trouble with the British, they're always underrating their opponents, and that means——' He interrupted himself to ask: 'Can I have plain water instead of soda, Mrs. Worth?' And Robin said, 'Of course,' and Ruth said, 'I'll get it,' and turned toward the pantry as Jerry went on: 'That's why they keep getting licked. They thought they'd won in Libya, and now the Germans have pushed them clear back to where they started from. They lost in Norway and in France, and now, by God, they've put three or four divisions into Greece to take a licking there!' There was a sudden heat in his tones. 'Just check back on what England has done and you've got a recipe, ready-made, on how to lose a war. Convince yourself that your enemy can't win. Tell yourself you're invulnerable. Minimize his successes and magnify your own. When one of your allies is conquered, say she was a hollow shell, or a false friend, or that she was betrayed. Never admit your enemy is a great military power. Scatter your forces. Act as if you thought ten armies of twenty thousand men, even without cooperating, could beat an army of a hundred thousand that works together. Let the enemy force you to fight on fronts where he has all the advantage. Fight a defensive war. That's been England's policy so far—and she's hardly won a skirmish yet.'

Ruth returned and gave him his highball and said smilingly: 'Still talking war, Jerry?'

Mark was struck by something in her tone, and Jerry looked up at her in an almost guilty fashion, and Ruth nodded, laughing down at him. 'Go on,' she urged. 'Go on! Tell them.'

Jerry was red and white by turns, and Mark looked at Robin and saw her smiling; and Jerry said feebly: 'Oh, my God, Ruth, I can't!'

So Ruth laughed again; and she faced Mark. 'Remember when I asked you to marry me, and you said you'd be a father to me instead? Well, Father, Jerry wants to ask your permission . . .'

But Jerry at that came strongly to his feet. 'Permission be damned!' he cried, grinning at them all. 'I'd like to see anyone stop me.' His arm was around Ruth. 'We're going to be married, the middle of May,' he said.

So there was a pleasant tumult for a while, and Ruth told them: 'I did it, really, in self-defense. I'd typed his whole darned book once for him, and he changed it all over so I had to type almost every page again, and then he started to change it some more, and I realized he was just putting it back the way it had been in the first place—just anything to keep me working for him and with him every day—so I knew he felt about me the same way I felt about him, and that was all there was to it. Now I'm going to haul him out of his shell and dust him off and marry him!'

When they were gone, and Mark and Robin were alone, Mark said thoughtfully: 'That pleases me a lot. I feel almost as though I'd brought Ruth up; and there's always been something a little pathetic about Jerry, in spite of his wide knowledge and sound sense and his positive way of talking.'

'She told me about it upstairs,' Robin confessed. 'She's a sweet thing.' And she said: 'Jerry thinks she's just a poor working girl. She hasn't lied to him about it, but he's never asked any questions. She's going to let him go on thinking so. They'll live on what he earns. She says she doesn't dare tell him for fear he'll be scared back into his hole again.'

Mark smiled. 'I don't think she need worry. Jerry's too genuine himself to be overly impressed by anything as unimportant as money.' And he said: 'She needs him as much as he needs her. They'll each do the other a lot of good.'

She came to kiss him smilingly. 'Of course,' she agreed. 'That's the way with all proper marriages. It's bound to be.'

7

(May 1941)

Tony wrote, in mid-May:

> Dear Dad—You asked if I knew what comes next. Well, we'll finish here in about three weeks. The exact day depends partly on where we go from here. I'm going to apply for multi-motored. I'm a little overweight for the P shooters. If I get it, I'll probably be sent to Ellington. We will definitely (as definite as the Army ever is) get five days and probably more; and I'll come home.
>
> Of course something may happen to prevent. Most of the fellows here seem to think we're getting closer to a shooting war all the time. The Greeks are done, and nobody knows where the Germans will hit next; but did you notice that deal that gives us the right to send troops to Greenland, and Churchill said the other day that when he said 'give us the tools' he meant for us to deliver them in England. With the Atlantic patrol operating, sooner or later

a German submarine is going to sink one of our ships, and then—Bingo, and we're in!

It makes the crowd here pretty sore to read about the strikes all over the country. Six or seven million working days were lost last month by strikes, and a lot of them were in defense work. Why doesn't President Roosevelt do something about it, Dad? He could draft every man in essential jobs and then tell them they'll either work—on army pay, the same as other fellows their age in the army are getting—or go to jail. I don't see what right a fellow has to claim exemption from the draft because he's working in an airplane factory, and then refuse to work. Of course we're not really at war, and that makes a difference; but if we were, a man that refuses duty in a factory where he's working on some defense job ought to get it just as hard as a soldier who refuses duty. And that ought to go for the bosses, too, from foremen up to the president of the company. The Government gives its orders to capital, and it ought to give its orders to management and labor too.

The letter had been waiting—unopened—when Mark came home for dinner, and he was reading it aloud to Robin. He looked at her now, smiling, and commented: 'This is the first letter in which he's had much to say about anything outside his flight training. Probably that's coming to be an old story with him now.'

She nodded and he read on:

But President Roosevelt probably won't do anything. The trouble is he never fires anybody, and Ma Perkins is still on the job like an old hen protecting her chickens, and she won't let anyone say Boo! to labor. Well, there's nothing we can do about it, except do what we're told.

Oh, by the way, I had a letter from Ingrid the other day, and she's planning to come to the United States and become a citizen. She's coming to Boston sometime this month. Of course she has a lot of friends there, Betty Ritchie and so on; but I wish you'd ask her to stay with you—till she can get settled, anyway. You might like to write her and invite her ahead of time. Her address is—I'll have to look it up, but I'll put it in a postscript.

She says she's going to get a job in Boston. I don't know whether she will or not.

Lots of love,

Tony.

Mark finished and passed the letter to Robin. 'The address is here,' he said absently, 'if you do care to write.'

'I will, of course,' she agreed. 'I liked Ingrid—though she must be changed.'

Their eyes met for a moment in silence. Then he said smilingly: 'I didn't like Tony's overly casual "By the way," as though the request were unimportant.'

'He mentioned Ingrid often in his earlier letters,' Robin suggested, answering his unspoken thought. 'But he hasn't referred to her lately.'

'Is that a bad sign?'

'I liked Ingrid,' she repeated, and smiled reassuringly. 'So it seems like a good sign to me.'

She wrote to Ingrid as Tony had suggested, and the girl replied, gratefully accepting the invitation. 'I remember you very nicely at Hanover when you were Mrs. Kerr,' she said, 'and I am glad you are the same as Tony's mother now, and that I will soon see you and Judge Worth again. I will be coming, if you please, on the twenty-fifth, Monday morning. The train gets in at about eight o'clock, I think, but do not meet it so early because I will know how to come straight to the house. Thank you very much indeed.'

Robin did not read this letter to Mark. There was something in its tone, forthright and affectionate and completely unabashed, which seemed to her to say eloquently much more than Tony had yet told them. So she only said to Mark: 'Ingrid gets here the twenty-fifth. I had a nice letter from her.' And he understood from her tone that he was not to see the letter, and guessed from that fact more than Robin supposed.

But Robin wrote to Tony, and on second thought she enclosed Ingrid's letter for him to read. 'She's a friendly person,' she said. 'I suppose she'll only stay with us for a few days, unless we insist, and I'll hesitate to do that. After all, we've no claim on her at all, but we'll try to keep her till you come.'

She had a telegram from him, in quick reply:

> Don't try to kid me. You know the answer. If you let Ingrid out of your clutches, I'll haunt you. As soon as I get my commission, I'm going to marry the gal. Tell Dad, if you haven't already.
>
> Love,
>
> Tony.

8

(May 1941)

Ruth and Jerry were married on a Saturday afternoon, in the small church where—surprisingly—Jerry was a regular attendant. Mark and Robin were, except for the minister, the only others present; and afterward they all went for lunch to Jerry's home—which Mark had never seen. It was a very old house, and it had apparently been put together one room at a time, so that at almost every doorway there was a step up or down. The house from the outside seemed small, but it was in fact surprisingly large, with half a dozen rooms on the first floor and on the second, and two others on the floor above. The front door was flush with the street, a street where some traffic ran, with a cluster of stores not a block away, and a busy cross-street there; but behind the house a lawn and garden lay secluded and beautiful, with the dark, still waters of the river, dammed to furnish power for a mill in the village, at its foot. The garden was walled, and the house itself shut off the noises in the street, so that the spot was a quiet corner set apart from the world.

Jerry had been his own housekeeper, but whether for this occasion or from long habit, the rooms he used were scrupulously ordered. Half the house was unfurnished, or was used to store odds and ends, old New England chairs and tables and secretaries; or objects, many of them still in the crates in which they had been shipped, which Jerry had at one time or another during his travels acquired. Ruth, showing them these crowded rooms, proudly exclaimed; 'These are all my wedding presents from Jerry. He's forgotten what's in the boxes and packages himself! Aren't we going to have fun unpacking them?'

The used rooms were easy and delightful, books everywhere, some good old things, half a dozen choice rugs. There was a laughing reproach in Mark's tone when he said: 'Damn it, Jerry, why haven't I ever been here before?'

'Oh, no one ever comes here,' Jerry declared. 'Except Ruth, these last few months. And the Padre comes sometimes for a pipe and a drink.'

The minister—Jerry called him 'Padre' or 'Bill,' but he was the Reverend William Merrilee—lunched with them. He was a round, cherubic little man with pink cheeks and blue eyes and a crown of disorderly white hair; and he might have been any age past fifty. He was as merry as his name, with a quick, jolly wit and—even in his laughter—that quality which can only be written as one word, loving-kindness. Merely to see him was to feel that he liked you, or more than liked you; that he was your friend through thick and thin. Mark found it more and more true as he grew older that this trait in a man, this unaffected, uncritical, and undemanding friendliness was tremendously attractive. When as sometimes happened he felt also sadness in a new acquaintance, the attraction doubled.

And there was a deep sadness in Mr. Merrilee, a long sadness of which few were conscious, of which few knew the cause. His wife died when their baby was born. The baby girl survived, and Mr. Merrilee's sister came to live with him and to care for the baby. When Helen Merrilee was seventeen, Mr. Merrilee's sister reported to him that Helen had been seen, too often, with a young man named Donner who was—she assured her brother—the most infamous rake in Providence, where Mr. Merrilee's clerical duties then lay. She said he must speak to Helen, and he did so.

He and the child had never been close. He had loved her completely; but he had acquired from his own strict father and mother an attitude toward children based on the text: 'Whom the Lord loveth, he chasteneth.' So he had always seemed to Helen stern and forbidding, and she did not trust him in this crisis, defiantly standing her ground. She wished to marry Mr. Donner, and her father might have been weak and fond enough to yield; but some of the ladies of the parish combined with his sister to insist that he must not. He forbade Helen to see the young man again, and when she stormed at him, he threatened to lock her in her room. She collapsed in grief and woe, wailing that he was cruel and terrible, crying over and over: 'I wish I was dead! Oh, I wish I was dead!'

Four days later, by the entirely irrelevant accident of a ruptured appendix and peritonitis, she died. Thereafter Mr. Merrilee decided that the only important precept in Holy Writ was: 'Love ye one another.' That was forty years ago, for he was in his early eighties now. His career as a churchman had by worldly standards suffered from his refusal to be rigid toward evildoers, and his present church was shabby, his congregation small. But the men and women to whom he ministered were strengthened and comforted.

Mark told Robin that evening: 'There's a man I'd like to know better. We must plan to see him often.' She agreed. They had both been tremendously attracted to the jolly, loving, wistful little minister.

9

(May–June 1941)

Mark and Robin met Ingrid's train, and Mark stayed in town while Robin drove Ingrid home. She thought the girl, at least on the surface, not greatly changed; lovely with the beauty that comes from perfect health, with a clear skin and clear and friendly eyes. But there was a change not immediately apparent. Hatred and anger and the lust to kill had somehow taught Ingrid gentleness, and the sight of suffering had taught her tenderness and pity, and the certainty of Tony's love for her had taught her a calm, sure strength that was at once confident and humble too.

She said at once when she and Robin were alone: 'Tony says he has told you he is going to marry me.' Hers was the glad, surprised tone of one upon whom has been bestowed an unexpected and long-wished-for boon, and Robin understood this, and loved the girl beside her.

'I'm so glad,' she said. 'I always liked you very much.'

'Tony says his father will be glad, too.'

'Yes indeed, he is.'

Ingrid seemed to settle contentedly into her seat. 'Then that is nice,' she said. 'It would not be fun for any of us if Tony and I married and you did not like it.'

At the house, Robin would have put Ingrid in the guest room; but the girl said: 'Would it be bad, or make trouble if I slept in Tony's room? I want to be with his things around me.' And she said wistfully: 'You see, in Canada at Christmas, we did not know how it would be with us. We——' She hesitated, her cheek bright. 'I don't know how to say it, except we did not make love at all, even to talk. We were not even alone together hardly for a minute. So our loving each other is all in our letters since then, and I want him to come close to me, and in his room it will be like that, a little bit.'

She became at once at home with them and they with her; and she preferred from the first to stay with Robin rather than to accept the invitations which came from all her friends and Tony's. Robin suggested to Mark that a formal announcement of her engagement to Tony might relieve her of the necessity of declining so often; and Mark asked Tony's opinion. Tony's answering letter was written on the third of June.

Dear Dad—
    That's the thing to do, sure. I mean, announce our engagement. Of course we can't be married till I get my commission, and that won't be till late this summer. But that's all right. I've told Ingrid to go out with Chuck Little and Joe and the others and have some fun; but she says she'd rather stay at home, and if we announce it, they'll understand her not going out more. She says she likes to be where if she gets lonesome she can go up to my room and smell my clothes! Don't tell her I told you, but she sleeps with an old hunting shirt of mine. It's been cleaned, but she says it still smells like

me. She says her father told her once you could never really love a person unless you liked the way they smelled!

There was much more about Ingrid, over which Mark and Robin smiled in affectionate understanding; and then Tony wrote:

You see what the Luftwaffe did in Crete, Dad? There are no islands, any more. Some say that was just a dress rehearsal for England, but the English had no air power at Crete. Tackling England will be a different matter. Air power can always turn the scales, if it's unopposed by other planes; but a few good fighter planes can make a lot of difference. Look at what happened in England last fall.

The Luftwaffe has had things its own way in Europe. But wait till we get over there and take a hand.

I thought we might get into it when the Germans sank the *Robin Moor,* but we took it pretty calmly. We take the whole thing too damned calmly. We're becoming calloused to horrors. Look at what happens every time a ship is sunk, people putting out in open boats, and maybe being rescued after a day, or a week, or a month, and maybe never being rescued at all. Boats full of people disappear and you never hear of them again; and we don't think anything about it. A good many people have died of thirst on the Atlantic in the last year, died horribly after weeks of terrible suffering, and some have starved to death, or turned cannibal, the way the men from the *Essex* did when she was sunk by the whale a hundred years ago. Every once in a while I wake up in the night and think that somewhere out on the ocean, all the time, day after day, there are maybe five or six little boats full of men dying of thirst and hunger, and killing each other over a scrap of food, and eating the men who die first—and all because of this war, and it makes me sick.

I used to damn Hitler; but it isn't just Hitler, Dad. It's some blind, slug-gish force in men that makes them do things they don't really want to do at all. It's greed to get what you haven't got, or to keep what you have; it's lust for power or hatred of power; it's covetousness, and pride, and gluttony and sloth. It's all the deadly sins, working in each of us, moving us like chessmen, driving us like Gadarene swine headlong over the precipice. I don't think men shape their destinies at all. You know, Dad, I'm beginning to think none of these big things—wars and so on—matter. I think what matters, what makes us happy and unhappy, is the way we behave ourselves, in our own lives. If I don't brush my teeth in the morning, I feel a lot worse about it than I did when Hitler conquered Poland. If I'm sarcastic or mean to someone, I feel a lot worse about it than I do about what Italy did to France. And any day I do a good day's flying and am friendly to people, and—generally behave myself—I go to bed feeling warm and happy and comfortable.

We think too much. We ought to feel more. It's a lot more fun to just like people than to try to decide whether they've done something which was right, or wrong.

I see Roosevelt says he's not planning convoys. But the Atlantic patrol is the same thing, only we're not openly accepting the risks involved. If I were a German submarine commander and sighted an American battleship and heard their radio telling the British where I was, I'd sink the battleship in self-defense. If we're going to get in, I wish we'd do it, and not be such meeching hypocrites about it, waiting to yell 'outrage' the minute we get hurt.

What did Hess come to Scotland for? Are we going to seize Iceland now that she's cut loose from Denmark? Wasn't that hunt for the *Bismarck* a grand, terrible, dramatic, tragic, pitiful thing? Did you notice it was planes that got her, crippled her?

The real trouble with us, the reason we're not ready—mentally—for war, is because we've no positive, real, emotional reason to fight. Germany's fighting for something she hasn't got and wants. England—and the United States, for we're really in the war already—is just fighting to keep what she's got, to keep things as they are. That's not very inspiring. It's dog-in-the-manger stuff. We'll never be whole-heartedly in this war till we find a Cause for which to fight; something at once concrete and beautiful and good. And it won't be the *status quo ante*. It will be a dream, a vision of a new and better world; a composite vision formed of the many aspirations of many men, fused into one great beautiful common goal.

When we see the shape of that new world, the German soldiers will join us in fighting for it too.

Sorry to be so long-winded. I just got wound up. Take care of my Ingrid for me. In about a week now, we'll be through here, and I'll head for home as fast as the airlines will bring me.

Love

Tony.

There was a postscript.

Dad, if anything ever happens to me, read over this letter. It says a lot of the things you've taught me to believe. I love you.

Tony.

XV

Drang nach Osten

(*June–September 1941*)

(June 1941)

THE day the Army, to put an end to strike disorders there, seized the North American Aviation Company's plant in California, Mary Halstead's baby was born; and Ed, on his way home from the hospital that evening, came to tell Mark and Robin and Ingrid that Mary was perfect, and the baby, too.

'He was a little ahead of time,' he explained with a proud grin. 'But Mary said she wanted to do a hurry-up job.'

'She was always sure it would be a boy,' Robin reminded him.

'You can't fool Mary,' he agreed. He sat down, and she saw his brow beaded with perspiration in the reaction after these hours of strain.

'Highball?' she suggested, and would have risen; but Ingrid, always quick to save Robin needless steps, was already on her feet.

'Please, no, I will do it,' she said, and went toward the dining room.

'Tell us all about the baby, Ed,' Robin urged. 'Has he any hair? How much does he weigh? Any teeth?' While he spoke, her own eyes were glowing with bright dreams. Ingrid, returning with glasses, decanter, soda, and ice on the wide tray, seeing Robin's tender, listening smile and the gracious abundance of her figure, thought having babies was a beautiful thing. Robin had always been lovely, but never so completely so as now, when she sat thinking of Mary and of her own child soon to be; and Ingrid thought of Tony, and she was stirred in all her senses by this mystery in which she too soon would play her part. Her heart was high; for Tony, his work at Randolph done, would be here tomorrow, and for four full days, and in prospect those four days seemed eternal. Beyond them, time did not yet exist.

Ed sipped his highball, and after he had told Robin all there was to tell, he and Mark speculated as to where and when Germany's next blow would fall. There were rumors of a mobilization against Russia, but they agreed these were surely propaganda, meant to lull England into a false security. The Kaiser had died at Doorn a week or so before, and they remembered what an ogre he had seemed to be, twenty years ago; and Mark said:

'I wonder what his thoughts were? Do you suppose he mourned his vanished glory? Or was he perhaps content to be just an old man chopping wood for exercise? Hitler, they say, would like to be a painter.'

Ed laughed shortly. 'So he goes out and paints the world red!'

Mark caught Robin's eye upon him, watching to see whether this war talk would rouse him as it had in the past, and he smiled at her reassuringly. 'The war has receded into the background of my life, of my thoughts,' he confessed. 'Probably in the long run our own affairs are always more important to us than the affairs of the world. Now Robin and I go along much the same way day after day, happy with each other and with Ingrid here; and although I see the headlines, there are some days when what they say doesn't go below the surface of my mind; days when I hardly think of the war at all.'

'You always took it pretty calmly,' Ed agreed. 'I mean you—well, for you it was a problem in philosophy, or in world politics, or something like that; impersonal and abstract. It's pretty personal to me.' He was thinking of Edwin who had stumbled to death on the threshold of the war.

'I used to think of it always in terms of Tony,' Mark assented, answering Ed's unspoken thought. 'But now that he's committed, now that there is nothing left for him or for me to decide, I don't feel the same. I've none of the doubts and uncertainties which used to disturb me.'

Robin rose to go upstairs. 'But stay and talk with Mark, Ed,' she insisted, when he would have taken his departure. 'He'll sit reading for hours if you don't. Tell Mary I'll come see her in a day or two, and give her our love.' Ingrid went with her. It was always happiness for her to help Robin make ready for the night. When they were gone, Ed said smilingly:

'They don't come any better than those two—and Mary. Mark, you and I have all the luck!'

Mark nodded, looking after them. 'I remember the war never really came to life for me till the Germans hit Norway,' he reflected. 'I knew Ingrid was there.'

'Does she ever talk about it?'

'Seldom, and then very little.' He said thoughtfully: 'But Ed, we're getting used to this war, getting hardened to it. You know that line: "Vice is a monster of such dreadful mien," and so on. I've forgotten how it all goes, but the idea is, you get familiar with it, get used to it, and finally embrace it.'

'We're on the way to embrace this war, all right,' Ed agreed.

'The thing has a devilish attraction for the human mind,' Mark commented. 'We all like excitement, of course; and the idea of sacrifice appeals to us. Even the idea of sacrificing our lives stirs something in the average man—and woman, too. And, of course, men and women love to put on uniforms, like children dressing up. We in this country were sure, two or three years ago, that we'd never mix in another European war. Now we accept the fact that we'll have to.' And he said: 'I've believed from the first that we'd go in rather than see England lose; and I think Mr. Roosevelt has done a wonderful job in leading us to accept the idea of our eventual participation. But he couldn't have done it if there hadn't been in all of us a secret readiness.'

'It fascinates us, the whole show,' Ed agreed.

'So many forces combine to urge us into it,' Mark commented. 'Quite apart from our dislike of Germany's international bad manners and of her domestic tyranny, and forgetting for the moment our affectionate solicitude for England, we still feel ourselves outsiders, and that makes us restless! Then there's pride in our capacities, and a natural.desire to show them off.'

'Like a Freshman football player,' Ed suggested, 'watching the Varsity in a big game and wishing he could be in it.'

'Exactly,' Mark assented. 'Probably that's juvenile; but at least, we're not actuated by greed and envy.' He said thoughtfully: 'We're a contented nation, Ed. The average American has a way of life which—if you include his opportunities—approximates what he wants. It's hard to imagine a nation like ours ever being willing to risk what it has by going to war just to try to get more. I can't see us deliberately deciding to attack another nation in the hope of tangible gain.'

Ed nodded. 'I wish the rest of the world felt the same way.'

Mark said thoughtfully: 'The plain fact is that our national experiment—possibly in part because we've had lavish natural resources—has been a success. The people, the common ordinary people like you and me and like our choreman and Mr. Roosevelt, are on the average more comfortable, better informed, mentally and physically stronger than in any other great nation in the world. If in Europe and Asia everyone was as comfortable, physically and mentally, as here in North America, no

Hitler could lead them into a war of aggression. There'd be no more wars; or at least not until somewhere south of the equator another nation arrived at an armed and aggressive discontent.' He smiled. 'That's an Utopian ideal, of course, but it's sound. Contented nations are hard to lead into a war of aggrandizement. World peace can only be based on world contentment.'

'I'm not sure contentment is good medicine—except perhaps for cows. It leaves no room for ambition.'

Mark nodded. 'But somewhere there's a middle ground,' he insisted. 'Wherever you find a nation in which the will of all men rather than the will of one man determines national policy, that nation is slow to go to war. The sure road to world peace is the development of world-wide democracy.'

'How about disarmament?' Ed asked, but Mark shook his head.

'No. Disarmament is just an invitation to aggressors.'

'But in your world of contented cows there wouldn't be any aggressors.' Ed smiled. 'You're a philosopher, Mark, or a psychologist or something. But some day this business will outgrow your brain, and infect your heart.'

Mark said, after a moment, soberly: 'I wish it would, Ed. I'm tired of thinking about it. I'm tired of words.'

Robin and Ingrid, upstairs, could hear their low voices murmuring. After Robin was abed, Ingrid stayed awhile with her, talking of Tony and his imminent home-coming.

'I'm going to put him in the guest room,' Robin told the girl, 'and leave you where you are. There's no need of your changing for so short a time.' Ingrid had been from the first in Tony's room, adjoining their own, with a communicating door between. Sometimes she had dark and terrifying dreams, echoes of the days in Norway after the Germans came, and she might cry out in her sleep; so they left the door open, and when Robin heard her she would go quickly in to soothe the girl and comfort her; and in the darkness, only half awake, Ingrid clung to her like a small, frightened, sobbing child. In daylight, she never referred to the things she had seen, and she wore no shadow in her eyes. It was only when sleep relaxed her self-control that the deep scars of those dreadful days showed through.

2

(June 1941)

They went, all three, to the airport to meet Tony's plane; and when he came striding toward them they were standing together. Tony—as though Mark and not Ingrid were his beloved one—clasped his father in his arms and kissed him. He kissed Robin, too; and he turned then, almost abashed, to Ingrid. Robin, watching them, remembered what Ingrid had told her; that except in their letters they had spoken no word of love. They met like shy strangers now, Ingrid's cheeks glowing, Tony almost pale as they clasped hands, their eyes embracing. Tony said:

'Hello.'

Ingrid laughed a little. 'Hello, Tony.'

Tony grinned. He looked around at the many passers-by, and Mark guessed his thought; and Tony said urgently: 'Let's get out of here! Come on!'

So they all laughed in an equal understanding, hurrying to the car. Tony drove them home. Ingrid sat with him, Mark and Robin in the rear; and Tony caught their eyes in the mirror and told them how well they looked. 'Specially you, Robin. You always were wonderful, but you're stupendous now.' He smiled at her in the mirror, teasingly. 'I'll have to start calling you "Mother" pretty soon.'

Mark asked questions, and Tony told them the thousand things they wished to know; and Ingrid, close beside him, watched him with happy eyes that searched his countenance, examining each feature as though she were afraid some detail would escape her; and when he looked down at her, their eyes held for an instant and they laughed together, for deep reasons of their own, before he turned his attention again to the traffic in the way. Once Mark good-humoredly protested, bade Tony keep his eyes on his driving; and Robin, watching them thus completely happy, held Mark's hand and squeezed it hard.

When they came home, came into the house, Tony turned uncertainly; but Robin, wisely understanding, said at once: 'Tony, you're going to be in the guest room. Ingrid, you go show him!' So Ingrid caught Tony's hand and they raced up the stairs, laughing and contesting to be first; and Mark and Robin heard their quick steps as they darted into the guest room, and the door slammed.

Then the two in the hall below heard nothing more, and after a moment Mark chuckled contentedly. 'The rest was silence!' he said.

Robin kissed him. 'No reason why I should, but I just thought I would,' she explained, and kissed him again; and then, still in his arms, she looked toward the stairs. 'Bless them!' she whispered. 'Oh, please, God, bless those children.'

Tony's brief days at home were crowded full. There were so many friends who wished to do him and Ingrid honor; but Tony would accept no invitations, preferring always to dine at home. So Robin planned with Elin a buffet supper to which they could invite as many as they chose. Once Tony begged the use of the car and he and Ingrid left at dawn for a long day together. They drove to Hanover. The college year was over, but Ingrid wished to see Professor and Mrs. Vernon, Mike's father and mother, with whom she had spent her first winter in this country; and Tony, too, had many friends among the faculty. Mark wondered whether Tony might be made unhappy by thus revisiting the scene of Lucy's death, and he wondered whether Tony and Ingrid spoke of Lucy that day. He never knew, but next day, leaving Ingrid at home with Robin, Tony went out for an hour, and at dinner he told them all:

'I went over to see Mr. and Mrs. Pride for a few minutes, had tea with them. They were always mighty nice to me.'

'That's good. I'm glad you did,' Mark agreed. 'Mr. Pride and I sometimes lunch together. I've a real affection for him.' He asked: 'How's Mrs. Pride?'

'Why—she cried,' Tony admitted, meeting Ingrid's eyes so that Mark knew there were no secrets between these two. 'But I think it was mostly because she sort of felt it was the proper thing to do. I don't think she feels very deeply about anything.'

Mark was not so sure. It had seemed to him that Mrs. Pride, for all her merry lightness, must have had many tortured, prayerful hours when she saw her own follies live again in Lucy; yet perhaps this was only his imagination. Tony might be right in his estimate of her.

Except for the buffet supper, when the house was full of Mark's friends and Tony's, these four dined alone together. Mark and Robin usually went early upstairs; but Tony and Ingrid, having said good night to them, returned to the living room again, and it might be hours before Robin, who slept lightly nowadays, heard them come up, heard their whispered parting in the hall. And a little later, after Ingrid was abed, she was sure to hear Tony come softly from his room to kiss Ingrid good night, and quietly to open the door between her room and theirs, so that if dark dreams tormented her, Robin would surely hear.

The brief days, which in prospect had seemed so richly many, suddenly were done. When the time came for Tony's departure, Robin and Ingrid went with him to the airport; and Mark came from town to join them there and to drive them home. Ingrid gave Tony a smiling kiss and a long embrace for his good-bye, and on the way home she was composed and serene; but once they were in the house, she fled upstairs, and Robin quickly followed her and found her lying dry-eyed on her bed; and Robin sat down beside her, and then Ingrid's tears came streaming, and she clung to Robin, whispering in passionate tenderness and woe: 'If anything happens to him! Oh, if anything happens to him!'

Robin held her close. 'Nothing will, darling. Nothing will,' she promised. 'Don't you worry about Tony!'

'You don't know,' Ingrid insisted, suddenly tense in Robin's arms, her breath hissing as though her teeth were clenched to hold back a cry of pain. 'You don't know the things that do happen! You don't know! You don't know!'

'Sh-h-h, dear. I know Tony, and I know how much we all love him.'

'Loving doesn't do any good. Fathers and mothers and girls somewhere love all of them; but loving doesn't stop the things hitting them!' And for a long time Ingrid wept helplessly, till slowly Robin brought her peace. So at last she was quiet, and Robin made her lie down, and brought a cold compress for her eyes, and Ingrid looked up at her with a wry, small smile and said contritely: 'Oh, I am wrong to make you unhappy so, to make you worried about me.'

Thereafter what fears she felt she did not show.

Tony wrote them of his safe arrival at Ellington Field, and of his work. 'Life is a good deal easier, inspection also. The main job is flying and getting the hours as fast as possible.' He spoke of 'beam work' and night flights cross-country, and of practice with instruments, and in the use of oxygen at high altitudes; and once he had news of old friends.

> Who do you think I saw this last week-end? Ruth Rollins—Ruth Crocker, that is—and her husband. They called me up and we got together for dinner. I'd never met him before. He and Ruth are driving across the continent, taking their time; and they're planning to go on to Honolulu. Ruth's mother's there this summer, and she wants to see her, and Jerry wants to see what people there think about the Japs. They told me so much about the place that

I think I'll try to get sent out there. How'd you like to live in Honolulu, Ingrid? No skiing, of course, but I'll teach you to ride the surf at Waikiki—after I learn myself.

And he wrote of mock combat, and of playing hide and seek among the clouds, so vividly that they felt the keen, stirring beauty he described, shared with him the wide, pure freedom of the skies. Once he wrote to Ingrid:

I wish everybody on earth could see the things we see. Men would be a lot different if they could get away from the earth now and then. There was a great cloudhead today, rising ever so high and majestic, with the sun shining on it; and I flew past the face of it, not a mile away, and it towered to Heaven above me. You just couldn't breathe when you looked at it. You didn't have any physical sensations at all. You couldn't even hear the engine. You were all alone in a great, pure, holy, beautiful silence. It was like seeing God with His veil lifted.

Ingrid gave them that letter to read, and Robin saw her countenance transfigured as she listened while Mark read it aloud. Afterward without a word she took it from Mark and went out-of-doors and down to the summerhouse by the lakeside, and when they were alone, Mark said quietly:

'If the boy's to die, Robin, I hope it's up there, where he loves to be.'

She touched his lips with her fingers. 'Hush, my dear. Never fear for Tony. Please.'

3

(Summer 1941)

Through that month of June for a little while after the fall of Crete there was a lull, a breathing time; yet always the air seemed vibrant with the rumble of great distant guns. The United States closed German consulates, charging that they were centres of activity hostile to American interests. Churchill, speaking more for American than for British ears, said: 'United we stand. Divided we fall. Divided, the dark ages return. United, we can save and guide the world.' The proponents of Union Now seized upon this speech to put their program into more concrete form, to suggest a World Congress with twenty-seven American representatives, twenty-two British; and Bob Ritchie, discussing this with Mark, said drily: 'The trouble with that is that the Britishers would always be unanimous for Britain; but there'd always be five or ten Americans who'd vote England's way. So England would run the show.'

Mark agreed completely that any plan for formal union was unworkable. 'Most plans are,' he pointed out. 'Events have a way of disrupting them. After the fact, we say: "So and so happened according to plan," like a war communiqué.'

' "We planned it that way," ' Bob quoted derisively.

'And we try to persuade ourselves that we did,' Mark assented. 'But in fact, the event makes the plan, not the plan the event. Whoever wrote: "I am the master of my fate, I am the captain of my soul," was whistling to keep his courage up, a fox barking at the moon. We do pretty much what we have to do.'

'What Churchill talks us into doing,' Bob amended.

But Mark shook his head. 'No, we'll do what the event compels,' he insisted. 'The United States and England will in the future be forced to cooperate pretty closely. My father says we're bound to England, just as the British Empire is bound together, by ties of common funk!'

'The United States doesn't have to be afraid of anything except of making a fool of herself.'

'I don't think fear is the right word,' Mark argued. 'But we and England have common interests, and common ideals. For instance, England has cooperated with us in enforcing the Monroe Doctrine.'

'She didn't cooperate a hell of a lot when Maximilian grabbed Mexico.'

'All the same, if it hadn't been for the English fleet, we'd have had to fight for the Monroe Doctrine long ago. And there'll be other doctrines in the future on which we agree; and we'll cooperate to back those doctrines. That will be a free cooperation, to achieve definite ends—and to be dissolved when those ends have been achieved.'

Bob laughed. 'If we team up with England, we'll have to pull the bulk of the load,' he declared. 'She's lost the Mediterranean now. I tell you, old man, the British Empire's done.'

There was enough surface truth in this so that when in the third week of June Germany invaded Russia, Mark felt a sudden and tremendous relief, since it was clear that, at least for the present, England was safe. The experts—his nostrils wrinkled at the word—predicted that Russia would fall an easy victim; but Mark did not believe this. Distances would fight on Russia's side. The simple physical difficulty of transporting troops and supplies, of building highways and airports and altering the railroad gauge, would slow down even an unopposed German advance. He studied the map and decided that if Germany could seize and hold the line Leningrad-Moscow-Sevastopol, she might turn her forces toward England again; but until she should have achieved that position, England was secure.

And Mark, since concern for England's safety no longer beset him, found that the war receded into the background of his thoughts. Tony's letters, Tony's beloved Ingrid here with them every day, and the fact that his child and Robin's would be born in the late summer; these things were his world. Robin in the evening was usually as comfortably drowsy as a cat, and he might read aloud to her and Ingrid for a while after dinner, till he saw that she was asleep in her chair; and he and Ingrid would look at each other and smile, and then Ingrid would rouse Robin and go up with her to help her make ready for the night, and Mark would follow presently, so that he might not disturb her by coming to bed after she was asleep.

He was apt to forget the war, or to think of it as an abstraction concerning which he could speculate quite calmly. Once he and Robin were listening to a concert coming over the radio, and when it ended, it was followed by news bulletins. He would have turned this off, but he saw that Robin was asleep and feared the silence would wake her; so he listened till the news ended, and saw then that she had waked and was watching him.

'You were frowning, as you listened,' she said. 'What were you thinking?'

'I've been trying to decide why Germany went into Russia,' he confessed. 'The commentators talk about the Ukraine, the "black earth" there, good soil forty feet deep, and Germany's need for wheat; or they talk about the oil field at Baku and her need for gasoline. But I think they're wrong. She could have secured wheat and oil by peaceful means. I suspect this attack is a *quid pro quo* in Hitler's bargain with Japan. I believe he's undertaken to keep Russia so busy on her western frontier that she can't interfere with Japan in China. I suspect his attack on Russia is designed to turn Japan loose in the Pacific, so that Japan can tie us up there and stop our help to England.'

Robin asked drowsily, watching him with happy eyes: 'Are you going to start worrying about Japan, now?'

'Oh, I've stopped worrying,' he assured her smilingly. 'Everybody has. With Germany tied up in Russia, England's safe enough, for a while at least, and people in this country know it. They're not worried about the war at all now.

'But they're confused—emotionally confused—by the demand that they start cheering for Russia. Most of us don't like Russia. I doubt whether we ever will. And what with knowing that at least temporarily England is safe, and what with hoping that Germany may wear herself out against Russia, I think there's been a tremendous letting up in our willingness to get ready to fight Germany ourselves. We're like a Kansas farmer who has been watching a tornado approach his home, and sees it veer away in another direction. He feels safe again, and goes back to his plowing.'

He found evidence enough of this feeling everywhere. The drafted men in training were reported to be bored with making beds and building roads and digging ditches, and to be complaining that they were not given tanks and cannon and rifles and all the tools of war. Tom Sheffield spoke of this when he and Mark one day lunched together. Tom's mother had died a fortnight before, happy in having had her son for the last months of her life and in dwelling in her old home again. Tom still stayed on in the big Lincoln house and planned to continue to do so, but since his mother's death he seemed sometimes uncertain and confused, seemed forever to expect a rebuff, a harsh or angry word; and Mark thought he had lived so long under the complete domination of a woman—his mother and then Emma and then his mother again— that he was unused to stand alone, and moved haltingly, like one who has just laid aside crutches.

He spoke to Mark of the newspaper and magazine articles about low morale among the soldiers. 'But Tommy says his outfit is fit and keen,' he said. 'Ready for trouble and wishing it would start.' And he asked doubtfully: 'Do you think we'll send an army abroad? I see those English generals, Wavell and Auchinleck, say England can't win unless we do.'

Mark said reassuringly, recognizing the anxiety for Tommy's sake which harassed the other man: 'Don't take them too seriously, Tom.' He smiled. 'The trouble with generals, they're experts, and experts are usually wrong.'

'That's right,' Tom agreed with a wistful eagerness. 'The experts said Russia would be whipped in a month, and she isn't, is she? Germany certainly can't start any other campaign for a while.'

Most people, sooner or later, spoke of the Russian war; Bob Ritchie, whose temper had become increasingly uneven since his illness, damned Churchill and Roosevelt for the welcome they had given this new ally. 'It's shown up the rotten hypocrisy of the lot of them,' he declared.

'First Stalin was a louse and now he's a knight in shining armor. They make me sick!'

Elin frankly and openly exulted over every German victory on the Red front. Robin told Mark one night: 'We had a long talk about it this afternoon. You can't blame her, of course. Einar died fighting for Finland. The Russians killed him, and now Finland's fighting on Germany's side against Russia, so naturally Elin's cheering for them.'

'A lot of us will always cheer for Finland,' Mark agreed. 'But don't let Elin and Ingrid get together. I don't want them to quarrel.' They were careful to avoid discussing the war in Ingrid's hearing. Whenever Germany was mentioned, her color drained away and her hands clenched hard. She hated Germany as Elin hated Russia.

Mark had in mid-July a letter from Longstreet Dent in which the Mississippi man asked: 'How do you Boston folks take this Russian war? We've been taught down here to love Finland and hate Russia, so we're some confused right now. It's hard to turn us on and off like a faucet.'

And Mark's father wrote to say that the incipient war spirit in Ohio was dead. 'We might have gone along to save England,' he admitted. 'But England's in no danger now. Mr. Roosevelt will have a hard time persuading us to fight to destroy Germany. The *Robin Moor* business didn't make a ripple out here. The way it looks to us, Germany and Russia may wear each other out—and we hope they both lose. We're like the man in the tree watching the bear chase his wife and yelling: "Go it wife, go it b'ar!" '

This division of loyalties was everywhere in evidence, and Mark began to regard the war as dispassionately as if it were a case in court. But Bob Ritchie,. whenever they talked together, insisted that Mr. Roosevelt was still bent upon his policy of intervention, and his rancor against the President increased with every day. When Secretary of the Navy Knox said depth bombs had already been dropped by our destroyers, Bob was enraged. That we should repair British warships in our navy yards seemed to him a deliberately provocative act, violating all the laws by which we professed to set such store. Our occupation of Iceland, he declared, was as much an outrage as the German occupation of Denmark. A few days after publication of the news that Mr. Roosevelt had met Winston Churchill at sea, he came across the street after dinner to sit with Mark on the terrace in the twilight; and at once he spoke of that meeting and of the Atlantic Charter which the two statesmen drafted there.

'Franklin's usurping the powers of Congress,' he said. 'He's practically declared war!'

'I don't see it so,' Mark dissented. 'Everything he's done comes within his Constitutional powers.'

'Don't be that way!' Bob protested almost plaintively. 'The Atlantic Charter's no more nor less than a treaty, made without the advice or consent of the Senate. He committed us to help in "the final destruction of the Nazis' tyranny."'

'Not quite,' Mark corrected. 'He simply stated our national policy— as he sees it—both for now and for the future, after the destruction of Hitlerism.'

'Oh yeah!' Bob's tone was dry. 'Well that isn't what Churchill thinks. He told Parliament that he and Roosevelt have jointly pledged their countries to the destruction of Hitler.'

Mark shook his head. 'Churchill misrepresented, or misunderstood. Mr. Roosevelt merely said what he believes our national sentiment to be—and I believe he judged it correctly.'

'You're kidding yourself,' Bob said hotly. 'Man, we're being quietly diddled, that's the truth. We've soldiers in Iceland and Newfoundland and Bermuda and British Guiana—and all of them ready to shoot at the first head they see. We've given Germany plenty of reasons to declare war. Roosevelt is scared now that Russia will finish Hitler off before he can get us to let him play with the big boys—and Churchill's playing the same game, and laughing at us up his sleeve.'

Mark said good-humoredly: 'You remind me of an editorial I read last week.' He went in to find the paper, came out again and turned on the overhead light on the terrace where they sat and read a paragraph aloud:

> To the Europeans, the greatest victory will be to see us enter the war; to find the United States, when the war ends, prostrated in economic collapse, a shattered republic, ripe for the isms that have reduced the European nations to a group of jealous highwaymen bent on one another's ruin. The United States has everything to lose by war, and nothing to gain. Defeat would be disaster, and victory, even if achieved, can be charged off as a total loss.

'Who wrote that?' Bob demanded.

'My father,' Mark confessed, laying the paper aside. 'It's the Mid-Western point of view.'

'It's the only sane point of view,' Bob declared. 'Your father's a damned smart man!'

They had been friends for a long time, and Mark would not speak as strongly as he felt; but he was distressed by the other's violence, and he said firmly: 'I'm afraid you and I will never see eye-to-eye on Mr. Roosevelt, Bob. It's true that before Germany attacked Russia he had led our thinking to the point where we were about ready to ask Congress to declare war; but I think he was right, I think he's done a wise, great thing. I know you don't agree, but I have felt for a long time that if the pinch comes we must stand with England; and Mr. Roosevelt saw that long ago.'

Bob snorted, but Mark insisted: 'You know I've never been a Roosevelt man, and even now I think he fails to comprehend the size of the job ahead; but at least he's persuaded us that we must undertake the job! Maybe he hasn't prepared the country in material ways, but he has prepared the American mind. Give him credit for that, old man!'

Bob laughed shortly. 'You're as bad as my father!' he declared. 'He used to damn Roosevelt as loud as anyone, but he's all for Franklin's foreign policy. Only he'd like to see us get into the war right now!'

Mark smiled. 'I was never for Mr. Roosevelt,' he repeated. 'But I may have been wrong. Even his domestic policy has its points. Do you remember that book by Sinclair Lewis, *It Can't Happen Here?*'

'Sure, I read it.'

'I re-read it, last week,' Mark told him. 'It was published in 1935, the year before Mr. Roosevelt's first re-election. Its thesis was that we might find ourselves led into a bloody revolution in this country; a revolution in which the millions of unemployed elected a demagogue President who reorganized the country on the Hitler pattern. And Bob, that book was sufficiently plausible so that it was taken seriously.'

'Seriously, hell! A lot of people read it because it was full of sadistic butchery and they ate it up.'

'A lot of people read it because it was near enough the truth—or the possible truth—to scare them,' Mark insisted. 'The point was that with conditions in this country as they then were, what Lewis described could have happened here. But Mr. Roosevelt's internal policies have helped to change those conditions, Bob. Give the man credit.'

Bob stared at him for a moment in a scowling truculence. 'You're not a damned fool, Mark,' he protested. 'Even if you do talk like one.' He came back to his original point. 'Read the Atlantic Charter,' he challenged. 'If that's not to all intents and purposes a treaty—why, I'll vote for Franklin for a fourth term!' And he rose. 'Good night!' he said shortly, and walked indignantly away.

4
(August 1941)

For a while after Bob left him, Mark stayed where he was, thinking of what the other had said. Robin and Ingrid were in the living room, but he did not move to join them till he heard the telephone ring, heard Ingrid go to answer it, heard the quick happiness in her voice. Mark went in to meet her returning.

'It was a telegram from Tony,' Ingrid told them, radiant with delight. 'He's got his commission, and he'll be here Wednesday afternoon, and he says we must be married Thursday morning!' She came swooping to kiss Robin, to kiss Mark; she swung in a swirling circle around the room, pirouetting, her skirts flying; she came back to hug Robin tight, and they laughed with her at her happiness.

They had known approximately when to expect Tony, and Robin and Ingrid had been busy shopping and making all plans; but every plan had to be discussed and rediscussed now, and they sat late, going over and over the same ground again and again. Mark, watching Ingrid, realized that she had become this summer increasingly dear to him; and when Robin at last rose to go upstairs, and Ingrid would have gone with her, Mark called her back.

'Wait, Ingrid,' he said smilingly. 'I want to tell you something.'

'About Tony?' she asked quickly.

'About both of you,' he assured her. They faced each other, each of them for the moment grave. 'You know, Tony and I have been very close to one another since his mother died,' Mark said. 'Sometimes I've worried about him, as fathers will. Sometimes I've worried for fear he'd marry the wrong girl.'

She nodded in quick agreement. 'I did that, too,' she said, so completely serious that he dared not smile.

'I just want you to know, tonight,' he told her, 'that I'm not worried about that now. I'm glad and thankful you're going to marry Tony.'

For a moment she did not speak, but he saw her eyes fill. She lifted one hand in a helpless gesture, smiling then; and she said: 'All I know to say is—so am I glad, and happy, too, and most glad you have said that to me.'

She turned as though to go to Robin, then came back to him again, rising on tiptoes to kiss him softly, smiling up at him through glad tears. 'Just see how I am happy,' she whispered. 'To cry like a baby so.' And she ran away from him, hurrying up the stairs.

When presently Mark followed her, he and Robin talked a further while; and she said smilingly: 'I hope the baby doesn't come to the wedding. He's so bumptious it would be just like him to try to seize the spotlight; and I don't want anything to interfere with Tony and Ingrid.'

Mark smiled. 'I'm afraid my interests are divided,' he confessed. 'Tony and Ingrid and you and the baby; between you, you've certainly driven everything else out of my head.'

Yet this was not wholly true. When presently he turned out the light on the table between their beds, she quickly slept; but Mark did not. Thoughts of Tony filled his mind, and of the war in which Tony might one day play his part; and after a time he remembered what Bob had said about the Atlantic Charter, and—reflecting on that—he knew he could not sleep. He rose at last, careful not to disturb Robin, and in his dressing gown he went downstairs again and searched out a newspaper clipping containing the document signed by Mr. Churchill and Mr. Roosevelt, and read it through.

Since he and Robin were married, he had seldom written in his diary. Once it had served him as a companion; but he had Robin now. Yet tonight he found himself perplexed again, and at last, appraising the Charter to discover how much real meat it contained, he sought out the diary and began to write. His was a naturally judicial and dispassionate mind, and it was thus he wrote now.

> Re the Charter, take each point:
> First—that they (i.e., the U.S. and England) seek no aggrandizement. This is meaningless. England said—or would have said—the same thing in 1914, and yet she took some two million square miles (figures from memory, probably wrong) as her share of the loot.

He frowned as he wrote. Those who had seen him on the bench were familiar with that frown of concentration, of clear, cold intelligence, concerned only with fact and demonstrable truth. He lighted a cigarette, consulted the newspaper copy of the Charter, and wrote on:

> Second and Third—This is the old 'Self-Determination of Small Peoples.' Query: Then will Russia restore Latvia, Esthonia, etc.? How about the Sudetenland? Or the Gaspesian peninsula, for that matter; or one of our Southern states where negroes outnumber the whites. Obviously the principle of a plebiscite to determine the national character of a given region is not universally applicable.
> Fourth and Fifth—Are these perhaps appeasements, a hand extended to Germany? If (see Third, above) 'They respect the right of all peoples to

choose the form of government under which they will live,' will they say
Germany may choose the rule of the Führer?

Sixth—'After the final destruction of the Nazi tyranny they hope to see,'
etc. In spite of Mr. Churchill, there is clearly no pledge involved in these
words, no pledge to help destroy Naziism. Mr. Roosevelt has not denied Mr.
Churchill's statement to Parliament; but even so I feel sure Churchill—and
Bob—are wrong.

Seventh—Here is 'freedom of the seas' again; but England still claims and
exercises the rights of search and seizure. Try taking even an empty American
vessel to a German port, and see what happens. This clause is mockery.

Eighth—This is disarmament—but only of the 'aggressor nations.' Suppose
we disarm Germany, and then seek to dictate internal German policies. Do
we not become an 'aggressor nation' ourselves?

He paused again, re-reading what he had written, adding an inter-
lined phrase here and there, as though he were making notes on a brief
submitted by counsel in a case before him for decision.

And yet, when he had read what he had written, it did not satisfy
him. He shook his head in a sudden sharp discontent and began to write
again.

This dissection is empty business, with no contentment in it. An analysis
of the famous document leads nowhere. The Charter is words without meaning, except the meaning implicit in the meeting of these two men. I prefer
to cling to my own fundamental and basic certainty.

That certainty is that I do not want to see England lose, but this does not
mean that I want us to attempt to police the world; to interfere if, for
instance, the Czechs wish to separate from the Slovaks, or vice versa. I am
not even sure I want to see Germany again reduced to her condition in
1920-1922. As my father says, Mr. Roosevelt has a mandate to save England;
but I do not believe he has an equally definite mandate to crush Germany.

Mr. Roosevelt has a mandate from the people to save England as a measure
of self-defense for the United States; but if Hitler offered the world peace on
a basis of the security of England, the restoration of western Europe, and an
indemnity to the nations of western Europe—keeping for himself nothing but
a free hand in the east—I believe we Americans would want to accept it.

The weakness of Mr. Roosevelt's position is that he has not yet been able
to make an issue, a blood-tingling issue which would enlist the whole-hearted
support of this country. The Four Freedoms are merely words. Germany—
Germans—are fighting for a definite constructive plan. We are invited to
fight essentially to keep what we have, to keep the world as it is. That is not
enough. We . . .

His pen paused, for he heard a step on the stair, and as he turned,
Ingrid appeared in the doorway. In her night garments, her feet bare,
she seemed astonishingly small. He rose quickly as she came toward
him; and it was only then that he saw that, though her eyes were open,

she was pale and taut and she looked blankly at nothing. She brushed past him, going toward the French doors; and he realized that she was asleep. She touched the handle of the door, and he spoke softly.

'Ingrid!'

She whirled to face him, crouching, desperately tense; and—too wise to approach her—he spoke her name again. 'Ingrid! It's Judge Worth. Tony's father.'

She mumbled in terror: 'No, no, no!' She threw up her hands, backing away from him. 'No, no!' She backed against the door, frantic fear in her eyes, watching him as though he were a monster; but when he did not move to come near her, her protesting cry lost conviction, and her eyes began to clear. He saw that she was waking.

He said in reassuring gentleness: 'You'll catch cold, dear!' There was a Paisley shawl on the back of the couch and he took it and held it, still not moving for fear she might be frightened into flight, till at last, haltingly, she came to him and he put the shawl around her. 'You were walking in your sleep,' he said.

She drew the shawl close over her shoulders, blinking in a puzzled way. Then she nodded, shuddered, her teeth chattering. 'I was dreaming,' she said in a low, shaken tone. 'It was very bad. It was things I have seen.'

'Don't ever be frightened. You're all right now. You're all right here.'

'I know.' She nodded again. 'I'm so sorry. I have the bad dreams so much.'

'You're safe here, Ingrid.'

'Yes.' He saw that her brow was wet, and she was breathing quickly as though she had been running. A hard pulse pounded in her throat. He thought she might better wait awhile, for full wakefulness, before going back to bed.

'Sit down,' he said. 'I'm writing, but I'll be finished in a minute. Then we'll go upstairs.'

She obeyed him, curling her feet under her on the couch, the shawl warm around her; and he touched her shoulder reassuringly, and she looked up at him and smiled in a shy way. 'I ought not to trouble you so much,' she said.

'You never trouble me,' he told her. 'We all love you, you know.' He smiled. 'And Tony will be here tomorrow, remember.'

Her eyes quickened. 'He will, won't he?'

'He surely will!'

She made a little sighing sound, a hiccough like the echo of a sob, and he sat down at his desk and looked again at what he had been writing, seeing the written words through a red blur of wrath. He had broken off in mid-sentence when she appeared, and he looked back one paragraph, in puzzled wonder, as though it were hard to understand his own words. He turned the pages and read them through again, at first carefully and then in a sort of scornful haste; and at last, beginning at the beginning, he drew slashing lines down through each page, obliterating the whole. Then he set a crossed line under the last paragraph and wrote below it:

> I've come to my senses, thank God! What I have written above is nonsense, empty words, about a thing which cannot be put in words. Ingrid came downstairs just now, sleep-walking in a dream of terror. She was in Norway when the Germans struck there, and memories haunt her sleeping hours. Her coming made me see the truth! Perhaps I, too, have been sleepwalking for years; but I'm awake and sensible at last.
>
> I tried to write—above there—logically, judicially, calmly; but I was wrong to do so. The time for logic and calm reason is past! Some things men feel but cannot put them into words. There are no words for Hitler, ruling boys by prostituting the noblest virtues of man's heart—loyalty, service, sacrifice— to his own base ends; ruling men—and nations too—by the threat and the practice of secret, uncontrolled assassination at the hands of the Gestapo or by frightening the tender hearts of women. There is no fate for him but dreadful, swift, eternal death. The time for the calm judicial mind is past. This is the hour for emotion, for hot hate of this evil man. Let us go to this war, and fight it till his reeking footprints are erased from every conquered land.
>
> This war is not a war of ideas, of nations, of policies, of thought. It is Hitler's war against every individual in the world; and above all it is a war against boys like Tony, against girls like Ingrid. Seeing her terror tonight brought it home to me. There is a scar of remembered horrors on her heart which will never heal. The war did that to her, teaching her fear and hate, making her look on death and mutilation.
>
> And there are millions like her, young girls scarred by terror, babies driven insane by the shock of bomb bursts near them, boys and men and women killed, their arms and legs ripped off or shredded into tasselled stumps, their bellies opened, their skulls crushed like a nut under a heavy heel. Death is the least of all the dreadful things; for to live with a scarred soul may be worse than death. The old War did that to Robin's Davy, and to Robin, and to Dave, and to so many of the people I know.
>
> This is another war, and already it is worse than that one, and Hitler, none other, calmly and with calculation made this war. I hope to live to see him crushed like a spider under heel. God damn his soul to Hell!

He finished with a strong content, and sat for a moment at once trembling and appeased. He closed the book and laid his pen aside; and in the very violence of his own anger, as though it purged him, he found peace. Serene again, he turned to Ingrid, and he smiled.

'Now, bed?' he suggested.

She rose, came near him. 'It does good to me to be with you,' she said. 'When I am with you, I do not think there can be anything in the world that is wrong.' She shivered faintly. 'It is only when I am in my sleep, alone, that I remember those things.'

'After tomorrow, you'll have Tony,' he reminded her. Yet Tony would be here for so short a time. 'And from now on, even when he's not here himself, you'll have him in your heart for company.'

She nodded gravely. 'Yes, I know that, and it will be always so,' she said; and they went together up the stairs.

5

(August 28, 1941)

Tony and Ingrid were married in the living room at ten o'clock Thursday morning as Tony had wanted it to be; and from daylight on the house was astir with a happy excitement. Robin, the first to wake, lay quietly watching Mark in his bed beside hers; and then she heard Elin go downstairs, and then as the first rays of the risen sun touched her windows she heard Tony come from his room to Ingrid's. When he softly closed the doors between their rooms, he looked in and saw Robin awake; and he grinned like a boy, and she blew him a kiss. After the door was closed, she heard the low murmur of his voice and Ingrid's for a while in the other room; and then a car stopped outside, bringing Anna to help Elin in the kitchen for this great day. Then—the sun was well risen now—Mark woke, and they talked together, their voices warm with perfect happiness.

He and she had decided that the Reverend Mr. Merrilee, whom Jerry called 'Padre,' should perform the ceremony; and Mark and Tony had gone to see the minister the night before and had brought him to rehearse them all in that which was to be done today. Robin spoke of him contentedly.

'There couldn't be anyone better,' she said. 'I'd hate having a stranger do it. I want things to be completely perfect for these two, Mark.'

'Everything will be,' he promised her. 'Never fear.'

Elin brought trays for Robin and Ingrid, and Tony and Mark had breakfast together downstairs. Mark guessed Robin had planned it should be so, and he clung to this hour with his son, protracting it as much as possible. Tony, for all his maturity, had shy questions to ask, and Mark could answer them; and presently Tony said:

'It's like old times, isn't it, just us two having breakfast together this way.'

'Some fun?' Mark smilingly suggested, using that catchword which once had been much on Tony's tongue; and Tony said:

'Some fun!'

'I wonder how it would be to have a daughter getting married,' Mark reflected. 'Probably fathers are pretty well excluded then. And yet I think a son is much more lost to his parents when he marries than a daughter; but when a son marries, he becomes more like your friend than your son. He's the head of a family of his own, facing the same responsibilities and the same problems you've learned to face. And he has to face them alone, can no longer come to you and ask you to share his perplexities. Every man, certainly every married man, lives in some ways a solitary life, has experiences and anxieties he never discusses, thoughts he never utters, not even to his wife. For even after they're married, there's a deep gulf between man and woman, Tony. Men have a lot of worries they never tell their wives, because to do so would only make two people worry instead of one.'

Tony said warmly: 'I can't imagine anything I couldn't talk about to you.'

Mark was made happy by that word, but he said smilingly: 'There'll be things. For instance, when you and Ingrid are at odds, don't ever tell me. Young people, young married people, should keep their disagreements to themselves. If you ever told me you were disturbed by something Ingrid had said or done, I would tell you you were wrong, of course—no matter how right I thought you were—but at the same time I'd hate her for what she had done. By and by you and she would forget and love each other as much as ever, but I wouldn't forget. I'd always hold it against her. That's the way parents are. So never criticize Ingrid to me, Tony.'

Tony laughed. 'I can't imagine ever criticizing her to anyone,' he declared.

'I love her, too,' Mark said simply. He told Tony about her dark dreams, about her sleep-walking. 'Be kind to her always,' Mark said, 'and by and by those wounds will heal.'

They were still at the table when Chuck Little arrived. He had driven

up from Hartford, starting at dawn, to be Tony's best man; and Elin
gave him breakfast, and then Robin called Mark to come and dress.
'Because there'll be no chance for you up here after Ingrid starts to
dress,' she warned him. He left Tony and Chuck at the table, and when
he came down they, too, had disappeared into the guest room upstairs
to dress and wait there secluded till the time came.

Mark was alone for a while; but he could hear Robin and Ingrid
moving to and fro overhead, hear their happy voices. Then Jan, who by
her own request would be Ingrid's maid of honor, came across the street
and stayed a moment with Mark, lovely in the bright gown she would
wear, before she went up to be with Ingrid and Robin and left him
alone again.

Mr. Merrilee arrived a little after nine, and he wished to instruct
Chuck Little in his duties as best man; so he and Mark went up to
the guest room, and Mark stayed there with them till he heard the doorbell and descended to greet the Halsteads, Ed and Mary and all the
children. Ed carried the baby upstairs and called Robin to inspect his
son. Mark and Mary, watching from the stair foot, heard Robin agree
that young Edwin was wonderful, heard her say laughingly:

'But hide him away till after the ceremony. It's hard enough waiting
for mine as it is, without seeing how sweet they are. Put him here in
Elin's room.' Young Edwin would sleep there serenely throughout the
proceedings.

Before Ed came downstairs, Bob and Nell arrived; and Nell and
Mary went up to be with Robin and Ingrid, and then Tom Sheffield
appeared alone, for Tommy was in camp in North Carolina. Will
Ritchie, too, was in the army now. Tom and Bob compared notes about
their sons. Tommy, enlisting as a private in the regular army, had been
transferred to an officers' training camp; and Tom spoke of him proudly,
hiding his unadmitted fears. Will in his last letter reported that he had
volunteered for training in a parachute outfit; and Bob told them this.

'Nell says the Army'll be kept busy paying bills for breakage for him,'
he said laughingly. 'She says he's sure to land in a greenhouse every
time he jumps.'

They were all sufficiently under the strain of the occasion so that they
welcomed the chance for laughter; and Ed said: 'One thing sure, they
won't have to teach Will how to fall. He's been doing nothing but prac-
tise falls all his life.' They labored the point, making much of Will's
awkwardness, clinging to the subject as though afraid of silence, till
Ruth and Jerry Crocker arrived; and then Betty Ritchie made an

entrance, a little superior to all this excitement, as though there were something juvenile about it, applauding Robin's arrangement of the flowers in the polite and kindly tone one uses to applaud the antics of a child.

Mark was perspiring faintly as the time drew near. Listening to the labored conversation of the others, he had a faint smothered feeling, and he felt the thumping of his heart and tried to relax, to free himself from the intolerable tension of this waiting. Then Mr. Merrilee came downstairs, in his vestments, ready to perform the ceremony; and Mark's heart pounded hard as he introduced his friends to that kindly little man, till Mr. Merrilee's quiet serenity eased and heartened him.

Presently thereafter Nell and Mary appeared. Nell's first glance was for Bob, as though each time they met she feared since his illness to see some sorry change in him. Their coming was like a signal, and every voice was lowered and the little group rearranged itself in a half circle around the room, and Elin and Anna came to the dining-room door and stood there watching the stairs. Mark could see them from where he stood, and he beckoned Elin to come nearer, but she smiled and shook her head and stayed for the present where she was.

Mr. Merrilee produced his prayer book and crossed and stood with his back to the fireplace, waiting, beaming as he faced them all. Robin came down the stairs alone, and after a moment Tony and Chuck Little followed her. Tony looked all around, smiling at everyone, completely at ease; but Chuck was pale and drawn, his hand forever seeking his coat pocket to make sure the ring was safe. They took their places beside Mr. Merrilee.

There was neither piano nor organ; but Ann Halstead—she was sixteen, tall and lovely, her dark hair sedately smooth, her stormy beauty for this occasion tamed—stood where she could watch the stairs and near her mother; and after a moment she and Mary began to sing softly the wedding march from *Lohengrin*. Mary's voice was a true contralto, Ann's a clear soprano which had already had some training, and they blended well.

Then, Jan and Ingrid, Jan leading, came sweetly down the stairs. Mark saw Jan's eye, as she entered, go straight to Tony, just as Nell's had gone to Bob awhile ago; but Jan's were full of gladness and joy, with no reservation in them, and Tony smiled and so did she, and Mark thought Jan's affection would always be a thing Tony could treasure, and he hoped it would not rob Jan of her own happiness some day.

When Ingrid saw Tony, her step seemed to quicken, as though she could no longer endure delay; and she came swiftly to his side.

So after a moment, when they were all hushed and still, Mr. Merrilee spoke quietly. 'Dearly beloved, we are gathered here together in the sight of God . . .' Mark, standing—since he would give the bride away—close behind Tony and Ingrid, let his eyes rest on Tony, watching Tony's ear, and the flat curve of his cheek; and the minister's voice went gently on, serene and rich and calm. So he turned at last to Tony with the question, and the familiar words were strong and proud. 'Wilt thou love her, comfort her . . .' Mark remembered that Ingrid in her dreams had sometimes sore need of comforting. 'Honour and keep her, in sickness and in health; and forsaking all others, keep thee only unto her, so long as ye both shall live?'

Tony's voice was perfectly natural, clear and sure.

'I will.'

Mr. Merrilee spoke to Ingrid, and then Mark had his brief part to play, and he fought to keep his countenance as composed as theirs were. And then, echoing the minister, Tony was saying:

'I, Anthony, take thee, Ingrid, to my wedded wife, to have and to hold from this day forward, for better for worse, for richer for poorer, in sickness and in health, to love and to cherish till death us do part . . .'

Till death us do part! The words were like a heavy blow. Every pulse in Mark's body seemed to come pounding in his throat, to blur his eyes so that he could no longer clearly see Tony's straight shoulders and proud head and the clean line of his jaw. Tony looked down at Ingrid while he spoke and her eyes were turned to him, each speaking to the other as though they were alone here; and their young countenances were transfigured.

Then they were all murmuring together in the prayer, and so it was done, and Mark went straight to be with Robin; for those sombre words were thudding in his heart and he turned to her for reassurance, while around them everyone talked at once, their voices and their laughter mingling.

Mark watched Tony and Ingrid, bound that nothing should cloud their last few moments here. Ingrid was as gay as any, yet always her eyes turned to Tony, waiting for the sign from him that they might go. They were to take the car, their plans their own; and they had been married in the garments they would wear.

But first they must taste the dishes Elin and Anna passed, and cut the cake, while Chuck Little saw the bags safely in the car. Then Ingrid went up to put on her hat, and Tony to bring her down, and Robin produced boxes of gaily colored paper rose petals, from which everyone dipped handfuls, and then Tony and Ingrid came running down the stairs and across the living room through the bright shower and the proud and tender cries. Chuck had already turned the car, waiting in the driveway, to face the street. Everyone followed them that far, and Tony helped Ingrid in, and took his place beside her and meshed the gears. The car leaped ahead.

So, they were gone, and Robin laughed in a great relief. 'Well, there!' she said. 'That's done!'

'Alone at last,' Bob chuckled.

Mark said nothing, but he was content, remembering the happiness that had transfigured the countenance of his son.

6

(August–September 1941)

The day Tony and Ingrid were married, Russia announced the destruction of the great dam on the Dnieper River, to keep it from being useful to the conquering Germans. The Nazi troops had crossed that barrier stream in several places, and the *Drang nach Osten* went clanging on. The Finns captured Viborg, and Leningrad was brought under attack, and Mark said thoughtfully to Robin:

'I remember when Russia invaded Finland, she said she could not tolerate Finnish fortifications as near Leningrad as they were on the old frontier. If she hadn't seized that territory, Leningrad would probably be in German hands by now. Stalin plays a pretty wise game.'

But Robin refused to discuss Stalin, or Germany, or the war. 'I've lots pleasanter things on my mind right now,' she declared.

Tony and Ingrid returned late Sunday night, after Robin and Mark were abed; but Mark heard the car, heard the garage doors open, and went down to let them in. They came to sit side by side on Mark's bed, facing Robin while they told their travels, each interrupting the other, their voices blending in a rich harmonious antiphony, their eyes forever meeting, their hands touching; and Robin and Mark listened and laughed and loved them greatly; and when these two had said good night at last, Robin said:

'They're so completely happy. Do you notice how Ingrid has changed?

Physically, I mean. Her cheeks are smooth and full and glowing—and Tony's too—as though they were fairly swollen with happiness.'

He chuckled. 'They act as though they'd just discovered a wonderful secret which no one else in the world had ever guessed before!'

Tony had two days at home. He was under orders to report to Mitchel Field. 'So I'll be able to come over for week-ends,' he promised. 'This is just temporary, or I'd take you with me, Ingrid. I think I'll be sent to Honolulu eventually; and as soon as I'm settled there, you'll come out and be with me.'

The night before his departure, when Ingrid went upstairs to help Robin make ready for bed, Tony stayed awhile with Mark. Both of them clung to their hour together; but they spoke of impersonal things, and Mark found himself deferring to Tony's opinions, and while they talked he thought Tony was a man now, not only because of his marriage, but because he was an initiate in warlike mysteries where Mark could never follow him.

Tony was more than ever convinced that air power was the decisive force in modern war. 'Planes haven't done all I thought they would,' he admitted. 'But they've done plenty; and wherever either side has been able to seize and hold command of the air, that settled it.' He set forth facts like a demonstration. 'Twenty-four hours after she attacked Poland, Germany had command of the air, and that finished Poland. When she attacked Norway, she held command of the air over the Skaggerak, and that prevented England's Navy from interfering with her troop transports. When she won command of the air over the Norwegian ports, England had to get out. Her command of the air beat Holland and Belgium and France.'

'But not England,' Mark suggested. Watching Tony he saw how the other's youthful countenance had assumed firm, lean, strong lines; and he thought that the soft and tender boy he had known was become like a tempered blade.

'Not England,' Tony agreed. 'Because Germany never won command of the air over England—nor even over Dunkirk! It isn't just planes that win battles, Dad. It's command of the air. Germany had it in the Balkans and in Greece and she had it in Crete, so she won the Balkans and Greece and Crete. Even in the Russian campaign, whenever Germany has command of the air, she sails. Then, when her armies get so far ahead that her fighter planes can't command the front line, the army has to wait while air fields are built and organized, up nearer the battle front, and then they go on again.' And he said strongly: 'This is an air war, Dad. The side which wins and holds command of the air will win every battle—on land or sea!'

They talked till Ingrid, ready for the night, came down to join them, sitting on the floor at Tony's feet, leaning back against his knees; and Tony rumpled her hair while he talked to his father, till Mark at last rose.

'Well, I'll go along up,' he said. 'Robin never really gets to sleep till I come.'

'We're coming, too,' Tony assured him, rising; so Mark bade them good night and stayed behind for a moment, going out on the terrace, quietly grateful for this hour with his son, before he came in and turned off the lights and followed them up the stairs.

Tony left next morning, hopeful that he could return for the following week-end; but that evening he telegraphed Ingrid:

> Orders to Randolph right away as instructor. Sorry not to have the week-end. Love, love, love to all three of you. Tony.

When Robin's boy baby was born, two days later, Mark stayed all night at the hospital; and he came home at dawn to tell Ingrid and Elin all was well. Elin gave him breakfast before Ingrid came downstairs, and she brought the morning paper to lay beside his plate. The headline read:

U S WARSHIP ATTACKED BY SUB
FIRES BACK AS TORPEDOES MISS

Mark's eye ran through the first few paragraphs. The *Greer,* an American destroyer, had according to the Navy Department been a target of German torpedoes and had replied with depth bombs. The *Greer* was undamaged. Whether the submarine had been disabled was as yet unknown.

But Mark thought that did not matter. In any case, the shooting war was on.

XVI

Shooting War

(September–December 7, 1941)

I

(September 1941)

ROBIN came home from the hospital when the baby was a scant three weeks old, and she flatly refused to have a trained nurse in the house even for the first days. 'Danny is a perfectly healthy baby,' she told Mark in smiling pride. She had insisted that the newcomer be named after Mark's father, whom she had from the first liked tremendously. 'Nurses are all right to make sick people well, but I think having a nurse around all the time is just as likely to make well people sick.'

Elin agreed with her, and Ingrid, too; and between them they tended the newcomer as though he were a fragile treasure, precious beyond price.

The week after Robin's home-coming, Jerry Crocker and Ruth returned from their summer's absence, and Ruth came one afternoon to see the baby. Robin, knowing how Mark enjoyed talk with Jerry, asked them both for dinner on the following Saturday; and she bade them come early so that Jerry, too, could meet the new master of the house before Danny was put to bed.

They arrived at half-past five, and after his supper, the baby was briefly on display. Jerry, uneasy as men are apt to be when confronted with this human phenomenon so universally enchanting to womankind —quoted Phillips Brooks. 'Well, now, that is a baby!' he declared, emphasis on the verb; and Robin was content, and Mark caught Jerry's eye and they smiled together in a common masculine understanding while Robin and Ruth and Ingrid all trooped away upstairs to put the baby to bed. Jerry grinned then and asked in a cautiously lowered tone: 'Did I say the right thing?'

Mark laughed. 'I didn't hear any complaints. Robin seemed delighted.'

'I'm no judge,' Jerry confessed. 'So my opinion wouldn't be worth anything; but I imagine he'll turn out all right.'

They meant to wait for the others before starting cocktails, but there was a long delay and they could hear three feminine voices all going at once abovestairs; so they made a start, and Mark said: 'I'm glad of a chance to talk to you, to get your impression of what people are thinking about this shooting war we're in.'

'I've two notebooks full of stuff, just since the *Greer* was attacked,' Jerry told him. 'We landed in San Francisco that day, and I talked to a dozen people, a couple of newspaper men, a taxi driver, a man who sold me some pipe tobacco, the garage man where we'd stored our car, people at random. They all said substantially the same thing; that the *Greer* was in waters where submarines were operating and so she had to expect it. They weren't excited. We were in Los Angeles when the German statement came out, saying the *Greer* had dropped depth bombs before the torpedoes were fired. That contradicted our Navy report, but people—the ones I talked to—believed the Germans. They said Mr. Roosevelt was trying to make a case, to get us into the war.'

'Were they against going in?' Mark asked.

'Yes. But they were willing to go ahead as we've been going—and quite ready to accept the possible loss even of naval vessels in patrolling the sea lanes.' Jerry went on: 'We were in Denver when Roosevelt made his "rattlesnakes of the Atlantic" speech, and most of the men with whom I talked there thought again that he was just trying to drum up war sentiment. No one took seriously his claim that our sending warships and soldiers to Iceland was self-defense. They don't yet feel that Germany is any threat to us, out there. When Knox made his Milwaukee speech, saying that our naval vessels had been ordered to attack German subs on the convoy routes, we were in Lincoln, Nebraska; and the people there were strongly against that policy. Many were definitely pro-German.'

'Do you think it possible,' Mark suggested, 'that your own feeling influenced what they said to you?'

Jerry shook his head, smiling. 'No. As a matter of fact, I don't agree with them, not now. As long as we weren't in the war, I was for staying out; but now we're in it, actually if not formally. It's too late to discuss anything but how to beat the Germans.'

'I'm glad to hear you say that,' Mark said warmly. 'My own feeling has crystallized this summer, Jerry. For a long time this war was a question of ideas, with me; but not now. It's become a question of emotions. I just plain hate Hitler and want to see Germany smashed.' He smiled a little. 'Remember the German Hymn of Hate in the last war. Gott Strafe England and all that. That's the tune I'm singing now— against Germany.'

Jerry nodded gravely. 'I'm coming to it myself.' He looked toward the stairs. 'I think being married has made the difference in me. Wars are hell on our women, Mark. After this war, any way you look at it, the future will be tough; but it will be intolerable unless Germany is beaten —and unless we help, she won't be.' He added warningly: 'But there's still a lot of opinion on the other side. Not many men west of the Alleghanies accept the plain facts of the case today. And mind you, they didn't say so just to agree with me. When I want to lead a man to speak out in meeting, I always state a point of view from which I hope the other fellow will differ, so that we can start an argument. Then I try to get him a little mad—and so I find out what he really thinks.'

'Get who mad?' called Robin, from the stairs, descending; and Ingrid and Ruth were with her, and Mark mixed fresh cocktails. At dinner Robin led Ruth and Jerry to talk about Honolulu. 'Tony's at Tampa, now, instructing,' she said. 'He went to Randolph first, but they sent him to Florida, and he's not sure how long he'll be there. He's hoping to be sent to Honolulu soon.'

Ruth said: 'Well, of course it's wonderful there. We were with Mother, or at least we stayed at her hotel.' Mark looked at Jerry, understanding that he must by this time know that he had married a wealthy girl; but if Jerry did know, certainly it had made no difference to him. 'She's having a lot of fun, has some bridge-playing friends and she's planning to stay there all winter. She seems to me to have grown a lot older since Father died, but she's living the way she wants to.' Ruth looked smilingly at her husband. 'She didn't know what to make of Jerry,' she confessed. 'Sometimes his language is a little—startling.'

They all laughed, and Jerry said: 'But Ruth's smoothing me down, working off the rough edges.'

'We saw Mrs. Sheffield, too,' Ruth told Mark. 'But she didn't recognize me. She was in a cocktail bar, with an unattractive-looking woman. Mother says she's the local scandal. She tries to flirt with all the young Navy men, and she's drinking all the time, much too much. And Mother says she's very hard up, forever borrowing money from everyone she knows, so they all avoid her.'

Mark remembered that Tom's divorce had been secured on the basis of a cash settlement; and it was not surprising that Emma's extravagance had thus soon made an end of her resources. He was sorry for her. Certainly she had deserved no sympathy; but he had known her a long time. Thinking of Emma, he had missed what Ruth was saying, but now he heard her add:

'. . . and of course Jerry was busy most of every day, talking to people everywhere.' Her eyes flashed smiling toward her husband. 'He's the greatest man to talk you ever saw.'

Mark asked: 'What did you talk about, Jerry?'

'Why, people in Honolulu don't talk about anything but the Japs,' Jerry assured them. 'There are more spies and counter-spies in Honolulu than there ever were in Monte Carlo in Oppenheim's best days. You'll find someone trailing you from the hour you arrive, Navy or Army Intelligence, or F.B.I., or the little yellow men. There are so many Japs in Honolulu they get in your hair. There's a Jap in every crack in the woodwork.' He added: 'And the Navy is itching for trouble. They wanted to fight Japan as long ago as 1931 when the Japs went into Manchuria, and they're sure we'll have to fight to stop her in Indo-China.'

Mark enjoyed the evening with Jerry. After dinner, leaving the others indoors, they sat on the terrace for a while; and Mark said thoughtfully: 'You know, Jerry, you and I have arrived at the same end, but by different roads.' Jerry looked at him inquiringly, and he explained: 'I mean, at the conclusion that we must help beat Germany. You believe that now because you feel Mr. Roosevelt has led us so far that we're committed; and I . . .'

Jerry interrupted. 'I go farther than that,' he amended. 'I think he's done right to commit us.'

Mark nodded. 'So do I,' he agreed, and he explained, looking through the window into the living room where Ingrid sat with Ruth and Robin: 'I've been working toward that conclusion for a long time, but until a day or two before Tony and Ingrid were married, I was still . . .' he smiled. 'I was still the thinker, like Rodin's figure, trying to weigh each day's events. And then suddenly the essential truth was brought home to me.'

He hesitated. 'Ingrid was responsible,' he said. 'You know she was in Norway when the Germans struck there, fought against them as a guerrilla for a while.'

'There seems to be a lot of that in Europe now,' Jerry commented. 'This shooting of hostages in France, and the Yugo-Slavs haven't quit yet, and I see there's trouble in Moldavia and Bohemia.'

Mark nodded. 'And her experiences left their scars on Ingrid,' he said. 'She has nightmares, and bad dreams.' There was a smouldering heat in his tones. 'And it came home to me suddenly that all over Europe there are millions of girls like her, girls and young men, whom Hitler by precipitating this war has condemned, not necessarily to death nor even to horrible physical suffering, but to what is worse; to mental torment from which they will never wholly recover, which will leave its traces on their whole lives.'

'The last war did the same thing.'

'Of course,' Mark assented. 'The last war left its traces on most of the men I know. On Ruth's father, for instance. Has she told you?'

'Yes.'

'And on Bob Ritchie, not only physically, but I now think mentally, too. He is bitter against Mr. Roosevelt, and I think that bitterness is largely the result of a sort of subconscious horror at some of his memories of the last war, which makes him foresee what this war will bring. You probably know scores of men who served in the last war; and few of them were able to come back to normal, simple ways of life again.

'Hitler's let loose the same thing in the world today, in a more dreadful form, because he turns his bombers loose on men and women and children who are absolutely defenseless.' He made a sound that was only half a laugh. 'He's brought all of us already to the point where we are glad when English bombs strike Berlin and kill women there, and frighten German children into hopeless maniacs, as English babies have been frightened. He's beginning to shape us in his image. That's his greatest crime. It's not so much what he does to English babies; it's that he makes us eager to do the same thing to German babies!' He looked over his shoulder and saw through the window Robin sitting by the fire. 'I've a baby of my own upstairs. That brings it home to me. He's reduced me to such a state of mind and soul that if one of his bombs harmed my baby, I'd be glad to read of German babies slaughtered. There's his unforgivable crime; the fact that he has not only turned the beast loose upon the world, but he has roused the beast in each of us. He has made us ready to cheer the news that an American-made plane dropped American-made bombs on Berlin women and children and babies. Oh, we don't put it so explicitly, even in our thoughts. We say: "The English bombed Berlin. Hurrah!" But those bombs we're cheering killed men and women and children. He's made us rate our beastliness a virtue, made us pray it can match his.' He made a slow movement with his clenched fist. 'So God damn that man to eternal Hell, forever and ever, Amen!'

For a moment Jerry did not speak, and Mark was trembling from the emotions his own words had evoked in him. He lighted a cigarette with shaking fingers. They heard Ingrid laugh, in the living room; and Jerry said in a quiet tone:

'You're taking it hard, Judge.'

Mark tried to smile. 'How's the book coming along?' he asked. 'Doing any more on that?'

Jerry shook his head. 'I got off on the wrong foot,' he said, in a thoughtful tone. 'I was trying to nail down the facts, the day-to-day facts, the actual events which have led up to this war; but now I've decided facts don't matter. The real history of these ten years will be the history, not of what happened, but of what Americans thought was happening, and of their developing mass opinion about world events. In the long run, a generally held opinion is more important than all the facts you can muster.'

Mark laughed shortly. 'Opinions be damned! Facts be damned! It's emotions that will settle this business now.'

2

(October 1941)

The day after the *Kearny* was torpedoed, Tom and Mark and Bob and Ed dined together in town. Mark was the first to arrive at the club, and Tom Sheffield came in just afterward. Tom asked: 'The others here?' Mark shook his head, and Tom said quickly: 'I'm glad of that, Mark. I wanted to talk to you, see what you think.' And he said: 'I've had a letter from Emma. She wants to come back to me.'

Mark, after a moment, was not surprised. He remembered what Ruth had said. If Emma were in need, it was like her to hope to resume her hold on Tom. He asked: 'Where is she?'

'She wrote from Honolulu, but she said she was coming as far as Chicago, gave me her address there.' And Tom added, as though he were pleading her cause: 'It was a tragic sort of letter, Mark, full of regrets and remorse. I can't help feeling sorry for her. Emma was foolish in some ways, about money especially. But—we married each other for better or for worse. What do you . . .'

He broke off as Bob and Ed came in together, his glance warning Mark to be silent. Over cocktails the talk turned at once to the *Kearny*. Ed thought this incident would surely lead to a declaration of war. Tom had no opinion, but Bob strongly disagreed with Ed.

'We don't know all the facts yet,' he insisted. 'Remember the first report on the *Greer* said the submarine fired its torpedoes without provocation. It wasn't till three or four days ago that the Navy admitted that the *Greer* trailed that submarine for hours, and that a British plane dropped depth bombs on the sub—or tried to—before the sub ever let go her torpedoes. So the sub probably thought the *Greer* dropped the depth bombs. You couldn't blame her for fighting back.'

Mark held his tongue, unwilling to become involved in any argument with Bob, afraid what he might say; but Ed answered him.

'She could hear the *Greer*,' he pointed out. 'Unless the *Greer* were over her when the depth charges were dropped, she would know a plane had dropped them.' But Bob ignored this.

'The fact is,' he insisted, 'we've sent our warships into a combat area, claiming it's necessary for our defense to do so; and they're bound to get hurt. The *Kearny* had orders to shoot at any sub she saw; the sub shot first, that's all.' And he said, in a derisive amusement: 'I'm a little sorry for Roosevelt. He's trying so hard to work us up to war pitch, or to get Hitler to start a war, or something; but we persist in keeping calm, and so does Hitler.'

Tom said doubtfully: 'Don't you think one reason we refuse to get excited is because the newspapers keep telling us Germany can't win? People don't reach the fighting point till they get scared, or mad.' His eyes met Mark's meaningly. 'And when they're not scared or mad any longer, they get over wanting to fight, like husbands and wives.' The little man, Mark guessed, wanted to take Emma back. He was pleading her cause. Tom had always been dependent upon women, but now his mother was dead, and he was lonely, ready to forgive Emma if only to relieve that loneliness. Mark answered the other's appealing glance with a reassuring smile; and at the same time he echoed Tom's words.

'The newspapers have a lot to answer for,' he agreed. 'They've consistently played down bad news, played up good news. They've catered to our wishful thinking, and fed our delusions of grandeur, and assured us that we can win a war in Germany by building tanks in Detroit, and planes in California, without ever sending men to fight.'

There was a sardonic wrath in his tones. 'If you want to lose a war, it's easy enough! Persuade yourself that your enemy cannot win. Tell yourself that you are·invulnerable behind your Maginot line, or your fleet or the Atlantic Ocean. When your enemy is advancing, assign to him a fictitious "schedule" under which he must capture a certain point on a certain day;.and if he is a few days.late, say he was defeated. Whenever your armies or the armies of your allies are forced to retreat, keep insisting that the beaten armies are still "intact."'Scatter your forces. Act on the theory that·ten armies of twenty thousand men, even without cooperating, can beat one united army·of a hundred thousand men. Let your enemy force you to accept battle in places where he has a ten-to-one advantage in transportation. Fight a defensive war.. Oppose dynamic thought with passive ideologies. Oh, it's easy enough to lose a war!'

His voice hardened with rising anger at his own words. 'I was slow in realizing what we must do. At first I thought we ought to prepare, and I thought we ought to help England with supplies so she could beat Germany. The newspapers said that was all we needed to do, and Churchill said the same thing, and I believed it.

'But I don't believe it now. Not any longer. The war is right in our front yards now, and we've got to mix in. I didn't always feel so. I could see a German case, as well as an English case. I looked at the thing judicially.'

Bob·chuckled. 'Sure! Old "There's-something-to-be-said-on-both-sides." That's you!'

'It was me,' Mark admitted. 'But I'm past that now! I'm not judicial-minded any longer. I want to see us whip Germany. Her success is built not only on armed strength, which I could forgive and even admire; but it's also built on treachery, and on an avowed policy of making promises only to break them, and on frank lies, and on a planned campaign of murder, the murder of innocent hostages in France, the murder of children wherever her planes can find them, the machine-gunning of panic-stricken, unarmed men and women. I want to see Germany smashed, flat; and I want to see us do it.'

He had never spoken so strongly to them before, and for a moment they were all silent. Then Bob challenged in a dry tone: 'How, Mark? What's your program? How will we go about smashing her?'

Mark wiped his lips with the back of his hand, spoke more quietly. 'This war—we're already in it, in an unadmitted, hypocritical fashion—can't be well fought by us if it is just dropped in our laps by Washington. We've got to make it our war, not Washington's war. As a matter of fact, I believe Washington is way behind the country. Congress wouldn't declare war today, but I believe the country is ready for war, ready for sacrifice, and work—for Churchill's blood, toil, sweat, and tears. The people are just waiting till someone puts their will into words. Mr. Roosevelt won't do it, or can't do it—possibly because of Congress.'

'Congress isn't worth the powder to blow them up!' Ed said calmly. 'They're a hypocritical bunch of peanut stealers! Everything they do is done for votes. Take the tax question. Everyone knows that the way to control extravagance and hold down inflation is to make it impossible to spend money; and the easiest way to do that is to put a hundred per cent—or a two hundred per cent, or a five hundred per cent—sales tax on non-essentials. But will Congress pass a sales tax? Not they. Or maybe Morgenthau won't let them. This business ought to be paid for as we go along. Every spare dollar every man can get hold of should go into it. But all the damned Congressmen can think of is trying to find a tax that won't offend too many voters!'

'Well, we elected them,' Mark reminded him. 'So if Congress is wrong, we're to blame! Next year, I'd like to see us try to elect some real men, throw out that bunch of trimmers in Washington, put in a Congress that is for war to the hilt!'

'Next year's a long time ahead,' Tom suggested.

'There's a long war ahead,' Mark retorted. 'Five years, perhaps ten.'

'What you want is a Congress that will rubber-stamp Mr. Roosevelt,' Bob protested.

'No,' Mark told him flatly. 'I admire Mr. Roosevelt. He's done a good job in seeing what was coming, and in leading us to accept it. But I certainly don't want to see a Congress that blindly accepts his leadership. Too many politicians—possibly he's one of them—confuse loyalty to individual leaders with a higher loyalty, a loyalty to their country. I want to see a fighting Congress, fighting mad, loyal to just one thing —the determination to beat Germany at whatever cost to the individual, to the party, to the heads of Government. There's only one issue in this country today: To beat Germany or not to beat her.'

Bob asked in a sardonic tone: 'Did you ever think we might just tend to our own business?'

'Our business for the next few years is going to be war!'

'John Lewis wouldn't agree with you.'

'He will, in time,' Mark insisted. 'Of course, Mr. Roosevelt is a labor President, but Bob, this is labor's world—if we use the word labor in its broadest sense. The men who work with their hands have in the last two thousand years become increasingly informed and articulate; and they were always the majority, and we all believe—I think—in democracy, in majority rule. Labor, the majority, rose to power in Germany, and in Italy, just as the workingmen rose to power in France a hundred and fifty years ago.

'But in those countries labor, though strong enough to seize power, was not wise enough to use the new weapons they had seized; so out of some preliminary chaos there emerged in each case a dictator—Napoleon, Mussolini, Hitler—and in each case these dictators crushed labor, or reduced it to a debased and willing servitude. The condition of labor in Germany and Italy today is worse than it was a quarter-century ago, or fifty years ago.

'In our country, labor—I use the word again in its broadest sense as meaning all men who work primarily with their hands rather than with their heads—seized power without bloodshed; but here, too, they largely delegated power to one man. Yet, because we in this country have had a hundred and fifty years of free and orderly government, they made a better choice. They chose not a war-mad gangster, but a man who, however much you may object to his measures, had fine dreams and tried to make those dreams come true. The result has been that nowhere in the world has labor ever made such strides as in the United States in these last eight or nine years.'

Bob laughed grimly. 'I'll say so,' he agreed. The others did not speak, and Mark went on:

'But the way of life which Hitler has forced upon us threatens to nullify those gains, either indirectly, by compelling us to meet him on his own terms, or directly, by conquest. German victory means the reduction of labor everywhere in the world to the wretched status of labor in Germany and Italy, forced to work for a subsistence wage, denied the right to strike, denied education and the chance for advancement. In Germany only the select few, chosen in youth, are granted even a modest education. All others are condemned from boyhood to be soldiers, mechanics, workers, and to be no more than that for as long as they live.

'The United States and England are the last remaining obstacles in the way of the enslavement of workingmen everywhere. Labor is politically powerful in England, and ours is a labor Government today, because we're a democracy and labor has the votes. You've heard about the Wave of the Future. Well, this is the real wave of the future, the rising tide of labor's power all over the world. It's labor in England, and in the United States, and in Russia, which will win this war; and they'll win it not only by working but by fighting. And they'll be working and fighting not for themselves alone, not only to preserve and to extend their own new-won freedoms, but also to release the enslaved laboring classes of Germany and Italy.'

Even Bob was now soberly attentive, and Mark concluded: 'There's the whole history of the last two thousand years; the history of the gradually increasing political power of the man who works with his hands. That rising tide of labor power has had its setbacks; but each time the wave has risen higher after those setbacks; and it will continue to rise. I tell you the new world will be labor's world—and labor is ready today, not only here but in Europe, to work and to fight to make that world—once they see the future clear.'

When he finished, no one spoke, but after a moment Tom Sheffield leaned eagerly forward as though he had remembered something long forgotten.

'By gorry, Mark,' he cried, 'I know another man who says the same thing. Matt Clancy, Mary's father. You met him at Tommy's wedding. He says that's what this war is all about. I mean, it's labor's war, to hold what they've won so far, and to hold the right to go on fighting for more things. He says Hitler's crushed labor, and so has Mussolini. He doesn't like England, but he says English labor is all right. He says labor in England forced the Government into this war, forced England to fight Hitler because they saw that Hitler wasn't just the enemy of Poland. He was the enemy of mankind everywhere.'

'He's right,' Mark said strongly. 'This isn't just World War II, against Public Enemy Number One, as though we were going to have a World War III and a World War IV and so on indefinitely. This is the War for Mankind! If we lose it, then labor will lose all it has gained in a hundred and fifty years.'

Bob laughed harshly; but Tom Sheffield spoke in an eager haste. 'That's what Matt says. None of us here really know anything about labor—not at first hand; but Matt does. He and I have seen quite a lot of each other since Tommy was married, and specially since Mother died. I go over and have dinner with him and his mother. She's a grand old dame.'

'I liked him,' Mark agreed. 'And her too.'

'He liked you,' Tom assured him. 'He's spoken of you a dozen times. But what I started to say, Mark, he thinks you ought to be in politics.' And he said challengingly: 'Mark, what you said awhile ago—why don't you run for Congress yourself?'

Mark was so surprised that he did not answer; and Bob laughed and said: 'Not a chance, Tom! Remember what Daniel Webster said? "I have given my life to law and to politics. Law is uncertain, and politics is utterly vain."' He told Mark strongly: 'And that's the weak spot in your idea, Mark! You talk about electing a strong Congress, but you'll have to find able men willing to run before you try to elect them, and no man good enough for the job is willing to take it. You know damned well you wouldn't take it on a platter!'

Mark said thoughtfully: 'I'm not so sure. We're drafting men for the army, and drafting capital, and management; and I think we ought to draft men for munitions work—men unfit for combatant duty—in order to release able-bodied men for the army. Why not draft men for Congress too?'

'Draft them?' Bob laughed. 'You have to fight off the candidates as it is.'

'Maybe that's the trouble,' Mark urged. 'Our Congress, House and Senate, should be the real directing power in this country. The decay of Congress is responsible for the rise of the executive power; not the contrary. Suppose we had a national "Win the War" organization, neither Democratic nor Republican, with a platform capable of inspiring a fierce and universal approval, and a strong candidate in every Congressional district, and in every state where a Senate seat is open. A campaign on that basis would get results. Some good men would be elected, and the nation-wide vote even for defeated candidates would have its influence on Congress—and on our future ways.'

Bob chuckled. 'I'd like to see your platform,' he declared. 'You'll have to satisfy everybody, and that will take a platform as long as *Gone With the Wind*.'

But Tom said eagerly: 'Mark, will you have lunch with me and Matt Clancy some day soon? Talk this over?'

'I'd be glad to,' Mark said, with a sense that he was committing himself to something irrevocable, and a deeply satisfying certainty that to do so was fine and contenting. He turned to Bob and smiled. 'As for a platform, that's simple,' he said. 'Just four words: "Let's Win the War."'

3

(November–December 1941)

Tony had hoped that Ingrid might soon come to be near him; but he was ordered first from Mitchel Field to Randolph and then to Tampa and then back to Texas and then to New Mexico, and his orders were changed so frequently that he could make no definite plans. These many transfers made Mark realize how completely Tony and hundreds of thousands of other young men had ceased to exist as individuals, had become simply units in a mass, like the cells in the human body. Tony had applied for service in Honolulu, and hoped the application would be granted; and early in November he wrote Ingrid that his chances were good, and that he would surely be given a week's leave and be able to come home before he left. But early in November he telegraphed from San Antonio:

> Ordered to Honolulu at once. No leave. Tough break, but no help for it. Writing. Love, Love, Love to all three.
>
> Tony.

Robin took the telegram over the phone, and she was reluctant to tell Ingrid Tony's news. Ingrid just then was out on the terrace where little Dan in his perambulator was taking the sun. Instead of going to her, Robin telephoned Mark, repeated Tony's message to him.

'He sounds pretty upset,' he commented. 'It's hard for Ingrid.' And he asked, 'Is she all right?'

'I haven't told her,' Robin confessed. 'You know, Mark, she hasn't written Tony about their baby. She's been waiting to tell him when he came home.'

'I'll try to get him on the phone,' Mark decided. 'Perhaps she can fly out there for a day or two with him before he leaves.'

But he telephoned half an hour later to say that Tony had already departed, one of a group of pilots who were being ferried West in a transport plane. 'He'll be in California in the morning,' he said, trying not to let his voice betray his feeling that there was something irrevocable in this departure for faraway places.

Robin felt this, too, but she had to tell Ingrid the disappointing news. Ingrid took it evenly. 'He has to do what they say, the thing they think has to be done,' she said. 'I know that is what he wants, even more than seeing me. That is right, too.'

Tony's letter came two days later. It had been written in haste; and after explaining his new orders, he added:

> There seems to be more excitement down here since the *Reuben James* was sunk. Before that, we went along pretty calmly—except that everyone was sore at Lewis over the coal strike. As far as the war was concerned, we knew we were helping the English Navy a lot. Thirty-five British ships have been repaired in our navy yards already. An English naval intelligence

man was here the other day, and he says the English are tremendously impressed by the speed with which we make repairs. He says we fix up their ships in half the time it would take to do it in their own yards, the yards where the ships were built. So I guess some of our labor is on the job, in spite of Lewis.

But since the *Reuben James* was sunk, there've been all sorts of rumors about what we were going to do next. Germany claims our destroyers have been attacking her subs, and the men here think she keeps saying that because Japan has agreed to come into the war if we attack Germany. Maybe that's why I've finally got orders for Honolulu!

I hate not seeing Ingrid or any of you, but I'll send for Ingrid as soon as I know how things are out there. Love, love, love, one for each of you,

Tony.

He added a postscript. 'You can write me at Hickam Field out there.'

Robin said in laughing protest: 'He didn't send his love to my baby!' Mark smiled and reminded her that Tony had never seen his small brother, had not yet realized his existence.

'Besides, babies don't mean much to young men his age,' he pointed out.

Ingrid cried happily: 'Yes, they do! You wait till you see how he is with ours!'

That evening they all wrote him long letters. Mark in his referred to one he had just received from his father in Ohio; and he explained:

He says people out there want to see Hitler beaten, but that they dislike Mr. Roosevelt so intensely they're against anything he wants. But he thinks they would consent to war, rather than go on with this continued uncertainty. I've heard publicity men use the phrase: 'The Engineering of Consent.' It seems to apply to our national state of mind today. We've been engineered into consenting to the war; but we need more than that! Consent is a passive state. We will need to arrive at some real enthusiasm before we can go ahead and win. Our consent has been engineered by a campaign of fear, on the texts 'You can't do business with Hitler' and 'Our salvation depends upon England'; but we don't really believe either statement. A man with a talent for it can always do business; and as for our salvation, if our salvation depends on anyone but ourselves, we're already lost!

I've been led into a move which may have extensive consequences. My notion is that we must make every effort to elect a strong, war-minded Congress next year. I said so to Tom Sheffield, and he insisted that I talk it over with Matt Clancy—you remember, he's Tommy's wife's father, a shrewd, able, likeable Irishman—and Matt wants me to run for Congress next year, thinks I can be elected. I've said I would do it if I saw a chance to make a good race, win or lose, and if some sort of national campaign were organized to elect Congressmen on a 'Let's win the War and to Hell with Everything Else' platform. Clancy thinks it can be done, and he's in correspondence with Jim Farley and Smith and Landon and Willkie, discussing it; so I may find myself in politics 'for the duration.' Don't speak of this in your letters. I haven't told Robin yet. She'll think I shouldn't do it, that it would be bad for me; but it may be something I can do to help things along.

Incidentally, Tony, Tom and Emma are married again. She asked him to take her back . . .

He hesitated, wondering whether to tell Tony what he thought Emma's motive was, then decided not to do so. She might conceivably be sincere. So he went on:

. . . and he is lonely and incomplete since his mother died. They were married in Chicago and they'll live in the old house in Lincoln. Tom bought it back from Ruth, you know. I don't expect much of Emma; but perhaps Tom is better able to handle her now.

Another bit of news. Nell tells me that Chuck Little is paying attention to Jan; has been up to see her at Merryfield. Nell says Jan likes him a lot. They had a good time together the day you and Ingrid were married.

He read this last paragraph to Robin for her approval, and she commented smilingly: 'You've always thought of Jan as being just a little heart-broken over Tony, haven't you?'

'I suppose I can't imagine any girl not being in love with him,' he admitted.

'Don't worry about Jan,' she advised him. 'She's a splendid girl, and much too sensible—and too charming—to be foolish about Tony.'

So Mark let it stand, and he wrote another page or two, about Ingrid and how well she was and how fond they were of her; and about Danny, describing how he throve every day; and about Robin; and he quoted from memory parts of Will Ritchie's latest letter, which was packed with hilarious accounts of Will's misadventures. He wrote of himself: 'I'm as well as a horse, haven't felt so well in years. In fact we're all perfect here, and happy in our pride in you.'

When he finished, Robin and Ingrid were still writing; and he waited for them to be done, and sealed each letter separately, and put airmail stamps on them and walked down to the mailbox on the corner. The night was fine, cold and clear. He thought Tony might even now be in the air on his way to Honolulu.

Tony's first letter after his arrival at the islands was addressed to Mark, with a sealed enclosure for Ingrid. It came a day or two after England opened a promising new offensive in Libya. Churchill told Parliament the attack had been five months in preparation. 'At last,' he said, 'we meet our enemy equally well armed and equipped.' He predicted a quick decision, possibly within a few hours. Mark, although he remembered the earlier British drive in the same region, which had furnished hopeful headlines for a while, only to be cancelled by a swift German counter-stroke, nevertheless took Churchill's words at their face value; and he was in an optimistic mood when Tony's letter came. Tony wrote:

> Dear Folks: Well, I've been here two days and it certainly is a lovely place. The Travel ads don't do it justice, but nothing could—neither words nor pictures. You'd better all come out with Ingrid when the time comes and just settle down here.
>
> As I say, you can't do this place justice, so as far as the scenery is concerned I won't try; but I can tell you something about the general set-up. We're based at Hickam Field, and we're kept busy with practice blackouts and alerts and so on. When the alarm is given, every available plane takes the air. Everybody has instructions what to do in case of a Jap bomber attack. Patrol bombers are flying all the time, and every day except Sunday we have training flights—what they call the inshore patrol—clear around the island. We have Sundays off, mostly—and Saturday evenings, of course.
>
> No one out here has much to say about Germany. It's all Japan. They think Germany's too far away to matter here. The Navy is worse than we are about the Japs. We don't take them so seriously. The Hawaiian militia is mostly Japanese. They're at Schofield Barracks. They even have some Jap officers. We have Japs around Hickam Field right along, workmen and so on. The Navy doesn't allow any Japs at Pearl Harbor, and no ships can come within three miles of Pearl Harbor without being challenged. There are destroyers patrolling all the time. The Jap fishing fleet isn't even allowed near Diamond Head. But in spite of being so careful, most of the Navy wives have Jap maids, and Jap servants, and there are Jap waiters in all the cafés and hotels, so they can get an earful any time. They were all a little amused out here when Churchill said that if the Japs attacked us, England would declare war within the hour. They say the Japs won't dare start anything, because the Navy can smash Hell out of Japan in two months.

Robin said, interrupting for a moment: 'I know how the Navy feels. Nell took me to a meeting for Chinese Relief in town the other day, and Admiral Yarnell was one of the speakers. He said we were going to have to fight Japan, and he said, as far as he was concerned, the sooner the better.'

'Ed feels the same way,' Mark agreed. 'He gets it from Navy men.' He turned to the letter again, read on. There was much more, news of Tony's good health, his investigation of living facilities for himself and Ingrid. 'As soon as I'm sure what's best to do, I'll write or cable,' he promised. 'I hope Ingrid can be here for Christmas, and I think I can work it out all right.'

Time of Peace

Mark wrote him, a few days later:

Dear Tony: Your letter interested me a lot. Of course we here feel about Japan as people out there feel about Germany; that Japan is far away, any danger there completely unreal. The headlines today say: 'Hull Gives Tokio Final Terms,' and that the choice of peace or war is now up to Japan; but Hull's note, the papers explain, was really a 'blueprint for peace in the Pacific.' I'm sure Japan doesn't want trouble with us. When Germany invaded Russia, I thought she might have made a deal with Japan to keep Russia busy so that Japan could go ahead in China; and certainly Germany has kept Russia busy. She looks like capturing Moscow any day now. Maybe a part of her deal with Japan was that if we declared war on Germany, Japan would declare war on us; but we're no nearer war with Germany than we were when you left. Mr. Roosevelt made light of the *Reuben James* sinking, said we had to expect such things and that it would make no difference in our policy toward Germany; and people here accept that point of view. We're already in an undeclared naval war with Germany, because Hitler claims that our defense area is his offense area, but no declared war is in sight—unless by his decision.

I personally believe our policy is weak and almost cowardly. Our Navy has orders to shoot, and so have the Germans—but so far as we know, the Germans are doing most of the shooting. If we've sunk any submarines the Navy doesn't say so. But undeclared wars are unworthy of decent governments. If we have a right to do what we're doing—and I think we have—we ought to say so, and go to war against anyone who tries to stop us.

I think the trouble is, Mr. Roosevelt feels he can't get a declaration of war from Congress, so he's trying to force Germany to declare war on us. I'm in favor of everything we're doing, but I'd like to see us do more. I want to see Germany smashed, and I want to see us help do it; but not in the hypocritical left-handed fashion in which we're trying to do it today. The Navy men who are risking death—and who are dying—out there in the Atlantic must wonder sometimes, rather bitterly, how long it will be before we have the courage and the honesty to come out in the open and back them up with all our power.

I suspect we're deceiving ourselves by thinking that a defensive war will win, just as we think the Allies won the last war. As a matter of fact, the last war was never won—or if it was won, Germany won it. It was lost by France, standing on the defensive. The defensive is always a losing fight. As soon as Germany was forced to go on the defensive in 1918, she knew she could not win—so she surrendered. She knew surrender was better than defeat. This war we must win, win on the battlefield, by overpowering and destroying the German armies, the German war machine. If we're going to go on fighting on the defensive, we'd better surrender now—as Germany did in 1918. The only way to win a war is by offense, by pounding the living daylights out of the enemy.

The war between the states was won not at Gettysburg—that was a defensive battle—but on the offense, by Sherman's march to the sea, by Grant at Vicksburg and in the Wilderness and at Richmond and at Appomattox.

Peace after Gettysburg would have been—on no matter what terms—a defeat
for the North, just as the last peace was a defeat for France and for the
Allies. It is said that Stanton's policy delayed our victory over the South, that
he did it deliberately because he believed a long war would smash the South
and end the question of secession forever, because he wanted to see the
North aroused to a relentless policy. Perhaps he was right. Certainly that war
between the states did forever settle the secession question. This war must
settle Germany's future. We're still saying: 'We must not lose this war.' But
it's time to begin to say: 'We must win this war!' and set about doing it;
openly and avowedly, mustering every man and every factory for the fight.

   If I sound like a stump-speaker, forgive me. Maybe I'm practising for the
Congressional campaign next year!

   God bless you. We all think of you constantly, even in our dreams.

                                                            Your Father.

During the days after he mailed that letter, Mark followed the news
from Washington with a faint concern. The Japs were sending troops
into Indo-China, Roosevelt asked for an explanation, the British sent
soldiers and warships to the Far East, and Premier Tojo said Japan
would 'purge England and the United States out of East Asia with a
vengeance, for the honor and pride of mankind'; but Mark reassured
himself with the reminder that our Navy could surely handle any
trouble in the Pacific. Nevertheless, he and Robin avoided the subject,
Robin because she hoped he was not worried for Tony's sake, Mark because he was unwilling to confess his uneasiness.

By the fourth of December, when Tony's next letter came, the crisis
seemed to have eased. Tony wrote jubilantly that he had made his
plans for Ingrid to join him. He had taken an option on a small house
which he was sure she would approve. 'But if she does not, we'll look
for another,' he said. 'They'll hold it for me till the first of January,
but I want her here for Christmas. If she wants to fly all the way, fine.
You'll have to figure out the best time for her to start, from that end.
It can't be too soon to suit me!'

And of the routine of his days he said:

   We're right on the job out here. The talk is that Hull's note demanded
that Japan withdraw from China and Indo-China, and everyone here says
Japan will take that as an insult, and will fight to save her face. The Navy
thinks she'll attack Thailand, and that then we'll have to step in. They've
warned us to look out for sabotage here. Alert Number One, they call it.
That means all our planes are concentrated, and under guard and ready to
take off in fighting trim at four hours' notice. We're—that is, the Army is—
operating the aircraft warning system from four till seven every morning. I
don't know why they don't do it all day, but the thing they're really watching

for here is a Jap rising on the Island. There's no danger of an attack from outside. At least everyone says so. I wouldn't be surprised if the Japs tried it, the way they did at Port Arthur, but everyone says I'm nuts, so probably I am.

There was more, about Ingrid and their plans, and next day Mark consulted the air lines and made her reservations. She would leave on Monday, the eighth, fly to the coast, go by boat from there; and she and Robin spent all day Friday shopping, all day Saturday with needle and thread and iron in order to have everything in readiness.

'She's so excited she can't do anything for herself,' Robin told Mark that evening. 'It would be fun to go out with her, wouldn't it; just arrive with her and surprise Tony.'

'Perhaps we can go in the spring,' Mark agreed. 'Let them get settled down in double harness first. They'll have adjustments to make, you know.'

'We didn't,' she reminded him smilingly.

'We made our adjustments beforehand. After all, they've only had a few days together. Even their courtship was done by mail.'

'Yet even a few days can be packed full, in times like these,' she said thoughtfully. 'We don't always realize it—but we're living so tensely and so intensely, living a little above normal pitch, that even a moment may hold much.' She touched his arm. 'They've already had in their two lives a full measure of—full living.' She smiled. 'I expect their few days together last summer held as much happiness as most people's whole lives. They'll always have those days to remember. The rest of their lives will be like an anticlimax.'

He bent to kiss her. 'You're sweet, Robin. Every day with you is a new climax of happiness for me. I know what you're thinking, what you're trying to say—to reassure me. But don't worry about me. I'm not—worrying about Tony. No matter what happens, I'll always have him, richly and proudly and completely.'

'I want no—unhappiness ever to touch you, my darling.' She clung close for a moment, then smilingly met his silent kiss again.

Before he went to bed that night, Mark wrote Tony a letter to go by airmail, telling him Ingrid's plans, and he continued:

Things here go along in the same old way. John L. Lewis agreed to arbitrate the coal strike, after Mr. Roosevelt named the arbiters. I suspect Lewis was sure the decision would be in his favor before he accepted arbitration. Tokio's answer on Indo-China was conciliatory, and everyone seems to think the Jap crisis is over. I read a letter from one of your Dartmouth professors in the *Herald* this morning. I've forgotten his name, but he's somewhat of an

expert on sea power. He says we could base a fleet on Singapore, Manila, and
Guam and blockade Japan into submission very quickly. He sees no danger
of a Jap attack on the Philippines, says our fleet would cut the supply lines
of the attacking force; and he's sure there's nothing of a decisive nature which
Japan could do. I distrust experts, but I suppose he's right, since you say
the Navy says the same thing.

Robin and I think we may take a vacation this winter and come out and
see you. Some fun, eh? Remember when you were always saying that? We
have so many happy memories in common, you and I. I don't suppose any
father and son were ever closer. It's a long time since I told you this, but
there's no harm in saying it again. I've always been proud of you, and proud
of having your confidence and love. You've made me happy in so many ways.

Robin and I are very much in love with Ingrid, Tony. Be good to her,
and we'll see you in February or March, and some day you'll bring her back
home and we can all be together again. I love her, and I love you.

Your Father.

He added a postscript, smiling as he wrote, copying some words off a
card in his hand:

> They've finally reached your number in the draft board here, and a card
> came for you today. It reads: 'You are hereby notified to report to Doctor
> Hammersmith at City Hall for physical examination at seven P.M. on Tues-
> day, December 9, 1941. Failure to do so is an act punishable by imprison-
> ment and fine and may also result in your immediate induction into military
> service.' I shall appear and make your apologies and explain to them that you
> are otherwise engaged.

He walked down to the corner to mail this letter, and it seemed to
him as he turned homeward as though the letter were already in Tony's
hands, as though Tony were already reading it. More than ever in his
life, though thousands of miles separated them, he felt himself tonight
one with his son. Letters were not needed between them. He knew that
if Tony were awake—and he was, of course, for it was still daylight in
Hawaii—Tony was surely thinking of them here, of Ingrid, and of
Robin, and of his father. He looked at his watch. Half-past ten. That
meant say five o'clock in the afternoon in Honolulu. Saturday afternoon. Probably Tony would go to dinner with friends somewhere,
dance with a pretty girl or two, tell them about Ingrid, return to his
quarters presently and think of Ingrid soon to come to him, and of
them all here, and so go happily to sleep and wake to a fine new day.
He came home and went upstairs; and Robin, already abed, lifted her
arms to give him good night. He was at peace with himself, serene and
unafraid.

4

(December 7, 1941)

After midday dinner on Sunday, Robin and Ingrid put the baby to bed for his nap, and then Robin made Ingrid too lie down. 'You need to rest after meals, dear,' she told the girl. 'And specially now when you have this long trip ahead of you.'

Ingrid said in dreamy happiness: 'I do not think I will sleep at all. There is too much excitement in me.' But Robin sat down beside her, stroking the other's head, making Ingrid close her eyes, till she felt the girl relax and saw that her breathing was soft and regular.

She went downstairs. Mark was at ease on the couch, a book on his lap, a little drowsy; but he looked up and met her eyes and smiled. She asked: 'You mailed your letter to Tony, didn't you?'

'Yes, last night.'

'I think I'll write him and let Ingrid take it.' She sat down at the desk and her pen began to run. After a while she heard a sound from the couch and looked that way and saw that he, too, was asleep, but a little later he woke and sat up in a quick way and she asked:

'All right?'

'Oh, yes,' he assured her, and chuckled and said: 'I dreamed about Tony. He was right here, came into the room and woke me up by kissing me, the way he used to when he was little, laughing at my surprise. It was one of our games.'

She smiled, returning to her letter. 'Nice dream,' she said. 'Weren't you lucky to have it!'

'Some fun,' he agreed, and resumed his reading.

Later they heard Ingrid in the room above them, heard her feet touch the floor. Robin had just finished her letter to Tony, was about to start another to her father.

'What day of the month is it?' she asked Mark. 'Father always likes his letters dated.'

'The seventh,' he said. Then they both looked up as they heard Ingrid running down the stairs. She came in, wide-eyed, radiant, looking all around; and then her eyes shadowed. Robin asked:

'What is it?'

Ingrid laughed breathlessly. 'I woke up and I thought I heard Tony's voice,' she said. 'Saying my name. I thought he was here. I was still asleep, maybe. It seemed so real, I almost believed it.'

'He's in all our thoughts so much, no wonder we dream about him,' Robin said. She looked at her watch. 'We've missed some of the Philharmonic,' she told them. 'It's twenty-five minutes past three. I was afraid the radio would wake you, Ingrid. Turn it on now, will you? It's on WEEI.'

Ingrid went to do so, switching on the current, tuning to the station; but when the tubes warmed enough so that they could hear anything, the Philharmonic broadcast had just been interrupted, and a news flash was coming over the air.

THE END